sur

sur

antonio soler

Translated from the Spanish by
Simon Deefholts and Kathryn Phillips-Miles

Peter Owen

Peter Owen Publishers
c/o Pushkin Press
Somerset House, Strand
London WC2R 1LA
www.peterowen.com

Translated from the Spanish *Sur*

ISBN 978-0-7206-2107-5

A catalogue record for this book is available from the British Library.

Cover design: Benedict Richards/Graphicacy
Typeset by Octavo Smith Publishing Services
Printed and bound by Clays Ltd, Elcograf S. p. A

MINISTERIO
DE EDUCACIÓN, CULTURA
Y DEPORTE

SECRETARÍA
DE ESTADO
DE CULTURA

This work has been translated with a subsidy from the Ministry of Education, Culture and Sport of Spain

I'm talking about the modern city, constantly being rebuilt and destroyed, today's novelty being tomorrow's ruin; a city that's inhabited or, rather, co-habited in streets, squares, buses, taxis, cinemas, restaurants, concert halls, theatres, political meetings, bars, tiny apartments in huge buildings, the enormous, ever-changing city, reduced to one room measuring a few square metres and as endless as a galaxy, a city that we can never leave without straying into another one that's identical even if it's different; the city, an immense everyday reality which can be summed up in two words: other people.

– Octavio Paz
Sombras de obras

This was our daily experience,
A simple, sepia image of life,
Shitty reality,
As patient as a sniper.

– José Luis González Vera
'The Slow Suburbs'

The author would like to thank Raquel de la Concha, Ana Lyons, Beatriz Coll, Manuel Longares, José Damián Ruiz Sinoga, Mar Llorente, Lidia Rey, Blanca Navarro, Joan Tarrida, Simon Deefholts and Kathryn Phillips-Miles, Abner Stein, Peter Owen Publishers – and, of course, Dr G.

María del Mar,
South, north, east, west,
A compass rose

The dawn light spreads across the sky like tepid milk, engulfing everything. Rooftops, sleeping trees, gleaming cars. It's a whitish brightness that erupts suddenly and rapidly in a thick, misty explosion. It stains the clouds and hangs down around them. You can hear the day arrive, panting, its heavy breathing pausing for just a moment, as if the earth were about to stop and start turning backwards before resuming its orbit and bringing in the new day.

The night hasn't cooled the asphalt down. It's still there, hot and sleepy, slithering beneath its feverish crust. The sun rises inexorably. Life is coming to the boil. The hours of reckoning have passed and with them the triviality of death. The day begins. Insects are scratching away at the soil.

The city's apartment blocks, houses and warehouses have petered out by now along that stretch of the Avenida Ortega y Gasset, and plots of land and boundary walls enclosing only derelict land have taken over from industrial estates. A solitary palm tree, electricity pylons, a half-painted boat alongside a wall in an abandoned garden. The overhead signage on the BP garage emits a momentary flicker of light, fluttering inside like a bird.

A man in green overalls is walking across the forecourt between the petrol pumps. He's got a face like a fish, with no chin and hardly any neck. He scans the area with his beady eyes. There isn't much to see. The monotony of summer, a passing car and, on the other side of the roundabout, advertising hoardings: a man and a woman apparently naked in bed under a sheet; he's behind her with his arms wrapped around her, and alongside them the strapline REDISCOVER YOUR PASSION WITH A NEW MATTRESS. There's another one, half torn off a few days back, leaving a glimpse of a white vehicle, the Volkswagen logo and a word flapping on the torn paper: **Caddy**. The two hoardings in the middle are half hidden behind a tree. You can just make out a red car and the words **Spirit of the** MEDITERRANEAN emblazoned over a photograph of some idyllic beach.

Further on, behind the hoardings, is the outline of a long red building several storeys high. The pump attendant doesn't know what it is, even though he's been working here for years. He can also see a green patch near the advertising hoardings, a cluster of unkempt reeds like the ruffled hair of someone who's just got out of bed, with bad breath, like the ground itself.

What the man with the beady eyes can't see is the most important thing of all. It's what his colleagues are going to discuss with him and some of his customers will ask him about for the rest of that day and the days that follow.

The man can't see the path that starts at the foot of the hoardings, a path edged with dried-up weeds, thorny plants and bits of rubbish scattered among the semi-urban stubble. A crushed beer can, plastic tangled up in the frazzled vegetation, bits of brick and glass and faded paper, cables, rusty wire. The soil all dried up and grey, dusty and overheated.

The small path goes through the waste ground and up towards the red building in the distance. It carries on to some featureless mounds, and in the middle of those there are two remaining sections of what must once have been a concrete wall, which seem to have arisen from the earth itself, planted there like a pair of standing stones, and someone has painted, in large letters, the word **WAS** on one and, on the other, in slightly smaller letters, the word **BUEST**. And it's there, right at the foot of the second concrete block, that the brown bundle is lying. Seventy-five kilos, curled up in a ball.

It feels strange. Counterintuitive. The bundle, the body, seems at one and the same time to be immobile and yet trembling, moving, as if it's whispering or thinking out loud.

It's in an almost foetal position. Only an outstretched leg breaks up the pattern of the antenatal posture. Beneath the seething mass of ants swarming over him, it's possible to make out that the man is bare-chested, covered in dust. His trousers are grey; the right leg is hitched up almost to his knee. The ants are also at work there, just as they will be on his other leg, hidden beneath the trousers, although his left foot is missing a shoe and there's a dark stain, a bruise that's almost black, on which the insects are concentrating all their efforts, like the cells of a genuine super-organism.

The ants belong to the species *Linepithema humile*, the so-called Argentine ant. They are small, reddish, completely omnivorous. They live in the soil, beneath timber, beneath floors. They kill other insects and wipe out all the other species of ant in any territory they invade. Here they are forming a crust over the fallen body, finding a way into every fold of the skin, penetrating orifices, boring, cutting, dragging, communicating anxiously, avidly, greedily; one hundred and thirty million years to arrive at this point of efficiency and precision.

The man's skin is pasty, straw coloured, sallow. His eyes are half open, and a hundred ants are drinking greedily at the edges of his eyelids. His eyes are a greyish blue. Eyes that once looked out on snow-covered fields in another continent, eyes that once awoke to see his son Guillermo in his cot, eyes that once shed tears of joy the first time they saw him. When life was wonderful. The insects are working away at his eyes, organizing themselves into a chain to delve into his ear cavities, entering the labyrinthine depths like potholers, burrowing into his scalp, prowling inside his nostrils, entering his mouth and returning with their booty of saliva and residues of benzodiazepines (diazepam, bentazepam, lormetazepam) and alcohol (vodka, gin, tequila). The man's breathing is shallow, and it's barely possible to discern any movement of his diaphragm.

On the other side of the roundabout, beyond the path and posters where a man has his arms wrapped around a woman (who is pretending to be asleep) and a red car races beside a beach by an emerald sea, a car pulls up, a young man gets out and with a smile he asks the man with the beady eyes and green overalls, 'Lolo, did you notice that someone's knocked over the sign? The one on the roundabout. It's flat on the ground. Did you notice?'

And the man with the beady eyes and the face like a fish and the green overalls says, 'Oh!' and feels that the day has begun.

Ismael's scissors are weighty, pointed and sharp. Ismael's scissors are handled carefully, with considerable precision. They cut through the cloth in a straight line. First a clean cut, then they turn and make another cut in the curtain at a sharp angle. With the third cut, a new triangle is formed, which falls to the floor between Ismael's bare feet. His feet are almost buried in triangles, all approximately the same size.

Ismael is very young, burly, with muscular arms, a broad, fleshy back and a fixed stare. He's concentrating. He started off cutting up the sitting room curtains from the bottom up. First the curtain on the right. From the floor up to eye level. Now he's working on the other curtain. He's cutting from left to right. He's meticulous, facing the window, bathed in the light that, without the curtain to block it out, is streaming into the sitting room with increasing ferocity.

He started cutting early, before daybreak. He went into the kitchen, gently opened the knife drawer. He took out two. The longest ones. He lined them up and measured them. He took one in each hand and felt their weight. Then he put them down on the worktop. He drank some water out of the fridge, straight from the bottle, a long slug, leaning his head right back, and then put the knives away. He took the scissors out of the same drawer and wandered around the flat. He looked at his mother's empty bed. Night shift. A large bed like a raft, floating in the darkness. He imagined his mother naked with her legs spread apart. Then his father. And then the Other Man. The Other Man had also been there. With his dick. Ismael nodded.

He went into the bathroom. He saw his silhouette in the darkness of the mirror. He took the towel that was hanging by the washbasin and left the room. As he passed by his brother Jorge's bedroom he gave the closed door a kick. 'Gorgo!' He smiled when he heard his brother give a start, the bed making a noise and Jorge spluttering, sleepy and scared. Then silence. Fully aware that his brother was awake and would be half sitting up, motionless, watching the door from his bed.

Ismael went to sit on the sofa in the sitting room. And he started cutting the towel into triangles, robotically, focusing all his attention. He cut up the towel, he cut up the cloths he'd found in the kitchen, he cut up one of his mother's dresses that had been lying on top of the bed and he cut up Jorge's running shorts. Everything into equilateral triangles or, at least, acute triangles. Then he started on the curtains, taking his time, just as lost in thought as when he made the first cut in the towel, studying the material and occasionally looking out over the street with the same concentration as it became increasingly visible in the first light of day. The birds sped past the window, five storeys up, tracing a web of straight lines, an invisible, obsessive network over the treetops, in among the windows and the orange awnings of Calle Juan Sebastián Bach.

The sun lands on Ismael's feet, the triangles of beige cloth, the warm snowflakes falling to the floor beside him. The sun's rays are making the windows opposite glare, turning them into reflectors. Over there, three floors up, he sees an old woman come out on to the terrace and sit down behind the railings. 'Over and over again, all day, every day, in your cage, in the zoo, until you drop dead or until I do you in, you old slut.' And he carries on cutting things up, calmly, almost cheerfully.

The smell of thyme. The Runner runs and cuts through the shade of some pine trees, sunshine, the shade of a carob tree, sunshine again. Sweat. Freedom. The perfectly rhythmic tapping of his trainers on the asphalt, increasing pace and speed. He runs, fast and light footed, carried on the wind.

The Runner descends the gentle slope of the street that used to be called the Camino de las Pitas and is now known as Calle Julio Verne. He comes out into the open, accelerates, forces a sprint, the bright glare swamping everything, and everything on the point of becoming distorted, on the point of breaking up. When his body tells him that he's pushed himself far enough, he redoubles his efforts and increases his speed like a wonderful, long scream, ten, twenty, thirty metres more, and when he achieves that and everything is stretched to the maximum he carries on running for another ten or twenty metres.

He stops, and the blood suddenly returns to his body in a great wave;

his heart fills his whole body, takes over his whole anatomy and then disperses and concentrates into small clusters at his temples, in his neck, in his abdomen.

The Runner bends over, rests his hands on his knees and breathes deeply. The smell of the countryside returns, and the heat of the morning and the electric call of the cicadas, so early. He straightens up and starts walking. He looks at his Fitbit. 56′09″.

He walks, jogs, a gentle run. He goes past the Los Olivos school buildings on the right, behind the metal railings. Three priests are kicking a ball around on the football pitch, laughing and larking about like a bunch of children. 'Like a dawn chorus' is what he'd like to say to them. He feels another urge to take off and run at full pelt, but he does precisely the opposite, stops jogging and continues on his way at walking pace.

'REJOICE IN CHRIST, THE NEW LIFE, THE ETERNAL GARDEN OF EDEN', that's what they used to write on the blackboard, always in capital letters so you'd know it was the One and Only Truth. 'Whatever you're doing, never think that someone else has done it before,' Father Isaías Abril used to say, 'and when you're kissing a girl, never think that someone else has kissed her before but rather that you're the very first one and you're opening up the world and life itself. That's how you should appreciate things, everything in moderation, nothing to excess. Because the alternative path leads to vice and depravity and will make you disappear from Christ's sight. Disappear for all eternity. Do you know what that means?' And, of course, as he was saying that he was imagining the words WORLD, HISTORY AND LIFE in capital letters. And Vice and Depravity. Invisibility. Hair combed back in a high quiff with yellowish highlights, perhaps touched up with a few drops of hydrogen peroxide alone in his room, in the endless nights in the priests' residence behind the school. His tinted glasses. Talking ten to the dozen, brought up on the plain somewhere in Salamanca or Palencia, making a big thing about progress. Girls, kisses, youngsters, vice. Disappearing for all eternity.

The Runner strides onwards. He sees a fresh bit of graffiti on the wall that runs along the street. I LUV YOUR LITTLE BUM. The first time. Father Abril could have gone on endlessly about that, too, in capital letters, and the path to vice. The sound of the priests playing football fades out. The Trinitarian trill.

He spots his motorbike in the distance. His heartbeat's back to normal, his sweat is like a second skin, the air seems to enter his lungs not just through his nostrils and his mouth but also through the pores on his chest and sides, penetrating his T-shirt, his ribs, his veins, that pink sponge used in anatomical drawings to represent the lungs.

He uses the rest of the distance to his bike to do stretches. Calves, quadriceps, hamstrings, flexors.

When he's right beside the motorbike he sees the patch beneath it, the drops of oil. His worst fear. 'Sod it!' He crouches down, touches the oil with his fingertips. 'Sod it! I'll have to scrounge off Mum again.' He pictures his mother's bedroom, the chest of drawers. The pairs of knickers and scarves, the little bundle of banknotes.

He stands up, looks back at the open fields and the school buildings, now visible again. He opens the top box, takes off his T-shirt and puts on a clean one, white with a slightly frayed neck. He puts the sweaty T-shirt in a plastic bag. He breathes deeply. Stretches his flexors. Tells himself that everything will sort itself out sooner or later. It'll sort itself out. He crouches down again, inspects the oil stain on the ground. He looks at the inscrutable engine jutting out from the dirty frame. Piaggio.

Before he closes the top box he looks at his phone. Two missed calls and a WhatsApp from Jorge. Gorgo. He opens it.

Cdn't make it bstard bruv rippd up runng shrts all in bits.
Spk l8r

The Runner rubs at the oil patch with the sole of his trainer. He inspects the muddy clots. He gets on his bike and turns on the ignition. It sounds OK to him. It sounds the same as usual. And the morning is opening up. Like Aladdin's cave.

The ants work away tirelessly. They identify the points of maximum extraction with least effort from the human quarry that's been offered up to them. Their language is chemical. A volatile trail of pheromones.

Different levels of pheromones mean different things. The glands that produce them never stop working. They emit an antediluvian Morse code, perfected over the course of millennia. An alphabet of twelve basic meanings. Alarm, recruitment, trophallaxis, sexual arousal, caste, etc.

The colony forms a frenetic network all around the body that is lying among the dried-out bushes at the foot of the concrete monolith with those five letters **BUEST** written near the top. Over the course of the last few minutes the man – Dionisio G.G., as the local papers and other media outlets would describe him over the next few days – has slightly changed the position of the fingers of his left hand. There have also been some autonomous reflex movements in his stomach.

The temperature has risen by three or four degrees, and the *terral*, that hot wind, reminiscent of a heater about to burst into flames, spreads through the city and takes possession of the derelict sites, the stones and walls, licks at windowpanes and turns the metal blinds of shuttered shopfronts into sizzling grills, envelops people in an almost palpable, tactile aura and melts the asphalt.

The traffic's getting busier on Avenida Ortega y Gasset, and a scrawny individual, clutching a guitar by its neck, is walking across the patch of waste ground towards the two concrete monoliths, as yet unaware of the body covered in ants. Meanwhile, on the other side of the city, in the district known as Los Pinares de San Antón, a man who's occasionally crossed paths in Amelina Marín's notary office with the man who is currently being eaten by insects, is stretched out on a teak-framed deckchair, fiddling with the leaves on a nearby bush. He's tall. His receding hair is combed back, and it's going grey. His chin is almost square, and he has a high forehead. He's wearing an outlandish Hawaiian shirt.

'Céspedes is what all my friends call me, and my employees, too. Why would you want to call me anything else, and why do you want to know the name I was christened with?'

That's what the man is saying to the woman who's lying in the deckchair next to his. She's young, and the two of them are alone in the garden, near the swimming pool. They've been up all night. He's in good spirits and carries on talking.

'Céspedes. Everyone calls me that, from back when I was at school:

employees, clients, people at the bank, and if I were sent to prison that's what they'd call me there as well. Why would you call me anything else, when everyone apart from my mother calls me that? Even my wife does. What's up? Why are you looking at me like that?'

She's looking at him with her mouth open wide, sizing him up and smiling with her eyes as she runs her tongue over the back of her teeth, slowly, as if counting them.

Céspedes goes on. 'Do you think it's odd? Or were you going to say yes if I told you the name on my birth certificate? I've spent the whole night by your side as if I were on guard duty, and there you are, just like an ice maiden – something straight out of the fridge anyway.'

'Was I going to say yes? Yes to what? What do you mean by that? A quick fuck?'

'That's your term, not mine. I'm talking about what makes the world go round, you know, the mutual attraction of the planets, gravitational forces and cellular wavelengths, everything, amino acids and children's ghost stories, Freudian fantasies and everything that makes a man feel attracted by a woman like a tiny pin being sucked into a huge magnet, the ones with more energy than they can cope with. We're cosmic dust, Carole. Men I mean, not women.'

'You're so cute.'

'I'm simply accepting my status as a tiny pin and nothing more.' Céspedes looks up at the trees opposite and runs his fingers through his hair, trying to push it even further back. 'But, like I told you before, I'm more than happy to carry on chatting to you chastely, just as we've been doing all night.'

'Do you think I've got more energy than I can cope with, Céspedes?'

'I can see it in your eyes.'

'So what does that mean? Having a quick fuck is just something you do, and I'm like the girl in the box office telling you whether or not you can buy a ticket to enter? "If you say yes", that's what you said. Well, isn't that great? And then you say we've spent the whole night talking. Well, when our host introduced us it was at least four o'clock in the morning and then you went chasing after the woman in the silver heels who left you high and dry, and it was at least half past five by the time you sat down beside me to stare at the moon.'

The woman sits up, tilts her head to one side – her hair dangling like a dark, heavy curtain – without taking her eyes off Céspedes.

'It wasn't the moon I was staring at; it was the back of your neck, and you were looking at the moon. That's a different thing altogether, don't you think?'

But the woman doesn't respond. She half closes her eyes and looks around, stretching her long neck, and yawns. She's yawning just at the same time as, ten kilometres away, the guy who's walking across the patch of waste ground clutching a guitar by its neck is climbing up a small mound and sees the whole of the first concrete wall, not the one that says **WAS** but the one that has **BUEST** written on it at the top, and he carries on, blinded by the sun in the same measure as he's blinded by the adulterated heroin and cocaine that's running through his veins. He walks across the stony clay, through a sea of weeds and plastic, tin cans and pieces of brick. And that's how, while he's still moving, while he's still moving forward, our hallucinating hero first of all mistakes the prone body for some wire mesh or a dead animal, perhaps a goat, and then for a dusty bundle of something that's been dumped, until he's right up close, when he feels the powerful morning heat bouncing back from the concrete wall, and he focuses his eyes and understands. He's shocked and he understands, all at once.

Carole, the woman who's yawning, lies there with her head to one side and her hair hanging down like a soft pendulum. The temperature in that garden is six or seven degrees lower than it is in the ants' waste ground. Over here you can hardly feel the *terral*, and there's a faint aroma coming from the pine trees, and the man, staring into her eyes, says, 'I fancy you. God, I really fancy you. I've always fancied women like you, although I've never, I've never really met one, but I've always, from what I've read and from what I've fantasized about, I've always known that women like you existed, and here you are right now, and I feel like a castaway on a desert island who's found the key to a safe full of millions of euros over on the other side of the world, honestly, yes, honestly, or do I look like I need to lie to you or even want to?'

Carole gives him a sarcastic glare, with one eyebrow raised and a half-smile.

He continues. 'I can feel it right here, in my heart, in my gut, and it may be too late for all that, but it's fine, I'll treat it as a gift anyway, even if you're still there looking at me with that expression on your face, or precisely *because* you're looking at me like that. I recognize you. You're one of them. You're one of those very few women, maybe only one in every two hundred square kilometres or whatever but spread very thin, and they've always given me the slip, always. Whenever I went into a room they'd leave through the other door, and whenever I got on a train they were always on a different platform, or it was the coward in me whispering in my head that those inaccessible women I was searching for were the ones who had just left through the other door or the ones on the other side of the glass when it was too late to speak to them or go up to them, they were too far away so I could allow myself to dream, to fantasize. But not any more. Perhaps I had to go through everything I've gone through just to be here and tell you all about it. Now I'm not looking at you from a train or sitting in another car at the traffic lights or on the other side of the road, you're sitting next to me in this ridiculous place, this morning, and anything's possible now after quite an absurd night and day and month and life. I don't want to go on about it any more, but I don't want you to float away like a soap bubble either. I've said enough, I've already scattered a few petals on the steps of the altar, don't you think? And I'm not trying to make something out of it. Don't look at me like that. Sometimes a person says what he feels, more or less, but that's it basically.'

Céspedes stands up, the deckchair creaking as it is freed of his weight. He puts his hands on his hips and stares out at the swimming pool, completely absorbed, as if the swimming pool were his past. Then he turns around and looks up at the house, towards the balcony overlooking the garden.

'Did you know that they shot a film here in this house – or part of a film?'

'People have been telling me that all night. The owner and God knows how many others. They ought to put a marble plaque by the door.'

'Yes. And did they also tell you that the scene was – or one of the scenes was – a sort of orgy, and then one girl ended up committing suicide in the garden and Juan Diego was sitting beside her crying? It must have been right here on this bit of lawn.'

'They spared me the details. So there was an orgy here, group sex or something? Who's Juan Diego? Another friend of yours, like them?'

'No.'

'No what?'

'No to everything. There wasn't an orgy and he's not my friend and I hardly know anyone here, one of the owner's friends or maybe two, that's all, I was forgetting you're French and you don't know who's who in this country. A little girl lost in the woods, running away from the wolf and being French or half-French or three-quarters French she wouldn't know any sad little Spanish actors.'

'The thing about the little girl lost in the woods, is that a special turn-on for you? You already told me that one last night.'

'No, it's just something about you. I'd like to know what kind of wolf you're running away from, though it could just as well be the wolf that ran away. Juan Diego's a huge actor, my family almost worships him when he appears on TV. He played Don Juan and did all that kind of thing, you know, with the guys in tights and starched collars, but he had him down to a T, he was like a method actor . . .'

'Very interesting. Back to what we were saying, since you won't tell me your name, can I call you Cespedito? It sounds right. It goes with your style.'

Céspedes looks down at himself in his Hawaiian shirt, Bermuda shorts and boat shoes.

'That's a bit of a cheap shot. On the other hand, your name really does sound right, I even like your name, Carole. And this,' he says, looking down at his shirt again, 'this is the uniform you're given when you've been kicked out of your own house, that's all.'

The woman shrugs, still smiling. 'Yeah. Another local custom.'

'Yes, you see?' He sighs and pulls a face as if he's tired. 'I've been away from home for two days, and I feel as if I've been released from a cage. Perhaps my wife thinks she's shut me out of my nest by closing the door behind me, and I'm outside in the open air with too much space. Freedom is very confusing.'

Carole watches him. Céspedes raises his eyes to the heavens, and to

Carole his chin looks even more square, his mouth half open with his big teeth. She's looking at his wide shoulders and his solid back when Céspedes turns around again and goes up to the edge of the swimming pool still mumbling something that she can't understand. Somehow she's growing rather fond of this man.

Jorge, Ismael's younger brother, the coward, who didn't turn up for the Runner's training session this morning, hangs a right on Avenida Juan XXIII and turns into Avenida de Europa, fiddling with the air conditioning. The blast of air pumping out of the ducts gets hotter and hotter. He slams the dashboard with the palm of his hand. *Heap of shit. My cousin and his shitty car!* He looks up, swerves to avoid some idiot coming straight at him who's sounding his horn noisily *fuck you!* turns into the entrance to the patch of derelict land used for parking, flicks the indicator and reverses into the vacant parking spot. *Fuck his mother!*

Jorge gets out of the car, a Renault Kangoo with the back windows blanked out to form part of the bodywork with signage for his cousin's business printed over it in a semi-circle, **MOLDURAS Y MARCOS FERRER** (Ferrer's Mouldings and Frames), with the address, **Avda. Europa 45**, cutting across the top. On one side of the lettering there are two artists' brushes, one crossing the other like the crossbones on a pirate flag. On the other side there's a logo, very badly drawn, supposedly a cherry tree sprouting a few leaves and some things that are probably meant to be cherries but look more like meatballs. Jorge stifles the urge to give the car a kick. He makes do with thumping the logo, which makes a sound like a muffled gong. When he turns around he sees Vane, the girl from Calzados Famita, the shoeshop, getting out of her car.

'What's up? Don't you like your wheels? You're going to put a dent in it like that.'

Jorge smiles and looks around *fuck everything!* and inspects the panel he's just thumped.

'No, it's not that. There was some moron back there looking for trouble,' he says, nodding towards the far end of the avenue. He's ashamed to admit that the air conditioning doesn't work.

He stands there, squinting in the sun, waiting for the shop assistant to get her handbag and something else from her car. Curly hair, straw-blonde, straight out of a bottle. White leggings. Jorge takes the opportunity to admire her behind *she must be wearing a thong* and wonders whether she's sweating and thinks about the taste of his girlfriend's sweat. He turns around just as the shop assistant gets out of the car completely and nudges the door shut with her hip.

When she comes up to him, Jorge realizes that she's taller than he is. *Fucking high heels.* Nothing ever works out for him. Never. His brother Ismael is fifteen centimetres taller than him.

The smell of burned stubble wafts up from either side of the patch of waste ground. Right then the smell seems sensual to Jorge. Marijuana. Incense sticks. They walk along together, Jorge trying to follow a straight line, the shop assistant, in contrast, zigzagging a little, clutching a blue folder, her handbag nestled on one side. She's wearing pink lipstick. It's thick and creamy. Too much. She has dark eyes and eyebrows and yellowish hair, curls bouncing across her bronzed forehead. Jorge's erection reaches maximum rigidity when he notices the streak of black eyeliner.

'You're a bit early, aren't you?'

The girl puts on a pair of sunglasses, transforming her face, making her look older *and even more stunning.*

'Tell that to my boss. We're up to our eyes getting everything ready for the sales. I was here until half past one last night, and all I got was a lousy rum and coke from the bar on the corner.'

'What a pain.' Jorge screws his face up, pretending to be upset. *He probably wants to hump you.* He pictures the back room in the shoe-shop, the smell of leather that hit him when he went in there one afternoon. He imagines the blonde girl lying on the table with her legs wide apart, her arse on the Formica tabletop and the shoeshop owner standing in front of her. He remembers the sight of his girlfriend's nipples two nights back as she lay there with her eyes half closed, saying, 'More.'

'But he's not a bad person. Basically.' The girl smiles, raises one hand and waves her fingers in the air as if she wants Jorge to count them or something.

'What?'

'Ciao. I'm off to get some cigarettes. Bye for now.'

'Yeah. See you later, Vane . . . *Vane*. He could repeat her name a thousand times. *Vane, Vane, and she was right here looking into my eyes.*

Her hair bounces against the back of her neck in time with her footsteps. Her deep-pink blouse sways, and the white leggings cling to every millimetre of her legs. Stilettoes. Jorge stops at the curb, lets two cars go by, crosses the road. He remembers the moron tooting his horn. He goes past the shoeshop window. SALE!!! UNBEATABLE OFFERS!!! And he turns to look at the shop assistant's now-distant figure. The bell rings. There's no one in the shop. They're in the workshop at the back. He goes around behind the counter, towards the back room. His cousin's talking to Pedroche.

'Good morning.' Jorge wonders whether that's the first time anyone's ever said good morning here. It's like at school when he'd go to the headmaster's office to be told off for something his brother had done.

His cousin looks up, and his lips curl into something vaguely resembling a smile. 'How're things, mate?'

Pedroche is sitting on a high stool and looks at him out of the corner of his eye, and the only thing that comes out of his mouth sounds a bit like 'Hmmm'.

'Air con's broken on the car. Doesn't work.'

His cousin looks at him as if he hasn't understood.

'Are you sure?'

'Nothing but hot air.'

'For crying out loud, I don't believe it! I only got it fixed last year. What have you done to it, mate?'

'The year before last.'

'What d'you mean, the year before last? It was last year.'

'The year before.'

Pedroche butts in from his corner without looking up from the frame he's putting together. 'The year before last, Floren. Paquito drove it over there, may he rest in peace.'

'You sure it's not working? It's really hot today. You probably put it on max, you're so antsy, and you stripped the thread and it's flipped on the heating.'

'It's not working. It's got nothing to do with the thread.'

'Did you collect the money from the hotel for the mouldings? From the Valleniza?'

'Yes, in the evening, after we closed.'

'Good. Leave it in the till with the invoice. Did they give you any hassle?'

Jorge shakes his head. His cousin comes towards him, almost brushing against him. Jorge feels nervous, but there's no reason to be. Floren glances over at Pedroche and whispers, 'What a sight! Don't ask him what happened to his face.'

'What?' Jorge frowns, reassured but confused.

His cousin whispers, 'I'll tell you later. His wife beat him up. Don't say a word. I'll tell you later.' Then he turns towards Pedroche. 'OK, I'm off for some breakfast. You coming?'

Pedroche makes a vague affirmative gesture without taking his eyes off the frame he's working on, and it goes without saying that he utters his favourite word 'Hmmm' but quieter than usual. He puts down the glue brush. He cleans it meticulously and carefully puts the lid back on the bottle as if it contains high explosives.

He slowly gets down from his stool and takes off his blue apron. He hangs it up. Stubby legs. Chubby. He's the same height when he's off the stool as he was when he was sitting on it. He walks towards the door.

As he passes, Jorge can see his injuries. His cheek is grazed and scratched. On the top of his head, almost in the centre of his bald patch, he's got two plasters that don't quite cover his swollen skin, which is bright pink. He's got a black eye. Looking at his back, Jorge thinks he can see some scratch marks under his shirt collar as well.

Jorge turns back towards his cousin with a frown and a quizzical expression, but Floren ignores him and opens the shop door. Pedroche's squat figure follows him quietly. Like cattle being led to the slaughter-house. They hit them on the head with a mallet, or at least they used to. Apparently they electrocute them now. It makes no difference: they still have convulsions when they're being gutted. They slump to the floor releasing thick clouds of steam. Pedroche closes the door behind him. The shop bell, from China or wherever it was manufactured, makes the usual nasty tinkling noise. Vicente, the halfwit from the butcher's shop, says the sound of it makes him want to pee.

Jorge waits a few seconds. Then he goes to the till and opens it. He takes the money out of his wallet and puts it in the till. He also takes the invoice his cousin mentioned out of his wallet and unfolds it. He checks that the numbers he's falsified tally with the cash he's left in the till. He hears a woman's footsteps on the pavement. *Vane.* But then the woman whose feet are responsible appears on the other side of the shop window. She's middle aged, short, and she's wearing men's trousers. Jorge has a flashback to the shoeshop assistant bending over, her body half inside the car, her lips, a lock of hair across her perfect forehead. *Perfect.* Her eyes all made up behind her sunglasses, a body in the night.

He takes out his phone. He notices that the Runner's seen his message but hasn't replied. *He'll be pissed off. Another one to add to the collection. To the pile of shit.* Like his brother, like the moron blowing his horn, like the concierge with his face like a sheep. *Electrocuted.* Like his mother, who can't keep Ismael, the bastard, under control. *Vane.*

He opens the photo gallery on his phone. He taps on one of his girlfriend on the beach. Topless. He zooms in, concentrating on her mouth. Her lips. There's the scar in the corner of her mouth, on the left-hand side, small but prominent enough to make her look slightly severe, even when she's smiling, like in the photo. Jorge likes that scar, the effect it produces. *If she didn't have one, I'd make one for her with a knife.* One day he told her, 'If you didn't have one, I'd make one for you with a knife,' and she laughed and at the same time she shook her head, flattered but also feigning repulsion. 'If I had the money I'd get rid of it. I'd get plastic surgery.'

Jorge returns the photo to its normal size and then homes in on her breasts, zooming in, studying her nipples, her areolae, their creamy colour, their smoothness, little explosions. *Baby volcanoes.* He slowly returns the photo to its normal size, displaying the full volume of her breasts. *The weight of them, they're heavy. And smooth and soft.* He can see the folds of her abdomen and then her bikini bottoms, bright orange, and the top is scrunched up *like a dog that's been run over* and cast aside on the towel.

Jorge goes back to WhatsApp and taps on his girlfriend's name. He starts typing.

what you doing?

He stares at the screen, at his girlfriend's tiny profile picture. He doesn't like that picture, but she won't change it. He starts typing again.

where R U?

He pictures her at home, talking to her mother, that soulless and insincere woman. The phone vibrates. It's Gloria.

sleeping, sweetie

Jorge pictures his girlfriend's bedroom, in darkness, he remembers when he saw her there when he went in to wake her up two weeks back. Her mother looking on from the dining room, and he was calling her, 'Gloria, Gloria', her leg peeking out beneath the sheet, up to her thigh, and as she turned over he saw her Hollywood wax.

in the nude?

no, just sleeping

That's awesome! Her pussy, naked. Her thigh, her groin, the sheet.

Jorge puts his phone away. His cousin Floren and Pedroche are leaning on the bar in La Esquinita. The temperature's rising on the patch of waste ground opposite the bar, where the cars are parked and where until a few years back there used to be huge Campsa fuel tanks looming up like ancient spaceships. The *terral* is spreading out across the city, over the pavements and the rows of shop windows and the cars' metallic bodywork and the asphalt. A desert wind, bone dry, curling up cardboard and shrivelling timbers, drying them out, expelling every last trace of moisture from everything, making the furniture contract. It blows slowly, like a menacing beast, taking over streets and enveloping passers-by in its furnace-like breath. It's a more gentle wind in Los Pinares and on the sheltered, prosperous side of the city, and it gets stronger on the plains where the population has spread, in Portada Alta, La Barriguilla, the Viso estate, Los Prados, the San Andrés neighbourhood, La Luz, La Paz, Virgen de Belén. One enormous greenhouse, a warehouseful of humanity.

The *terral* runs down the ravines formed by the smaller rivers, the alluvial zone created by the sands and clays of the Tertiary period, engulfing them. The soil is absorbent, ideal for the process of humectation and desiccation, swelling with the rain and contracting in the dry heat like a cornered animal, under the *terral* wind that befuddles humans and stimulates insects. On the patch of waste ground opposite the BP garage, the man being eaten alive by ants is now completely exposed to the sun. His temperature is almost forty degrees, and the ants are scampering around, determined, as steadfast as machines, and a few hundred paces away the man who was walking towards the concrete monoliths clutching a guitar is now talking to the other man at the petrol station, the one with a face like a fish who's wearing green overalls.

'He's just lying there, next to those pillars, the ones over there,' says the man with the guitar, and he points towards the waste ground, towards the advertising hoardings where a man and a woman are sleeping on the best mattress in the world, where a red car appears to be flying alongside a Caribbean beach.

'There, next to that concrete thing,' he says, pointing with his free hand, waving his arms around and his guitar bumps against one of the pumps *boing* and bounces off, while the other man looks at him suspiciously.

'What do you mean, what concrete thing, where?'

'I've just told you, boss.'

'Calm down, calm down, tell me exactly what you mean without getting uptight, OK?'

A few minutes earlier the guy with the guitar had gone up to the man lying on the ground and was mesmerized by the swarm of ants, and he'd taken a few steps back and looked about and started walking towards the other side of the petrol station and then gone back and poked the man on the ground's foot with the tip of his shoe, then he'd gone up even closer and patted his trouser pockets looking for a wallet or a phone and hadn't found anything, he'd shaken the ants off his fingers, hadn't wanted to put his hands in the man's pockets *fingerprints, DNA, they can do all sorts nowadays* then looked around again, and there, in the distance, in the window of the building overlooking the waste ground he thought he saw a human figure, hiding *they've seen me*, and he looked left and right and then there wasn't anyone at the window *they've seen me, and they'll grass me up*, and he'd carried on walking and then finally, timidly, he'd changed direction and headed towards the green BP sign.

'Jesús! Jesús!' The man in the overalls calls over to the shop. A young man appears. 'Jesús, call the police. This bloke's saying something about someone lying out there on the ground covered in millions of ants.'

A few customers come over, attracted by the shouting and all the commotion. The man with the guitar looks left and right and then stares at the man in the green overalls so much he almost goes cross-eyed.

'I don't want any problems, boss. I've made my report.'

'That's fine. You wait here.'

'I was going for a crap, boss, and then suddenly I found him there.'

'That's OK. If you want to, you can have a crap in the toilet over there. Knock yourself out. Just don't mess me about.'

'Crawling with ants like he was dead. He was like a sack of cement, boss, with all that dust. What was I supposed to do? He was just lying there.'

'But he's not dead,' one of the onlookers states rather than asks.

'I don't know. I was going for a crap.'

'Going for a crap or sniffing around,' the man in the green overalls says under his breath. 'It's anyone's guess what he actually saw.'

'Sniffing around? What do you mean? No need to insult me. What do you know about sniffing around? I'm minding my own business, and I find him there with all the ants. He could have been stabbed.'

'OK, when the police get here, you tell them that or whatever.'

'It's nothing to do with me any more. It's none of my business. He's lying there, next to one of the walls or those concrete things, over there by that thing you can see behind the hoardings.'

'We ought to go and take a look,' says one of the onlookers.

The man next to him shrugs his shoulders. The man in the green overalls tells everyone to stay where they are. He repeats that it remains to be seen whether the man with the guitar is making it all up as a wind-up and because he's high on drugs.

One of the customers laughs. 'Do you think he might be?'

Another one shakes his head, squinting over towards the two concrete monoliths. 'You can't actually see anything. It's too far away. We'll have to go and take a look. Bring some water, Manolo,' he says to his companion. 'Get a bottle from the car in case we can do something.'

The man called Manolo gets a big bottle of water from the car, and the other man looks over towards the waste ground using his hand to shield his eyes.

The guitar man's no longer listening to anyone, and he's looking from side to side. He tries to pluck up some courage. 'This is too much! I'm going for a crap. I find this guy on the ground, and I come over here and people want to screw me around. I should have just gone and left him. Instead I draw the short straw for being Mr Nice Guy.'

'Didn't you say you needed a crap? Well, go on then. I don't want to be screwed around either, so back off.' The man in the green overalls places his feet apart like a boxer. He's feeling good for the first time that day, or maybe that week.

The young man looks out and calls over to the man in the green overalls from the shop doorway, 'They're on their way, Bartolo. And an ambulance, too.'

'Bartolo? What kind of name is that?'

'What's wrong with you?' says the man in the green overalls, moving towards the guitar man, who takes a step back and goes off towards the toilets talking incessantly in a voice that's getting louder and louder.

'"What's wrong with you?" he says. Sod this for a game of soldiers. Take me for an idiot? You've got a nerve, firing off insults and taking your problems out on everyone else.' He goes into the toilet. 'I'll have a crap all right, you bastard.' He leans his guitar against the wall. 'But I won't be able to go now anyway, what with that dickhead and the other bastard crawling with ants.' He looks at the washbasin, the soap dispenser, in the corners. Impossible to hide anything there. 'Just my fucking luck.' He opens the cubicle door, takes a wrap out of his pocket and carries on looking. He tries to remove a tile that looks a bit loose; his blackened fingernails scratch at the edges, but he can't get it off. He hears voices outside. He reaches towards the basket that's there for used toilet paper, takes out two or three pieces, feeling sick. He unravels one. 'Fucking bastards.' He pulls off a sheet from the toilet roll balanced on the cistern, rolls up the wrap in it and then covers the little package with a bit of used tissue. The voices come closer. 'He hasn't left, has he?' says a policeman almost from the threshold of the toilet door. 'He's in there,' says the dickhead in the green overalls. Bartolo. He's got a nerve.

The guitar man bolts the toilet door shut and quickly drops his trousers.

'Hey, you, are you in there?'

'I'm having a crap, for fuck's sake.'

He pulls the chain, gives a fake cough and places the little bundle into the basket then covers it with another piece of used tissue. He puts his trousers back on noisily. 'And what with this bloody heat, what a load of shit.' He makes a gulping sound, coughs and opens the cubicle door.

Doctor Galán is walking down the corridor, where she meets Blasco, a nurse, a seasoned veteran, who stops in front of her and tells her, 'The guy in orthopaedics with the tibia and fibula is ready whenever you want.'

'OK, I'm just going to make a phone call, then I'll come and find you.'

I'll come and find you. Anyone can see right through me, that worried look in my eyes, a stone falling down a well. A stone falling that never stops falling down that vertical tunnel, waiting in vain for the splash in the water. That's the feeling dragging Dr Galán down, a stone in endless freefall down her chest cavity where no light has penetrated for months, years. *Not even a trace of natural light. Just artificial light and only artificial light, every day. Dioni. He disappears, and I'm the one who's lost my way, stuck in a labyrinth, lost.*

She's a tall brunette with greenish eyes and round cheeks. Her hair is tied up in a high ponytail. Her sensual full lips are caught in parentheses between two expression lines. Dr Galán, accident-and-emergency specialist, mother to an apparently well-behaved teenager, wife to a lawyer with a brilliant past, Dionisio Grandes Guimerá.

She walks into her on-call room, takes out her phone and puts on a pair of black-framed glasses. She looks through her contacts. **Julia M.** She taps the screen. Julia answers on the sixth or seventh ring, and there's a sound of clothes rustling, a deep, sleepy sigh before someone speaks.

'What's up, Ana?'

'Were you asleep?'

'No, well, it doesn't matter, I'd just dropped off.'

'You haven't heard anything then?'

'So you haven't either? Nor me. That guy who sometimes bumps into him when he's out on a bar crawl hasn't phoned back.'

'I see.'

'I left him three or four messages, but no answer, then I fell asleep. So now . . .'

'I see.'

'Hang on, he's just sent me a message. I'll have a look.'

'Yes, do.'

Dr Galán looks at the X-ray on the desk, the light-blue colour of the bone and the black line of the fracture.

'Ana? He says he hasn't seen him and doesn't know anything.'

'I see. Well, I don't know. I'm going to . . . I'm going to call the police.'

'Really? The other times . . .'

'It's been two days. More. Since Tuesday . . .'

Silence.

'Something's happened.'

'I don't know, Ana. I don't know what to say, to tell you the truth. I'll get dressed and come over.'

'No, don't worry. I'll wait a bit longer.'

'I'll have a shower and come over.'

'Something must have happened. It was always going to happen. That's all.'

'I'll be half an hour.'

'I'll let you go. Don't worry, I'll let you go.'

'I'll be there in half an hour.'

'Whatever you like.'

Dr Galán presses her thumb on the picture of the red telephone, cutting the line. She's tempted to phone her husband again even though she knows that once again she'll hear the automated voice telling her that the phone's switched off or out of range. She looks at his picture on her phone. He's smiling but sad. Bitterness with a sweet smile. Now his lips are covered in ants, his skin is yellowish and dull under the sun on the waste ground. Men driven crazy by the world.

She takes off her glasses and looks over to the window, the view of the car park dissected by the blind's slats. She takes a deep breath, rubs her hands on her cheeks, strong fingers *just like me, strong*, and she leaves the room.

Men driven crazy by the world, the Runner thinks to himself as he takes the stairs two at a time up to his flat. Calle Martínez de la Rosa, a narrow building, a dark stairway. *Just like being nowhere, this flat, this street, these people.* The block is painted white, surrounded by low houses, and it's near Calle Barón de Les. The Runner goes up through its innards until he arrives at the fifth floor. The door on the left. The peephole's scratched, and the outline of the Sacred Heart emblem belonging to the previous owner is still etched into the dark varnish. *A year and a half, two years there. It'll be there for ever.* He opens the door and goes in.

There's a smell of cooking. *So early.* He wants to gag.

'What a stink.'

His mother hasn't heard him, she hasn't understood what he said, doesn't even look up. She's chopping up some vegetables to go into the steaming pot.

'There you are. You've been a long time.'

'It's the bike.' The Runner goes down the narrow corridor, leaving his mother and the kitchen behind him. And the smell.

'What?'

'The bike! It's bust again.'

He sees his grandmother sitting on the leatherette sofa.

'Hi.'

'How are you doing, son? So the motorbicycle's broken down again?'

'Yep.'

His mother pokes her head into the corridor, drying her hands on her apron, glasses perched on the end of her nose, as if she put them there just to annoy the Runner. 'What's up?'

'Nothing.' The Runner sits down on the edge of the bed and takes off his trainers.

His grandmother turns her head and shouts down the corridor, 'It's the motorbicycle. It's broken down again.'

His mother comes in. 'Will it cost much?'

'I don't know. They'll let me know.'

'Did you take it to Leandro?'

'Why Leandro?' The Runner gets to his feet, and his mother looks at the impression he's made in the bedcover.

'Look at the bedspread. I've told you a thousand times not to sit down as soon as you come in all sweaty. It leaves a stain, and here's me like a housemaid.'

'For Christ's sake!'

His grandmother chips in, 'He's tired after all that running. It won't leave a stain.'

'It's not you who has to wash it.'

'I've done more than my fair share of washing, and in this home, too.'

The Runner's mother ignores the old woman, leans back against the doorframe again and speaks to her son.

'So you didn't take it to Leandro? He's a neighbour, he's got his own bike shop and garage just next door. It's a very nice shop.'

'I don't know him. I took it where I always go, back where we used to live, to Niño del Sordo.'

His grandmother's wriggling in her armchair, trying to turn it around. *Like an astronaut lost in space.* She can't bear to be left out of the conversation. 'And you walked back all the way, son, after your run?'

'He'd have caught the bus. You caught the bus, didn't you?'

'What bus? There aren't any buses over there. What about the boiler? Didn't I ask you to turn it on for me? Now the water will be cold for my shower.'

'It doesn't take a minute to warm up. You have your juice, and it'll warm up. Anyway, what with this heat . . . but it doesn't take a minute, you have to pick holes in everything and find fault, and I can never do anything right.' His mother goes off down the gloomy corridor towards the kitchen, towards the stench. 'The juice is nice and fresh.'

The Runner turns on the boiler. It reminds him of an old Russian space capsule that's been patched up, with its seized-up temperature gauge and evidence of several coats of paint. He leaves the bathroom and goes back to sit on the edge of the bed, sees his grandmother's profile, her hair in a bun, her black housecoat with little white patterns on it. *Protozoans.* Yellowing flesh dangling from her arms. *Like a corpse.* And her hand with its shaky fingers stroking the brown leatherette.

'How's it all going down in Cape Canaveral, Grandma?'

'How's what?'

'At Space Command? How's it going? Are you landing on the moon any time soon?'

'Come off it now with your silly jokes,' she says, smoothing down a crease on her dress. 'So what are you going to do with that motorbicycle now? You'll need it if you land yourself a job.'

The Runner sighs deeply, suddenly feeling like his blood has silted up. *I don't want to live like they live, I don't want their life, I should go somewhere, I don't know, go off and be reborn as someone else somewhere else.* He stands up, goes towards the bathroom.

'I don't know, Granny, I just don't know.' And he closes the door.

The Runner's grandmother sits there deep in thought. She leans over slowly and peers out in the direction of the kitchen. Her hand is shaking. She puts on her best voice and calls out softly, obsequiously, 'Antonia.' *I know she heard me.*

She waits. She looks towards the corridor, then calls out in a slightly stronger voice, but still obsequiously, 'Antonia.' *She's a bad one; she's always been a bad one.* 'Antonia!'

'What? What's wrong?'

'The television.'

'Why all the shouting? What's wrong?'

Why all the shouting indeed; she's always having a go at me.

'Can you switch it on for me so I can watch *La Mañana*?'

'All this shouting, and that's all it is! I thought there was a fire or something.'

'No, there isn't any fire. It's just to take my mind off things. If I watch Silvia, it takes my mind off things.'

'You could switch it on yourself. You'll end up going to your grave and still not knowing how to turn on the television. You don't even know how to use the remote.'

Always going on about dying if she doesn't mention it maybe she'll explode and everyone has to die when their time comes, like Anita, only twenty-nine and look at her.

The Runner's mother presses the button on the remote; the old woman repositions her chair, her jaw trembling.

'There you are. The TV's on.'

'Look, it's Silvia.'

'That's all I'm here for, to listen to this nonsense.'

The Runner gets under the jet of cold water, like needles piercing his skin, the echo of voices on the television coming through the walls – *Here in the studio with us today is the leading specialist . . .* – clapping, his mother's voice passing by the other side of the door *that's all I'm here for, to listen to this nonsense*, the water feels like a brief moment of freedom *everyone drowning, everyone, men driven crazy by the world, and here's me still in my cage tomorrow.*

The Runner gets under the jet of water. He'd like to sink beneath the surface, make himself crystalline, escape down the plughole beneath his veiny foot. He has a vivid recollection of a rainy night that winter, his night-time uneasiness allayed by the raindrops tapping against the windowpane. The Runner and his thoughts are all water, a colourless liquid, water slipping away obediently on a journey to the centre of the earth.

The Runner is thinking, the birds are tracing a tangle of invisible lines across the sky, the ants are working away like metallic machines, like lifeless pieces of equipment, and men are wandering around and are working like men, wearing themselves out, getting bored, tired, lost, and in the bar on the corner, La Esquinita, Pedroche shakes his head like a dull pendulum, like a spinning top that's run out of spin and says, 'No, I just can't do it.' He shakes his head and opens his fleshy pink eyelids, slightly purple in one corner, opens his eyelids just as, on the other side of the city, an energetic, mature man called Céspedes looks up and watches, through the branches of a monkey-puzzle tree, the streaks of blue sky where the summer birds are practising their frenetic movements, their geometry, and says, 'Come on, let's go, I'll treat you,' and the young woman looks at him, half sarcastic and half surprised, pretending she's a heartless woman, the hard young woman who's seen it all before, and asks him, 'Where? What for?'

'No, I just can't do it,' says Pedroche, shaking his enormous, bald, injured head slowly, like an ox. His moustache is blondish, almost ginger.

'I can't live, carry on living like this with that woman.' His voice is soft, the tone bitter. 'Each day she gets worse. I was tricked, I was tricked well and good. They saw me coming way off and saddled me with a lunatic.'

Floren is leaning against the bar, watching him. He raises an eyebrow, and the other man turns towards the window, looks out at the street, chewed up by the sun, the hot air disturbed by the passing cars, the flat plain extending beyond the patch of waste ground, the improvised car park, the brown and yellow weeds covering that stretch of barren land in the middle of the city.

He's got a head like a hippopotamus, thinks Floren, *or an enormous pig, a nice pig, with his injuries and bruises.* Floren focuses on Pedroche's beady eyes, light green but cloudy, which might have been attractive in another face, and as he studies them carefully he feels embarrassed, and to dispel his embarrassment he starts talking. 'I don't know, mate, she's had other crises like this one before, what can I say? You're the one living through it, so what can I say to you except be patient?'

'No, I've had enough, I . . .' Pedroche looks from side to side. 'It's over.'

'Once you've had a chance to cool down a bit then you can think it through. Don't do anything hasty in your state, the first thing to sort out is the money, get that back and the jewellery and then let everything calm down.'

'Eighteen hundred euros, can you believe it? The rings are worth a fortune, they were her grandmother's, and the bracelets and some earrings I gave her when we got engaged. I was tricked like a real dickhead.'

'Well, the priest isn't going to keep it all, he knows, he'll know that she's not right in the head, and he'll give it all back to you, he's not going to keep the money. Do you know where he lives or what you're going to do? Go and see him at the church?'

Pedroche looks defeated, stares at the remains of his tonic water, down in the dumps. Floren's scared he's going to burst into tears. He looks at the waiter and thinks it's just as well he's with some customers at the other end of the bar.

Floren wants to bring him out of himself. 'So then, what are you going to do? Go to the church? If you like I'll come with you, we'll both go, the two of us.'

'Either that or I'll find out where the priest lives from the woman who runs the newspaper kiosk, though he should have given it back to me as soon as she gave him everything, eighteen hundred euros for charity and whatever the rest of it's worth, for the needy she says, and when I say, "It's my money that money's mine," she goes and takes her boot off as calm as you like as if it was something normal or she'd been thinking about it since Christ knows when and I thought she's got something in her boot that's hurting her or it's because it's too hot I don't know why she's wearing boots in this heat, wearing boots in the summer, and as soon as she's got it off, wham, she grabs it by the leg and, wham, that big fat heel in my face, on my head, we nearly crashed and there's her: wham-bam . . .'

'OK, yeah.' Floren's scared his friend's going to burst into tears or have a fit of rage.

'I was driving, and she's hitting me like there's no tomorrow, like she's trying with all her strength to kill me with that heel and calling me a mangy dog, a selfish pig and a bastard, she kept on and on with the bastard thing, and if I hadn't managed to stop the car we'd both be dead.'

Pedroche is panting as if he were still driving, and his wife, Belita, were still hitting his head and face and arms with her boot, in the middle of a summer's evening, near the sea, with the clouds stretching out like puffs of cotton wool then fizzling out like a dog's drool around a trace of the moon that only just dared to quiver on the horizon, that tunnel.

*

For the second time Céspedes tells the taxi driver to turn the radio down *. . . the young man, nineteen years old, originally from Somalia with a Norwegian passport, based in London . . .* The taxi driver, before reaching over to the volume button on the steering wheel, calmly examines Céspedes in the rear-view mirror . . . *killed an American woman and injured five other people on Wednesday night . . .* The taxi driver takes the opportunity to take a look at the young woman, Carole, who's sitting next to Céspedes. Then he presses the button and turns down the volume just a bit . . . *the police are working on the theory that it was a random act . . .*

Céspedes stops staring at the taxi driver's reflection in the rear-view mirror. He feels a buzzing in his groin. He buckles under the sceptical look the young woman gives him. He manages to take his phone out of his pocket. Damn. He looks at the screen. Julia.

. . . psychologically disturbed. A Spanish family that was walking through Russell Square . . .

'Fucking hell, what a pain, she's such a bore, she's sent me twenty messages.'

'Well if you don't pick up you're going to end up with thirty before you know it. If you like I'll cover my ears. Or stick my head out of the window. Is that all right, taxi driver, you don't mind if I stick my head out of the window?'

. . . the area where the attack took place was back to normal by yesterday morning . . .

'I can't tell if you're being serious or joking, madam, or is it miss?'

The buzzing persists, the phone quivers in Céspedes's huge paw.

'No, it's not a joke.'

'Listen I don't need any problems, you see, you may not realize it, but this is a very tricky job.'

. . . the senior officer in Scotland Yard's counter-terrorism squad, Mark Rowles . . .

'Turn the radio off would you, please, just turn it off.'

The taxi driver, no longer looking in the rear-view mirror, decides to obey.

. . . the investigation, which aimed to

Céspedes runs his thumb over the screen and lifts it to his ear.

'Hi, Julia.'

'Didn't you see my messages?'

'Yes, damn it, and I sent you one back, I'm not completely useless. And if this acquaintance of yours has ended up homeless . . .'

'He's not an acquaintance, he's a friend, a good friend of my brother's.'

'It makes no difference, Julia, even if he was the brother I never had.'

'Yeah.'

'I can't do anything. I'll have a look and see next week.'

'And no question of us meeting up, obviously.'

'Next week.'

'Anyway, try and make contact. Give him a call, at least.'

'I'll try.'

'OK, good. If you find anything out call me. It's serious, otherwise I wouldn't be breaking your balls about it, OK?'

'OK.'

Céspedes presses the red button to ring off. The young woman looks at him. Céspedes shrugs his shoulders. 'What?'

'Nothing.'

They go past the old warehouses at the port. *The boats' yellow sadness*, Céspedes recalls a line from the poet Juvenal Soto. He whispers, 'The boats' yellow sadness . . .'

The woman looks at him, without letting on whether she's understood or even heard what he murmured. The taxi driver turns off the extension of Muelle de Heredia into the Avenida Ingeniero José María Garnica. They leave the port's cranes and stacks of containers behind. The taxi driver can see the outlines of Céspedes's powerful head and the woman's long, dark hair against the white light coming through the rear window.

'She's a friend who wants to sort out half the world's problems, or maybe the whole world's problems, except for mine.'

'From what I can see, you ought to call yourself "Céspedes and his Affairs". Get one of those little badges and pin it on your chest,' says Carole.

Julia Mamea. Julia in another taxi, four or five years ago. Fifteen hundred, two thousand nights ago. Sitting between him and Ortuño. That smile with the sad eyes that he'd already recognized perfectly by then and identified as an expression not of reluctance but desire. The night flashed past the windows with the flickering of the street lamps, and Céspedes kissed her again, her soft lips, her saliva, the tip of her tongue. When he opened his eyes he saw Julia's hand on Ortuño's thigh and, still kissing her, he exchanged glances with his friend. He made an affirmative gesture with his eyes, granting permission, and Ortuño's hand moved up to Julia's breast and rested there like a weightless bird, caressing her right breast, feeling its curve with the palm of his hand while Céspedes put his fingers on her other breast and moved them gently like somebody looking for something delicate, a thread of cotton, a contact lens, underwater. Julia, when she realized she was being caressed by both men, breathed out deeply, moaned as if an old pain had returned to some part of her body, pushed her hips forward and without opening her eyes withdrew her mouth from Céspedes and turned towards the other side to offer it to Ortuño. Céspedes and Carole are in an almost identical position to Céspedes and Julia that night.

The taxi driver asks them, 'Shall I drop you by the side?'

'What?'

'Shall I drop you by the side of the station or do you want to go around the front?'

'By the side.'

The taxi driver makes a turn. He stops at a traffic light. Julia separating her mouth from Ortuño's mouth and leaning her head back in the seat, in between the two men, looking up at the roof of the taxi, noticing the intermittent lights passing over her face as they go from the light of one street lamp to the next, then half closing her eyes and placing a hand on one thigh of each man.

Céspedes notices a motorcycle parking bay, a blonde girl taking off her helmet and shaking her long hair in the sun. The yellow sadness, boats, fury. Ahead, on the right, is the María Zambrano railway station, a grey building with a white clock on one of its side extensions. *A giant's wrist.* Julia's breathing, opening her mouth as if she were a patient, two of his fingers entering her vagina. On the left, the bare bricks of the House of the Little Sisters of the Poor. The sun throwing everything against the asphalt on the other side of the windows. *The world lies on the other side of the goldfish bowl.*

The taxi stops to the side of the station.

'Do you need a receipt?' There's a hint of sarcasm in the taxi driver's voice, but not in the look he gives through the rear-view mirror.

The other taxi driver was watching, too. He was watching as Ortuño unbuttoned Julia's blouse while Céspedes was kissing her and she gave herself up to it all, limp, as if she'd lost consciousness.

'No. I don't need a receipt. I'm not on business.' *Prick.*

'OK.' The taxi driver takes the opportunity to have a last gawp at the woman. He puts the radio back on.

Austria believes that Turkey lacks the sufficient democratic standards necessary to . . .

Céspedes takes some scrunched-up notes of all different colours out of his pocket. He hands the taxi driver a twenty-euro note. The driver accepts it, taking his time. *The Austrian chancellor, Social Democrat Christian Kern . . .* Carole gets out. As she opens the door a scorching blast of air sweeps into the car. *The European Commission has to open its eyes to this fact . . .*

'Close the door for me, please, the heat's coming in,' says the taxi driver, looking directly at Céspedes for the first time, turning his head.

Céspedes, holding his gaze, pushes the door further open with his foot.

. . . considers the negotiations with Ankara which began eleven years ago to be over . . .

'You must have lots of money and lots of fun and lots of everything except for good manners and education.'

'Education and leisure.'

. . . in his opinion these negotiations are now just a diplomatic fiction . . .

'What?'

'Education and Leisure. One of Franco's ministries. You listen to the radio all the time and you didn't know that? Or are you deaf?'

. . . Turkey's democratic standards are far from . . .

'Céspedes!' The woman has leaned over so she can look into Céspedes's eyes. 'For crying out loud, I don't believe it, picking a fight with a taxi driver!'

'Lady, I've not done anything to offend you.'

. . . since the frustrated coup d'état . . .

'My money, the change.'

'Here it is and next time don't expect me to pick you up.'

'I know who's going to pick *you* up.'

'Céspedes, for crying out loud!'

Céspedes drags himself across the seat and puts one foot on the pavement . . . *thousands of suspects have been detained* . . . He pauses at the end of the seat and looks at the taxi driver.

'Get out or I'll move off.'

'Go on then,' he says, looking him straight in the eye.

'Céspedes!' She straightens up, takes a step back and walks away from the taxi.

. . . *a state with shades of totalitarianism* . . .

'Count yourself lucky.' Céspedes gets out of the car, closes the door, and the taxi driver's voice is lost behind the glass.

The air is suffocating, and Céspedes feels as if he's gone into a kind of dry-cleaning tunnel. The heat evaporates his anger in an instant. He's arrived in another world with a different light. Carole speaks to him without realizing that everything that went on in the taxi already belongs to a distant past.

'What are you playing at? Do you think you're going to get me on a train with you if you start acting the tough guy with the first person you meet?'

'Carole.'

'First you have a wild idea of travelling five hundred kilometres for a spot of lunch and then you start mixing it with . . .'

'Carole, I'm sorry.'

'I'm honestly not sure.'

'Let it go. Forget about it. Can you press the off button up here' (touching his temple) 'and forget about it, please? Look, there's the House of the Little Sisters of the Poor. Do it for them.'

Carole looks at him with one eyebrow raised. The other taxi driver stared, too; he watched the men's hands, he watched Julia's breasts popping out over the top of her bra, out of her blouse, he watched her with the hunger of a starving man, and he watched them with the hatred of a cornered beast. Hunger and hatred. Her nipple between his fingers. Charity.

'Come on, let's go.'

Céspedes takes her by the arm and tries to guide her towards the station entrance, tries to lose the past, to move forward, forget about Julia, that night, his wife, the front door to his house, locked, the dog barking beside him, his wife's voice behind the door, the dog's vomit, his face reflected in the window, his life behind the net curtains, the treetops swaying in the garden as if they were going to vomit as well, the exchange of words and reproaches, everything left behind at least for a day, for a couple of hours or for ever. *Stick a knife in it and let it sink, an inflatable mattress sinking in a swimming pool choked with chlorine, that's my life, let me breathe.*

'Come on.' He's let go of Carole's arm, now he's just looking at her and then looking at the station entrance. *My knife those eyes my knife and my salvation, today is the only thing I have and the only thing that matters, let today last for ever.*

Carole slowly looks away. Carole takes a step, Carole goes forward, and Céspedes feels the scorching air like a blessing before the automatic doors open *open sesame* and they go into one of the corridors in the retail centre, which is the way into the station and the platforms.

Ismael opens one eye, and the first thing he feels is thirsty and then immediately on top of his dry throat, or perhaps because of it, he feels furious, as if someone were prodding him and trying to get him up off the sofa, but he holds it in, not knowing where he is and barely knowing who he is, all he can feel is this scratching in his pharynx and a sharp pain in his spine.

His mother takes a step backwards, and he makes an effort and doesn't move. He recognizes her and stays where he is, lying down in spite of the pain in his neck and his anger and thirst. He looks around the curtain-free sitting room. Just one scrap of cloth has escaped his scissors, hanging down from the rail like a shorn miniskirt.

She's average height, her hair dyed a sort of mahogany colour. She's Ismael's mother and Jorge's mother, divorced, the intermittent lover of a man whom Ismael calls the Other Man and whom he's only seen from a distance a couple of times when he's come to pick her up, and, peeping out of the window, he's seen his car, a red Nissan Leaf with a number plate ending in 8. He's dark skinned. Younger than his mother? Yes, younger than his mother.

Her name is Amelia. The few friends she's got call her Amel, and when she hears that name she feels slightly sophisticated, transported ridiculously (half a step) towards a life that she once might have had. Amel. She has a vaccination scar on her upper arm, an anachronism belonging to her generation, a soft crater, a hypnotic whirlpool in the bronzed smoothness of her skin. Her eyebrows and lips are perfectly made up. She works as a receptionist at the Hotel Los Patos.

Half asleep, she opened the front door to the flat after her night shift, and the sweet premonition of her darkened bedroom with the blades of the ceiling fan silently rotating was instantly shattered when she found the triangular remains of a towel on the hall floor. *Ismael.* An electric alarm ran through every brain cell when she saw those small triangles scattered all over the floor. Snowflakes of disgrace.

Like Hansel and Gretel, Amelia followed the trail of cloth triangles from the front door along the corridor to the kitchen and the sitting room. She was just as distressed as the poor woodcutter's children, lost in a much deeper and darker forest than those abandoned siblings, with no moonlight to guide her home because this flat, these walls, this furniture, the glass cabinet with the gilt-edged wine glasses, the glass ceiling light, the dining room table with its ever-so-elegant arched legs, this was her home. And her home also contained the devastation that crushed her spirit. She was angry and frightened as she saw her eldest son lying asleep on the sofa, holding the scissors, the heap of cloth triangles carpeting the cheap flooring and the remains of the curtains dangling like a ridiculous rag over the sitting room window. Home. Amel. Real life, and that son of hers, who was now looking at her, eyes bloodshot with sleep, squinting from a yawn which was a sort of endless muted scream. *Those full lips. Nobody else in my family has lips like that.*

Lips like a fillet steak. Ismael. God has listened. The first born. Not sitting up properly, half lying down, half naked. Like the sitting room. *Like our life.* Home. And now his mother's asking for an explanation, feeling shocked or pretending to be shocked *because how can he possibly shock me any more?* And Ismael twists his head around, looks at the scrap of curtain still hanging there, the banner after the battle, Ismael smiles, laughs, he can't help laughing, aware of his own genius, his brilliant intuition, how easy it all is, how easy everything can be if you let yourself go, how life can flow and become wonderful, an everyday miracle, just by letting the liquid drive of one's impulses follow their course. Ismael, wrapped up in his beatific state and his mother uncomprehending, not wanting to open her eyes and comprehend. *But don't you realize? Don't you realize? And you say you're my mother. That you know who I am. What world are you living in?*

But Ismael's not laughing or smiling any more. He's looking down at the floor, and he's still silent, but his silence no longer contains any hint of happiness, he swallows the silence like a drowning man swallows water, he stifles the words that reverberate through his mind and come out on his tongue, still silent, as if he were still sleeping, as if he weren't there, and he feels thirsty again, his back's hurting again, he's hot again and he doesn't know where that blast of heat's come from, his mother seems to have brought it in from somewhere, from those places she goes to. *Which bed did she screw in? He'll have screwed her in the car. Pretending she's angry because of the sodding curtains and the shitty towels when the truth is she's angry because of me, for having me, for me being her son.*

And that's when Ismael gets up, almost jumps to his feet, and the first words he says are, 'I'm not drunk. I'm not drunk! I'm not drunk yet, but I want to get drunk. It's like you're forcing me, it's like you won't be happy, it's like you're forcing me, so you can be right and you can be satisfied and happy saying look, see, I was right, I know, I know, and you know nothing, you know fuck all! That what you know. Plain and simple.'

And he brings his face up level with his mother's, that mouth, those lips that nobody in Amel's family ever had before, but there they are, will always be, they grew inside her belly, through a multiplication of her own cells and the flow of her own blood *invaded by a venomous seed left inside me, and it grew into a tree.* In the middle of nowhere. Solitary trees battered by the wind and cowering in the sun. There are rivers flowing beneath trees.

'What I do know is that I can't take it any more.' That's the only thing that Amelia manages to say in the face of her son's anger, and he takes a few steps away and then turns back and stands beneath the last vestige of the curtains, and the latent memory of the urge to laugh that he felt moments before he saw the rag flashes through his mind, but the memory immediately turns into a black bird in flight, swooping down, entering his mouth, getting stuck in the middle of his chest, digging around like his mother, and his mother sputtering, 'What about the pills?'

'The pills?' As if it were the worst possible insult, that's how Ismael takes it – God himself heard her – thinking, firmly believing that his mother said those four words simply to hurt him. 'That's like me calling you a slut,' he says, his eyes open wide. He hesitates and then opens them wider. 'Or worse. Worse than me saying it. Like I was doing it to you.'

His mother would like to burst into tears, but she's overcome by bewilderment, how scared this son of hers makes her feel, this individual who was her son. And she feels like asking him, *Like you were doing it to me? Doing what to me?* But she senses the shadow of genuine fear and rejects that murky path and opts for an easier route.

'What do you mean, Ismael, what on earth do you mean?' she asks at the same time as fresh doubts flash across her mind like supersonic planes, and those questions are, *What's happening to him? What's happened to him? When? How far will he go?* And the conclusion, much slower and wiser, *That's it, he's lost, it happened a long time ago, and there's no way back.*

And it's true. Ismael is lost. Much more lost than the woodcutter's children in the story and much more lost than his own mother. Lost in a more distant forest with birds that don't just eat the breadcrumbs but also the pebbles that she herself, rather than her son, has tried to leave in the forest, sinking them into the ground so that he can find the path again, the way back home. Their home.

'Poisoning me.' It's like he's imitating a madman. That's how the expression on his face looks. A poor imitation. Only, he's not imitating anyone.

'The truth is I've tried.'

'That's what you want, you want to poison me with that shit. You and your pills. You and that psychologist, and me stuck on the bus all day going to the clinic, coming back from the clinic, listening to you and her asking me about my father, stupid bitch asking me that. And you just sitting there.'

'I've tried,' and now Amelia does start crying, she breaks down weeping as she pictures herself searching for her son, her child, in a dark forest. 'Yes, I've really tried.'

'Don't cry!'

Amelia feels weak, her legs feel weak, as if weeping required all her energy and her muscles, her tendons, and even her bones had stopped working so she could weep. Her whole body immersed in childlike sobs. Total distress. And again she repeats the same words, like a source of nourishment, a lifeline that she and her weeping have discovered to feed her, to stay afloat on the rough sea.

'I've tried. I've really tried.'

'Don't cry! For fuck's sake!' And he bangs the table, a resounding blow that captures his mother's attention, trapped at the other end, and now it's just a matter of snapping her out of that stupid sobbing. 'You've been out all night. Next time . . .'

'For God's sake. I've been working, Ismael, for God's sake.' She's still crying but it's less focused, less intense, less liberating, she's back in the real world with all its noise.

'Next time I'm going to drink that bottle of alcohol in the bathroom and see what happens.'

'I've been working. Do you know what that means? Working all night to –'

'Working? Since eight o'clock? You went out at eight o'clock, it was still daytime, and now, what time is it now?'

'Don't I have the right to be more than just a housemaid to the pair of you?'

'What were you going to say earlier, that I don't know the meaning of work? What about the two months I spent in that hotel kitchen? And for what? Why didn't you find me a job at your hotel? It had to be that other place. You put me there in the worst place with those people as a punishment, knowing they were going to fuck me around.'

'As if I could, as if I knew what was going on in all the hotels in the world. You weren't there more than two weeks, what with days off sick and . . .'

'Oh, you know it all, the whole bloody lot, you know everything, don't you? And what were you going to say, go on, spit it out, about days off sick and what else?'

'And with you getting drunk is what I was going to say. How many times did they catch you drinking on the job? Cooking wine, brandy, anything they had in the kitchen, if you weren't going to do any work it would've been better not to go in, and if you didn't go so much the worse, and me trying to cover for you.'

'Come off it, all those little shits grassing me up and making up stuff. You don't know what they were like.'

'I know very well. I worked there for three months. As soon as I saw you there when I went to see how it was all going I realized I'd made a mistake. All those bottles, you spent more time drinking than working.'

'That's what those bastards wanted, that's what they said, all of them fucking me around and you . . .'

And blah blah blah, and blah blah blah. The heat's coming in through the walls, filtering through the cracks, twisting all the timbers. Ismael gesticulates, he and his mother move on to a familiar chapter, the same one as always. The river's stagnated. There's no longer any risk it'll burst its banks. There's the shredded curtain, the heated glass through which you can see the building opposite. The sky's becoming thinner like a stretched skin, like a sheet of blue plastic that's pulled too tight and at any moment it might be ripped by the swifts' crazy zigzagging. The Calle Juan Sebastián Bach is a mechanical ballet of cars, reflections and noises, and beyond, perhaps five kilometres away as the crow flies, leaning on one of the admin desks in the Clinical Hospital's emergency department, Dr Galán says, 'I know it's him.' And she says to herself, *That's it, it's finally happened.*

People are standing around the man who's covered in dust and ants and talking to each other. Intense cutaneous pallor, dry skin and mucous membranes, dull corneas. Dehydrated. There's an ambulance parked on the edge of the waste ground and a man and a woman wearing blue trousers and tops. The hospital has already had a call from the ambulance so they can prepare for his arrival. There are enough details for Dr Galán to feel certain that the dreaded moment has arrived. Even though there are no documents and no one can yet put a name to him and there's no physical description other than that he's a middle-aged, grey-haired man, she knows it's her husband. That's what she tells Quesada, the doctor who answered the call from the ambulance. They're still there on the waste ground, or they were three minutes ago, Quesada tells her. He's holding the notes that the nurse has just taken down. Dr Galán takes the sheet of paper and reads it.

The patient must have been unconscious and out in the sun for more than a day given the advanced state of dehydration and lack of response to verbal instructions. Unconscious, hypotension. Agonal breathing. Weak and filiform pulse. Covered in dust and small ants which almost entirely cover the remains of dusty clothing and the smaller cutaneous folds. No sign of external injuries. Everything seems to indicate that the patient has suffered a serious case of heatstroke after being unconscious for one or two days for reasons unknown and being exposed to temperatures in excess of forty degrees.

Quesada hesitates. Dr Galán looks him in the eye. They're old friends. Quesada resorts to his usual calm manner to resist her look. And she tells him, 'Leave him to me. It's him.'

'We'll do it together,' says Quesada.

And she shakes her head. 'Tell them to get the emergency room ready. Is Ramiro on duty?' Dr Quesada says he is. And she says, 'Tell him to come, tell him to come with me, and thanks. Julia's coming over, I've spoken to her. She must be on her way. Thank you.'

'Ana,' says Quesada. And she shakes her head as she walks towards the entrance to A&E. Those days spent with Quesada and his family in the peace of the countryside seem a long time ago. So do those summer nights during that other summer when she would go out on her terrace and the fragrance from the nearby trees wafted up to her like an offering. A silent choir. She would lean on the balcony rail smoking a cigarette as she watched the lights in the distance, those twinkling lights suggesting other people's lives and a harmony that came up to her home like a gentle wave. The world was right there, and she could sink her feet into its warm waters. Back then she was still unaware that he, her husband, had another life. Another life that was now bringing him here in an ambulance, covered in dust and ants.

Dr Galán walks down the corridor bathed in aseptic light. Ramiro, the nurse, catches her up. He looks her in the eye. He doesn't say anything. *He already knows. Quesada's told him that the patient being brought in could be Dioni, that I know it's him.*

To avoid Ramiro's gaze, to avoid her own thoughts becoming muddled, Dr Galán says, 'Julia's on her way. We'll get everything ready.'

'Whatever you say. Intravenous drip?'

'Yes. And the defibrillator monitor, to check vital signs.'

'What?'

'I'll tell you as we go along.'

'Gastric lavage?'

'Perhaps. I'll tell you as we go along.'

'OK.'

They go into the emergency room. Ramiro walks over to the middle glass cabinet and opens it. Dr Galán is reflected in the glass.

If I'd only known how to play it. If I'd only known long before that it was all a lie, that those business trips were a cover, that those nights when he was supposed to be staying late to prepare for a complicated trial he was really going out looking for men, or maybe he was already seeing Vicente, perhaps everything would have been different. It was all so hopeless later on. When I found out what was happening in his life, in my life, I felt it was already too late for anything, too late for divorce, too late for talking, too late for staying with him in some other way. Wishful thinking, hoping for an easy way out or for fear of the future being written in stone and all I had to do was to put up with it, to hold out, to sympathize with him, to love him. An efficient mother, an efficient doctor, an efficient wife, that's how excuses are made for everything. And it was all emptiness, and I was on my own in the middle of the emptiness, just as much then as now.

Raimundo, the guitar man, throws his head right back and finishes off his bottle of water. 'I can't believe how hot it is. Thanks a lot, boss.'

The policeman, leaning on the bonnet of his patrol car, is watching him with a certain amount of condescension but not much curiosity. The garage's customers look at them both suspiciously as they go inside the shop.

'So tomorrow you'll come by the police station, don't forget.'

'I won't forget, boss. I don't want any hassle, but I'll do my bit. I've proved that, haven't I? I came over here and that guy's going to survive thanks to me.'

'I don't think he's going to survive, thanks to you or anyone else.'

'Yes but, you know, boss, I did all I could. I could have just disappeared.'

'Whatever you say.'

'One thing, you guys couldn't give me a lift into town, could you?'

'We're not a taxi service, in case you hadn't realized, Facundo.'

'Raimundo.'

'Whatever, we're still not a taxi service, Raimundo.'

'Come on, boss, I mean, I've stayed here all this time, and I should've been with my mate by now working to earn a bit of cash, come on, boss, it wouldn't cost you anything.'

'We're not going into town, and we're not a public-transport service, how many times do I have to tell you?'

'That's harsh, boss. I mean, it's so I can work. It's part of your job to support the transport service, isn't it? Even though you're not a public-transport service, and all I want is to earn a bit of cash with the guitar.'

'You really don't give up, do you?'

The policeman half turns towards the inside of the vehicle he's leaning on.

'Gabi.'

'And with this heat it's going to kill me walking into town, boss.'

'Yeah, yeah. Gabi.'

'It's so I can work.'

'Yes, for crying out loud, I think I've got that. Gabriel!'

A man in plain clothes gets out of the car. He's dark skinned with a beard.

'Are you going into town or close by?'

'Yes.'

'Do you mind giving our friend here a lift?'

'Where are you going?'

A passing customer from the petrol station looks at the plain-clothes policeman and stops. 'You're the policeman in the papers, aren't you? Congratulations.'

The guitar man looks at them suspiciously.

The customer holds out his hand to the policeman. 'You're Gabriel Muñoz, aren't you? I've seen you in the papers. You're a lifesaver.'

'Yeah, that's right.'

The customer goes off towards the shop. The guitar man asks him, half admiringly, half suspicious, 'Are you famous? Did you nick a lot of bad guys or what?'

'Come on, I'm in a hurry, if you want me to give you a lift.'

The man in the green overalls comes over, holding a newspaper. 'Bartolo,' murmurs the guitar man.

'Would you mind signing this for us? Something like this doesn't happen every day around here.'

The man in the green overalls unfolds a copy of *Sur*, the local newspaper. On the front page, spread across four columns, is a photo of the policeman who's now in plain clothes. POLICE LIFEGUARD HERO.

The guitar man looks surprised and lays it on thick.

'Wow! What's this? Full on!' he says to the uniformed policeman, who's still leaning on the bonnet. 'Look and learn, boss!'

'OK, lend me a biro. It's like a carnival here.' The plain-clothes policeman wants to get it over with.

The guitar man tries to read, 'Police lifeguard hero Gabriel Muñoz, an officer . . .'

'Get off, you idiot.' The man in the green overalls pushes him away.

'Calm down, fella,' says the policeman, taking the biro from the other garage employee who's holding it out to him, looking back and forth between the policeman and the newspaper as if he still can't take in how this man can be in two places at once.

The guitar man starts reading again.

'. . . officer . . . who was off duty, rescues two young swimmers who were on the point of drowning on Playa de la Misericordia. No way! That was you, boss!'

'Thank you very much,' says the man in the green overalls looking at the autograph proudly, as if he'd saved the two youngsters from the sea himself.

'OK, let's go. Tell me where you're headed.' The plain-clothes policeman starts walking towards a car that's parked in the shade.

'If you just let me make a call for a moment, just for a moment, I'll let you know.'

'OK, make your call.'

'No, I mean, can you lend me your phone just for a moment? I haven't got one. Just a moment, so I know where my mate is, and I'll hang up.'

'For crying out loud, fella.' He pulls his phone from his jeans pocket. 'Come on then, make your call.'

'Thanks, boss, I mean, Gabriel.'

Raimundo takes the phone, looks at the screen, moves his lips. 'Six five three six seven – what was it? – six five three six seven two.'

'Don't you know the number?'

'Yeah, yeah, that's right.'

He dials the number. It's answered on the fourth or fifth ring.

They're in a pedestrianized zone in between some three-storey blocks, and at the end of Calle Archidona there are a couple of wooden benches in the sun and some small trees that can barely breathe.

El Tato's phone vibrates in his pocket, making a sound like an anti-aircraft siren.

El Tato's sitting on a stone bench protruding from the wall scrawled with graffiti: KUKI **ANAIS KUKI**. He looks at the number he doesn't recognize and slides his finger over the screen. 'Who is it?'

'Raimundo. Is Eduardo with you?'

'Where are you hanging?'

'I've been having some hassle. Is Eduardo with you?'

'He's with Juanmi.'

'Who? Where? Is Eduardo with you?'

'Yeah, here, over there.'

'Call him over, tell him to get on the line, quick.'

'Chinarro! Chinarro!'

'Tell him to get on the line.'

'He's coming, for fuck's sake. Chinarro! Where are you?'

'I'll tell you now. You won't believe what a bummer. The guy was crawling with ants, just lying in the middle of a field.'

Eduardo Chinarro has got up from the bench he was sitting on with Juanmi and La Penca and walks calmly over to El Tato. He takes the phone.

'What are you up to, Rai? Where are you?'

'Where are you?'

'In Portada, with El Tato, Juanmi and La Penca.'

'Portada? Mate, we were going to go and work.'

'Cool. Where are you? I lost track of time. He's got some amazing dope . . .'

'What the hell are you doing over there?'

'Even Oreja came over, you know, from the Daltons.'

'OK, OK.'

'The Daltons, Rai. He pulled out his gun and he stuck it in Juanmi's face. Where are you?'

'I'm coming over.'

'Juanmi's got some amazing dope.'

'Who the hell is Juanmi?'

'Juanmi? He's an old mate from . . .'

'Wait for me there.'

'Listen, so I shouldn't go into town?'

'Wait for me there.'

'But where are you, Rai?'

'Wait for me there.'

'OK. Hello? Rai? Rai?' Eduardo Chinarro takes the phone away from his ear and stares at it resentfully. 'It got cut off or something, Tato. Where's Rai?'

El Tato takes a long draw on the spliff and holds down the smoke. 'I don't know.'

'He's coming over.'

'Yep.'

'That's what he told me.'

'Ahhh.' El Tato releases a light-bluish cloud.

'It's like my head or my hair's going to catch fire with this heat, don't you think, Tato?'

Eduardo opens his mouth. He's missing some teeth. He looks over to where Juanmi and La Penca are sitting. Eduardo smiles and strokes his scrawny goatee. He claps his hands twice and clicks his heel and starts singing in his gravelly voice, his face contorted and the veins on his neck engorged.

'*Tiene mi Cuba un son y una cantina . . .*'

'Fucking hell, Eduardo,' El Tato complains, 'don't start.'

'Wow, what an artist!' Juanmi laughs from the bench on which he's lying almost supine.

'If you don't shut it the Daltons really will come, you dickhead.'

Eduardo turns around, indignant. 'They were already here, Tato, before you arrived. Oreja was here, or his brother, and he pulled out his gun and told Juanmi, "Shut it, or I'll sort you out."'

Eduardo is walking with a twisted gait, bow-legged, murmuring in a slightly musical tone, '*Hecha de caña y ron y agua marina*'. Then he raises his voice and changes his tone. 'Hey, Juanmi, I bet you shat yourself when you saw that gun, yeah?'

He sits down next to Juanmi and gives him a slap on the thigh. Juanmi is skinny, thin as a rake, and his limp hair hangs down over his cheeks. He's freckly and almost blond.

'You shat yourself.'

'Yeah, sure, you can see I'm still shaking.' Juanmi lifts his hand up and makes it shake like someone with Parkinson's.

'Isn't that right, Penqui? She says not.'

La Penca raises an eyebrow and at the same time draws on her Marlboro, tugging at her strappy yellow top and flapping it back and forth to let some air in. She blows into her cleavage, you can see her breasts through the smoke, a greenish tattoo, a bird, near one of her nipples.

'Eat my pussy, Eduardo,' she says, looking the other way. 'Ugh! There's La Segueta. Sit up straight, Juanmi, La Segueta's coming.'

Eduardo looks in the same direction as La Penca and laughs, imitating a schoolchild, 'Sit up straight!'

A woman is coming towards them from the blocks at the end, she's close to the bench, and she's heard what La Penca and Eduardo have said. Her son is Rafi Villaplana, the Marquis of Portada, Cardboard Face, Golden Boy and all the other nicknames they can come up with in the neighbourhood. La Penca still remembers the day her brother was arrested for the first time, how La Segueta arrived at her flat with her shopping bags to have a snoop around, without a bra, her massive boobs hanging there, the weight of them stretching her T-shirt, which was stained with spots of grease or something. With half a row of teeth protruding from her lower jaw and the other half just bare gum. 'It couldn't be as revolting as that if she flashed us her pussy,' the man in the kiosk used to say.

La Segueta's mouth is half open, displaying her extraordinary laughing gear, her boobs are bouncing around, and she's dragging an old blue shopping trolley that's falling to bits. She stops a couple of metres before she gets to the bench on which La Penca, Eduardo and Juanmi are sitting. La Segueta is short, with a broad face, juvenile eyes and eyelashes in the centre of the chaos, her hair a silvery bleached blonde.

'I can see you two are going to do well in life, and as for you, Aurori . . .' Aurori, alias La Penca, continues to stare straight ahead, irritated. 'Your mother would be so proud to see you there.'

'Mind your own,' La Penca whispers, smoking her cigarette.

Juanmi stifles a laugh, bending over on the bench, supple, double-jointed.

'That's right, you laugh. I bet you picked this one up at the university . . .'

'Just like you,' murmurs La Penca and throws her cigarette butt on the floor and treads on it, flaps the neckline of her yellow top, the green bird peeping out. 'I bet you go back to Oxford to do your shopping.'

Juanmi stretches out his legs as if he's having a spasm and pulls them back in, bends over and unbends trying not to burst out laughing or pretending to hold back a laugh that isn't really there.

'Yuk! Who the hell is she, man? Dracula's bride? Oh, hilarious.'

'Shameless. You've got no shame.'

'Don't overdo it, Juanmi,' Eduardo scolds him. 'For fuck's sake, Juanmi.'

'Have you seen Mariano?' Mariano's wife, alias La Segueta, Encarnación Molledo, Encarni, Encarnita, Rafi Villaplana's mother, the one with the noisy guts, Dracula's bride, asks Eduardo. 'Did you see him this morning?'

'He was in La Amistad, Encarni, a short while back.'

'Having a beer, I suppose?'

'I don't know, Encarni. He was asleep. And how's Rafi?'

Encarni, Encarnita, La Segueta has started walking off. Her shopping trolley looks like it's melted in the heat. 'My Rafi's out working, which is what you lot should be doing – not hanging around here.'

'I thought he was working nights, Encarni? I haven't seen him for ages.'

La Segueta stops and reveals her array of teeth and gums. 'Rafi's head of personnel, and the head of personnel doesn't work nights, that comes with being head of personnel. That's apart from his own stuff.'

'Wow, Rafi's the real deal, but he still works at the Hotel Los Patos, doesn't he, Encarni?'

'He's the big boss there, you better believe it, Eduardito,' says La Penca, looking up and squinting at the sun's reflection in the window of her apartment.

The woman moves off, ranting and raving under the sun, drooling the words Envy, Envious, Green with Envy, and away she goes with her boobs swaying from side to side like silent church bells, shopping trolley melting in the sun, her discoloured hair glowing like a saint's halo. La Penca thinks about her father, that pig, behind the window, fast asleep. She pictures the apartment right now, the sofa with its worn-out fringes and tassels, Yubri, her brother, ensconced in the bathroom, sitting in the tiny bathtub, filling it entirely with his corpulent body, his pimples and the hairs on his back, Kuki lying in front of the door waiting for someone to take him out, the sink piled high with dirty plates, the photo of her dead mother with two plastic roses embedded in the frame. La Penca opens her mouth, breathes in a mouthful of scorched air, looks up even higher at the heat-crazed birds *they'll soon be dead*; it's so hot everything seems unreal.

'Do those birds die in the winter, Tato?'

El Tato looks up as well. 'They go away.'

They go away. Eduardo stands up, has a stretch, lifting his arms towards the sky. It looks like he wants to separate his head from his body the way he twists it.

'Tato, did Rai say when he was going to come over?'

El Tato leans against the wall, shaking his head.

'You look like you're in front of a firing squad like that, Tato.'

La Segueta, a hazy outline in the sun, crosses between the parked cars, heading for La Amistad, and there, in a shop doorway, she'll find her husband with his head to one side, just like he's been shot in the side of the head and is spluttering with death spasms, snoring, sitting on the metal chair on the pavement that Palmiro the shopkeeper has lent him with a newspaper, also borrowed, resting in his lap.

'Where do they go, Tato? The birds?'

El Tato shrugs his shoulders. 'They just piss off,' he says and spits on the floor.

La-la-la-la-la. Eduardo closes his eyes, raises his arms and starts clapping at head height, singing *la-la-la-la-la.*

The scrawny trees are still firmly rooted next to the bench they're sitting on, their ridiculous vertical shadows barely reaching them, ambulances are arriving at hospitals, their ear-piercing sirens cutting through the hot air. *This is where Portada Alta begins.* The abattoirs with their rivulets of blood and water running down the gutters, steam sticking to bodies like a second skin, and there he was in the middle of it all, a cigarette butt between his lips and the animal at his feet, its legs convulsing almost comically. 'That's how I found him.' That's how Aurora, La Penca, found her father, the day she went to tell him that her mother had died, three days' growth on his face, his eyes bulging more than ever, threads hanging off the shoulder straps on his vest, his feet in the gutter, surrounded by a rivulet of water and blood. The abattoir, men bleeding out, the blood running through thin tubing, cannulae, tubes, filaments, sprinkling over the operating-theatre floors, saturating cotton swabs, staining sheets, resting in plastic bags in the darkness of fridges until they are taken out again and fed like a snake through different tubes into different veins. 'Mummy,' she said, and her father understood, with the knife in his hand, the brownish blood on his chest, her mother dead, abattoirs, those blue shadows of skinned animals, trains crossing empty fields,

La-la-la-la-la.

In the AVE high-speed train – a white tube – Céspedes is drinking from a plastic cup, the ice diluting the whisky, and he's studying Carole's almond-shaped eyes, and again he thinks, *I've always liked them, always liked those eyes,* eyes that he'd never seen until the early hours of the previous night but which had always lived inside him, or that's what he felt or what he would like to feel now, he felt that or something like it in the middle of the night when she gave him that look, half ironic and half fascinated, the sarcasm a roundabout way to get close to him, like a challenge, those pupils, that narrow almond of an eye, and the tone of her voice coupled with that look, the black trees in the garden, the glare from the swimming pool and the voices reverberating down below, and there he is now, looking at the yellow fields through the window barely forming a blurry border dividing the glass, a Rothko painting, the sky, the fields, the corpses travelling in the glass,

La-la.

'For fuck's sake, Eduardo, bitch, weren't you supposed to be going somewhere?'

'How can I go anywhere? They don't give as much if you don't have a guitar, Tato, and anyway Raimundo told me to wait for him here *la-la, la-la-la-la-la.*

The Runner takes his blue-covered notebook out from beneath his mattress, stretches out on the bed, turns the pages and wishes that his life was like that, a train taking him away, to wander aimlessly, no fixed destination, to have a life and live it, to have problems, disappointments, ups and downs, but not this, not this place stuck in the middle of nowhere with people who gave up on everything a long time ago, trying to make progress in a dead-end street, waiting for the days to come and go like a succession of empty envelopes, the train, 294 kilometres per hour, endless rows of olive trees that suddenly burst into view through the window and a wall of orange clay advancing on the carriage that seems like it's going to jump on to the train and devour it, *Jonah and the whale,*

Céspedes breathes in, small cemeteries, a sensation of being in a covered wagon, the world coming and going *playing with us like a yo-yo, and whenever it likes, without us hearing its footsteps or seeing its shadow, it'll have wolfed us down and we won't be here and we won't know that we're not here, to hell with this poor man's philosophy.*

'Tato, do you know where Rai was calling from?'

'No, Eduardo, he didn't say.'

Ambulances, heat, La Segueta looks at her husband, sleeping, snoring, the sun scorching his feet, which are only half inserted into his shoes, the green-and-purple protuberance of his veins, and Dr Galán is also looking at her reflection in a window, she's seen the ambulance arrive, she knows it's that one and she knows that the person inside is Dioni eaten up by ants, eaten up by himself, and she walks down the corridor as if the floor and the walls were also made of glass, that light that sick people have, the Runner reads what he wrote a few days ago: *My father came home one night with some orange fish, he was clutching a large jar to his chest, and I was still half asleep, and I thought that the fish were swimming in his lungs, inside my father* – then he looks up from the notebook. *Maybe one day I can write something that isn't a lie, something like the air that I'm breathing in this room,* Dr Galán didn't want to go to A&E reception, preferring to wait in the emergency room, Ramiro's there beside her, avoiding her eyes, examining the bed, the fold of the sheets, the intravenous drips, the vasoactive drugs, *And I stared at him, I stared at him as if my father had died and was coming to reveal the unknown to me, the fish were swimming around in his transparent chest, but not even that,* the Runner hears the hum of the television, a voice announcing the end of the world, La Segueta touching her husband's shoulder,

Mariano, Mariano,

she's disgusted as she touches him, as if he really were a corpse, and her husband opens one eye, returning from the great beyond,

Trains go past, the music of the dead, empty trains go past,

Céspedes sounds serious, Carole looks at him with one eyebrow raised, and he carries on reciting lines by Juvenal Soto,

Empty trains go past, yes, that's how it goes, empty trains go past, on their way to the ports where time is stored,

Mariano opens his mouth like a fish, his face is huge and ruddy, his eyes are small and a greenish colour, he's bald except for a scrappy grey tuft towards the front. Mariano leans back in his metal chair with its hot frame, the aluminium slats embedded in his fifty-nine-year-old flesh, coughs and smiles back in response to his wife's contemptuous glare,

On their way to the ports where time is stored, the time that I don't have,

'Give me some money,' says Encarnación, Encarnita, La Segueta, and Mariano's smile turns into a surly expression. 'Money?'

Céspedes is still wearing a sad smile, Carole's eyes look into his, and for a moment all the cynicism disappears. La Segueta repeats her demand, displaying her bizarre set of teeth. 'Yes, money, that stuff I have to give to the people in the shop if you want to have something to eat, money, the stuff you put in the fruit machines.'

Mariano bends down and grunts, attempting to put on his shoes using his finger as a shoehorn, and his voice from down there sounds like a snore, as though he'd gone back to sleep. 'I've got no money left, I gave it to you, I gave you some money last week and yesterday another twenty euros. Hasn't Rafi given you anything?'

La Segueta shuffles her shopping trolley back and forth, nervously. It's made of canvas, a dull-blue colour. The canvas looks like Juanmi's doped-up eyelids.

'Twenty euros? Fifteen. And that was the day before yesterday, yesterday I had nothing. You've spent it on the fruit machine, all your money's in that machine again. Those little fruits have frazzled your brain, and Rafi's working, he's not at home and he needs it for his business, with everything he's doing.'

'Yeah, yeah, yeah,' says Mariano, sounding bunged up and sitting up in his chair, giving up on his shoes, heels hanging out as if they were flip-flops, the fake leather of his footwear like a rogue animal, then he bends over again, 'Yeah, yeah, yeah.' Mariano curses his fate. 'Why doesn't the girl go out to work? Why doesn't Rafi make a contribution? And Migue should contribute more than he does.' He likes the word contribute. It sounds distinguished, lending him an aristocratic superiority, an educated man, he always refers to his school certificate like it was an Olympic medal. 'More than he contributes. They're all adults now, all of you are adults, you should leave me in peace.' The same old words, the same old voice and the same old glare from his wife, La Segueta, her mouth half open. Back on the train Carole realizes that the only thing that works with this man is irony, sweet cynicism, she realizes that to communicate in any other way they would both have to take a step back, go back to the moment in the early hours of that morning when they exchanged their first words, perhaps their first looks, and now no other form of approach will work, the fragile house of cards that they've been building with their fundamentally ridiculous form of sparring would collapse into the void, so Carole takes a mental break, forgets about the lines of the poem that Céspedes is reciting incorrectly (or deliberately moulding to suit his own purpose) and says to him, 'Still making up poetry at your age, Céspedes?' and Céspedes, who has understood the game and Carole's internal thought process responds on the same level, 'Well, you see, it's the whisky, it takes me back to my youth.'

'Or to your adolescence, at least,' she replies, and he nods and looks back at the blurred landscape, the silent howl of naked speed – *not even the fishes could swim any longer in the stagnant water in that chest, they opened their mouths and drowned. That's how I saw them a few days later, floating in the water with their white stomachs, and that's how I saw my father's eyes, his stubbly beard and his unkempt hair, like a needle sinking in a goldfish bowl* – and the city, too, is a silent howl, and those who live there could also be needles sinking in a river's current, La Penca puts a fresh cigarette between her lips, half closes her eyes, the leaves on the trees hang above her, immobile, tense, and the wheels on the stretcher carrying the man from the waste ground make a slight squeaking sound in the silence of that part of the hospital, *a needle sinking in a goldfish bowl*, and the visitors make way and the medical staff look on professionally as Dionisio Grandes Guimerá and his ants go past en route to the emergency room where his wife is waiting for him, the route of the condemned, and La Penca smokes her cigarette, El Tato looks up at the birds, the Runner reads and Chinarro clicks his heels,

La-la-la-la-la.

*

Julia Mamea drives her car out of the side exit of her garage on to Calle Compositor Lemberg Ruiz. The light looks like molten silver to her. She rummages in the glovebox for her sunglasses but can't find them. It's so bright. Her hair's still wet after her shower, dark waves that are almost black or sometimes even a kind of deep blue or purple. She turns into Avenida Obispo Herrera Oria and heads west.

After speaking to Ana, she went back to sleep again but doesn't know for how long. Before leaving home she got two messages from Ana:

Man found on waste ground, severe dehydration, several days in the sun, unconscious, very serious.

And this one a minute later:

Grey hair, approx 50. Sure it's him.

She knew it was going to happen, me, too, really. She knows it's him. Ana's sure. It must be him. She pictures him. Julia pictures Dioni's body lying on a plot of land, one that she knew on a side street off Calle Martínez Maldonado that's nothing like the open waste ground full of mounds and stubble where her friend's husband was actually found. She pictures Dioni's grey eyes and his smile, his sad, slightly bewildered smile, a mask to hide behind, the same as putting a sign on his face saying CLOSED. *And all because of a fuck, all this pain because of that. What does it matter? What does it matter, when it comes down to it, who he does it with? He's going to die, he might die because of that, because other people don't like where he does it or who with, whose genitals he likes touching or licking, we're all mad and one day everyone will understand that.*

Julia rolls down the window to let a bit of a breeze come in. A blast of heat, a red-hot howl forces its way desperately through the window. She rolls it up again. She flicks back a lock of hair from her cheek. *I'll get it cut and bleached,* she catches a glimpse of her reflection in the rear-view mirror and pictures herself with short, bleached hair, pale blonde. Would it make her features stand out? There are fine lines around her mouth. She's forty-six years old, as of last month. A car overtakes her very fast and ostentatiously on the right and the driver gesticulates at her. *Idiot. His mouth and features look like Céspedes's.* She thinks that perhaps she ought to text Céspedes again. Give him a bit more time perhaps. *He can be such a shit when he wants to be.* She feels like rolling down the window again, the air conditioning isn't having much of an impact. She resists the urge. *I never wanted to get my hopes up, I always knew, right from the start, and in his own way he was honest with me, even though he's dishonest, he's been honest with me. Right from the word go, he told me he was married, he never hid the fact, and he thought that completely exonerated him from any blame or responsibility. What a prick.*

They met at the vet's four or five years ago. Julia was there with the puppy she'd bought for her son, and Céspedes was there with his. They had to wait for almost an hour and spent the time talking, not about the weather or the names of their dogs or about the pets they used to have, but about all the crazy ways you can find to while away the time when you're kept hanging around. Céspedes was amused and sensitive and suggested that as she was a nurse she should vaccinate the dogs and then they could leave.

Then they bumped into each other again at the vet's a month later. They both felt it was fate, and she said she would like to see him in his office to ask for some advice. She took particular care getting ready that day. She put on her lipstick in the lift on the way up to his office. Céspedes realized it was a signal when he saw her red lips, a message written in lipstick and addressed to him. But until the time came to say goodbye, he was only interested in explaining how she could sort out her property problem. Julia was disappointed, and on her way out she brushed her hand over the cover of a book on the desk and read the title. *The Advantages of Travelling by Train.* 'That sounds like fun. Is it a novel?' she asked. 'Yes.' 'Is it any good?' 'I think so. I haven't started it yet, but I've read other books by the same author. He's worth reading. I'll lend you one if you like.' Julia said yes half-heartedly. Céspedes told her that the books weren't in his office, he just had books for work there and one or two he was in the middle of reading, but they could meet up in his studio where she could choose from some two thousand books. A little refuge in Cánovas del Castillo. I go there to read, to do nothing, to watch the cranes in the port, the ships leaving port. 'I see. And do you just watch the ships leaving port and not the ones coming in?' 'Yes, only the ships leaving port.' 'That's very romantic, don't you think?' 'No, not really, but now that you've mentioned romantic, you've given me an idea – there's a book you'll really like.' 'Don't give me a weepie with characters in capes.' 'No, don't worry. It's set in the Salamanca District of Madrid, and it's about the twentieth-century bourgeoisie. It's brilliant.'

Julia's passing the sports complex on her right, the *frontón* court with its green wall, trees overhanging the fence. *He'll be there by now, Ana will know by now, yes she'll know by now.* She stops at a traffic light. An obese woman is walking across the road beside a young girl and both of them are laughing. *Thirty-eight degrees, and, as those stupid sods on the radio say, it feels like forty-three.* The traffic light turns green.

Julia and Céspedes were in a small room lined with books, standing beside a table with several piles of books. Julia was flicking through a book that Céspedes had given her, the pair of them standing next to each other. Her body was just a few centimetres away from his. She turned the book over and read the back cover: *the upper bourgeoisie of Madrid awakens following Franco's death.* She flicked through the pages again and looked up. 'I'll take it.' He turned around a little, avoiding touching her body with his but close enough so that he was face to face with Julia. He moved his head slowly towards her as she said, 'That's not why I'm here,' and they started kissing. She was so keen, it crossed his mind that she'd wanted to do it since they met at the vet's.

Another traffic light. On the left are the low-rise apartment blocks of Portada Alta. On the right, under an orange awning, there's a shop with a sign which says BAZAR ALIMENTACIÓN LA AMISTAD and a woman with bleached hair is standing next to a man sitting on the type of metal chair that bars put out on the pavements. The woman is moving her mouth as if she were chewing gum and she's got a large shopping trolley beside her. The man, who is wearing beach shoes, is complaining. We know they are Encarni, alias La Segueta, and her husband Mariano, or El Mariano.

He had kissed her neck, pressed his hard groin against hers, gently, very gently, fondled her breasts and had looked into her eyes before saying, 'Come on.' He took her by the hand and led her into the room with the blinds down, partially shaded, and she thought, *He had everything ready*, with the bed made up, everything as it should be. And she thought, as he was undoing her blouse, as he was gently caressing her bra, her nipples, she thought about what she would do, if she would let him get on with it and she'd just feel pleasure at being penetrated, moderate pleasure, or whether she'd explain to him what she needed to have an orgasm. *It depends on how it all goes, on how he is*, thought Julia, but when they were still standing up with their arms around each other and he touched her pubis and squeezed it delightfully, when he pulled her knickers down and took his time, with the patience of a watchmaker, tenderly caressing, moistening, slowly plunging his fingers into that viscous mucus, she decided that she would, even though it was their first time. That day she also wanted her reward, her fill of pleasure.

As she drives down the street shrouded in white light, the buildings becoming fewer and fewer, Julia remembers Dioni at Ana's last birthday, the sadness in his grey eyes, and she wonders what these last few days must have been like, if he'd wandered from place to place, if he'd been attacked or if it was all an accident or an attempt at suicide, suffering because of his closet homosexuality and giving up after the relentless passing of the years.

She told Céspedes just as she had told so many others after he had penetrated her, expertly, using almost all the different possible types of rhythm, looking into her eyes, but unquestioningly, enjoying desire but not wanting it to end. She waited for a moment of less intensity, their two mouths very close together, looking into each other's eyes, an aura of mutual understanding and happiness.

'If I want to come, I have to do it in a particular way. Do you want to give it a go?' He moved his face away and his eyebrows moved in an unmistakeable sign of acceptance at the same time as he asked, 'What do you think?'

Julia stops at the Sandro Botticelli roundabout, an all-enveloping light is turning the coloured cylinders on the roundabout pale, the cars are circulating as if they're on a merry-go-round. She drives on to the roundabout and follows the road towards the hospital. A row of trees, another roundabout, white sunshine, buildings in the distance, the city beginning to break up.

'You have to lie down like this, on your back.' Céspedes obeyed, Julia lay down on her side next to him, one elbow on the pillow, placing one of her breasts close to Céspedes's mouth, 'that's it, and I lie close to you, that's it and you put your hand, put your arm underneath me (Julia lifted her hips, a faint citrus smell) and place your hand behind, that's it, slip a finger inside me (all wet, an open wound) and another finger behind, that's it, that's it, and you suck on my nipple, suck my tit (she put her nipple in his mouth, she put her fingers in her mouth and smeared them with saliva, an expert) and I'll pull you off, yes, that's it, yes, yes, yes, that's it, I love your fingers, yes, that's it, that's it, more, more like that.' She slurped with her mouth, sucked in air through her teeth like an inverse whistle, and Julia moved gently, repeating the word 'yes' as Céspedes moved his fingers, in and out, he made an effort and sucked on her nipple, he licked, nibbled, and Julia tensed up still repeating the word 'yes' until it turned into a kind of hoarse, muffled, spasmodic, intense and astonished howl. As if it were the first time that she had conquered that pleasure dimension.

'That's what makes you really unique, that great gift you give to a man coming like that,' Céspedes told her years later. So poetic.

The lift has a faux-antique mirror, a bit of gilt in an effort to give it a touch of distinction that's spoiled by the excessive rattling, a sinister clanking of chains and the distant hum of a motor that's threatening to give up the ghost.

Ismael's at the back of the cabin, aware that this is a commanding position in the lift. His mother's standing side on to him, absent-mindedly studying the bottom of the mirror. Her shoulders are bare with half her back exposed, and she's wearing that chiffon dress with an orange print that Ismael hates, a hemp bag hanging from her shoulder with the edge of a pink towel poking out. The beach. Ismael watches her from his superior position. He looks at the back of her neck, which is completely exposed because of that haircut that he finds so distasteful. He finds it insulting, offensive, to him personally, to his family, to everyone, *like a slut*, the smoothness of her skin and her hair clipped short on her neck and long at the sides, falling in curls. *She's looking at the ground like a sheep searching among the pebbles for some grass to eat, and now you're going to lie down on your back on the beach like I saw you that day stretched out on the sand.*

That day Ismael saw his mother lying on the towel, asleep, her sunglasses crooked and her bikini top undone, the straps that should be tied behind her neck to hold it up lying on her chest and a nipple poking out from one of the cups that had slipped down. Ismael standing up on the sand, his shadow falling over his mother's face and her just lying there with her mouth half open, breathing deeply, recovering from her night shift. *And who knows what else and everyone passing by gawping at her, she looks like she's fallen asleep after having sex.* He was tempted to prod her with his foot. But after staring at her for over a minute he turned and walked into the sea, as if he were walking down the street, and when the water reached halfway up his body he immersed himself completely, bending his knees, then turned again immediately and got out. And then without bothering to look back at his mother he carried on walking along the beach towards Sacaba, keeping an eye out for Canijo.

In the lift, 'How old are you, Mum?'

Amelia, without moving her head, her chin buried in her chest, raises her eyebrows and looks up at her son, who isn't smiling as she expected but looks serious, and she can't tell whether what he just said is a question or a reflection.

'Don't you know?'

Ismael shakes his head, looks at his mother's bare shoulders, and she feels embarrassed, ashamed, she wishes she had them covered up. The lift gives a violent shudder, and Amelia feels liberated, grateful for this brusque landing that snaps her out of it.

'Have a look at my ID card the next time you rifle through my things looking for my purse.'

'I saw your purse once and I opened it and I didn't look at anything, I wanted to see –'

'Yeah, yeah. So why are you asking how old I am all of a sudden?'

You don't understand you don't understand you just don't get it, you're too old to dress like that, but you don't understand, you're the one who doesn't know how old you are.

They walk towards the entrance to the building. Amelia in the lead, her back divided softly into two smooth, bronzed dunes. Ismael behind, looking at her, his face full of hate, his bottom row of teeth showing as he speaks.

'I wanted to see if you had a winning ticket, that's why I opened your purse, I'm not interested in what you've got, not in the least bit interested.'

'In that case I don't know why you have to go looking.'

The street appears like an off-white stain behind the door's glass panels.

'Bloody pain.'

'Yes, it's a bloody pain when people go through your bag and open your purse and snoop on your phone.'

'Phone? So you didn't say anything to us and you just went and bought a new one with a lock on it, that fingerprint thing.'

Amelia, her hand on the doorknob, stops and turns to face her son. 'I shouldn't have to say anything. Jorge doesn't rummage through my things.'

'As far as you know.'

'Yes, and the thing with the telephone is precisely because you go poking your nose in where it doesn't belong.'

'As if I care. What was I going to find? A photo of him? Or one of you that shouldn't be seen?'

Amelia doesn't reply. She stops for a moment so he can take full stock of the look of contempt on her face. *Little shit.* Ismael holds her stare, making sure she can see just how little he cares. Amelia opens the door and a waft of heat invades the hall, as if the street were on fire and a cloud of invisible hot embers had crowded in.

The pavement is a hot plate. Amelia clutches the handles of her bag, pulls down the sunglasses she was wearing above her forehead.

'I'll see you later,' says Amelia, raising an eyebrow. 'And please, Ismael, please . . .'

'OK, OK.'

Ismael turns around and starts walking towards Avenida Velázquez. His mother watches him, makes an effort and asks him, 'Where are you off to, Ismael, where are you going?'

Ismael shrugs his shoulders and carries on walking without acknowledging her. His mother watches him then turns and heads in the opposite direction. She bumps into Saray, the neighbour on her landing. They talk without stopping, their voices getting louder and louder as they get further away from each other.

'What a day, Amelia, what with this *terral*. Eh, girl?'

'Tell me about it.' *Twenty years younger than me, and she always has to call me a sodding girl.*

'We're going to roast. And you down at the beach, why not, if you've got the time?'

'I've earned it, on my feet all night.'

'Yes, it's all right for some. Cheerio, sweetie.'

'See you later.'

'How's Ismael?'

Ismael? Mind your own business and let's see if your dick of a boyfriend can give you another bun in the oven.

Amelia doesn't reply, pretending she didn't hear. She's reached her car and clicks the electronic key. She burns her hand on the door handle. The car's been out in the sun, roasted, scalding hot. She gets in, burns her hand on the steering wheel. She starts the car and puts the air conditioning on full, then gets out of the car and waits until it's tolerable. She can see Ismael in the distance, almost at the other end of the street. He's standing on the pavement, stooped over his phone. A solitary figure. *My son.* Better not to think about it. She gets in the car even though the temperature inside has barely dropped.

THE RUNNER'S DIARY

(Imagination not crushed by routine and repetition, by statistics) (by the law of probabilities) (in other words by recollections, memory + false memories)

What would it be like to walk down the street without doing anything else except walking down the street? Ignoring everything, moving forward, not stopping for anything, not letting anything affect us (divert us), seeing how everything passes by without us stopping like a train running down the track, nothing outside except insects crashing against our armour plating, driven forward by a current, an external energy or at least something much stronger than our curiosity (curiosity is just another insect so leave it behind). Simply moving forward. Nothing else. Pathetically following schedules.

That's what lots of people do. Lots of people I know. At least they seem to. (Like when I'm running on the track, nothing exists except for the run, your stride, your rhythm, your breathing, saving your energy in order to run more. Everything begins and ends with you.)

But children do stop. They're always stopping. They examine holes, turn over an insect they find on the ground, pull off one wing, then the other, then they want it to fly. They look at their own distorted faces in hubcaps, in a motorcycle's chrome mudguard, they look at themselves in shop windows and can't recognize themselves. They end up being suspicious of themselves. They pull faces and examine themselves, as if they were also insects, they try to see who they are and what they're like in shop windows. What life has in store for them or what they don't remember.

They could be anything, anything is possible. Almost possible. Almost anything. And they suspect, some of them suspect. Those who aren't too bewildered (those who aren't too certain, those ones).

They're right to be suspicious. I'm still not certain. That's my purity. It's the only type of purity I've got.

I remember back then. That house was my home, I still call it home, that house where other people are living now, people I don't know. It was my home and at the same time it was a tunnel. I remember the light in the yard, the sun on the floor tiles making them hot. I remember the heat, how I would burn myself when I took off my sandal and put my foot on the ground and tried to keep it there. All that brightness and the sun bouncing off the white wall. But more than anything when I think of home I remember the darkened rooms. People sleeping, breathing, my sister, my mother, my father or at least it seemed like it was them lying in the darkness, covered up like bundles, suddenly moving an arm or a head without really being them, they moaned, they were blind people lost in a corridor running parallel to the corridor where their bodies were and where I was, too, and all of a sudden they opened their eyes, someone entered their bodies and they recognized me, sometimes they took a few seconds, and then they said who they were. I was barefoot and at that time the floor tiles were freezing cold. And I'd look from a distance at that tall, narrow piece of furniture in the entrance hall, with its mirror I was scared to peer into. That one more than other ones. The hall that divided everything up, and, although no one was ever there, all the breathing that went on in that house and in other houses, in other tunnels, seemed to converge right there.

I remember a glow on my bedroom wall. I shared a room with my sister. The two beds were separated by a dark hole. The glow was there every night, shimmering on the wall as my sister was sleeping. The glow came from the street outside, it came across slowly and up towards the ceiling (now I know that it wasn't possible, it was the light from a street lamp that was nailed to the wall opposite, nailed, fixed in one spot and unable to move, but I could see its reflection moving in the same way water overflowing from a bathtub moves across the floor, like a tongue).

I was awake. I was awake and anything was possible. I wasn't a train, I wasn't a machine with armour plating. I used to stop everywhere. I wasn't on the running track, I wasn't running a 400-metres race. I didn't know what anything was and nobody taught me. Nobody told me: no one knows anything, they pretend, and you must pretend like everyone else pretends, one day you'll have to come face to face with questions alone, one day, one moment, and then you won't exist any more, there won't be any questions or answers, everything will be over, but until then pretend, fake it, live, breathe, walk down the tunnel as if the sun were shining.

I was inexperienced and now I'm an expert in inexperience. Back then, at that time, everything was alive and anything was possible. Even in broad daylight. I'd see a shadow flit along a wall and the shadow could be a hundred different things. A man, a woman with her face covered, someone or something completely unknown. Shadows were a question in themselves. People could do things way beyond what was known. Your house could suddenly turn into a diseased tree. Anything could happen. A man could walk past the window and scare you rigid, because you hadn't seen him in detail, because logic hadn't taken root and the world hadn't solidified. Whatever the man was carrying in his hand might be a knife. And the knife might be there to kill you. My father came into the room and he was a man and a threat and a mystery and goldfish could swim around in his chest. That's how I saw him or thought I saw him when I woke up and saw him in the bedroom doorway, in the shadows. His face blurred, a face that could have been any other man's face and a light that seemed to come from inside him and which was a reflection of the hall light in the huge jar he was carrying in his arms, with orange fish. Behind him were voices. My mother telling him to come away, to let me sleep, and he would laugh, without coming into the bedroom.

I had seen a man bleeding to death at the side of the street. Sitting in a doorway, his legs outstretched, deathly pale but smiling. One shoe was missing and there were bubbles of blood coming out of his mouth. He'd been run over by a car, and he looked drunk rather than injured, with his eyes half closed, half unconscious and like he was running, with that same expression but with the bubbles of blood, and the people gathered around him were making faces, looking as if they expected the worst. He survived, it wasn't serious, and one day, several months later, my father pointed him out to me and said 'that's the man you saw when he was run over' and he survived because he just had a few broken ribs, but one of them had punctured his lung, the lung is like the bladder inside a football that inflates and deflates and one of the man's lungs was punctured like a football gets punctured. He survived.

Two or three years earlier my father took me to see the body of someone who'd drowned. We were somewhere near Calle Salitre, the word went around and he grabbed my hand and took me over there. We saw him from the Puente del Hierro at the mouth of the river. What I remember is leaning against that metal railing, watching men coming and going from a distance. I remember the mounds, like dark-coloured, solid dunes, and in between them were these puddles that looked very deep. They said it was a boy who'd drowned. They'd fished him out of one of the pools and they'd covered him up with a tarpaulin. I thought he might get up, at any moment that bundle might pull back the tarpaulin and stand up and stop being a bundle. Like people do while they're asleep. Or maybe I'm thinking that when I remember it now. But what I'm sure of is that these things happened, and anything could happen at any moment. The boy was playing on those mounds one minute and a short while later he was lying still under the tarpaulin. You could change into something else. Then the dead man was my father. A bundle in some room at the hospital, wheeled in on a stretcher, alone in the basement. A bundle I didn't see. That's how it was. All of a sudden people could be sitting on a doorstep making bubbles of blood with their mouths, deflated inside, or lying under a tarpaulin or in a basement. What my mother used to talk about was people who'd died in their sleep, and she'd say that was the best thing that could happen to anyone. She still says so. And if she's near my grandmother she says it with an even greater sense of pleasure. My grandmother's got a weak heart. She takes pills and she shakes. I'm sure she also sees shadows and bundles at night when all the lights are out and she listens to the rest of us breathing.

Julia drives along Calle Jiménez Fraud, and the hospital building comes into view in the distance among the trees. The last traffic light in the street turns red. It's the light that gives way to the Metro along the stretch that's been turned into a tramway. She remembers being with Céspedes on the Metro one morning. She can't remember why they took it. The car had broken down, yes, that was it. *He never misled me, he never promised me anything or talked about divorce like so many others did, he never even told me his wife didn't understand him. He didn't tell me either that he was going out with other women, but I knew he was. Saying very little, we knew everything about each other, everything we can ever know about anyone else. I ended up thinking that his wife knew, too, and looked the other way. She's kicking off now because she caught him in the act, and she's thrown him out.*

The Metro carriages rumble past. A young man looks out at her. The dried-out scrub shakes as the train goes past. Julia's once more aware of how hot it must be outside. The traffic light turns green. *And he was completely up front about the Ortuño episode. He knew I'd like it, and I did. He was kissing me and looking me in the eyes that night in the taxi when the other guy started touching me as we went through the Cerrado Tunnel, the lights whizzing past like a merry-go-round, one of them licking my neck and the other kneading my breast as if it were made of clay, the taxi driver watching through the rear-view mirror, I held his gaze for a second, just enough, as Céspedes was unbuttoning my blouse, just enough for him to realize that I wasn't embarrassed and that I wasn't a working girl on the job either. I was a lady, and that turns them on even more.*

Julia parks the car. An ambulance is going towards A&E. *It can't be Dioni, but if it is Dioni Ana will be in the ambulance with him.*

She's right. Dioni isn't in that ambulance. Dionisio Grandes Guimerá arrived at the hospital in an ambulance that didn't have the necessary equipment to treat him. Blood tests haven't been done, they don't know his oxygen saturation levels or his ion levels. From experience, they know that the patient is suffering from a serious electrolyte imbalance and that he's lost bodily fluids, but they are unable to provide any statistics or details. Straightforward transport, nothing more. His wife, Ana Galán, and Nurse Ramiro González were waiting in the emergency room.

Ana Galán waited in silence with her hands in her pockets. When the stretcher came into the room and she saw his hair, his forehead, his arched eyebrows, she confirmed he was her husband. All Ramiro noticed was an involuntary twitching in the muscle around her lips, which happened again, although more pronounced this time, when they took the sheet off to reveal hundreds of tiny ants scurrying across the white fabric and still delving into the folds of her husband's skin, rooting around in that yellow, dried-out skin.

From that moment onwards, everything was automatic and fast. They knew exactly what steps to follow and talked less than on other occasions.

Julia quickly covered the distance between the car park and the entrance to A&E under an unrelenting, scorching sun. Her hair seemed to dry suddenly, immediately. She saw Nurse Blasco's face from a distance, her eyes staring at her, and she knew *Dioni has arrived, it was him*, she hurried even more.

Dioni has arrived. Dioni has arrived, and Céspedes is travelling in a white train at three hundred kilometres per hour in a Club Class seat. He's looking out of the window at the grey blur of some holm oaks, Carole's nodding off beside him, and he remembers a long-ago trip with his wife, a swimming pool and his daughter walking around the edge, she put her foot in the water making it ripple gently. Dioni has arrived, his wife is sponging his body with some gauze, getting rid of the ants. He's been connected to monitors, four electrode monitors have been stuck on his chest, the Abbocath connected to the drip delivering the saline solution through a peripheral intravenous line that Ramiro quickly set up as soon as Dioni arrived. The pale, grey-brown landscape and the trees flashing past the window, torn out by their roots, evaporating into thin air. *Moving forward, advancing*, Céspedes thinks back to yesterday morning, pictures himself with his forehead leaning against his front door, his wife's voice behind the door. 'It's over, never again, I didn't deserve this.' *That string of hackneyed phrases learned from films, melodramas*, learned during all the time wasted in front of the television (at his expense) and chatting with her friends at the club. Dioni's vital signs are heralding his death. Dr Galán and Nurse Ramiro have seen it all so many times that they cannot be mistaken, agonal respiration. *This is it. This is the moment we realize he's dying, while all the people outside are waiting to hear what's going on, mice running in their little wheels, their own internal wheels.* Dr Galán goes through the statistics again: temperature 40.2 degrees; blood pressure 90/50; heart rate 36; oxygen saturation level 63. *Hypoxemia*, now scientific terms are applied to emotional language. *How callous.*

The Runner's dozing on his bed with his diary notebook lying on his chest; Ismael's loitering on a side street off Calle Juan Sebastián Bach, pretending to look at his phone, but he doesn't take his eyes off the shop doorway opposite, watching who goes in and out, looking for Consuelo la Giganta, waiting for her, and while he's waiting he looks at the mannequins in the window, he knows them down to every last detail (light-blue blouse, tight white trousers, lime-green T-shirt, yellow skirt) just as he knows down to every last detail each segment of the green sign hanging above the shop D'SKANDALO MODA Y COMPLEMENTOS. He watches, takes a few steps and then watches again, while his mother walks along the beach, now close to the seashore, and his brother, Jorge, Gorgo, the baby of the family, the worker, who's head over heels in love with Gloria, Jorge who's scared of his brother and looks at photos of his girlfriend on his phone, listens to what his cousin Floren (who he's been ripping off for the last six months on the invoice payments) tells him about what happened to Pedroche. Up until now we only know a few details.

'You're not going to believe this, it's really heavy. What d'you think happened to Pedroche, how he got those injuries to his face and forehead? It was his wife, Belita. Yeah, it was her. But why d'you think she did it? If I tell you you're going to fall off that stool. You know she's got the hots for that priest she goes to, where she goes to mass every day? Pedroche says he's a pretty-boy, tall, and he's got all the young girls drooling over him, at least the ones who go to church. Well she goes and takes nineteen hundred or two thousand euros that Pedroche had at home. He says he always has some cash hidden away between the pages of an encyclopaedia for a rainy day or for emergencies, it's one of his hang-ups, and she discovers his hiding place, and she's taken the money and put it in an envelope, yesterday or the day before, I'm not too sure when he said it was because he was telling me and I was thinking how can this guy put up with all this crap? Anyway, the thing is, Belita, what a ball-breaker, she goes and takes all the cash and, wait for it, that's not all, she also takes all her jewellery, think about it, the engagement ring Pedroche gave her because in her family they're all so old fashioned with their airs and graces and they wanted everything done formally, and poor old Pedroche had to go the whole hog when they got married, just imagine, the rest of them desperate to offload the mad cow. I can picture him now with that innocent face of his staring at the floor soaking it up without a clue what he was letting himself in for, and the whole family knew that she was off her nut, and when they took her away they told him she'd gone to see her aunt in the country or she was with her mother at a spa. Anyway, the thing is, she goes and gives it all to the priest, the priest himself or the sacristan or an old woman who does the cleaning there, anyway she hands it over to someone in a bag, the cash and the sodding engagement ring, some holy medals on gold chains and, wait for it, not just one or two bits of stuff, it was everything she had, all her mother's earrings and her grandmother's stuff and she says this is a donation that she has to make to the parish and the priest, whatever his name is, and off she goes, and that night when Pedroche goes to put some more cash in or get some out from the sodding encyclopaedia he finds all the money's gone, he says he felt a sudden rush of blood to his head and his face turned as red as a tomato, you can imagine, and he says I must have made a mistake, no worries, and he takes a deep breath and grabs another volume of the encyclopaedia, the next one along, opens it, nothing, the money's not there, mate, then he really starts to flap, he puts the book face down, and the next one along and the next one, and nothing, he goes through all ten or twelve volumes, then the light goes on in his head and he says, bugger me, it's Belita, she's seen me putting the money there or for once in her life she's done a bit of cleaning, and who knows where she's put it or she's taken it to the bank, he calls her phone, she doesn't pick up, and now he's really panicking, you know what he's like with money, just imagine it, he calls her again, voicemail, "Belita, call me," and he says again, "Belita, for Christ's sake, call me," and the fourth or fifth time she picks up as calm as you like and says, "Sugar pie!" every time I hear her call him sugar pie I swear it makes me cringe, so anyway he says to her, "Did you take the money that was in the house?" and she's like, "Money, what money?" and he's desperate now, "My bloody money, the money that was here," and she cuts in, "Sugar pie, why don't you come and pick me up? I'm at my cousin Auxi's place, and I don't feel like waiting at the bus stop in this heat," and he's like, "But where's the money?" and she's like, "Are you coming to pick me up or not?" so he leaves the house and gets in the car, and he's thinking, bugger me, that woman, what the hell was I thinking hitching up with her and all that stuff, and he gets there and she's not outside, he calls her on the entryphone, "Belita, for Christ's sake, come downstairs," and she's like, "Oh, sugar pie, don't be like that, I'm just saying goodbye," so he waits for quarter of an hour stuck there in the car, and it's getting dark and he's desperate, another ten minutes go by he calls her, "Belita, for Christ's sake, I've been here an hour," and she says, "I'm coming now, don't be like that, the thing is she's feeling poorly, and I was just telling her a story," and he's like, "Story, for Christ's sake, that's why you made me come over here, for a story?" and she's like, "They're going to hear you all over the whole block, I'm coming down now, and you mind your manners," and eventually she appears, and you wouldn't believe it, he says, "What are you wearing?" she's all dressed up for winter almost in a heavy skirt she never takes off for love or money, platform boots and walking in slow motion and complaining, "Your manners, I couldn't say goodbye to my cousin properly, the poor girl she was almost in tears the way I had to rush," and as soon as she gets in the car he says, "The money, where's the money you took? Tell me, where is it?" and she says, "Pedroche, keep your eyes on the road, the poor girl, the state I left her in all because of you and your hang-ups, and now you come at me with this, all you think about is yourself, so utterly selfish," and he's driving and looking at her sideways, I can see him, I can just picture him, and he says very quietly, holding it all in, "Just tell me, Belita, now when we get home you give me back the money, it's money from work, from customers, money I have to pay back," and she's like, "And a liar, too, 'money from customers', since when do you collect money from customers?" and he says, "Belita, you'll give it back as soon as we get home, and we'll forget about it," and she's staring at him, and she says to him, "I haven't got it any more, it's not ours any more," and Pedroche gets more and more worried, "What do you mean? What have you done with my money?" "Your money? So I don't count? I never count for anything, that's what you'd like, for it to be all about you, you're so selfish, like now you drag me out of my cousin's house shouting down the intercom so the whole street can hear," and he says, "Belita, for Christ's sake," you know how he drives, all hunched over the wheel, "Belita, for Christ's sake, what do you mean?" and she's like, "That's right, just like you to get hot under the collar, making my life impossible, and hiding things all over the place, like a weasel, like a magpie, and stuffing money that isn't yours in between books." "What do you mean that isn't mine? Whose money is it? I work for it," and she goes, "It's God's," and he says, "What's God's?" "It's God's, it belongs to God, like everything, everything belongs to Him, and we owe it all to Him," she says, and, of course, he can't handle it any more, and he goes, "Fuck me, you're crazy, you're so crazy you're off the scale," and she's very calm, I can see her now with that face taking up half the car, and she goes quiet, and he notices out of the corner of his eye she's making a strange movement, and he sees her taking off her boot, and suddenly, without saying anything, she starts whacking him, holding the boot by the soft part on the leg, wham-bam-bam-bam, fucking hell, mate, she's going to kill the pair of them, Pedroche there hunched over trying to hide behind the steering wheel, they're on the ring road and there's heavy traffic, and she's giving him some with that heel with all her strength, and the car's swerving from side to side, so fucking heavy, mate, until he pulls in at a bus stop and manages to stop, and his seat belt only gets stuck, and meanwhile she's giving him some wham-bam-bam non-stop, Pedroche says, fuck me, like a machine not shouting or saying a thing, just hitting him as viciously as she could until he manages to undo the seat belt, she was hitting him on the hands while he was trying to get it off, did you see how one of his hands is half purple, all covered in bruises? Well, then he gets out of the car, and what do you think the crazy bitch does? She gets out after him, it's over the top, mate, what a laugh, you have to laugh, and she goes hobbling after him with a boot on one foot and the other one bare, and she still gets him with two or three wallops, and the people at the bus stop, apparently a couple of lads and an older woman are there with their mouths hanging open saying, hey, what's going on? This massive woman holding a boot and hitting this tiny little guy, and his forehead's already bleeding, he says his whole face was covered in blood, he needed five stitches, and he goes running off, the car with its doors wide open and people looking, and she's going after him, but she can't keep up any more, of course, it must have been a sight, her with a boot in her hand and telling him, he says she was telling him, "You're a bad man, that's what you are and what you've been ever since I met you, a bad man," and the people at the bus stop are just stunned, and she comes back and sits on the bench and says, "Good evening," and starts putting her boot back on as calm as you like, and when she's put it on she goes off down the pavement click-clack-click back home, and he's there holding his head, still wary and watching from afar, he says the two lads from the bus stop came over and were asking him if he was all right, but they were a bit nervous, naturally, they probably thought he must be some kind of abuser or a drunk or whatever, and he was just there with his head down, you know, like a wild boar, "No, I'm fine thanks, it's nothing, just a cut, that's all," and he got in the car and saw her in the distance and headed straight for Carlos Haya Hospital, of course, because the cut had opened up a vein or something, and he says his shirt was totally soaked in blood and his face looked like his skull was cracked open, but, anyway, they stitched him up, he told them he'd fallen down some stairs, he says the nurses were looking him up and down, but obviously he looks like butter wouldn't melt, so they're not going to think he's a thug or anything and not in a million years that his wife has given him a hiding with one of her boots so, well, after this spectacle he leaves the hospital and, of course, he heads off home, and just picture what he's like, cursing Belita's mother and thinking what the fuck's she done with the money and on the other hand saying, let's see what I find when I get home and what kind of state she's in, if she'll come at me with a broom handle or a knife instead of her boot, man, she's crazy, but no, he says he got back and she's lying in bed wide awake but in bed and looking at the ceiling, have you been to their place, have you seen the bedroom, well the bedroom's like something out of Dracula, I don't know how to describe it, very old fashioned, I mean, old fashioned but, like, gloomy or ancient looking, all very dark with black wooden furniture, and the bed's like it's been made up for a corpse at a wake, you know, and these heavy curtains from a century ago, well anyway, Pedroche puts his head around the bedroom door, and she's lying there like nothing happened, "You're a bit late, aren't you?" and, of course, he doesn't dare, he doesn't know how to approach her, he says to me, "How am I going to talk to her about that performance in the car? Maybe she'll kick off at me again, but then I couldn't just pretend nothing had happened because I was still trying to get my head around the thing with the money," so he says to her, "No, I dropped by Carlos Haya," he says it like that, just like he'd gone to a bar to see a friend, no big deal, "I dropped by Carlos Haya," and then he says she turns over a bit like this and looks at him, she's staring at those plasters and says to him, "Your egg and chips are on the table," you know, she does him fried eggs in the afternoon and leaves them on the table, just imagine a fried egg five or six hours old, and he eats them, but yesterday, when she said that, he just stood there in the doorway as if saying, what am I going to do, eat the egg or what the fuck do I do, and he finds some courage and says, "OK, I'll eat it now, Beli, but tell me one thing because it's important, and I'll have to sort out the thing with the money, Beli, because it's important, we need that money, that money's for –" and she cuts him short, "The money's not there any more, forget about that money because we don't need money or jewellery," and he's like, "What d'you mean we don't need it, Belita?" and she says, "What for? So it can be hidden away in some books, with all the shortages in the world and all the poor and things that need to be done, why do we need those bits of paper stuck there like pages in a book?" "It's not like that, Belita," he's petrified, standing there in the doorway, he doesn't dare go in, and he says she starts to get angry again and sits up in bed, and she says, "Let's leave it there, there are things we don't need and other people do, so that's enough of that, you went on at me this afternoon at my cousin's, and now you're going on at me again, so go and eat your egg, and if you fancy it there's that pork loin you like in the fridge," and he says that, half going with the flow, he tells her, "Yes, yes, I'll eat the egg in a minute, but jewellery, Belita, what jewellery do you mean?" and she says as calm as before and turning over on to her side, "My mother's jewellery and the rest of the family's, or are you going to tell me that's yours as well? And the engagement ring was mine, too, though I wish I'd never seen it, but it was mine," and Pedroche seeing her there, that huge lump lying on the bed, it's a wonder it doesn't buckle under the weight, all he can say is, "Yes, well, those are your family's things, and so you've given them to him, have you, to the priest, for the poor?" and then he says she turned around in a bit of a rage and says, "No, not to the priest, to the parish, or I suppose you think that everyone's just as selfish as you are, he doesn't want a thing for himself, and the few times I've mentioned giving him some money he's always said, put that in the collection plate or give it to the Little Sisters of the Poor," so Pedroche realized that it was completely impossible, he says he went into the sitting room and stayed there all night dozing in an armchair, he didn't even stretch out on the sofa, waiting for the next day so he could go to the church and speak to the priest and tell him, "Listen, Father, I know my wife left some money here and some of her family's jewellery, but the thing is, she's not well, I don't know if you realized, I mean she's got problems what with her nervous breakdowns and stuff, and I know there are no bad intentions on your part, but would you be kind enough to give it back because she'll be the first to repent in a week's time or when she realizes what she's done, and she might come here to ask for an explanation or whatever," he had his little speech prepared, and first thing in the morning he was there at the church door, and this man appears, I reckon it was probably the sacristan, that was this morning, and Pedroche says to him, is the Father in, Father Sebastián (I think he said Sebastián or Julián, I'm not too sure), and the other guy obviously, seeing him there with the plasters and the black eye, and he's thinking what's this one after? And he tells him he doesn't know what time he's going to be there today, if he's going to be there at all, because he had to do some things over in Los Asperones or somewhere, and Pedroche's getting really annoyed now and asks him if he knows where the priest lives, and he says he doesn't, somewhere near by, between the church and Cruz de Humilladero, in other words he's telling him to leave him in peace, and when Pedroche comes a bit closer to him he starts off with, "Listen, don't come here and start making trouble or I'll call the police right now, listen," and so he hangs around for a bit walking up and down by the church door, and then he comes here, and he's desperate by now, you can see the way the land lies, look at him, he's probably talking to her sister or that cousin of hers, I don't know, mate, his life must be hell, I told him I'd go along with him this afternoon to see the priest, I can't just let him go on his own, and we'll see what the priest says, who knows what he'll come out with, what with the jewels being hers and the money supposedly is both of theirs if they're married, I don't know, maybe the priest will say, your wife knew what she was doing when she gave me this so it will stay in the parish funds or whatever, my mum used to go to that church, and she said he was a really nice lad, the priest, although there's no denying he had them all a bit crazy for him treating them like they were all marchionesses, yes milady no milady and all that stuff, and besides, by all accounts he's a bit of a looker, my mum said he's like a film star, that priest, a film star like Gregory Peck, my mum said, Gregory Peck, he was a bit like George Clooney back in the day.'

He's not intubated. He's being given 100 per cent oxygen. Dionisio Grandes Guimerá is an organism that is becoming extinct. Ants are still wandering around on the sheet. Dr Galán carefully removes them as if that were her job and this were a way to cure her husband, to make him recover, have another opportunity, a new life. Julia came into the room a short while ago. Dr Galán only sees her right then, standing to one side, behind her and next to Ramiro. And, a short while before, Ramiro will have told her in an almost inaudible voice that the possibility of brain damage is very high and that the patient's (Dioni's) Glasgow Coma Score is very low, oxygen saturation level 63. 'No resus,' he whispers. 'They're going to let him go.' Ana and Julia know that's what he'd want, what Dioni would want. To put an end to it. To put an end to a nightmare that has yet to peak, to pass through his body, all that tangled mess of suffering, through a narrow filter, through a bottleneck leading nowhere. *The ripples made by a pebble in the water becoming smaller and smaller.* Dr Galán squashes an ant between her fingertips, and Julia rests her fingertips on the doctor's shoulder while Amelia spreads out her pink towel and can feel the throbbing heat of the sand through the material, that feeling of peace and life.

And her son, her son Ismael, can see the green dress that Consuelo wears every day when she goes down to the shops. She's called La Giganta.

She's tall, big boned, with an olive complexion, dark eyebrows and her hair styled and dyed like Marilyn Monroe's. She has dark eyes and a smudge of blue eyeshadow on her eyelids. That's the external packaging. Consuelo la Giganta must be around forty-five. She's married to a disagreeable character who's also tall. A character who only says hello to people he knows personally. In the lift he looks down from on high without acknowledging anyone else in the cabin. That amazing cabin where Ismael always hopes to bump into Consuelo. They have a son, also aloof, who's three or four years younger than Ismael. Dark haired, with his mother's bright dark eyes. Ismael is mortally offended to see those eyes in the boy's face. It makes him feel like he's witnessing a profanity, a sordid act.

They live on the sixth floor. One floor up from where Ismael lives with his mother and his brother, although their flats don't occupy the same vertical area of floor space. Ismael would like it if Consuelo lived in the flat immediately above theirs. He'd like to listen her footsteps as she walked across the floor, to hear the toilet flush, the taps running, the echo of her voice struggling to cross the barrier of fake marble, concrete and lime that separates them. Even so, sometimes Ismael thinks that he can hear noises coming from Consuelo's flat and even from Consuelo herself. A voice, the very particular pitch of her voice, her tone. It's a gentle tone, earthy, the sound of a voice in a narrow tunnel. Some nights he can also hear the clickety-clack of Consuelo walking around in her heels when she's getting ready to go out with her husband. They go to El Palustre social club. Ismael has heard her talk about the club a few times, and once he realizes that she's there, talking and laughing with other people, it holds a morbid fascination for him.

La Giganta has dark lips and small teeth, not very white but nice and straight. They've acquired a yellow tinge from her cigarettes. Sometimes, leaning out of the kitchen window, Ismael has also seen Consuelo's naked arms hanging out the washing above her head. On these occasions Ismael turns his torso around, twists his neck, and can see her brown arms, her fingernails painted a deep red – almost brown – her fingers moving through the air as if they were sending out a coded message as they peg out the washing. Ismael leans out even more so he can see more than her forearms, more skin, and he manages to snatch a view of her elbow and occasionally her firm biceps and even her armpit, that sacred, off-white, greenish-grey, unfathomable cavity, when the house-coat La Giganta uses indoors flaps open and exposes a glimpse of her dark bra and her bra strap, always black, that Ismael always imagines when he gets into the lift with her.

One afternoon as he came out of the lift he met her in the entrance hall. Consuelo was sitting on the concierge's chair. Ismael had no idea what she was doing there. When she saw him, Consuelo asked him for a light, smiling, her mouth twisted and her dark eyes clouded over, *she always looks as if she's coming*, putting the cigarette in her mouth, gently placing the mottled filter between her lips, and, like an idiot, he told her, 'I don't smoke, I haven't got a light' and carried on walking out into the street, unnerved, feeling that he'd missed an opportunity, The Opportunity, and as soon as he reached the street he sprinted over to the kiosk and desperately asked for a lighter. 'Blue or red?' the man asked, ensconced behind a barrier of sweets and magazines. 'I don't care.' 'Red?' 'I don't care, yes, red.' He dropped a coin, kicked it away and ran back, coming to a halt just outside the entrance and went in smiling. Consuelo was smoking her cigarette and chatting to a neigh-bour. Ismael took two steps towards them, stopped, looked at the letterboxes, removed all the advertising leaflets from theirs, rolled them up and stuffed them in his back pocket just as the neighbour was saying goodbye to Consuelo. Ismael went up to her, smiled and showed her the lighter. 'I found a lighter,' he told her and she, in turn, showed him her cigarette. 'Me, too,' she said and she took a long drag on it, looking at him intrigued. Was she challenging him? Ismael stood still for four or maybe five seconds, *suck my cock and swallow my juice, you whore*, he almost said the words out loud, for an instant that thought, those words, were so powerful that he thought he had actually uttered them or that she, Consuelo, without his needing to utter them, knew exactly what he was about to say, what he was actually saying, what that silence meant, those seconds when everything was held in suspense, when he could see himself grabbing her by the neck and pulling her towards him, towards his crotch. Until she said, 'What?' and he snapped out of it, came back to reality and once again saw that he was still standing there with the red lighter in his hand, and she had the cigarette in her mouth again and was now looking out towards the street, towards the glare and movement behind the glass. Ismael, not knowing what to do, had already taken a step towards the lift, had already opened the door and was standing there, seeing his reflection in that mirror which had reflected back Consuelo la Giganta's image so many times, on which he placed his lips, kissing the glass, licking it.

His mother is lying on her back on the towel she's just spread out. She places both hands beneath her back and undoes her bikini top. She pulls down the straps, and pulls down the cups. She lifts her neck – with a forced expression on her face that contradicts her feeling of well-being – and makes sure that the strip of cloth covers her nipples. Not beyond the areolae. She lies back, relaxes her expression, lowers her sunglasses from her forehead and places them over her eyes. The blazing sun prickles her body with a million sharp needles while the proximity of the sea makes her feel relieved, almost refreshed. That gentle, murmuring purr.

One of these days, one of these days it'll happen, Ismael told himself, slightly swaying, going up in that mirror-lined cabin, thinking that one day he'll kiss those lips and those arms and those hidden nipples that he imagines are as dark as her lips. That's what he thought then and what he's thinking now as he keeps watch over the entrance to D'SKANDALO.

La Giganta goes out at the same time every morning to do her rounds in the neighbourhood, rarely deviating by more than five or ten minutes. And almost every day she goes into that shop to chat to the owner. Sometimes Ismael goes over to the shop window and sees them inside. They laugh and cluck their tongues. He doesn't know what they talk about. He doesn't know how they know each other or why Consuelo goes in there so often. Once, Consuelo's husband went into the shop, and they both came out quarrelling and looking serious. Her husband spat on the pavement and walked in front of her, and she walked behind staring at her husband's shoulders and the back of his neck with a calmness that Ismael interpreted as scorn. Ismael's family also joked about Consuelo's husband. La Giganta's husband.

Ismael gets annoyed when his brother and his mother call her La Giganta. He masturbates as he whispers her name, Consuelo. He lies in wait for her every morning, from Monday to Friday. On Saturdays Consuelo's schedule is irregular, unpredictable. On Sundays the shops are closed, and if he's lucky he hears the sharp tic-tac of her heels through some part of the ceiling. Sometimes, from his window, he sees her cross the street with her husband and get into their car, a Peugeot 406 with one of the back doors dented in a collision. From up there, Ismael can see Consuelo's legs through the reflections in the windscreen. Sometimes her legs are sporting a pair of black trousers. Her legs are too thin for her body. It doesn't matter. Ismael's not interested in her legs. The sound of the car fades away at the end of the street, and the rest of Sunday is empty.

He's never seen her outside the neighbourhood. Everything's focused on just a couple of streets and three or four shops which Consuelo goes into and emerges from moments later. Carnes Castilla, El As de Pan or the little supermarket in Calle Manuel de Falla. Sometimes the fruit shop or the roast chicken shop in Plaza Mozart find a way into her itinerary. Almost every day the tobacconist's, although this visit doesn't count, it's too fleeting, as if the tobacconist were waiting for her with her packet of Marlboro ready, and La Giganta grabbed it with the speed of a relay runner. And always D'SKANDALO. That's always the last call Consuelo makes, and the duration of her visit is unpredictable.

Ismael spends minutes and minutes watching the shop's green door sign, its windows and the mannequins. These minutes can stretch and grow longer, and at such times Ismael feels as if he himself is being watched, spied on from every window, by every passer-by, by every acquaintance who sees him from a distance and, above all, by the concierge of his building, who's often leaning against the entrance doorway to his building, watching, with his arms folded. *Fucking parasite.*

Ismael pretends to look at his phone, make a call, receive calls, makes as if he's talking to someone, chooses Canijo or his brother or his mother as the person he's supposedly talking to, or the dickhead in the kitchen at the hotel where his mother found him a job. He walks towards some place or other in the street, changes the tone of his voice and his observation point, at the kerb or on the corner. Until all of a sudden he sees La Giganta's washed-out hair, green dress and brown arms in the shop doorway, and he starts walking.

Everything is measured. His movements are synchronized with La Giganta's slow walking pace. He knows that if he sets off from the corner of the street at a fast stride they'll coincide at the entrance to his building, assuming Consuelo doesn't bump into some neighbour and stop for a chat. If this happens, Ismael slows down, curses, takes his phone out again or stops to look in a shop window and watch his quarry out of the corner of his eye until the rhythms of the chase are reinstated. His heart is like a whistle, or a fluid that expands and flows throughout his body.

The objective is to be in the lift with her for thirty seconds. He walks into the building two paces behind Consuelo, and Consuelo has already guessed who those silent footsteps belong to and whose shadow she can sense behind her. The concierge sees them come in and watches. *He knows, the bastard knows, and what do I care if he knows, the whole world can know about it for all I care.* And then, the ritual. She looks at him and smiles, she says 'Hello' and he replies. They wait for the lift and he's praying that no one else will arrive. She looks at the light showing which floor the lift is on, the ceiling, he looks at her. Her nascent double chin, the black smokiness of her eyes, her almost bare shoulders and her bra strap peeping out from under the sleeve of her sheer dress. The curve of her breasts, although not overly full, two green dunes.

They go into the lift, she's always at the back. Without asking, he presses the button for number 5. The number is white on a black background. Thirty seconds of silence, anticipation, the prelude to what will happen, that day or some other day. Both of them are aware of it and say nothing. She sometimes plays around with the mystique of the situation when she says, looking pleased, and only very occasionally, 'We seem to bump into each other a lot, you and me,' to which he responds with a monosyllable or simply with a smile that he hopes will speak volumes, will send a clear message. And the shudder of the arrival as the lift stops and he looks at her again before going out. And the frustration, that dull rage when he suddenly finds himself on the landing outside his flat, not knowing why he's missed this latest opportunity or what he's doing in this lonely place, listening as the lift door opens on the floor above and feeling that he ought to be at Consuelo's side right then and not where he is now, hearing her footsteps, the keys jangling, the door opening and then after two or three seconds closing, right then he ought to be squeezing her against the door after closing it, placing his mouth in that cavity between Consuelo's neck and shoulder, running the palm of his hand over the two green dunes made by her dress, wanting to tear off her clothes but putting off the moment of seeing her naked body, covered only by the hypnotic geometric outline of her bra, to touch her skin in the same way that he touched it that day, one day when his desire entered the world of reality and Ismael couldn't tell if he was dreaming or experiencing a different reality, as if some strange passage had led him into a future world or a dream and so, swept along by a sensation similar to being extremely inebriated, moving like bodies move under the water, he stretched out his hand, straightened his index finger and his middle finger and while Consuelo looked idly on as the floors went past he slid his fingers over her naked arm, a gentle incursion over ten or fifteen centimetres of Consuelo's skin, and for once she seemed surprised and she asked him, 'What? What's going on?' genuinely intrigued, just as the lift swayed and stopped at the fifth floor, and Ismael, still submerged in the depths of the ocean or transported through a narrow tunnel of his own imagination or time itself, pushed his hand against the lift door, like a hatch opening out on to reality, and walked out.

And so, in the hope and also the certainty that one day his dream will come true and he'll finally be alone with Consuelo – watching her leaning against the door half naked, slowly removing her bra and showing him a dark nipple, leading him down a corridor he's never seen before into a darkened bedroom, throwing herself on the bed and whispering in his ear, *Fuck me, like that, like that, Ismael, fuck me*, and today, Ismael, suffused with this flight of fancy, is waiting for Consuelo to come out of the dress shop called D'SKANDALO, ready to go up with her in the lift, hazily thinking that one day something will happen, that at some point she'll break through her wall of ice and will say to him 'Come up with me,' or she'll just press the sacred number-six button.

And so, just like every other day when he spots her, Ismael's heart also melts today when he sees Consuelo la Giganta in her sheer green dress walking through the La Paz neighbourhood.

And so, on this August day, the *terral* tears remorselessly through the city, sweeping down streets and enveloping them like an imaginary, invisible monster that disrupts routines and enfeebles and shatters people's minds.

And so, swept along by blind, pheromone-fuelled obedience, in a temperature of forty-two degrees, on the patch of waste ground on Avenida Ortega y Gasset thousands of ants are scurrying around, searching for the trail left by their companions who have been taken away together with the body of Dionisio Grandes Guimerá. They're scurrying around in an ever-increasing web, marching across the scorched earth, dodging bits of plastic that have been softened by the sun, advancing through gigantic mounds of rubble, dried-out scrub, burned-out trees, fragments and remnants of buildings from a bygone age. An archaeology comprising masses of cement, scraps of plaster, desiccated cigarette butts, bits of glass, drink cans, flattened aluminium with a few surviving marks – a string of strange, discoloured letters – like the ancient carcass of a boat that has run aground. Swarming, climbing, descending, searching, communicating with each other, and in their nervous exchanges they experience something vaguely similar to frustration and alarm. Many years' worth of food supplies, the inexhaustible pantry consisting of Dionisio Grandes Guimerá's body, have vanished into thin air and, like the cells of a single organism, they are seeking a way to reverse this disappointment, a way to make the mirage reappear.

And so, like the chains of that lift in which Ismael's fantasies rise and fall, Raimundo Arias's thoughts and words clank and crunch, whispered, masticated, furious and filthy. Agitated like a tormented ant, he's meandering through that small labyrinth formed by the streets of Portada

Alta searching for his colleague Eduardo. His guitar is weighing him down and impeding him, just as he's weighed down and impeded by life, the day, the heat, the glaring light and poverty. He can't stand wearing these cracked shoes, that's what he hates most of all. And for all that he rubs the top of his shoe on the back of his other leg and rubs it viciously, the grooves and wrinkles are still there, caked in the putrescence and yellow dust from the patch of waste ground, with his bunion pushing his shoe out of shape and the soles worn out by the hundreds or thousands of kilometres he's tramped in search of sustenance and smack.

You can judge a man by his shoes. That's the only good advice his father ever gave him before he hanged himself from a hook in the dining-room ceiling rose. His mother found him there, his sickly, ungainly body taking the place of the four-bulb light fitting that his father had carefully put on top of the table before he strung himself up. What he couldn't prevent was the evacuation of his bowels, the hanged man's final mucky act that sullied his farewell to the world, the oilcloth cover on the table and one of the four lamp shades. His shoes, on the other hand, were muck free. Gleaming, freshly polished. Spick and span. Not like the ones his son is wearing now as he walks over the pink-and-white paving and scorching asphalt of Portada Alta until he comes across El Tato on a bend in the road in Calle Papamosca.

Feverish, indignant, Raimundo asks, 'Hey Tato, where's that bastard Eduardo?'

And El Tato, with the dilated eyes and faraway look of a hashish smoker, says back to him, 'Eduardo, he's such a pain in the arse.'

'Where is the stupid bastard?'

'Eduardo?'

'No, my fucking sister! I don't believe it! I come across a dead man in the middle of nowhere, and they nearly fucking nick *me*.'

'Dead man?'

'Totally dead. Heavy or what? Then one of the cops gives me a lift in his car.'

'Hey, Rai, you're something else.'

'So where's that wanker Eduardo?'

'Nene Olmedo's place. He was heading over there with Juanmi and

La Penca. Nene Olmedo turned up, and the three of them went off with him.'

'No way! There's something wrong with that guy, inside his head. Eduardo! I'll kill the bastard!' Raimundo waves his guitar in the air violently.

And, still muttering 'I'll kill the bastard' and 'Fuck this', Raimundo Arias starts walking off, not wanting to listen to what El Tato is saying to him, 'Hey, Rai, give me a tune on that guitar.' 'Fuck you,' Raimundo replies through gritted teeth not even knowing himself whether the insult is aimed at El Tato or Eduardo Chinarro. And still muttering and disgusted by the state of his shoes (El Tato was wearing a spotless pair of Nikes) Rai crosses Calle Ave del Paraíso with his guitar over his shoulder, then he crosses Calle Colibrí, too, and goes into the Parque de la Peseta in search of his partner.

And so the train crosses the almost empty *meseta*, the white worm in which Céspedes is travelling with Carole's sleeping head and her perfumed hair resting on his shoulder. *This sackful of dreams, this life which won't be close to mine and that I won't see again, I'll have today and tomorrow and within a week or, if I'm lucky, a month from now I'll end up on a platform, and her path will take her away at three hundred or a thousand kilometres per hour, her life ahead of her, until it's her that's left on the platform at another station in the year 2042 or 2050, if she's lucky, if she's not covered in a black shroud, covered over and carried off.* Rusty boats, black sheets, a dog vomiting and running off under the rain, street lamps and yellow lights in the windows at night, Julia's face which suddenly morphs into Carole's, a hotel room, and he's walking in the dark between pieces of furniture he doesn't recognize. The borders of sleep bring unconnected images into Céspedes's mind.

He opens his eyes, and there, replicated on the four or five screens in the carriage, is the face of that actor whose name he doesn't recall; he's also walking down a dark alley, treading in puddles that throw up reflections as if from another world, and he stealthily takes a silver pistol from his jacket pocket. *I don't know if this is freedom or the prison gate closing behind me.* Suddenly, a life with no mooring ropes. Céspedes runs over the past few days, the past few hours in his mind, goes over them with the distraction that comes from a sleepless night, a lazy, almost pleasurable leeward drift that leaves him still lethargic but with his mind alert, electrified. If right at the start he'd told that moron, that conceited head of personnel at the Hotel Los Patos Ortuño introduced him to, Rafi Villaplana, to sling his hook, right now Céspedes would be sitting beside his swimming pool holding a dry martini poorly mixed by his wife or maybe planning a September getaway with her, choosing a hotel somewhere in Copenhagen or Amsterdam, half bored and half enticed, Elisa choosing the hotels and him agreeing with a calm indifference. *At the end of the day that stupid ambitious clown has screwed me over well and good if this is what being screwed over is like – or is it what I wanted, what I've been seeking for God knows how long?*

That stupid clown with his back-combed hair, trousers hoicked up above his waist, with his upper-class manners and his working-class background, son of the wonderful toothless Segueta, who, in order to win Céspedes's favour and smooth the path for what he considered to be the deal of the century, lined him up with that woman his wife caught him in bed with, well, not exactly in bed, no, on the desk, screwing her on the desk. 'Natalia Ibáñez,' the idiot said by way of introduction, 'my confidante, my right-hand woman.' And he sucked his teeth, who knows whether by way of a swagger or to announce one of the skills boasted by the woman who from then on Céspedes and Ortuño would call 'Ibáñez the Sword-Swallower' or simply 'Ibáñez'. *Nails like a whore and an arse like a filly.*

'My job at the hotel's just temporary, I'm focused on something very different.' That's what Villaplana said. 'As I said, Céspedes, just temporary, and you're a role model to me, I'm telling you straight, and I don't give praise lightly, a real example.' Resident of Portada Alta, raving lunatic, Rafi Villaplana was speaking with the certainty of someone who uses bullets instead of words. That was how he'd got hooked up with the English girl who, according to him, had a father with plenty of money to invest.

Saying that his job at the hotel's just temporary and Céspedes asking for reports and confirming he'd been working at the same hotel for fifteen years, having arrived as a bellboy and having worked his way up the ladder, obsequious to his employers and aggressive towards his peers. 'We're going to do this, Céspedes, I guarantee it. You put up your share, and my father-in-law (my future father-in-law) will cover the rest, he just has to see that I've got your commitment, that we've got the infrastructure and we're not – that I'm not – a simpleton. He's got investments in half of England, but he doesn't know how things work over here, he started at the bottom, not right at the bottom but as a foreman, and after five years he had his own foundry, after seven years he had two, and after ten years he was a big fish within the sector in Gloucester, metal carpentry, he's clever, and we can trust him, Céspedes, isn't that right, sweetheart? Céspedes can trust him and he can trust us, too? And you as well?' And then Villaplana touched Ibáñez's thigh, slid his hand to the inside. *Familiar territory explored with tongue and dick*, thought Céspedes.

And it was the ease of it all that sank Céspedes, that lack of importance and almost lack of interest in Ibáñez, that apathy which led him to commit an indiscretion which he had never made before. The feeling that with this semi-whore with pretensions he wasn't breaking any laws or betraying anyone's trust was what led him first to bring her home and give her a Bailey's (that muck was the only thing she'd drink) while he collected some documents from his office, and that was what then inspired him to sit her on the desk, pull down her knickers and screw her right there. And that was how, with his trousers around his ankles, his shirt unbuttoned and hanging over his arse, Ibáñez moaning like she must have thought a cat in heat would moan, that was the scene when Céspedes's wife, with a broad grin, popped her head around the door, just her head, and said, 'Hi there, honey.' And then she didn't say anything else. Her head stayed there, without a body, cut off at the neck by the doorframe, the expression that had started as a grin starting to wither, transforming into the muscular contractions of someone retching just before they throw up, while Céspedes *the worst thing about the whole stupid incident was me with my trousers around my ankles, what a bummer* turned around, still erect, and tried to take a few steps in no particular direction, impeded, leaving Ibáñez's pussy exposed, and her idiotic face, her moans now morphing into the screams that cats really do give when something is just too much for them. Four, five seconds? Probably Señora Céspedes's head wasn't there any longer than that. But we all know that time is a relative measure, completely meaningless in situations where emotions are intense.

And so Ismael watches the determined (and at the same time leisurely) progress of Consuelo la Giganta up Calle Juan Sebastián Bach, along the pavement on the side with odd numbers. And so his mother sinks into a deep stupor, her hair and her bikini dripping wet after the quick dip she's just taken in the cold and almost crystal-clear water. Playa de la Misericordia. Amelia appreciates the towel's warmth, the heat filtering up from the sand through the material, damp and warm at the same time. She blesses the breath of air that, on this part of the beach, near the seashore, forges a path between the fresh sea breeze and the muggy heat, passing over her and caressing her skin like a soft tongue. She closes her eyes, and the world disintegrates, reality fragments almost with the same precision with which her son Ismael cut up the curtains, the towels and every scrap of material he could lay his hands on between the small hours and sunrise. Triangles, scraps that scatter and fly across the sand until they hit the tiny breakwater that barely disturbs the water with a timid murmur. And one of those triangles carries an image of Rafi. The latest row, with her telling him, *Never again, I'm warning you, never again*, knowing that her words had lost their power, that nothing she might have said could get through to Rafi Villaplana. A blind alley.

She knew it from the very first day. From the moment he suggested going out to lunch to try to resolve – that's what he said, resolve – the problems that had arisen with the new receptionist in a relaxed way. Amelia knew that this meal was unnecessary and that it never would have taken place if she had been a man. Villaplana never needed to consult anyone about anything, it never took him long to resolve disputes. And her impression was confirmed when lunch turned into dinner at the last minute. She knew that the meeting would be even more protracted. She took a lot of care over her make-up, chose the silk blouse and the trousers that suited her best of all. She knew he had something of a history, but on this occasion she wasn't going to be the victim, she would be the predator, Amazonian, free and independent. Aware. It was more than two years since her husband had left. She'd rebuilt her life, or at least she'd saved it from becoming a complete shipwreck. She'd had to find a job, her younger son had also made it to the lifeboat that his cousin had offered him in the framing and mouldings shop and her other son, Ismael, was flailing around helplessly between violence, alcohol and despotism. And so she was going to allow herself a bit of fun with this personnel manager who was rather a dandy, somewhat past his prime but attractive and self-assured. Everything was perfect, she reassured Queta, her colleague who worked in admin at the hotel. 'I can tell you from my own experience: give him a wide berth,' her friend had advised her. 'I don't have any expectations, all I want is a bit of fun.' Yes, that's how it was.

And so she found herself in the quicksand. She who'd been free, independent, Amazonian, emancipated and even a rebel woke up one day to find herself tied down as firmly as Gulliver when he woke up in the land of the Lilliputians. Only her strings, Amelia's strings, were viscous and slimy and it was impossible to undo the knots. It was as if the string and the knots were made of the same substance as Rafi Villaplana himself. *I haven't tricked you, Amelia, you knew right from the start, you know it's the truth.* That was the one and only, firm and unshakeable argument that Rafi Villaplana hid behind. Right from the start, at that dinner in El Higuerón, he told her he had a fiancée. And with a seductive smile that left the door open to irony and even sarcasm, shaking his head, he added, 'Fiancée or something like that, who knows how it'll turn out?' And he turned away quickly and looked towards the horizon, a tarry mass, a muddle of sea and sky, just as he muddied the trail of his emotions, always zigzagging between what was certain and what was possible, what could be seen and what was imagined.

And so Amelia falls into the labyrinth that opens up before her as soon as she closes her eyes. And so the trains and the ants run their course, and so the waves break again and again on the beach, persistent, shattered and docile, almost silent, creating a murmur that doesn't bother anyone. Just like the tide and just like the ivy that keeps rising up in Amelia's chest but never reaches her throat. Giving in every time Rafi calls, pining when she hasn't heard from him for a few days, jealous when she sees him chatting to a female guest or another employee who's younger than her. Without the will to leave him, without the strength to free herself from the tangle that's tying her down. Where else would she go? And why? It's all so tiring. Shallow. Some children are shouting and splashing about, and Amelia can't tell any more if they're really there or just part of her dream.

And so a dream comes to an end with pin-sharp clarity, and for the first time since her husband entered that room, filthy and at death's door, Dr Galán holds his hand. The dream she had wanted to be a part of is over and the reality she had wanted to ignore has kicked in, and now, when it's too late, it's inescapable. For the first time that day she touches her husband in a non-medical way, without checking his vital signs, without looking at the monitors, the pulse oximeter or his score on the Glasgow Coma Scale. And so she takes his swollen hand in hers and, at the same time, with a twitch of her shoulder she rebuffs Julia's outstretched hand. She rejects pity or anything resembling it. Now more than ever. And she doesn't even reply to Julia's soft voice behind her. 'Do you want us to go? Shall we leave you alone for a moment?'

The distortion of death. Dioni's face transformed by the mask and the days of neglect. His eyes half closed. Dr Galán has seen too many people die in this room. Now she knows. She can hear Ramiro and Julia's muffled footsteps at they leave the room. She sees their two silhouettes out of the corner of her eye. What sort of private moment does Julia imagine she can have with this body that will soon be a corpse, what kind of comfort can she find? She could turn around and ask her. But, no, she knows she must hold her tongue. She was the one who wanted her life to be shrouded in silence. So open minded, *always deceiving everyone, always frightened, the bold doctor, the fearless one, and always there in my corner returning to my corner just like when I was a little girl and didn't dare go outside, afraid of the other children and grown-ups with their hugs and giving thanks when night came because then being afraid was justified and I didn't have to hide or pretend to feel faint or have a tummy ache, just as later on I had the excuse that I was the only one, with my patience and stoicism, who could keep the peace in our home, for my son, or was my son just an excuse? That's a scourge I've still got to beat myself up with, you've given me everything, Dioni, the scourge, turning your back on me and now you're right here.*

And so she takes Dioni's dying hand and strokes it, looks at his cracked, dried-out lips, his shrivelled yellowish skin, the electrodes and the monitors, the rhythm of death on the screen, the drip that will make it pain free, almost sweet. And Dr Galán thinks of the moment when she will have to talk to Guille, her sixteen-year-old son. Too much life ahead of him without a father.

And so Guille, stretched out in a hammock in their garden in Calle Sierra Pelada, struggling with the heat beneath the trees, draws on his spliff and dozes off, watching that Peruvian maid his mother's just hired stripping the sheets off his bed upstairs. *That stain from last night, not even JuanCa's dog would poke that, when I see JuanCa I'm going to tell him, I'm going to tell JuanCa, wait till you see the Peruvian.* And he pictures himself with JuanCa, telling him, 'You've got to see the car crash of a maid my mother's taken on. She's got a head this wide, the bitch is half a metre tall and her tits look like they've rolled down from Machu Picchu. I bet you my balls that even a complete dog like you wouldn't poke her.' And Juno and Loberas, the three of them in stitches, and JuanCa saying, 'Line her up for me, and I'll let you know; before you turn your back I'll have shot my load twice.' 'I'll give you a photo of her, and I bet you twenty euros that you couldn't get a hard-on, you dirty dog.' Machu Picchu! Guille gets the urge to call out to her from the hammock, 'Machu Picchu!' And just the idea makes him giggle, a soft, pleasant, irrepressible giggle, as if a river had opened up inside him and those two words were the most ridiculous thing that anyone could ever have imagined or invented. *How can people not realize that? How can they say those words and keep a straight face as if nothing has happened?* And so Guille swings in the hammock with the spasms of his stifled giggles, his eyes brimming with tears as he looks at her ridiculous little outfit, the pink uniform that his mother has foisted on the housemaid and thinking about JuanCa. *What a dog, Machu Picchu.*

And so the Runner wakes up drenched in sweat, the notebook he'd been writing in scrunched up under his chest. The plaster Virgin that his mother placed at the head of his bed, next to the photograph of Sebastian Coe, reminds him fleetingly of a dream he'd been having. A darkened house and a man lighting up the rooms with a candle, maybe he was a priest, Father Abril, and the memories that came back to him as he was running past the school?

The Runner can't hear anything coming from the other side of the door, not even the murmur of the television or his mother's complaints *with luck, they've gone* and he feels an enormous relief, a flicker of pleasure at the thought of being alone in the flat, like on Sundays when he hears his uncle's voice echoing along the narrow corridor. Proud, vibrant, loud. Ridiculous and at the same time adored by the Runner, that man represents freedom. He takes his mother and his grandmother out of the house for eight or ten hours at a stretch. They go out to the countryside, and his uncle and his mother scour riverbanks for wild asparagus and other bits and pieces and identify plants and birdsongs, while his aunt and his grandmother natter away on a pair of deckchairs in the shade of a eucalyptus or an olive tree. And, if the stars are aligned, if the Runner's sister is spending the weekend with her fiancé, he has the empty, silent flat all to himself. And Lucía. And this will happen very soon, next year, when his sister gets married and every time his mother and his grandmother go out the flat will be all his. But that idea, the very idea of staying there another year provokes a wave of darkness inside him, dark ivy creeping up his chest. *I'm the one who has to leave, open the door, breathe and put an end to all this.*

The Runner turns over on to his side, rests his cheek against the sheets and remembers the last time he was with Lucía in this very bed, the light was almost the same, the net curtains filtering the glaring brightness of that day, a silent Sunday afternoon. But it's not the memory of Lucía that takes root and flowers inside his head. It's that fleeting image, that mental evocation of the empty house that leads him back to that other house, *his* house, after his father's death, when everything became temporary and nobody was quite sure what would become of them a year or even a month later. It was all so precarious that even the furniture started to move around, bedrooms changed occupants in strange rotation that ended up with one of those bedrooms being left empty, without any furniture at all apart from two chairs and a table top propped against the wall, displaying its chipboard underbelly and its antediluvian stains. That empty bedroom became the Runner's refuge. A few cushions on the floor, the window shutters half closed and hours in the semi-darkness, listening to music, although he'd never been a fan of any particular band or orchestra. Sitting on those cushions he would read under the weak light filtering through the shutters. Books that Canijo would lend him. And his dreams. A future that knew no bounds. There was no hint that would let him guess what it would be like, but he envisaged it being very far away from there. Different. And the jumping. He'd take a run-up and jump and hit the wall with his foot, as high as possible. Then he'd mark his record with a pencil. Again and again. Nobody, neither his mother nor his sister, appeared to notice all those footprints on the green paint. He'd jump furiously, raising his leg higher and higher, bordering on two metres and breaking his fall as best he could. He stopped running. When Santi Cánovas and Ángel called him to go out training he didn't pick up, or he made up ridiculous excuses, obviously untrue. Santi Cánovas spent a whole afternoon sitting in that room with him. He was the only person to ask him about those footprints on the wall. He jumped with him once or twice. He lost his membership to the athletics club. He tore up his membership card. He would read, sitting there for hours on end, and he jumped.

Now, on this suffocating day with the *terral*, he reflects that what he was doing back then was similar to what some other adolescents do, self-harming by cutting themselves with knives or burning themselves with a cigarette. He remembers that empty bedroom. He remembers the strange light fitting that appeared one day hanging from the ceiling in the room when all the furniture rearrangement was going on. Another one appeared in his mother's bedroom. That one was purple. His uncle must have fitted them at some point. Not the one with the echoey voice – the other one. The one whose voice was reedy like a flute and who always carried a screwdriver in his shirt pocket. He used to fix everything. An obsessive fixer. Plugs, electric irons, televisions, watches, computer keyboards, fuse boxes, locks, blinds, coffee makers. And as he screwed and unscrewed he'd talk away in his voice that sounded like a flute. He must have got those light fittings from some shop run by one of his friends, some shop selling household goods, and brought them to his sister-in-law as an offering, a starting-block for the emotional and financial recovery of the family unit. Regeneration. The Runner opens his notebook and reads the last few lines he wrote a couple of days ago. *I don't know where to look. Better not to look anywhere. Better not to look up. Although I know that if I spend any more time without moving, everything will move around me. Including Lucía. I run and I don't go anywhere. It doesn't matter if I run in a straight line, I always end up running in circles around the 400-metres track and after running ten kilometres I'm still in the same place, or fifteen or twenty metres ahead of where I started. Or fifteen or twenty metres behind.* The Runner sits up. He opens the drawer of his bedside table. There they are: his biros, arranged in order of diminishing thickness. He selects an intermediate one. He's tempted to cross out what he's just read. He puts it in brackets. He looks at the light fitting again. And he starts to write.

THE RUNNER'S DIARY

The light fitting. Hanging there from the ceiling and looking like a UFO. It's shaped like an eye and hangs (dangles) from a short black cable. Instead of illuminating it seems to be watching. It throws out a feeble light. A low-wattage bulb, which is made even weaker because of the dark bottle-green glass with indentations that are meant to be for decoration, its aesthetic essence to remind us of our poverty. A charity lamp. My mother's pride and joy. Two little lights. That's what she called them when they suddenly appeared hanging there and I asked her. She looked at me sadly (I'm not sure whether she was sorry for me or for herself) when I told her that they looked like two UFOs and, what was more, they were blind UFOs, two small black holes that sucked up the apartment's limited amount of light. She didn't say so, she didn't answer me, but I know she thought that if I didn't like them I could get a job and buy some really bright new lights. She took pity on me and held her tongue. And her pity turned into a hook, a butcher's hook that ended up making my guts bleed. With the pus of remorse. I wonder if she would feel the same, if she ever feels sorry when she has a go at her own mother. When she rations her television time or makes fun of her for her favourite programmes. When they go out to the countryside and they brag about climbing up the steepest and stoniest hills while my grandmother stays down below, sunk into her deckchair crocheting and she, my mother, when she comes down victorious from the mountain with her bunches of herbs and tells her she would have been better off staying at home if that's all she wants to do.

That's where I come from.

I come from that magma, that nebula. Not just from that body, not just from the darkness of that body or the depths of that veiny white belly, floating in liquid, I come from that madness and that rain of meteorites she produces non-stop inside her mind. I am descended from that wounded pride and that similarly wounded humility. From that arrogance which is capable of cornering and destroying her own mother and that humility which folds and melts when faced with ridiculous objects like those lamps and the person who brought them. And the stiff cable from which they're suspended. That discipline. That's what she's like and that's the plasma that she injected into me and fed me with, it was imprinted in my cells, controlling me ever since I left her uterus.

The light (what it represents) (write more?)

My mother says that when I was small the world was full of UFOs and people who saw UFOs. There were always people on the TV who'd seen strange lights in the sky, descending, gyrating, ascending, by the side of the road, in remote houses out in the country. Almost everyone was sure that civil aviation pilots, and of course military pilots, had seen them. They were in on the secret. Lots of people admitted they'd been abducted. Taken inside those spacecraft through very powerful beams of light that sucked up their bodies. That's what happens to my mother. She's abducted or she escapes, goes to the other side, disappears, and then we see her transformed. She goes from one extreme to the other. Without passing through any intermediate point. The exemplary, humble woman and the woman who persecutes her mother. I'm ashamed to write it down. I feel like a traitor. I am *a traitor. Infinitely worse than her. A wretch. Because I'm more intelligent than her, because she's made an effort for me to be better than her and everyone else and all I can manage is to be much worse. Because I only get the first version, the exemplary mother. She forgives me, apologizes for me, sticks up for me against my sister, against my aunts' knowing looks and questions. 'Hasn't he found a job yet?' they ask, happily, persecuting her in turn. They look at her and they look at me. Their sons, my cousins, have been working for two, four, six years. They've got cars. One of them has bought a flat, another one is going to get married. They go on holiday, they travel. They give their mothers presents: they show my mother their watches. I steal from my mother.*

That's my gift to her. I open her wardrobe drawer, lift up the handkerchiefs and underwear and see the little bundle of notes. The amount I take depends on how thick the bundle is. If I'm desperate I don't notice how much is there. On two occasions, as far as I know, my mother has accused my grandmother. The word she used back then was hypocrisy. My grandmother gives her all her pension every month except for the fifty euros she gives to me. On those occasions my mother accused her of giving with one hand and taking away with the other. It didn't occur to her that it might be someone else who was taking money from her drawer. She couldn't imagine it was me. It isn't that she didn't want to think it, she just DIDN'T think it.

I don't need to be abducted by the crew of a UFO or any other bastard. I can transport and transform myself. I'm my own black hole. I swallow myself, gobble myself up, and I don't know where I'm going. I'm the shadow transmitted by that light. I'm everything that gets lost along the road. The breadcrumbs that drop to the ground when bread is broken, crumbs that never find their way into anyone's mouth and benefit no one. The crumbs that are carried away by ants or swept up with a broom. The seed that the priests talked about at school. Not the bad seed, but the seed that falls on stony ground and grows there.

Are these the thoughts provoked by that light? What it embodies? What I reflect back on it, because the light, that lump of glass and that cable that looks like a riding crop, they don't embody anything. What's the opposite of that light? Is there anything on this planet, within my reach, that could produce the opposite effect or be an antidote to the light's virus?

HER LADYBIRD, HER TATTOO, HER ANKLE, HER LEG, HOPE. HER.

Yes, the ladybird Lucía has tattooed on her right ankle. On the inside. That drawing embodies peace. Solace. (write what I feel) (the feelings it gives me)

But the light fitting is always present. It's screwed into the ceiling, and I come back here every night, I come back underneath it. When I go to sleep and when I wake up it's floating there in all its sadness. It's the last light I see each day. It's the first thing I see every morning. It reminds me of the life I've led, step by step. And afterwards, when the review is over, *it says to me, 'Go on, get out of bed now if you can and carry on in your rut, you and I know your measure, your lack of worth, I am your fate and your future, too.' It reminds me who I am. What I haven't got. The life I could have. What I don't dare imagine so I won't get depressed. Stuck to the ceiling, like the triangle encompassing the Eye of God. Vigilant in case I leave the sphere of darkness.*

Lucía has a ladybird about one or two centimetres long (more like two) tattooed on the inside of her right ankle, just above the ankle bone. She had it done before I met her. It's not a good tattoo. There's barely any shading to give it depth, and unless you look at it carefully you could easily think that it's a drawing that some amateur has sketched with a biro. Perhaps that's where its secret lies, perhaps it's that innocence, that freedom, combined with Lucía's skin, that fills me with such emotion, even with happiness. That faith in the good things and, in a manner of speaking, as my uncle might say (the one with the strong voice), that faith in life.

There's no red in the tattoo (just a thin outline of what would be the wings and the shell, which is almost a pale pink) and the ladybird's spots aren't black either. It's all blue. Just blue ink and skin. I remember when I first used to sit on the benches along the seafront with Lucía and how she would wiggle her leg nervously, up and down, swinging it on her other leg and how the ladybird went up and down, and I saw the confirmation of a distant promise in that movement. The fact that being with me made her feel nervous filled me with emotion. The fact that she made the same movement several months later when her brother was so ill made me feel the same again. Her bare foot, her open sandals, the gentle sway of her pale calf and the ladybird swinging back and forth.

I followed the path the ladybird might have taken closely. It would climb slowly along the bridge, along that smooth motorway of her calf towards her knee and there it would broach the rounded bony obstacle and go on to the flat expanse of her thigh, avoiding the delicate wheat, those soft, golden, almost invisible hairs on her skin, solitary strands, the smooth expanse, the pale desert above the thigh, that space which isn't thigh or groin or even hip, with the chasm on one side and the shadow of the pubis on the other, that trimmed hedge behind which the entrance to another world is hidden, and following, following up towards the thorax, towards that destination that always beckons, climb the gentle staircase of ribs and along the silky dune of her breast as far as the simple monument embodied by her nipple and contemplate the marvellous landscape from its peak, that extension of hills and valleys, bumps, invisible pores, moles like planets, dips and abandoned courses, then follow the path in a harmonious descent to the hollow created by the collar bone, clamber over that modest obstacle and embark on the ascent of her neck, now shaded by a forest of hair, those waves, those pale, curly locks, an abundance of wheat surrounded by darker highlights, culminating in the ascent of her chin, and from this headland, looking out towards the red barrier of her lips, that elastic crater which widens into a smile, the incarnation of the future and reality (that is, what I consider the future and reality, uncertainty, which I never quite reach and which runs away from me, the same way as life runs away, like the days run away, just as the landscape falls behind me when I'm running without going anywhere) her mouth, reality, the future, my fate in the depths of that cave from which her teeth peep out like damp stones, that archaeology of white stalagmites and stalactites, climb up in the shade of the side of her nose and then, yes, truly arrive at the chosen place, the ultimate destination, the estuary of her eye, the watery shore, the gaze on which everything depends.

The light tells me that this might come to an end. That this also has an expiry date. And that one day that light will be turned off for me. Her eyes will no longer gaze at me, the ladybird's swaying will rise and fall in its nervous to and fro in the presence of a different voice. Lucía might also get bored. I know that. I can sometimes feel that on those evenings when we don't go anywhere, but her voice makes me calm, her words show she understands me and her eyes want to console me. I can feel it, I'm afraid of it. I don't need the light to tell me that; it's the broken tooth in the cog which sooner or later ends up breaking the machine.

Fucking motorbike. Niño del Sordo has told me to have the cash ready. He doesn't know how much – whatever his father says. Now I can't even give Lucía a lift home, today or tomorrow or for who knows how long.

*

'Hey, Rai, maestro, how's it going?'

Raimundo's knocked on the door two, three, four times with the palm of his hand, and it's only just been opened by Nene Olmedo, who looks him up and down with a surly, contemptuous expression on his face. The guitar, his skinny arms, sunken chest, face full of angles and corners, bulging eyes. Nene Olmedo pulls a face that Rai can interpret whichever way he likes. The owner of the squalid dump turns his back and says, 'Come in and close the door, for fuck's sake,' and that's when he hears Eduardo Chinarro's voice from the depths of the pigsty, 'Hey Rai, maestro, how's it going?'

'How's it going, Rai, who told you we were here?'

Raimundo doesn't reply. He takes two or three hesitant steps, the guitar bashes into something, *clunk*; he stops and waits until his eyes get used to the semi-darkness.

'Did El Tato tell you? I told him to tell you, Rai.'

'There you go, shooting your mouth off, dickhead. Why not put an advert in the local paper?' Nene Olmedo goes back to where he was sitting, a mattress on the floor, next to La Penca.

'Just El Tato, Nene, I didn't tell anyone else. He's a mate of yours, isn't he?'

As he begins to make out the faces in the room – Nene Olmedo, La Penca, Eduardo sitting on a crate of beer and another guy he doesn't recognize who's sitting on the floor near Eduardo with his head against the wall, asleep – the smell in the room hits Rai full in the nostrils. Sweat, bleach, smack, cigarettes. And the heat. A dense fug descends like lead from the ceiling. The small window at the back is closed, the glass painted white a thousand years ago, but now it's turned dark orange, almost brown, decaying light filtering through.

'Yeah. A real mate. We're all mates, but you have to keep your eyes open wider than your sister's arse.'

Rai can see the needle sticking out of Nene Olmedo's arm. The spoon, the lighter and the powder are on a small stool in front of him. La Penca, his Dulcinea, is watching him out of the corner of her eye, and Rai understands. Fuck her.

'For Christ's sake, Eduardo. I'm not working with you again, not even if you went down on your knees and begged.'

'Hey, Rai, what's up? Come on, Rai, what's up now? I told El Tato to tell you. We said, I told you on the phone, Rai.'

'I'm up to here with it. Fuck you, Eduardo!'

Eduardo Chinarro gets up from the crate, looks around, his gravelly voice more gravelly than ever. 'That's enough, Rai, that's enough, for fuck's sake . . .' He squints, the veins on his neck swell up like drainpipes, he walks over to Rai who bares his teeth, like bitches do when they're defending their puppies.

'Whoah now, whoaaah!' Nene Olmedo screams from his throne, from his grimy mattress, 'not in here, you can piss off out of here right now, piss off!'

Eduardo Chinarro, his face contorted, is still staring at Raimundo Arias, thirty centimetres from his face, the veins in his neck pumping. Raimundo nods his head over and over again; rather than agreeing, it looks more like he's got Parkinson's. Juanmi, who was asleep, wakes up, sniffs, coughs, looks around without knowing where he is, retches, burps, contains himself, looks as if he's going to laugh.

From his throne Nene Olmedo gives him a kick in the ribs. 'Owwww!' the other guy moans, but it seems the pain hasn't stopped him wanting to laugh, on the contrary, he doubles over in a stifled laugh, flips right over, falls to the floor in a semi-foetal position and laughs with his mouth wedged to the floor.

'Now you're all getting totally out of fucking order,' the syringe hanging from his arm like a broken pendulum.

'This is a bad scene,' says Rai with his chiselled face, like an Amerindian.

'Bad scene, my arse, dickhead,' says Nene Olmedo. He looks at La Penca, talks to her in a different tone, like an accomplice. 'Come on then, babe.'

Juanmi's gone back to sleep, stretched out on the floor with a smile on his face, completely flat out. Nene Olmedo tightens the strap on La Penca's arm and a vein appears. 'Shoot!' she says.

And Rai looks at his Dulcinea's hair falling over her shoulders, as tangled as his own emotions. Her yellow top, firm round breasts. He remembers her on Playa de Sacaba, laughing, the sun blazing, and the pair of them taking a dip in the water. Eduardo and Eduardo's sticky breath, which Rai breathes in through his mouth like engine exhaust, don't bother him any more. He sniffs. Squares his shoulders. Turns around.

'Come on, Eduardo, arse in gear. Let's bounce.'

He opens the door and goes out. Eduardo snaps out of his paralysis, still breathing heavily. *You don't know who I am, this guy doesn't know me, the next time I'll make you eat your words, I'll make him eat them,* he mutters, swallows saliva like someone swallowing a pill, shows the gap in his teeth like a lion without a roar and turns back and says, 'See you, Nene, see you around, Penqui. Cheers, mate, you're a good mate.'

No one replies. He goes out, following in Raimundo Arias's footsteps. As he gently closes the door he takes in the scene. Juanmi on the floor by the steamy window, Nene Olmedo manoeuvring the needle in La Penca's arm while she's gazing at the ceiling, open mouthed, disconcerted, as if there were something up there.

Rai walks rapidly down the middle of the street, blasted and overwhelmed by the sun. His guitar is like a piece of old furniture dancing beside him. Eduardo follows him on the pavement, in the shade. And, no longer in a whisper, he says, 'The next time you're going to eat your words, Rai, I swear on my dead mother.'

Rai doesn't reply. He carries on walking at full speed. Eduardo follows ten or twelve metres behind. They cross the Parque de la Peseta. The shade of the trees calms them down. They skirt around the children's playground. A boy aged five or six, sweaty, sitting in a Wendy house, is sipping a can of Fanta. He breathes in, tilts his head back, anxious to get the last drop. Without stopping Eduardo gives him a piece of advice on his way past, 'Watch out, kid, you're going to cut yourself like that.'

The boy, still holding the can to his lips, looks at him with his eyes popping out as he carries on slurping and making a noise like a broken vacuum cleaner.

'You'll cut yourself.'

A man emerges from the shade with his shirt unbuttoned and his gut hanging out.

'What's your problem? What did you say to my son?'

Eduardo stops, his face contorts, he looks at the man, who's still coming towards them, the boy stops slurping, but his eyes are still wild and he's still holding the can to his lips. Rai carries on walking and calls out, 'Let's go.'

'What do you want with my son?'

'Why should I want anything? The boy's going to cut his mouth open the way he's going at that Fanta can. Why should I want anything?'

'I'll cut your bloody tongue out if you don't sling your hook.'

Eduardo looks at him open mouthed, genuinely failing to comprehend. Rai tells him again, 'Let's go,' and waits.

The father carries on with his tirade. 'Are you one of those queers who likes children?'

Eduardo doesn't react. He carries on watching as the man approaches. 'There's no need for that,' says Eduardo.

'What, what did you say, joker?'

Rai's turned around and comes towards them. He speeds up, his mouth twisted. He grasps his guitar by the neck like a baseball bat and almost screams, 'Fuck off. Fuck off and die! You rancid piece of shit!'

The boy takes the can away from his mouth for the first time, but his mouth is still gaping, bright red, almost as wide open as his eyes. The father puts his hands up as if instead of a guitar he was being threatened with a firearm. 'Whoah, whoah!'

Rai reaches him, makes as if to hit him with the guitar, and the man covers his head, and that's when Rai takes the opportunity to give him a kick, he kicks Daddy in the thigh, and then he whacks him with the guitar *clunk!* right in the ribs. Eduardo Chinarro steps in like a vigilante and also grabs the guitar neck.

'Leave it, Rai, leave it! Can't you see he's just a stupid moron, the wanker?'

The man takes a couple of paces back, and, emboldened by Eduardo's intervention, he starts breathing faster, his gut going in and out like a bellows, 'And you! You two! Come back here again and I'll smash your guitar into little pieces.'

Rai goes towards him, and Eduardo pulls him back.

'Come on now, Rai! Mate! I thought we were going to do some work? Come on! Don't bother with that stupid piece of shit.'

Raimundo Arias hasn't once taken his eyes off the man in the open shirt, who's now touching his ribs where the guitar made contact.

Rai feels another mad surge of rage. 'Get out of here. Piss off, you fucker.'

'You what?' says the other man, taking another step back. The penny's dropped that Rai's really manic, better to back off, while puffing his chest out, even if just a little.

'What d'you mean, *you what*? Fuck off right now, or I swear I'll kill you right here.' Rai bares his teeth. 'I said, piss off!'

That's when they hear the boy moaning, a kind of inverted scream, as if the boy, his mouth open unusually wide, is breathing in all the sounds of the world.

The father, clutching his side in order to justify his retreat, goes up to the boy and slaps him on the hand that's holding the Fanta can, which falls to the ground, and that's when the boy stops breathing in and exhales with all the strength of his lungs and screams, 'Nooooo! Noooo! Noooooooo!'

'Look, Rai, look at the kid, the little brat, let's get out of here, Rai.' Eduardo grabs Raimundo's arm, looks at him sympathetically as if it's Rai who's crying. 'Come on, Rai, the guy's a shit and that's that.'

But Rai's still staring at the man. He watches as he picks the child up in his arms, and the boy's shaking his head hysterically, possessed, horrified by the loss of the empty can. Apocalypse Now.

Finally Raimundo, maybe unnerved by the strident dissonance of the boy's screaming (he's a musician after all), gives in, turns around and lets Eduardo lead him off, and they continue on their way. Behind him, heading in the opposite direction, he can hear the boy's desperate wailing, and in one of the brief intervals between sobs, the father's voice breaks in, 'If I see you around here again, you flea-bitten bastard, it'll be two against two.'

Rai tenses up, but, to calm him down, it's Eduardo who reacts, and he turns around and says, 'You're really looking for some, aren't you, big daddy?' and he searches around on the ground. 'Don't show your faces around here again, you cocksucking paedos,' the man shouts, still walking away.

The child's howling and shaking, Rai stays rooted to the spot and Eduardo finds what he was looking for: two or three granite chips, the size of pebbles and nice and sharp. He snatches them up, ignores the fact that they're so hot they burn his hand, and begins a short, powerful run-up, like a javelin thrower, and just like a javelin thrower he suddenly breaks his run and releases. The projectile flawlessly traces a perfect parabola: focus, directrix, parameter, axis, angle, radius vector, combined with the appropriate strength and direction, $y = ax^2 + bx + c$, make the stone land at the feet of the intended target, literally at the feet of the man with the open shirt and protruding gut. He lets out a howl and a curse and, seeing that Eduardo is getting ready to launch another projectile, lumbers off at an ungainly jog, the child staggering along behind and, in spite of everything, still wailing.

The second projectile reaches the general area, the combined mass in the distance comprising father and son. The sound of the impact is a dull thud. From where Rai and Eduardo are standing it's impossible to be certain exactly where it's landed. They make a calculation based on the noises they pick up. First there's a moment of absolute silence, nothing but a motorbike with an unmuffled exhaust breaks the overheated silence of the surroundings. Then comes the father's yell, a kind of elongation of the 'e' vowel, tattered and shattered into various bits in order to insert several 'ohs' at full volume, as if, in some kind of primal fashion, he was trying to imitate the sound of an electric saw or something like that. And then comes the echo of his first words, 'You've killed him, you've killed him, murderer, murderer, you've killed him, you've killed him,' etc. (always multiplying each statement by two). 'Murderer, murderer', the double-dip cadence persists alongside the boy's worrying silence and Eduardo Chinarro's worst fears; he's now regretting his poor aim and the millimetre-fine imprecision that's made the stone smash into the boy instead of the father.

Eduardo screws his eyes up and tries to make out the scene. There's too much heat, too much light. The trees are holding their breath; the plastic benches and children's play apparatus are about to melt. Eduardo looks at Rai, who has also turned around, watching the events with curiosity. Eduardo shrugs his shoulders. He relaxes his hand and lets the third stone, the stillborn projectile, fall to the ground.

The child's father's desperately wandering from one side of the path to the other and lifts up a hand that's soaked in blood. From a distance you can see that his shirt also seems to be stained red. Then he stops in one spot and resumes the chant that he'd abandoned for a few moments (you've killed him × 2, murderer × 2, criminal × 2, etc.), but, more to the point, while this litany goes on, the child's exasperated howling starts up again, grows louder and louder still, with renewed strength, brimming with health, at the top of his lungs or even twice as powerful as that.

Eduardo's pupils dilate, he looks up to the sky and lets out a cackle which infects Rai, 'Let's go, Rai. Let's get out of here, cuz.'

The pair of them start walking in the direction they were originally heading when they came across Fanta Boy. They go at speed, leaving behind the latter-day land of the Garamantes. Eduardo says in a whisper, 'What a bastard!' while in the distance the said bastard calls the police and starts off again about murder and paedos.

'He can go screw himself, can't he, Rai?' Eduardo's throat is rasping.

Raimundo Arias doesn't respond to that enigmatic statement but to an earlier remark. Deep down, there's a Cartesian side to the man. 'What made you call me cousin all of a sudden? Whose cousin?'

Chinarro's reply is worthy of a wise man. 'How should I know?'

The passengers start getting their things together, and the stewardess announces their imminent arrival at Madrid's Puerta de Atocha station, and, although she asks that passengers remain in their seats, they all rush to disobey, desperate to be the first to set foot on the platform.

Carole's head is still resting on Céspedes's shoulder. She opens her eyes and looks out on the world as if she's woken up in a spaceship. 'You bastard, you've abducted me,' she whispers.

'What?' Céspedes looks at the top of Carole's head out of the corner of his eye, only managing to make out a fuzzy blur of hair and the tip of her nose.

'I said, you've abducted me,' she yawns and closes her eyes. 'I'm so tired, my God. Tell the guard to let us stay here for another hour.'

A tall, bronzed man in a lightweight jacket looks down at her from his 1.85-metre height with a mixture of scorn and desire. Carole opens one eye and looks up at him, makes him look away with her Cyclopean eye. It appears this was the stimulus she needed to finally rouse herself.

She sits up, looks out through the window at the cables and mini-pylons and the grey tones that announce their imminent arrival at the station.

'Have you worked out where you are?' Céspedes asks her.

'More or less,' Carole replies, absorbed by the concrete landscape.

'Good. And do you know who I am?'

She turns towards him. It's the first time she's looked at him since she woke up *Christ, she's beautiful* she shakes her head gently from side to side. 'I don't have the faintest clue about that, believe me.'

Céspedes breaks into a broad grin.

'You're laughing, why are you laughing?' says Carole with a frown.

'No, I'm not laughing.'

'What are you like? And I'm the fool who's playing along.'

The train comes to a halt. Céspedes and Carole are drowning in a sea of people's midriffs, suitcases being taken down from the luggage racks, people shuffling forward, holding back their urge to escape.

Carole lifts her arms above her head, stretches and arches her back.

Céspedes makes a gesture with his head, pointing towards the door. 'Shall we make a move, young lady?'

Concrete pillars, a procession of people, suitcases wheeled along making dodecaphonic music with their bearings, dry heat, drowsiness, a milky light. They walk along with the crowd. Céspedes has a feeling of intense freedom. He knows it's ephemeral. *Floating on a cloud of concrete, a block of granite that at any moment will tumble headlong into the abyss, in free fall.* The freedom of those who throw themselves off a cliff, the prerogative of those who no longer have to be held accountable because what they can be held accountable for adds up to zero or infinity.

Tomorrow is the twenty-second century, just behind every mountain, no one suspects or even cares what's lurking there. Céspedes gets on the escalator close up to Carole. He can smell her back, her long hair. Once, many years ago, a woman asked him, 'Why are you staying the night with me here and not going home?' *Because of the scent of your hair,* he thought, but he made up some other excuse.

They start walking. Carole and Céspedes beside her in his Hawaiian shirt, Bermuda shorts, boat shoes. They amble along with the travelling carnival.

'Do you do this often?' Carole asks, cocking an eyebrow.

Céspedes knows what she means but asks, 'What?'

Carole doesn't reply, she looks him over with a mixture of irony and scorn.

'Do you mean, invite a woman out to lunch?' Céspedes chooses a middle path, neither giving in nor responding to what he was really asked.

'Five hundred kilometres away?'

'Less often than I should. I do it less often than I should.'

'Because you need a madwoman to do it with?'

'Anyway, before we go to lunch, we're going –'

'And you don't find one every day, obviously.'

'First of all we're going to a place, if you'll allow me . . .' Suddenly his wife's face flashes up, rounded, clearly defined, much more real, much plumper than if she really were there beside him pulling along one of those suitcases.

A chasm opens up in front of him. The ants proceed in an orderly fashion. They identify with each other, they know their mission. Céspedes has stepped out of the line for a moment, he's lost the pheromone trail.

Neither his wife nor his daughter. There will be no blackmail. There will be no skulking in the shadows. Not, at least, while he still has daylight. His phone vibrates in his pocket. He doesn't take it out. Freedom not only not to answer it but also not to be bothered who's calling. Escalators. The scent of that hair. Carole's rhythm. In the distance he can see the station's glass frontage, the taxi queue, and Céspedes has an unexpected flashback to that religious text where there was an interminable queue of people, they were souls, the priest said, waiting for the Last Judgement. *John the Apostle and the Seven Churches of the Apocalypse.*

He's not going to nag any more, he's not going to call him again. That's what Rafi Villaplana's saying to himself. *Screw Céspedes. I'll make it happen with or without him.*

He runs through his contacts on the phone with his thumb as he drives along. Amel.

Amel. That affectation of hers, wanting people to call her Amel. As if dropping two letters means she's escaped from the shitty life she's got and will always have, she was born in the gutter and she'll die in the gutter, however much she can wiggle her arse, that's just normal, innate, there are women who've just got it in their blood since they were sucking on a dummy, they might go for twenty years or forty like her without realizing it, married, with her little hubby, the boyfriend she had when she wore her hair long and she was still called Amelia Martínez Robledo or Rebollo or whatever she was called, and suddenly, bang! one day it happens, something changes inside them, a gland or a rush of hormones or neurons that make connections, like when a car thief hot-wires a car, like the bastards who stole mine and slashed the seats before they dumped it, they make that connection, and everything that was there bottled up starts to flow out, and, boy, does it flow, fucking hell she gets mad for it, she has me there like a fish on a hook, each day a little bit wiser and more like a tart, making the most of it because it's not as if her looks are going to last for much longer, her arse is already starting to sag, and the moment she lets herself go her arms could be as flabby as a blancmange, those biceps, unless she lifts more weights than Mike Tyson or she buys all her tops with long sleeves, then she'll look for someone else like me, younger than her, not her tits, hers are like rubber, the bitch, she really gets me going when she stands up and walks around the room, around the bed, like a vulture looking for something to eat, and the way she looks at you while she's sucking you off, as well as your come juice she wants to swallow your brain, she wants to swallow you whole, that has to be in the blood otherwise there's no way, not like La Nuri, she really put on airs, and even though she made herself up like a whore it was like what she was doing was making you paella or cleaning your dick, screwing her was like playing a game of cards with a child, all fake, but this one, this one knows what it's all about, but all the same I'll get rid of her, I have to get rid of her by September at the latest, I can't lose sight of the timing, I really can't lose sight of it, before September, Jane's father doesn't miss a trick with his eyes like a fox, that's my future there, I've got to make the leap, that bastard Céspedes could smooth the way for me, but if he doesn't it'll be the worse for him, we'll meet again sooner or later and then he won't be looking down his nose at me, he thinks I don't notice how he looks at me, he thinks I'm a loser, personnel manager for a hotel on the coast, and by the way he always gets the name of the hotel I work at wrong, he says Las Golondrinas, Los Gansos, and once he even said Los Pollos (very funny), and I laugh, sometimes I correct him so he feels better, Los Patos, and other times I bite my tongue, he thinks I'm just going to carry on doing what I'm doing, that I'll stay there until I retire, or perhaps I'll climb another rung up the ladder but still basically just a muleteer, and that idiot Ibáñez has just screwed him up, going to bang him in his own house, and the wife catches them at it, she's got the brains of a mosquito, and he thinks he's so clever, he's had a couple of riding lessons and now he wants to be the champion, screwing trash like her in his own home, well, now you have to pay the price, champ, and the lengths he goes to to avoid me, this crap about picking up the phone when it takes his fancy and not picking up when it doesn't, saying, 'What is it, Rafi?' as if he were saying, 'What the fuck do you want? Keep it short because I've got more important things to do than chatting with you about your fantasies,' I'm noting all this down in my little book, he doesn't know who he's messing with, I'll chew him up and spit him out and his mother, too, this is my big chance, and I'm going to grab it with both hands, this is going to happen, simple as that, I've been working for my living since I was fifteen years of age, first in the market at Huelin, swallowing shit, and since I was seventeen at the hotel, doing a bit of everything, what no one else wanted to do, holding out my hand for tips, carrying luggage, washing down the kitchen, guarding the place at night, seeing how everything worked and earning respect, getting promoted, first to receptionist then head of reception then head of personnel, I've been the backbone of that hotel, the management's attack dog, kicking out anyone who didn't toe the line, the troublemakers or anyone the bosses didn't like, that bastard Domínguez, pretending to be the victim and then behind everyone's backs going to the papers, rummaging through my bin to see if he could find anything to compromise me, waiting for me at my front door at six o'clock in the morning in his car and following me everywhere one day and another time slashing all the tyres on my car, again and again, until the company gave me a special payment to buy covers for them, and the scratched paintwork and silicone in the front-door lock to my apartment twice, and the others, people I've helped, I know they won't be there when it's my back against the wall, I gave Gamal money from my own pocket, a whole month's rent, and I said pay me back in six instalments, no interest, and I brought him to María Luisa, the Mexican lawyer, to sort out his papers, he's a good worker and he's grateful, but what can I expect from him? A bagful of dates as a present? Or Seoane, I promoted him twice in three years, and he lives like a king, thanks to me, and Covaleda, I hired him when his business went bust, he was homeless, out on the street, the bastard, and then he paid me back by putting pressure on the management, screwing me over, I know what I'm playing at and who I'm playing with, Jane's father is going to go back with a good impression of me, he has to, and he's going to soften his stance, I've already won her mother over, but I know I have to round it off, that when I turn my back she still looks at me and says to herself, 'What's this one after from my daughter,' but she can't help laughing at the things I tell her, I'm sure she thinks to herself, 'If I were twenty years younger this one would be keeping me happy in a different way,' I can tell, and she appreciates the fact that I speak English, she wasn't expecting me to be able to joke with her in English, and I don't hesitate and splutter like the guys who can trot out fifty or sixty words, I'm not Rafael de la Fuente with his Cambridge accent, and I don't need to be, but I do make an impression, I have to do well, and other members of my family better smarten up their act, it's like they don't even realize what's at stake for me here, my mother has to get her teeth sorted out once and for all, drop her ridiculous objections that it's going to be uncomfortable eating with false teeth or an implant or whatever, it'll cost a fortune, but she can't be opening her mouth and displaying those gums as if she were a street beggar, for Christ's sake, she needs to buy some new clothes, my father can pay for them for once, and then the noise her guts make, like a drain, whenever she gets nervous, the day she met Jane she sounded like a fucking toilet flushing, and I've tried to get through to her in all sorts of ways, 'Mummy please try eating some different food or don't eat anything at all or go to the doctor's or something,' and all she does is laugh and show off those nightmare teeth and put her hand on her stomach as if there were a revolution going on down there and she could calm it all down like that, it's a fucking joke this shitty neighbourhood, it's chewed us up, we're not really like this, we never were, and it's reached the point where it's time to leave a distance, my mother doesn't understand, she knows she's not like the others, but she's let herself go, through boredom or whatever, she's let herself go, mixing with those people all day and letting them into her secrets, it doesn't matter how many times I tell her, 'Keep your distance, Mummy, keep your distance, don't you see that we can't be getting mixed up with their problems and crappy lives, are you going to get into a fight over whose turn it is to clean the stairwell or who's knocked over the rubbish bins? Hold your head up and put these people in their place and don't go mixing with La Puri, for Christ's sake, or those other women gossiping about whether El Petuso's daughter's taking drugs or whether the girl from fruit shop opposite's pregnant and who's the father, as if we cared about all that, didn't I buy you that television with a 32-inch screen so you could watch it to your heart's content? I haven't seen you turn it on once,' my father has, yes, he spends the whole day in front it watching the football or whatever else is on, and if there are scantily clad girls he'll sit there half undressed himself, joining in the striptease, rubbing his hands like he's about to tuck into a huge meal, he doesn't care which team it is or which little whore's showing off her tits, he's there in the middle of the sofa in his underpants, like, the other day I came in, and he's sitting there in his underpants fast asleep with a hard-on, a bloody great hard-on sticking out, I don't believe it, how embarrassing, and then he asks why I'm shouting at him, 'For fuck's sake, Dad, I might have come back here with Jane, and you're sitting there in your underpants, if I'd come back with Jane . . . what a sight, you're really showing us at our best, aren't you?' and he's there looking dumbfounded still half asleep with his eyes all red, and he's smiling, and he says, 'I'm feeling a bit randy, Rafi, that's all.' Randy? For crying out loud, and then he goes and says, 'As if you come back here with your Jane every day – don't make me laugh.' 'I come when I need to, and if I don't come so often it's because you might be here putting on a show, don't you get it, Dad?' I wanted to tell him, 'Watch out, your dick's going to jump out, for fuck's sake, if you shift an inch it's going to jump out, and that really would be disgusting. Don't you understand that?' When it suits him he does, when he wants something he's always gone for it, there's a guy like that at the hotel, and it'll only take me two days, the first day I'll make him sweat, and the second day I'll really screw him over and the third day he'll be back in the dole queue, and he just sits there on the sofa with his arms folded, his hairy gut a flabby grey bulk, the TV on full blast, and he's acting like I've offended him or like he can't understand it, staring at the screen and ready to have another argument, I had to point to the door like a traffic cop before he got up and went to his room, I'm not surprised my mother doesn't want to sleep in the same bed as him, slouching along more flat-footed than ever and the few remaining hairs on his bald pate standing up straight in protest. 'And don't turn the TV off, don't you turn it off!' I felt like smashing the remote against the screen, but I counted to five and steadied myself and carefully took the remote and gently pressed the off button, and, even though it made me feel sick, I smoothed out the indentation he'd left in the sheet my mother uses to protect the sofa, running my hand over it with as little contact as possible, it was all warm, it made me want to throw up, but as I did it this feeling of tranquillity came over me, and it was like I'd put on a pair of stilts and I could see everyone from about a metre above their heads like I often do at the hotel, although this time, as it was my father, instead of the stilts, I should have been looking down from the Eiffel Tower, and not even then, each time I see him snoozing in that shop doorway in the middle of the street against the wall as if he'd been shot sitting down, they shoot some people like that, snoring, I've seen him more than once, 'For Christ's sake, go up to the flat if you want to have a sleep, you slob, you've got a bedroom all to yourself after all,' and on top of that he complains that the room's only a box room, it's tiny, in his sixty-odd years living day to day and hand to mouth he's only earned a pittance, and he thinks he deserves an imperial suite? The last time I saw him I felt like kicking his chair away and tipping him out into the middle of the pavement to teach him a lesson, I went into the shop (Bazar la Amistad it's called, what a stupid name), and I told the stupid moron who runs it, I told him, 'Don't let my father go to sleep in the doorway, can't you see what a bad impression it makes? It's not good for you, and it's not good for us, OK?' And the shopkeeper says, 'He's not doing anyone any harm. Mariano comes home worn out from his night shift, and he has a little snooze, what does it matter, what harm does it do anyone for the man to have a rest under the awning in the shade? And, after all, he's your friend,' and the stupid prick has a laugh, another one who's all dimples, and finally he says, 'This shop is called La Amistad, which means friendship,' and I said, 'To hell with friendship *and to hell with the night shift, do you think I didn't know he works nights?' as if I'd never seen him set off for work or found him stretched out on the sofa with his shoes in the middle of the floor and his tie undone, I used to go in and have a good look around on the ground floor, and then I'd sit on the edge of the table and he wouldn't wake up until the fourth or fifth paper ball landed on him, sleeping like a pasha, and he'd say, 'Rafalito lovely to see you, I'd just put my head down for a bit, fancy a coffee?' And off he'd shuffle to the coffee machine in his sandals, and he'd sit on the sofa yawning, always sleeping always eating, eating and sleeping like an animal and with his one-arm bandits and the TV, that's all his life consists of, but at least he doesn't go around the neighbourhood socializing, if he's not in the sodding shop or feeding the machine with coins in the bar, he's in front of the television or snoring in his bed, and nothing else is worth shit, his only saving grace is that he can be polite in his own way when he wants to be, even if he breaks your balls going on about the same four things over and over again, 'I managed to bring up a whole family with just the Senior School Certificate,' and he shakes his head as he pronounces the word 'Senior' so that his audience can say, 'What a modest man,' and also because he considers himself the Einstein of the family, the only one to finish his baccalaureate, for all the good it's done him, but he did, and I didn't finish mine because I had to be rushing here, there and everywhere, at least his guts don't make funny noises, the way he stuffs himself it would be odd if there were room for any noises, and he can get by in English, so all those years working in reception have been of some use, I must buy him a tie because otherwise he'll turn up in front of Jane's parents wearing a tie with the company logo, he doesn't give a monkey's, with the knot all loose and the top button of his shirt undone, although at least he can put on a bit of show, which is more than I can say for my brothers and my sister, she blows hot and cold depending on what day it is, and as for her boyfriend, he's sensible, he'll just about do, but he really thinks he's someone with his little books and poems, and my sister's head over heels, but it makes me want to say, listen Estafanía, this guy's father owns an ironmonger's shop about fourteen square metres in Calle Mármoles so don't get ideas that he's royalty or can walk on water or anything, and above all don't think that he's anything special just because he sits up straight in an armchair as though the thought of leaning back in it made him feel sick, he'll do but that's about it. My brothers, you wouldn't believe what I've been landed with, Pepe better not show his face, he's turned out like his father only worse, with any luck he'll be off with that woman of his in the countryside doing their organic stuff, whatever, he's bone idle and he can't tell a lettuce from a turnip, all he knows about it is sitting in a rocking chair in the shade of a carob tree, and if there's a bottle of gin handy so much the better, the day he was showing me around what he calls his smallholding, 'Look at my smallholding, Rafi,' with his straw hat and sandals and squatting down to see how his pumpkins are coming on, pulling up weeds and talking about fertilizers and pesticides and that woman of his following behind not saying a word, as if we didn't know what she was thinking, she can't stand us, and Migue following his drift and asking him about watering and the irrigation ditch they want to dig, and in the car on the way back I had to tell Miguelito, 'Listen, don't you realize that this whole set-up is just crap, and one day when we least expect it our little brother will say to hell with the whole shebang.' It's better if Migue keeps his mouth shut, if the other one has taken after my father, this one is like they really did find him on the doorstep like we used to say when he was little boy, 'Miguelito, some gypsies left you on the doorstep,' and Pepe and I would say to Mummy, 'Mummy, why did you bring the gypsy boy into the house? When he grows up he'll rob us all and he'll put shoe polish on our sister's dolls,' and he'd start to cry like an idiot, and the more he cried the more Pepe and I would laugh, we'd make him look in the mirror and say, 'Can't you see you've got gypsy hair?' and it was true, and no one knows where it came from, I think my grandmother used to say that her grandmother, or was it her mother, was a half-mulatta from Brazil, it's anyone's guess, what's certain is that we're all quite light skinned and he looks like a gypsy, but he didn't inherit the brains, these gypsies and mulattos are always pretty sharp, but he doesn't know his arse from his elbow and he doesn't really seem to care, although now he wants to copy me, but he doesn't know where to start, he wants to brush up his accent a bit, and he's bought two or three pairs of half-decent trousers and he stands up really straight when he's talking like someone with their head screwed on tight, but the things the kid says, at least Pepe's got a bit of a brain, but this kid, however many times he's told his handful of friends to call him Jaime instead of Migue (what a great idea of my father's to call him Miguel Jaime Sebastián Ricardo, as if the boy were the son of a tsar) but, however much they call him Jaime the boy can't help being a dimwit, he's a good lad but there's not a lot to him, let's see if the job he's landed in the barracks can shake his head up a bit, poor Miguelito, what a state, but that's how it is, it's the same as it is with the employees at work, I have to win the game with the players I've got, a draw's not good enough, here we have to beat Jane's father 5-0, he knows we're not Bill Gates's long-lost cousins, but we've got to impress on him that we're not part of the rabble, we know where we stand, and the things we've let slip by taking our eye off the ball, we're going to pull them back, step one, my mother's teeth, knowing what class you come from is in the blood, just like Amelia knows where she came from, so it's all the same whether my parents are living in Portada or up there in Limonar for the time being, sooner or later they'll be out of here, my dick of a father can get a loan from Sepúlveda or wherever, but they'll be out of here, and anyway, on this visit Jane's parents aren't going anywhere near the house or the neighbourhood, I don't care what they think, and if there has to be a family get-together I'll bring them to the apartment in Los Álamos and say it's my parent's home, we'll put out a few photos of them, and that's it, I'll call Céspedes again for the last time, he can't just leave me high and dry, the bastard, with the shitty day I've got in store for me, and I'll have to speak to her, Amel-Amelia Martínez, I've got to speak to her today or tomorrow or next week, the day I speak to her I'll jerk myself off first or I'll get her to jerk me off like a whore, yes, why not, like a total whore, and if she breaks my balls I'll give her such a slap, she's where she is in the hotel because of me, and she knows it, oh yes, she knows it, if I have to give her a slap then I'll do it, she can stamp her foot and burst into tears, but anything more than that, if she comes out with threats or says she'll turn up in front of Jane, I'll crush her, we'll see if she wants to gamble with her job, with the food on the family table and that lunatic son of hers, if she wants to go back to the dole queue and ask for scraps let her break my balls when the moment comes, when she sucks me off for the last time with her face like a whore and those eyes that look like they're going to burst with pleasure and melt.*

*

Dr Galán goes out into the corridor, leaving behind her husband, the mask, the catheters – and the capsule that the emergency room has become. Her eyes meet Ramiro's. The doctor breathes, whispers. Ramiro nods his head vaguely and goes into the room that she's just left. So, what shall I tell Guille? That his father's still breathing? And he might say, 'So what? Of course he's breathing.' 'Yes, but he'll only be breathing for a few more hours. You need to prepare yourself, we all need to prepare ourselves. Me, too.'

Dr Galán looks around. Julia's disappeared. *She'll be propping up the coffee machine, befuddled, trying to make herself wake up, her day off interrupted by one of Dioni's whims.*

She makes a decision and takes her phone out of her pocket. Contacts: **Guille**. She stares at those six letters. She puts her phone back in her pocket and walks down the corridor. Soft voices, footsteps, the noises of the outside world get louder and louder as she gets closer to the exit. A searing heat greets her as she steps out of the door, and that steaminess that seems as if it's about to set her hair and skin on fire envelops her. She imagines that her ponytail is like a torch on the point of bursting into flames. She likes the feeling, that almost unreal, disproportionate heat. A hallucination that removes her from the world.

She leans against a car, and, although it's parked in the shade, the metal is hot and almost burns her through her scrubs and her knickers, but she stays there. She takes out a packet of cigarettes. Winston 100s. 'Smoking seriously damages your health and the health of those around you.' *Life seriously damages your health and the health of those around you*, she thinks, and a faint, sad smile almost appears on her lips. Dr Galán lights a cigarette. She breathes in the smoke as if it were salvation and then feels the weight of her phone in her pocket again. *Just another second, just another moment before it all kicks off.*

She takes a few drags, chucks the cigarette on the ground and squashes it. Her fingers clutch the cigarette packet again, but she releases it before taking it out of her pocket and takes out her phone instead. She shades her eyes with one hand to see her contacts. **Guille** appears on the screen again. She gently taps on her son's name . . .

. . . and her son's walking slowly up the hill, which is starting to level out, the terraced houses on Calle Macizo del Humo are on his left and, on his right, a chicken-wire fence allows a view of treetops, roof terraces, in the distance a green expanse scattered with tiny buildings and the bare reddish-brown earth rolling down across a series of hills towards the blue sea.

He'd only left the house ten minutes ago, and as soon as he went around the corner and started climbing up the ramp to Calle Sierra del Pinar he was already regretting not having taken his moped. He's wrapped his beach towel around his head and imagines that he's a Bedouin and that a Moorish girl with Mónica Ovejero's eyes is doing a belly dance for him, when his phone vibrates in his bathing trunks' pocket. He thinks it's Loberas, who's waiting for him at his house so they can go to the swimming pool. He sees it's his mother calling. *What a pain.* He doesn't pick up and walks on dazzled under the sun with his phone buzzing in his pocket.

He doesn't want to hear his mother going on about his father. He knows he's been away from home for two or three days. He doesn't care where, he doesn't care what's going on between them or if they're going to get divorced or why they haven't yet. *They're abusing me.* They're selfish. *They're not going to use me, just leave me alone, this fucking heat.*

Guillermo Grandes Galán (neatly trimmed fringe, sloping shoulders, tall, gawky, looks like he's got knock knees but hasn't, looks like he's got flat feet but hasn't) has no idea of what's going on at home and doesn't suspect anything either. Nor does he want to. Sometimes his father stares at him. From his bedroom doorway, without going in or out. He wants to say something, he wants to spill the beans. Divorce, illness, whatever. But he doesn't go there. And he's not going to make it easier for him. He doesn't want any extra hassle. From his father or his mother. Each of them should face up to their own shit.

The heat. *You can touch the air, it's half melted.* Guille has an idea that if you struck a match the air would burst into flames. *Sweet,* like the explosions in films, a great big red-and-yellow flower filling the air. He'll say to Loberas in a minute, *Loberas, can you imagine striking a match and the air goes boooom and it bursts into flames, everything destroyed? Even Piluca's arse would go boom and Juno's hair would stand on end like a hedgehog.* His phone starts vibrating in his hand again. His mother. *Yes, you can call as many times as you like.* Guille stops outside the door to Loberas's terraced house. He presses the bell. A line of disciplined Argentine ants (identical to the ants that have been feeding on his father) are diligently climbing up beside the entryphone in a straight, narrow column. Guille takes out his lighter and sets the ants on fire, they evaporate. *The air isn't on fire, but we'll make an exception for you just to fuck you up a bit.*

'Yes?' Loberas's voice crackles over the entryphone.

'Come down, you wanker. I'm giving you a free pest control job.'

'What pests?'

'Your cousin's pussy. Come down, for fuck's sake, I'm melting here.'

His phone starts vibrating again. This time it's a WhatsApp. His mother.

'Fucking hell, what a drag.'

'What pests?' Loberas's sleepy voice is distorted by static.

'Are you coming down or what, mate? You were the one who wanted to go to the bloody swimming pool.'

'I'm coming, I'm coming. One Loberas, on its way!' Another vibration, another WhatsApp from his mother. He swipes down on the home screen without going into the app, so his mother can't tell it's been read. Call me. Urgent. *Yes, take a seat, I know all about your emergencies and your crap.*

Mummy's emergencies and crap. His mother wants to tell him about his father's medical condition. And to some extent, how it's all come to this, how everything has come down to a room in a hospital where his dying father's spending his last few hours. She'll only tell him some of what she knows. *He doesn't need to know everything, everything I know, the little I know, now or ever*, his mother thinks. *If I hide it from him he'll never really know his father, but that's happened to all of us, the truth doesn't have to be a knife.*

The little I know. Dr Galán doesn't know and so she won't tell her son that it all started one day long ago, around 1975, also a hot summer's day, when Dionisio Grandes Guimerá, whom everyone in the neighbourhood was beginning to call 'the Talent', was on the beach at El Candado. He was there because he'd struck up a friendship with a boy from a good family at school whose father (a businessman and town councillor) was a member of the yacht club. He and Enrique Rodríguez weren't only friends at school. They shared books, they went to the bar at the Faculty of Economics together and spent time talking to people involved in clandestine movements. They would go off to the El Agujero reservoir with some of Enrique's friends, Meliveo, Paquito Arteaga, El Pajarito. They would lie down under a tree, smoke, talk about girls. Dioni listened to them, and being with those kids from a certain social élite playing at being bad boys made him feel part of the centre of the world.

Enrique Rodríguez had been expelled from two private schools and sent to the local high school as a form of exile or punishment. No sports facilities, no buses to take him from his front doorstep to school and no mollycoddling. His father had condemned him to the living hell of mixing with the lower classes that he himself hailed from. But what his father thought of as a punishment was a kind of paradise for Enrique. No monitoring, freedom. No priest to note down his absences from class. Some of his former schoolmates had fallen from grace in the same way, and now they shared the same classrooms and escapades. Enrique held court. And they'd accepted him as a diligent boy but one who at the same time had a touch of genius and who was always ready to play along with them.

Dionisio Grandes Guimerá skilfully combined the dissolute habits of his new friends with achieving distinctions in most of his subjects. Over the course of the year he'd discovered that he wanted to be a lawyer. And also that summer, at the end of his first year of friendship with Enrique Rodríguez, he made another even more important discovery. It happened on the beach at El Candado.

Enrique, Meliveo and El Pajarito were stretched out on their towels with two girls they'd just met. Inmaculada Berruezo and Vicky Leyva. Blue bikinis, teenage bodies. Enrique and his friends compensated for their clumsy attempts at seduction with a skilful use of irony. Dioni, the Talent, immersed up to his thighs in the water, could hear them laughing behind him and could picture his three friends, each showing off in front of the two girls in their own way, and it was then, when he turned around, that he saw the boy, a stranger, walking slowly towards him along the shore. The water gently lapped over his feet. At a certain point the boy changed direction and went into the sea. He walked on until he was up to his knees, close to Dioni, gazing at the horizon.

He was a bit older than him, maybe two or three years. He'd never seen him before. He didn't know who he was. But at that moment Dionisio discovered his own identity. A curtain was drawn back from in front of his eyes. The sun's reflections in the water and the fierce glare meant he couldn't see clearly, but everything was there. There was a mirror behind the curtain. And the unmistakeable image which that mirror reflected back was of himself. The revelation of a calamity and a fundamental truth. The boy ignored Dioni, he was an intruder, someone who definitely didn't belong to the club. Bronzed skin, attractive pink nipples adorning a pair of pronounced, hairless pectorals. And those swimming trunks. Tight, white, immaculate. And that bulge, that discreet but prominent bundle, with several powerful knots, bulking out the stretchy material.

Dionisio looked away, he wanted to focus on the horizon, on the temperature of the water, on that sailing boat, also white and also gleaming, which was setting off from the small quay. But in reality it was as if he were unable to see and unable to understand anything: the water, the boat, the sun, the laughter and a whole morass of memories and feelings that suddenly came tumbling out, rolling across the water like a paper streamer unfolding, revealing the side that had been concealed up until then. That was who he was. There it was, unveiled, his true nature. He was different. He knew it. The message came from way back, and that boy, that intruder, that proud boy from the wrong side of the tracks was merely the bearer of the news, the messenger.

There he was, sent by who knows who but with a clear mission. A dark annunciation. He never forgot the image of that young man's body. For Dionisio Grandes Guimerá, as the years went by, that memory would also call to mind those characters in American films who are sent by a court to catch some individual unawares and serve them with a subpoena so they can't then evade justice. They've held out their hand, they've touched the piece of paper, there's no way back. Archangels on the side of the unknown.

He never knew whether, there on the beach, he had felt desire over and above the sensation of emptiness or if that was something he imagined as he relived the moment. In any case, every time he remembered the young man's body, his chest, his smooth bronzed stomach, his swimming trunks with that bulge, he felt the temptation, the urge to go up to him or to have gone up to him, to have kneeled down in the water up to his shoulders, get up close to the smooth silky material of his swimming trunks and press his cheek and his lips against it. Touch it. Feel those protuberances with his fingertips, his whole body rocked by the gentle lapping of the waves on that glittering white and brilliantly sunny day.

The boy walked off. In the same way as he'd arrived. Silently. The messenger. Dioni watched him climb the steps that led to the car park. A small area bordered by discoloured rocks and the club's wire fence. A short while later he heard the rapid backfire of a motorbike without a silencer. He watched through the wire fence as he passed, his shirt flying open behind him on either side of his naked chest like the flag of a country he didn't know.

He stayed on the beach. Transformed. With that unknown weight, that new burden, as new as the world was new. The light, the sea, his friends' laughter, which came from the void. He caressed the surface of the water with incredulity, took a few steps, his feet sliding on the muddy sand of the sea floor. He was a different person.

He went back to join his friends, now suddenly transformed into strangers. The girl called Inmaculada looked at him with a smile, smoking a cigarette, her big, greenish almond-shaped eyes half closed. On the other side of the glass. She and Enrique, covered in freckles, pale skin, like an abattoir worker, Meliveo with his mirrored sunglasses, always bubbling over with enthusiasm, El Pajarito, the other girl, they were all on the other side of the glass. 'Yes,' he said when Vicky asked him if the water was good, 'Yes.' And he smiled appreciatively, but he might just as well have screamed or spat in her face. He felt abandoned, lost overboard. He wanted to go up the steps, run, disappear under the sun. He looked at Inmaculada's breasts, trying to make out the outline of one nipple, then the other, he remembered her nipple with its large aureole when she dived into the water with Enrique the previous week and when she came out of the water her bikini top had slipped, he remembered his erection, and it was a consolation, it felt like a victory over the boy in the white trunks, a victory over himself. He carried on looking at the girl hoping to be stimulated, lowered his gaze to her stomach and stared at her thighs, her crotch, her mons pubis covered by the thin blue cloth of her bikini, and his eyes met with hers staring back at him coldly and she slowly brought her thighs together, never taking her eyes off him. It didn't matter that he quickly looked away, he could feel her cold stare, and, despite the fact that it was full of scorn, to Dioni it seemed the clearest sign of innocence that he'd ever come across in his life.

His period of confusion was beginning. Welcome, welcome, they said from the balconies, from the pavements, from deep inside his head. The chorus of the damned. Dioni lay face down on his towel. He pressed into the hot cloth. Beneath him was that heat, which seemed to come from the centre of the earth. The dark sand, his eyes closed, the noises, the voices, the laughter, the dampness of his still-dripping body, the salt water and the sun with its rough caress, his breathing, Inmaculada's breast, her nipple bursting out of her bikini, the white swimming trunks, Inmaculada kissing the messenger, their mouths joined, their bodies and now, yes, a firm erection, a splendid tautness pressing it to the heat of the sand and the earth. So many years ago.

The taxi was cruising along the half-empty boulevard in the heady August light. Carole looked out through the passenger window, one eyebrow arched, and Céspedes tried to interpret that image, that unadulterated arrogance, that life force. *I wouldn't know whether to screw her or kneel in front of her and weep, and I shan't do either, it's too late. I'll let her go, she'll go, tonight, tomorrow, it's all the same, this is my stop, that's what matters, the train will carry on without me, who knows what I'll come across in the future on those platforms, in the tunnels around the station. The tunnels, the underpasses. Yes, I'll still have the local trains, short journeys, scenery that's all too familiar, those sad beds, those bodies, just as lugubrious as mine, phantoms like me knowing they're on the final stretch before they give up altogether. It's on its way, it will be here soon enough, that day and that moment's already starting to show on the horizon. Now I shall remain here, now I can see those eyes without drawing on my memory, the basket that's increasingly full with so much dirty laundry. I'm here, I can see her, her small forehead, that eyebrow that looks like a brush stroke, no, more like a silky artist's brush, poised, dangerous, a bow ready to launch its arrow.*

He'd given the taxi driver a specific address, Calle Serrano 51, as well as the route, but Carole didn't know where they were going. All she could do was make a sarcastic comment, 'A bit early for lunch, isn't it?' And Céspedes had answered, 'Yes, you're right.' The sweet shade of the trees caressing the car's windows, alternating with flashes of sunlight and glare. The car makes a start up Calle Alcalá, and Céspedes remembers what he had read a few weeks earlier in that book about anarchists, how three of those crazies were going along this street on a motorbike and sidecar, lining themselves up behind Eduardo Dato's limousine and opened fire, killing him by shooting blindly through the boot. Céspedes couldn't recall whether the book mentioned the month it happened, if there would have been this heady light and the buildings' façades would have been like a dead mirror. The taxi approaches the Puerta de Alcalá, takes the bend smoothly.

'This is where they killed Dato. What do you think of that?'

Carole carries on staring out of the window. 'That's fine with me.'

She's perfect, so perfect that you'd have to be on your guard twenty-four hours a day, and even then it wouldn't be enough, in a different time I'd have tried, whatever – the taxi driver carries on, skirting around El Retiro. Carole looks over at Céspedes, sidelong – *whatever* – not wanting to ask, but intensely enough to communicate her unease and to let him know that an error on his part could cost him dear. *Yes, she's perfect, she knows it and can't help telling the whole world about it every second of the day.* Calle Velázquez. It's another life. Céspedes remembers the times he spent in the Hotel Wellington, that night with Malcolm and Lago, and even further back when he was at university, back in his youth, that freedom that he never really made use of, never really explored. It occurs to him that there was a time when he was innocent, too. *No, not exactly innocent, just inexperienced.*

The marble façades, another hint of drowsiness and another waft of scent from Carole's hair. *That scent is the stuff of dreams and possibly an armful of tragedies, half my life suddenly recalled thanks to a combination of shampoo, a rush of blood and the musk or spores or whatever that shiny head of hair contains, my affliction, my weakness that has made me follow aromas, looks, lips, tones of voice, intuitions, insinuations, shadows, rather than actual sex, I could explain it to my wife, tell her, no, listen, I didn't betray you for the sex, I did it for the scent of her skin or to get off on how she raises an eyebrow, yes, that's why I had my dick stuck in Señorita Ibáñez's pussy, I could explain to her it wasn't so much that woman's hair or her eyebrows let alone her voice that interested me in the slightest but rather it was a matter of routine, screwing that silly woman was the least important thing, the least damaging thing for our marriage and the least fraudulent thing I'd done in a long time, yes, that's it, explain it to her and the dog, each would understand as well as the other.*

The taxi turns into Calle Serrano, Carole yawns, puts her hands together as if to pray, puts them like that between her thighs and looks sleepily at the shop windows as they pass by the taxi like a merry-go-round. *For a start, just to begin with, I'd have to explain it to myself, go into that reservoir up to my chin, begin to swallow water and mud, not speaking as if I myself understood why I did what I did, where that sense of abandon I succumbed to came from, rolling downhill thinking that actually I was going up. Going up into a hole. Better just to leave it there. That's it, that's the only thing I could say to her without lying either to her or the dog or myself. That's it, that's how it was and that's what I've done.*

The taxi comes to a halt at the same time as Céspedes's phone announces the arrival of a new WhatsApp message. While he pays for the ride and Carole gets out of the taxi, another message arrives. Céspedes gets out. *Talk about timing, who the hell could that be?*

'Just a second.' Céspedes points to the opposite side of the road, wanting to distract Carole so that she doesn't realize their real destination.

He gets out his phone, almost dropping it.

Carole gathers her hair, lifting it up and revealing her neck, with her arms raised, and says something about the heat. Céspedes clicks on the green WhatsApp icon. Julia. *What the fuck does she want now?*

Can you do me a favour?

Fuck, I don't believe it, what a ball-breaker.

This woman's crazy.

'Just a moment, I'm sorry,' he says to Carole, who's turned around and is looking at him in disbelief. 'One second.'

'Is it your grieving wife or your bit on the side? Don Céspedes, the troubled one's bit on the side?'

'No, it's just an idiot, I swear to you, honestly, the biggest idiot you could imagine,' he says as he types away.

'Yeah, yeah, you mean one of your bits on the side.'

A new WhatsApp arrives.

Sorry to be a pain but like I said is urgent. Not to mention a tragedy. One of my friends eaten alive by ants, half dead

And, following this absurd message, another one:

U ok?

What the fuck is she on about? Céspedes knows he might regret it, but so what, he's written the message totally fucked off and he presses the send button, he's got to find a release for the bitter taste Julia's left in his mouth, *let her pay for it, let them pay, action reaction action reaction and then at the final reckoning the Big Lottery will adjust the balances.*

'Sorry, Carole, I'm ready now.' Céspedes tucks the phone away in a pocket in the leg of his Bermuda shorts, one of those pocket's that's almost level with the knee.

'You'll hear it down there, too, even if you put it in your shoe you'll still hear it. And you'll pick up.'

Céspedes doesn't reply. He takes her by the arm and she looks at the façade they're standing in front of. Banco Santander.

'Have you brought me all this way just to use an ATM, Céspedes? A few kilometres too far, don't you think?'

'Of course, but this is my favourite ATM, it plays Wagner as it hands out the cash.'

'Wagner? As in Woody Allen and Poland?'

'The very same.'

'That's a bit vulgar. It doesn't sound like you, Céspedes. Or does it? And you know what's worse? You're infecting me, you're making me come out with ridiculous things because deep down what I want to say, what I think is, what am I doing here?'

Carole stops in her tracks and makes Céspedes stop, too.

'And you know what happens when a girl asks herself that question, don't you?'

They look each other straight in the eye, he nods, feels the phone vibrating against his leg with a new message, is tempted to take it out and smash it against the pavement. 'You're right. That's the worst question, the prelude to a full stop. "Lovely to have known you, but that's it."'

Another vibration. *I bet that's Julia. She'll be pissed off. Sod her. Why doesn't everyone just fuck off and leave me in peace?* But he doesn't reach for the phone and look at his messages – ? ? ? ? – what ? – he looks into Carole's eyes instead, puts his hand on her cheek, covers her earlobe with his fingertips, buries his nails in her hair and says, 'Forgive me. Look on it as a brief parenthesis, how can I put it, a farewell to a friend, a brief parenthesis, a day full of real mental relaxation.'

'What sort of friend? Listen . . .'

'A friend for one day, whatever, that doesn't matter. A day in the life, nothing more than that. I'm going to be serious for a moment, nothing extraordinary, but what I really wouldn't like is for you to look back on this as something vulgar, and, although there have been some things that might make you think like that, forget about them, don't take any notice, all I want is for you to remember the best version of me, and please forgive the other one, he's the scrapped version of Céspedes produced by fifty-five years in the automatic shredder, but behind or beneath that there's something more, at least there used to be, I can assure you. Just that. We understood each other, you got who he was last night as soon as we exchanged our first words.'

'There's a limit to what anyone can understand, Céspedes. You must have learned that by now.'

'Yes, and that's all this is about, so for one day we don't pay too much attention to ourselves and we forget or we make ourselves forget about that fucking dotted line that tells us where we have to go in life and what the next step will be, the next word, the next meeting and the next coffin. You might be really young, but you know how it works a lot better than I do, for fuck's sake, Carole, I only have to look in your eyes, you're saying it loud and clear, you've got a sign on your forehead that's two metres high.'

'If you say so.'

'Yes, I do say so. Tomorrow we can go back to the dotted line and carry on filling in the picture, what's expected of us, of me at least.'

She looks at him. Her eyebrow arched. Her lips are tightly pressed together, making an expression that could be interpreted as a yes.

'Anyway, the day's slipping past like the wolf in the fairy tale, sneaking along the corridor leading to Grandmother's room, there's not so much left for you to endure, and, even if it's just because of the law of probability, there'll be fewer opportunities for me to put my foot in it, that's combinatorial, a scientific fact, the best consolation.'

Céspedes takes her by the arm. They walk along the empty pavement. Streets like tubes, dead trees.

'And since we're here please excuse another vulgarity, but this is where I brought you, don't think I'm some kind of pimp, I'm just someone who's lost his way and wants you to have a memento of him, that's all.'

A white shopfront, two box trees trimmed into cones, one on either side of the door and a sign above it: *Chopard*. Carole looks at Céspedes quizzically, he makes a gesture of apology and points to the entrance, whispering, 'Please.' They go through the glass door etched with a *C*.

They're greeted by the silence of the jeweller's shop and a lungful of cool air. The exquisite floor with its brown geometry floating on a background of pale wood. Armchairs upholstered in blood-red fabric and bunches of flowers to match. The display cabinets look like parts of a spaceship. An elegant hostess appears from nowhere and does her best to ignore Céspedes's outfit (Hawaiian shirt, Bermuda shorts, worn-out boat shoes), measures Carole up and prepares herself for the possibility of having to despatch with some degree of consideration the barbarians who through error, ignorance or arrogance have dared to burst into her temple.

'We'd like a watch for the lady.'

The high priestess continues to size the pair up from behind a friendly smile.

'White gold? Rose gold?' Céspedes almost says it directly in Carole's ear.

'Perhaps.'

'Perhaps,' Céspedes repeats to the employee and smiles at her, and at the same time he opens his eyes wide in an exaggerated way and chews a little bit of the shop's refined air, much like Jack Nicholson when he's interviewed by the head of the asylum in *One Flew Over the Cuckoo's Nest.*

For one brief moment the god Pluto's subaltern feels she needs her boss, but she reacts, she pulls herself together and enters the arena. She doesn't want to end up as the casual victim of a mistake. From that moment on the strange couple are treated like the heirs to Buckingham Palace or the relatives of some footballer who may recently have landed in the capital.

'Please.'

She sits them down comfortably and begins to show them different pieces. White gold, rose gold, watches with concentric circles encrusted with diamonds. Carole's wrist receives the sophisticated artefacts while the employee recites her poem, the Happy Diamonds collection is characterized by Chopard's famous dancing diamonds *spoken like a parrot, you think we're third-rate passing trash who probably won't buy anything* thirty-two-millimetre quartz, this is rose gold (do you see?) it's eighteen carats, that's right, the phone starts vibrating again against Céspedes's leg *the ants*, the ants spring to mind again, and now he seems to read Julia's message, but he can't quite understand what it means, *eaten alive by ants, what the fuck, what the fuck does that mean, is that for real?* the telephone stops vibrating, 'This is a very striking piece, as you can see, the face and hands are all one colour' *matching her bra or at least her bra strap* Céspedes looks at Carole's shoulder, the emerald-green shadow of her bra strap *I'm also being eaten alive by ants, the whole fucking world* 'The watch face is made of agate, and, as you can appreciate, it extends right across the diameter of the case' *the whole world is like a million or a billion ants' nests, and all these ants' nests are ready and waiting to descend on us, waiting for the moment to start eating us starting with the feet or the eyes* Céspedes looks out at the street across the empty room, the cars pass by silently on the other side of the glass *why is Julia telling me all this, she could send it in a group WhatsApp because it's something that concerns us all equally, or perhaps she sent it to me because she knows, because she can sniff it in the air like only a woman like her can sniff out rotten flesh, am I next?* 'Hmm, this one,' says Carole lifting up her wrist, letting her arm float in the air like a cardinal whose hand you are obliged to kiss, 'Yes,' the high priestess affirms, 'it's beautiful, it's a variation, deep black, onyx, the effect of the diamonds dancing around the face is unique, the whole range of brilliance is heightened against that background, spectacular, you won't regret it,' the shop assistant smiles happily, just as she would with two regular clients. The time has come to see whether this is all a joke or if the scruffy man in the Bermuda shorts is an eccentric who will actually pay up. Carole raises an eyebrow inquisitively, shows Céspedes her wrist adorned with the black jewel and the hypnotic dancing diamonds, 'Onyx,' she says, and Céspedes confirms, 'Onyx. Perfect.'

Out on the waste ground the ants' nest murmurs, roars, bellows. The scout ants, the ones that take risks and venture into the unknown, are not the young ones. They're the older ones, the ones that are worn out, sick, the ones that no longer represent a serious loss for the colony. They climb up mountains of clay, clamber over the super-heated pebbles, sniff around, sample a piece of abandoned gauze with traces of saliva and blood from Dionisio Grandes Guimerá.

The patches of waste ground murmur, roar and bellow under the punishing sun. 'Rai, I'm going to drop dead, mate, I'm going to die with this heat,' Eduardo Chinarro says in his gravelly voice to Raimundo Arias, who's walking ahead of him, and without turning around says, 'Who is he, I want to know, who is that piece of shit?'

Three, four, six ants are walking dizzily over the bedsheet. Ramiro extends a finger and gently crushes them. He looks at the empty slits that Dioni's eyes have become, a boiling yellow mass, almost brown, his farewell to the world. There he is, on the other side of the mask, hidden behind that diving mask, a scuba diver with no oxygen and no water. The lift's innards whine and crunch as the door closes, and up it goes to the unattainable paradise on the sixth floor, to Consuelo la Giganta. Ismael's anger roars and dissipates as he accepts the inevitable failure of every morning. It wasn't worth waiting on the street corner gauging the La Giganta's steps with the precision of a watchmaker, which shops she went into, how long she would take, and then finally to bump into her in the entrance hall, calmly opening the post box as she exchanged a few words with the concierge *why the hell do you have to talk to that scumbag, Consuelo, when I'm here waiting for you?* watching her out of the corner of his eye and putting the junk mail back in the post box at the very moment she passes by him, her smile, her tiny teeth *she looks like a whore*, clunk, closing the post box and joining her to wait for the lift together. 'This wind is really something, isn't it?' 'Yes,' he replies, hanging on to her every word and imbuing his monosyllabic response with the same warmth and friendliness as if she'd said to him, 'Today's the day I'm going to let you fuck me.' Then disaster strikes, the fat lump of a woman from the fourth floor appears. She's wobbling from side to side, a metre and a half from one hip to the other, a mummified leg poking out of each corner of that tent of a skirt (black, as though she were in mourning) which looks like it was made from a length of cloth she found discarded by the roadside, and she says good morning and how hot it is, talks about the owner of the butcher's shop and his accident and all the break-ins in the flats, how you have to be so careful, about her daughter who lives in Switzerland and the letters she sends her on the computer, how cool it is in Switzerland where there are no robberies at all and how it's going to be even hotter tomorrow and we're at the very gates of hell and no one can bear it and we'll all have to move to Switzerland or the North Pole although people say the North Pole's melting away and it's all because of the Chinese. All this in the short wait in the entrance hall, and then in the brief journey in the lift for four floors. Then, one floor alone, barely two and a half metres, to look at Consuelo and her twisted smile and then get out of the creaking box cursing life and all the while hoping that the fat lump of a woman from the fourth floor will die. The lift crunches, shudders, the building shudders, Ismael's teeth crunch.

The sun overpowers everything. The stones are burning, and anything metal, like the bodywork of parked cars, spits out heat. The very air is on fire. It's as if a magnifying glass is focusing the sunlight and chasing people down the street. Jorge looks out of the window at work and over to the patch of waste ground on the other side of the street and thinks about his girlfriend Gloria, *she'll be awake, she'll be in the shower*, rivulets of water and foam trickling down her thigh, like the day he watched her having a shower while he was sitting on the bidet and she was beneath the water, her skin as smooth as a statue incarnate.

The Runner goes into his mother's bedroom barefoot and opens a drawer in the chest of drawers. Underwear, worn-out flesh-coloured bras, knickers, the melancholy of all that lace, exotica on rotten flesh. That drawer is like a mortuary, and the Runner puts his hand in as if entering a crypt. Profaning graves, lifting up tombstones, with the smell of a recent death, his hand rifles through the funerary clothes seeking out the money. There they are, the banknotes, like children sleeping in the depths of a cave. His fingers will bring them out into the light of the day and will give them to the mechanic, *El Niño del Sordo*, to the guy at the Repsol garage, to the waitress tonight who'll charge for his and Lucía's drinks. He closes the drawer and averts his gaze from that flesh-coloured underwear, from poverty, from his own destitution. *My mother was once a woman, too; some mothers are still women, Jorge's mother for one.*

Jorge's mother is stretched out on Playa de la Misericordia, dozing in the sun. All around her people are selling ice creams, smoking, chatting, swimming, drinking, yawning, children are running around, chasing one another, screaming and splashing about, and Jorge's mother, Amel, Rafi Villaplana's lover, sees it all through a flimsy but solid veil, a veil that cuts her off from all the din and turns it into a distant, soft echo. The waves gently crashing, salt crystals floating in the air, the earth is a rocking chair that doesn't stop moving. The breeze lulls her to sleep. It's as though it's ageless and time doesn't exist.

She's sweating. Her body is a slow, heavy engine, breathing with a long, passive, sustained asphyxia. Belita touches the cross that Father Sebastián Grimaldos has blessed for her (she almost forced him to do it) next to the baptismal font. She kneeled down and kissed his hand.

It smelled of cigarettes. Belita Bermúdez has viscous memories; her past is submerged in a pond. She's peering through the picture window in her flat and contemplating the huge expanse beneath her. She has a round, fleshy face. Her chubby cheeks are out of proportion, and her mouth is small and closed. A tiny moustache made of droplets of sweat. Round, sleepy eyes that stare expressionless into the distance, at that horizon on which the roofs of the warehouses give way to an arid piece of level ground between Avenida Juan XXIII, Avenida Europa, the Dos Hermanos district and the agglomeration of blocks and building plots that fade into the distance on the right. An almost visible, stifling heat is rising up from that level ground; it seems as if it's at boiling point.

Belita takes it all in, impassive, sitting at the window, ten floors up. Her hair is matted, divided into two mountains, two solidified waves, the Red Sea parting not to let Moses pass but a broad parting from which thick, dark roots are sprouting, a thick head of hair that abruptly changes colour after two or three centimetres and becomes a kind of dark wheat, limp and tinged with orange. As if an unrelenting sun, as if a biblical curse had dried it out, like a ruined crop, a cornfield frazzled by drought. She opens her small mouth and swallows a slow lungful of oxygen. Her knees are pressed together and her ankles are wide apart. Black shoes with a block heel. The skin on her legs is a whitish, sickly pink. She once dreamed that she was pregnant. She had the dream while she was awake, and she dreamed it for several weeks, months almost. She was forty-two years old. Pedroche eventually believed her, even had a flicker of pride. A child. Belita was transformed into a happy woman, or almost happy. She looked at her belly in front of the mirror, naked. She looked at her belly like she's looking at the patch of waste ground now, covered in weeds and parked cars. Her enormous white belly. She watched it grow. Pale, veiny, soft, drooping down towards a dense pubis, a deep abandoned reed bed. She felt her breasts, looking for any sign. She even said that five drops of milk had come out of the left one. It was a happy day for her. For Pedroche it planted a seed of doubt. Belita went out and bought baby clothes and a cot. And when Pedroche began complaining that all these purchases were premature she started hiding her new acquisitions: dummies, rattles, socks, baby clothes and bibs were hidden under sheets, camouflaged between towels, squirrelled away in saucepans. She told her cousin Auxi about the advice the doctor had given her. She told Pedroche about the advice her cousin Auxi had given her. Everything pointed towards an easy pregnancy and a comfortable birth. Her personality softened, the look in her eyes became more human.

'They say that the same thing happens with dogs, to bitches,' Pedroche confessed to his friend and partner Floren. 'It's a phantom pregnancy, that's what they call it, and their periods even stop, although I don't know if that happened to her, she says it did and she says that what she had was a miscarriage even though the doctor says it wasn't, it wasn't a miscarriage or a pregnancy, nothing, it was all psychological and that was all. The doctor, apparently, never confirmed the pregnancy. What she told her cousin and me was all made up, all in her head.'

Pedroche stopped and looked thoughtful, studying the frames, the pictures he was working on, with the same remoteness as his wife is now looking at the expanse of roofs, industrial warehouses and empty plots stretching out in front of her.

From then on, from the time of the pregnancy affair, everything got worse. Much worse. For several months Belita didn't set foot in the street. Almost a month in bed, recovering from what she sometimes called a miscarriage and other times a birth. She developed dark, almost purple, bags under her eyes. Her mouth became smaller, her lips thinner and her face larger. That was the medication. Someone must be to blame. 'Who's to blame, oh Lord?' She said that often, to her cousin Auxi, Pedroche, anyone who went to visit her. Her cousin's children were scared of going into her bedroom. Belita cried when she saw them, and even so she stretched out her hands towards them and said, 'I love you so much, your little cousin was going to love you so much.' The children looked sidelong at their mother as she pushed them towards the bed to kiss the monster.

From that point on Belita thought of herself as a mother. She also knew what it was like to have a child, and, what's more, she knew what it was like to lose one. A mother's grief. The day of the miscarriage, the birth, when her period came, Pedroche found her sitting on the bathroom floor between the toilet and the bath, the floor stained with blood, and her hands, the toilet bowl, the washbasin, everything was covered in dark reddish-brown streaks. She'd been crying, but when Pedroche arrived she'd calmed down. Not exactly calm, but calmed. As though she'd sunk into a dream. Her legs were stretched out on the cold floor (it was December) her skirt rolled up and her vagina like a dead animal between her thighs, bleeding. The first thing Pedroche did was to cover up that image with a towel. 'My child, my child,' said Belita. The child was that blood clot staining her cotton knickers, which she picked up and showed people – her cousin, and the phantoms of her brother, her parents, her uncles and aunts – all of whom she must have imagined were there by the bath, pressed up against the bidet, ghostly, silent, like her dead child.

It was a tough Christmas. Belita spent hours sitting on the sofa, wrapped up in a woollen dressing-gown. The television turned off, in mourning. She wept in silence. She wouldn't allow Pedroche to take her hand to console her, to stroke it. She was tormented by the strains of Christmas carols, the birth of Baby Jesus, season's greetings that people exchanged in her presence, the happy sounds that came in from the patio and the stairwell. All the windows closed, everything had to be closed, everything in darkness. 'Like my child,' she said to Pedroche. And that's what she did. Windows, shutters, curtains. Everything was in semi-darkness when Pedroche came home from work. Belita's bulk on the sofa would look strange in the gloom. Pedroche would turn on the light not knowing what he was going to find. And she would be there, with her mouth open, her head bent over and her eyes rolled back, asleep. Or pretending to be.

'I think she does it to shock me and also to make me feel guilty about the child, the pregnancy that never existed,' Pedroche confessed to Floren. 'She gets up, doesn't say a word to me, and goes to the bedroom dragging her feet, like she was going to the gallows.'

Pedroche stretched out his time at work as long as he could. Sometimes Floren would be driving past their premises after eleven at night and would see a light on in the back, in the workshop. When Pedroche got back home there was no longer even a fried egg, like Belita used to cook for him four or five hours before he arrived. On the last day of the year Pedroche sneaked a few sips from a bottle of cider. He emptied the rest down the sink. He also looked out over that empty, dark expanse, with lights in the distance. People who were living their lives.

He'll come, and He'll give me everything, Father Sebastián is forever saying it, every day in every mass he tells me with his own lips, he tells me He knows me and He knows, and He knows, He knows us and He could forgive us, He could forgive us all, but He won't do it, I ask Him on my own behalf and I ask Him on behalf of those that He's not going to forgive, those who are out there in the world. Belita Bermúdez, ninety kilos of dormant matter, submerged in amniotic fluid, in a gentle wave rocking her *the world and the people out there.* The world is an enormous waste ground, cars that pass by silently, down there, Belita watches them from twenty-five metres up. Those tiny beings, those insects, each with their own lives, their houses, their families and their feelings, at least that's what Father Sebastián tells Belita. 'The world doesn't end with us. The world is a miraculous chain, my daughter, miraculous.' *A chain that ends with me because of him, he can't give me a child, a child who doesn't leave me, a child who calls me Mummy, and place it in the world with all of them, with all the others, but being my son, being him, being me, a part of me my life.*

Father Sebastián Grimaldos is snoozing in his flat in Calle Amarguillo. Leatherette sofa and a heavy, carved sideboard. Bare walls and blinds half lowered. Dog collar on the floor beside him. Shirt half unbuttoned. Head slumped to one side. Dreams. Heat. A spoon in his hand. On the coffee table, next to an out-of-date newspaper and a book, *Gran Granada*, the remnants of a vanilla ice cream he'd bought in Valentino's ice cream parlour on the way home. A fly is buzzing at the window.

The sun is like a dagger; the air is like a lunatic's feverish thoughts. Inside people's homes the timbers dry out and creak and moan, dull and muted.

'I think my head's about to catch fire, Rai.'

Raimundo walks through the labyrinth created by the building works for the Metro. They've gone past Plaza Manuel Alcántara and they're going up Avenida de Andalucía, Eduardo Chinarro trailing behind by five or six metres. Their feet are burning from the asphalt, the insides of their trousers are dripping with sweat, the cloth sticky and rigid.

'This isn't normal; the heat's so intense I'm even starting to get into it, know what I mean, Rai? So intense it's like everything's going to explode. How can you wear socks, Rai? Are they wool, Rai? Fucking hell, slow down a bit.'

Chinarro's shirt is completely unbuttoned, billowing around.

'There's no need to rush, Rai. The punters will still be there.'

Raimundo mutters and jabbers and utters insults under his breath and presses the searing-hot guitar against his side. 'The punters will still be there, he says! Of course the punters won't be there. They'll all be gone. Or are they going to hang around just for you?'

Eduardo shakes his head, speeds up. He's sweating. *My head and my balls are about to catch fire, for fuck's sake!*

'If you hadn't got mixed up with those people we wouldn't have to rush.'

'I was waiting for you, Rai.' He almost catches him up, almost gets alongside him.

They go past the Tax Office building. Ahead of them, enveloped in a smoky-grey fabric, dirty, overheated, looms the empty Post Office building. Ghostly, victim of a rare case of aluminosis, a monument going to rack and ruin. Like a natural disaster surrounded by the building works and fences and the disproportionate heat. Trapped in an enormous spider's web.

'And who the fuck is that guy?'

Eduardo frowns. 'What guy, Rai? The one with the boy and the Fanta? How should I know? Some dickhead.'

'No, I mean the one who was there with you and La Penca.'

'Oh him? Whoah, that was Nene Olmedo. He's got connections, Rai, you better watch your step with that one. And the other one's just a kid.'

'He'd better watch his step with me.'

'Yeah. That, too.'

They walk on, taking long strides, Rai in a straight line, Eduardo slightly staggering.

'That, too, Rai, a man has to watch his step with you, too.'

Rai looks over at him for the first time in a long while, screwing up his right eye, focused. That means a question is on its way.

'Nene Olmedo is in with the Daltons, Rai, the Portada crew and the Barriga crew as well, you know, Rai, they pull big stunts like robbing banks with guns, and no one dares lay a finger on them. They're like reptiles, Rai, cold as ice. Word is that doing a bank job for them is like going to buy a lollipop.'

'And this guy goes with them, on the raids? Or does he just hang out shooting smack and selling shit on the corner?'

'They've got bikes that go like shit off a shovel, I've seen them messing around in Portada, and you wouldn't believe it, Rai, just imagine when they're doing it for real,' Eduardo holds forth, Raimundo suffers in silence. 'So I don't think Nene Olmedo goes with them on the raids, but he hangs out with them, or so he says. Their bikes are like the ones you see in the movies, Rai, all dials and numbers and stuff. And they've got stashes all over the place.'

'Stashes, my arse.'

'You know, stashes, where they hide their guns and the cash, and the number two, I think, the number two in the Dalton gang is a black belt or even higher, Rai.'

They go over the bridge, a bed of concrete beneath them. A river with no water, a dried-up vein. They go into La Alameda, sheltered by the shade of the giant trees.

'Wow, this bit of shade's so cool, eh Rai?'

'And this Nene, is he a black belt, too? Sounds to me . . .'

'No . . .'

'Sounds to me like he's all mouth, just a piece of shit.'

'No, not El Nene, it's best not to mess with that lot, Rai, although he's not a bad guy, he's just, like, an arsehole, but he's OK, Rai, and La Penqui, what she must have seen in him or liked is the way he carries himself, but they didn't do anything, Rai, all it was is that we were having a laugh with the other guy, you know, the other guy who was there, he's a good laugh, his name's Juanmi, or that's what they call him. I don't know who he is.'

'I don't give a shit about him.'

'No, of course, me neither, Rai, I don't give *two* shits about him.'

*

Yes, no one really cares, almost as little as Raimundo Arias and Eduardo Chinarro care who this Juanmi is, but if anyone would like to know (his story isn't long, but it's quite interesting), I'll mention that his full name is Juan Manuel Ares Ruiz. He's clocked up around a quarter of a century and is from quite a well-to-do family. His father was a doctor, an ear, nose and throat specialist, and his mother is an ex-teacher who took early retirement and then spent her time looking after her depression and vaguely threatening suicide. Juanmi has left several jobs. He ostentatiously took out a white handkerchief to wave goodbye to several job opportunities that came to him through contacts, connections and favours owed to his father. He also left university in his second year. Philology. Why was he studying philology? Only because back then he was hanging out with a sullen and reclusive friend called Veloso. Veloso fancied himself as a poet, or that's what he made out. He used to write, but no one knew what he wrote. Train timetables? (He liked going to the station and watching poetically as the passengers came and went.) Recipes? (He said he loved cooking.) League tables for the girls' tits in his class at uni? (He gave them a penetrating and continuous optical assessment.) Well, whatever it was he wrote it all down in a Moleskine notebook and then stared up at the heavens. No doubt about it, he was a poet. Juanmi didn't dare ask him what he was writing or what he was thinking. No one asked the half-mute Veloso anything. He went into the heart of the Dantean wood, he was going to meet his own personal Virgil and, so that this Virgil would be able to recognize him (a Virgil that in the best-case scenario could be Antonio Gala or Mario Benedetti), Veloso wore a hat with a medium brim, grew a thin moustache and an even thinner goatee. At university they started calling him El Fino. People of a more rebellious nature simply called him Cantinflas. But let's not dwell on Veloso with his Moleskine on his path to the heart of lyricism. If we don't much care about Juanmi's story, forget about Veloso's. Juanmi understood that the poetic wood was too impenetrable for him. He lost the urge that had driven him to university and found shelter with two people who would play an important role in his dubious journey. These were precisely the people who had christened Veloso Cantinflas. Alfonso Pallarés and Víctor Calero. Two scoundrels. Pallerés had an arse like a woman's, and his tongue would flick in and out of his mouth like a snake when he spoke. He was particularly prone to doing this when he was talking about women or one of his nights of excess. His two favourite hobbies. And, if they went hand in hand, so much the better. He was a likeable flatterer, a charlatan who boasted about his vocation as a smooth talker. Calero tried to imitate the tongue thing, but it didn't quite come off, he had no charm, not for that and not for anything else. Whatever Pallarés did well, Calero made a mess of it. He was an apprentice. He was killed in a road traffic accident a few years later. One of his most brilliant discoveries was that on roads, streets and motorways there were many more bends to the left than to the right, and he enthusiastically defended this position. He was killed on a straight piece of road, but when his body was thrown out of the car which he himself was driving (without a licence) it traced a perfect curve until it went headlong into a milestone which (such an act of providence) had the number twenty-one on it, his exact age at the time. But let's not get ahead of ourselves. Juanmi, our Juanmi, hooked up with these two characters. Pallarés and Calero. He saw in them a beam that lit up the murky path towards transgression in different and promising dimensions. An unknown landscape for our gullible Juan Manuel. Pallarés knew *Don Juan Tenorio* almost off by heart (yes, be amazed, be very amazed) and, what's more, apart from the ending, his aspiration was to follow the romantic outrages committed by its protagonist down to the very last detail. Calero said he was Captain Centellas, 'a great lover'. Although he put on airs, Calero was actually Chuti, Señorito Pallarés's dogsbody. The plan was either to make girls fall in love with them or take advantage of the girls and then abandon them treacherously. To humiliate, deceive and then spill the beans. If they could get something from the victim along the way, so much the better. If she ended up seeing a psychologist, better yet. When Juanmi hooked up with these two bad photocopies of Casanova, Pallarés was at the zenith of his evil ways. He was going out with a Norwegian girl and sleeping with her mother at the same time. The daughter knew nothing about what her mother was up to; the mother apparently did know about her daughter. Or that's what Pallarés said, with his tongue flitting about like a butterfly in the spring. That's poetry indeed, our gullible Juanmi said to himself. And when Calero took him to the Llano de la Trinidad to find 'gear', he saw the shimmering face of poetry even closer up. Brown powder, which according to Calero was coke. Cocaine for smoking. Forget about putting stuff up your nose, because then you've got to live with a platinum septum, said Calero to Juanmi the apprentice. Centellas Calero wanted Juanmi to be his Chuti. But no way. To cut a long story short, Calero asked Juanmi for the cash, and Juanmi pilfered some from home. Daddy cursed him and threatened to throw him out. Mummy said he was a poor little thing, looking at her husband out of one eye while the other searched out the drawer with her tablets, the knives and the window she would throw herself out of if anything should happen to the boy. Life is so cruel. Yes. Juanmi paid (or rather, his father did), Calero scored and the two of them, Juanmi and Calero, were floating. And, what about Pallarés? No, nothing of the kind. Pallarés's feet firmly on the ground. To Juanmi's surprise, when he offered him some of the stuff so that he could join them on their amazing trip, the much-admired Pallarés looked him up and down and turned his back. 'See you, mate.' And when Juanmi turned to Calero he summed it all up for him in one short sentence: 'You're an idiot.' 'Why?' Well, because Pallarés never got involved ('just say no' as people said later). A lot of violent words, a lot of wrong-doing and a lot of getting off with girls, but Don Juan's apprentice was crystal clear about this. Calero was indulging in his addictions behind his spiritual leader's back. Juanmi racked his brains trying to find the north star. And then, when he found out that Pallarés was not only comfortably passing all his subjects like a French pole-vaulter but that he'd started studying law as well, his compass rose went crazy. Pallarés was the worst person out there. The most evil person in this wasteland. And so? God helps those who help themselves, his father sometimes said. Exactly. So, poor Juanmi lost someone else. Pallarés was already just a dot on the horizon. Juanmi's race towards the moral orphanage became furious. His own private version of the Indianapolis 500. Daddy also said goodbye a few months later. Prostate issues that even Dr Torrecillas couldn't cure. For Mummy, his death was a kind of cure-all, like the 'balm of Fierabrás' in Don Quixote. Not only did she stop hiding tranquillizers in the strangest places at home but she also stopped taking them. Windows were no longer an inevitable portal into the void and gas could have other domestic uses than asphyxiation. Doña Brígida (I'm even telling you her name now) got her act together. She finally managed to help her only son. But Juanmi had already cut himself adrift. In the time between his father's death and his mother's resurrection, our hero managed to get his hands on some of the family money. Not too much as, although Doña Brígida's life was turned around, her finances weren't. Even so, Juan Manuel, now the little man of the family, got his hands on enough cash to become independent. Or that's what he thought. A small apartment overlooking the sea in Pedregalejo, a few months making out to Calero that he was the new Don Juan because he was generously paying for everything for the two of them. A few girls set foot in that apartment and a few crazies, too. Someone stole a small wad of cash that Juanmi kept in the bedside table drawer. A girl on an Erasmus scholarship, a mate or a whore because a few representatives of the oldest profession in the world also found their way there. His vocation was to be wicked, but his destiny was to be a fool. There wasn't much let-up. Calero had his fatal encounter with milestone twenty-one a few weeks later on a little-used B-road. Another farewell. And now Juanmi was all alone in the world because his mother was no longer the understanding lady who constantly indulged him. Apart from the occasional piece of advice and the odd bit of cash, Doña Brígida gave her son very little. She was needed as a Samaritan in other, higher places. Charities, food banks, holidays for widows all claimed her input. So, he was neither Centellas nor Chuti nor the Knight Commander. Juanmi was a 21st-century version of a street porter. And if the male character from *Don Juan* was notable by its absence, let's not even mention the female role. The closest that our friend got to an Inés was a web page where a girl dressed as a nun, with a cigarette dangling from her lips, urinated copiously on a man who was apparently thirsty for justice and nun's pee. So Juan Manuel Ares Ruiz ended up as nothing more than a poor devil and, if only out of pity, we should cut him a bit of slack. There's only one path to happiness left for Juanmi. The comforting powder that his friend Calero had provided for him until now and that Juan Manuel has to go out and buy in person for the first time. He recognizes the usual supplier, the skinny nervous guy who gave Calero the wraps while Juanmi waited in Mummy's car. The supplier offers, and Juanmi buys like this:

'Smack?'

'Coke.'

'Coke?'

'Eh?'

'Not smack?'

'No,' stammers Juanmi, 'coke, like Calero used to buy. He's dead.'

'Smack.'

'No.'

'Listen, mate, what's your problem?'

'Nothing. I just want what you gave to Calero.'

'Smack.'

'Smack?'

Oh! For all those months, who knows how long, Juanmi hadn't been taking cocaine. That brownish powder was something called smack, junk, heroin. Impossible? No, nothing's impossible when it comes to Juanmi. Smack, then. Well, what can you do about it? In his own way, Juanmi has broad shoulders and can cope with almost anything. It's basically a case of letting himself go downhill. Smack? Well, smack it is. All the demonization and gossip about it were just old wives' tales. Nothing had happened to him so far, and nothing would happen to him. What was more, and this was the big excuse in the kind of pinball machine that is Juanmi's head, smoking isn't the same as shooting up. Off you go then, Juanmi, the world is yours for the taking. You can imagine the rest. A downwards spiral towards limbo, his life revolving around the magic powder, pilfering and stealing from his mother. The great Juanmi still believes he's not an addict because he can control it and he sometimes manages to stay clean for one or two weeks, enough time for him to believe that he's not hooked and so he can get high to celebrate, just as happened that day of the *terral* when he was chatting with Eduardo Chinarro and then Rai saw him dozing in Nene Olmedo's place, and neither his story nor his life mattered to anyone.

Rai and Eduardo pass through the labyrinth of metal fences, walls, plastic posts and other obstacles thrown up by the Metro building works.

'Look at them. Fancy working in this heat, eh, Rai?'

Raimundo looks sidelong at Chinarro. The screech of a circular saw cuts through the air, and they can't hear each other speak. Rai's opened his mouth, but Chinarro doesn't know what he's said. *Some crap about La Penqui,* Eduardo thinks to himself. *What's the betting he's still going on about that dickhead or licking his wounds over that bit of skirt?* He walks beside him through the cacophony of circular saws, passing cars, and the white dust rising several metres into the scorched air and then falling back down as microscopic snowflakes.

And yes, Eduardo's hit the nail on the head, Rai's still thinking, still imagining, still picturing La Penca in Nene Olmedo's arms, *she's all over him*, Raimundo the guitar man thinks, but the image of La Penca in that hovel releases a few drops of sulphuric acid that eat into his stomach. He walks briskly through the dust storm and the racket, and at the same time he desperately wants to stop in his tracks, turn around and go back. He imagines himself bursting in there, tipping over the table, grabbing that bastard El Nene by the neck. The more he dwells on that urge the more determined and faster he walks. *Knock his head off and then what?* He doesn't want to think about it. He hurries Chinarro along, he wants to get La Penca out of his mind, eradicate her like an infection. He knows what she's doing right now. *Fucking little shit, I'll rip his heart out, fuck him up well and good.*

Yes, she's all over him. La Penca's been left all on her own, floating in that gloomy room, under her back are a few cushions that move and seem to slide across the floor like clouds slide across the sky, she herself is a cloud, dilating and contracting, fraying at the edges, parts of her melding with the air and disappearing, Nene Olmedo's mouth is a red door that leads into another room, inside his body with tunnels and vaults and El Nene's panting is coming from a long way away, bouncing off the walls and coming back to her, it's a secret language she vaguely knows, like the Morse code of his languid thrusting, he's inside her, part of her, with the dry bloodshot eyes of a fish, Nene Olmedo is an eel that not only fills her vagina slowly and entirely but also expands throughout her whole body, filtering through her capillaries, penetrating and occupying the tiniest cracks in her skin, filling them, flooding them, and it's there in the throbbing she feels as her nails meet his flesh, on the inside of her teeth, in the roots of her hair, bursting through her tear ducts, spilling over in a sticky patina of sweat that their two bodies have produced, on which Nene Olmedo is sliding, their skin and their bodies are like soft, gelatinous rubber. Yes, she's all over him, La Penca is floating on the cushions, her yellow top rolled up around her neck, and she vaguely wants to be strangled, her dog bites her nipples, she half opens her eyes and looks tenderly at the naked lightbulb hanging from the ceiling, and now Nene Olmedo is licking her neck, his hot breath enters the tunnel of her ear, and he moans, moaning like a man weeping, enters, withdraws, doubles up, moans, there's so much sweat between the two of them, such a loud slurping noise it's like a haemorrhage, so much sweetness, and La Penca, letting herself go, closes her eyes again, hears El Nene's faraway breathing, touches herself, moistens her fingers with that fluid and making a superhuman effort from the other side of the world, asks him, 'Have you come your load yet?' And although she feels an uncontainable urge to laugh she can barely manage to open her mouth in a nondescript expression that she would like to have been a smile.

Guille watches her. Mónica Ovejero (fifteen years old, long hair, chiselled features) is standing up. She's talking to Trini's mother as though they were the same age, like one of those neighbours who come to the pool in one of those multicoloured sarongs, a wide-brimmed hat and a foldaway chair. Mónica is also carrying a large basket on her shoulder; she's wearing gold sandals, and she's putting her weight on one foot and then the other, her hips going up and down as she gesticulates. Loberas doesn't seem to be aware of anything; he's sending WhatsApps to Juno and, not taking his eyes off the screen, he says, 'The stupid fuckface doesn't have a clue, I tell him we're here, and he says he's tired, the bastard.'

Mónica Ovejero is slim, almost blonde. She looks like a model. JuanCa says her legs are thirty metres long.

'What about JuanCa?' Guille asks, pretending to be interested.

Mónica's stopped talking to Trini's mother and, softly sinking her feet into the lawn, she heads towards them. Guille starts to get nervous and pretends to be annoyed when he asks Loberas again, 'What's up with JuanCa these days? He's always ducking out of things. I've had it with him.'

'He's not coming.' Mónica's shadow is looming over him. Loberas looks up in surprise. 'Hey, sweetie! What are you up to?'

'I'm flying in a hot-air balloon, can't you see?' She drops the bag on to the lawn, stretches her neck so her long hair falls naturally over her back.

'Don't be sarky. Good thing you look more beautiful every day.'

'Yeah, yeah. Grab the end of my towel.'

'Of course, I'll grab hold of anything that's yours!'

'Grab the end, that's it.' Mónica, in contrast to her good looks, has a somewhat rasping voice.

'Where's your brother?'

'He's a fuckwit.'

'Steady on, girl. Have you two been fighting?'

'I don't fight with garbage.'

'What a prick!'

'Worse than that.' Mónica sits down on the towel, takes off her T-shirt, shakes her hair and gathers it for a moment at the back of her neck in an ephemeral ponytail that opens out instantly into a thick curtain.

She's in a white bikini, her shoulder blades gently outlined, as if painted in watercolour.

Guille watches her, aware that he still hasn't said a single word since Mónica arrived. He didn't say hello. He should have done. Now he gets it. He always realizes things a few seconds after everything's happened. She could have asked him to help her spread out her towel, he was probably nearer than Loberas. It's as though she hadn't seen him, it's like she hasn't even noticed that he's there. And Loberas saying, 'You look more beautiful every day' and 'I'll grab hold of anything that's yours' and Loberas doesn't even know her as well as he does, and she replies without batting an eyelid, like she's known him all her life.

Mónica gathers her hair at the back of her neck again and lets it go. Guille's heart beats harder, he tries to think of something to say but it all gets muddled, he starts talking, then he stops, waiting for right moment to butt in, and, without knowing why, he blurts out a string of words that don't have anything to do with what he'd planned, surging up as he speaks, as if engendered spontaneously by the contact of his tongue with the air and nothing to do with what he wanted to say.

'Trini's mother's looking fit,' and, seeing that his words have made Mónica stop playing with her overabundant hair, he raises the stakes, 'so fit I'd like to poke it inside her and not stop for a week.'

He feels like a man with balls of steel, speaking so confidently, but then he hears, or thinks he hears, Mónica whisper 'Imbecile' at the same time as she throws him (and this he does notice clearly) a sideways look full of contempt.

But he can't stop now, Guille laughs and nudges Loberas. 'Wouldn't you, too, Loberas?'

'Wouldn't I what?' His friend doesn't know what he's talking about, he's totally immersed in his phone.

And now, he can't tell if it's an echo or if Mónica's said it again more clearly, 'Imbecile.'

A dark wave ripples through his entire body. He wants to say sorry, say it was only a joke, that he hadn't really meant to say what he'd said and hadn't actually said it, they were just words, sounds to show that he was there. He'd have to start again. Mónica would have to be speaking to Trini's mother again, and when he saw her arrive he'd say, 'Hi, you're looking pretty' or 'Wow, looking good' or just 'Hi, Mónica, where's your brother?' But no, everything had conspired against him, Loberas acting soft, grabbing the end of the towel and telling Mónica how good she looks because he doesn't do it like a man, he does it like a girl touching another girl's hair and asking her what conditioner she uses and what lovely skin she's got, and Mónica, after saying 'Imbecile', shakes her hair again, yes, again, as though she were the only person in the world to have hair, as though she were the chosen one out of the entire human race to be the Queen of the Tresses or was a full-time walking shampoo advert. And then she lies back on her towel with her face to the sun, just as remote as if she were on the other side of the world.

Guille understands like never before that everyone looks after themselves, and, if they can, in passing, stick it up your arse, they will. He retches, a dirty retch from deep down in his diaphragm, like when the drain in their garage was blocked and a black liquid started welling up from it. He feels sick with indignation. *Stupid cow with her fucking hair and her tits that aren't really tits, she doesn't stop fiddling with that crappy bikini as though she were hiding treasure inside or as though she were Trini's mother, who the fuck does she think she is, and that bastard Loberas there, what's he thinking about, JuanCa's the one who should be here, I was going to pull her down a peg, revolting little rich bitch, look at her, now she's wearing her sunglasses, and she's putting on a face like she's on a photoshoot 24/7 and no one's even looking at the bitch. I'll take them down a peg, her and Loberas. I'll make her pay, I'll make them both pay.*

'He's not coming.' Loberas looks up from his phone.

'What?'

'He's not coming now. Later.'

'Who's not coming where?' Guille still has a vacant expression on his face.

'Where've you left your brain, man? JuanCa.'

'So much the better.' *Fuck you all.*

Guille's phone vibrates in his pocket. He still hasn't taken off his Bermuda shorts. *JuanCa's calling me.* No, it's not JuanCa, rather it's those fateful four letters M-A-M-A. He doesn't answer, puts the phone on the grass. To the ants it's a UFO, the intergalactic threat from outer space, *that's all I need.*

Piluca closes the metal gate at the entrance to the pool enclosure. Blue eyes, almost transparent, chubby face. She's Mónica's inseparable friend. Guille and his friends know them as Jekyll and Hyde. She comes towards them waving her hand left and right, she's like a head of government or something like that or, as Guille thinks, *one of the three kings on a Twelfth Night procession, she and her friend are on a permanent procession, and, by the way, she's pug ugly.*

She reaches them. She and Mónica do their girly coochy-coos and all that crap. Mónica's ecstatic to see her, overwhelmed after such a long separation (probably one or two hours; they spend their whole lives putting on make-up and trying on clothes in each other's houses) they laugh, whisper in each other's ears and laugh again. Loberas tries to stick his oar in, and they ignore him. He's also passed over to the world of non-existence, the limbo Guille's inhabited since Mónica's arrival. Loberas, orphaned, asks Guille if he's going to have a swim. *I hope you drown, you wanker*, Guille thinks, but all he says is, 'Nah,' and then he says, 'Later.'

More arrivals. More characters. Mónica's brother appears (she raises a scornful eyebrow, he gives her the *bras d'honneur* behind her back). He's accompanied by Juno. He bumps fists with Loberas and Guille. Mónica's brother says he's got a game of *padel* tennis lined up and he doesn't even sit down. Juno takes off his T-shirt, messing up his enormous bouncy quiff, and goes for a shower straight away. He doesn't say hello to anyone. *At least he's got a pair of balls and didn't even look at Mónica, so fuck her.* Fuck her, because Mónica does look at Juno, twice, and puts her sunglasses on her forehead, wearing a big smile, ready to chat, and the smile freezes on her mouth when her Apollo with the quiff goes off for a shower and then, his muscles shivering from the cold water, he runs across the pristine lawn and dives like a dolphin into the turquoise water not giving a shit that diving is prohibited by the house rules. He pulls half a dozen powerful strokes, gets out and spits out a jet of water like a fountain in the park, at the same time rearranging his prodigious quiff. Mónica and the ugly pug whisper in each other's ears. They're talking about Juno, of course, but it sounds like they're also whispering Guille's name. And not only that, Piluca turns around and looks at him, looks at Guille, and smiles. Are those bitches talking about him? Are they comparing notes? What the fuck is all this about? And at that moment his telephone rings again. Guille looks at it and can't believe it. It's his mother. What's wrong with everyone? And now it happens, now he passes his thumb over the screen and his life changes for ever.

'Now what is it?'

'Guille . . .'

'What the hell is this about?'

'Guille . . .'

'What the fuck's going on?'

'Don't talk to me like that.'

'For Christ's sake, with all your calls it's like being hassled by Interpol.'

'Guille.'

'I'm on holiday, aren't I? Isn't that what we agreed?'

'Guille, Guille, listen, something's happened. Did you –'

'Yes, Mummy, and I didn't stay in bed all morning, and I didn't break anything.'

'Shut up and listen to me, listen Guille.'

'I'm listening, for fuck's sake.'

'And don't talk like that, please don't talk to me like that.'

'Well then, don't call, for fuck's sake! Why d'you think they invented WhatsApp?'

Piluca turns around to look at him, Mónica does so out of the corner of her eye.

He feels grown-up, he thinks he's found a stunning riposte, brilliant. 'If you don't want to hear me then don't call me.'

'Something's happened.'

'It always does.'

'To your father, to Daddy . . .'

The anger, the repugnance, the trail his parents leave behind like snail slime. 'All your problems, I'm on holiday, didn't we talk about that?'

'Daddy . . .'

Brilliant, energized, firm. Like an executive. 'I don't want to know what's going on or not going on between the pair of you.'

'Your father is dying.'

'You what? What did you say?'

'Your father is dying. He has only a few hours to live.'

'But what are you talking about? What . . . ?' *Not this shit, no, what's going on, what is this, I'm at the swimming pool and everything was normal, what is this?*

'Listen, I'm sorry, Guille.'

'It can't be true! Fuck!'

Piluca looks at him and Mónica, too, not just sidelong now. Even Loberas looks up from his phone.

'Yes, it's true, Guille. I wish it weren't. Listen. Uncle Emilio is going round to the house. He'll pick you up, and then both of you come here. I didn't want to tell you this way but you –'

'Where?'

They stop looking at him. Juno pulls some powerful strokes in the swimming pool, cutting through the water like a shark.

'At the hospital, I'm at the hospital. I'm sorry, I didn't want to . . . I didn't want to tell you like that, it's the pressure, I'm sorry, Guille, forgive me.'

'Was it an accident?' Guille lowers his voice, suddenly shy.

'Er, no, something like a . . . a shock. Uncle Emilio's just back from his holidays, and he's on the way, he'll be at the house within an hour. Are you at home?'

'What? Yes but, yes. And is it definitely so bad, so serious, might it not be?'

'It's very serious, son, but you go home. If you want I'll come home – shall I come?'

'No, no, I, no. No.'

'I'll tell you everything when I see you.'

'No, no.' *Fuck don't just leave me high and dry, always always always it's your stuff, all your shit, and now he's dying.*

Juno gets out of the pool, he's placed his arms on the side and launched his body out of the water as if he were made of paper, weightless, he could have carried on ascending, flying into the sky. He stands up and arranges his quiff, his swimming trunks, his muscles.

'Did you hear me, Guille?'

'Hmm.'

'You can't . . .'

'And why do I have to go?'

'What do you mean, he's your, well, no, Guille, we'll see, I'll speak to your uncle, don't worry . . .'

'OK, and what do I do?' *You've been doing this to me since the day I was born, and now . . .*

'Listen to me, Guille.'

'I've got to go.'

'You're going? Where?'

'Home.'

'But didn't you say, you told me, aren't you at home?'

'Not right now, no.'

'Guille, please, wait for your uncle.'

'Yes, at home.'

He hangs up.

As if by magic, like in a time warp, Juno has joined them and is sitting on a corner of La Piluca's towel, his arms wrapped around his knees. He's talking, showing his teeth. Mónica flips her sunglasses up and down, from her eyes to her forehead and her forehead to her eyes, touches every corner of her bikini, ties up the straps and then does them again. Everything comes closer and then backs away, like Mónica's sunglasses going up and down, everything in front of Guille is in constant motion. And then it stops, it's fixed, more fixed than ever, much more intense, nearer, the whole world is stuck to his face, goes in through his eyes, lock, stock and barrel. He can see everything all around him just like in science classes when they explain how an insect sees, a fly stuck on the enormous window of the world. Everything's there, and he's there, too. He won't be able to hide. Where did he get the idea of hiding? *From my father? I haven't done anything. I'm here.* Terror. A pendulum. And suddenly he thinks, darkly, *Nothing's happened, everything's the same.* Trini's mother is laughing, children are splashing in the baby pool, a small plane with a banner advertising a concert is flying past. There's nothing, not the smallest detail, to indicate that something, something serious, something important, has changed in anyone's life. Everything is inside his head. A voice, some sounds that have gone in through his ear. He might have imagined it, it could be a dream. But no, the phone vibrates again in his pocket. He's not going to answer. He doesn't need to look at it to see who it is. Not even that. His mother's not even going to give him a ten-minute truce, ten minutes in which the summer will carry on the same and the most important thing that might happen would be that JuanCa would turn up or not, or that Mónica didn't repeat the word 'Imbecile'. No. There she is, calling him and calling him again, wanting to drag him along, involve him, stuff him into the same hole she and her father have stuffed themselves into. And suddenly the pendulum gives another lurch. *My father's going to die.* The telephone stops vibrating. *Can it be true? They say that, and then they'll save his life.*

Loberas has cracked a joke. Guille knows it's a joke, but he can't quite work out what it means or what exactly has been said. He smiles. Juno is looking at him, asking him something, this guy always asks questions, always gets straight to the point.

'What's up?'

And Guille smiles again, and Juno asks him, 'Has something happened?'

And he replies, 'What?'

He can feel Mónica looking at him and that Piluca bitch, and he considers going for a swim. That would be the best thing. A swim. *Go for a swim and my father dead, how? Fucking hell, I didn't ask, did I ask?* He feels like crying. He'll have to, sooner or later. *Will I have to? When everyone arrives? When he dies. Shit.* Shit, he pictures himself in a sea of black suits and ties *one of my father's ties; I should be crying*, his father's wardrobe, a coffin, his father inside and the family. He sees them all, his Uncle Emilio and Aunt Emilia, his cousins, his grandmother, Great-uncle Pedro, Pérez Palmis, everyone from the club, Grace Jarvis, his mother's friend, who'll come over from the States, the people from the lawyers' office, his father's business partner Carlos San Emeterio, a whirlwind, a whole merry-go-round of faces. *And these people, Trini's mother dressed in black with her tits, fuck no, he's dying, is he dead yet? Right now? At this very moment? Kneeling down, my great-uncle and the Jesuit, I'm not going to pray either, everything's gone soft.* Loberas is writhing with laughter, he's rolling around on the grass pretending he can't control it. *Did she say a shock? But what does that mean? What happened? And what about Dublin? Dalkey, the beach, Sarah's laughter. Will I be able to go to Dublin? What about the house? Will we still be able to live there? A flat? Where? Fuck, what is all this?* Guille sees different neighbourhoods, streets he has walked down without noticing anything, streets with balconies. *My mother earns a fortune, my father, Daddy, will I never see him again? I don't want to see anyone die my mother won't make me is that what she wants? They say that Bores's father wanted to get out of bed, and he screamed, and he wanted to lie down on the floor. Dublin?* He sees aeroplanes, an airport, the boarding bridge, a queue of passengers waiting to get on the plane, a stewardess smiling at him. *They were always on about money.* There's too much saliva in his mouth, and feels faint, he turns around, puts his mouth to the ground and spits, releases a long dribble on to the grass, on top of an ant, *I baptize thee,* the ant starts swimming in the saliva, scuba diving, Guille turns around, it's too hot, he sits down again, too much light, and the whole world's blinking like an indicator on a car, nausea from the pool, the smell of chlorine and all these people. All these people will stop, this afternoon or whenever, they'll stop still and they'll say his father's name and they'll talk and talk about him and his mother, they'll say they saw him. He was there at the swimming pool, the poor boy, and he had no idea, more saliva, his gums, his teeth all seem to have turned into saliva, and Juno looks at him again. *That bastard, nothing ever happens to him, he's like rubber inside and out.* Juno frowns, raises his chin and a shoulder all at the same time creating a powerful question mark. He shakes his head and against his will opens his mouth, but he reacts in time, he doesn't say anything, he smiles and sucks and spits. This time he doesn't just release the saliva he spits it out, in revulsion. *Am I fainting? What the fuck is happening, they're playing a bad joke on me, he can't die, they're going to put him in a coffin.* And then he says suddenly, 'I'm off.'

Juno frowns even more. Loberas, almost yawning, asks, 'So soon?'

and argues, with scientific precision, 'But you haven't even had a swim yet. You can't go now, man.'

But Guille is already on his knees, he doesn't know why he's kneeling. 'I have to go.'

And again the machine in his head plays tricks on him, those fluids, those electrical impulses that make him say what he doesn't want to say, and he says, 'My father.'

Loberas smiles and asks him, 'But weren't you talking to your mother?'

'My father's had an accident,' yes, that's it, he's said it. 'My father's had an accident, and it's very serious, very bad.'

That's it, there it is, liberation, it's all OK, the world is still turning, the oxygen enters his lungs, children are splashing about in the baby pool, the sound of laughter, he can speak and move and everything's the same as before, all the same, only Loberas's mouth is wide open, and all his features, his eyes, his nose, his teeth are all compressed with the same expression those cartoon characters wear when they've been impaled, everything's just the same except that Juno's also got down on his knees as if he had some powerful springs inside his legs and they've pushed him towards Guille, followed in his wake by Piluca's pale, shocked eyes, both her little hands placed over her mouth covering the skilful work of her orthodontist and attracting, obviously, Mónica's sweet, attentive, compassionate gaze. So close to glory. 'My father's going to die.'

A hundred thousand million.

'A hundred thousand million. That's how many people have been needed for you and me to be walking quietly along this pavement, waiting for a taxi, suffocating in this heat, and you, dear Carole, with your pretty watch on your wrist. A hundred thousand million, so my dear, dear Carole, let's not let them down, we mustn't let that whole chain of people's efforts, births, blood, sweat and tears, dreams and deaths go to waste, for it to have been nothing more than a ridiculous endeavour resulting in a couple of ridiculous lives. You're not like that. Let's live and breathe. You know how to, that's why we're here, that's why you're here now.'

'So when did you learn that stuff about thousands of millions, or have you made it all up? In your coffee breaks at the office or . . . ?'

'No. There are these things called books and a man called Edward Wilson.'

'But the real question is why? So you can bamboozle young girls out on their own in the woods after you've bought them a watch?'

'Yes, that's right, you've guessed it. I always knew you were special.'

'Yes, very special, but going through that shopful of wonderful watches and stones hasn't shed much more light on you apart from the fact that I'm very grateful to you, but I don't think that's what you're after, gratitude.'

'Of course not, what would I do with that?'

'You're doing it for yourself, out of vanity or whatever, pride.'

'Yes, you're spot on about it being selfish, but it's nothing to do with vanity.'

'And not so I'd admire you either, because at the end of the day I might even play at being offended.'

'You can play at being whatever you like, but what's important is how you really feel. And offended, Carole, you've no reason to feel offended, it's something as innocent as giving you a peck on the forehead. It was something I wanted to do and you liked it, so everyone's happy.'

'Not to mention the people in the shop and that silly cow. How much did it cost you?'

'No, please. It's not –'

'Yes, I know it's not important, but I'm just curious. Five thousand?'

'Carole.'

'More?'

'Do you like your watch? Are you enjoying this walk, wilting in the heat, here beside me?'

'Less? No. The little girl lost in the woods knows what the fruits of the forest are worth. I'm not going to admire or despise you any more or any less, and I'm not going to like it any more or any less . . .'

Céspedes takes a receipt from the pocket of his Bermuda shorts and holds it away from his face so that he can read it: €8,850.

'Four thousand four hundred and twenty-five. Happy now? All clear?'

'Just as happy. Crystal clear. Céspedes's labyrinth is clearly defined, a labyrinth with no taxis in it. It's so hot! Isn't there one single taxi in this city? I haven't even seen one that's occupied.'

'That's what happens when you get on trains with strangers. But that's what life is like, a whole string of trains. Sometimes the wrong ones,' Céspedes drops his ironic tone, 'and we only realize when it's already too late.'

'My plan is not to get on too many wrong trains in life. Not to drag too many suitcases along platforms, you know.'

'I thought I was going to catch mine, too, the right train, and it was going to take me further, I was on the ball, I'd seen my father, a good example not to follow, but quite some time ago I realized that, in spite of being on the ball . . .'

'I'm not you.'

Céspedes smiles. 'No, you're not.'

They both look around again at the same time, looking for a taxi that, like Godot and JuanCa, never arrives.

'No, I was never a little girl lost in the woods. I didn't have time for that,' Céspedes adds sarcastically.

'Are you going to tell me a story about a little boy who struggled to overcome his cowardly (or simply wretched) father and then slayed the dragons and the rich kids?'

'No, you've already told it, in greater detail than I was going to give you, too.'

Céspedes puts his arm up. A taxi's indicators start flashing, and it pulls up smoothly at the side of the pavement.

'Your pumpkin carriage awaits, my lady.'

'How many people, how many millions of people did you say? How many million grandparents do we have?'

'A hundred thousand million.'

'So there would have to have been twice as many in order to bring a taxi over here a bit sooner, don't you think?'

'Indeed, Your Highness.'

And so the white vehicle, that carriage made out of plastic, aluminium, steel and glass, disappears in among the other poor metallic monsters following the dark and burning hot asphalt track, with three people inside, three descendants from those thousands of millions of hominids, cave dwellers, cannibals, explorers, peasants, blacksmiths, sailors, dreamers, wretches, heroes and scaredy-cats. The fifty-five celestial spheres of the universe revolving above their heads, life's scythe, the unsolvable conundrum, crossing the sky in an endless riot of colour and blood.

Yes, that's what Céspedes is thinking as he sees the reflections, the trees' shadows, ground-floor windows and pedestrians flash by, erased, lost for ever, brothers, souls, you who have wandered these same paths throughout time, unaware that you are pilgrims, that's what Céspedes is thinking, unkempt, exhausted (up all night like a naughty boy), yes, a tired old dog like him, no sleep last night, doing battle all day, the weight of his years hurting his back, his muscles going numb, short of breath, a cornered animal, yes, who is he to talk about lives capable of not letting down thousands of millions of people, souls, pilgrims, bastards like him with no clear direction beyond their own belly buttons, that bespangled god made out of clay, forever lighting candles at his own altar? Which ones? Yes, which particular times would he say were the high points of his life? The ones that nourish him on sleepless nights, the lifeboats he swims towards when half awake. His daughter, yes, there's one. His daughter in the garden, him watching through the window, and the little girl walking through a clump of daisies, a cloud that briefly blocked out the sun and darkened the sky, and he knew then, in that transient shade, that it had all been worth while and he could cope with it all, yes, he was at the apex of his life, nothing could destroy that moment, it was registered in the archives of the universe. Very good, yes, and what else, Céspedes, what else? Yes, there's more, there's more, one day in autumn walking along the banks of the river Henares, the ground covered in leaves, the sound of his feet, and Vicky's feet dragging through the piles of dry leaves, laughing the pair of them, and that friend who was with them, laughing, he doesn't recall what they were laughing about in the cold, there was a dog, the sound of a dog barking coming closer, a labyrinth of trees, youth, and the future stretched out there at their feet under that carpet of yellow leaves inviting them onwards because it was all going to be theirs, what did their precarious situation as students matter, that effort, all that toil that arrived from home as a modest but punctual money order on the fifth of every month, a shy letter from his mother and a piece of advice from his father, that happiness beneath the trees, that plenitude. Anything else, Céspedes? Yes, only last night, at daybreak today, next to this woman, looking into her eyes and tenderly knowing that my time is already up but still feeling the vigour, the heartbeat of an old lion, or a large cat at least, a fox that has learned how to seduce and bamboozle ravens of a very different type and size, still alive, perhaps more alive than ever, inhaling the perfume of the living, the rapturous presence of life. And there are also days with his wife, yes, of course, that afternoon when he saw her on the other side of the street, when she was waiting for him but hadn't seen him, alone, in a black overcoat, long hair blowing in the wind, a woman in the heart of the labyrinth, and he knew that he loved her, fully, vibrantly, yes, and those days they spent in a cabin, that peace, the breeze carrying a scent of dry pasture, and the look in his wife's eyes that seemed in total harmony with the light, the sensation of not wanting to be anywhere else, yes, and a Christmas that really felt like Christmas, his daughter, his mother, his wife, an open fire, Dickens, the business was going well, flourishing as if by magic, every wind blowing in their favour, Paris, Turin, Milan, money that came and went leaving a glittering trail, and the biggest treasure was feeling free of worries and cares, that sense of absolute lightness. And on the other side? Yes, there was another side, in Céspedes's mind those other memories were kept in a shadowy zone, hidden behind the shadow of a wall that divided his memory. The side in which he kept memories that shone in a different way, much more diffusely, dishonestly, *the dark side that Father Isidro talked about in our spiritual discussions, sodomy, the scar around his neck, the glasses typically worn by a priest, red lips, he said it in the silence of the chapel. Those men practised sodomy, they were on the dark side, and you, Father Isidro, do you practise it as well or do you just feel up little boys' legs and tell them as you told me, 'What a lovely pair of trousers,' while you stroke the cloth, my thigh?* The dark side, moonlight. *They deceived all of us.* Yes, Julia's shadow crosses that zone and the shadows of one or two others. Elvira and those nights in Barcelona. He remembers one night, after leaving a sordid, gruesome strip joint. The echo of her stilettoes on the wet pavement and a dark weight attracting him towards the floor, the smell of petrol and rain in the heart of cities, wet cardboard, bloated cigarette butts, damp walls and doorways. That also seemed to float on the islands of his memory. Shipwrecks, yellow fields and blue terrain illuminated by the moon and neon lights. And Julia? Yes, of course, she is also an island in the dark waters of his memory.

Now Céspedes feels a small pang of remorse. He's tempted to look at his phone, he thinks he's received new messages. Maybe from Julia. He shouldn't have sent her that WhatsApp totally fucked off, but it's done now. No. He doesn't look at his phone. He doesn't do anything. Better to let himself go, better not to go back over that absurd story again. No islands. A life is a continent. A life can't be worth so little or be condensed into just a few seconds. Over the course of more than half a century there must be moments, days, months in which everything was lived much more intensely or coherently, yes, that's it, when it will all have had a deeper meaning than a few clouds passing over a garden that's suddenly left in the shade, whether his daughter was there or not. His daughter's significance is much greater, the scope of that significance is much broader and deeper than just that image beside a flower bed when she could barely stand up and couldn't even talk. A stroll along a riverbank thirty years ago, a woman masturbating in a strip club under the cock-eyed gaze of four or five men. Games with Julia Mamea, starting with the taxi ride with him and Ortuño, so many nights, faces, bodies, images, alcohol, fleeting moments of squalor and splendour, all that is nothing, *nothing but small change, the essence, the truth is something else, a continuum, a river, that's right, a river, a liquid expanse, an underground river that threads and joins it all together, yes.*

Better to let go of those ideas. Perhaps it's just because he's tired, because of the exhaustion that's built up after three days of wear and tear and stress. His wife barring him from the house. And at work, the investment company's poor performance, the penultimate gift. He tells Carole, 'Do you know what I've been most afraid of throughout my life?'

'You?'

'Yes, me.'

Céspedes would say she was looking at him with a mixture of curiosity and irony, but she ends up saying, 'No.'

So tired. Céspedes looks out of the window for a moment, then back at Carole.

'Well, I always thought it was fear of not being good enough.'

'And now you think it's something else?'

'Er, not exactly. I've refined it, pinned it down. I've always been afraid of tomorrow, that's what it is.' The woman is about to ask a question, but Céspedes interjects, 'Not an abstract tomorrow, not the future, but precisely the day I'm going to experience tomorrow. To have reached this point and to be good enough tomorrow.' Céspedes smiles with his square jaw, his large teeth, his powerful forehead. But he has the weak eyes of a dreamer. The breeding ground of fear.

Yes, happiness is possible. Happiness, or whatever it is that's called happiness, is something that Floren, Jorge's and Ismael's cousin, experiences every day. Every day he gets out of bed wrapped up in that cotton wool and every night he goes to sleep curled up beside it. Happiness is embodied in María del Carmen, his wife, and his daughter Carmencita, the same name as a brand of powdered saffron. Some people might think Floren goes through life wrapped in sticky candyfloss just like you get at fairgrounds. They may be right, but when he finishes work, when he pulls down the metal shutters at his business, Floren feels serenely and resolutely happy. Running on greased rails along a track with very gentle curves and barely discernible slopes.

So while his other colleagues, people in neighbouring premises, fellow practitioners in the art of odd jobs and small business, find their way to La Esquinita, the bar on the corner, for a bottle of beer, a shot of something, a chinwag and the freedom, the immense freedom, to be uncouth, to be real men, he prefers to go straight home, discreetly, with a smile on his face, to his flat with a view over the TV aerials, roof terraces and empty building plots. His paradise. Because everything he sees in the company of his wife and daughter is paradise itself. On the downside, Floren won't be party to his colleagues' conversations. He'll miss the details of Benito's sexual exploits (Benito's the only bachelor in the group) and, above all, those of Boss-Eyed Manolo, divorcee of good character, who rebukes Benito for his unsavoury habits and who, to the envy of the married men, gives the lad some sound advice. 'No no, lad, what you're doing's really bad for your health, drinking and one-night stands, I mean, that's all right for a laugh, but that's as far as it goes, all that stress trying to find a decent bit of snatch, if it'll be nice and tight or if it's too wide – it does happen, you know – or if she'll catch you by the short and curlies and introduce you to the brat she had with some other guy or her cousin or even her mother, and even if she doesn't introduce you to anyone she'll be going on about the hassles at work and her previous boyfriend or her ex, that's the worst thing, having to listen to how she's got over it all now and what an angel she was and what a bastard he was, and meanwhile you're knocking back the G&Ts, your liver's swollen and sick of how you treat it, kicking back at you, and there you are like a right Charlie looking at your watch, and it's going so slow you think maybe the spring's broken, it's a mess, and you'll never get those hours of sleep back, a right mess. No, not me, no way, the first few months after we separated maybe, until I saw how the land lay, and I said to myself, whoah, Manolo, don't go there. No. What I do every Friday is I go for supper at Quintana's bar, a nice bit of sirloin or a sea bass, top notch, and Quintana's missus cooks like an angel, if it's sirloin she does a sauce with it made out of, er, made out of something or other, but you lick the plate like it was one of the apostles' sandals, and if it's sea bass, a nice bit of garlic and some olive oil Quintana brings back from his village, I have a good feed, nice and quiet, a couple of glasses of good Rioja, rice pudding made by Quintana's missus, full of vitamins, one of the best, you know, I eat like a lord, and then I get a taxi like a lord, and bingo, there I am in Calle Don Cristián. And La Loren's got me a little love nest there, all set up with a little bird, a little bird I've chosen on the internet, are you listening? I see a little bird on the internet and how much she weighs and her measurements and whether she does it doggy fashion, all that stuff, and say "That one", and on Friday there she is waiting in her thong or her whatsitsname with all the lace, we have a nice G&T – not too strong – and I check her over, see what condition the chassis is in, how firm the airbags are, all that stuff, no hurry, no pressure or nothing, no stories about the kid's school or that her mother-in-law's evil or her mother-in-law's a saint, none of that crap, she behaves herself, I get my end away, and by half past twelve or one o'clock I'm in my own bed, as healthy as you like, and meanwhile you're there destroying your liver, all roused up and watching them come, that's not a life, Benito, you're going to kill yourself, lad. And I've told all the rest of you the same thing, and I've also heard that one or two of you have been spotted over there, of course, when you've got a bit of time to kill or you're taking a compressor to be fixed or something, or say you have to visit a customer or even at breakfast time, in other words, out on the razz like poor Benito here.'

And he toasts his own speech by raising his glass of beer and knocking back half of it in one go. And that's just the prologue. The speech is the aperitif to other long monologues in the course of which we learn about all the latest football signings and how the size and thickness of the female pubic area these days doesn't match up to the perfection reached twenty years back, those carpeted pussies, as Boss-Eyed Manolo calls them, and the big revolution in hybrid cars and the decline of the diesel engine.

Floren gathers all this vicariously on his coffee breaks when one or other member of the conversation club comes up and mocks his habit of rushing off home to his wife and daughter every day. 'You'll end up like the rest of us,' they tell him. And he smiles and sometimes he promises to have a few drinks with them. Yes, tomorrow, and tomorrow he'll say the same thing.

The beatific state, the happiness that really does exist but which doesn't have much to say for itself. Unless it's a passing moment of bliss, very different from Floren's. For example, what the Runner experiences when he's with Lucía or when he thinks about her. Because in his case, that ephemeral proximity to fulfilment has a double edge, because it's irresolvably linked to a fear of loss, a premonition of a future disaster, sometimes imminent. The pleasure an inhabitant of Jericho might have experienced when he heard the perfect music of the trumpets just before the first hairline crack appeared in one of the walls of the room where the listener, a music lover, was enjoying the heavenly performance before the walls came tumbling down.

Yes, Lucía provides the Runner with the only moments of peace in his life, and at the same time Lucía's real or imagined presence can lead him to the lowest depths of dejection through his fear of losing her. But how little that fear matters and how flimsy it is in the monumental presence of Lucía, when her gaze and her words dispel all the dark thoughts. 'Look at me,' she says. 'Look at me, silly.' That's all. And then he feels like a golden boy, and he knows he can cope with anything. Even with losing Lucía. She's a dynamo, a battery, a fountain of light he'll always carry inside him. He even imagines himself many years from now – on his own or with someone else, older or elderly, here or on the other side of the world – remembering her and remembering her energy, the feeling of completeness she gave him.

It's a different kind of happiness, or maybe the same kind of happiness, only distorted. A malfunction, but at the end of the day it's a beneficial force, capable of lifting the spirit, like air bubbles rising happily, desperately, towards the water's surface. Yes, that exists, too. Floren's blissful life exists, and the Runner's sublime moments exist and Lucía's as well, that mystery she holds inside her, but the Runner can only glimpse vague traces of it. Bubbles seeking the surface. Fish, drowned men, amphibians, submariners, machines, monsters releasing the oxygen pent up inside them. The whole city releasing bubbles. Hundreds of thousands. Lungs, gills, capsules, bottles, cylinders. Living tissue and rust, each emitting their desperate or jubilant signals.

Yes. Dionisio Grandes Guimerá also knew a double-edged happiness in his youth, or at least he went through periods when fulfilment and despondency seemed to be shackled at the ankles. At the time, someone told him that life was like a merry-go-round. That may well have been true, but during his dark days he imagined his wooden horse carrying on plunging downwards until it smashed through the carousel floor, its hooves dragging along the ground, broken, the piston or whatever it was that should have been making the horse go up pushing it even further down. Heading towards the centre of the earth. A wooden horse sunk up to its neck. At those times Dionisio Grandes Guimerá, diligent student, the Talent, felt like he was living on the fringes of the world and, even then, he could already discern the possibility of an abrupt exit from it.

Those were the years when he lived at 25 Camino de Suárez. They had a flat at the back. His father would get up long before daybreak and go in search of his van. Sounds from the bathroom while he lay stock still pretending to sleep. Then, in the silence of the early morning, he'd hear the hoarse rattle of the van's engine and the sound of its tyres on the wet asphalt. Winter nights. That sense of relief as he listened to the noise of the van, an Avia with 'Frutas Grandes' painted haphazardly on the sides, driving away out of his life, taking his father to the wholesale market. Until the boomerang came back with even greater force.

It was about this time when he started to break away from the gang: Enrique Rodríguez, El Pajarito, Meliveo, those people. Very occasionally he'd get a call from Enrique, inviting him to some party in Arteaga's house. He was once there on a Sunday evening. Arteaga's parents had let him and his brothers have the top part of the house. A room with two huge flags on the wall: Great Britain and the United States. Semi-darkness. Girls and cheap gin. Plans to travel around the world on a motorbike. Not getting trapped by the system. Playing at being bad boys. Dioni's presence was barely noticed. Music. Confusion. One or two heavy drinking sessions. One winter's evening he was kissing a dark-haired girl. She seemed pretty drunk, too. Years later Dioni recalled her vomiting on the pavement. Street lamps reflected in puddles. Feeling really sorry for her as he helped her tidy her hair. Lost, the pair of them.

He was studying law. That was what mattered to him. That's what nourished him. He hadn't felt attracted to anyone else like he'd been to that boy on the beach in the white swimming trunks. At least, not with the same intensity. Not with such intensity. He shied away from the inner voice that tried to get him in the corner and ask him, 'Am I? Am I?'

He met a girl. Ángeles. Blue eyes and dark hair. She was on the same course. They kissed. He wanted her. His fellow students almost respected him. The Loner. And back in the neighbourhood: the Talent. His mother exaggerated his academic achievements in the lift and at the corner shop. For Dioni the question was basically one of staying the course. Trying to make sure his father's van didn't blow up, that the painful trickle of customers carried on buying from his shop, avoiding the fruiterer's closing down before he finished his studies. A race against the clock in which days became months. Ángeles's blue eyes. Pale blue. One Sunday he brought her home. His parents had gone to spend the day at the allotment. He let go of her hand in the entrance hall, intimidated by the stare of a passing neighbour.

His home seemed strange with Ángeles there. The table, the torn leatherette on the arm of the sofa, the photo of his grandfather. The smell. He felt like a visitor, too. She sat on the edge of the bed, looking at the floor. He looked at the bedspread, which suddenly seemed old, its pattern discoloured. But he was in seventh heaven. Her face was like a Native American's, with high cheekbones. Everyone on campus said she was beautiful. Possibly. In any case, she seemed to have more bones in her face than was usual. He was in seventh heaven, yes, right there in the centre of it. That feeling lasted for days. Or that's how he remembered it.

She was wearing a pink bra. With silky bra straps. Satin? Her cheekbones. Wavy dark hair. He kissed her, a bedspring creaked, like the voice of a dead man, taunting him. Her mouth was like a whirlpool in a river. Catching whatever came near, voraciously. Like fish do, like nature does. He undid her blouse. Pink. Two moons. She put her fingers on the back of his neck, stroking his hairline. She was guiding the blind man. That scent. Her skin, the trace of perfume. They didn't speak. She lay back on the bedspread. The creaking and the sadness of that fabric on their skin. The curtains fixed and dry as columns. Dioni lost his vision. The mattress, the curtains, the plaster statue of Christ all ceased to exist. She knew. Ángeles knew the ropes. She lifted her hips, hoisted her waist off the bed to allow her jeans to slide down her legs. The imprint of the belt on her stomach, a few marks in her flesh, a highway across her skin. The pink lace was also there, carving diagonally across her thighs. It was there beneath the lace, that presence of musk. That honeytrap. 'You,' she said. That's all. Her eyes just as blue, her mouth red, almost smiling. You. And he understood, undoing the first button of his shirt. She smiled. Was she an expert? She climbed over his back, towards the headboard, and pulled off the bedspread. Her naked shoulders on the sheet, the satin bra strap. He leaned over her. The way animals drink. And her fingers on the back of his neck again and her whirlpool mouth. Her tongue was like a man overboard trying to escape from the current. Flailing around like people who are drowning flail around in the water. It darted into his mouth looking for safety. Walls of water. He stood up, his trousers on the floor. Ángeles's gaze. Her pink knickers had disappeared. The musk, the hillside of short, frizzy grass. Black grass flattened by the wind. She wasn't smiling any more. Expert. She took him in, held him, almost like a mother at first, then like a policeman. Seizing him. Writhing and squirming and caressing him again. Was this what it was like? Was it always like this? That anguish, that somnambulant desperation that seemed to take hold of her. Her eyes closed, mouth open. Writhing in a nightmare she didn't seem able to escape. And saying 'Yes'. She said 'Yes'. There was an open wound down there. The same warmth as a wound, of blood. That viscous dampness. She wrapped herself around him skilfully. She raised her legs, enveloped him with them, his lower back, his buttocks. Ángeles's pupils stared into his eyes for just a moment. A question? He sought refuge, hid himself in her hair. The way fugitives hide behind trees. With the same anxiety. The wound, fingers, hands down below. In the opening. Soft fruit. Hot. Saliva. That's what it was. That's what it was like. That mouth, so dark. That hungry beak. Was he inside? Stinging. He was in. It fitted. The tight walls, a narrow corridor. She pulled her face away. Looked at him with an expression a bit like fury, scorn. It turned into a kiss, a nibble, a moan preceding a scream. Down there, that red-hot poker. A wave, salty water, a whirlpool wrapping around you and dragging you, stones, pain, sun and salt in your face, a sea creature's tentacles, back underwater, fingers, nails on his shoulders, stinging, blood? teeth, his mother's face, a dream, light in the window, a transparent eye and that sound of a puddle, was it always like this? She knows, does this only happen to her? Or all women? She scratches him, hits him, green veins, rocks her head from side to side, against the pillow, fingernails, pain, rocking, drowning, epileptic, epileptic? No, so that's what it's like, the bones in her face disarranged, jumping out, hiding, tensing up, she stops rocking her head, relaxes, opens her eyes, looks at the ceiling, almost smiles, a new glint in her eyes, and she says again, 'You', now as a plea, 'You', the tide goes down, ebbs away, still moving, 'You', her legs' embrace, the rhythm increases again, a cradle rocking, the tunnel widens, the sound of each thrust into the puddle, he sinks, like that, inside, inside, light, no pain, it softens, the liquid of his bones mixes with the light, he comes out of himself, disappears, returns, disappears, that field, the white sun, disappears, returns, back in his body. The room, the bedspread, the smell. Her fingers in his hair again, as if they'd always been there. The sounds. He noticed her heart beating beneath that pinkness, beneath her skin and her smell. Four brief knocks on the door.

It never happened again. Ángeles never went back to that house again, back to that bed. The bright white sun was turning dark. The fluid sensation solidified, crystallized. Granite. Cold. The process lasted a few days, maybe. She didn't know why. Neither did he. He only knew that he didn't want it to happen again. He didn't like her. He decided. He looked at her at the bus stop, and he knew. *I don't like her, no, I don't want her to touch me, I don't want her to kiss me.* An autumn afternoon, already getting dark. She had some raindrops on her forehead. When she put her fingers on the back of his neck he made an effort not to pull away. And the sentence was cast upon her.

Empty. The world had never been so empty. Just him and the world. A depopulated planet. No one around him. Empty. Hollow. A vagabond within four walls.

When Dionisio Grandes Guimerá looked back on that period it was always connected to darkness and the night. The semi-darkness of the corridor in the flat. The dim light on the ceiling at the end of the afternoon. His parents' shadows. Blurred books. Stretched out on the sofa in the early hours. Listening to his father snoring behind the door and his mother's short gasps. The night's dark wall. Masturbating into the wash-basin. The boy on the beach's nipples, Ángeles's tongue, stinging, the bulge in his swimming trunks, musky flesh and tears, the satin bra strap, the cradle rocking.

He thought about it in the silence of the early morning. His head resting on the ripped arm of the sofa and the balcony in front of him. Flying past four floors. The true void. Ending it all. From the sofa he could see the dark windows of the building opposite. Dead mirrors. All those people there, waiting. He dozed off with that image seared on to his retina. When he opened his eyes he met his father's bright stare, the glare from the bathroom light making a yellow cubist pattern on the wall. His father on his feet, unshaven. Pyjama top open, hair, flesh. 'What are you doing here?' He barely murmured. 'I fell asleep.' And his father giving orders in a whisper. 'Go to bed. What are you doing here?' His muscles wasted. He looked at the balcony out of the corner of his eye, like an old accomplice, and headed to his bed. His father splashing around in the bathroom. The smell of his bed, dozing off to sleep, it might have been two minutes or fifteen minutes later, the hoarse rattle of the van going off into the night. Frutas Grandes.

Then Ramón Ranea came on the scene. With his pock-marked face. His hair all frizzy, like Ángeles's pubic hair. Frizzy and patchy. He was repeating the year. Sitting next to him. Walking beside him along the corridors, asking him things. In the cafeteria. He arrived on campus half crucified on a motorbike with oversized handlebars. His arms outstretched, his face impassive and a cigarette hanging out of one side of his mouth.

'Lobito, bored out to 125, Enduro handlebars.' Ranea introduced his bike as if it were his girlfriend, or at least his dog. 'I'll give you a lift home.'

Dioni shrugged his shoulders. Straddled the bike. A short seat, their bodies together, Dioni clutching some metal tubing behind the saddle. As he leaned back to grip this bar his crotch was pressing too hard against Ranea's body. He sat upright again.

'Don't move around so much. Better if you hold on to me,' Ranea advised, like a professional rider. He put his hands on Ranea's shoulders, to placate him.

'I can't move like that, better around my waist,' Ranea continued, instructing him in the art of motorcycling.

He grabbed him around the waist, trying to suppress his sense of touch. For a long time Dioni remembered the texture and the smell of Ranea's timeless corduroy bomber jacket. Stiff, like cardboard. A particular aroma of stale sweat and the cigarette stuck between his lips wafted on the wind from the moment Ranea jumped on the kickstart. He left him at his front door and hardly said goodbye before he went off, the motorbike backfiring.

No. It was impossible. Dioni could never imagine getting close to Ranea in the same way as Ángeles. Kissing him. That image was like a vaccine against his doubts. The pock marks, his beady eyes, half asleep, his scent, the random bits of stubble peering out of the craters on his cheeks. And yet, there it was, there was his shadowy presence when he ejaculated over the porcelain of the washbasin. A vague presence that

Dioni wanted to put down to the way their bodies had rubbed together, to the constant presence of that unexpected, half-mute companion. He was certain. He could never go up to that face, close his eyes, kiss him.

But it wasn't like that. Everything turned out differently. Ranea's family – comfortably off despite what Dioni had inferred from Ramón's appearance and his scruffy clothes – owned two antique shops and also had some premises in the city centre, in Calle Fresca, where they stored some pieces of furniture and which Ranea used as a place of study and refuge. 'When my three brothers are in the same room they make more noise than the rest of the world put together,' Ranea, deadly serious, had told Dioni on the first day they went there.

It was a mess. Piles of pictures, pieces of furniture stacked up in pyramids, one on top of the other, lampstands, metal shelving, several filing cabinets. At the back, a window that was far too small, so that the electric light had to be on all the time. Ranea's books were lying on a lacquered green table with very elegant legs 'in the style of Napoleon III', he explained to Dioni. 'My father says that studying at this table will stimulate outpourings of wisdom, or some crap like that.'

Roman law. They opened their books. Each of them at one end of the table. Ranea spread out his notes all around him and muttered to himself. After a short while he went and stretched out on a sofa upholstered in gold damask. 'If I fall asleep wake me up in an hour.' He fell asleep immediately. Deep breathing. Dioni looked around the room, studying everything carefully. Walls of stacked furniture, urns, clocks adorned with carvings, mirrors – one of them cracked, reflecting back the shadowy atmosphere of the room, divided in two – *Ireland* – he thought.

There were two heaps of books on top of a table similar to the one he was sitting at. He got up without making a noise and went over to them. He picked up the one on top of the first pile, bound in green leather. *Dante and His Circle.* He opened it. 'THE NEW LIFE. A while after this strange disfigurement . . .' Next to the books there were two framed sketches. Fine strokes. A tree, a moon, a young man, was he crying?

'García Lorca.'

He turned around with a start. Ranea was standing beside him.

'Did you wake up?'

'No, I'm asleep. This is all a dream.'

'Ah, I hadn't realized.'

'They're drawings by García Lorca. That one and that one. Signed. There's his signature.'

'Oh, yes.'

'If you've got a hundred thousand pesetas you can take one away with you.'

Ranea's breath was similar to the smell in that place, concentrated. Confusion. Too close.

'OK, I'll take them both. And the other ones.'

'I don't know how much the other ones are or who drew them. Let's see.'

He turned it around and tried to read in the half-light.

'Moreno. It's written in pencil. Five hundred years ago at least. Can't make it out. Moreno. Moreno Villa.'

'Ah.'

'Do you know who he is?'

'No.'

'Me neither.'

Ranea carried on looking around. As if it were the first time he'd ever been there, too.

'I'm not going to study any more.'

'No. OK. Me neither.'

'I'll take you home then.'

'No, what for?'

'So you don't wear out your shoe leather or waste money on buses. You've got to save up to buy those drawings, remember. Grab your books.'

The clean night air. The noise and smoke of the motorbike and Ranea's usual farewell, barely making eye contact. The red rear light disappearing into the darkness.

The second day at the storeroom Ranea put down his books and notes on the Napoleon III table, but he didn't even sit down. He went off to the back of the room, losing himself among the pieces of furniture.

Dioni heard him opening drawers, rummaging around in the metal filing cabinets.

'Aren't you going to study?'

Banging on a drawer supposedly stuck. Silence, and then, 'Yes, coming now.'

'I'm happy to leave it for today if you like.'

'I'm coming now. It was here, my father had it here, but I can't find it.'

'Find what?'

'No, nothing. We'd better study. Or pretend.'

'Pretend what?'

'Yes. Study. We'd better study.'

He could still hear Ranea moving around between the pieces of furniture. But when he emerged, he didn't go to the study table but to the gold damask sofa. He sat down, looking at his fingers, as if he were counting them.

Dioni underlined his notes. Ranea spoke to him.

'So will you want me to drop you back home later?'

'Well, I don't know, I hadn't thought about it. Whatever.'

'Your chauffeur, at your command.'

'What? What's up?'

'Nothing, only joking. You know, I enjoy it. Riding the bike. Taking his lordship wherever he wants.'

'Yeah, yeah.'

Ranea sniffed, tilted his head back, looking at the blackened ceiling. Dioni tried to go back to his notes. The best thing was to get out of there. Wait a short while and then go. And not come back. Ranea, it was obvious now, was an idiot.

'Do you fancy Milagros?'

The idiot still had his head resting against the back of the sofa, but he'd lowered his gaze and was looking at Dioni with his eyes almost closed. Dioni took his time to reply.

'Milagros?'

'Yes, Milagros, in the third year.'

'Oh, I know who you mean.'

'Obviously. Do you fancy her?'

Dioni sat there looking at Ranea, trying to guess where he was coming from.

'Everyone fancies her, that's why I'm asking you.'

'Not me, I hardly know her.'

'You don't know her? They call her Strawberry Lips. Have you noticed her mouth? She was in my class last year. Do you look at her, because she looks at you, even though you don't fancy her and you know she's not for you?'

'What? What do you mean?'

'The other day I noticed she was looking at you in the cafeteria, laughing, with the other girl, the tall one. Pricktease or what . . . ?'

'If you say so.'

'Aesthetically, of course, you want to look at her and even touch her to see if she's real. But fancy her, you don't fancy her.'

'Whatever you say.'

'Obviously. Food for other sparrows.'

He stopped talking. They both stopped talking. The air felt thick. What was he doing there, that's what he'd written in his notes: 'What am I doing here?' Remorse, a dull hatred. And he saw it. He knew, or he guessed. That's why he was there.

Ranea was rubbing his hand over his crotch, palm open, in a circular movement. Like stroking an animal. Ranea staring at his own hand. Dioni staring at the sheet of paper, the isolated words, the indecipherable scrawl of his own handwriting, being aware of Ranea's movements in his peripheral vision, his blurred outline sunk into the sofa. Leave. No. He could still pretend. He could still act as if he hadn't seen anything. Guilt.

The point arrived when it was impossible to pretend that he couldn't see him. Ranea had opened his flies and extracted from inside his trousers a member that was now erect, vertical, like a small stake had been stuck in his belly, and Ranea himself was observing it with a somewhat puzzled look, a frown on his forehead. Then he asked Dioni, 'Have you ever tossed off with your mates?'

'No.'

Dioni had now looked up from the desk. He looked Ranea in the face, trying to keep his gaze at eye level.

'You mean, not very often?'

Ranea now moved his erection from side to side, holding it by the base. Waving it, heavily, slowly.

'Seeing who can shoot the furthest, who can shoot the most and all that. Haven't you ever done it?'

'No.'

'Do you want to give it a go?'

Now Dioni looked at the penis. Thick, wide, dark. Just for a moment.

'No.'

'But you don't mind if I rub mine a bit, do you?'

'No. You do whatever you want. I'm leaving.'

'Come on, you're leaving just because of this?'

'No, but I'm leaving anyway.'

'Not even out of curiosity?'

'What out of curiosity?'

The beach, the waves, that sunny day, was that it? That clean air and this squalid darkness.

'To see it.'

Ranea started to move his hand very slowly up and down his penis. Dioni gathered together his notes and put them away in his folder. His erection was as hard as Ranea's. His body rebelling. Mocking him.

He stood up. Almost at the same time Ranea got up from the sofa and came towards him, with his hands in the air and his prick sticking out, almost completely horizontal, pointing.

'Come on, Dioni, for fuck's sake, does this really bother you?'

'No, not me. No.'

Ranea stopped close to the table. His penis bobbed up and down, driven by its internal muscles, by contractions in his groin.

'Come on, don't go, I'll put it away. We're good mates, that's all. Nothing wrong with that.'

'It's just that me, personally, I don't.'

'OK, it was just so we could have a bit of fun. Look, it's doing acrobatics now.' New oscillations, now more exaggerated. 'It's got a life of its own, you know what I mean?'

A smile, a step closer.

'I was having a look earlier, I remembered some magazines my father kept in the drawers, girlie mags, American girls, fucking.'

Ranea's prick was brushing against the table. A blind animal exploring its surroundings. Near Dioni's books, near his hand.

'It's just like yours, touch it. You'll like it just as much. Hold it.'

Dioni, head lowered, heart stood still, all too slow. He could smell Ranea, the same essence as when he was clinging to him on the motorbike. It was still all a secret, for all that Ranea was scratching at the wall, like a terrier. *Nobody knows, nobody knows anything. He'll know. Only he will. He already knows, the first day he sat next to me he already knew.*

'And then I'll do it for you, hold it, feel its weight.'

Dioni was like a statue, frozen to the spot. He would have liked to shake his head. Or nod.

'What do you think's going to happen? You won't turn into anything, it's nothing. Look.'

He shook his head, very gently, and Ranea came a bit closer, half a step, and the blind beast brushed against Dioni's fingers. A dog without a coat, hot, almost burning, smooth and clumsy. Yes.

It was easy, straightening his fingers to touch the febrile, docile skin. An animal, take it in his fingers, cover it over, it was thicker than his, squeeze it gently, forget about Ranea and his breath, his odour. All his surroundings concentrated in that touch, on that burning weight between his fingers, that animal seeking him out like he was its owner and not wanting to let him go. Stroking it, softly, stroking, up, up, down, very slowly. Not paying any attention to Ranea's words, not listening to him.

'Yes, like that, you see? That's right.'

Ignoring him. As if he were a different body, another being, independent of that blind, powerful animal filling his hand, with a life of its own, quite apart from Ranea and his voice and clothes and pockmarked face. He was its owner. Give it to me. And he kneeled down, yes, beside the table, next to the books and papers, everything forming part of a past that was already remote, all in the distance, kneeling on the shore, on the beach, that sunny day and that bulge in the white foam that now appeared naked in front of him, looking at him with its single eye vacant and blind, he brushed it against his cheek, pressed it against his face, so many years later, making up for lost time, yearning for it, opening his mouth, shaking off Ranea's hand from the back of his neck, and his fingers in his hair, opening his mouth, yes and touching that burning heat with his tongue, cradling it in his tongue, moistening it with his saliva, a wounded animal, blind rebel, hard, rigid, and enveloping it, opening his mouth to receive it, take it, inside his lips, with the live flesh in his mouth, that contact between two skinless bodies, Ranea's voice coming from elsewhere, 'Swallow, suck,' and him, yes, swallowing, sucking, sucking, a desperate suction, and savouring, obeying and that's the greatest discovery, yes, obedience, 'Swallow, eat me, bitch,' the taste, rubbing it against his lips, strawberry mouth, waving it next to his face like a badly aimed arrow, brushing against his cheek, his smooth chin, and it enters again, strong, entire, retches, withdraws, enters, licks, sucks, tenses, Ranea moans, shudders, thrusts, mouth full, bitter, withdraws, sprays, hot, drinks, spits, chokes, waves, a noise, Ranea, his voice hoarse, the books fall off the table, he opens his eyes *this is who I am*, warped darkness, furniture on the ceiling, pain in his knees, the taste, Ranea pulls away, he breathes, dizziness, the prick still quivering, agonizing, drooling, a white blotch on his trousers, and he, yes, he as well, his own trousers damp and sticky, on his knees, empty, hollow, stripped of any internal matter, regaining reality, and suddenly he feels like all the dams have burst and this filthy surge entering into every pore of his body, turning into anger, discovered, soiled, enslaved, that black matter filling him up inside. He looked away from Ranea, from his moribund organ, from his face, silting up, Ranea spoke, incoherently, trying to make a joke. Better not to look at him. He gives him a tissue, short fingers, more odour, cleans himself up. He leaves the tissue on the grimy tiles. Picks his books up off the floor. The secret's out. Now everything depends on this guy, on Ranea, on his round eyes, on his silence.

And there were others, others like Ranea. A retch, the bitter taste filling his whole mouth again. Ranea could talk, and others could work it out as Ranea had done. His secret. What he thought was his secret. He can deny it. He can leave it behind. The desperate desire for the days to fly past, for time to distance him from there. Everything was now on the other side of a new partition. Was this life? Partitions, windows, walls. Closed doors, gaps through which the undesired could seep. Dioni was sure that it was always going to be like this, and he was afraid of it, too. And at the same time another possibility came to the fore, the trace of an iron will on his inner horizons, a tool he could use to change everything. Yes. Everything depended on him, and he was the absolute master of his own will. What had just happened had been a revelation of sorts. A warning. A necessary step. Now he was determined to control his life. He could do it. Nothing like this would ever happen again.

And he left, driven by that impulse. Disgusted and reborn. 'No,' he told Ranea when he insisted on dropping him back home. 'No. It's over.' He was the stronger one. He knew it now. He went out into the night, walked down that narrow street, almost brushing his shoulders along the two side walls that seemed as though they were about to join together, a funnel, solemn bells, shadows, he emerged into the open air, Calle Larios, the cars' red lights reflected in the puddles, making squiggles. His groin feeling cold, clammy, a memento. A hangover of shame. Calle Compañía with its blissful semi-darkness, his solitary footsteps. It didn't matter that it would always be like this, that all the streets and all the nights and years, his whole life would be a solitary walk. Solitude was like a refuge, like paradise. He was the master of his own path.

Desolate, isolated, children of nowhere, they walk, groan, die, laugh. Animals are bleeding out in the abattoirs, the slaughtermen smile and die of obscure diseases, their hands holding the cables, electrodes and knives, surrounded by the disembowelled beasts and the steam from their intestines hanging in the air. The insects carry on scrabbling at the earth, burrowing into the lives of humans, walking through walls, perforating, chewing and looking up at the sun. 'Tell me where we're headed, Rai.' The man with the twisted neck and the bulging, exhausted veins, Eduardo Chinarro, begs for mercy. 'Where are we headed, Rai?' So much sun. The shadows are melting and sticking to pedestrians' feet. Passers-by, stick figures shimmering at the traffic lights, ghosts. The air is burning, forever burning. 'Why do you love me?' the Runner wants to ask Lucía. 'Tell me where we're headed.'

'Why did you love me?' The Pandora's box of fear springs open. At the crematorium the Runner also saw a dead man on the other side of the screen. A display window for the dead. A dried-out yellow face peering out from the coffin. White cloth, silk or satin? His father's face nestled in fake fabric. They burn the coffins. That charcoal, those black lumps that they put in an urn afterwards. That's where his father went, inside his urn, and they put the urn in a bag from El Corte Inglés. What a joke. Walking along beside his mother, and there's his father in a plastic bag brushing against his knee, under the trees in the crematorium gardens.

They're in a taxi. The world's going by on the other side of a window, the trees' shadows and the underside of their leaves barely glimpsed, fragmented by speed, sparkling in the window. *There goes my life, there it will stay. Leaves.* Carole's eyes are sleepy as she's talking. The glint of fatigue. *She won't be here tomorrow.* Céspedes feels the weight of his own body, a bag filled with a heavy liquid. *That's what I am.* Ah, life, yes, all that panting. And those people passing by on the other side of the glass, walking along the pavements.

The smell of cooking in the stairwell, grubby handprints on the paintwork. Children's hands on the walls, old muddy footprints, ink, scraps of rubbish on the stairs, and La Segueta walks up heavily, groaning, a flabby machine, a beast determined to find her lair. Gapped, serrated teeth, sagging udders, silent church bells calling worshippers to a miserable service. 'You've thrown our money away. It's always about you, no one but you, and the rest of us here at your beck and call.' Mariano, the hen-pecked husband, climbs the stairs behind her. *This pain in the arse, this bad dream, and she won't stop talking, she can make me a meal and let me have the spare room, the small bed that smells of cocks, Penca, my cock, how's that little whore doing with her dark-brown cleavage, she was wearing that yellow top today, what a pair of tits, she could come back here, come on in, Penca, come in, sweetie, sit down so I can have a good look at you when you bend over and the way they bob about with no bra.*

Raise the chalice, offer it up to God, my life and my body, the motionless curtains. Father Sebastián yawns, reflects that anxiety is an elusive little beast. *I dreamed that I was dying on the altar, I was dying and I wasn't dead, or did I think I was?* His phone is buzzing. The sound of cars going by, crossing Calle Unión. Machines in heat. Perforated? The ants are rummaging around on the ground, they can taste the corpse, saliva full of sugar. Vodka, barbiturates.

'Give me something to drink,' a boy beside her says. 'Give me something to drink.' Amelia, lying on the beach, awake, opens one eye and hears the boy's voice and the gentle sound of a wave breaking, a light snore and a pair of glass bottles clinking together and a man's raucous laughter and a woman shouting, 'Hang on!' and another wave rumbling and the boy repeating 'Give me something to drink' and the sound of an engine and a man saying 'We won three nil' and another man laughing and some music, Camarón de la Isla, and a shout and people splashing about in the water and another wave sucking up pebbles and dragging them along, Amelia opens the other eye, her head feels heavy, so hot and thirsty, 'Give me something to drink,' a pain in her neck, what time is it? Lunch, Ismael, the curtains, the towels, the scissors. The psychologist, the office or centre or whatever it's called in Calle de Trinidad Grund. Consulting room. Plastic flowers, old magazines in the waiting room. *I'll have to take him back there; it might at least calm him down a bit.*

The cigarette drops heavily on to the rough asphalt surface, studded with sharp gravel. Smoking in the car park, crammed with burning hot metal. Dr Galán's hair falls over her face. *Nothing will ever be the same again.* The same as what? Who you were, the lies we built our world on? Tightrope walkers. Trapeze artists. A photograph, that's all that remains of that time. Dioni, his blue polo shirt, teeth and laughter. Innocent laughter, and the wind in his hair. Guille hidden behind his fear. Her peering into the abyss. 'Will they come for me?' says an injured man into his phone, a bandage encasing half his head. A turban. A&E. I don't know what happened, one minute I was standing up and the next I was on the floor. 'Are they going to come?' A scrawny tortoiseshell cat ambles along in the sun. Sick or mad. *They'll come for us all, like the old song goes, they've already come for Dioni, or was it a poem?* They weigh the internal organs, measuring the disaster, calculating the calamity down below. The autopsy room. Death's caretakers. Weighing scales and mortuary drawers. Steel and chrome. *La raison de la mort.* Not its meaning. The meaning of weeping, its melody. All these people interpreting its anthem, self-taught, weeping. Life behind partitions. Ants with white heads, beasties in the darkness diving underground. Delving around for us. And sometimes, yes, delving around inside us. I've seen it. A hotchpotch.

She wipes the white dribble off her stomach with a scrunched-up pair of knickers and feels like her entire being consists of the world itself. Aurora Perea Pemán. La Penca. She opens her eyes, sees Nene Olmedo beside her. She thinks about her home, her brother Yubri, about to go to prison, and her bastard father, always with the stink of the abattoir on him. 'It's my profession,' he says proudly. 'I feed the world.' His home. It's his home. The dog chews the furniture, twists his square head with its staring eyes and clamps the leg of the dresser in his jaws. And he chews the splinters he extracts from the furniture diligently and methodically. Plastic flowers in her dead mother's picture frame. Her father asleep in the thick heat at the back of the narrow flat. It oozes sleep, the room stinks of rancid sleep, the whole flat, the saucepan on the stove giving off thick steam just like that unshaven man's breath as he dribbles into the pillow while his son Yubri stares in complete absorption at his phone and kills pixels, blood-stained stick figures.

La Penca half closes her eyes, calmly examines her shaved pubis, her strip of fuzz, her little moustache pointing towards her belly button at one end and at the other towards that pink flesh, reddened, still open between her sweaty legs. 'Have you been fucking me a lot, Nene, have you?' Her pussy's so funny, it makes her laugh to look at it. Nene Olmedo is sitting facing the wall, examining the whitewash, meditating on the existence of other worlds, devotee of extra-terrestrials and abductions. He believes in them just as he believes in Christ the Captive, tattooed on his back between his shoulder blades. Nene Olmedo's Christ gesticulates and makes faces when he scratches his back without ever taking his eyes off the wall. A decayed landscape. The arid surface of his beloved extra-terrestrials. La Penca, Aurora. Her clothes scattered across the squalid room, semen-soaked knickers in her hand. She picks up and drops and picks up and drops the packet of Marlboro, everything like rubber, everything soft and remote, everything OK, La Penca, Aurora, manages to lift a cigarette to her lips and then, even more laboriously manages to work the lighter mechanism, applies the flame to the cigarette for too long and burns it, scorches it, there were still lumps of something in the urn holding what were supposed to be her mother's ashes. Then she discovered, they knew vaguely, that those shits at the funeral parlour or the crematorium or whoever, those people, would burn bits of wood and plastic and any old crap and would give it to the families so they could go and solemnly scatter the rubbish over the fields or beaches or terraces where the deceased had supposedly once been happy. They placed them at the feet of saints, statues of the Virgin, along with photos of real corpses, and they weren't their remains, it wasn't them, it was just ashes from old bits of furniture. Penqui, Mummy wasn't Mummy, Mummy was that stuff they say on the radio the people at the funeral parlour handed out, Yubri squinted, Yubri didn't feel the same disgust she'd felt when she grabbed a fistful of that granulated dust. Penqui, what you thought were bits of bone were just lumps of stuff. Yubri felt bitterly resentful, and so he bought some petrol, five litres in one petrol station and five litres in another one and five litres in another one and five litres in another one. Twenty litres. And he set fire to two hearses and the front of the funeral parlour. And he was recorded on four security cameras operated by various neighbouring establishments and businesses. Yubri's chewing on cold octopus while he's killing pixels, and the dog's chewing the furniture. Peace. The ash falls on to Penqui's chest and throat. 'Nene. What happened to that lad who was here with us?' Nene Olmedo makes a supreme effort to tear his eyes away from the wall. He looks around the room, maybe transported to another galaxy. He emits a bestial sound – 'Nnńdrra' or something like that – and La Penca looks at her cigarette end and her fingernails with a double layer of varnish. 'Juanmi? His name was Juanmi, he was over there, did he fuck me, too, Nene?' 'Nnndrra.'

They fly together in flocks then scatter, filling the sky with sharp angles. Swifts, swallows, creatures with a beak open in search of food. Insects in the air. That's what death is like. A bird that flies with its mouth open to catch the mosquitos that cross its path. Without any skill or judgement. 'Give me life,' a sick person said to Dr Galán just a few days ago. In the same way as you speak to God or the saints. Work a miracle, give me life. With their yellow eyes and different bags of liquid hanging by their bed. The rainbow of the dead. And there goes Guille on the road to Mount Calvary. Going up the hill to the private housing estate. He's accompanied by his Martha and his Mary, his Simon of Cyrene and his Judas. Guille in the centre of the fire, in the centre of the *terral*, that heat that breaks thermometers. Mónica Ovejero looked at him with her almond eyes when she heard the news, put her hand on his shoulder, the other on his cheek. Piluca folded his towel, gathered up his things, helped him on with his sandals. She didn't wash his feet. Loberas, a weak apostle, could only blaspheme. 'Christ Almighty! His dad's going to die.' High drama at the swimming club, a life-and-death story. Tragedy in a bikini and smelling of sun cream. Birds also fly around these parts. The procession proceeds on foot. Juno dispossessed of his powers. His muscles useless. And as they passed by Trini's mother, Piluca stopped beside her and broke the news, a messenger of death. The teenager has all the experience of an adult. She's buried two grandmothers in just one year. She whispers the appropriate words. A wise old woman in her teens. Cù Sìth.

Guille and his crew go up a street named after a painter, but his Calvary is over on the other side, on a street called Calle Sierra Pelada. A stone-built house. Reeds and bougainvillea. The family home, Dioni's home, the doctor's home, the martyred child's home. It's now public knowledge that Guille's uncle will pick him up there. Shortly after they leave the swimming club heading for Guille's house, a white 4×4, a Volkswagen Touareg, almost runs down the absent-minded Loberas. The front passenger door opens and, without explaining how she left the swimming club or managed to get to her car so quickly, Trini's mother addresses the retinue. 'Get in, child. All of you get in, and I'll drive him home, for God's sake.' None of this going on foot, none of this walking, no getting tired out or exhausted, he's got a big ordeal ahead of him. All the exhausting rigmarole that comes with a death. Tears, bitterness, fear. The pain, all the different emotions, being overwhelmed. No getting tired out. The swimmers get in, their slender legs, their pointy bones, adolescence, the anxiety of their first encounter with death, the abyss that beckons. The car's CD is playing a tuneful number. Trini's mother's dark eyes searching in the rear-view mirror. 'Yes, my mother called, she told me.' And off they go, a firm grip on the steering wheel, tanned arms. The road to Golgotha in a Volkswagen.

And now, yes, now he would kill the old trollop. He'd slice off her ears with the sharp kitchen knife right now. With the scissors he'd used to cut up the curtains and towels and dish cloths, the sheets and the table napkins. Triangles. Now all he feels is disgust. Ismael. It was a soft wank, his cock only semi-erect. One of those that end too soon, resulting in drowsiness and apathy, and after fifteen or twenty minutes curled up in bed, off to raid the fridge and binge manically. It doesn't matter what or how much. Eat, swallow, fill the void, the hollow that stretches from his head to his feet. He feels like smashing the glass on that picture in which he caught his reflection. As if it were someone else laughing at him. That's what his shadow looks like in the glass. He'd kill the concierge, that bastard with a face like a horse, standing there like a ram, leaning against the doorway. Watching. What's he watching? One day he'd lie in wait for him in the alley. Wearing a balaclava. Like a giraffe, with his long neck and tiny head. Consuelo going past him and the bastard watching him as he goes in behind her. He'd wring his neck and spit in his face. Ismael likes to boast about his imaginary murders. When the old man from the amusement arcade died he told Federico from the lottery shop and the man he buys gin from in the supermarket that he'd killed him. He told them he'd split his head open with an axe and the old man had suddenly come back to life and how the bastard's eyes moved like glass marbles and then his mouth creaked open like an old door and he lay there stiff. The truth is that the man was found dead, but the paramedics said it had been a heart attack, and although his nose and his jaw were broken and he had a cut on his head it must have happened when he fell down the stairs in the arcade. Ismael also likes to say he's going to do in the old woman in the fur coat, La Marquesa. 'I'm going to rape her, and then I'll hammer a nail into her head to put people off the scent and out of curiosity, it's something I've wanted to do ever since I was a small child.' That's what he says when he's in a good mood. Not like now, when La Giganta's nowhere to be seen. Twenty-four hours, twenty-three and a half, he'll have to wait until tomorrow when Consuelo goes out of the front door again in her green dress to wander around the shops. Simply because she feels like it. Not for any reason. Hours, days, weeks piling up, and the lift keeps going up and down, its heavy door falling like a sentence, one more day, another day and another week, and she's going up on her own every day in that wobbly box, ascending through the hollow, sucked up by the steel cables, by some motors hidden away in some dark place, taking her to another life on the other side of that door and those walls behind which she takes off her clothes, eats, breathes, fucks and showers (her black knickers, her smell, her dark eyes looking sideways when her husband gets on top of her, what does she say to him?). More days, more time, more hanging around on the corner looking at his phone pretending to talk to somebody, inventing snippets of conversation, 'Yes, I'll be there, I'm here, I'm waiting, I told you, yes, I'll mention it, no, the one working there's my brother, my brother Jorge, Gorgo, yes him.' He pretends to listen and nods his head. 'Yeah, yeah.' Sometimes he doesn't even pretend, he puts the telephone to his ear, and that's all. Reluctantly, wearily. Looking back defiantly at anyone who looks at him. Another day. More time, maybe go to the bowling alley this afternoon or just to the bar and then, then wherever, then get some money and go back to that place, whatever that street was called, in the town centre, the whisky bar with the Colombian girl with the big tits and black nipples. And meanwhile back here the old woman perched on the balcony opposite, looking at what? Why does she have to look at anything, the old bitch? Every day.

And now his brother will be back. His mother will be back. Tired. Both of them will come back. They'll sit down, and they'll look at him, pretending, they really do pretend. They don't dare to look at him straight; they're scared, and they pretend not to be. Hiding their contempt. Mummy. Little brother Gorgo. He remembers when his mother gave him that name. She'll have forgotten all about it, but he remembers, he remembers only too well, how she would lean over the cot, pointing at the bundle of wool smelling of sour milk, a face with chubby red, almost purple, cheeks peering out, saying, 'Look at your little brother Gorgo,' yes, she called him Gorgo. 'Look how handsome your brother is.'

Jorge, Gorgo, smiling, listens to his cousin Floren. 'Here's the latest on Pedroche,' says Floren, his eyes shining with laughter. 'He's spoken to the priest, who says he's going to give him back the money, nearly two thousand euros, and the jewellery, just as well the priest's a decent sort and doesn't want to hang on to it, he could have said, "I don't know what you're talking about," and kept it all or said it's a donation for the church, you know there are some real vultures about, but no, the man says he'll sort it all out and they've arranged that when we close up tonight we go to the church and he'll give him everything back, and to look after his wife, she's a good woman blessed with the love of God and all that, fucking hell, he says she's a good woman, that's because he didn't see what she did to Pedroche's face, anyway, mate, let's see how it all works out, I'm going to get some lunch because I've got to go to the bank before I go home, so you lock up.' Floren goes out. For a brief moment his outline seems to evaporate on the other side of the window, then it goes back to its usual shape and disappears.

Jorge examines the waste ground on the other side of the window, looking out between the frames and samples of mouldings, at the car park, that flat horizontal expanse where the cars look as if they've been dumped like pebbles in the sun, sleeping beetles, and the frazzled weeds, a half-dried-out tree, its leaves stuck in the air, completely still. He dials the Runner's number. He'll meet up with him tomorrow. For a run along the Camino de las Pitas. The countryside, the morning air. Or maybe on the track at the sports complex, wherever the Runner wants. Six rings. The Runner isn't picking up. Maybe he's pissed off because he stood him up this morning. He's a bit odd. Sensitive. Almost never says anything more than necessary. He does his warm-up routine. The Runner likes doing his stretches at the steeplechase water jump. On his own. He looks at you and makes you think there's something the matter, that you've done something wrong. He never says what. Jorge thinks the Runner looks down on him. So, to try and ingratiate himself, he asks him about people he'd heard being talked about when he used to run with Granero's team. People who've run on that track and who the Runner might have known, even though he was younger than them. He asks him. Like that morning by the basketball court. Doing pull-ups on the bars. There was a scent of eucalyptus, and the wind was moving the leaves and making them rustle, and it wasn't just a sound, it was an emotion. Metal plates. Grey leaves and the wind passing through them. The Runner stretched his arms and then hoisted himself up until his chin was on the bar. Ten, fifteen, twenty. Is it true that Azulay was the best at the 400 metres back then? What about Soler? The Runner, no longer on the bar, just stared at the track's red surface.

Those runners had been there on sunny afternoons, with the fairground megaphone. Not the best, the best 400-metres runner who had ever raced on this track was Felipe Vicaría; he really was good. 'Vicaría,' Jorge repeats. He hadn't heard of him. 'Yes, Vicaría. More power, more belief, more determination. He had a really strong finish; the other two kept better pace, Azulay much better, I think he ran in the Olympics or whatever was on at the time, the University Games, but Vicaría was the best.' Jorge fell silent, staring at the track as well and watching the Runner out of the corner of his eye, not wanting to point out the contradiction and not understanding how someone who could run faster than another could be worse. And the slower one better. The Runner's obsessions, the tunnels inside his head. But training with the Runner was good, he knew stuff, suggested training routines, not just jogging, not just breaking balls like the Sunday runners. Vane. The sales assistant in Famita's shoeshop. She clicks past their shop window in her high heels, *teasing*. White leggings. Arse clearly delineated. Her behind passes an empty picture frame and for a second looks like a picture. She doesn't look inside the shop. She must have a boyfriend. *She's one of those who walks around as though no one else existed, they've got it all worked out in their heads, they know what they want, they've known all about it two years before you even had a sniff, that's why she's walking around like that just looking straight ahead, until they want to, and then it's worse, they look, and already you're on your knees.* The shop assistant crosses the street, on to the patch of derelict land that's used for parking. Her hair bobs up and down as she walks. She's wearing sunglasses, chewing gum. The sunshine makes her look small. Jorge counts the banknotes again. He walks to the back room. A smell of glue and varnish. Night-time on the beach, cold sand, Gloria looking into his eyes and asking him, 'Do you love me?' Again. Asking him again. Asking for confirmation. Same old story. The cold sand beneath their feet, and he's hugging her. Yes. Easing down her thin bikini. Her nipple tasting of salt.

The whole flat smells of boiled pasta and raw meat. The whole flat seems to be boiling over. Bubbling away in a slow cooker. The windows are open, and the stifling heat is overpowering everything like a despotic master. Everything is reduced to other-worldliness, to foreignness. No, not foreignness, more like a visceral rejection, precisely because the disorder, the smell, that conglomeration of sensations, are all too familiar. Rafi Villaplana closes the front door, which leads directly into the living room. The sofa is covered with an old sheet so the corduroy upholstery won't get spoiled, the armchair is lined with plastic, and the seat is graced by a crumpled T-shirt and a sock. The coffee table (tubular legs painted red and a light-coloured wooden tabletop) is the flat's signature card. It's a compendium, a Noah's Ark bearing everything. Two ashtrays crammed with cigarette butts. The small mounds of ash spread across the dirty, crowded surface when a gentle gust of hot air bursts into the room. Some loose sheets from a newspaper, a plate with the shell of a hard-boiled egg, a crumb of egg yolk spilled on the table. A crumpled packet of Fortuna cigarettes, another half-full packet, boxes of medicine, a nail-trimmer, a coat-hanger, a spoon, a salt cellar, some knickers and, beside them, like a totem in the midst of this shipwreck, a white metal frame with a photograph of Rafi Villaplana. A corporal in the regular army with a stiff moustache, a cruel mouth and tassels dangling from his red cap because of the deliberate way Corporal Villaplana is tilting his head. The collection of bric-à-brac continues on the shelves of another piece of furniture attached to the wall that matches the coffee table. A Bible with a black cover on the top shelf is guarded by individual photographs of the Villaplana Molledo siblings. Two of them are immortalized in plastic frames adorned by rococo filigree. Acanthus leaves and misshapen ivy curl around Pepe (straw hat shading his blue eyes, pock-marked face, cocksure smile, checked shirt open to the waist) and the same foliage wraps around Estefanía, La Niña (shy eyes surrounded by white eyeshadow, focused gaze, unhappy that she's being photographed, pink V-neck top revealing the first sign of breasts, freckles). Migue, now known as Jaime by his new friends, poses within a bamboo frame with a dopey smile, curls, dark eyes, long eyelashes, smoking jacket, shirt with starched collar poking out over a bow tie at Valderrama's wedding and, finally, a new appearance by Rafi, now in an artificial wooden frame, with a happy smile, in the workshop at the Universidad Laboral, dressed in a blue apron, so many years ago, when he still didn't appear to have realized that he was really the great Rafi Villaplana. And below them, shelves of chaos. A library comprising

And in the Third Year, He Rose Again, a book with no spine, two small porcelain plates, a bottle of cough mixture, an empty beer bottle, a pair of sunglasses, a bowl of copper coins, a statue of St Jude with a sprig of dried parsley at his feet, a ceramic beer tankard (chipped), **Erinnerung an München**, a sock, a plastic gondola with a bit of wire holding the gondolier's arms in place, with a plug draped over an empty flowerpot. An abandoned sandal on the floor pointing towards the kitchen, like an atrophied weathervane. Home sweet home.

Rafi Villaplana hears his mother splashing about at the kitchen sink and her voice asking, 'Rafi? Is that you, Rafi?' 'Yes, Mummy.' At the end (the doors to the kitchen, bathroom, bedrooms all lead off a narrow space that the Villaplanas call a corridor), at the end of the corridor, then, his father can be heard snoring, having just nodded off. Rafi, feeling guilty, notices his father's highly polished shoes, the most comforting sight to be found in that flat. Expensive leather, English design. His mother's head and torso peer out of the kitchen. 'Is that you, Rafi?' 'I've already told you, Mummy.' 'Do you want to eat now?' She exposes her gums, the half-empty row of teeth, like an insult. Better not to look. Better not to see the revolting udders stretching her top at the level of her stomach, fried tomato stains all down her front, hair uncombed and a bit greasy. Rafi's tone of resignation when he says, 'I'll eat with the others, Mummy, why else would I be here?' And his mother, now back in the kitchen, shouting back, 'Your father's had an egg and gone to bed, Pepe, too, because he had the day off today and he's been down at the beach, I don't know if La Niña is coming back for lunch now, she's gone, she's gone off for something or other or to see someone, and I've already, I've already been eating as I go along.' Rafi peers around the door. His mother's chewing. She swallows half a glass of beer in one gulp. 'This heat's unbearable, isn't it, Rafi? This *terral*.' She smiles. That gap.

Yes. It's all so bleak, why on earth did he come here? None of this can be fixed. Not even a hundred dentists. A thousand miracles. Cana, the centurion's servant at Capernaum, Bartimaeus of Jericho, Malchus' ear and walking on water. You'd need all the miracles put together. Rafi remembers when he was an altar boy. Father Liébana, the unconsecrated hosts, the money scrounged for the collection box. You'd need a miracle worker, a lion tamer, an iron hand, Rafi thinks, to fix all this. To hone and sharpen, clean up and polish it all. The centurion's ear and my mother's teeth. Reinstated. 'Mummy.' 'What Rafi?' 'Nothing.' *Bring Jane's parents here? Yes, why not, they could come on a glorious day like today. My mother could come out to meet them with her decoration of fried tomatoes, that gap, her droopy tits, the zip on her skirt undone and beer by the litre. And my father in his underpants, sprawled out in the back room or on the sofa, snoring so loud he could make the walls fall down. They're not going to set foot in here. And Jane as little as possible. Never again. And if Jane has aspirations she'll have to understand. Yes, she'll have to understand that behind all the nice things there's the effort of self-improvement, climbing each step of the social pyramid and all that shit. Talking about where her grandfather came from, the man was picking up scrap metal on the bombsites after the war in the London suburbs, Birmingham or wherever. Yes. But how's she going to understand? How can anyone who's always had everything, double helpings of everything, understand? They can't. Because what her family and Jane herself have to understand is that my parents, my family, are not what they seem. They mustn't just look at the surface, at appearances.*

Appearances, that's what Rafi Villaplana sees, leaning in the kitchen doorway. His mother stirring the tomatoes in the saucepan, wiping the sweat off her forehead with the back of her hand and pouring herself another glass of beer. Things are not what they might seem at first sight, neither he nor his family belong to this bleak neighbourhood and these run-down blocks of flats. The neighbourhood went downhill with them inside, but it used to be different. So this is all somewhat temporary. Something that's happened, that happened in the past and is going to be sorted out. *I'll sort it out even if it breaks my balls.*

The rumble of passing cars is behind him. The dazzling sun beats against the glass door. It clunks shut with a sound of heavy metal and glass. He goes into the unexpected coolness of the hall. Head down, prudent, silent. The tired sound of his own breathing is Pedroche's only companion. He breathes out through his nose, he's sweating through every pore of his body. His bald pate is an expansive plain sown with beads of sweat, so abundant that his head looks like a frosty field. The dressing on his wound is coming away and has turned pink around the edges. Broad shouldered, short, his stature reduced one step lower by his state of mind, weighing heavier than the law of gravity, than all the universal laws. He's walking along like a nervous dog, accustomed to strangers throwing stones to scare him off. The priest has been reasonable. He'll give it all back. And he'll keep it a secret, he won't tell Belita that he's given her donation back to her husband. Maybe, just maybe he should let him keep something, a small amount, a sign of cooperation. A hundred euros? Fifty? Fifty's not enough. A hundred, and a promise from the priest that he won't say anything to Belita. Not even in confession. She's the one revealing secrets in confession, not him. Let the priest tell a lie, let him sin like the rest of us. Surely with his good looks he's sinned more than once. They say he did it with Nani from the kiosk; they saw her going to the sacristy all the time and coming out with a big grin on her face. Bar-room gossip. Pedroche kept his ears open and his mouth shut. And when they asked him he shrugged his shoulders and said, 'Anything's possible.' And the others carried on laughing and shouting. Wickedness.

The person he definitely hasn't sinned with is her. Belita's gone downhill. When Pedroche first met her she wasn't bad. Tall, nice figure. What he liked most about her was her figure. Her attributes. That V-neck blouse she used to wear that got really tight. You could only guess what one of those breasts would weigh. Quite a lot. And her hips. And quiet. She was nice and quiet. They followed the same route every evening. Decaffeinated coffee in the Café Rey Pelé, a stroll around the Torre Vasconia and its neglected flower beds, along the boundary wall of the Deaf and Dumb School. Holding hands, her leaning into him a little, gently so they could kiss. Him holding her tight, supporting the weight of her chest with his own. Blunt instruments. So much promise. And over time he would map out the profile of those two enormous protuberances. His hands trembled from desire. Greed. Wear your V-neck blouse, he'd ask her. And, indifferent, she'd give in and would turn up wearing it or, just as indifferently, would make an excuse, 'It's in the wash,' or she'd complain, 'People will think I haven't got any other clothes, all because of your filthy obsession.' A slow kiss, her strange scent of old lemons, and him not just mapping out her breasts now but groping them until she'd say to him, impassively, 'I don't know what you're hoping to find there, always the same, I don't know what you get out of it. Let's go.' And they'd continue along the same old route without saying a word. Pedroche erect and resigned. Trusting in the future. Belita walking along like a blind woman who knows her way. Back through the little garden around the Torre Vasconia, Avenida de San Sebastián, a short section of Calle de Eugenio Gross and Calle Antonio Jiménez Ruiz until they arrived at number 3, where she lived. That dark, unreachable corridor (a new erection, a new frustrated fantasy for Pedroche). First floor. Belita wiping her feet on the doormat, a kiss on each check. End of story. Hook, line and sinker.

What a waste, a kind of madness or blindness. Deception. The way they trapped me, she and her family. All of them around that table. And I was the meat to feed to the crows. A gullible country boy. The daughter married off. The pills I didn't see, the doctors I never knew she saw. The spas. More like asylums. Everything so mysterious. And me going along with it. Until I got here. They put me in a cage and threw away the key. She swallowed it. Like everything else. The lift carrying Pedroche to the tenth floor shakes and rattles. Suburban skyscraper. Abrupt halt. A creak. Slightly cold sweat. On his forehead, on his back. On his legs, too. The landing. And now her. Seeing her. What she might say. *That priest. He was reasonable. Smug, almost cocky, wanting to be reasonable but making me feel like a fool. He'll be like that with the women. Superior but pretending he isn't. If I were in his shoes I'd have had them all. He must have done it, too, with the ones he wanted. They do it as well, they're only human. Men like everyone else. Or with boys, they do it with boys a lot. Everywhere they go.* Pedroche looks at the Sacred Heart on the door. If it were real silver it would have been stolen. The druggy on the fifth floor. Or anyone. Keys. Don't make a noise. Pedroche has another look at the figure of Christ. His crown of thorns. Healing hands. Two fingers raised, ready to bless or maybe trying to attract a waiter's attention. The bill please. And the complaints book. Better not blaspheme. Not now and not ever. Pedroche's tempted to cross himself. But he doesn't.

He opens the door carefully. Everything's quiet. No noise, but he can feel a presence. The hall's in semi-darkness. A black shawl hanging from the coat stand. The hall mirror is a pool of murky silver that doesn't reflect anything. Pedroche thinks of all the things that mirror's seen.

What it's reflected. The calmness of the nights, the passing of shadows that he couldn't see. The world of the sleeping. The mirror used to belong to Belita's grandmother. She'd look at herself in there. She and other people, in a different home. Lots of dead people. They've been there. In the stories they say they're on the other side now, looking over here, where we are. Waiting for us. Pedroche puts his keys away carefully without making a sound. Nobody should enter their own home this way. But lots of people must. Sneaking in like a thief. Knowing that the person waiting for them hates them. The same as you hate them. It's only a matter of measuring the degree of loathing. He takes two steps forward and peers into the living room, his rubber soles squeaking like a new-born kitten. If she's in she'll know he's back already. The living room's empty. The curtain is flapping slightly. The windows are open. Has she jumped? A flicker of hope. No. If she'd jumped he'd have seen her down below, the ambulances, police and a sheet on top, the blood. *I don't want her to die, or maybe I do, I want her to leave, shut up, go away, disappear. Like diseases disappear. I want to breathe with healthy lungs. She might have jumped while I was in the lift.* Ten floors. The impact. Would he have heard from inside the lift? Eighty-five, ninety kilos from ten floors up. Weight, velocity, acceleration. There was a formula for it. Would she have screamed on the way down or would she have gone quietly, tight lipped as she is? Into the void, through the void, towards the ground. With her face. The air buffeting her fat cheeks. Pedroche's tempted to go to the window and look out. But he knows she hasn't. That nothing's happened. There'd be a particular noise, cars braking, voices. Or silence. That contained silence, like an electricity cable. You'd hear the tension, not the usual noise. Engines, rubber on asphalt.

He peers into the kitchen. A plate with an egg on it. As though a hen had laid it right there. Or a conjurer. He looks back at the mirror. All Belita's ancestors trapped in there. All their madness. That's what she imagines when she looks into it each time she leaves the flat or each time she comes home. 'What's your name?' Once he caught her unawares, standing there looking into the mirror and asking 'What's your name?' with the same apathy as if she were asking a child who was knocking door to door selling raffle tickets or something. Pedroche froze, uncomfortable at having interrupted her, but she wasn't in the least bit bothered. She looked at him with the same indifferent expression she'd worn when she was interrogating the mirror, and he was the one who had to look away.

The bathroom door is also open, but there's no one in there. The corridor's shaped like the letter Z. At the first turn there's a large earthenware jar containing some dried sprigs of something or other. It looks funereal. His father's burial. The row of headstones and empty niches waiting for tenants. Open niches, gaping wide. Trees swaying above the wall, beautiful, bright green. Cloudy, blue-grey sky. Family, cousins. Comforting him. A brotherhood of orphans. So warm, knowing they won't see each other again for another few years. One of them will be missing. And the rest will gather to put him in one of those niches. The corridor. The longest section is empty. A shoe, just one, there in the middle, pointing at Pedroche. Medium heel, worn down, crouching like an animal hiding from a predator. He walks on. The small guest room (where no one has ever slept, where Belita put the cot and two nursery pictures that are still hanging there) also empty. Pedroche is tempted to go back to the kitchen, to the living room. He knows she's in the master bedroom at the far end. He senses her presence. And he knows that however careful he's been she'll have heard him. His breathing, his shoes squeaking. A living being bringing warmth to the flat. Yes. He takes some more steps. He sees her from the bedroom doorway. Lying on the bed, dressed in black. Not quite on her side nor entirely on her back. Eyes closed. Bare feet. Veiny old marble. White with a bluish tinge. She opens her eyes, leaving them half closed. Unsurprised. Eyelids heavy with medication and contempt. And her eyes, that weak light. The disproportionate cheeks, distorted by her position, tiny mouth, ridiculous lips. She looks at him. Pedroche also looks at her and makes a gesture of assent before looking away and turning around. The abandoned shoe is now presenting its back. He passes to one side of it. He feels the heat again and the gentle noise coming through the living-room window. Sickness. God bless every corner of this home.

Céspedes is ruminating in another taxi. *I'm rolling along, I'm a lame horse, not working properly. My brain is dictating new movements to a tired body. Low frequency, short wave. Radios, noises. This tiredness is an ache that's creating knots throughout my body. And I have to untie them, right in front of her, without her noticing, without her realizing that what I'd like more than anything is to go to a hotel, any hotel, a boarding house or the Ritz and lie down on a bed. Sleep. But I have to carry on and follow the script I wrote first thing this morning. So that she doesn't confuse improvisation with disaster, a little adventure with the most ridiculous stupidity. The most absolute absurdity.*

And along they go. Castellana, María de Molina, a boundary wall, hedges, glass panels. An elderly lady half collapsed under a bus shelter. goiko grill, *SOMO*, metal chairs and tables on the pavement, DELICATESSEN. A sign with a green border Avenida de América, another below it on which Carole only manages to read Plaza. The merry-go-round of life goes by the taxi window like a streamer. Carole sees trees being left behind. Some more isolated pedestrians. The sun drawing shadows with Indian ink. She and Céspedes have been expelled from paradise. Or, worse still, not even allowed in. Paradise in the form of a restaurant. Céspedes's outfit is an unpardonable sin. And mentioning Alfonso is no help at all (Señor Alfonso Durán – absent). 'He isn't here,' the maître d', or whoever he was, told him with a polite but indifferent expression, suspecting that as well as being scruffy he's probably under the influence of alcohol or some other mind-altering drug. 'Don't you recognize me? Haven't you ever seen me here chatting to Alfonso?' The man tells him that it is exactly out of respect for Señor Durán and the other customers honouring the restaurant with their presence today that he might be kind enough to go home and change, that the house rules are more than happy to accommodate 'smart casual' but sadly not beachwear. It's not a matter of questioning his personal taste, but what might be accepted in other establishments is not acceptable here. In the same way that one wouldn't turn up on the beach wearing a tie. Please try to understand. It's not because of you and even less because of us, but rather because of our other customers who wouldn't understand. They'll happily reserve him a table, of course, for whatever time he would like to choose. Carole tells Céspedes to find another restaurant. No. Céspedes will not accept them being treated like pariahs, however entertaining it might be. And this time providence places a taxi for hire right outside the restaurant. 'Take us to El Corte Inglés, the nearest one.' 'Calle de Serrano?' 'Whichever, the nearest.' Carole leans her forehead against the window until they arrive next to the large grey bunker. Cubist, semi-cubist. Window displays. Photographs of an idyllic summer. Air conditioning, escalators, gentlemen's outfits. Céspedes looks for an assistant and the assistant looks for a suit. Navy blue, pin-stripe. 'And a tie,' says Céspedes to the shop assistant. 'A tie?' Carole asks him, looking at his Hawaiian shirt. 'Yes, a tie. If they want to fuck me about, we'll show them.' A tie with a pattern of tiny camels is the one he selects. Céspedes ties a knot in one of the mirrors while the shop assistant prepares the bill, watching him suspiciously. A huge knot. Carole looks at him sceptically. 'What she's looking at,' Céspedes thinks, 'is her own reflection. She's trying to look in from the outside, wondering, "Can this be happening? Am I really here with a fifty- or sixty-something man I don't know who's trying to get one over on a waiter, maître d' or whatever the little shit at the restaurant calls himself." Well, yes, sweet-heart, here you are and you've come five hundred kilometres, a thousand if you include the return leg, to have lunch with a man you don't know who's almost twice your age. Didn't you want to play at being a bit naughty, ironic, sarcastic, corrosive? Well, here's a bit of irony personified. One metre eighty, eighty-seven kilos of irony. Irony in the shape of Céspedes. Céspedes in a downwards spin, Céspedes in free fall. Who could have foreseen it? Four weeks ago, four days ago. A door opens, and the house of cards goes flying. The door opens, and there's my wife, and me with my trousers around my ankles and my dick stuck in the wrong hole, not the right one. Even Julia's offended. Bombarding me with messages about ants, people with problems who need to be helped, saved. Me saving anyone in my current situation, that really is the purest irony.'

Julia sees Ramiro rush past. She follows him with her gaze, peers down the corridor and watches him run. She knows. Cardiac arrest. End of the road. Ana Galán's walking at a normal pace. Her eyes are bright. Julia walks eight or ten paces behind her. She notes her firm shoulders, the back of her neck, dark hair gathered in a ponytail. Even today she seems haughty. Her distance has made people who don't know her dislike her. She'll break down tonight or tomorrow. Once this whole ritual that's starting now is over and she can close her bedroom door.

Dioni was there, hidden behind the oxygen mask, wired up to a set of monitors that were no longer giving any readings. Excluded. On the other side. Dirty feet pointing to the ceiling. An ant climbing up the purple summit of a toenail. The Everest of his big toe. Dr Galán at the head of the bed takes off his mask. His real face. *When did she see her husband for the first time as he really was? When did she discover who he was, what her husband was really like?* Julia wonders. Dr Galán stares at one of the monitors. Ramiro stands behind her. Possibly ready to catch her if she faints. *As though he didn't really know her*, thinks Julia. And she, Dr Galán, carefully places the mask on top of the monitor she's been watching, turns it off and then looks at her husband, places her index finger on the dead man's lips.

THE RUNNER'S DIARY

I don't know why I wrote this: I've seen my father's still, blue-and-green face in the fire. I shouted out to him but he didn't reply . . . it was raining drops of blood, and hands emerged from the puddles or there were reflections of hands (the puddles were mirrors), there was a beaten-up bike and a skeleton.

I wrote down a dream that I didn't have. (Thinking that someone was going to read this?) (The reason for writing, importance of writing, me as a writer, delirium, impossible dream?) Reality, truth: I dreamed something like that but not exactly that.

This is what I actually dreamed about: I dreamed about a fire, and everything else was jumbled up. I could feel my father's presence, but I didn't see him. I knew he was in that dream or that the dream belonged to him. Something like that. That I was in one of my father's dreams. It was night-time and there were shadows. That's the only thing that seems accurate to me now (accurate within what was dreamed) on reading what I wrote back then (two, three months ago?). Yes, that and the certainty that my father was dead. That is the essence of what I dreamed. That my father was dead, but at the same time my dream was something that he had dreamed or somehow belonged to him.

NOW. Now I think what this home would be like if he were still alive. What would the rules be? Could I live like that? What would he have made me do? In the dream I felt that my father was my enemy. Someone who was interfering with my life, a threat. Would I be stealing money from my mother now if he were alive? Would I be lying in this bed now, waiting to be fed a meal after being out of work for a year? Thirteen and a half months. Would I really want him to be here and not behind a slab of cheap marble? His full name, two dates and bye-bye. Blotted out.

Lucía looks at his photograph and says, 'I would so like to have met him. What a man.' My mother's sister never tires of saying how she would hang on to his arm and say, 'Brother-in-law, take me to see a film tonight.' My mother listens to her without saying a word, proud and at the same time contemptuous. She knows how to combine those two things, pride and contempt. The young woman (barely out of her teens) parading around with her sister's husband. 'I fancied him more than my own boyfriend.' That's what she says. My mother hates her, but not because of that. She's flattered by that. 'I took what you couldn't, that's what you can't get over.' She hates her because she was their mother's favourite. She hates her, admires her and loves her. She lays into them both on account of how much they love each other. They should pay for it. They leave her out in the cold. At some point they left her outside, and she dug the trench where she lives now.

She likes to think that I'm there, too, it doesn't matter that I don't shoot or shout. Or if I'm lying in the officers' hole waiting for my boots to be cleaned or something like that. But she pictures me wearing a gas mask like her and a uniform like hers. If I told her, if I mentioned trenches and all that stuff she'd sit there looking at me with no comprehension. She'd laugh at my jokes. My remarks. One of my remarks in the mouth of any other member of the family might get them shot at dawn. Shot twice. Or a hundred times. Like she does her mother. Every morning, shot in the same place. Tied to the armchair. In some places, I think, they shoot people sitting down. Sitting down with a target pinned to their chest. She doesn't give her a coup de grâce*. She keeps the old woman alive so she can shoot her again the next morning. (Can she really love her that much?)*

Yesterday we watched that film about the First World War. Black and white. Lucía looked away in the final scene when they shot the wounded man on the stretcher and all that. As though we were right there. We'll go to France in the winter. Look out of the window and see grass and frost and domes.

My father. That was what we were talking about. The times I felt he was a complete stranger, an intruder. The first time, I remember, I must have been five or six years old. In a bar on Calle Mármoles. He and his friends. He was always surrounded by those people I didn't know. They'd pinch my cheeks, run their hands stinking of tobacco or petrol through my hair. They thought it was funny how I'd shudder after they'd given me a stroke. Like a dog. They'd laugh and give me another stroke. I don't remember what I did that day. Why my father got angry. Perhaps it was something I refused to eat. That was something that often happened with my mother. But he didn't know what I was used to eating, he was always out somewhere or my mother fed me at a different time. He picked me up and shook me. His face with that black stubble. Black hair. Hard eyes. Eyes that women liked. He picked me up and shook me. And he hoicked me up level with the bar in one go and sat me there in the middle of bottles and glasses of beer. There were numbers written in chalk and pools of water. My clean trousers. And then he shouted straight in my face and gave me another shake. I don't know what he said. I don't remember why. But I do remember perfectly well what I felt. Attacked by a stranger. In the hands of that person. Everyone laughed seeing me there, trying not to cry. His friends. Everyone found my efforts funny except for him. There was no fire, and it wasn't raining drops of blood. But it was worse than that, just being there, among those people.

If he were still alive now, he wouldn't be that stranger. I would have become accustomed to him. I did become accustomed to him. He wouldn't be a stranger. But that power of his would still be present. I'm sure that he forgot all about what happened in the bar that same week, that same day. But the seed of that incident, its after-effect, would still be floating there between him and me. Because it was already there, before then, that was just the trigger, because back then I already knew what our roles were. The invaded and the invader. The tyrant and his victim. Death freed us from that shadow. Freed me.

My sister's his representative on earth. His spirit's representative. The way she speaks, the way she looks at you. An ever-present reminder. Daddy wouldn't have wanted that, Daddy wouldn't have liked it, Daddy would have said. She'll be gone soon. She'll get married to that boyfriend of hers who's the complete opposite of our father. Maybe she's doing it in order to fulfil her role. Agent of the invader, the controller.

She'll be back soon, she might already be in the lift. With all the office politics. Medina, the useless colleague who won't let her breathe. Mateo, the boss who understands her but not well enough. Her salary. When she gets married, she says, things are going to be tight. She can't do any more to help us. She doesn't look at me. She looks at the television as she talks. Calmly. But she's spitting out every single word at me. She thinks I should have stayed on at that firm where they used me as a messenger, as a dogsbody. Her friends. Working in an office. Working in an office meant lugging boxes up from the car park. Standing there with my arms folded, not being told what I was supposed to be doing. Going down to fetch them coffees. Because they were all very busy. Going around schools and neighbours' associations asking for the committee director or chair to persuade them to work with us. With them. She asks me if I've been out for a run. Every day. And then she pulls a face. She looks at my mother. My mother keeps her head down and eats her lunch. My grandmother says something she shouldn't. I steal from them.

When I get to where I want to be they're not going to believe it. If I get there they won't believe it.

Smoking, burning, cooking. Bits of offal fall into the frying pan, fish are sliced up, roe and guts removed and thrown into the waste bucket or dropped on to the floor to mingle with the cigarette ash and butts and vegetable peelings. Wings and trotters and bloody claws are slashed off with cold steel. Rai strums his guitar. He plays an intro for the contorted Chinarro. Frying pans, saucepans, griddles, ovens, hot plates, both electric and wood fired. Eduardo lowers his arms, spreads his legs like a deformed weightlifter and starts singing the first notes of his perennial song. His carotid artery, jugular vein, tendons, all the vessels leading to his brain and his eyes expand so that his gaping mouth can release that blast of crackled voice. Created by beer and rum and salt water.

Calle Bolsa. Tables with white tablecloths and barrels from a fake cellar invade the street. Eduardo Chinarro's voice and the din from

Rai's guitar intermingle with the noise from the diners and busy waiters at the Rescoldo restaurant. The occasional tourist looks up from their plate and watches the farcical performance. The regulars raise their voices so they can be heard over the racket and chew their food. Ismael chews his with a crooked grin. Victorious, defiant, head tilted back, he watches his brother concentrating on his macaroni. 'Macaroni, Gorgo, again, that's what you get here, isn't it? Lots of macaroni.' 'You've always liked that,' his mother retorts in self-defence. 'Of course I like it, I like it loads and so does Gorgo, isn't that right, Gorgo? Look how much I like it, watch.' Ismael stabs at the macaroni, forcing more and more on to his fork and puts them into his mouth, stabs at more of the pasta tubes in tomato sauce and stuffs them in on top of the previous forkload, cramming his mouth, and sputters, 'And bwead, I like bwead, too.' And he adds a bit of bread to the overload of macaroni. He's talking with that warm mass of food on the point of spilling out of his mouth. 'Gogo, too, Gogo likes bwead.' His mother, Amelia, tries to assert her authority. 'Ismael! If you carry on behaving like a pig I'm leaving the table, no, you can leave, and you can eat in the kitchen.' Ismael's soft eyes look watery because of the blockage in his mouth. He chews ostentatiously, and Gorgo eats, aware of the flecks of sauce on the faded leaf pattern of the tablecloth. Pedroche rehearses a speech, tries out a facial expression, goes over in his head what he's going to say to Belita, how he's going to look at her if she appears in the kitchen, if she looks at him. He rehearses how he's going to look at the priest and what he's going to say to him, restrained, careful, what he's going to tell him about his wife's delusions once the money and the jewels are safely in his pocket. My wife, you know, my wife. My wife is that monster that sleeps beside me and who one night, you know, Father Sebastián, one night she might sneak out of bed and smother me with a pillow or take a knife from the kitchen or from under the mattress and stab me, Father Sebastián, that family of hers were so hard on her, like a murder of crows, all sitting around the table, all keeping their mouths shut. And they all got together to say the rosary, too. The oil catches fire in the frying pan, sulphurous flames from hell leap up from the pan to avenge Pepe Pedroche's blasphemous thoughts, and the flames envelop the piece of meat, which rears up like a wounded animal and looks at him. Don't use water. No water. A plate, a lid, something to smother the fire, to cut off the oxygen supply, to stop her hearing, knowing, smelling, appearing in the doorway. Let her sleep, let her sleep for ever, let her sleep at the far end of the flat. At the back. Rafi Villaplana is eating, sitting on the edge of the sofa, his tray on the coffee table that he himself cleared of ashtrays, cigarette packets, boxes of medicine, ripped-up newspapers, dirty plates and eggshells. He's eating and listening to his mother talking to him from the kitchen. 'And you know what I say, don't you, Rafi?' 'Mummy, Mummy.' 'What?' 'Mummy, keep your voice down, he'll hear you, you'll wake him up and that's all I need, for crying out loud, another bloody scene.' 'Nah, he won't wake up, it would take an earthquake in China to wake him up, he sleeps all night, he does next to nothing when he gets to work and then he has a sleep until the morning shift gets there, whatshisname told me, you remember him, the nasty one with glasses, one day I went to pick him up to go to Paco's, and he says to me, "You wouldn't believe how well your husband sleeps. Some mornings I really have to shake him, like a little baby," of course, he said it with a bit of side, he's a nasty man, that one, or at least he used to be (didn't he die?), you know what, Rafi, he only got the job through a connection, and you know what, I've had it up to here with your father, the lying bastard told me he didn't have any money, and when he went to sleep I looked in his wallet and he's got sixty euros, two twenties and two tens, I left him one of the tens, and let's see what he says when he wakes up and finds out, he'd better not come at me with "Where's my money?" if he didn't have any, "Didn't you tell me you didn't have any? So now what's happened? Did it grow on the money tree, or were you lying to me?"' 'Mummy, listen, Mummy, please, let it go.' 'He doesn't understand, you know what I'm saying? You know, Rafi?' Rafi Villaplana takes a sip, eats and chews and drinks and has another sip, and while he's listening he thinks things over. He thinks about business deals, he thinks about his ambitions, he thinks about labyrinths, his father, his mother, his siblings, that bastard Céspedes, Amelia, his fiancée's father, he looks at his watch (TAG Heuer, blue dial, stainless-steel strap). *I can afford it. It's a statement.* It's a statement that he's always thinking about, and it comprises two chapters. Chapter 1: I can afford it. Chapter 2: I deserve it.

The *terral* races along the deserted streets and alleyways, licking the buildings and the closed windowpanes. Anyone living here knows that faced with this wind it's better to shut yourself away, steam slowly between four walls and not confront the all-consuming, stifling heat head on. Close the windows, bolt the shutters, let the wind go down the street like a curse or a plague without coming into contact with it, without letting it inside. A northerly wind that runs along the riverbeds in search of the sea, along the suburban alleyways, sweeping over buildings, people, cars and trees. Covering them with a dry patina from the desert. The insects are the masters of the world, sensing the arrival of paradise. Elytra, antennae, wings, carapaces, exoskeletons, jaws, chirping, flying, buzzing through the air and above the overheated ground. Alighting on animals, dead or alive, overseeing the world, bits of broken bottle, faded paper, dried-out scraps, mummified branches and calcinated shoots. Kitchen full of smoke, Pedroche's eyes watering, listening out for noises in the corridor. La Penca slowly climbs up the stairs in her block of flats. Calle Papamosca, a clatter of plates, the smell of cooking from behind closed doors. La Penca calmly makes her way up. The concrete handrail has been repainted. Mustard yellow. Spatters of paint on the floor. The flecks on the tiles moving around like an ants' nest that someone's just kicked over. The memory of Nene Olmedo between her legs slowly dripping down her thighs, or at least that's what it feels like. It's all jumbled up then it all starts coming back, and now, halfway up the stairs, she can once again feel Nene Olmedo's mouth, his teeth clashing against hers, the taste of Nene's tongue, his saliva, is it saliva that's running down her thighs or is it just her imagination? He'd got his come all over her stomach, so what's that dripping down below? She opens the door; the key turns easily. The door has been repainted. Mustard yellow over brown, brown over green. She sees all the coats of paint, all the different doors. The smell of the flat, the smell of Kuki who runs up to greet her, vaguely happy, lazily wagging his tail. Drunken old dog. He sticks his nose between her legs and La Penca hits it with her knees. 'Piss off, dog.' Kuki sneezes, shakes his head, looks at her suspiciously and sneezes again. Yubri shouts out from his lair, 'I'm hunnngry, Penqui. Penqui? I've had two of those little chocolate-cake things and a packet of olives that were in the cupboard. Penqui?'

And La Penca looks at her mother's picture and thinks it's her mother speaking to her. She looks at the splinters scattered across the floor that Kuki has bitten off the leg of the sideboard. She looks at Kuki, who's still shaking his head after that blow from her knee and is enthusiastically chewing on the varnished splinters that are stuck in his teeth, in his dirty palate. She aims a kick at the dog who, despite his lack of agility, easily manages to dodge it. 'I'm hunnngry.' It's the high spot of his performance, when Eduardo Chinarro launches his final warble, like a Christ with neither church nor apostles. He bows low and blesses his audience as they chew their food indifferently. The pickings are slim when Rai passes the hat around, or rather, proffers the back of his guitar among the diners like a collection plate. A few spare coins for the destitute. Rafi Villaplana eats, chews and thinks things over as his mother makes an appearance in the living room and his sister opens the door and greets him unenthusiastically. Ah. A greeting Rafi responds to with a glance. His sister's trousers are far too tight. Dressed to impress a dirty old man, Rafi reflects as he chews. Belita's praying, 'Don't abandon me, don't leave me alone on the path, don't give him the Devil's tools,' moving her old doll's lips, lying in bed, licking away a bead of sweat that was about to go into her mouth. *Amen. Grant us peace, grant us forgiveness.* The retinue scales the garden steps, sits down in the air-conditioned living room. Guille, Mónica, Piluca, Loberas and Trini's mother. The housemaid appears, uniformed and well informed. Her knowledge of Don Dionisio's fate is betrayed by the tears that are making her eyes glisten. Too much grief for such a short period of service. She offers them a snack while they wait for Guille's uncle. She's tempted to say 'young master Guille's uncle', but she's wary of overdoing it. Her upbringing in the Andes didn't teach her much about protocol. Guille looks from one side to the other. They sit down. The house looks different, like another world. Piluca takes him by the hand. She's also tearful. Mónica just looks at him, pressing her knees together. Downy golden hair on bronzed adolescent legs. Her T-shirt barely covers her bikini bottoms. She hasn't been taught the protocol of death either. On the mantelpiece there's a photo of the man who they think is nearly dead and is dead already. He's crossed the river. Trini's mother takes control, places a hand on the servant's shoulder and guides her to the kitchen.

Loberas tries out facial expressions. He looks at his phone, thinks about what it will be like when his father dies, what it would be like if his father were dying now. The coins are clattering around in the guitar. Just a little. Rai pulls a face. 'Niña, are you going to have something to eat?' Rafi asks his sister. She responds with an expression that might mean yes. 'Don't go into the back bedroom, your father's asleep in there,' her mother warns her. 'There's a surprise,' the daughter replies. 'He's probably pulling himself off.' 'Is this the kind of language that poet of yours teaches you?' 'Leave it out, Rafi. Try a different tune for once.' Rafi Villaplana wags his finger censoriously as he watches his sister go out into the corridor, taking off her blouse, revealing her back, the rear-view geometry of her bra. Rafi looks away, drinks, swallows. And a sudden breeze of fresh air sweeps up the river Guadalhorce, an illusion that will suddenly free up people's thoughts, diffuse their anger, uncover a glimmer of hope and then it immediately turns into a mirage because the *terral* will wipe out that fresh breeze and redouble its efforts, its eagerness to ignite the air and reduce everything to cinders. The insects are labouring away on all the scraps of waste ground. The ants are carrying off their burdens, exchanging pheromones, the flow of language. They haul away small corpses, dying wasps, former brothers in the family tree, heading for the larder. Ismael raises his voice, proposing a toast to his mother and his brother. Just to intimidate them and make them feel small. Gorgo persists with his strategy of burying his head in the sand, head down, avoiding eye contact. Ismael thinks his brother's just pretending to be afraid. It's more than three months now. Three months since Ismael last hit him. Two punches in the stomach and a threat. Ismael's mother watches him out of the corner of her eye. 'Yes, let's drink a toast to the old woman across the road, the bird behind the glass in her cage, who still hadn't died this morning – do you think they feed her on canary seed, or what else would she eat?' The new taxi comes to a halt, the new taxi driver takes the fare, and Céspedes opens the door for Carole. Her ladyship taken back and forth in her carriage under the relentless sun. Céspedes, sporting his new blue pin-stripe suit, camel-motif tie over his Hawaiian shirt and boat shoes, leads her to the restaurant door. Floren hungrily cuts up a piece of meat that's leaking a trace of blood, the pink juice spilling delicately on to the porcelain plate, and as he cuts the meat he asks his daughter Carmencita, 'Did you have fun at the swimming pool, did you?' And the little girl nods her head enthusiastically while her mother tries to feed her a piece of chicken skewered on a dangerous-looking fork. 'Did you?' The little girl carries on nodding her head manically, testing the elasticity of her muscles and her cartilage, the room swims around, and the mild vertigo makes her shake even more. 'Hey, hey, Carmencita. Be careful with that fork, sweetie pie,' her mother warns her. The little girl stops, raises her eyebrows just like a patient in a psychiatric hospital and says, 'Yessss.' 'Yes?' says her father, chewing the slightly bloody meat. 'Was it fun or was it loads of fun?' he continues with the interrogation. 'Looooads of fun,' the child replies triumphantly, as she gorges herself on chicken. 'Brilliant.' Julia's holding on to Dr Galán's arm, and they leave the room where her husband is lying. 'What do you want to do?' Julia whispers as they go down the corridor of white lights. 'Do you want to go home and see Guille?' The doctor shakes her head and feels obliged to utter her first few words as a widow, her new life. 'Not yet . . . not yet,' she seems to repeat in a low voice. 'Shall we go to the cafeteria?' Julia asks, looking at Dr Quesada, who's walking a metre behind them as though she were asking him rather than her friend. He makes a gesture with his head, pointing to the ceiling, in other words, upstairs. And Julia twigs and asks her, 'Shall we go up to Quesada's office for a while?' Ana Galán shakes her head. 'The cafeteria?' Now she nods her head, half closing her eyes by way of an additional explanation. And Julia turns around again to look at Quesada. Pedroche the downtrodden hero opens his mouth and swallows a mouthful of cooked egg. He fiddles about with a piece of bread while the egg disintegrates between his back teeth and his tongue, the soft jelly of the egg white, the earthy, aromatic denseness of the yolk spreading throughout his mouth, that damp cave with its stalactites and stalagmites and cavities, the subterranean river of his tongue. And when all that remains of the egg is a fetid mist lingering in the grotto of his mouth, Sesame opens again, and Pedroche pops in the mangled piece of bread and at the same time looks over at the small picture hanging on the wall next to the fridge. The little house in the country, sheep tarnished yellow by steam from cooking, clouds from a different era. 'Where can you drop me off?' Guille hears Mónica saying from the sofa. Her legs are no longer so tightly squeezed together, and she's sitting more comfortably. She even seems to have forgotten that she's in the house of a deceased or pre-deceased person. Guille had got up to go to his room in search of a thicker shirt. He doesn't feel so good. Trini's mother had pronounced, 'If you like we can turn the air conditioning down or turn it off, darling.' He had declined the suggestion and went up the wooden stairs to his room. More in search of the comfort of solitude than cotton. To be free from all the looks, from those furtive eyes lingering on him, exploring his reactions, his feelings. Or what he ought to be feeling. Nothing. Let them all talk away on the other side of the wall, that's what he feels. And let them stare at him as if he were mounted on the wall in a frame. An abstract painting they don't understand. And he hasn't got a clue about the rules, how someone who is about to become a semi-orphan is expected to behave. And he stayed up there, in his room, looking out at the horizon clipped by a cloud of purple-and-white bougainvillea streaming down the hill in their splendour, a cluster of trees filtering out the harshness of the sun, the orderly roofs and the sea in the distance, curving majestically. Like a groan ending in the letter A, a whole series of hoarse As, surging up from the depths of a mine, Eduardo Chinarro's song comes to an end once again, now in among the tables of two restaurants: La Barra and La Reserva 12. The guitar and the coins, the *terral* and a volcano burning inside his exhausted throat. Chinarro's panting, and the gap made by his missing teeth becomes the absolute owner of his mouth. Charity, my friends. Céspedes and Carole make themselves comfortable at their table. The dim light enveloped them as soon as they walked across the chequered floor at the entrance. A game of chess. The ostentatious tie resting on his ransacked chest, Céspedes's powerful forehead and jawline; Carole's tired, beautiful eyes, black eyeliner with a devilish flick at the corners. *Acushla machree.* Opaline air, honey-coloured atmosphere. The silence of luxury. A menu open in their hands. Cerebral phase. Ismael is still wearing a lost smile, now a little too forced, he's bored with livening up the meal. Without the curtains that he chopped up this morning to serve as a barrier, the light penetrates areas of the room it doesn't normally reach. Sun on their three silhouettes. Glaring sun reflected in the cocktail-bar mirror, walls that are accustomed to a velvety light are now brightly glowing. Jorge can feel the weight of his phone in his pocket. Thinking about Gloria, his girlfriend, again, and Vane from the shoeshop passes through his mind once more. Leggings, eyebrows, sun-tanned back. Ask Gloria to get some blonde streaks in her hair. Their mother's trying to say as little as possible so that the equilibrium isn't shattered, so that Ismael doesn't snap out of his calm state and Jorge doesn't challenge him, even if it's just with a glance. The Runner sinks a spoon into his soup, scoops up chickpeas and liquid in the same way as the authorities scoop up refugees from a sinking boat on the television screen. When she arrived, his sister talked about the office, her fiancé and the dress she's going to buy. She whispered with her mother in the kitchen and sang to herself in her bedroom. Her head is full of her wedding and her future happiness, when she'll leave this flat and will only return occasionally as an outsider. Someone who'll view them from the other side of the glass. The Runner's mother gets up, goes to the kitchen, comes back bringing trays and plates she'd forgotten. They eat in silence. Grandmother spills half of each spoonful of food in the middle of her plate before the spoon has even gone beyond its circumference. Her hand is shaky and so, too, the mouth receiving communion. The only words are spoken by a special correspondent sent to Greece and the presenter in the person of a blonde woman looking concerned. The only other noises are a slurping of liquids, water pouring into a glass, soup sloshing around mouths, a shipwreck and waves of green beans and chickpeas in the four pools of soup. Juno and Montse, his mother, enter the house of misfortune. She's not properly dressed, bikini straps peeping out from the edges of her summer dress. 'As soon as Juno told me I came rushing over here. I was about to go to the beach with Fonsi, but when he told me the news . . .' she says to Trini's mother before she gives her a kiss on each cheek, almost on her ears. And then, in a whisper, 'What happened then, tell me, what happened?' Trini's mother shrugs her shoulders and raises her eyes to the heavens by way of explanation. Juno, composed again, back in his role of exemplary mourner gives Guille a hug, forgetting that they were hanging out together little more than half an hour ago. He kisses everyone: Mónica, Piluca and Trini's mother, and he also asks, 'Where's Trini?' 'With her uncle in Bomben,' he's told. Juno nods, wearing a responsible expression, approving this information as he goes back across the room to find his friend Guille. He sits down next to him and pats his thigh then gently flicks his head so that his recently washed quiff returns to the position long rehearsed in the mirror. The housemaid appears with a tray full of sandwiches. She bears it aloft, ready to make an offering to the gods. Or to the dead. Father Sebastián and his window, beneath it the Sinai desert in the form of an alleyway and dirty asphalt. This is my kingdom, and you are my Lord. Dr Galán's sunk in the metal chair in the cafeteria, opposite Julia and her staring eyes, Quesada and silence. *Where shall we go? Why doesn't it rain and wash all this away?* Images on the TV news, men and women crammed into a tiny boat. These are the poor wretches coming in search of jobs. The sea swallows them up and no one says anything. We are selfish by nature. They sell arms. Rubbish. And then they come and kill us. That's what they do. And we look on. Yes. That's right. They keep their mouths shut. They don't say anything. The Runner's grandmother is shaking more than before. *If you looked at me like that woman is looking at me, then everything would have been different, that's what I'd say to my wife*, Céspedes says to himself. Strong jaw, grey eyes. He opens his mouth, breathes, wants to forget, looks at Carole, another dream, something that will never happen. They eat. The Runner is eating, his old friend, the best 400-metres runner, Felipe Vicaría, is eating, Consuelo la Giganta is eating with her tiny teeth, Rafi Villaplana's sister is eating standing up in the kitchen, they're all eating. Everyone's eating, the wind's eating and the ants are eating, they're eating vegetables, dead scraps, chopped-up animals, fish drowned out of the water, boiled greens and cattle that have bled out, Guille's eating a cucumber-and-honey sandwich, Piluca's eating and Pedroche's eating. Molars and jaws. Dr Galán is opening her mouth and taking a first sip of the bitter fermented yeast, thinking of her son and the dead man, the dejected Céspedes silently takes his first mouthful of food, happy Floren is eating and watching his daughter eat, fearful Pedroche is eating and Ismael is eating the last spoonful of buttermilk. Food slips, slides and slithers down everyone's throats. Heading into a dark pit. We'll all see each other there. Chinarro's watching his benefactors eating with a clatter of spoons, plates and street life. They're indifferent and know nothing about his art and can't even speak his language, and they'll never return, and someone says 'Hallelujah!' and hugs an old acquaintance. El Tato is chewing his hamburger in Mon Rou and watching the empty ambulances go by. Nene Olmedo is sharpening a stick and some smoke goes into his left eye. Me, too. People are eating on the beaches, in offices and at petrol stations, in hospitals and on patches of waste ground, in beehives and the cossetted houses of El Limonar, at the entrances to markets and on the streets, under pergolas and sunshades made out of cane, in hostels and hotel terraces, in glass cages. The entire city is eating and chewing.

Pharynx and oesophagus. The voluntary phase is over. Stomach, pancreas and transverse colon. The factory in motion, enzymes dissolving the work of culinary artists and their wares. Transforming their handicraft into digestible matter. A tube with one sole objective. Ingestion, digestion, absorption. Mechanics and chemistry working together, a shower of hydrochloric acid drenching the captive foodstuffs, flooded passageways and cells. Chyme, bolus, flow. Proteins break down, the inner muscles of the gastrointestinal wall move into action like skilled workers in the absence of their master in pursuit of the objective and earning only the minimum wage.

The clock seems to stop for a few moments. The atmosphere becomes one degree heavier. Thermometers make an effort and rise a few tenths of a degree. Chairs scrape, serviettes tumble, ashtrays smoke, liqueurs are spilled and the diners get up from their tables befuddled, while others continue with their heads bowed, praying to hunger, brandishing forks and spoons with a mixture of discipline and joy.

The empty streets, hospitals, children, traffic lights changing colour, trees, façades, mute effigies, dead reflections in the windowpanes, laughter on the seashore, mermaids' bodies naked in the sun and a golden cross rearing on the horizon, everything is encompassed in this drowsiness that has suddenly overcome poor Pedroche's head as he sits on the Formica chair. A light-blue chair, flecked with white. The monster is sleeping or lying awake, but she's there, at the back of the flat. Bodily fluids carry out their solemn role, and the streets yawn.

*

The Runner can feel his skin sticking to the leatherette sofa. He tugs his running shorts down a bit to stop his thighs touching the hot plastic. His grandmother shakes her head, then does it again, very quick, short shakes. It's a sign that her emotions are getting jumbled up because of her Parkinson's.

'Yes, that man, the one on TV, he looks like that other man who did something like that, not the same thing because it was something else, but it was just as terrifying.'

Her daughter, rather disparagingly, points out the contradiction as she takes the tablecloth off the table. 'If he didn't do the same thing then he did something different. You just love the sound of your own voice.'

Grandmother's green-veined hands and the skin tags on her neck don't stop shaking. Her eyes are sparkling beneath the mask of her years.

'There you go again, you don't know what I'm going to say, but you're already telling me I'm wrong.'

'I don't know what you're going to say? Haven't I already heard all about it a million times? "They used to call him the Vampire" and the whole story.' The Runner's mother disappears down the corridor. 'The tablecloth's going in the wash, I don't know who's responsible for all these stains. It was clean on today.'

'My God, that woman!'

'When did all that happen, Grandma?' The Runner tries tugging at his shorts again.

'She's so tiring. And prickly.'

'When was it, Grandma? The thing with the Vampire.'

'What? Well, well it all happened at least sixty years ago, or fifty-something years ago. I was a young girl. I'd had your mother, but your aunt hadn't been born, or if she had she would only have been two or three years old. Hang on, she *had* been born, because I used to take her to the butcher's with me, that's right, and then when the man's picture appeared in the newspaper, she used to say "Mummy, bogey-man".'

'Where did you live back then?' asks the Runner's sister, who's still sitting at the table, her eyes full of sleep.

'We lived near by, that's why we used to see him, in Postigo de Arance.'

'Is that the name of the street?'

'It's the narrow street that goes from the river to Calle Carretería. I walked past where we used to live last month and nearly dropped down dead when I saw our building had been demolished and there was a wall around the site. I loved that place.'

'We lived in Calle San Bartolomé,' prompts the Runner's mother as she comes back in, 'otherwise how would you have seen or heard about anything?'

'That's right, it was Calle San Bartolomé because all the pipes in the building were being fixed; it was just temporary, and your father's cousin rented it to us, but we actually lived in Calle Postigo de Arance.'

'So, what happened? What did that man do?' The Runner remembers the story very vaguely, something he might have heard about when he was a child.

'Well, I'll tell you all about it. It was a winter's night, sometime after the Day of the Dead. You have to imagine what it was like back then. There were hardly any street lights, the buildings were dark and you could hear people's footsteps as they went down the alleyways. It'd been raining for days and days, and the river was on the point of bursting its banks, such a noise. I was fast asleep in bed when I heard your grandfather say, "Something's happened." I opened my eyes and saw him standing at the bedroom window looking out on the street. "Something's going on; there are lots of people." It would have been around three or four in the morning. I got up, and he was right, there were people, blurry shadows, on the other side of the piles of rubble behind our building. "Now it's stopped raining, I'm going to go and see what's happened," said your grandfather. "What do you mean?" I said. But he was already putting on his trousers and coat on top of his pyjamas, and I was curious to find out what had happened. Cars were beginning to arrive at the plot behind our building, and you could see legs and very long shadows on the walls in their headlights, people in their dressing-gowns, tousled hair, standing there as if they were all going to be taken prisoner. I thought perhaps it was something to do with the river. But no. They were all looking at something else entirely. I saw torch beams moving around and realized that one of the cars was a police car and that the people walking around among the piles of rubble were in uniform. You can't begin to imagine the effect it had on me, all alone at home, when one of those lights shone on a bulky shape covered over with a sheet in the middle of the plot. I can still see it, and I can still feel that cold streak running up through my body; it chilled me to the bone. The icy finger of death.'

The Runner's mother stops washing the plates in the sink for a bit and pokes her head into the corridor. 'We could all do with a bit of that iciness today.'

Grandmother shakes her head scornfully. 'You're mixing up two very different things. I wouldn't want to feel that iciness for anything in the world. When your grandfather came back he was in a bad way. Really shaken up. It was the smell. He was right there, at the front. He'd gone up to the little bundle when they took the sheet off and shone a torch on it, and there was the young girl lying in the mud. He saw her little face and thought she was about eleven or twelve years old because it was Angelita, and she had a lovely face even though she was already a young woman. That image stuck in his head. Her hair was all sticky with mud and other stuff, blood or whatever, her eyes weren't quite open and they weren't quite shut and her nightie was bloodstained down below, and she had one white hand with her palm turned upwards towards the heavens, that's what he told me thousands of times, that hand was like innocence itself, and, right beside it, the great big bloodstain and the hole in her stomach, the torch lighting up her glistening intestines that had spilled out into the mud.'

The Runner's sister gets up from her chair and sits down on the sofa next to her brother. 'Did you know her? Did you know the girl?'

'Yes. Yes, of course we knew her. There was a man there that night, and we saw him lots after that going around and asking questions. He was a policeman, and his name was Machuca. Very bony. Big and strong but bony, young, tough, bald even though he was still young. Looking at every detail. Rather than looking at the girl he was watching the people gathered there. He went up to two or three of them. Jiménez was one of them and that man, the one from the glassware shop . . . What was his name? A tall blond man.'

'Amancio!' shouts the Runner's mother from the kitchen.

'No, Amancio was the electrician, the one who found her.'

'The electrician was Aurelio!'

'Aurelio?'

'No, it wouldn't have been Aurelio!' The Runner's mother comes down the corridor drying her hands on her apron. 'He'd been in the area for years. I remember taking Daddy's radio to him, on the corner of Calle Salvador.'

'Oh yes. Aurelio. Amancio's the other one.'

'Oh yes, Aurelio,' the Runner's mother imitates her. 'If you're going to tell the story, and we all know it inside out already, at least do it properly and don't make things up.'

'Right, well, there we go, after so much time the names aren't really important. The thing is that the policeman Machuca was standing in front of them, staring at them. He took it all in, you could see in his eyes how he was taking it all in. He didn't even glance at your grandfather.'

'Daddy had the face of a saint; you could easily tell he was a good person.' To his grandmother's annoyance, the Runner's mother has stayed in the living room, leaning her hip against the back of the sofa, looking completely indifferent to the conversation.

'That policeman and his boss, in plain clothes, they were talking to Aurelio the electrician because he was the one who found Angelita. Aurelio had got out of bed to have a glass of milk and couldn't believe what he could see from his window, so he went across to the derelict site, lit a match and went over to the white bundle, lifted up a corner of the sheet and recognized his neighbour Angelita's face.'

'Was she already covered up with a sheet, on the site?' The Runner looks surprised.

'Yes, I'll explain later, the thing is that Aurelio ran over to Leonor's place, or was it the hairdresser's?' She looks at her daughter. 'Who was the one who had a telephone?'

'The hairdresser, the hairdresser. Don't you remember, we used to go over there on Sundays and give her two pesetas . . . ?'

'It was a five-peseta coin.'

'. . . two pesetas or a five-peseta coin, it's all the same, and then we'd phone Uncle Ramón in Albatera?'

'And he phoned the police.'

'We went there every Sunday; how could you forget it? The thing is, you can't remember anything and you jumble it all up; you say one thing and then something else.'

'I'm off.' The Runner's sister makes as if she's getting up off the sofa and looks at her brother. 'It's impossible to understand anything. Tell me later what happened to the girl, the policeman, the electrician or the hairdresser.'

The Runner shrugs his shoulders. His mother gets cross.

'I'm not allowed to say anything. She can go on about what she thinks all the time, and you just lap it all up. I say something and all you do is pick holes in it and say "I'm off". I'm the one who should be off because I've got loads of stuff to do, and I don't want to be wasting time on all this nonsense.'

The Runner's mother goes back down the corridor to the kitchen; she's snorting and muttering, and her words can't be understood properly in the overheated living room. The leatherette is eating the Runner's legs alive. Grandmother's shaking reaches 8.2 on the Richter-Parkinson scale. She doesn't say anything for a while until the earth stops shaking. Her grandchildren respect the silence. The Runner's hands are underneath his thighs; his sister is looking out at the sun being reflected in the window opposite. Grandmother leans forward and looks down the empty corridor. She pulls a face of resignation.

'Who were the girl's parents? What did they do? I mean, what jobs did they have?' asks the Runner's sister.

'Her mother had died, and no one knew who her father was. The girl lived with her grandmother, her mother's mother, very poor. That night, on the derelict site and around the whole neighbourhood you could hear a loud roaring noise coming from the end of the street, it was coming from the embankment. The river was muddy and the water level was really high, it was dragging along uprooted trees, rocks and dead animals. We all thought it was going to burst its banks. There was so much noise and so much water every single day. The noise was there when you woke up and still there echoing in the background when you went to sleep. It was like the echo was in your head. It was really striking. That's what your grandfather said when they went to collect Angelita's body and put her in the hearse, you could only hear the men's footsteps splashing in the puddles and that noise coming from the river, the rocks crashing against the embankment. It was pitch black. That night it seemed like dawn would never come; it arrived very slowly, as if the light of the day didn't have enough strength to wipe out such a black night. They were already making inquiries that night. The police were questioning people in the street and people living in some of the nearby buildings. That policeman I told you about, the young one, Machuca, he went after Jiménez, tall and gawky, he seemed like a good man. They said he went after him and asked him for a light, nothing more, on the corner of Calle Cruz del Molinillo. And then he asked him, as if it were nothing, if he knew the girl. The butcher said . . .'

'The butcher was Jiménez?' The Runner's sitting on the edge of the sofa.

'Yes, yes, he was. That's what I was saying. What was I saying?'

'The policeman who went after the butcher.'

'No. Errr no, oh yes, well I don't know.' Grandmother looks down the corridor, frightened of any criticism coming from the kitchen, but there's not a sound. 'Yes, so anyway, that night the police found out all about the Vampire. A few weeks before, perhaps when it started raining, I don't know, people said they'd seen a figure in a cape walking around the streets at night, especially around Calle Cruz del Molinillo, around derelict sites and also walking across the roofs of some of the buildings. He was wearing a hat, like this, sort of pointed, with a peak and all dressed in black. That's when they started calling him the Vampire of Calle Molinillo. They said he'd attacked a boy, although no one knew who the boy was. And they said he'd sucked the blood from a dog, a dog on a site full of rubble, they said the dog had puncture wounds in its neck. So, when Angelita turned up dead, lots of people said it must be the Vampire, the Vampire of Calle Molinillo.'

'The police wouldn't have believed that,' the Runner looks at his grandmother sceptically.

'No, they didn't, they said, they said . . .'

'And what about the girl's grandmother, what did she do when . . . ? How old was the girl?' asks the Runner's sister, making her grandmother even more confused.

'Well, the policeman, Machuca, he must have been, I don't know, men looked older back then.'

'I mean the girl.'

'Yes, yes, I know who you mean. She was fourteen years old, that's right, although she didn't look it. Girls looked older back then, all of us did, we had to grow up faster because life was hard in those days and it was all like that. The policeman, he and his boss, the inspector or whatever he was, went to see Angelita's grandmother, Doña Agueda. She knew all about it because Señor Andrade had told her. Señor Andrade was the pharmacist. Señor Laureano Andrade Andrade. He helped the family out, which wasn't such an odd thing to do back then in the neighbourhood, in that neighbourhood. He was well-to-do, and I think he'd been Doña Agueda's fiancé (or wanted to be) when they were very young – the thing is, he was there with the grandmother when the police arrived.'

'She would have been devastated, wouldn't she?' The Runner's sister smothers a yawn. A wasp is buzzing at the window.

'Well, no, actually, she wasn't. It was very strange because that woman, either she was ill from way back when or she was depressed because of how her life had turned out. She seemed very strange, and that night she was acting as if she were drunk.'

'She wouldn't be behaving normally if her granddaughter's been killed.' The Runner's sister's eyes are watering, from drowsiness, from the suffocating heat.

'Of course, that was the impression she gave, but people said she was completely devastated only she didn't show it on the outside. Mr Andrade, who was tall and as thin as a rake, a redhead – you could tell he'd once been a redhead because he was one of those people with pink eyelids, his skin covered in freckles – was giving her a herbal tea, and she was eventually able to talk to the police and tell them she didn't know how the girl ended up on the site, that she'd been fast asleep when she went to bed. Everyone thought that woman had been ill some time before what happened to her granddaughter. A week or I don't know how many days before all that, she'd fallen asleep in Antonio's shop, the grocer's, she'd sat down on a sack of lentils, like the ones you used to get, and she gave everyone a great big shock because they thought she was dead because she went to sit down, and her head bent over, and when they called her name, nothing, no reaction. They had to move her and she opened her eyes as if she'd arrived from another world, saying, "Oh, I don't know what came over me." She didn't last much longer after what happened to her granddaughter, even though Don Laureano looked after her so well right until the end, as if he'd really been her husband or at the very least her brother-in-law or something like that. And so, what was I saying? Oh yes, they were asking her questions, about her neighbours, if she'd noticed anything odd, apart from the story of the Vampire. Because right from the beginning the police said that whoever had done it had to be a neighbour or someone she knew. And that suspicion only became stronger once they realized that the sheet, the sheet used to cover her up, came from her own bed. It was the electrician who found her . . . Aurelio, wasn't it? Aurelio. The strangest thing about it all is that he said she was already covered up with the sheet when he found her, and it wasn't him, like everyone thought at the beginning, who'd covered her up. Very strange. They started asking if anyone had seen anything that night. They asked your grandfather that night, too. They put him in a police car because it had started raining again, cats and dogs. The police car made another impression on him. He was very impressionable, your grandfather. The police took it all very seriously, treating everyone as if they had a gun stuffed inside their clothes. He said there was a strong smell of petrol in the car, and it was all smoky from their cigarettes. He told me (one of his funny things) that the smell of petrol inside the car came out of Machuca's breath and lungs, or that's what it seemed like to him. Those men were used to dealing with people's dramas and calamities every day, the worst of everything, but you could see, I could see how upset they were about what had happened. The worst of it all came to light a few days later. To begin with it was things people were saying in Antonio's shop or in the butcher's, but then the policeman himself said the same thing to one of the people he was interviewing.'

'One of the people he was interrogating.' The Runner's still following everything carefully. His sister's fallen asleep.

'Yes, that's right. So, what did I say?'

'Nothing, it doesn't matter.'

'They'd cut out the girl's private parts, her organs.'

'Her genitals?'

'Yes, they'd been cut out.'

'Fuck.'

'It was really horrible. That's when people started talking about the Vampire even more. A big story came out in *Sur*, the local newspaper, too, "The Vampire of Calle Molinillo" in great big letters. And a blurry photo that looked like a stooping man, dressed in black or dark colours walking over a rooftop in Calle San Bartolomé. In the newspaper you couldn't tell what colour clothes people were wearing and you couldn't tell if it was a person or a blur, but it did look like a person and one wearing a cape. The journalist, Roche, was very famous, and your grandfather knew him, too, he went to the site many times, asking questions and making enquiries, and there was even an American, Daniel Murphy, a friend of the journalist's, who later went to work at a place called El Pomelo, who was wandering around the neighbourhood wanting to know all about the Vampire. Back then it was really unusual to come face to face with an American, but the thing is, everything was really strange after that girl died. The nightmare went on for days and days. It never stopped raining; your grandfather said the water was like thick drool. It wasn't really, it was only rain, but it rained morning, noon and night, all day long, and you could hear the river embankments shuddering. And they kept on seeing him. After Angelita was found on the abandoned plot people saw the Vampire everywhere. Some said they'd seen him climbing down from a balcony, others saw him looking out of a window or on a rooftop terrace and some even said he'd appeared in a little girl's bedroom, and when she woke up he was at the foot of her bed. Of course, he was seen in Calle Molinillo, too. And everywhere else, all at the same time.'

'It was psychosis,' the Runner stands up, 'collective psychosis.'

'No, yes, no, are you going out?'

'No, I'm just stretching. I'm sticking to it, I'm sticking to the sofa.' The Runner takes two steps forward, turns around and sits back down.

'It wasn't collective because I for one never saw anything.'

The Runner's sister opens one eye, frowns and closes it again.

'So, what happened?' The Runner searches for a cooler place on the sofa.

'The rain never stopped, although it did ease off. But the noise from the river could be heard louder and louder in the neighbourhood, echoing and groaning, noises that seemed to be coming from the buildings' foundations – and that's not just because of what your grandfather said, it was like a constant rumbling noise, you could even hear it on the ground floor of buildings; it must have been because of the drains, and it made everyone really worried. It was as if the earth were about to open up and swallow us all. The council, it would have been the council, sent some men around to put sandbags on the embankment because some cracks had appeared in the walls and water was seeping through. We feared the worst. A flood like the time when it burst its banks . . .'

'And what about the girl?'

'No, first of all she has to present the daily weather report, if she remembers; she doesn't even remember what she ate yesterday, and she remembers what the weather was like every day more than half a century ago,' the Runner's mother pokes her head around the kitchen door.

'What do you mean I'm not going to remember. It's not every day a girl gets killed, your own neighbour.'

'But you hardly even knew her.'

'So, you know who I knew and who I didn't know, do you? You were just a little brat playing with paper cut-out dolls all day long. You never even looked up from them, putting a dress on one, then another one, then a different one again. Your father got worried and said we'll have to take those bits of paper away from the child, worried he was.'

'My father! My father was the only one who loved me. Of course he was worried. He was the only one who would have been.' The Runner's mother got as far as halfway down the corridor, her hands wringing her apron, perhaps wanting to be wringing a neck.

'That's right, and you cried so much at night. Telling your father to stay with you because the Vampire was coming, you wanted to come into our bedroom every night, and you never stopped crying.'

'You'd frightened all the children with your gossip. Don't you see? A hundred years later, and you're still going on and on about it. Now she'll say something about my father . . .' The Runner's mother starts retreating towards the refuge of the kitchen again. She's indignant, and that makes her movements seem erratic, rather uncontrolled.

The Runner's sister opens her eyes. 'For crying out loud.' She stretches her neck as if it's hurting her. 'You can't even sleep for five minutes in this flat. I'm tired from work. What time is it?'

'Early!' a voice from the bunker of the kitchen yells out.

A few moments of silence. Just heat. The wasp isn't on the window-pane any more. The Runner's sister rubs her forehead with both hands, her elbows raised. She's returned to the world. *Not for long*, thinks the Runner. *She's probably got a calendar, and she's marking off the days left in this flat. That's what I would do.*

'Who killed her?' asks the Runner's sister with her eyes closed.

'I can't remember if it was one or two days after that night when that policeman Machuca saw the butcher Jiménez. Machuca had gone to collect his boss's umbrella – he'd left it somewhere, I don't know where – and he saw something in Jiménez, perhaps because he was in a hurry and looked a bit sneaky or because of his apron which was covered in blood stains. And he would have remembered him from when he asked him for a light that night, and if he asked him for a light and went after him it must have been because he smelled a rat, suspected something or sensed it, like people say they can. Machuca gave the inspector his umbrella, crossed the street and saw Jiménez go into his butcher's shop. They used to call it the Establishment. I don't know why. Everyone used to say, "I'm going to the Establishment." I don't know. Machuca went into the butcher's Establishment very calmly. He didn't say anything, not even good morning. There were two or three customers there, and the boy who helped Jiménez out was there, too. He was a nephew. A nephew? Nephew or cousin, cousin or son of a cousin, one of his family at any rate. He waited for Jiménez to finish serving the customers, who all left knowing that something was up because of the man in the uniform who was staring at an almanac with a photo of a black pig and a faded picture of Christ the Captive that was there framed in the middle of those yellowish tiles. I can see it all now. They said Machuca didn't reply when the butcher said good morning to him, and that he just stood there looking at everything, and while the boy stood still, Jiménez continued cutting up pieces of meat, getting on with his work, until the policeman said to him, "I thought I saw the Vampire in the street. You haven't seen him around here, have you?" The butcher, without stopping what he was doing, replied, "As you can see, I'm working." This rapid response didn't go down well with the policeman at all. The whole neighbourhood started talking about it, because the butcher's assistant told them afterwards, and he was looking from one man to the other more and more anxiously. You see, the police or men like that policeman Machuca pick up on these things straight away. Machuca asked the butcher point blank, "Haven't you heard about the little girl, Angelita?" And then Jiménez stopped what he was doing. "How could I not have heard about something like that? What's more, you saw me that night. I gave you a light." "Yes. Jiménez, that's your name, isn't it? Manuel Jiménez Pineda," said the policeman as he read out from the framed municipal licence that was hanging on the wall next to the almanac. And he slowly went over to the counter display, looking at all the meat and offal set out there, and, as if he were talking to himself, asked what the innards of a man or a girl would be like, do men and girls have the same things inside them as the animal innards on display? He looked at the boy, and the boy, with his eyes on stalks, looked at his uncle or his cousin or whoever he was. And what Jiménez said was, "I'm just a worker, and I don't get mixed up in anything." "So, you're a worker, are you? Well, do you know that the man who killed the girl and cut out her insides was a worker, too, someone working with meat, offal and intestines?" Machuca had sniffed fear in the air, the way a dog can, that trail that only a dog can sense. The boy, who never stopped talking about it all later, looked around, frightened, towards a corner in the back room where the cold-storage room was and a few other things. The policeman started moving even more slowly, like a fox, and speaking in a low voice, "I'm a worker, too. I wear a uniform, but I'm a worker, or do you think I'm not?" "I'm not saying anything," said Jiménez. "What about you, lad, have you got anything to say?" he asked the boy, who'd shown no sign of being aware of the policeman's existence up until then. The boy was all hunched over and didn't say a word. Machuca turned to the butcher again and said, "Do you think someone would have the balls to do to me what they did to the girl? Stab me then have some fun cutting out my innards then wandering around as cool as anything talking about vampires, Dracula and Frankenstein? Do you think so?" And the butcher kept his mouth as tightly shut as the boy's. Machuca went behind the counter and paid no attention to Jiménez when he said,

"Hey, where do you think you're going?" And he looked inside the back room where the boy had been looking. There was a bloodstained sack in a bucket and beside it, hanging on a hook, a black overcoat. Then Machuca goes and says to him, "Why don't you try doing to me what you did to the girl, come on, give it a go, you piece of shit," and he came out with all the insults under the sun.'

'So, that's what happened?' said the Runner, 'the policeman guessed the butcher was the killer just like that and just because he'd seen him wearing his apron?'

'Yes, because of his apron, because that first night he thought he was acting very strangely and he saw the overcoat or the black cape and the sack.' The Runner looks towards the silence of the kitchen. *She really could jump off the balcony one day, out of pride.*

'But, what was in the sack?'

'The sack? But anyway, it wasn't "just like that" in any case, I don't know what I was saying, the policeman Machuca and all the others were asking questions all around the neighbourhood, they knocked on doors, searched everywhere and looked at clues, and the policeman would have seen some other things apart from what he imagined or where his instinct led him, the footprints found around the girl or whatever. Did I tell you it was all muddy? How should I know? It's police stuff.'

'OK, but what was in the sack?'

'The sack? Nothing, just his things, a knife, tongs, things he used for work, and they were all covered in blood.'

'What happened next?' The Runner's sister looks at the time on her phone. 'I've got to go. Can you give me a lift on your bike?'

'It's broken down. It's still early, isn't it?'

'I've got to get there a bit early, there's a mound of paperwork. I'll give Quino a call and, if he can pick me up, I'll stay, otherwise I've got to go now.' The Runner's sister gets up, stretches and walks towards the kitchen looking at the calendar on her phone.

The Runner asks, 'Did he say why he did it? Did he confess?'

'What? No, nothing like that.'

'Did he rape her?'

'What he said was, what happened was . . .'

'Was it his cousin, the young lad?'

The Runner's grandmother shakes her hands, she's trembling in several different places.

'No. What he confessed was, the only thing, when he saw the policeman acting like that, the only thing he said right there in the Establishment, when he realized what might happen to him was, "When I arrived Angelita was already dead." Machuca punched him so hard it could have split his face in two. The lad, that cousin, jumped over the counter thinking he was coming for him as well and ran off, then passers-by started poking their heads around the door, then when the word got out a whole crowd gathered outside the Establishment, more police arrived, Machuca's boss and loads more people. When they took Jiménez out of the shop to put him in a car, the police had to protect him because everyone wanted to rip him to pieces, shouting "Murderer, Vampire". Children were saying, "The Vampire, they've caught the Vampire." You can't imagine what it was like.'

'And then what?'

'What Jiménez said was that he found Angelita dead, with all those injuries and a soaking-wet sheet beside her. It really chilled him to the marrow to see her like that so he covered her up with the sheet.'

'And he went home without telling anyone?'

'Yes, it was all going around and around in his head, and he didn't know what to do, and by the time he'd decided Aurelio had already told the police,' she lowered her voice, 'or was it Amadeo, the electrician.'

The Runner's sister comes back and sits down in the same place as before. The same place she's been sitting since they moved into the flat. The Runner has never seen her sitting anywhere else, except at lunchtimes. *She doesn't want to get infected.*

'Quino's coming to pick me up.'

'And why didn't he say so straight away?'

'So, the whole Vampire thing hasn't been solved yet?' The Runner's sister stretches, her arms brushing against the picture hanging on the wall behind them. A bridge, a house, a river. Snow. Everything's grey apart from an orange glow coming from one of the windows of the house. Since childhood the Runner has often dreamed of being behind that window himself.

'Because what Jiménez said was that he'd committed a crime that he was prepared to pay for, and the thing is, for a few months he'd been buying animals at a farmhouse up in the Montes de Málaga that didn't have a health inspection certificate from a man who'd had problems with his animals being sick from some disease or another, and the butcher said that the animals were all right even though there was no certificate. He slaughtered them there himself out in the countryside and even took his knives and equipment with him. The police discovered a back yard at that farmhouse where there was still blood and hairs beneath a tumbledown roof, and the butcher used to bring them back to the Establishment at night, and if anyone had seen him at a distance with his overcoat, walking close to the walls and with a sack over his shoulder (the stuff about the hat and cape were made up), they came up with the Vampire thing.'

'Did he walk up to the Montes?' asks the Runner with a distant look in his eyes, thinking about something else.

'No, he used to take his motorbike with a sidecar, and so that it wouldn't make a noise he used to park it on the other side of the river on Avenida Dr Gálvez Ginachero or somewhere near there and then walk back to the neighbourhood. Walking around with contaminated meat is a bit of a problem.'

'Just imagine.' *All that meat and entrails bumping around in the sack, the knives, animals bleeding out in the middle of the night, their legs tied together, dumped on the ground waiting their turn, smelling blood, lambs, rabbits or chickens, feathers and hair, hands at work, howls and fear.*

'He thought the story about the Vampire was amusing to begin with, and he'd even told some customers that he'd seen the Vampire walking around the embankment. Even his cousin, or whoever he was, had gone out at night wearing the overcoat and walking around the empty sites (just for a laugh) so that from a distance people would think he was the Vampire. Even though he never went to the farmhouse with the butcher, he knew all about the dodgy dealings. They found half a sheep's ribcage and four skinned rabbits (or they could have been cats) in another sack, and, of course, people in the neighbourhood said they'd found a sack full of the entrails and remains of other girls and who knew how long Jiménez had been selling those over the counter at the Establishment. It all went completely crazy. People were taking laxatives a week after eating what they'd bought there, other people went to get blood tests to see if having eaten human flesh would come up in the results, and, seeing how sombre Jiménez looked, everyone took it as proof of his wickedness. Your grandfather, in addition to Roche the journalist, had a friend at the Natera police station who told him that they questioned him long and hard but couldn't get anything more out of him. There was one policeman – his name was Márquez, but everyone called him El Tenazas – who interrogated Jiménez all day and night. They kept him there for days on end, not letting him sleep and feeding him tablets to calm his nerves. People said all sorts of things, like they hit him with wet towels and iron bars on the soles of his feet. The man from the farmhouse, the one with no inspection certificate, said it was true that he'd sold him a few beasts out of necessity but that he didn't know anything else. They roughed him up, too, and when they let him out of the police station three days later even his wife didn't recognize him. And the cousin, the young lad who'd said he knew all about the animals and the underhand dealings but nothing about the other stuff, couldn't confirm a thing and knew nothing about what had happened at the butcher's because on the night of the crime he'd been in bed with a high temperature and a doctor even went out to see him and the doctor backed him up and everything.'

From halfway down the corridor the Runner's mother asks her daughter, 'Aren't you going to be late?'

'Quino's picking me up.'

'You'd have been better off lying down in your room for a bit and not listening to that load of rubbish.' The Runner's mother turns around and heads toward the kitchen. 'What's the point?'

'What a pain . . .' whispers the Runner's sister. 'What happened in the end, Grandma?'

'In the end? Well, in the end . . .' She looks down the corridor, lowers her voice, trembling. 'You've no idea what a pain she is, being here with her all day, pounding up and down that corridor!' She wipes her mouth with a tissue, puts it in her housecoat pocket and takes a breath. 'In the end, at the trial, they explained that Jiménez had somehow taken Angelita from her house by giving her something or threatening her, and that this must have happened on other occasions, and after raping the poor girl he killed her and then opened up her belly as if she were one of those animals in his sack. He was given a very long sentence, I can't remember if it was a life sentence. But the thing is he died. From some terrible disease two or three years after being locked up. People said that the other prisoners made life very difficult for him and he had to put up with a lot in there. And things were left there. Until eight or ten years later, after the girl's grandmother had died and no one remembered anything about the Vampire of Calle Molinillo or Angelita or anything, and Don Laureano died.'

'Who?'

'Don Laureano Andrade Andrade, the pharmacist, the man who used to help out Angelita's grandmother. And he left a will. And when the notary went to read the will he found everything there. He took it to the police, although there wasn't any point. Nothing could be done. What the will said was that Angelita had become his lover on her fourteenth birthday. She was his lover.'

'The girl? At fourteen? Did she want to?' The Runner's sister frowns.

'They were different times.'

'What about him, the pharmacist, how old was he back then?'

'Well, he would have been almost seventy. More than sixty-five definitely. These things happened. He would have got around her somehow, with presents and crafty little tricks, talking to her and telling her things, we just don't know.'

'But what happened? Why did he kill her?' asks the Runner.

'Don Laureano . . .'

'She's still calling him "Don" Laureano.'

'And what should I call him?' Grandmother looks at her granddaughter, trembling.

'The paedophile.'

'Well, whatever you want to call him, he gave sleeping tablets to Angelita to give to her grandmother to make it easier for them to get together. As soon as her grandmother dropped off to sleep, Angelita left for his home or, as some people said, Don Laureano came to their home, and that's where they did it with the grandmother all drugged up rather than sleeping on the other side of the wall. She always looked weak and confused, and some people thought it was because she was old and others thought she was ill. It was already that winter with all the rain and the noise coming from the river, those long weeks when it was all so dark and one day followed another without it really getting light and it never ever stopped raining. Angelita got pregnant. Don – I mean, the pharmacist – wrote down all the details in his will. He made the girl take a strong pill that would make her have a miscarriage, and that night she had a haemorrhage and there was no way of stopping it. They didn't have a phone at home. So, she tied the sheet around her belly and went to see him so that he could do something about it. But, however much he tried, he couldn't stop the bleeding. He gave the details of everything he tried in his will and also said that Angelita was really frightened and wanted him to call a doctor and go to hospital, and he told her to wait and that he'd try this and that, and then she said that if he didn't call someone she'd walk to the hospital herself. He didn't want her to make a noise, and in desperation she opened the front door to go to the hospital and there he was in front of her with a knife in his hand. In his will he said he didn't know how but he'd already stabbed Angelita in the stomach and felt obliged to finish what he'd started and stabbed her again and again.'

'He didn't know how, oh yes. So the knife moved on its own, did it? Bastard,' said the Runner's sister in disgust.

'And then . . .'

The entryphone rings. Their mother's talking in the kitchen. 'Yes, dear, yes, she's here, I'll tell her, I'll tell her right away. Quino's downstairs. He's come to pick you up. He's double-parked.'

'OK.'

'Hurry up,' the Runner's mother's voice sounds triumphant, as half of her own mother's audience will now be gone. 'Hurry up, or he won't wait.'

'Don't panic. He'll wait for me till the cows come home.' The Runner's sister gets up. Without looking at her brother or her grandmother, she says to them, 'See you later.'

The Runner's sister goes into the bathroom, and the mirror light clicks on. The tap. Grandmother's hand is trembling as she looks down the corridor, and there's a brilliant sparkle in her eyes. The Runner realizes how she might have been thirty or forty years before, strong, full of life and now harassed and bullied. The Runner starts talking to swat away things he doesn't want to think about.

'So much for the Vampire. It was the old pharmacist all along.'

The light clicks off. The sister comes out of the bathroom. The sound of her heels reverberates down the corridor, they can hear her in the kitchen saying goodbye to her mother.

'She'll be taking an apple from the fruit bowl. She takes one every afternoon because she's on a diet for her wedding,' the Runner's grandmother explains, as if he were a stranger.

The front door opens then closes. There are a few moments of silence.

'As if she needed to go on one. Young people nowadays,' says the Runner's grandmother getting comfy in her chair. 'Diet, indeed.'

Without quite getting up, the Runner lifts his legs up from the leatherette and notices how the drips of sweat cool down when they come into contact with the air, despite how hot it is in the small living room.

'And then?'

'What?'

'The Vampire, the pharmacist.'

'Oh yes, him. I don't know how many times he stabbed her. When he saw what he'd already done he told himself, "I have to kill her, I have to kill her," and then he couldn't stop,' she bends over again, looks down the corridor and lowers her voice. 'What on earth is your mother doing? You can't hear a sound. Even if I know something, I'm not saying anything, I'll keep my mouth zipped. You can only talk about what she wants to talk about, and me with my mouth zipped.'

'Don't pay any attention to her.'

The Runner's grandmother bends over and looks down the corridor trying to hear any incriminating sound.

'It's worse if I don't pay any attention to her. It's always worse whatever I do. Sometimes I wish I could pop my clogs.'

'No, don't pay any attention to her.'

His grandmother, the skin on her neck trembling, leans back and smiles. She shakes her head and holds back a laugh. 'What on earth can she be doing in there so that she can't hear me. She goes mad. And she's so pig-headed. Always contradicting me, she's like a guard dog. I go over there, "Woof!" I do something, "Woof, woof!" And she doesn't stop, I want to say to her, "Calm down a bit, dear." I know she's not a bad person, but she's so pig-headed, then she comes and asks me if I'd like a bit of broth and to put my legs up because they're swelling up, but I bet she goes and tells you that nothing of what I've told you happened the way I told it. Anyway, this is what I was saying, Don Laureano wrote it down, and it all came out in the newspapers. He said his mind went blank after the first cut with the knife and that then a voice was telling him he had to carry on. He killed her in his flat. Then came the job of cutting out her organs. I reckon it must have been so no one would find out about her pregnancy, as back then there were no blood tests or anything, and also so that no one would suspect rape or something like that. He took her to that patch of waste ground and left her there. The policeman Machuca said... Ah, I didn't tell you, your grandfather, who walked everywhere, knew a shoeshine boy, like the ones you used to see, everyone called him El Rata, and he used to polish Machuca's shoes, and I think Machuca used him as a snitch and got tip-offs from him. Anyway, El Rata told your grandfather that when they found out about Don Laureano's will the policeman said, "Who knows what really happened?" and that he'd never liked that old man from the pharmacy, and that he might have made the whole thing up to show off that he'd made the girl fall in love with him, and what did it matter if he passed himself off as a murderer if he was already dead, and, in any case, he didn't have any kids or anything, just a couple of nephews he left a few possessions to, and he gave one or two other things to the Little Sisters of the Poor.'

'He was making up for it.'

'Huh? Oh yes, he was making up for it, he'd have been washing his soul out with soap before the Last Judgement. But, however much the policeman Machuca said that, it was also to get rid of the problem that he'd made a mistake with Jiménez the butcher. Just as Don Laureano had written down, they found the pair of knickers Angelita was wearing that night, bloodstained, greenish-brown stains and beside them a medium-sized kitchen knife in his flat. Everything was in a drawer in a sideboard almost within sight of the cleaning lady. They also found one of those small saws with a bit of iron on top hidden under a floorboard.'

'A fretsaw?'

'A what?'

'A fretsaw.'

'I suppose. And a few bits of lace and little bows like the ones on women's underwear and a photo of Angelita taken shortly before she died.'

'What was the photo like?'

'It was a normal photo, like all the photos back then, passport-sized but a bit bigger, and what the policeman Machuca said to El Rata, trying to justify himself, was that they hadn't exactly done anything wrong by locking the butcher up because who knew how many people he'd made ill with that contraband meat he was selling, no one even knew what animals it came from or what condition it was in and who knew how many people had been saved from poisoning by Jiménez because he'd taken him prisoner. He told the shoeshine boy, and the shoeshine boy told your grandfather, "The butcher was a bastard, you only had to look at him, just like you Rata, you should all be hung up on a hook, just like everyone like you." That's what he told him. And that's what happened, that's the story of the Vampire of Calle Molinillo. It all had such a big effect on us, the never-ending rain, the noise from the river echoing around the neighbourhood, days when there was no proper daylight and everything remained dark. There had never been a time like it in our neighbourhood before.'

Jorge gets up first. His brother Ismael watches him. Ismael is almost the same height sitting down as his brother is standing up.

'I'm off,' says Jorge by way of a goodbye.

'Will you be late tonight?' his mother asks.

And, his back already turned, he shrugs his shoulders and grudgingly responds, 'I don't know.'

The click of the door. Freedom.

'What about you?' It's difficult to tell whether Ismael's thick lips are smiling or sneering as he asks the question.

His mother guesses that it's the latter. And she knows what's coming next.

'Am I what?'

'Are you going to be late?'

'I'm working.'

'Ha! Ha!' Ismael bares his teeth. 'Ha! Ha! Ha!'

They stare at each other. His mother defiant. Tanned skin, almond-shaped eyes, hair shining and giving her a dark, reddish aura in the sunlight. Ismael pale, wavering between sarcasm and rage. Still undecided. He'd kill them all. Some nights he thinks about it. Not his mother or Gorgo. But, if he could be certain, if he knew that the police wouldn't catch him and nothing would happen, would he kill someone? The old woman across the road? The concierge or Consuelo's husband? Or that shit who's screwing his mother? Definitely. A few of them. How? A knife? A hammer.

His mother's saying something to him, the usual stuff. '. . . and what do you think I get up to, eh? Tell me. Answer me. One minute you're foaming at the mouth and the next you want to be treated like you're normal.'

Ismael's knee thumps the underside of the table, the glasses shake, the knives and forks rattle on the plates and the empty Font Vella bottle tumbles over in slow motion.

He stands up and strides across the sun-drenched room.

'That's right, storm off, that'll solve everything. Banging and crashing and storming off until one day . . .'

All alone. Plates, breadcrumbs. The remains of the curtains hanging in tatters from the rail, a tattered pennant in the aftermath of a battle. So many battles. Every day. She sees a few triangles of cloth that have escaped the broom, on the floor, behind the standard lamp. She remembers the first time he did it. It was her leopard-print shirt. She found it cut neatly into pieces in the waste bin in the bathroom when she went to throw away some cotton wool after taking off her make-up. She wasn't particularly surprised. It was a sign announcing they'd reached a level that she'd seen coming for a long time. That day she went to his bedroom, furious. He was asleep. She turned around. The next morning, silence. She couldn't find the right moment to say anything. The days slipped by. When her husband left she felt liberated. For quite a few weeks. She told him so not long after he'd gone, when they'd arranged to meet up so that she could give him some documents: his passport, a chequebook, bills. 'When you left I felt as if the windows in my life had suddenly been opened.' Yes. Until the nausea came. Desertion in the form of corrosive acid, a drop on her skin or running through her veins for every memory of her husband.

Her two sons gave her neither comfort nor company. Ismael with his aggression and Jorge with his kind of autism. His shyness. She had never worked before, and the first job she found, as an office cleaner, didn't help much either. Friends, other divorcees, all that sadness. Better off on her own. The first man she went to bed with, or at least, the first one she had sex with, in the back of a car, one August evening. Another August. The windows wound down, the sound of waves and the smell of the sea permeating the car. She can't remember his name. There were several more. Trying to erase some memory or other. To cleanse herself or muddy herself. Or just to have fun. And then the withdrawal. Her friend Dori. Dinners on the promenade, country walks she found so boring. Then another man, a decent man, a widower, so nervous the first time he brought her home he almost broke down weeping in her arms. I need time, he said. As if anyone didn't need time. Loads of time.

Then came working at the hotel. As a cleaning lady, housekeeping, cleaning the rooms. Villaplana appeared. She remembers him. The first time she met him. She was bending over a bathtub, and he was standing in the doorway to room 513, watching from the corridor, next to the housekeeping trolley. Sizing her up. All he said, more as a statement than a question, was, 'You're the new one.' 'Yes.' She turned off the bath taps and stayed there on her knees. He gave a slight nod, ambiguously, and went on his way without saying who he was. She knew already. Rafi Villaplana, head of personnel, back at work after an appendix operation. She kissed the scar, like a schoolgirl. The first night. The apartment in Los Álamos. The sound of the sea and her naked in front of the net curtains, looking at the moonlight shining on the water. Shimmering. *I felt like a woman, and I hadn't felt like that for a long time, Rafi, so I want to say thank you.* He was lying down in the semi-darkness, his legs vaguely accented by the moonlight, his head and body lost in the darkness, the red glow of his cigarette indicating where his face was.

Paloma, Palomita. Back then there was a Paloma, Rafi Villaplana's official fiancée, whose parents owned two perfume shops and four or five premises they leased out. The Aguilera empire. Amelia heard about Paloma just when Rafi was opening her cage in order to devote himself 100 per cent to chasing after the English girl, who was seriously rich. At least, her father was seriously rich. He broke it off with Paloma, and Amelia knew that sooner or later he would do the same to her. *I never promised you a rose garden.* It's true, Villaplana never promised Amelia a rose garden. Not even a mysterious promotion at work, which Amelia never knew who to thank for. Whether it was down to Villaplana himself or to Yolanda, the head of reception who was about to retire. Much as her furious colleagues put her meteoric rise from cleaner to receptionist down to her having been in Villaplana's bed, it was never really clear. What Villaplana giveth, Villaplana taketh away. That's what La Turbia, the one-eyed woman from the laundry who had seen Rafi take his very first steps on his career path, used to say. 'That one was biting before he even grew any teeth,' she would say.

La Turbia, Rafi, accumulated images of nights in Los Álamos spring to mind as she loads the plates into the dishwasher. Rafi's tense, skinny arms pressing on the bed, poised above her, his face, his teeth. Drowsiness comes like gas seeping into her head. The sound of the front door closing. Ismael going out. Too hot. Amelia leaves the glasses on the worktop, closes the dishwasher door. She washes her hands in the sink. Rafi's threat. What will become of her when he disappears? What lies in store for her? *Back to nights out with the girls? Another widower or more divorcees, a whole raft of numbskulls until someone half-decent turns up? Do I have the strength to go through all that? I don't know.* It's cool in the corridor. She goes into the bedroom. Semi-darkness. Windows closed, blinds down. Her bed a white island. She takes off her top, breasts still firm. *My best feature. And my skin. I'm very attractive. People say so. And I notice. How they look at me.* She stretches out on top of the sheets. A sinking sensation. Set the alarm clock. Rafi's smile, a narrow street, stone walls, somewhere she's never been, streets with steps, voices on the beach, Jorge's hand on the table, his fingers kneading a piece of bread. Tom Thumb.

*

Plaza del Siglo. The off-white cobbles are a dizzying jigsaw. The heat makes them a blur, and the lines seem to dance around, let loose from reality, running into one another. Several industrial-sized black plastic bags and a few squashed cardboard boxes are piled up next to some large rubbish containers, topped off with an abandoned bedside table. Peeling varnish gleaming, almost melting, in the sun. Eduardo Chinarro examines it carefully. Twisting his head around, like a dog hearing his master's voice.

'It's all right, isn't it, Rai? That table. My mother had one just like it at home.'

'That thing's got to you, and you've come over all homesick, haven't you? All romantic over a bedside table.'

'You're not joking, Rai. Romantic. Like that crooner, Nino Bravo.'

He's thinking back to the years he spent living in Carranque, Plaza de Pío XII, with its orange trees. A balcony overlooking Calle Virgen de la Estrella, and you could see the square and that church that looks like it's out of a naïve painting. Chinarro's memory of a house, some pieces of furniture immersed in murky water. A slow-moving river swept it all away. First his father, then his mother. Stuff.

'The world's full of stuff, know what I mean, Rai?'

'What sort of stuff, though? Stuff made out of what?' Rai's taking shelter from the sun in the doorway of a branch of Unicaja bank. 'Stuff made out of what? There are plenty of wankers, though.'

'All sorts. All sorts of stuff that people leave behind and stuff they've got in their houses and then that stuff wears out, and when they die their kids throw it out and give it to other people, and then they give it away, and after that, where's it going to stop? Where does it all end up?'

'That thing's really got to you. It's just a bedside table.'

'I've thought about it a lot, loads of times, all the stuff there must be in the world – think about it, Rai – and there's more and more stuff, plastic bowls, broken toys, gadgets.'

'That's right, gadgets, they use old things to make new things: recycling.'

'There's loads of it, Rai. More and more, and the factories are making more and more of everything, they never stop.'

Those plates and cups on the sideboard, all painted pink, the tapestry of a lion in the dining room, his mother's clothes, shoes, her black purse with the two little metal balls, glasses, comb, pots and pans, towels, the box where she kept the photos (and what about the photos?), a medal belonging to his dead brother, the one he never met.

'There's a load of stuff in the world, Rai, you can laugh, but there's an enormous load of stuff.'

What happened to it all? The stuff that got thrown out and the stuff that their cousin La Sorda took away, and Remedios, their neighbour, who was with his mother right until the end (she must be dead, too, by now), she must have kept a good few things and must have thrown the rest out. All that stuff must be somewhere, broken or decomposing.

'If I told you, I mean, if I told you how much stuff there was in my mother's house when she died, and there were still some of my father's things, some glasses and stuff like a transistor radio, one of the old-fashioned ones, loads of stuff, all that has to be somewhere, obviously. Even if it's in bits it must be somewhere, or am I wrong? They're not going to make it disappear by magic, Rai, am I right or am I wrong?'

'Can you stop breaking my balls?'

'Chill out, Rai, I'm only making conversation.'

'Conversation? Some conversation.'

'A conversation between two people.'

'What a day. I find a guy who's dead or half dead, eaten alive by ants, the poor bastard, and the cops are doing my head in, never mind the rest of it, and then you're not where you're supposed to be, and I end up meeting that shit Nene Olmedo, La Penqui does a number, then the Fanta guy with the kid and now you with the nonsense about the bedside table, for Christ's sake, and no one can spare a euro, and with this heat frying my brains, you know it's enough to make you soak yourself in petrol and light a match.'

Raimundo Arias has propped his guitar up against the wall, beside an ATM. Despite all the moaning, his anger has passed. He feels like everything is fading all around him and that he himself is starting to blur, melding into that cacophony of noise, violent light and overwhelming heat.

Raimundo Arias is slender and extremely bony. Prominent cheekbones and an aquiline nose, an exaggerated nose. It looks as if his body is harbouring more bones than are necessary. Olive complexion with eyes sunk into dark hollows shining brightly. Long hair, parting like a pair of curtains to reveal a broad, aggressive forehead. A face full of prominent features, corners and cavities. He opens his mouth and displays a set of teeth that are whiter than expected, reasonably well formed, as if they're intruders in that riot of bones. His bird's-eye-print shirt is open to the waist. His sternum looks like a barbecue grill, hairless and sickly. Skin and bones. He strokes his scrawny chin, then his hand moves down his neck, avoiding the disproportionate lump of an Adam's apple. He adds and subtracts. He's making financial calculations. He announces the results. 'We haven't made half of what we usually do. What a load of shit.'

'It's the heat, Rai.'

The shortfall. 'And what's more, after me losing what I've lost, what I had to leave in the toilet in the fucking petrol station.'

'So, like we said, we'll take a trip up there when everything's a bit quieter, Rai, and we'll snaffle it back. You can stick your hand in that basket with all the bog roll.' Chinarro chuckles, stretching his friend's tolerance to the limit.

'Yes, I'm going to stick my dick in it, too.'

Eduardo displays the gaps in his teeth as a sort of endorsement, yes, but then he goes back to the thoughts that are troubling him.

'How many people are there, Rai? Do you know?'

Raimundo's beginning to get bored.

'How many people are there where?'

'In the world, in the whole world.'

'How should I know, why are you asking me?'

'But you often say things like that and how much politicians earn and all that stuff. How many? How many millions?'

'In the world? On the planet?' Rai looks at the tables full of diners on the terrace of the La Reserva del Olivo restaurant as if that could provide him with an approximate calculation. 'Fifty thousand million. Or more if you count the Chinese.'

Chinarro tries to assimilate this number. He tots things up in his head, approximately, and approves the figure.

'So then say, let's say that at least half of them have got a bedside table . . .'

'What the fuck? I don't believe it. I'm going to take that fucking bedside table and stick it up your arse.'

'It's a conversation, it's because of what you were saying, look. Just say there are twenty thousand million bedside tables, and after a year a load of people get tired of them and buy new ones and the next year more people, and that's apart from the ones growing up and buying a flat and getting a bedside table, and forks, everyone's got at least six or ten forks in their house, and toothpaste, fifty thousand million tubes and next month another fifty thousand million, and then there's the old . . .'

'Old people haven't got any teeth.'

'I mean the old tubes, the ones that have run out, then they stay in the world like all the other stuff.' Chinarro stops and thinks, his face contorted, paralysed in a sort of deranged smile. 'Who knows?'

As for not knowing, he doesn't even know where his mother's remains have gone. He received a letter, back when he still used to go and see his cousin, La Sorda, who'd give him a hot meal once or twice a month. A letter from the cemetery saying that if he didn't pay who knows how much they'd take his mother out of her niche and put her who knows where. Jumbled up with some other bones, Chinarro supposed. With other people. He took the letter with him and kept it for months, several years, in his windcheater pocket, then in a plastic bag in his backpack. By now the writing was faded and the paper crumpled. He didn't read it again, but every now and then he looked at it. As though it were a photograph of his mother. The only thing he had left of her.

'Let's go to La Cosmopolita and not waste any more time.'

'Really? Over there? There's that waiter there with a face like an old witch, he'll make us clear off, Rai.'

'You just do your thing and stand your ground.'

'OK. And then we can grab something to eat, can't we, Rai? I'm famished.'

'You're the boss. Come on, we'll finish early and drop by Las Papas del Museo.'

'What, Las Papas again, Rai?'

'We can go to the Ritz if you like, as long as you're paying.'

'No, seriously, Rai, what about a hamburger?'

'Right then, let's go.'

They leave the shelter of the doorway. Into the full heat of the sun. The soles of Chinarro's sandals immediately start burning.

'Rai, did you know it was a nun who invented barbed wire?'

Ismael feels the weight of the three darts in his right hand. In his left he's holding the tincture he prescribes for himself on these occasions. A short glass three-quarters full of gin and an ice cube. He looks at the dartboard. He examines the ten or twelve locals currently in the Bar Danielín on the corner of Calle Ravel. He empties the glass of gin. A long, slow draught. He's not in a hurry. He likes to make the most of every single thing he does, enjoy it to the full *like a proper gourmet.* He sometimes watches television for fifteen or eighteen hours at a stretch. He's well up on the culinary sciences.

He leaves the glass on the bar and signals to Danielín to fill it up again. And he completes his order at the top of his voice, 'And a Red Bull.' He takes two steps back. Two steps to the side. Two customers are almost encroaching on the imaginary straight line between him and the dartboard. He breathes noisily through his nose, curls his upper lip. He leans back and throws the first dart. Violent, forceful, strong. The dart whizzes past the head of a man in blue overalls, who turns his head in surprise, hardly able to believe what's just happened. The other man did see Ismael make the throw.

'Fuck! What the fuck?' the man in the blue overalls says, looking at the dart stuck in the board.

Ismael approaches the bar casually. He picks up the glass that Danielín has just refilled and drinks slowly, emptying a third of it. He pulls a face, puckering his lips. He leans on the bar. Looks at his colourless drink. The floating ice.

'Hey!' says the man in the blue overalls, about fifty years of age, his hair combed back to his crown in a series of waves, a swell of salt-and-pepper hair. He tries to attract Ismael's attention, but he ignores him. 'Hey, you!'

Ismael picks up the can of Red Bull. He throws his head back and drinks. Slowly. The whole can.

The companion of the man in blue overalls, short and squat with an enormous head, quietly asks his friend to keep his cool. Tries to calm him down.

'Leave it. He's a nut, can't you see? So what's happening with the union, nothing new?'

Nothing. There's nothing happening with the union, but that moron with the darts has moved away from the bar and is looking at the dartboard again, out of the corner of his eye he sees he's still got darts in his hand, and from the dumb expression on his face and the lifeless expression in his eyes it's obvious that he's quite capable of throwing more darts. And he does. But on this occasion Ismael has moved over more to the left and the dart passes more than a metre away from the man in the blue overalls. A distance calculated to cause discomfort but not enough to make the man square up to him. An apparent gesture of goodwill. He's backed off a bit. He's just a bit scatterbrained, that's the message. Until the next dart.

Ismael waits. He studies the dartboard with a semblance of innocence, the two previous darts embedded fairly close to the bullseye. That wanker in the blue overalls. He takes aim. He's a happy man. Or the opposite, the complete opposite. But he's here, large as life, full of air, full of life, full of energy, pure energy, heaven, hell. He throws. He throws with a lot of force, as if instead of aiming for the bullseye he'd like to bury it in the wall, split it in two, destroy the board and Bar Danielín and the whole fucking works, all that joy, that strength released by his arm and projected into the dart. And the dart passes barely fifteen centimetres from the workman's head. The overalled man in blue. The incredulous man who opens his eyes without making allowances for madness and who feels compelled to join in with it, condemn it, now strongly supported by his friend, who has seen the dart's copper head, metal point and blue feathers pass by like a crazy rocket so close to his companion's head, so close to his own nose, and both of them start towards Ismael, who's eager to receive them into his arms, submerge himself in contact with these men, in their smell and their blood, these fools that life has so generously placed within his reach, saying the same things everyone says to him, 'Bastard, piece of shit, lunatic, if I'd moved an inch you would have taken my eye out.' They shit on his mother, they want to smash his face in, wipe it out, just like he wants to smash theirs in, break the spider's web, tear the sheet and pass through to the other side, free and ebullient.

He clamps his left forearm around the neck of the poor wretch in the blue overalls, sticks his head under his armpit and throws a right-hand punch at the other man's temple, the one with the enormous head, who wobbles around like a Weeble. The man in blue jams his elbow into Ismael's stomach and side and he, the lost boy, the child in the maze, by way of counter-offer, bites him on the head, on his forehead.

The bar breaks down into a cubist painting, everything falls apart, just as nine days earlier the walls and mirrors of Bar Tamarindo fell apart, just like a month and a half ago the pictures on the walls of the Numancia were moved and disturbed, or three months ago the darkened walls of the Onda Pasadena. Ismael sees and hears the other customers shouting and backing away all around him, just like in those other places they shouted and pushed and backed away while he aimed a kick at the groin of the brunette's boyfriend, the one in the black leggings with the big tits that he'd rubbed up against twice, at the same time as he nutted the guy who'd pushed into him as he passed by and then refused to apologize, breaking his nose, the same way as he's now hitting the man in the blue overalls in the face. The man's head is still wedged under his left armpit, and his right fist is smashing upwards with continuous blows into the snorting man's eyes, nose and mouth. Everything's full of light, such a pure light, from a different time, from so much truth.

The man with the enormous head kicks him in the thigh, and a random punter jumps on his back in an attempt to restrain him, manages to do so, and they crash against a table, the three glasses and a coffee cup that were on the table shatter on the floor, a Coca-Cola bottle bounces along the floor, clink-clank-clunk, Ismael tries to smash the back of his head into the punter's face and receives more blows from the workman in blue's elbow, weaker ones, Ismael releases him in order to concentrate on the one who's holding him from behind, throws himself backwards against the bar, trying to crush his assailant, almost does so, the man who was holding him releases his arms, the one with the enormous head comes towards him, Ismael moves, shakes himself free, the man with the enormous head kicks him again, near the groin, Ismael lands two punches on him, one on the left ear, one on the neck; the man in the blue overalls is bleeding from the mouth and nose, and the bite to the head that Ismael gave him is also weeping, the man can hardly stay upright, he feels as though his feet are walking on the ceiling rather than the floor, Ismael turns and looks at the man who was behind him, a skinny lad, it seems impossible that he could be that strong, he's almost bent double, holds up his hands as though Ismael was pointing a pistol at him halfway through a B-movie, the world starts to regain its usual boring proportions, the boat steadies itself, everything settles back in its place, the faces of the shocked customers appear out of nowhere, he hears Danielín's voice, shouting.

He's right in front of Ismael, short and sinewy. *He's got a pair of balls even if he's an old man of fifty.* He says things that all the old men and losers say, 'Who's going to pay for this, what's your problem, what the fuck's wrong with you, don't you dare pull another stunt like this on me, you're not setting foot in here again as long as you live.'

And, feeling magnanimous, out of pure friendliness towards Danielín *I'd so like it if he were my uncle or an older cousin or my grandad,* he tells him, 'It was them, they started it, you saw me, didn't you? I was just throwing darts, and they were giving me dirty looks right from the start. They think the whole world belongs to them and no one else can breathe in case their lordships get upset.' And, catching sight of them, seeing the one in the overalls sitting on a chair, unable to stand, and the one with the huge head pretending to be held back by another customer, seeing those dregs of humanity, Ismael loses the calm attitude he'd shown towards Danielín and feels a new wave of energy rushing up from the soles of his feet to the top of his head. 'Bastards, I'll see you outside, I'll see you outside, and I'll rip the heads off the pair of you.'

He feels like crying, a deep sense of anguish, a sadness making his legs buckle, forcing him to sit down like that shit in the blue overalls, sit on the floor and split his head open on the tiles *bits of brain and broken glass and blood* and the image of his blood on the floor, his own body lying there, rekindles his fury, and he pushes Danielín (he was still talking to him, reminding him of his obligations, rights, money, work, breakages). He pushes him aside and turns towards the bar, searches among the papers, glasses and cloths and finds the beaker where the darts are kept, takes one with green feather flights, turns back, looks towards the man with the fat head, who has read his intentions and hobbles towards the toilet door, opens it, and Ismael throws the dart and the instant the fugitive closes the door the dart sinks into it next to the little figure of a man.

They don't throw him out, they don't hit him any more and they don't go near him. Ismael kicks a chair and heads towards the door of Bar Danielín, in Calle Ravel, near the junction with Calle de Wagner. Only Danielín walks a couple of steps behind him, telling him that he's going to call the police, 'don't even dream of coming back here', he's going to file a report. And once he's back out in the street, as Ismael takes a burning mouthful of heat, that's when the bar owner, with a rush of courage, shouts after him that he knows where he lives and that the police will be around to see him.

The sun bouncing off the shop window opposite and the blazing hot air are disorientating. The gin sloshes around in his head as though his skull were a glass about to overflow. He looks at Danielín without listening to what he's saying. He waves goodbye to him. He touches his right eye, which is injured, a slap from the man who grabbed him from behind or maybe the shit with the fat head. He feels a flash of anger when he remembers him, feels the urge to go back to the bar and kick down the door to the toilets if the guy is still hiding in there. He can see him smashed against the white tiles, eyes wide open, blood on the tiles, the police, a judge, his mother in one of the visiting booths you see in the films *that bastard* and he sees him again, now lying on the toilet floor, the porcelain broken and the bastard dead, blood everywhere. But he carries on walking, advancing along the pavement, walking through the curtain of blazing hot air.

He turns into Avenida Velázquez with its dazzling light, the bustle of cars and dull grunt of a passing bus. He feels his neck, which is also injured. A slight bruise. Nothing like the night at the Numancia. That night he ended up in A&E at the Carlos de Haya. Six stitches on the top of his head, two in one eyebrow, one on the bridge of his nose. Bandaged wrist. Police statement, trial pending. Nothing to write home about. And, of course, nothing like the carnival last year when he was locked up for two days, and his grandfather, who was still alive at the time, had to use all his influence as a former captain in the artillery to get him released from the police cells and not get taken to prison.

His lawyer still tries to scare him with the same story, that this time they'll find him guilty and he might go to jail. His mother tries, too. 'That's where you'll end up, you in there and me left with the shame of it all, queueing up with the gypsies and the neighbours pointing their fingers because you do whatever you please, you'll learn your lesson in there, they'll take you down a peg or two and no messing around with psychologists and all that nonsense. You'll learn your lesson all right.'

Ismael retches, he leans over with one hand against a wall, but he doesn't vomit. The bitter taste of the gin comes into his mouth and a sickly hint of Red Bull. He spits it out. It's sticky. He thinks of the food they gave him at the police station that time. That green mush. Cream of bile, that's what the loser in the cell opposite said. 'It's from that copper's wife, they did an operation on her bladder last week.' Another retch. He carries on walking.

Only his grandfather. He was the only one who didn't give him grief apart from his brother, his brother didn't either, but that's because he's a coward. His grandfather would give him a wise look, speak to him in a low voice, say the right things. When he got him out of the police cells he gave him a pat on the shoulder, not to congratulate him, but as though he were an old friend who was going through a difficult patch. He didn't say a word on the way back home. He just drove the car and that was that. Ismael could relax. Everything was so new after being locked up. There were so many colours, so much movement in the street. People went wherever they liked without realizing what that meant. His grandfather seemed to understand it all. They made the journey like two grown men. His grandfather wearing a pair of aviator sunglasses, freckles on his bald pate and one arm outstretched, gripping the top of the steering wheel. It was only when he dropped him at the entrance to the flats that he asked him, 'Are you OK?' And he said, 'Yes.' His grandfather tilted his head back slightly to point to the front of Ismael's block with his chin and said, 'Go on up.' 'Are you not coming up?' Ismael asked him. And his grandfather shook his head. 'No, I've already spoken to your mother. You go up, we'll talk later.' Ismael waited in front of the entrance and watched the car drive off.

He spits out saliva. He goes into the sun, the bus waiting at the bus stop closes its doors, Ismael, runs, bangs on the door with his open hand. The driver looks at him through the window, weighing him up, he bangs again. The driver opens the door. He gets on. He searches his pockets for his bus pass, puts it in the reader, without making eye contact with the bastard of a driver. He goes down the bus, the air conditioning penetrating every pore of his body. He breathes it in. It feels like poison. The bus pulls off and weaves around, and the liquids slosh around in his brain again, and there's a bitter taste in his mouth.

Trini's mother has turned towards Guille, cupping her face in her hands. Her eyes are wide open. Seven or eight bright-red fingernails on her cheeks like exclamation marks. Two long self-propelled teardrops are suddenly running down Mónica's cheeks. Juno says, 'Oh my God!' and Montse, his mother, shakes her head as she's speaking to Guille's uncle, and then she says, 'No, Emilio, he doesn't know, we didn't know.' But it was too late.

He'd already told them unwittingly, unaware that nobody there knew yet that Dioni had died. 'Isn't it awful, dying like that?' Those were his first words when he saw Montse, his beloved Montse, who had almost cost him his marriage. But the old pseudo-secret romance and grief over his brother-in-law's death were put to one side when he realized that with those words he had broken the news to Guille that his father was dead. To Guille and to everyone else who was overcrowding the living room of this house in Calle Sierra Pelada.

Emilio took his hands off Montse's shoulders and, with his arms in the same position, almost like a zombie with his will submerged in a strange twilight zone, he crossed the room and went over to the sofa where, likewise strangely submerged in a thick liquid, his nephew Guillermo awaited him.

Guille stands up in slow motion, can smell his uncle's scent, that male aroma, slightly citrus, musky, then the contact, his shirt, his summer jacket brushing against his cheek, what it would be like to kiss a man, that roughness, lips, tongue, disgust. His uncle's hands on his back, that heat. Over his uncle's shoulder, Guille sees the crowd of people who have crammed themselves into his home, all silent, focusing, looking at him, he sees Trini's mother, brown, her hands still on her face, her dress, still damp from the swimming pool, riding up, exposing her tanned thighs, he sees Montse, Piluca shaking her head and weeping with a great sense of the occasion, very professionally, adult to the core, he vaguely hears the words his uncle utters close to the back of his neck and which he only vaguely understands, 'Be a man, it will get easier, we're here for you, your mother,' he sees Marcus, the English teacher, the class he was going to give Guille now suddenly converted into a wake, he sees Loberas, who looks away, taken unawares doing something shameful, death, he sees Asunción Arnedo with her husband, the American with the blue-black hair, and he doesn't know how it's possible that they're all there unless it's because of the incoherence you find in dreams, he sees another of his mother's friends, Maica Terés, and her two children, Maiquita Cabeza, who observes the scene with her eyebrows raised, perplexed, and Currito Cabeza, the diminutive *padel* tennis champion who came to play on the court in the neighbouring development and who is now clinging tearfully to his mother's waist, sensing the presence of something beyond his mother's control, beyond the world of the living, he sees two men he doesn't know, he sees Juno with his jaw manfully clenched shut and he sees Mónica with her two long teardrops refreshed but without screwing her face up at all, without disturbing her studied pose on the sofa, her legs gathered together to the side like one of those goddesses they learned about last year at school.

Guille breaks away from his uncle, who now tells him, 'Your mother's on her way if you want to spruce yourself up a bit, in case we go, if you want to see your father or if not whatever your mother says or whatever you think, in any case, there's no rush.'

That's it. He's crossed the threshold. But he doesn't feel anything. He's hollow. A ball floating on the water. The others do feel something. The others seem to see something that he can't perceive. They look at him like he's wearing fancy dress without realizing it. They've said things, they've uttered words, some are even crying, but nothing's changed. The same sun, their neighbour Cristóbal's motorbike backfiring as usual as it climbs the hill, happy, alive. But there's Juno, who gives him another hug and says, 'Stay strong, mate.' And he bows his head and shakes it slightly, pretending to be affected or at least upset, more upset than he really is, pretending to keep it under control, pretending he's distressed and being brave. What would happen? What would happen if he went up to Mónica now and kissed her on the mouth? If he crossed the room and gave Trini's mother or Montse a hug and touched their breasts? Would he be forgiven? They'd say, 'Poor boy. No, Guille, no. Come, come with me, son.' And they'd lead him away with a hand on his shoulder like an old friend, the same as Juno now with his muscly arm around his neck. 'Come on, mate, you can do it.' That's what they say to Currito Cabeza when he's playing a match; that's how Juno, Loberas and he spur each other on when they're downing shots in JuanCa's basement. What about JuanCa? Where is he? Where's he got to? He'd like to ask Loberas. He wants to see the face he pulls when he hears his father has died. He wants him to see him like this, surrounded by all these people, all hanging on whatever he says or does. And who are they, those people, who are just arriving, who are they? A blonde woman, a man somewhat younger than her in a pastel-coloured jacket. Whose friends are they?

Jorge goes into his girlfriend's flat. The coolness of the air conditioning. The furniture seems to have grown inside the flat. They've taken vitamins. Everything's too big for these narrow rooms. The dark Formica of the cocktail bar jutting out from the wall like a monster that wants to take over the whole room, the coffee table, sofa and the two armchairs that accompany it all jammed in together. *Invasion of the mega-furniture*, from the moment he went in there for the first time Jorge always has the same impression.

'Sit yourself down and shut the door or we'll lose the cool air,' Gloria's father tells him. There's a circle of hair around his bald spot, his face is bloated, the white hair on his chest wants to scale his rough-skinned neck.

'No, we're going straight out, Gabriel,' Jorge replies shyly, closing the door.

'Sit yourself down, these women take for ever to get themselves ready. Where are you thinking of going in this *terral*, anyway? It's nice and cool in here, eh? That machine works a treat,' he says, pointing with his chin to the air-conditioning unit protruding over the top of a sideboard.

'Out and about. We'll go for a walk and then we'll have a drink or something close by. Yes, you can really feel the heat.'

'Sit yourself down.'

Jorge lifts one leg in order to climb over the arms of the sofa and the first armchair, which are rammed together. Then the other leg. He hates being short. He thinks Gloria's father asked him to sit down just to put him in this predicament. He sits down. Gloria's father grunts and looks Jorge up and down critically. There's a smell of cooking. Or is it his future father-in-law's breath?

'Aren't you working today?'

'Yes, now, I'll be working in a minute.'

Gabriel breathes heavily through his nose, opens his mouth as if he'd like to yawn but doesn't. He twists his neck to loosen it up or something like that. He was obviously asleep when Jorge called on the entryphone. Jorge imagines that Gloria had opened the door in her bra and panties. He's seen her wandering around the flat like that more than once. The sound of her bare feet and her rushing from one room to the next in her underwear. Sometimes with a blouse or a skirt in her hand, covering her chest.

'You're with your cousin, aren't you?'

'I'm what?'

'In the shop, with your cousin, working.'

'Yes.'

'And is he doing well, with the frames and that? Does that make enough for a decent living for all of you?'

Jorge shrugs his shoulders. It occurs to him to say that there aren't that many of them, just the three, his cousin, Pedroche and him, more when they hire Sedeño, and as well as the frames they install mouldings and doorframes, but what for? He looks at the big cocktail bar. A hippopotamus. Gloria's father looks at him out of the corner of his eye. The smell of cooking is coming from him, Gabriel. Stale cooking. Stews and basements. He remembers when he was a little boy and he and his brother Ismael used to go into the flooded basement in the military barracks where his grandparents lived.

Jorge's still thinking about that basement, trying to block out the question Gabriel's asking him for the second time, 'So, your brother, how's he doing, has he calmed down at bit or has he got into any more scrapes?'

'He's good, no, good.'

'Did you know that Ramírez's son knows him? You know, from Los Mártires?'

'Ramírez?'

'*Uh, Wamirey.*' Gloria's father is running his tongue over his back teeth, he's just been to the dentist. 'Yeah, Ramírez. The welder. Villanueva's friend.'

'Oh, you mean Toto.'

'Toto, yes, him, Villanueva. A friend of his, Ramírez.'

They hear Gloria's footsteps approaching. She appears. *The purple one, the top I like.* Her hair's freshly straightened, gleaming, like it always is after she's been to the beach, *it's the seawater*. Her top shows off her shoulders and arms, lightly reddened by the sun. Tight. *Her purple mountains my Everest, my Mulhacén.*

'Shall we go?' She also looks at her father out of the corner of her eye.

'Yes.' Jorge goes to stand up and his knees bang into the table.

'He gave him a good one.' Gloria's father turns to the side to get a better look at Jorge's face.

'Pardon?'

'Your brother, he gave him a hiding, a really good one. Ramírez's son.'

'Daddy, let it go.'

'I'm talking to him. Having a conversation.'

Jorge manages to get to his feet and places one leg over the arm of the sofa, straddling it.

'Didn't you know?'

Jorge's flummoxed, he doesn't exactly know who he's talking about.

'He did what? Who did you say? Who was it with? Toto?'

'Toto! It's hardly going to be with Toto!'

Gloria takes Jorge by the arm, tugs at him.

'Hang on,' says Jorge, losing his balance between the sofa and the armchair.

Gloria looks exasperated.

'I was going to fall over!' Jorge says by way of apology, planting his leg on the other side. Terra firma.

Gloria goes out into the corridor, saying, 'Sunglasses!'

'Me, I'm pleased with how mine have turned out. José Manuel in the Military Academy and Gabriel working over in Mexico.'

'Yeah.' Jorge dreads the conversation about his future brothers-in-law. Hearing Gloria rummaging in drawers and faffing about trying to find her sunglasses he tries out a counter-attack.

'The one for junior officers, is that right?'

'*Ib de cadamee swat matter.*' Gabriel's exploring his molars again. He untangles his tongue and repeats, 'In the academy, that's what matters. Wearing stripes. The first ones are the important ones, the rest of them will follow. Stripes. I should have re-enlisted myself.'

'Yeah.'

'And Gabrielito's about to land a contract in Miami, on TV. He's really made it big. He'll make us all rich.'

'Do they still do that sort of thing?'

'What sort of thing?'

'Soaps and stuff, and cartoon strips with photos, isn't that what your son used to do?'

'No.'

'Photos like a cartoon strip and then they put the words in bubbles, like in the cartoons . . .'

'No, no.'

'Really?'

'To hell with that, that's what he started out with. Years ago.'

'Oh, I thought . . .'

'No, no.'

Gloria's footsteps echoing in the corridor, purple top appearing from the beyond.

'Ready.' She's wearing her sunglasses on the top of her head, leaving her forehead bare. *She looks like a real tart like that, a bit like Vane.* 'Let's go, then.'

'All that stuff was years ago.'

'Daddy, we're off now.'

'That was when he first arrived in Mexico. These days . . . I'm telling him about Gabriel, about the Miami contract.'

'Yes, I know,' says Gloria impatiently.

'You know, but he doesn't, I'm telling him now, and what you said about the photo-soaps, that was just at the beginning, when he was starting out.'

'Yeah, Gloria told me. He did modelling and all that funny stuff.'

'No, no. He didn't do modelling, he did some auditions. It wasn't modelling and that's not funny stuff, anyway, what made you say funny stuff? It's not just the girls who do it. But now he's going to be on TV, this programme, it's going to be a massive hit.'

'Daddy.'

'For crying out loud, girl! You sound like your mother.'

Gloria folds her arms, sticks out her hip, twists her neck around. She stands there in a statuesque pose staring towards the hideous cocktail bar, or maybe she's looking at the kind of niche where there's a framed photograph of the aforementioned Gabriel, fair haired, affected, with a bow tie, foulard and a quiff. In an adjacent niche there's the other brother, sporting a military beret and a furrowed brow.

'OK then, bye for now.'

Gloria unfolds her arms, pulls her top down (her breasts surge up from the purple depths like two radiant buoys) takes a couple of steps, and she's there already with her hand on the doorknob, flicks her neck (nearly breaking it) to reposition her hair and opens the door. A spectacular wave of heat infiltrates and charges into the flat like a drunkard, crashing into the cocktail bar, bouncing off the walls.

'And what I was saying about your brother, what he did to Ramírez's son, he'd better watch out because they're still talking to a lawyer, and he might get his come-uppance. No one should go around doing that sort of thing, and if they do they should pay for it. It's not right.'

'Yeah, OK, bye then.'

'Close the door, we're losing all the cold air. Close it.'

*

Céspedes's phone is vibrating insistently in his pocket. He drains the last sip of whisky, lets the ice gently burn his upper lip. Carole warns him.

'Summer pests,' she says. 'Aren't you going to answer? Is it fear or good manners? If it's good manners then don't worry, answer, better to get it over with once and for all and let them stop hassling you.'

'Sorry.' Céspedes bends over in the seat to get his phone out, at the same time pointing out his empty glass to a waiter, asking for a refill. 'I don't believe this bastard,' he says when he sees the screen.

Carole half closes her eyes. She lets herself sink into the restaurant's cosy ambience, the perfect temperature. Céspedes runs his finger over the screen. His monosyllable conveys reluctance, scorn, the desire to humiliate, provoke. Contained anger. The monosyllable is almost an insult.

'What?'

'Céspedes, it's Villaplana. Rafi.'

'What?'

'Sorry if it's inconvenient, but there's some information, I've got some information about that deal, and I can assure you it's important, you should take it on board before you make a decision, and it could be really good news for us . . . Céspedes? Can you hear me?'

'Yes, I hear you, I can hear everything, I can even hear the coins tinkling in your pocket.'

'Ah, OK.' The tinkling sound stops, and Villaplana's tone of voice becomes firmer, he tries to sound more dignified. 'Well, to cut to the chase, what I wanted to say is that I've found a geologist, an expert who can draw up some reports that support the transaction.'

'A geologist?'

'Yes, an expert professor in –'

'And why would we want a geologist?'

'He's a professor who's worked in Israel, at the university.'

'Who?'

'Ruiz Sinoga.'

'What?'

'How do you mean?'

'What are you saying?'

'Ruiz Sinoga.'

'José Damián?'

'I beg your pardon?'

Carole opens one eye. Sweet Polyphema observes her Galateus with a mixture of curiosity and censure. Céspedes makes an effort to lower his voice.

'What the fuck are you on about?'

'Do you know him?'

'You mean Fernando Arcas's friend?'

'I don't know who that is.'

'I do. Him and his friend.'

'And?'

'And what?'

'Yes, I mean what's he like, the one I told you about?'

'You're a pain in the arse, Villaplana.'

'Céspedes, what's up? A geologist can draw up a report on the land, can't he?'

Carole now opens both eyes. She leaves them half open. In spite of everything she likes the sound of the ice cubes that the waiter's dropping into Céspedes's fresh glass, and the liquid pouring over the crystallized water.

'OK, so what's wrong, then?' Villaplana asks, unsure whether to be haughty or concerned.

'Do you really think Sinoga is someone whose palm you can grease and then everything's sorted?'

'There's a proper way to discuss things. I'm not some country bumpkin, Céspedes, don't get the wrong idea about me.'

'Of course not. You're a suave individual. I'm sure you won't turn up at his office at the university with a couple of hookers or throw a brown envelope on his desk. You've got class, but it seems you don't understand that some people also have principles, and they live up to them.'

'You, for example?'

'I'm not talking about me. I'm talking about the people you mentioned. You know? You're, I mean, you could be a nice guy, Rafi, to have a few drinks with, a bit of chat, but that's it. That's all. If these are your big ideas, don't move away from your neighbourhood or your hotel and just stick to scheming with your suppliers and taking a nice skim off your employers. But save your story for your father-in-law.'

'That's enough, Céspedes. I'm offering you an opportunity.'

'Thank you. But let me tell *you* something.'

'What?' Rafi Villaplana tries to mimic Céspedes with his monosyllable.

'You can stick your opportunity where the sun don't shine.'

Céspedes cuts the line and throws the phone on to the tablecloth. Carole observes him from the other side of the table.

'A friend of yours?'

'A very close friend.'

'I noticed the affection.'

'Yes, I suppose you did.' Céspedes lifts the fresh glass of whisky to his lips. He takes a sip, trying to make the whisky wash away the bile.

He takes a sip and he wants to believe that the whisky, Carole's sarcastic look and the relaxed atmosphere of the restaurant are the only tangible reality, something much more solid than his previous life, lost down an enormous drain. The telephone conversation he's just had is a distant residue of that other life. Seaweed dredged from the sea floor, washed up on the shore and rotting in the sun.

Carole flicks her head. Her hair falls over one shoulder, and she asks, 'What now? Where are you going to take me now, oh man with no compass?'

'Now?'

'Are there trains going anywhere else?'

Carole sits there, observing him. She looks like she feels sorry for him. A lost dog she's given something to eat, and now she'll have to send him on his way. Céspedes picks up on where that look is coming from. *No, there are no more trains, you already know that.*

That solid world, the whisky, Carole, the restaurant, a world that will last barely a few more hours. That's what he knows. He's on the other side of it all. There may be a passageway, a crack, some way of getting back to the former world. But just the idea of doing that, the image of his home, his office, his secretary, his wife, fills him with despair. It's better to finish his drink slowly, better to end his time with Carole. Here and now. It's a point in time on one day at the beginning of August. Nothing more.

This is the point in time on one day at the beginning of August. Even though Jorge and Gloria are walking in silence along the shaded side of the street they can still feel the heat of the asphalt burning through the soles of their trainers. As if they were walking over hot coals. They get to Calle Bisbita, go out into the sun, into the small open space with the palm tree. Jorge takes Gloria by the hand to cross the street. She shakes herself free.

This is the point in time on one day at the beginning of August, and Gloria asks Jorge why he had to mention her brother to her father, all that stuff about the photos and whether he was a model, knowing it would wind him up. Jorge shrugs and says, 'I don't know.' This whole labyrinth, all these dead ends that his girlfriend carries around in her head. He keeps schtum. What the fuck does he care about her father, always on about his kids, that semi-pansy in Mexico who's now saying he's going to Miami to carry on poncing about, and the other moron who thinks he's Rambo's cousin.

They get to the benches, a bit of shade. They sit down. The purple top is stretched over Gloria's breasts, and that's more than enough for Jorge to convince himself not to say what he's thinking, and he bites his tongue; that's why he's here late in the afternoon one day in August. Out of charity. He takes hold of Gloria's small fleshy hand again and leans towards her. He tries to kiss her on the lips. He only manages to brush his lips across the scar at the corner of her mouth. He smells that shower gel, that freshness which, when it blends with Gloria's skin, creates a scent that disturbs him and makes him remember her taste and smell those times when he's been on top of her, with his mouth buried in her neck and her shoulder and her hair. The same thing happens with that scar, that pale streak that accentuates the expressions of scorn or displeasure that she makes with her mouth, which reminds him of the times she moans and shuts her eyes, and it's her closed mouth, the scar, that reveals all her sensuality and pleasure, all that exuberance that she does her best to swallow, to keep inside her body, choking, doubling over. A monster inside her body that shifts her bones out of place and leaves her exhausted. Soft, submissive and briefly not herself.

And now she's here beside him, flustered, set hard in one of her silences, lost in the depths of her inner self. Her scent floating in the air like a buoy on the waves, her shoulders, her thighs tightly squeezed into her jeans, her feet with toenails painted a deep blood red peeping out between her sandal straps.

Her shoulders and her voice are shaking because Estefanía Villaplana has appeared out of a nearby doorway and has told her something about a concert, something that the two of them should have spoken about days earlier, Jorge gathers. The pair of them laugh. A laugh that Gloria saves for other people. Something Jorge's not allowed these days, he doesn't know why. Estefanía keeps her distance. She's got a pretty mouth. She's standoffish and shy, and she lingers there in no man's land, neither coming nor going. For the nth time she says, 'OK, I'll give you a call,' and then she raises her hand and, finally, off she goes. Shoulders tense. Short steps. The sun swallows her up. And Jorge says to himself, it's that girl's brother who's fucking my mother. He wonders if she knows. If she knows then Gloria must know, too, and he wonders what's hidden inside her head, which is now so close to his. It will all change; he'll find a way through that labyrinth. And he's the last person to want to talk about the business with his mother.

Gloria breathes noisily in through her nose, as if she were drawing a line under something. Who knows what private chapter. She takes a packet of Marlboro out of her back pocket and removes a spliff, a misshapen white cylinder between her short fingers. She smiles at Jorge. He looks into her eyes, a reflection of the sun and eyelashes in a pool with green flashes. Yes. Promises back on track, oxygen freely expanding once more throughout Jorge's body, not so taciturn now, he gets out his Bic lighter (red, like Gloria's nails) holds it to the end of the spliff that's hanging out of the lips of the girl he loves, presses the blue button and the obedient flame burns the paper, the strands of tobacco and the small lumps of hashish, so close to that scar, so close to the promises held by that afternoon in August.

The scent of the hashish, Gloria's scent, her lips around the misshapen cylinder and then a thin waft of smoke unfurling, barely visible, from her slightly open mouth. A gentle breeze of that lazy, overheated, asthmatic air rustles through the top branches of the palm tree beside them, making a soft noise like a soothing wave of happiness. Jorge knows that peace has been restored and, along with peace, the prospect of taking Gloria to La Kangoo bar and feeling the texture, the softness, firmness, rebelliousness of those breasts in the palms of his hands, both outside and inside the purple top. He knows he will see Gloria's eyes misted over with desire, the despotic scar tensing, that he'll have Gloria's tongue in his mouth and Gloria's mouth and tongue going down towards his groin, sucking and licking while he fondles her freshly brushed hair, the heat from the back of her neck, that dark field of wheat.

And with slightly trembling, expectant fingers he takes the spliff from between her steady fingers and puts it to his lips and inhales. Heat and a knot in his lungs. The promise, Gloria's smile.

And it's there, on that bench in the shade, in that scorching heat as an August afternoon rolls by, that Jorge, Gorgo, Ismael's unfortunate brother, the sleeping Amelia's younger son, notices El Tato coming around the corner, making a feint as he dribbles with an empty Coca-Cola can and, following slowly behind him, Nene Olmedo, spoiling El Tato's careful control of the can. 'Nene,' says Gloria and takes another drag. Her eyes are already shining, slightly reddened, when El Tato stops in front of them and says, 'Gloria, how's it going, gorgeous. Hey, have you met Nene?' Gloria smiles and dips her head, as submissive as a fairy-tale fawn.

And Nene Olmedo arrives, a few paces behind El Tato. Savannah lion. Wolf of the forest. And he sizes up Tom Thumb Jorge, the beautiful Gloria, the weight of her tits in that purple top, the golden tan on her shoulders flowing down her arms like a gentle waterfall and, he assumes, also over her stomach, thighs and back.

'Fancy some?' says Gloria, stoned, stretching out her almost perfect arm with the spliff held in a pincer grip. 'Obviously,' El Tato replies, and he takes hold of the burning spliff in his rough paw (brown fingers, nails battered by several days' dirt and grime) and lifts it to his dark burgundy lips, wedged between a scraggly moustache and a ragged goatee. He swallows, holds and speaks from inside his chest. 'Weak,' he says. And holding out the half-finished joint to Nene Olmedo, he asks Gloria with his eyes if he can invite his friend to share in the treat.

'Of course,' she half whispers with a frown, taking it for granted that the mild drug is common property. And Nene Olmedo, in a black T-shirt, scrawny arms, all nerves and tendons, takes the spliff and gives it a short, sharp, professional toke. Fast and furious, a self-definition. He hands it back personally to Gloria, leaning over more than necessary, deadly serious, with the tip of his tongue poking out between his thin lips as if removing a strand of tobacco.

'You're José Manuel's sister,' Nene says, and it's an assertion rather than a question. By way of reply, Gloria lifts the now softened and discoloured spliff to her lips and takes a deep drag (a deep drag for her), looking Nene Olmedo straight in the eye, and it's then that Jorge, ignored by everyone, intentionally declared invisible by Nene, moves his hand into his girlfriend's (and the intruder's) field of vision and takes the overheated butt between his fingers. Even then he doesn't merit a glance from Nene.

It's El Tato, a second-division player, who suddenly notices him, identifies him and says, 'Jorge, what are you up to? That resin's OK, but do you want to try something stronger?' And Jorge rolls his eyes like an underworld pro, patronizing. 'Obviously.' And so he's blessed with the charity of a sideways glance from Nene Olmedo, who rolls up the already rolled-up sleeves of his short-sleeved T-shirt, right up to the arm-holes, and turns to ask the (now floating) Gloria, 'And is José Manuel back on leave soon?' And, her scar tensing up and her lips undulating like the arms of an Arabian dancer, she says, 'I don't know. He never says anything. He turns up one day and disappears the next, just like that.' 'That's his style,' Nene Olmedo agrees, placing one foot on the bench, right in the middle of the space separating Gloria's thigh from Jorge's.

And this is the point in time on one day at the beginning of August that the *terral* is now lord and master of all it surveys. It's in control of people's heads, gaining access through their pores, their ears and any other open orifice in the body of any human being, beast, machine, house, door, crack, window, gap, wound or running sore. Everything in its path is dried out, blazing, who can say whether more alive or dead. Disturbed, disrupting in the way that fires disrupt mountains, streets, buildings, awakening and disorientating people's minds.

And so Dr Ana Galán gets out of her friend and colleague Quesada's car, walks across the crumbling asphalt, goes up the steps, not knowing whether she's climbing up the scaffold or coming down from it, closely followed by Quesada's shadow, puts her key into the burning-hot front-door lock to her house, a widow now, a widow for the first time she enters the deceased man's house, the dead man's life, the remains of the shipwreck or the booty of liberty, the coffer still sealed. She goes in and comes face to face with the funeral crowd, the chronic frenzy of a wake, the unexpected grimaces of grief when they see her. The word has spread, the news of death and disaster has done the rounds, although nobody actually knows the circumstances. Only grief flows back and forth like a misty substance and sometimes like a corrosive liquid.

A foot, an old Nike trainer with no laces, that's the flag that infantryman Olmedo has planted between Gloria and her boyfriend Jorge. His foot, his leg, tight jeans almost sewn into his bare ankle that's tanned, almost black, twice as bony as Nene Olmedo's bony face and bony stare. Bony and sinewy like street dogs, the ones that always understand what's going on a few tenths of a second before everyone else. Jorge is completely shut out. Gloria's purple top is now like a stab wound in his chest, like his girlfriend's naked arms, like her bright, velvety eyes or the scar that now seems soft, floating on the surface of her skin and her lips.

Ana Galán's glistening eyes search for her son in the midst of all the people who have invaded her home. Among the pained expressions she spots her brother Emilio, feels and represses disgust at the sight of him talking to Montse, overcomes the knock-back and heads towards him, and before he can give her a hug she asks, 'Where's Guille?' 'Upstairs, in his room.' And, as she hugs her brother, she opens one eye and sees Montse with her face contorted in grief, almost on the point of weeping *and she's the one who almost broke up his family and got him turfed out on the street without a job, and him risking everything for a bit of pussy, for one he liked more than the one he already had, like Dioni after an arse or a dick, dragged along, dead, stop thinking about it.* She can think about vengeance another day. For now Guille is the focal point of her grief.

'They're dropping like flies in this heat,' Julia Mamea hears someone saying behind her in the hospital car park. She looks around and spots two auxiliary nurses, one of them chubby, her arms separated from her body like the wings of a duckling learning to walk, the other skinny and long legged. They disappear into the maze of shiny, baking-hot cars. Julia looks up and sees the grey building. It beams reflections from its windows like battle cries. Dioni's corpse lies in its belly. The enormous shredder is set in motion. Tomorrow the crematorium. She gets into her car, which has already been idling with the air conditioning on. The temperature's now bearable. She looks at her phone again, runs her thumb over the screen. She's tempted to send another message to Céspedes. Bastard. She drops the phone on the passenger seat, releases the handbrake. She has to go to Ana Galán's house. Beneath the plaster cast there's a wound. And when Ana decides to take off her armour she'll probably need her there. She knows it won't be today or tomorrow, but it's better to go and see her, to let her know that she'll be there when she's needed.

The streets are deserted, and on the other side of the glass Father Sebastián Grimaldos observes the alleyway, the wall of windows and blinds, the bleakness of an empty city *in the hands of God*, and he compares himself with a fly that has landed on the window beside him, motionless, exhausted after trying in vain to get out through the glass *soon it will try again and start buzzing, and maybe I'll kill it.* The fly, his contemporary, *the two of us co-existing at this moment in time in eternity, in this same place and this same instant within the immense expanse of time, brothers in arms, absurd thoughts with the heat and time of day muddling the mind, that man calling to claim back his wife's donation, that poor madwoman, watches, jewels, envelopes, banknotes, when I was in the seminary I thought about the missions, and the missions came down to this, a sad alleyway one afternoon in August, the supreme test I could be put to, so like the void, hounded by that crazy woman, the confessional can also be a fortress under siege, we're persecuted there, too, and it can also be a prison cell, she flung herself to her knees making the whole confessional shake – Moby Dick – and she told me, 'I have sinned, Father, I have wickedly sinned against the sixth commandment,' and she told me, before I could even ask her, she told me that she'd been thinking about having a child with me, ever since she came to my first mass she'd thought about it and wanted it because that was the natural path and also the quest for a pure being, our child, she said in a whisper, illiterate suburban enlightenment, my God, and as if that wasn't enough, I tried to make her stop talking, that was my duty, but she kept saying that she knew it was impossible, that she knew but she wanted to confess it because it was something that pained her deep inside and she felt a lot of pain and at the same time she wanted it and she was always going to want it and that's why she was seeking comfort or a cure and that as well as the innocent desire to see a child born of her womb and the seed of a pure man her body was beyond her control and pleaded with her to satisfy that thirst, it demanded it, however it was achieved, poor madwoman, and she said that in the bath, 'In the bath, Father,' she said, 'in the bath I use the handle of my hairbrush to satisfy myself, with my mind thinking about conceiving, Father, but I satisfy myself like that with the handle of my hairbrush, Father, thinking about and desiring what I shouldn't, what I can't have,' with her breath wafting through the grille, with the smell of her body and her monstrosity, refusing to obey me, refusing to shut up, 'Father, forgive me, forgive me, it's a torment for me as well, I'm a slave to this demon, it won't let me go, however much I implore it, and I get tempted to punish myself, but you're the only one who can help me,' what a crazy idea, coming to a church when she should have gone to see a psychiatrist, to a lunatic asylum, and she's carried on like that ever since, although at least after I threatened her with not being able to hear her confession I managed to get her to leave out the details, not to tell me about hairbrush handles and all the stuff she calls 'dirty things', for all that the child, 'our child' as she calls it, is a desire that assails her, an impossible desire, at least she recognizes that, 'platonic' she says, 'platonic', the worm she must have inside her digging tunnels in her brain, the poor pain-in-the-arse lunatic, it's all so sad and all so nearly comical like that other woman confessing to me that she masturbates with a stick blender, and me speaking from deep in my chest trying not to burst out laughing, she'd discovered the advantages of the gadget's vibrations and she'd lean against the worktop with the blender between her legs until the attachment caught her skirt and tore it to pieces and almost sliced through her femoral artery or something like that, luckily she only had a few superficial cuts, so she said, and from then on she did it without the steel attachment, just with the gadget's main handle section, this was her 'intention to reform':*

taking off the attachment with the blades so she could masturbate with it wedged between her thighs standing up in the kitchen grasping the sink, and she felt remorse, she said, lots of remorse, or that other lunatic who every time there's a crime reported in the paper thinks he might have committed it but he can't remember, and he comes in full of repentance, Lord above, this is my parish, this is my mission, what I thought of in the seminary as a long road to redemption, this is what it was, this is where my dreams of the apostolate have ended up, these are the sheep of the Good Shepherd, my consolation, so who can blame me if I see Lorena, make love with her, try to hold on to a bit of life and humanity in the midst of all this nothingness, in which I'm beginning to see my fellow men as shop dummies, bowling pins to be knocked flying by some dark ball, and I can't step through the glass that cuts me off from the world either, all I have is those afternoons with Lorena, only those times, and the peace and reward of a few grateful parishioners who believe in me, in what I say, in what they said to me, yes, this is my parish and this is my flock, truly, God is the least of my worries.

'This dope is much more powerful.' That's what El Tato said as he passed the joint to Jorge, and that's what Jorge is repeating now, 'This really is powerful,' as he tries the new spliff made by El Tato's own hands. He wants to ingratiate himself with El Tato, and he also wants to make his mark with Nene Olmedo, who's still on his feet, coming and going, pacing around an area of four or five square metres of paving stones, like a caged animal, placing his foot on the bench between Jorge and Gloria, twisting his neck to loosen it up, taking hold of Gloria's hair and lifting it to his nostrils. 'Your hair smells good, baby, it smells like jelly babies only better,' he tells her, and Gloria, to the delight of the sidelined Jorge, who has been wondering whether he should intervene, snatches it back from him, snatches back her own freshly washed hair from his hands and glares at Nene Olmedo, who smiles, feline, alley cat, and carries on looking at Gloria, whispering something, humming something to himself, with his picaresque smile, confident that he's got her in the palm of his hand, and El Tato saying, 'Great stuff,' passing around the joint, the third or fourth one, great stuff.

Nene Olmedo looks directly at Jorge for the first time and says, 'You're such a lucky guy,' and Jorge, unsure whether it's because of those words or to prove that he was able to infiltrate the universe of someone almost legendary like Nene Olmedo, a friend of the Dalton gang, experienced in holding up banks, or at least, in bag snatches and police cells, retorts with the confidence of a film star, 'That's no lie, bruv.'

And that, along with the excessive heat and a porosity that makes everything volatile, and a belief that Gloria is hot stuff but belongs only to him, along with the friendly banter from El Tato, leads Jorge to loosen his tongue and start blabbing. He blabs about the day's big event, not about his brother Ismael and how he cut up all the curtains in the flat into equilateral triangles, but about Pedroche and how his wife battered him on the head with her boot and left marks all over his face and his bald pate. He laughs, Jorge laughs about what he didn't laugh about this morning as if he'd only just heard the news, as if he were seeing now for the first time Pedroche's swollen, bovine face with the sticking plasters, watery eyes and half-closed eyelids. 'Fucking hell, all he needed was a cowbell, one of those big bells they put on cows. What an arsehole.'

And El Tato laughs. 'His wife? You mean his missus gave him a hiding? What's wrong with the guy? That's well bad.' Jorge laughs, laughs until the tears roll down his face, doubled over on the bench. Shaking his head, trying to say more, breaking out into laughter again as El Tato looks on expectantly and Nene Olmedo looks on in scorn, mumbling to himself, 'Snotty little brat.'

And that's when he spills the beans. That's when Jorge lets it out that this nobody he works with is married to a lunatic who's given the local priest all the jewellery she had in the house, her rings, her chains, everything she and her family had, not to mention a whole wad of cash, she went off her head and gave it all to the local priest, and when her husband asked her what the fuck have you done she goes and takes off her boot, she's wearing boots in this blistering heat, and then she gives him some, bish bash bosh, with her boot in his face and on his nut.

'And the guy let her do it?' El Tato asks, genuinely perplexed. And just the image of Pedroche getting hit with a boot makes Jorge speechless once again, little Gorgo, and he doubles up once again on the bench, and he bumps against Gloria who, after laughing a bit, is now looking at him and feeling uncomfortable. Jorge half sits up, shaking his head, looks at the floor and bursts out laughing once again and finally manages to say, 'No.' Just one word before another cackle, dribbling, half choked, and then he says, 'The guy was driving,' and then he's overcome by another laughing fit, and El Tato laughs, too. Nene Olmedo looks on open mouthed. He's no longer restlessly pacing up and down within those few square metres around him.

Dr Galán hugs her son, pressing him against her body, and her son, frightened and all his confidence gone, lets himself go with the current down an unfamiliar river.

'Until he stopped the car, she kept on hitting him until the car stopped, they were in the car driving along, and she took off her boot, and she's taller than you, Tato, she must be at least one eighty, or she looks like it in her boots, and he's as short as me, and she started hitting him, not shouting at him or saying anything, she just takes off her boot and bish bash bosh, fucking hell, hilarious.' El Tato looks at him with his eyebrows raised. 'Fuck me!' he says. 'They could have been killed in the car, just as well the guy with everything kicking off managed to pull over and get out and run off, fucking hell, what a scream,' says Jorge, his laughing fit now apparently under control.

'What a fuck-up! But what happens now? Does the priest get to keep it all? What are these people like?' says El Tato. Jorge sniffs, wipes his mouth, suddenly feels the renewed presence of heat. 'No, no way,' he replies. 'So the priest's cool?' El Tato asks. 'He's going to give it back to my cousin's partner, he's had a word with him, he's cool.' Jorge reaches out his arm to El Tato, who's holding a fresh joint, and now Nene Olmedo's interest is piqued, and the joking and playing with the girl's hair that smells like jelly babies and her tits and all the rest of it is over, all that stuff is always going to be there, not like the jewels and the cash belonging to the chump they're talking about.

The tone of Nene Olmedo's voice, just the tone, is still one of mere curiosity when he asks Jorge, 'And the cash, how much did you say it was, how much did she give the priest?' 'A whole wad of cash.' 'A whole wad. How much?' Jorge feels an intense but passing wave of nausea, and he improvises, exaggerating so he can carry on feeling important, without paying attention to Gloria or understanding why she's digging her elbow into his ribs. 'Three thousand euros, more or less, probably more.' Nene Olmedo stares at him, as hard as Gloria is staring at Nene, and now he's the one reaching out his arm for what's left of the spliff.

Guille is released from his mother's embrace. Neither of them is crying, and he thinks that something's amiss. That things shouldn't be like this. They're alone in his room, and he wants to escape. He wants to run away before she starts talking. He doesn't want to ask, and he whispers, eyes fixed on the floor, 'Uncle Emilio's already told me it was his heart.'

'Where's he going to hand it over, where's this priest from, which church?' Nene Olmedo asks slowly. His eyes are also shining. Gloria says, 'We have to go.' Jorge now senses the danger. He looks at her. She's about to get to her feet. Nene Olmedo gestures with the palm of his hand and the gesture is sufficiently clear to make Gloria stop. She stays where she is, and Nene, stooping slightly, repeats the question to the befuddled Jorge, 'Where?' 'I don't know, he's from around there, the priest. I think it's the church on Ronda Intermedia, on Calle Unión, isn't it? But I don't know how he's going to hand the things over, maybe in the church, honestly, man, I've got to go to work, we've got to go.'

'Well, if you don't know, find out,' Nene Olmedo replies calmly. 'OK.' 'No, not OK, call him, call him up.' 'But how am I going to call him? What would I say to him? I can't.' Gloria stands up, 'Let's go.' And Nene takes hold of her hair again. Only now he doesn't lift some tresses gently to his nose and nor does he care if it smells of jelly babies or mint. He holds it in his fist, up in the air, and without pulling too hard he lowers his hand and makes Gloria sit down, following the direction of her hair. Jorge rouses himself, or tries to, from the dream he was dreaming, looks at El Tato hoping for support, some explanation, but all he finds is a blank stare of indifference.

'Call the guy, that arsehole,' Nene Olmedo orders. 'Me? But I don't know his number or anything.' 'Well call your cousin and get it from him.' Nene Olmedo narrows his eyes a bit, there's something that doesn't quite add up. 'So I'll ask him just like that, will I? "Listen where are you meeting this priest and what time?" He doesn't even know that I know about what went down with him, he told my cousin in confidence. If

I call him he'll say "What the fuck are you talking about?" and he'll have a go at my cousin and he won't tell me shit.' Fear has loosened Jorge's tongue, and Nene Olmedo has to hold his hand up in front of the windbag's face two or three times before he stops talking.

Nene takes a step back, curls his lips, does gymnastics with them, puckering them and then stretching them, then he says to Jorge, OK then, he should go to work and when he's at work he'll find out all the details, ask his cousin or whatever, but he'll find out where and when the priest is going to hand over the jewels and the cash to the arsehole, and then he'll call him as soon as he finds out.

Pale, nausea rushing through his stomach again at high speed, Jorge agrees, his hands pressed against the stone bench, heat entering and leaving his body. He agrees and says, 'OK.' He knows he's completely fucked. He holds back a retch, mouth full of saliva, forces himself to swallow, turns to Gloria and says, 'Let's go.'

It's Nene Olmedo who replies. 'No, she's staying with us until you call.' 'What?' says Jorge, stunned, thinking once again that he must be in the middle of a bad dream. 'Give me your number, and I'll call you so you have mine.' Nene has already formulated his plan. 'But what do you mean about my girlfriend staying here?' 'Give me your number, shortarse.' The feline creature that Nene Olmedo carries inside him appears again, and everyone sees it. Even El Tato, who decides to intervene and says to his friend, 'Let her go, we've got them tabbed. Gloria lives just around the corner in the street up there. Our friend here's going to be sensible, isn't that right?'

Jorge nods his head, not very vigorously because the nausea's rising up from his stomach again or coming down from his head, and it's gathering in his throat. His mouth fills with saliva again. Gloria looks at the floor. Jorge doesn't know if his girlfriend is angry or scared. Judging from the tension in her arms, those pure golden, burnished columns, she's angry. Nene Olmedo starts moving his lips back and forth again and finally says to Jorge, 'Give me your number.' Jorge recites the nine numerals; Nene taps them into his phone. A whistle comes from Jorge's pocket. 'OK, now you know what you have to do and what's coming to you if you call me *after* the priest has handed over the stuff; then we'd have a big problem with the girl, you and me,' he says, and he takes a long, thin screwdriver with the handle wrapped in tape out of his back pocket.

'Obviously,' El Tato echoes, like a notary, 'it couldn't be more crystal clear, and our friend here is going to do the biz, I mean we bump into each other every day around here, isn't that right, Jorge? And Gloria, too, and we know where she lives, where she goes, even where she buys her tampons, so everything's crystal clear.' Gloria and Jorge get up from the bench. The purple top, her prize-winning tits, the scar in the corner of her mouth like an old promise, all of it now is just a source of humiliation.

A prisoner of the *terral*, head bowed and fuzzy, Gorgo walks away, feeling wretched. The shiny head of hair gleams beside him. The paving stones symbolize the impossible hieroglyphic in which he's lost. Speechless, he and Gloria walk along the streets, low-rise buildings on either side. He knows that his silence and hers stem from two underground rivers that are leagues apart. Surface run-off is making his own river overflow. *I'm not going to lose her*, he thinks, dazzled by the flashes of light bouncing off windows and car windscreens. *I'm not going to lose her over this*, and he retches violently.

Guille rushes out of his bedroom. He leaves his mother behind. He doesn't want to know. They've never told him anything, and he's never wanted to know, that was the agreement, and it's still in force whether or not his father has died. They can keep their noses out of his life. They can stick with their own. His father's had a heart attack. It was in a remote place. After a few days away from home. He was on business, or he'd had a row with Guille's mother. That's their affair. He wasn't murdered. That's more than enough. Knowing why he was there, what they argued about behind closed doors or why they didn't talk to each other for days won't bring his father back to life. All that's over. His mother's not going to use him now to salve her conscience or whatever it is that she's thinking of. He's not going to take his father's place. His mother can forget about that. He doesn't have anything to discuss. Nor does his mother have anything to discuss with him. Before he left the room he sensed a danger greater than his father's death and the grief it might cause. A danger that he can't quite name, and what it is exactly he can't quite pin down, an animal out in the dark. Perhaps it's the danger of seeing his family, his own life, through other people's eyes.

SHE NEVER REALLY KNEW. THE DOWNTRODDEN WOMAN. These would be appropriate headings for the story of Ana Galán and Dionisio Grandes Guimerá. She never really knew. She guessed, she endured it and resigned herself to the inevitability of it.

She was a young doctor, attractive and talented. She had a brilliant career ahead of her. Disappointed in love. Nine or ten months previously she'd broken up with a boyfriend she'd met at university who was two years ahead of her and who had tried unsuccessfully to persuade her to take up nursing, as a career in medicine was not only unsuited to her intellectual ability but could also affect them as a couple and the harmony of their life together as a family.

So, having broken up with him, Ana was the mistress of her own solitude, which is the same as saying that she was the mistress of her own life. That's how she felt about it after breaking free from that inquisitorial boyfriend who for three years had tried to mentor her and watch over her every move and thought. She was beginning to feel that freedom was normal for her, and that was when that lawyer turned up at a dinner at a friend's flat. He was considerate. Reserved rather than shy. His thoughtfulness made him seem confident. Attentive. He always seemed to take a back seat, that's what Ana Galán thought right from the off, that night he was randomly seated beside her; whatever path the conversation took it was focused on her and her interests. He only talked about himself in response to direct questions, although it didn't seem to be a subject he found particularly interesting. Because he knew himself too well and because, although he was only three or four years older than Ana and most of the other people at the dinner, he seemed to have done a lot more than any of them could hope to do in the next few years. That was what his lack of self-centredness conveyed. Or that's what Ana Galán thought.

That's what she thought for several years. It all began in the summer. There was something in Dioni that her doctor boyfriend had lacked: a sense of humour, respect, intelligence. Although Ana wanted it badly, sex took a little longer to arrive than expected and was acceptable once it arrived. Gentle, lingering, uninhibited, sometimes bordering on transgression.

They were on the beach. *Masturbate* Dioni wrote on her skin with his finger. She was lying face down, and he whispered in her ear, 'Guess what I'm going to write on your back. It's just one word.' His index finger writing invisible letters down her backbone: M A S T U R B A T E. She smiled, her forehead resting on her arms, as she tried to guess.

'M, E.'

'No, not E.'

And Dioni wrote the letter with his finger on her skin again.

'M, A.'

'Yes.'

'M, A, L?'

'No.'

'F? Masfe . . . ?'

'No, it's not F.'

'T.'

'Yes.'

'Masta . . . Maste . . .'

Dioni slowly wrote the whole word again, and once more she tried to work it out. She turned her head around, surprised, when after deciphering the first six or seven letters she looked at him and said incredulously, 'Masturbate,' and she saw the look of heady desire in his eyes, Dioni bending over her and whispering in her ear, 'Do it.' She shook her head, looking around (a mature woman dozing, a couple fairly close by and a family more than fifteen or twenty metres away), and he kept on insisting, almost pleading, his lips brushing against her ear, 'Do it, no one will see you, just me, do it.' He was being driven mad with desire, and it was transforming him. It was beginning to drive her mad, too. 'Do it.' And without changing position, Ana lowered one of her arms, placed her hand between her body and the towel, closed her eyes and furtively began touching herself. He watched as the muscles in her arm tensed rhythmically betraying the movement of her fingers down below, he whispered in her ear, 'That's it, that's it, give yourself some pleasure, that's it.' The sound of the waves breaking and dragging away the sand, licking the seashore, the smell of salt and sun cream, the gentle breeze, his voice whispering in her ear, his lips brushing against her but never actually touching her, 'Go on,' his voice more insistent as the movement of her arm became more obvious and faster, when she frowned and opened her mouth revealing shiny saliva, her teeth, the whispering, brushing against her ear, 'That's it, that's it, let yourself come,' the feeling of his breath, and she let out a hoarse sigh and then one more, an inaudible moan, her eyes half closed, the world returning, her hand still underneath her body. She swallowed some saliva, opened her eyes and saw his face, smiling, coming up close to her, whispering in her ear, 'Whore,' and, for the first time since he stopped writing on her back, touching her, caressing her waist, kissing her temple.

Fantasies, imaginary threesomes, mild perversions. The occasional bit of fellatio in the toilets at a night club, sex toys replacing penetration, dinners with friends where Ana's knickers ended up in Dioni's pocket after he gave her a signal to take them off in the bathroom. Forays that gave way to periods of infrequent sex. The wedding and her pregnancy. The baby, Guille. The scarcity of sex almost turning into asceticism. Matrimonial routine. A few peaks when sex returned in a disturbing way.

Blindfolds, veils, fetishes, masturbation with the other one looking on, and then nothing. Sexually, Dioni had disappeared, and sometimes he also disappeared literally from that flat in Morlaco where they used to live. Then there were late-night meetings at work. Nights when Dioni came home in the early morning. Even then Ana Galán didn't suspect anything, no infidelity, no secrets. The prosperous life to which they were both becoming accustomed softened the edges of everything. The firm, consisting of Dionisio Grandes Guimerá and his two partners, grew in both prestige and profit. Dr Galán had already made her name as a talented young doctor. That velvety comfort was something that went beyond financial or social position, it cushioned the bumps and placed each of them where they supposedly belonged.

It was a comfortable life, and Dr Galán accepted Dioni's absences or quirks and put them down to traits in his character or how he led his professional life and the relationship with his partners and clients.

Not even when Dioni came back home early one morning just before dawn with his shirt all torn, a split lip and one eye closed, did Ana Galán suspect what her husband was hiding.

She'd heard him crashing about in the corridor and shutting himself in the bathroom. For a moment she thought he was drunk and that all the rummaging about was down to him trying to sleepily and clumsily find a painkiller to ward off the effects of a hangover, but, hearing the taps constantly being turned on and off, after a few minutes she decided to get up. She knocked gently on the door and said the obligatory words, 'Dioni, are you OK?' Then his thick voice behind the door, 'I'm fine, go to bed.' 'Open the door.' 'Go to bed.' 'Dioni, what's wrong? Please open the door. What's wrong?'

And this is how she found him. His right eye inflamed and a burst blood vessel, his lower lip split in two. The knot in his tie was all undone and his shirt ripped from the neck down to his waist. Dioni told her that two men had mugged him as he was leaving the office. He'd resisted, a little, 'but they were violent, they took my wallet and my briefcase. I found my briefcase on the corner. It was open and some documents were scattered on the ground, my wallet, too, but no money.' His voice was thick, and he was trying to play it all down. 'It was nothing, I'm going to have a shower. I didn't want to make a noise.'

She examined his injuries and suggested getting a few stitches in his lip. Dioni refused. Ana didn't even react when she saw that the blood was coagulated, which indicated that the injuries weren't that recent. When she asked him when it happened, what time, he replied it was around two. When he saw his wife's look of surprise, he apologized, saying he'd decided to lie down on the sofa in the office for a while, to rest up a bit, and that he'd fallen asleep. 'I'm going to have a shower. Don't worry, it was a scare, nothing more.'

'And what did the police say?' asked Ana, not wanting to go out of the bathroom and leave her husband alone again, not wanting to risk some other catastrophe. 'Nothing. I didn't call the police.' Seeing his wife's astonishment, Dioni added, 'Tomorrow, I'll make a statement tomorrow. I wasn't in a fit state for anything. These things make you depressed, that's the worst of it, you feel abused, humiliated, and, besides, I know what police stations are like at night.'

'But,' she argued, 'if they were lying in wait for you, if they've taken papers, documents, then they know who you are.' 'Don't start making things up. They didn't take anything from my briefcase. They must have thought there was money or something valuable inside it.' Ana went from concern to astonishment. Dioni, exhausted, reiterated his argument, seeing his wife refusing to move. 'They've taken my money, they've taken what they wanted, it was bad luck. Can I have a shower now?'

Ana still waited a few seconds before leaving the bathroom. She felt bewildered, trying to make a tiny bit of sense out of it all. And when he turned around and she saw the two or three bruises on his back and the dark stain, dried blood, on his underpants, she could hardly restrain herself from going back in.

She waited sitting on the arm of the sofa, smoking beside the window. Dawn was breaking. A pink light was running down the side of the building and making the windows sparkle with red. The bay was emerging out of the mist, its perfect outline becoming visible. It was a long shower. When she heard the shower shutting off, Ana quickly stubbed out her second cigarette and stood up. Dioni still took his time coming out, wrapped in a bathrobe. 'Can I look at you?' she asked, almost pleading. He refused with a gesture and said he needed to sleep. 'Please,' she said, 'your back, let me see your back.' Dioni turned around and let his robe slip down to his waist. Dr Galán examined a bruise at the height of his right scapula and some contusions a little further down above his kidney. She pressed the area carefully with her fingertips. 'Does it hurt?' 'Only a little.' 'I should take a look at it tomorrow, later today, at the hospital.' 'OK. If it's still sore I'll let you know.'

Dioni pulled his robe back up. Trying to force a smile, he said, 'Bad luck. It'll all be forgotten in a week or so. What bastards.' Ana didn't meet those words with the complicit smile that they seemed to require. 'I'm going to try to get some sleep, even if it's just for a while. In spite of those shits I still have to go to work tomorrow, today.' Dioni walked down the corridor as he was talking. Ana Galán made a big effort to get over that sort of embarrassment she never really understood and asked, 'What about the other stuff?' 'The other stuff?' Dioni replied turning around, proving that he had infinite patience, 'What other stuff?'

Ana turned her head and indicated the bathroom, she almost stammered, 'Your underpants, you had, there was blood, a stain.' 'It's not blood,' Dioni sighed deeply. He was silent for a moment and then carried on, forced to explain, 'When I was attacked everything went belly up, I went to pieces. What with them thumping me or because I was so angry, that's another reason why I went back to the office, my bowels let go, and I soiled myself a bit. Anyway, it's all terribly romantic. I really need to get some rest now.'

They went into the bedroom together. Ana Galán woke up after nine o'clock. Sheets of sun on the wall. The other side of the bed was empty. Dioni was on the balcony looking out towards the sea. The baby, Guille, was in his playpen methodically trying to behead a toy giraffe. Dioni's hair was wet. Another shower. *He wants to cleanse himself*, she thought. She asked him how he was feeling. She examined him closely. His eye with a burst blood vessel, his injured lip inflamed. A professional examination. 'No problems with your vision?' He forced a smile. 'No, doctor, I can see everything quite clearly.'

Quite clearly. When Dioni left Dr Galán rummaged around in vain in the dirty clothes basket. She looked in the wastepaper basket. All she found underneath the torn shirt was an empty tube of toothpaste and a toilet roll with no paper. *Has he hidden it out of embarrassment*? And she went into the kitchen. The rubbish. The bin was almost empty. The underpants had vanished into thin air.

Shall I ask him again? Ana Galán wondered, leaning over the balcony looking towards the sea. Silence. The breeze. *Why would he lie to me? Another woman, and that's why he was beaten up? Who was it? An accident, bad luck. They wouldn't be blood stains. He went to pieces because of the scare. He's not lying to me. He's not. He's never lied to me.* Rule it out. A bad night. Bad luck. Dioni's wounded pride, that's why he was being evasive, almost on guard. Men. Those simian instincts that are still a part of us. The females suckling the babies up in the trees and the males learning how to use clubs, strutting their stuff.

The incident was now above all suspicion. Wrapping herself up in a haze that diminished with the passage of time, becoming almost unreal. She was like that for a while until one winter's afternoon when she was passing the office that Dioni had set up at home she saw him with his back to her, looking out of the window as he was talking on the telephone. She was about to go in, but while she was still in the doorway she saw her husband's computer screen reflected in the mirror opposite. There was no sound, and a naked man was lying on a sort of rack in a squalid room, supposedly a dungeon; another man in a makeshift leather mask was sodomizing him. Ana looked at her husband again, and, on noticing her, he turned around and smiled at her without realizing what his wife had seen.

Ana went towards the kitchen, taking hesitant steps but with the dark feeling that the computer images had something to do with the attack on Dioni. Something to do with his life. Had she wanted to be blind to it? What was all that? What was going on, and what sort of person was her husband, what sort of family was her own family? Was it all a flash of intuition or a ridiculous idea? These were the shadows that began looming over Ana Galán. And she began slinking through a shadowy landscape full of uncertainty. She kept her mouth shut and blamed herself for her silence. Ana, the courageous woman who faced up to everything, the personification of self-possession.

That was the first discovery, when doubts started coming to the surface. And now, on this afternoon one day at the beginning of August, Ana thinks her son is going down the same path and fleeing, although he might not even suspect what he's fleeing from. A little ostrich. He rushes out of his bedroom and escapes out of pure intuition. There was no need, as Ana Galán was never going to reveal any secret to him. *Your father was crawling with ants*, she thinks as she watches him leave.

She's alone in her son's bedroom. When she half closes her eyes she thinks she can see ants. Ants crawling over ashen skin, twitching their almost invisible antennae on the sheet at the hospital, marching like diminutive robots over the stethoscope and defibrillator. Their food has gone. Dioni. She doesn't feel as though grief has overwhelmed her. She was prepared. But she does feel extremely tired. Much more exhausted than she thinks she has ever felt before. As a doctor, she puts it down to low blood pressure, not sleeping, the suffocating heat filtering through the open window in Guille's bedroom. The sea in the distance, too dark, too solid, and two isolated palm trees that must be just as tired as she is.

*

THE RUNNER'S DIARY

18 years old

BIRTHDAY AND WHO I WAS

I remember the day I turned 18 I was looking at my father. Perhaps he already had the worm inside him. Apart from the red rug, the fireplace that wasn't used (most likely unusable) and an arch that led out to the corridor, I don't quite remember all the details of the room (I do recall the fireplace because when I was small I used to sit there playing with my plastic toy soldiers, I made them climb up the walls around the recess, every brick turned into a ledge, every bit of mortar a cave, and in my imagination that was an enormous rock-climb and when the soldiers arrived at the top they would fight and they would always go over the side, I spent hours and hours squatting down in front of that fireplace, killing my soldiers and saving their lives). I don't remember the room well, but I do recall my father's face.

I can see every detail of his face back then (or at least, the face I think I remember). The skin of his cheeks had started to sag. A heavy curtain of flesh, a rough velvet (because of his stubbly beard) (when he was ill and he stopped shaving for several days his cheeks and his neck were like a field full of weeds and stubble, some bits frazzled by the sun and other bits still alive, straw, nettles, earth). He didn't smile, but neither was he serious. He went along with the little celebration that my mother had put together. It had occurred to her, the previous week or the previous month, that it wasn't every day that someone turned 18. I imagine that it must have been an important moment in her life. Ringing in the changes. Or discoveries. Or she thought so afterwards, looking in the rear-view mirror. That her life had changed that day. I don't know what she thought. It doesn't matter. That idea came and went over me like a cloud that doesn't produce any rain. But I did wonder back then what my father's 18th birthday would have been like. That man sitting over there.

Very different from my own, I knew that. A village near Valencia, neatly pressed trousers like in the photos I saw of him as a young man, white shirt, working since he was a teenager, confident, with his ridiculous sunglasses, standing next to those girls who looked as though they'd come straight from the hairdresser's (either because they worked there or because they'd been having their hair done with some heated contraption), all that. He and I are different both in appearance and in circumstances. But wouldn't he also have looked at his own father back then, when he was 18? Looked at him the same way as I did when I was 18? Sizing him up. Saying to myself, so you were someone who felt out of place, too, someone who had to elbow his way through, making space for himself? Otherwise they'd eat you alive. You're not so straight up and down and you had to learn the hard way. And there you are, still pretending. Or resigned. Defeated. Like everyone else, just surviving and riding the tide that sometimes propels you forward and lifts you up and at other times seems to want to drag you down to the depths. You're that boy. No sunglasses now.

I'd like to have seen a photo of his father when he was more or less the same age as my father was then, fifty-something. To imagine what my father could see or thought he saw if he'd looked at his father like I looked at him. If he saw his father as a man and not as his father. (By then my father was nobody, almost nothing, a link between his father and me. An errand boy. I still believed that I was the final link in that chain, not someone who, like them, had to leave a marker, an unknown message, a letter that no one had ever read and no one would ever read. It was just me. I was the purpose, I was the destination. Not an errand boy with a secret. An empty letter. A blank sheet of paper. An envelope with nothing inside. An envelope with a few grains of sand inside. I'm a messenger. We're all messengers.)

Now I know what I felt back then. It wasn't scorn or anger and certainly not hate. It was fear, or something like fear. Peering over a precipice (with the bones of everyone who'd thrown themselves off at the bottom).

Seeing my father sitting there. My sister and that friend of hers. My mother happy because of the birthday celebrations, basically worn out but pretending to be happy because she'd been planning the festivities for weeks or months. And my father looking around to see the cake arrive. In my mother's outstretched hands, like someone bringing an offering to the altar, like she must have seen them carry the cake happily to the table in some film (in the film they'd be in the living room in some enormous house with large windows opening out on to a garden with a freshly mown lawn). My cousin Andrés, Santi Cánovas (I used to train with him in those days, and it was through him that I later got to know Felipe Vicaría), *as well as my sister and her friend, those were the guests at the party organized by my mother. And me.*

Those days. My Munich trainers. Blue, with the white cross. They were a present from Santi, second-hand. The first spike in the toe of the right foot was stuck: you couldn't get it out, and the others should have been the same height, irrespective of whether you were running on a Tartan Track or a Mondotrack. I thought I could be an athlete, a proper athlete. The possibility was there anyway. The path wasn't barred. But it was fogbound. I wasn't like Santi or, later, like Vicaría or Ángel López or Azulay or Cortés. I was disciplined, I trained, I competed and I trained. But my discipline was different from theirs. I competed against myself. Not against the clock. Against myself. Civil War. Running, breaking my record, more running, breaking my record again, and at one specific point the war ended, I crossed over to the other side and then I was liberated, I was flying, I was no longer tied down. For a few seconds, sometimes for a few very long seconds, I escaped from it all, it was all a race, I was a race, the world was left behind, I crossed into another dimension. I was fast, much faster than the clock actually showed. I came first in my race. I could also be the one who never won. In my running dimension, only I existed, there was no one else around. I ran on a track along just one street.

I had an old photograph on the wall. Sebastian Coe wearing number 254 at the Moscow Olympics. He looks crazed in that photo. Not just because he'd won, not just because he'd crossed the finishing line, but because he'd also crossed the invisible line. Because he was on the other side. I wanted to cross that line. Occasionally I glimpsed it. And I wanted that line to appear in real life, too, not just on the track. If I couldn't cross it I could at least catch sight of it, know that it was there, and that I could run towards it against myself.

There was the other life. People like Cumpián, Padín, Sergio, El Mono who weren't into running. They went to university or were about to go, one or two of them had jobs. They used to drink, smoke, rebel. Without a cause. I didn't smoke, I didn't rebel. Sometimes I would drink. There was one night, in an olive grove, down some road. Sergio had taken his father's car without permission, I don't remember where we were going (a party or a village fair). We had a puncture, and we couldn't see a thing.

We got out. Sergio, Padín, Inmaculada, someone else. We were drunk. Sergio was laughing and trying to use the jack, sitting down on the asphalt. Padín was angry, the crickets, the stars, I was holding a bottle of gin and went off walking down the empty road. I threw the bottle into the distance, it made a dull thump on the soft ground, there were voices, laughter, Inmaculada calling my name questioningly, I left everything behind, clean air, just a murmur in the distance, I walked and my legs felt strong, and I began to jog, running gently on the tarmac, so gently, with such power, I ran without being aware of even a single atom in my body, I ran along the road, I ran along in the darkness, I was darkness, I was invisible, I'd disappeared, and I kept on running without breathing, floating, fast, the sound of my strides behind me and the sound was so soft that my strides seemed like someone else's, someone who was following me a long way behind, I cut through the night, I opened it up and became a part of it, a puff of air, the trees breathing, the sky's black lung, so fast.

They didn't find me. They didn't find me until hours later, when they were on their way back from the party or the fair, a bit lost. Inmaculada wouldn't speak to me, the others were asleep, Sergio was driving and laughing. He called me Loco, admiringly. It was the biggest compliment he could give anyone. Loco. It meant being different, with your own compass, indifferent to the path that everyone else was following. That was my place. I don't know when I realized that this could be my role, my disguise. The one who's different. I don't know if it was always like that or if it's a space I discovered in order to survive. And I've been in that space for a long time now. It seemed to be the right place for me, and since then I haven't stepped outside it. The odd one out. The liquid that finds it hard to mix. The disguise that separates you from the others, that distances you and without which you would now be naked. My cells have grown accustomed to it in such a way that they are barely able to mix, to combine as easily as the others do, the liquids.

I live in my capsule, beneath my skin and the membranes I constructed. I don't know when it all began, probably because of something insignificant, something that would seem insignificant to me now, because I was told off, or out of shyness. (Would my father have known before he died when the construction of the wall began? Would he have known there was a wall between us? Yes, it's possible that he at least knew that there was a wall, even if he didn't know why it was built, and it's also possible that he knew what material it was made of better than I did. There's no way my mother can know. Not when it started or why. Not even that a wall exists. She's not able to. She can't go down that road, it would be another failure. I'm a good person, that's the explanation, I'm innocent, I'm better. My sister doesn't care. Perhaps my grandmother is aware of something, she knows that I'm peering out of a window, that when I speak to them I'm peering out of a window, but that I'm living within those walls, that they can only glimpse a bit of me when I'm peering out and I'm speaking from the other side.)

Maybe that's why, because I'd chosen to distance myself a long time before then, I didn't tell my friends, Sergio, Padín, El Mono, that it was my birthday that day, or that my mother had organized a sort of party. Before I saw them I thought I was going to tell them, I was thinking about it on the way there, after I'd eaten my piece of cake, after leaving my father sitting at the table, I meant to have a laugh with them, tell them all about my mother's organized happiness, how ridiculous it had all seemed, but when I saw them I knew that actually I had nothing to say to them, because what happened behind those other walls, the walls of my home, had nothing to do with them, had nothing to do with them at all. It was the same as I felt the night I started to run through the darkness on the road among the olive groves and I was tempted to lift my arms up as I ran, to spread them out as if I were on a cross and to look up to the heavens with an expression of madness or joy, the same as Sebastian Coe in the photo I've still got in my bedroom, the one that watches over me when I'm asleep.

The night Julia took a ride in a taxi in between Céspedes and his friend Ortuño, maybe something between them changed, between Julia and Céspedes, that is. Or, at least, that's what she thought at the time.

Now, on this afternoon on one day at the beginning of August, Julia knows, and she's known for a long time, that she was mistaken and that nothing changed in that taxi when she opened her legs and gave in to Ortuño's desire, allowing his hand to slide between her thighs while she was kissing Céspedes. What she doesn't know is why, having just left the mortuary, driving through this thick and unhealthy atmosphere, she's constantly remembering that night now, as though it had some obscure connection with Dioni's death, with her friend Ana's cold grief.

Perhaps it's to do with the messages she's exchanged with Céspedes. Accepting that they've also run out of road. The other thing, the threesome that began in that taxi, doesn't have much to do with Dioni or Ana Galán. Her relationship with Céspedes didn't change that night either. She would have meant the same to Céspedes whether or not she'd allowed herself to be shared with Ortuño. She'd already been assessed. She would never occupy a different place in his life. Over and above the sex, she was his confidante, an archive of confessions, perceptions and loyalties deeper than those Céspedes could share with his wife. But the centre of Céspedes's life was elsewhere. Who knows where?

Julia had slipped into Céspedes's life as easily as slipping into water. Enveloped by that gentle resistance, a softness that tenderly squeezed and caressed. Walking out from the shore towards the horizon. No, nothing would have changed if she had closed her legs that night or pushed away Ortuño's hand. She didn't. She let herself go. She walked into the sea, into the warm water, the gentle waves. She parted her thighs slightly in response to his pressure, offering a minimum of resistance, testing the daring or desire of that friend of Céspedes's she had met only a couple of hours earlier. The taxi driver's eyes in the rear-view mirror. The taxi brought them to Céspedes's apartment.

Light from the street lit up the bedroom. Cars' headlights showed up on the ceiling in a kind of ellipsis that seemed to stop for a second and then suddenly disappeared tracing a diagonal line across the wall opposite the bed. They were all moderately restrained, by mutual consent. Céspedes went into the bedroom with her after he and his friend had taken off her blouse between them, lowered her bra licked both her breasts in tandem like a pair of well-behaved children.

Céspedes led her by the hand to the bedroom. His friend waited his turn in the living room. Céspedes reminded Julia about him as he moved around on top of her. 'He'll be along next,' he said. And Julia responded with a naturalness that made her more lecherous, darker, attractive. 'Of course.' 'He's going to fuck you, he's going to stick it inside you,' Céspedes whispered into her neck, and she dug her fingers into his fleshy back and accepted with a moan, 'Hmm, yes.' 'Do you like my friend?' 'Hmm, he's not bad.' 'Not bad?' Céspedes pressed the investigation further, taking his time, holding on, retaining the electric charge of ejaculation in his brain. 'Go on, don't stop, carry on,' Julia commanded. Céspedes lifted himself up, took his face away from the hollow of Julia's neck and looked into her eyes in order to pose the question, redundant but crucial, 'Are you going to fuck him?' 'Carry on,' Julia commanded, greedy, practised, focused on the present, suddenly distanced from the man's fantasy, 'Carry on, give it to me.' 'Tell me,' he asked, insisted, 'tell me.' Julia half opened her eyes, emerging from a distant dream. 'What?' 'Tell me,' he kept on asking, still writhing, slipping, inside her, on the fringes of the battle. 'Are you going to fuck my friend?' Julia consented with a sigh, almost a snort, half closing her eyelids, her eyes disappearing under water. 'Yes, yes, yes,' she said, drowning. 'Now?' 'Yes, yes,' and Julia's consent came out as a moan, doubling up, contracting into herself, trying to leave her body, contorted, lost and suffocated, opening her eyes a little, staring at Céspedes's face as if what she saw there was the face of an assassin, a madman, a stranger, until she seemed to recognize him, her muscles relaxed, and her limp, passive body continued to move languidly in response to Céspedes's thrusting, as he whispered to her. 'Now, he'll be coming in now, he's going to come and fuck you,' and Julia, regaining some mobility, ran her hands, her arms over Céspedes's back, trying weakly to pull him towards her, kissed his ear, his neck with a flicker of desire, a pale light reviving in her eyes, in her half-open mouth, swallowing saliva, revealing a glimpse of her teeth and she bit her lower lip, starting to groan again, gently, a little girl locked inside her.

And so, erect, voluntarily and with self-control, Céspedes pulled out, took a few disorientated steps about the room until he found a dressing-gown and left. When he got to the living room he made a signal to his friend, nodding towards the bedroom door. Ortuño passed him leaving a vacuum in the air and also an unanticipated pang of jealousy in Céspedes's stomach, an obscure tug that almost made him turn back on himself and stop his friend. He hesitated, Ortuño took another step, two more, three, behind him. Too late. His friend went into the bedroom, and Céspedes heard a whisper, Julia's soft voice and some words spoken by Ortuño that he didn't want to hear. The living room was lit up by lights from the port, by cars' headlights, the flickering glow of the whole city. *My life, that boat penetrating the sea's darkness, those torches glowing on the ink.*

Scarcely time to smoke a cigarette in front of the window, watching the stream of red and white lights along the Paseo de los Curas. Scarcely half a glass of whisky, and then he heard Ortuño bellow and then his voice, too loud, 'Wow, you're really good, babe, where did that bastard have you hidden all this time?' He was suddenly tempted to go and drag Ortuño out of the bedroom, but then came Julia's voice in a low murmur, whispering to his friend, the hint of a laugh, and a wave of dark, heady sensuality came over him again with a shudder. That laugh, that lasciviousness of Julia's was what led him back to the bedroom. And once again he crossed paths with Ortuño in the corridor, although now in the opposite direction. Céspedes avoiding his eyes, the other man smiling, unconcerned.

Ortuño, the one with the hollow eyes and the cruel mouth, Julia thinks now. She's driving up Paseo de Reding, Avenida de Príes, Paseo de Sancha. She's ignored the shortest route, letting herself be swept along by the merry-go-round of memories, deliberately delaying her next encounter with Ana Galán, who's now back at home, a widow, impenetrable. *Crafty Ortuño, who disguised his cunning by pretending to be thick, with a fake innocence, he'd give me little slaps after fucking, and I half suspect he didn't know how to show affection, quite the opposite of Céspedes, all nervous tension and electricity, too many volts, I know that now.*

'Your friend has been calling me trying to meet up,' Julia told Céspedes, propped up against the headboard of the very same bed several weeks after that threesome. Céspedes was putting on his trousers, his stomach powerful and hairy despite a clearly discernible flabbiness. He pushed his hair back from his forehead, his hairline receding on either side creating an acute triangle of hair, a hairy arrowhead. Céspedes stared at her for a moment, his jaw slack, and carried on getting dressed, calmly buttoning up his impeccable shirt. And it was only when he'd done up the last button and picked up his tie from the rocking chair that he asked her, 'And?' And Julia smiled, shrugged her shoulders. 'Just that. He's been calling me.' 'Yes, you told me, and what do you say?' 'Nothing.' 'Nothing? You don't say anything? You just hang up?' 'I tell him I can't, try to put him off. I wanted to tell you.' 'Do you want my permission or something like that? You want my permission, is that why you're telling me?' The smile withered on Julia's face. 'No, I'm just telling you. I don't need anyone's permission.' Now it was Céspedes who shrugged and started to knot his tie.

Bastard, Julia thinks as she drives along the street. On her right, in the spaces between buildings, she can see the seashore, people walking along the promenade in bathing costumes. Swarming in the heat, and she remembers the ants on Dioni's body, disorientated. The traffic light turns green, someone sounds their horn impatiently.

Julia started meeting up with Ortuño every now and then. It broke up the monotony and also brought something akin to warmth. Human contact, yes, and there was also something likeable, almost childlike, about Ortuño. Dull, clumsy and also tight fisted, but that was better than the coarseness of some men who seemed to be hiding behind a totally false persona. Conceited, in love with themselves, their tennis, their jet ski, their BMW or their Rolex (usually fake).

She didn't hide it from Céspedes, and Céspedes restricted himself to saying, 'Yes, I know,' when she told him that she'd seen Ortuño. She never found out what Céspedes thought about those meetings. The most he managed to add was that he hoped that the three of them could meet up again soon. And they did. When he called her to arrange one of these dates, Céspedes was laconic, informing rather than asking, 'And Ortuño will be there. OK with you?'

And they did the same as before. Apart from the scene in the taxi, they played out the same pattern as the first night, step by step. Julia sitting between Céspedes and Ortuño, Céspedes starting the session by leaning over her and kissing her as he undid her blouse, fondling her breasts and pulling them over the top of her bra, *the customs officer, the landowner who thereby granted permission to his guest, seated at the table of my tits.* And the other man obeyed, waited for the signal, licked and stroked until Céspedes whispered something into Julia's ear and they left their hungry guest there, waiting his turn while they fucked in the bedroom and Céspedes asked her the exact same questions as on the first night, 'Do you like that, are you going to fuck him, tell me, are you going to do it, and then you'll want more, then I'll come.' And she said, 'Yes, yes,' short of breath, excited, with her plaything Ortuño waiting to do his duty.

He'll never be as close as this to his wife, no matter how many pet dogs, daughters, business deals or houses they share, she won't have known this man like I do; he's more mine than hers, more profoundly mine than any of his other women could claim, thought Julia back then. Céspedes and her. And then everything that was beyond that. What nobody understood. On the other side of a deep river. It wasn't an idea with no substance. Céspedes had mentioned it on other occasions, when he confided in her his fears and desires, his secrets.

Desired, valued, satisfied. She and Céspedes. Enjoying the present. The present in a pure state, a voluntary renunciation of the future. Defying it, despite knowing that it, the future, would end up winning the game, defeating them both in one way or another. Each of them in a different way, perhaps more resoundingly for him, possibly also turning them against each other. But meanwhile they would dance to their own tune.

Now I know that the music's over, now the time has come, there's the sweet smell of putrefaction, open wounds, amputations. Julia does a ninety-degree turn, leaving behind her the sea and the tiny Calle Rafael Pérez Estrada, divided in two by a solitary tree, and starts up the Camino Nuevo. The first night that Céspedes and Ortuño brought her to that house they also made this turn and directed the taxi down this same street because it was the only route that Ortuño, an inexperienced driver, knew to get to his friend's house. Now Julia's destination is rather different, the home of Ana Galán, a broken woman, and her husband, a man who's slipped out of life by the back door. Under wraps, the same way as he'd lived.

Those ants, rooting around under his eyelids, disorientated by the desert-like chest, without a nest to guide them, appearing from behind or inside an ear, coming out of Dioni's hair and marching out from behind his neck, searching, maybe still gathering food, extracting it from that immense mine (were they eating, were they devouring him?), Julia tried to wipe those thoughts from her head, forget what she'd seen, Dioni moribund, more deathly than all the sick people she'd ever looked after who'd died in front of her, disturbed, relaxed, sleepy, calm, rebellious, shocked and stupefied. Better to leave it all behind, like those bad days she kept under lock and key that stayed in the hospital wards and corridors as soon as she got into her car and turned the key in the ignition. The afternoon, the sun, life, all those people walking up or down the hill on Camino Nuevo with beach chairs, towels, sandals, half naked, seeking shade from the trees, defying the *terral*, better to leave Dioni in his basement, close the doors, turn the key.

The first night they brought her to that house it was also summer. Those couples, married couples, stranded, open, bored, adventurous, playing at being bad. Pupils dilated, forced grins, glances weighing up the goods more than usually permissible. Insinuations, nervous jokes. A few predators pacing around outside the various groups. Maybe twenty people in all. Shortly after they arrived – Julia, Céspedes and Ortuño – a couple started to kiss in the corner of the large living room, the man (short with grey hair) slipping his hand down to her crotch, leaving it there, his hand cupped like a shovel, groping, delving into desire. The rest of them exchanging looks. Broken promise. The woman (taller than him with dark hair) after the man had lifted her dress enough to display her thighs and place his hand beneath her thong, took hold of his arm, made him remove his hand from that small nest of nylon and whispered something in his ear. The man turned to look at the people watching them, gave a wan smile and went off hand in hand with the woman to one of the bedrooms. A private affair. Murmurs of disappointment, a trace of laughter, the self-appointed stand-up comedian for the night doing an impression of some television comic, the path back to ordinariness left open but quickly cordoned off by the owner of the house, rushing from group to group and promising sexual nirvana.

The lights dimmed. A murmur rippled through the room and brought the majority of the guests out on to the terrace to watch as, down there, on the lawn, illuminated by the swimming pool's turquoise glow, a man was moving on top of a woman. Naked, the young, muscular man's buttocks rose and contracted, a worm crawling without advancing, moving incessantly on the same spot and, beneath him, a blonde mane of hair spread out like a puddle on the lawn, a mature woman, her legs rising up and clamping her *ephebos* around the waist, trapping him, stiletto heels moving back and forth over his buttocks, while the crowd observing from the balustrade held their breath.

Beside Ortuño a short, stocky individual ran his hand down the back of a woman who was leaning her head on her partner's shoulder. The woman smiled at the intruder, who lowered his hand and fondled her buttocks, she whispered something in the ear of the man who was with her, and he, looking at the man who was touching the woman, offered her to him, turning her around to face him. The man's hand then rose up to her stomach, running over the thin material of her low-cut blouse, the woman half closed her eyes, leaning back against her partner, who whispered something in her ear, provoking an ambiguous smile, while the guest undid her blouse and brought his mouth towards her dark, uneven, sad nipples.

Two or three onlookers gathered on that side of the terrace watching the impromptu trio. Julia, Céspedes and Ortuño returned to the living room with the rest of the guests. There, a woman in her early forties got up on a low table. She was blindfold, and she was gyrating in time to the music clumsily rather than sensually. She took off her clothes bit by bit, imitating a striptease from some supposedly erotic film. A small group was encouraging her. They fondled her, and it appeared that the game consisted of her guessing who the hand that was touching her belonged to. 'Bunch of idiots,' Céspedes whispered. 'She's hot,' Ortuño insisted, looking at the woman in her underwear who, in spite of the heat, was wearing a black suspender belt and flesh-coloured stockings. 'They look like support tights,' said Céspedes. 'She's hot,' insisted Ortuño. 'A bit sleazy, though?' Céspedes remarked.

Julia, in a green dress, her hair loose, walks slowly towards the table in the centre of the room, not the low one where the amateur stripper is gyrating, but a large rectangular table made of dark wood. On her way she undoes the zip down the side of her dress, stops and lets it slip to the floor where it remains crumpled with its emerald-green reflections, and she, in her high-heeled sandals and panties, also green, her back completely bare, takes a few more steps and stops next to a man who's been watching her from afar, tall, square headed, mature, watery eyes. From where Céspedes and Ortuño are standing it looks like Julia says something to the man, who follows her and watches as she places the palms of her hands on the table and waits for him.

Céspedes's staring eyes, Ortuño's half-gaping mouth, women stop smiling, the game of blind man's buff comes to a halt, the woman who's up on the other table takes off her blindfold to see why the room has fallen silent. The tall man kisses Julia on the neck, wraps his arms around her. Julia's hands are leaning on the table, offering her back to the man who has opened his flies, the music has stopped, Julia wiggles her hips, lifting them and the man penetrates her from behind, thrusting into her in a gradual accelerando, and her eyes are half closed, staring at the table, Céspedes and Ortuño moving closer among the crowd of spectators, Julia with her panties pulled down but still wearing them, the man thrusting into her from behind, firmly and without saying a word, her hands clutching the edge of the table, she gives way, lowers her body and leans her elbows on the tabletop, everyone watching, thirty pairs of eyes fixed on her, not looking away, men rubbing their swollen members through their trousers, a young man approaches from the other side, in front of Julia, and slowly gets up on to the table, agile enough to do so in slow motion, Julia making an effort to straighten up, lifting her breasts off the tabletop and regaining her initial position, rocking back and forth from the silent thrusts (only the rhythmic sound of flesh on top of flesh) the young man, who has kneeled down on the table, takes out his member and offers it to Julia, his dark and engorged penis brushing over her face like a dumb animal, Julia, rocking back and forth, tries to catch it in her mouth, like a game at a children's party, until she manages to trap it between her lips and suck it impatiently *such a slut, she's so hot*, Ortuño rediscovers her, marvels at having access to that woman being bent over by that man who's thrusting into her while she produces those muffled noises, dampened by the young man's organ as he grasps her head, thick fingers visible in Julia's hair, and a low moan from the tall man who's holding her by the hips, whose mouth approaches her back, his lips against her vertebrae, the man now gurgling and snorting, electrocuted, and it's then that she's the one to spasm, moving her buttocks backwards and forwards until the man pulls out, staggering like a drunkard, taking in air like an exhausted runner, and Julia's dark and glistening organ is empty, a siren calling to passionate sailors, Ortuño takes a step forward ready to cover the spot, but Céspedes grabs his arm and gives him a look that tells him to stop while Ortuño frowns, uncomprehending, and a fresh volunteer, a sturdy man with a scraggly head of curly hair trying to disguise a bald patch, steps up behind Julia, undoes his shirt to reveal a prominent gut, unbuckles his belt, takes a condom from his pocket and lets his trousers drop to the floor as he tears off the condom wrapper with his teeth, all the while staring at Julia's back and her buttocks, looks at the young man who's still kneeling on the table and nods at him, *stick it in*, everyone can read on his lips, everyone except Julia who's still focused on the young man's organ and who receives her new occupant with a gentle moan, the audience breathes out noisily in approval, and the two men slaving away over Julia exchange glances and mumble to each other, the young man tenses up, rigid, all eyes are on him, the more committed pornographers get closer to gather more details and watch him pull his dark member from Julia's flooded mouth as she drools with slime and saliva and more fluid splashes in her face, more semen spray, while the young man is about to fall off the table and the man who's inside her beats her rump with noisy slaps, *bitch on heat*, and now it's Ortuño holding back Céspedes, angry at the violence of the slaps, a couple leave the room, arguing with one another, dragged away by the phantom of female jealousy, voices fading into the distance as they argue, the back-door man also moans, shudders and pants, sinks his rigid fingers into Julia's buttocks as he lifts his chin towards the ceiling and snorts, his kidneys heave up and down, and he's still pumping away inside Julia, he shakes his head, his dorsal muscles contract, his gluteal muscles almost disappear as if they, too, had entered Julia's vagina and his entire body's going to disappear, and then he pulls out, pulls out rejected, doubling over on himself, falling on to his knees, pathetic curls abandoning all attempts at camouflage this close up, revealing strange scars and hollows on his scalp, and she, Julia, stays there, leaning on the table, head sunk between her shoulders, green panties straddling her right buttock in a knotted string, another candidate has stepped up to have a taste, but Céspedes has also come forward with her dress in his hand, and he's the one who puts his arm over her shoulder and kisses her hair, wipes away her sweat and possibly some other sticky substance with his cheek.

Julia drives along Calle Sierra del Co, carefully navigating the tight bends between high walls and bougainvillea, and thinks back on that other night, so long ago (not so many years but such a lot of accumulated time) riding in Ortuño's car after leaving the house where all that had happened. Hair damp from the shower, head leaning on Céspedes's shoulder, the silhouette of Ortuño driving, sitting on his own in the front of the car. The three of them silent. Ortuño's eyes seeking her out every now and then in the rear-view mirror, and she's caught up in a childlike sleepiness, street lamps winking overhead, not knowing where she was or where she was going. Distant memories of family excursions, curling up with the music and her parents' voices.

Julia arrives at Calle Sierra Pelada. The street is full of cars. *Funeral cars.* She imagines the visitors who've come to the house, imagines Dr Galán bearing up in the face of the invasion. Waiting for the moment she can collapse in a heap.

She steers the car up on to the pavement, parks and gets out. The scorching air blowing along the streets greets her violently. She walks in the middle of the road. Crumbling asphalt, studded with gravel, plants peering over garden walls expectantly, like dogs with their tongues hanging out.

When she gets to within a few metres of the Grandes-Galán family house the door opens, and before anyone appears she hears some stifled laughter. As she approaches, Julia sees a skittish, freckly teenager appear. He stops laughing when he sees her. Another teenager with an ostentatious quiff like a breaking wave and wearing a suit and tie follows behind him, and behind them, smiling, comes Guille who, when he sees her, stops and waits for her at the front door. His smile has faded.

Julia doesn't hesitate, she gives Guille a hug, kisses him near his ear and says, 'Darling,' but she feels that Guille, that those three lads are the masters of the situation. When they break the hug, Guille's not smiling any more. He's moving his lips nervously, his mates are watching, and he wants to match up, rise to the occasion. Julia asks him, 'Is Mummy upstairs?' And he turns, looking back into the house, 'Yes, and Uncle Emilio, I'm just, we're just off to get a breath of air, and then I'll be back here or wherever they want to go.'

'Of course,' says Julia, and she strokes his arm, half smiles at the other two, who are sizing her up as a woman, and goes in. *Mummy, is Mummy in? When did I start coming out with nonsense like that? Where's Mummy? Ridiculous.* Julia goes up the steps leading to the garden. From there she can see the street and Guille and his two friends again. They're going down the hill in single file, the one in the suit leading the way. A trail of ants. Years ago Julia saw them on a television programme, carrying those shards of green leaves they'd just cut with their powerful jaws, and she discovered that those ants were not vegetarian and the leaves were not their food. She knew that what she was seeing was the basis of a huge food industry and that the ants inside the nest would let that vegetal mass ferment until it produced a fungus on which they fed. Farmers, manufacturers, industrialists. Perhaps they were carrying bits of Dioni to cultivate in the darkness of the ants' nest underground.

On Avenida de Europa the sun comes out like a bewildered amateur spy. Jorge, the unfortunate Jorge, looks from side to side. He turns around, and through the workshop window he sees Pedroche stooped over the table, his cousin Floren beside him. He takes out his phone and taps in the number that Nene Olmedo gave him a short while earlier. Three rings and El Nene's voice, much softer than face to face, says, 'OK, what have you found out, how are they going to do it?'

'All I know, what my cousin told me, is that Pedroche, the one whose wife hit him, is going to the church to . . .' – he looks over his shoulder again – 'he's going there to pick up the things, the money and stuff.'

'Which church?'

'The one with the priest.'

'Yes, but which church? Where is it?' Jorge can now recognize Nene Olmedo's voice.

'I told you.'

'I don't know anything about churches. Which church?'

'The one on Calle la Unión, on the corner of Calle la Unión at the top end near Avenida Juan XXIII. There.'

'What time's he going?'

'Sorry?'

'I said what time's he going to the church.'

'When he leaves here, when he finishes work. That's what he told my cousin.'

'What time?'

'Half past eight, quarter to nine, around then. That's what my cousin said, when we finish work, he said.'

'OK. If you see them leaving earlier you call me immediately.'

'Yes.'

'And give me a description.'

'What do you mean?'

'What does he look like?'

Jorge turns around to look at Pedroche.

'Short, bald, I don't know, quite fat.'

'Like Clooney in the coffee advert?'

'What?'

'Take a photo of him.'

'I'll tell you now, he's got a small moustache –'

'I said take a photo with your phone and send it to me.'

'A photo?'

'That's right.'

'Right, OK then.' Jorge looks back at Pedroche, who's in exactly the same position as before. 'And he's got some sticking plasters on his forehead as well . . .'

'Send me the photo.'

'Yes, OK, understood, Nene . . .'

'What?'

'So everything's cool then, I'll send you the photo and everything's cool, no problem.' Jorge hesitates, raises his voice. 'Nene? Can you hear me? Nene?'

Jorge looks at the phone. Nene Olmedo has cut him off. He thinks about calling him back. Stretching out in front of him is the bleak parking area, incandescent cars, dust and dried-up weeds. He turns around once again towards the interior of the workshop, Pedroche and his cousin Floren. He looks at his phone, Nene Olmedo's number. He decides not to call him, runs his finger over the screen, searches for his girlfriend's photo. He finds the one of her on the beach topless. He thinks it inappropriate to dwell on certain parts of the photo just now, and he zooms in on the girl's face. The trace of a smile, the scar in the corner of her mouth gives a sour edge to her expression.

And so the diminutive Jorge goes into workshop of Marcos y Molduras Ferrer. Gorgo, the shy one, the sneaky, silent Gorgo. He goes into and through the workshop, holding his telephone in his hand. He doesn't pay any attention to his cousin Floren's comment about whether he's quite finished making secret calls in the coolness of the afternoon. Jorge gives him a stupid grin and stammers something about how hot it is. Pedroche doesn't look up from the strip of wood he's pasting with glue. He's breathing through his nose, noisily. Like he always does. A pair of bellows within. Jorge thinks about how he described him: short, bald, quite fat. Chubby, he should have said. Dopey, blondish, even though he's bald, his moustache a mix of yellow and grey. Old. A shit. That's it. That what he should have said, 'Someone who looks like a shit.' And Nene Olmedo would have understood. *Someone who looks like a shit, and you're another piece of shit, a cunt, a bastard, that's what you are, and you lay a finger on my girlfriend, if you go near her, I'll cut you.*

That's what Jorge's thinking as his mother opens her eyes in the suffocating heat of the siesta and his brother Ismael crosses Plaza de la Merced drunk beneath the trees stupefied by the heat, that's what Jorge's thinking as he leans over the work bench with his telephone half hidden behind his arm and pointing towards Pedroche and one, two, three times, the camera on his phone records what's in front of it.

He sneaks a look at the result. He deletes the first photo, in which you could only see the top part of Pedroche's head, the bald pate, the sticking plasters and a fluorescent tube. The second and third ones are practically the same. Pedroche's elephant profile, his trunk-like nose, looking downwards, his fleshy shoulder stretching his faded checked shirt. His brushes and the gilt frame he's working on lie next to him. Behind him, looking at the ceiling, like a saint contemplating the heavens, his cousin Floren. He chooses the last one.

He sends it to Nene Olmedo, and as he's doing so he mentally bombards him with a volley of fresh insults while his mother looks at the bedroom ceiling, stretches, thinks about Rafi Villaplana again and the assistant receptionist who's giving her problems. She'll have to get rid of her if she doesn't change her tune. She runs her hand with its painted fingernails (dark burgundy, almost black) over her naked body. She revels in the pleasurable feel of the fingernails on her skin, in the hard, invisible trail they leave beneath the twin mounds of her breasts. And she yawns as her eldest son, the deeply disturbed and inebriated Ismael, leaves the Plaza de la Merced behind him and, walking down the middle of the road, stumbling over the uneven cobbles, turns into Calle Conde de Cienfuegos and, as he goes past the graffiti-covered walls, searches for the bar he was in, how many weeks ago he can't remember. Camboria, he thinks it was called.

And in Las Camborias, Eduardo Chinarro is chewing the soft bread, stodgy meat, slice of onion, splodge of chemical tomato sauce and yellow mustard in his hamburger. He has only a handful of teeth to work with, and he's trying to talk at the same time as he swallows.

'Best just to stay cool over that sort of stuff, Rai.'

Raimundo Arias imitates him with a sneer on his face, 'Feff fuff tofay coo ofer fat fortof fuff, Wai.'

'For fuck's sake, Rai.' Eduardo swallows the mass of food in his mouth, tensing his neck and opening his eyes incredibly wide as a result of the effort and speed. His eyes are watering.

Rai looks at him scornfully and takes a long sip of his beer, no longer wanting to imitate the strangled sounds made by his friend, whose speech, now his passages are unblocked, is normal again, normal for him.

'For fuck's sake, Rai, you take the piss when I'm giving you sound advice as a mate,' he says, swallowing again, this time just saliva. 'You should drop all this business over Penqui and stop going over it inside your head.'

Rai turns to the waitress. 'What's the damage for mine?'

'What good do you think it's going to do you? Penqui's a great girl in my book, although now she'd be the worst thing in the world for you because of that shit Nene Olmedo, and you've seen how he is when he's with her, Rai, but the best thing is to just let it ride and stay cool over that sort of stuff.' He takes another bite (the penultimate) of the soft mush of meat and bread with its smearing of sauces.

'OK then, finish up, pay for yours and let's go.'

Eduardo's about to reply, but, fearing another round of imitation, he holds his tongue, chews and half swallows. He rummages in his trouser pocket. He takes out a very crumpled ten-euro note, smooths it out on his thigh and places it by the side of the plate. With his mouth almost clear he starts speaking again.

'Aren't you going to eat, Rai, not even a chip?'

Rai shakes his head. 'I'm not hungry. It's the heat,' he explains.

'OK,' Eduardo says to the waitress. 'Let's have the bill, sweetheart, and take for the Coca-Cola from yesterday, too. Your colleague said I could pay later, so tell her, tell her I paid,' and then turns back to Rai. 'You'll be hungry later.'

Rai grabs the neck of his guitar, which was propped up against the bar. He looks sadly through the window looking on to Calle Huerto del Conde. Ismael's coming along that street, *God has listened to me*, and, when he gets alongside a graffiti mural representing *Guernica*, a shabby individual with a clumsy walk, a face like a toad and a trumpeter's lips staggers out of Pasaje Lesbos. Noticing Ismael's angry glare the man, in his late fifties, looks away intimidated and mumbles an apology. 'What's your problem?' Ismael responds aggressively, coming to a halt in the middle of the road, as the other man, overweight, shaven head, dark skinned and sweaty, raises his hand by way of apology and says, 'Sorry, sorry,' and stumbles off in fits and starts, like a real toad. 'Arse bandit, shit face,' Ismael calls after him and then continues on his way in search of Las Camborias.

Inside Las Camborias Eduardo Chinarro is still persisting in trying to placate his friend Raimundo's jealousy and thirst for vengeance.

'It's the same thing, Rai, that happened to me and that girl Roberta. At first –'

'That was twenty-five years ago,' Rai says, still staring out through the window.

'Twenty-five, man, what's up with you, Rai? At first I wanted to . . . no it wasn't even four, maybe five years at most. At first I wanted to go over there and do her in and that piece of shit, Manolín . . .'

The waitress leaves the change on the counter near Eduardo, and he asks her, 'Did you take for the Coca-Cola from yesterday, sweetheart?' She nods. 'Cool, and tell your colleague, won't you? And the thing is, Rai . . .'

'Let's go.' Raimundo gets up from the stool he's been half sitting on and stops looking out of the window.

Eduardo, who's been standing up the whole time, picks up his change, says goodbye to the waitress without catching her eye, 'Cheerio, gorgeous, brilliant hamburgers. When I make it big you can be my personal chef,' and he follows Rai towards the door that opens on to Huerto del Conde.

In the doorway Rai bumps into the broad, slightly wobbly form of Ismael. His guitar brushes and resounds against the new arrival's knee. Ismael looks at Rai's sunken eyes, which are oozing a foul-smelling kind of sticky tar. Ismael sticks out his jaw, a prelude to a brief discussion which doesn't take place. Eduardo has placed his hand on Rai's back and gently forced him to keep moving.

They leave. They can feel the weight of Ismael's glare boring into the back of their necks. Ismael, the drunkard, creator of equilateral (or, at least, isosceles) triangles, out of cloth. Eduardo Chinarro has a thought after the fact. 'Did you see that guy, Rai? Itching for a fight, fucking hell, what a headcase, it's best to just get out of their way, that sort, and keep moving and not get caught up their problems, Rai.'

'I'll stick the guitar up his arse and shit on all his loved ones and his mother, too.'

'Come off it, Rai, there's no point. He's like the other stuff, Rai, with Nene Olmedo and Penqui. You and me we mind our own business, like me and that Roberta when I found out about the business with that bruiser Manolín with the bulging eyes.'

'Everything's such a drag with you, mate. Let's go up to the Cruz Verde.'

'Aren't we going to the Polivalente, Rai?'

'There's no point. El Negre's not there any more. And that wrap I put in the shitty bog-roll basket in that petrol station is miles away. I don't believe it, what a day, and this fucking heat, I've had it up to here.'

'When I found out I was so mad I even grabbed that big knife I've got at home. I thought, they've even been in my bed, I bought that bed with my own money, but then you think it over inside your head and you think, do I want to end up inside just because of those two, no way, he can fuck in my bed until it breaks, the pop-eyed bastard. As far as

I'm concerned he can stick it in every orifice. That's what's matters, Rai, whatever suits best. What matters is whatever suits best,' Eduardo Chinarro pronounces, pleased with his metaphysical discovery.

The two figures walk down the street, the sun tracing their outlines darkly and sluggishly on the breathless asphalt. The ghostly houses on Calle Lagunillas, graffiti-covered walls and closed windows escorting the peripatetic duo. The sizzling heat cooks the bare bricks, and in a low voice Eduardo Chinarro rehearses a song that makes his veins swell up and tells of a stolen girlfriend and a love that died.

In Las Camborias Ismael asks the waitress for a gin with ice, sizing up the empty bar and trying to remember what happened and who was there the last time he came. A siren's dark song has brought him to this place, but he can't see the body of the person calling to him through the fog. He stirs the ice, and it tinkles against the glass, which he raises slowly to his mouth and scares the waitress while his mother takes off her smooth black panties and steps into the shower. The jets of water break against her hair and turn it into a dark mass, the water forming pools, streams and torrents running down over her shoulders and over the udders where Ismael once suckled and Rafi Villaplana now wets his lips. Amelia thinks about him as she soaps and showers, with the scent of the gel, the foam and her memories and the desire for the link not to break, for the summer to last and for Rafi to look at her again with that cold desire, the cat that needs to eat, that needs her over and above his ambition, his interests, his fiancées and his business deals. *I'm your pussy cat, I'm your cave, I'm the one who gives you what you need and then, yes, come out and talk and plan and dream, but come back and lick up the milk that nourishes you, with your rough tongue, your claws always extended so you feel like you're in the jungle, playing at being a lion.*

Alley cat, lame feline, Rafi Villaplana leaves the front entrance to the block of flats where his mother lives. He's left her behind, without her teeth, La Segueta, with her sagging boobs, speechless bundles wobbling behind that top splattered with various sauces, like medals of the highest order bestowed upon her by pots and pans. Her magnificent eyes like an old-fashioned movie star's, washed up in a face ravaged by time and stupidity. In the hotbed of her home, La Segueta complains about the presence of her husband, the illustrious Mariano, just awake from his siesta, befuddled and sitting on the sofa in his underpants, yawning, the spare hair on his balding head standing on end, electrified, pointing at the ceiling, and his shining eyes fixed on the 45-inch Sony television screen. He's clicking on the remote control searching for a football match, even if it's not live, or a programme where some young lady is, as he likes to say, displaying her wares.

Portada Alta is a wasteland floating in the sun's glare. Dried-out bricks, blazing-hot walls, bits of clothing hung out to dry, starched by the sun. Anaemic trees, trunks sunk into their square pits, a refuge for ants, cigarette butts, plastic bottles and wrappers discarded by passers-by. Rafi Villaplana's shadow crosses the geometric puzzle of the dirty paving stones. There's the hint of a breeze, an atmospheric deception, a curtain of fresh air that immediately gives way again to the desiccating heat of the *terral*. And on a street corner, one shoulder leaning against the wall, Nene Olmedo is studying the photo of the no-hoper with the sticking plaster on his forehead, and near by, sitting on a stone bench, El Tato is smoking a joint, and, holding the smoke down in his lungs, he asks him, 'Nene, how much dosh will we get from this divvy?' and, receiving no reply from the pensive Olmedo, he smiles, exhales a cloud of smoke and displays the gaps in his teeth to the neighbourhood.

And relatively far away, some three kilometres as the crow flies, the Runner is thinking about Lucía. Her greenish eyes, her voice, which always comforts and understands him. The Runner thinks about Lucía's work colleagues, the supermarket manager, that Ricardo who's always smiling at her and, even worse, at him, when he sees them on the Runner's third-hand motorbike. And him sitting in his Audi A3 with his elbow poking out of the window, a cigarette hanging out of his mouth, his sunglasses and his fuckwit grin.

Lucía's faithful. Not just sexually. She despises the big cheese and the other little cheeses who flock around her. The guy on the delicatessen counter invited her to dinner a couple of months back, thinking that Lucía and the Runner had finished just because he hadn't been to pick her up from work for three days. Another motorbike breakdown. Lucía pokes fun at those guys when the Runner mentions them as possible rivals. She's touched by the Runner's jealousy, and he knows it. But he also knows, or rather, he vaguely suspects, that at some point the underground stream might come across other seams, trickles of water, siphoning through the rock. And he wonders whether Lucía's laughter might have been there on some occasions to console him, a way of driving away his dark thoughts, rather than something spontaneous. Not the absolute truth.

If I can't find a job, if the months go by and the months become another year, maybe she won't resist the onslaught. From those guys or from others who have yet to show their faces and who are the real threat. The Runner knows that he should leave all this behind him. Go around the industrial estates as suggested by Vilches, his mother's distant relative who works in a bank, who always seems to be washing his hands and who, the Runner is convinced, is trying to become a sort of stepfather, always getting up to welcome her when his mother goes to the bank to collect his grandmother's pension and her own, always seeing her to the door and waiting there until she disappears around the corner, ready for a final wave goodbye. A marriage of old people, pay cheques, pensions, retirements, medicines. Coffins and more pensions.

Go around the industrial estates and look for work in the warehouses, businesses, whatever they do and whatever the job is. Look for work. 'They'll take people on who show a bit of initiative, they'll try them out, at least,' says Vilches without really having any confidence in him, knowing that the Runner's not going to make that arduous tour around the industrial estates either this week or next week or ever at all.

'Running, forever running, that's not a career or a benefit, and how long has he been on the dole? Why did you waste a fortune you didn't have getting him that education with the priests so he could run, so he could spend all day running without getting anywhere?' That's what Vilches said to the Runner's mother. That's what he said in front of his grandmother, and that's what his grandmother told the Runner. 'Running and riding about on a motorbike, what kind of job is that? Living off charity, I wish I could do that, too. He's turned out pretty savvy. You've got to tell him that's it, draw the line, tell him to go and look for a proper job, on the industrial estates or wherever, instead of all that running like a moron.'

Running, breaking free from those lead weights someone strapped to his ankles, who knows who or when? Ballast – so that when the race comes he'll be lighter, fresher, cleaner. Yes. That time will come, just as in a few hours the time will come when he meets up with Lucía again. He'll go and collect her from work tonight. He'll watch her come out with all her colleagues, breaking into the first smile of the evening when she sees him. She loves him.

And the tattoo will be there, on the perfect curve of her ankle, always climbing and never moving, her ladybird tattoo. Her tanned skin. They'll walk together by the sea, where the breeze will sweep away this inferno of a day. A slow burn, windows closed, his grandmother's slippers dragging down the corridor, coming and going. Her own 400-metres track. She's not going anywhere either. The stale smell of cooking and detergent coming from the kitchen and advancing up the corridor like a down-and-out asking his grandmother for spare change.

Breaking free from it all. That's what the Runner dreams about and believes in. He'll be the one to hit the bull's eye, to leave fear behind and, together with the fear, all those beggars who swarm around Lucía. Tonight and every night. And there'll be a door, the door to a house he tries to imagine, a small house, a corridor that doesn't smell of cooking or stagnated time, a house with clean walls and a door that he'll close behind him each night, like a blessing, because inside, in the heart of that house, away from the world, there'll be him and Lucía, gaining time day by day, mountains of hours, nights without frontiers. That will happen. That's how he likes to picture himself. And that's how the Runner pictures himself in the slow progress of that August afternoon, reflected in the varnish of the wardrobe, that murky mirror.

Never accepted, always hidden. Avoiding people's eyes. Dragged along. Dioni. Hidden from himself. Camouflaged. Repentant, purged, tormented. Double lives, triple lives. A false-bottomed suitcase. Everything dirty and beautiful hidden down below, covered up, concealed. Buried. The performance starting from the time he opens his eyes each morning and continuing so many countless nights into the darkest tunnels of tortured sleep. Those men who would appear before him in the labyrinth of his dreams, sometimes liberating him, other times condemning him. Judged, submitted. Sometimes the truth was like retching, a putrid bolus that he had to vomit up and then, as a marvel of willpower or a total absence of willpower, swallow again, calling himself a coward, a man of responsibility, a traitor, a wretch, an honourable man. Free and obscure. Paying for his fleeting moment of freedom with kilometres of gloomy tunnels. That's how Dr Galán imagines her husband led his life. That's what she suspects. A coward. Incapable of breaking with either of the two worlds he felt tied to. His responsibility in tow, that neat, incorruptible sense of duty that he took to his grave.

Dismembered. That's the image that suddenly appears in Ana Galán's head. That primeval fear from some film she can't remember the name of, in which a man's limbs are tied to four horses and he's dismembered. That's what you did, Dioni, you did it to yourself, you were the four horses, only you did it slowly, so slowly that in the end it was ants and not horses who were there with you in your final hours.

A widow's speculation. Dionisio Grandes Guimerá taking everything with him to the grave: the secret of how he really led his life all those years he was married and how much bitterness or bliss that marriage held for him. A door that was never fully opened. Not even when Ana found out that he had a double life did she get a sense, through the tiny crack that fleetingly appeared, of what lay behind it. Ana Galán, such a courageous woman, hospital heroine, not daring to know more than was necessary. The mystery of that afternoon in August has been locked away for ever. Does no one hold the key? Wait and see.

It was a winter's night, moisture in the air, threatening rain. An icy wind was coming from the port and blowing up Calle Larios shaking the Christmas lights, which had just been turned off. Glass garlands and the perfectly aligned street lamps reflected in the shiny marble. Dionisio Grandes was walking along with a client, and the cold night, the end of the Christmas festivities and the prospect of a new year flooded his being with an uncharacteristic feeling of lightness. In Plaza de la Constitución he refused his client's offer of a lift home, and they went their separate ways.

Dioni chose to walk for a few minutes, in no particular direction. That's what he told himself and that's what was floating around in the rational part of his consciousness, but his footsteps were leading him towards Plaza de la Merced and, once he was there, feeling the pleasurable acceleration of his pulse and the disturbing presence of adrenaline in his heartbeats, he carried on towards the dive bars in Calle Madre de Dios.

He spotted him before he went into the bar, through the glass door. As he stood aside to let a couple of people leave, he saw Vicente leaning against the bar with his back to the counter, his eyes raised as if praying to the heavens. But it wasn't celestial glory he was contemplating, it was a television placed on a high shelf, showing some Apollo-like surfers doing acrobatics in the spume of some giant waves. He passed close by, and Vicente didn't even glance at him. 'Too much for me,' Dioni thought.

Too young, too attractive. High cheekbones and a square face, whimsical mouth, a headful of frizzy, almost blond hair. Strong. Broad hands and thick fingers in the midst of which you could hardly see the bottle of beer he occasionally brought to his lips, without taking his eyes off the surfers' somersaults or their bodies. Hypnotized. *A worker's hands*, Dioni thought to himself, sitting at a table at the back of the bar, also seeing the breaking waves reflected in the window, the foaming tunnels that sometimes swallowed the surfers.

Buy him a beer, tell the waiter to serve him one on his account and raise his glass of whisky from a distance by way of a greeting. Celluloid cliché, a fantasy that evaporated, giving way to frustration. A slow worm. Dioni's steamy mood had rapidly condensed in the corner of the bar. The solitary ice cube, nearly melted away, tinkled sadly in the last dregs of his whisky, the fine drizzle of the afternoon, so inspiring, now reduced to that small puddle.

The almost empty bar and a second glass of whisky that he only half finished. Dionisio Grandes paid his bill, and as he was putting on his coat with his back to the door, a friendly voice called out to him, 'Are you off already? I was hoping to get to know you.'

Over his shoulder he saw the smiling face of the youth at the bar. A hint of a smile, large, powerful teeth. Carnivore. He held out his hand, 'Vicente,' and then, rephrasing the question, 'Do you have to go?'

Dioni's nervousness, shaking his hand, saying his name, spluttering and at the same time aware of his spluttering and indecision, 'Well, yes, no, I was about to go, look you've made me all nervous, I was going to go, it's so dead in here and you were so absorbed watching the television, I was putting on my coat,' he looked at his watch hardly able to see where the hands were, 'but yes, I can, I don't have to go.'

Taking off his coat, an adolescent forty-something, queer, another whisky, bar now transmuted into a cabin on a boat that was sailing out to sea in the middle of the night, and if only this could last for ever. His heart beating fast, expanding in one single interminable pounding, a siren calling to the boats, all so easy.

Almost nothing in common, and all so easy. Almost twenty years younger than him, barman, supermarket shelf stacker, a casual worker in precarious employment, aficionado of action films. 'Sylvester Stallone? Do you really like Sylvester Stallone?' Dioni asked him happily, and his counterpart would say, 'No, not Stallone, his films, but the best, the best ones are the ones with Chuck Norris, those really are good; if you don't agree it's because you haven't watched them, and, in fact – no, don't laugh – in fact, he's worked with some of the best directors in the world. What are you laughing at? You're the type who likes everything with subtitles and preferably if they're talking in Czech?'

Easy, expert, Vicente. They left the bar together, and Vicente suggested, completely naturally, that they find a hotel because they can't go to back to his for the time being; while he's unemployed, he's living with his mother. Dioni stammered and confessed they can't go to back to his either, and Vicente, looking at Dioni's hand, said, 'Yes, I know.' 'You know?' Dioni asked looking in turn at his hand and his wedding ring, which he'd forgotten to take off this time. A smile. Married. A venial sin.

Hotel Carlos V, a room for a couple of hours. Two lovers. Dioni letting himself be led by this young man who treated him like a poor defenceless being and at the same time awoke and satisfied his desire. He satisfied it. Gentle, strong, despotic.

'You're like one of those surfers who was riding the waves, so strong and yet so gentle, floating where others would drown, carrying me on your surfboard, your magic carpet,' Dioni told him.

The pair of them propped up against the headboard, Vicente smoking silently, watching him out of the corner of his eye, replying in a low voice, 'You think about things too much. I think you overcomplicate things. Magic carpet . . .' and then he opened his mouth, not holding back a yawn which left a bright glow in his eyes.

'They're almost yellow,' Dioni said.

'What are?'

'Your eyes, they're almost yellow, greenish and almost yellow.'

'It must be because I'm tired,' he said, wrinkling his nose and frowning as if he were about to yawn again, but instead he lifted his cigarette to his lips.

Masculine, wild, a real man. Dioni studied his neck, his smooth chest (waxed?), hard pectorals that Dioni ran his hand over and down across his diaphragm, his belly.

'Christ, I'm so tired,' Vicente said, turning over to stub the cigarette out.

His fleshy back, defined dorsal muscles, shoulder blades sketching a strange geometric shape, a continent, and when he turned back he was wearing a smile intended to be friendly. Dioni picking up his watch from the bedside table and saying, 'I have to go,' pretending to be worried and in more of a hurry than he actually was. Getting out of bed, seeing the discarded clothes.

'Let's see if I can find mine. I hope I don't get them mixed up.'

'Fine by me,' said Vicente, stretching out on the bed. 'I'm sure your clothes are better than mine.'

Dioni lifted up a pair of underpants, 'Calvin Klein, for Christ's sake, you can't really complain,' and he threw them at his head, full of fun.

'From the market.' Vicente caught them in mid-air, reluctantly, looking provocatively at the naked Dioni. 'You're not at all bad, Daddy.'

'Daddy?'

'Naughty Daddy.'

'I'll give you Daddy.' Dioni made as if to approach the bed again.

'Go on, Mummy will be waiting for you, don't be a bitch,' Vicente said, dissuasively.

Dioni carried on getting dressed, nervously, just as he was feeling a few hours earlier when he saw Vicente watching the television in the bar. Indecisive, timorous. Should he ask him for his telephone number? Too much for me. One fuck and that's it.

'Aren't you getting dressed?' Dioni asked, doing up his shirt.

'Huh?' Sleepy.

'I said, aren't you getting dressed?'

'I'll stay here the night. Since you're going to pay for the room I might as well stay until the morning. You don't mind, do you?'

'No, of course not.'

'I don't fancy going back home at this time, with my mother, all the hassle, the life I'm leading, etc. etc.'

'Yes, of course.'

'I get told off, not like you, you do what you like, you old queen.'

'Yes, well, if you only knew.'

Response: yawn, grunt, stretch, muscly arm, eyes half closed.

Jacket. Coat, sidelong glance in the mirror. Nerves. A quick look around the room in case of something overlooked. A doubt.

'OK, then, Vicente . . .'

'Tomorrow I've got to take my brother-in-law to the airport to help him out, but the day after I'll be back in the surfers' bar, the guys with their magic carpets. That's what you said, isn't it?'

'Yes, well, the day after tomorrow, yes, but I don't know what time . . .'

'If not, I usually drop in there two or three times a week.'

A world full of meaning. Planets, constellations, everything aligned, in perfect order. The cold air going right down to the bottom of his lungs, even further, spreading throughout his body, taking pure oxygen to every last capillary in his despoiled, humiliated, exalted, replete body.

Solitary footsteps along Calle Cister, the cathedral floating in the night. The sound of water in gardens, the darkness of the bushes and again the tinkling of the Christmas lights, unlit, trembling in the wind. Everything was completely remote but at the same time everything was infusing his body, the universe circulating through his veins.

This is life, I'm alive, he said to himself, and he walked towards the taxi rank by Hotel A.C. Molina Lario in another deserted street. His footsteps echoing not on the cobbles in the street but on the floor of that narrow room where Vicente must still be sleeping. He was accompanied by the memory of the bedroom and by Vicente's presence, too, the first time he saw him looking up at the television now a distant memory. As distant as if he had met him months earlier. And Ana, his wife, even more distant. His home, Guille, that world he would enter in twenty minutes' time and which right now seemed to be on the other side of the world. As if it belonged to another dimension. On the other side of unbreakable glass. That's what it seemed like, that's what he wanted it to seem like, that's what he, Dionisio Grandes Guimerá, felt as he walked past the cathedral's main façade, pulling up the collar of his overcoat, under the drizzle that was once again shimmering in the air.

She's scattering seeds like the farmer in the gospels. The good seeds will find a place in the ploughed earth and will germinate, and the bad seeds will wither away on the rocks in the sun. But these are all infertile seeds, lentils spilled on to the fake marble floor in the living room.

Deum de Deo, lumen de lumine, Deum verum de Deo vero. Belita Bermúdez takes the lentils out of the packet and sprinkles them carefully in front of the window. Hacendado brand. *Genitum, non factum, consubstantialem Patri*, she prays. The lentils bounce between her bare feet while she mumbles a prayer in the silence of the flat and stares expressionless at the horizon.

The sins of the world. The treachery of mortals, the weakness of those around us, everything's out there. Such a commotion, so much going on inside their heads. Invisible horses galloping towards us all, trampling other people's work under their hooves. All that noise, all that violence dormant inside them, leaving our souls like a desolate land. Whole regions devastated.

Et incarnatus est de Spiritu Sancto ex Maria Virgine. Naked, ninety kilos of slow, flabby nudity. Pores, skin, tiny craters, pits and mounds, moles and lumps. The mechanical motion of her arm scattering the seeds as she continues her mumbling, *Crucifixus etiam pro nobis.*

She despises the man who has entered her and poisoned her without leaving a new life to germinate in her body and at the same time giving life to her. The breath of a child would be her own breath, its heartbeat would roll away the dirty, heavy, almost dead rock from the centre of her chest. Bad seed, that man was a bad seed, dried out, dead wheat, it's written on his face like the children of evil bear the mark of sin on their foreheads. Despoiler, a man from desolate lands flourishing and sleeping beside her, seeking only to satisfy his base instincts, dribbling and grunting with the same greed as pigs grunting as they roll around in the muck. She was his mud patch, she was the receptacle for his sin. His Sodom and Gomorrah. That pig.

Heavy eyelids, sluggish gaze. An enormous turtle without a shell, Belita looks at the empty packet of lentils she's holding and then looks out of the window at the empty afternoon sky. Full of invisible souls. Our ancestors' atoms. Looking down on me, you who once existed. *Judicare vivos et mortuos, cujus regni non erit finis.* Tiny lips in the middle of the disproportionate expanse of her face, soft white flesh. Lips moving, silently reciting from the depths of her memory the prayer she learned in that lost childhood. Underwater. Words returning to her, lips trapping the air in small bites. *Regni non erit finis.* A light down above her lips, her chin lost in her saggy cheeks.

She throws the empty packet of lentils up in the air, and it lands on the floor. A dead butterfly. Her naked back, a fallow island, almost a continent of white, pink, yellowish, slightly purple flesh. Blue. Her heavy arms, unseeing fingers and chipped opaque nail varnish. Her hands move slightly away from her body, exposing a round, sagging stomach, folds of skin and flesh hanging over her hidden pubis. That thin, musky down, almost insignificant, lost beneath her mountainous body, a side story in that desert expanse of skin. The kingdom of shame and humiliation. This is where you entered me, where you tried to debase me, lick me, make me like you and poison me with your vices, pig, that was the only reason you went to my mother with your face like a little lamb asking to marry me, to put that snake inside me, that lifeless poison you spilled in there, your rotten seed, he-goat, Satan. *Et in Spiritum Sanctum, Dominum et vivificantem.*

Belita kneels down, her soft fleshy knees sticking to the floor, and she can feel the ridiculous but painful penance of the lentils. The gentle torture, the suffering that purifies her and binds her to God on high. She looks up at the window and again sees the clear sky beginning to fade, break up. Children of the world, here I am, Father Sebastián, you know me, you know that I'm seeking purity and that I turn my back on sin and evil and fight against them. I'm not arrogant, it's not true what that man I married out of innocence and pity says. It was out of pity for my mother, not for him; he never deserved any. You know that and you know how much I've prayed, how much I pray now, how much I suffer and how many sacrifices I make and will still make. You are my guide, my purity and my truth. You bind me to Christ.

She raises her voice slightly. Belita's lips emit a sound in the stillness of the room. *Et unam, sanctam, Catholicam et Apostolicam Ecclesiam.* She feels purified by the words; her mind and her body, too, are cleansed by the prayer. The miracle wrought within her once more. Once more I am pure, once more I am cleansed. It's like when my mother said your teeth are like a princess's pearls, your eyes are the eyes of a good fairy and God loves you much more than all the other little girls. Yes, and she runs her tongue over her small row of teeth, lace coated in lichen, which shows through the purple hole made by her lips. And the devil incarnate also tried to enter through that hole, also wanted to put his vile flesh into that altar, Mummy, to profane my pearls, sully my whole body, that ugly man I married to make you happy. My sacrifice. My altar. And look at me now. Yes. *Credo in unum Deum.* Believe in me. Believe in me, Mummy. Believe in me because I believed in you and I sacrificed myself for you and for all of you.

The pain of the lentils is going through her skin and digging into her bones. She looks down at the floor, the seeds spread all around her. They will never bear fruit. She looks at her breasts, those round dead weights, a double oasis, barely tarnished by the rest of her ruined body, like an implant from another woman on to this ravaged body. The shadows of veins beneath the white surface, underground streams on this forgotten map and, in the middle, imported from another world, the dark aureoles around her nipples. Where no child will suckle, if you don't work a miracle, if I don't achieve purity, if you are not reborn in me like an animal in its mother, like all life on earth each day and each year. Yes. *Credo in unum Deum.*

Father Sebastián, I commend myself to you, to the generosity that lives and reigns in your heart and throughout your body. Rejecting whoever comes from the darkness and slithers around us, emerging from walls and sewers, living in the plumbing, between the walls, hidden in cracks in the furniture, in the pores of wood and plaster, waiting for their moment, waiting for our weakness.

Dead eyes. Limp muscles, the stark, purple, opalescent profile of broken capillaries, that skin, that desolate landscape, the eruptions of prehistorically shaven downy hair. Worn-out feet and uneven, chipped nail varnish. Swollen flesh, flesh from the slaughterhouse. They came for me, they handed me over, you handed me over, and I said yes. For all of you. It was the moment of sin. And now the reign of light shall come.

Belita raises her arms, raises them slowly and heavily until they are stretched out in a cross, palms raised towards the ceiling. And so, kneeling on the scattered seeds, with her arms outstretched, she remains in front of the window, in front of the sky. Ten floors down, laid out before her is that landscape where blocks of flats give way to warehouses, then the empty streets of the industrial estates, walls encasing empty building plots, the ravaged countryside on the edge of the city and beyond, on the blueish horizon, mountains that are fading as evening falls. And as two teardrops trickle slowly down her cheeks, Belita is still moving her small, thin lips and the forgotten pearls of her teeth. *Deum de Deo, lumen de lumine, Deum verum de Deo vero.*

They're walking along Paseo de Limonar under the shade of the trees. Aimlessly and happily. Excited by their encounter with death, the first time it has crossed their paths. There they are, trapped by a confusing vertigo that alternately envelopes and releases Guille with no sense of continuity. A rocket guided by his friends. Juno, with his quiff and his suit and tie, fiddles with his phone. Guille is tempted to ask him when and why he went home to put on a suit and tie. He supposes that Juno thinks it's the correct etiquette for a bereavement. And there he goes, the leader of their small pack, and he turns and tells Guille and Loberas, 'El Tuli is waiting for us at his place. He's on his own, and he's got some gear.'

Loberas makes a silent but abrupt victory sign, like a footballer after scoring a goal in a silent movie. Still looking at the screen on his phone Juno raises his other hand, asking them to be quiet and expands on the news. 'And Cabello, Isidro and La Lori are on their way there, too.'

'Cool! She's really hot! Brilliant!' Loberas thrusts his pelvis back and forth in an exaggerated manner, fornicating the air.

Guille catches the mood, begins to glimpse the age-old kinship between death and sensuality.

'Hey, did Mónica say she was coming?'

'Oh, and he's sorry about your dad, he's very sorry, and he sends a big hug, mate,' said Juno, ignoring Guille's question.

'Don't start getting all heavy about Mónica.' Loberas catches up with Guille and walks alongside him. 'Didn't you hear? Lori's coming. Brilliant! Sweet!'

Loberas does his thrusts again, still walking along and ignoring Juno who pulls him up, 'Jesus wept, Loberas!' and carries on looking at the screen on his phone.

The trio arrive at Paseo de Sancha. Out in the sun again they're hit by the *terral*, which now feels twice as powerful. 'Is Mónica coming?' Guille asks again as he crosses the road beside his friend Juno. 'I don't know. She said she'd call later,' Juno responds, resetting his quiff with a sharp flick of his neck.

Guille gives up, puts himself into the hands of fate and is struck again by the thought that all this is unreal and that at any moment he'll get a call from his mother to tell him that his father's just arrived back home and it's all been a mix-up. They made a mistake. And also the thought that they may be just testing him, that none of it is true and that's why he doesn't feel anything. Everything's the same as any other day, Loberas laughing, Juno's air of authority, the ordinariness of people they pass, the cars going by, even this heat, this never-ending curtain of burning gauze enveloping them, and that it's all the same as it felt this morning, the same as yesterday.

Even the erection he gets when he thinks about Lori and his simultaneous desire to see Mónica again are reassuringly everyday. It's only Juno's dark suit and tie and his white shirt that tell him that his father has died, but even that is too unreal to be true. But he knows it is. That this duality exists. He knows because he can still feel his mother's body pressing against his as she hugged him, her weight, her scent, and all those people in his house, that whole crowd, now just a distant memory, as remote from him as those dreams that are lost down some strange conduit and become part of the past, part of something of a doubtful and distant nature as soon as you open your eyes. Yes, but in spite of everything he knows, he knows that it really has happened, that his father is dead.

The thought takes shape in his mind suddenly. Almost violently. As if the coin that's been spinning around inside his head has finally dropped, tails up. Sharp and clear. He's going to tell Juno he's going back, that he has to go back home. He feels dizzy, detached from the world, everything could evaporate before his eyes at any moment, and right then, just as he goes to tap Juno on the shoulder, Juno does a little jump and shouts out, 'Cabello, you bastard!'

Back to reality. Nothing's going to evaporate, nothing's going to fade away.

There's Cabello, hugging Juno, his dark eyes, almost shaven head and that enviable dark shadow on his chin, unshaven for several days. He sees him. Cabello sees Guille while he's still hugging Juno. And now without taking his eyes off him, he forgets about Juno and goes towards Guille with his bright eyes, almost too dark. He gives him a hug. That masculine aroma, the rasp of his beard brushing against his neck. Cabello hugs him as if he'd been to a thousand funerals, as if every last one of his friends' and acquaintances' fathers had died and he had been there to offer them comfort, strength, respect.

Guille scarcely hears the words Cabello whispers to him – 'It's crap, man; chin up, be brave' – but he knows that Juno and Loberas are watching him, are seeing how Cabello, who's left Juno planted in the middle of a hug, who's not even noticed Loberas, is hugging him close, man to man, telling him things that the others can't hear, just between the two of them. And Guille feels he should respond, say that he'll be there for Cabello, too, that he can count on him for anything, at any difficult time. Shit, at least he didn't go home, at least he'd held out. You have to hold out.

And after the hug his friend is still patting him on the back and telling him, 'We'll get through this.' 'Of course we will,' Guille replies, trying to reciprocate the gesture but not quite reaching, his hand left waving in the air.

They set off again. They go down the steps leading to some local shops and head towards the building's main door. Cabello pushes a button on the entryphone. An electric buzz is the wordless response. They go in. In the lift Cabello focuses his attention on Guille once again, telling him, as he stares at the panel of numbers, 'My friend Chenchu's father died, too. He went off the road and crashed his car, a black BMW X5, into a concrete block, and the firemen had to cut him out.'

'That's heavy, Cabello,' Loberas chips in.

'They had to cut the car open with one of those circular saws they use. The guy's dying in there, and they're working against the clock, and there's a helicopter waiting and the whole circus, but in the end he dies before they can get him out. A bit of the engine went right through his chest, smashed it to pieces. Did your father have an accident, too?'

'No,' says Guille, hoping not to disappoint.

'Yeah, but with diseases and stuff it's worse,' Cabello pronounces. 'You wouldn't believe the shit my gran had to go through when she croaked it. Chenchu's dad had it far better. Even though you're ripped to pieces from one second to the next and then you're fucked.'

'This guy my dad knew, his car caught on fire with him inside, and when they got him out he was all burned up like a piece of toast,' Loberas says, no one paying him much attention.

Cabello whispers something in Juno's ear.

'My dad wasn't ill,' says Guille.

But the lift's arrived at their destination, and Cabello and Juno get out of the cabin without hearing him.

Tuli's at the front door to his flat, barefoot. He's wearing a pair of fluorescent-yellow swimming trunks several sizes too large for him and a T-shirt with a frayed neck that might have once been blue and is now off-white.

'Hey, bro!' he gives Cabello a theatrical hug.

Each greeting becomes successively less effusive. A quick hug for Juno, a nod of the head to Loberas and the same indifferent gesture for Guille, until Cabello, who's already gone into the flat, tells him, 'Guille's the guy whose father died today – just now, wasn't it, Guille?'

'Hey, man, stay strong,' Tuli tells him. His breath smells of vinegar or something similar.

'Yeah, today,' Guille replies to Cabello, but he's not listening any more.

Guille goes into the flat. As the door closes behind him he's hit once again by the feeling of everything being completely unreal and the need to go back home. He zigzags along the corridor, just as if he were in a dream, gets to a very uncluttered living room with almost no furniture. Cabello is sitting on a gigantic white L-shaped sofa placed in the centre of the room, with a cushion behind his neck, focusing on his phone, giving the impression he's been sitting there for hours. Guille looks out at the sea barely a hundred metres away, through the french windows that give out on to the terrace. It's intensely blue, clear, majestic. He looks at the outline of the coast, the light breaking up into a thousand colours. But he's not in the mood for aesthetic subtleties. The air conditioning must have been set at less than twenty degrees and, together with the vision of the water, it sends a shiver down his spine. He casts aside a fleeting image of his father in a morgue, on one of those trolleys you see in films or naked on a metal table. Autopsy? *He's there now, no, best not to, the sea, me here, Cabello, Juno, his black suit.*

Cabello's voice brings him out of himself.

'What a guy, mate, evil!' he says, clapping his hands together. Now it's back to Cabello just arriving at the flat, sitting on the edge of the sofa, excited by the surprise.

Tuli laughs happily at the compliments paid to him by his friend and shows his teeth, which could tear a human body in two. Tuli is tall and strong. He has an enormous nose. If Guille had that nose he'd have a massive complex about it, but in the middle of Tuli's face it's the perfect nose, the best on the market.

What Cabello's excited about is the appearance of a small silver tray – or something that looks like silver – on which Tuli has placed three enormous spliffs.

'They're like trumpets!' says Loberas admiringly.

'The very best grass, grown by the old man. How he looks after his son!'

'Your old man's a perfect friend! Does he really give it to you?' Loberas says, looking open mouthed at the tray and then at Tuli's face.

'As if! No way! I swipe it off him when he takes me out to the place in the country to piss me off. He's got it hidden in a big bed of tomatoes.' Tuli's forehead is seriously furrowed. Bad memories.

'Heavy!'

'And there's a Romanian, Caratescu or something, who keeps his tomatoes watered,' says Juno, showing off his inside information and throwing his quiff backwards with a violent flick of the neck. 'We were there last summer, weren't we, Tuli?'

'Awesome! A-fucking-one!' Loberas goes on raving.

Guille laughs, trying to join in the collective fun, although Tuli's expression is still soured by the memory of his father. Disorientated, Guille goes to sit down at one end of the sofa, near the french windows and the view of the sea, but right then Cabello hisses at him and pats the sofa to signal that he should come and sit next to him. He's been keeping an eye out, he hasn't forgotten about him. Guille's spirits lift. He feels like shouting out loud, like Loberas, 'Sick!' He doesn't, but as he passes by him on his way to sit at the right hand of Cabello the god, he pats him on the shoulder and says, 'Dickhead!' to which Loberas responds with a loud cackle.

Serious, formal, professional, magnanimous, Tuli lights the first spliff, standing in the middle of the room. The others look on in expectation. Tuli holds the smoke down in his burly chest, behind the curtain of his faded T-shirt. After a few seconds he exhales a hazy smoke, barely visible, and, at the same time as an intense aroma pervades the room, Tuli lets out a hoarse exclamation, 'Fucking brilliant!'

General ovation, collective joy. Tuli raises the joint so that the first person who wants to follow in his wake can take it, when the doorbell rings, reverberating through the whole flat.

Everyone looks towards where they imagine the front door to be.

'Your father?' asks Guille with a start, surprised at his own reaction.

'No way!' When he realizes it's Guille, recently semi-orphaned, who asked the question, Tuli softens his tone and explains, 'No way, my father's in Tunisia or Turkey, somewhere like that.'

The bell rings again.

'It sounds like an air-raid siren, Tuli, like the Japanese are invading,' says Cabello.

'It's from when my grandma used to live here. She was stone deaf,' Tuli explains, heading towards the door.

From the living room they can hear Tuli's voice, and then more voices, laughter, footsteps approaching down the labyrinthine corridor.

Tuli appears again at the doorway to the living room, followed by a scrawny, blondish lad, Isidro, and, behind him, La Lori. Long and very curly dark hair, pale skin, slightly almond-shaped blue eyes. She's holding Tuli's enormous joint between her lips, breathing in. All the lads salivate when they see her. They watch her firm breasts bouncing beneath her strappy black top while she inhales, her eyes cloudy. The smoke seems to circulate through her bronchial tubes and her enormous lungs, down her arms, down through her stomach, down her extraordinarily smooth, generous, white thighs, until it reaches the tips of her toes and then it embarks on the return journey, passing silently beneath the straps of her sandals, ascending her thighs, losing itself under her very short shorts and climbing up her body and neck before appearing deliciously aromatic and blurred between the radiant whiteness of her teeth. Strawberry lips, a magical gap between her two front teeth. Desire. Pure and sudden joy.

'You know everyone, don't you?' asks Tuli the host, taking the joint from Lori in his fingers and waving it around, offering it to any takers.

Everyone looks up and reaches for it, Loberas high-fives with Isidro, approaches Lori and kisses her on each cheek.

'You know Guille, don't you, Lori?'

Lori, taking the joint back from Tuli, looks over at Guille as she takes another drag she nods her head.

'His father's just died, only just now,' he says, presenting Guille's credentials.

Lori raises her eyebrows almost far enough to reach her wild hairdo, breathing in deeply at the same time. And at the same instant as a small waft of smoke emerges from her lips she manages to say, with a voice from the depths of a tomb, almost with a cough, 'That's shit!'

Guille nods. Cabello gives him a fraternal slap on the thigh.

'So how come you're here? Have you only just found out?'

Lori's eyes have suddenly gone bright. Not out of sympathy for the deceased and Guille's sudden semi-orphanhood, as Guille would have liked, but because of the joint.

'We got him out of his house. You wouldn't believe how many people were crowded in there and all of them with an attitude, either cut up or pretending to be cut up, all too much,' Juno explains to her, before asking, 'Pass the joint, would you?'

'Is that why you're dressed up like that? Wow, that's some serious shit.'

'For the funeral. I thought we were going straight there.'

'Straight there? Where?' Lori's about to have another pull on the joint, to see if she can understand it all better.

'Where they put the dead people, the cemetery, fuck it, I can't even remember what it's called. Pass the spliff.'

'What a nightmare.'

Lori goes over to Juno and hands him the smoking cylinder just as she spies the tray on the table with the other two joints waiting to be lit.

'But you've got some more over there. That's so mean!' She makes as if she's going to keep the one she's holding, but Juno has already swiped it off her.

'Come over here, Lori, I'll light you one all for yourself,' says Cabello, and he repeats the same gesture he made to Guille for her to come over and sit next to him, patting the sofa, now on the other side.

'Dirty old man,' says Juno, laughing.

'You're the dirty old man, only ever thinking about one thing,' Lori retorts on her way to the sofa. 'Fucking hell, it's cold in here, isn't it?'

'Tuli's invited a penguin along,' says Loberas, laughing at his own joke. 'Isn't that right, Tuli? We're going to feed it sardines. It'll catch them in the air.'

'That's seals.' Isidro, the blondie, looks half asleep, and his voice is sleepy, too.

'Tuli's penguins eat anything, even seals. Isn't that right, Tuli?'

Lori, an obedient local girl, sits down beside Cabello. Guille has been watching her approach, an imposing presence. More imposing, more inaccessible, more indescribable with every step. It seemed to him, he thought he saw, that as Lori sat down she and Cabello had kissed on the lips, or perhaps he'd been mistaken, or they'd made a mistake, he wasn't sure. But they didn't show the slightest bit of surprise or discomfort. They'd kissed on the lips, intentionally. Guille gets a hard-on.

He thinks he might wake up at any moment, in his room, on a winter's day, with all those clouds that seem as though they're going to come in through the window and get inside your head. He smells Lori's scent. It's more than a perfume, it's the scent of her body, her clothes and even the smell there must be in her house, the smell of her soap, what she eats, her breath. *The scent of her organism*, Guille iterates mentally. It's a pleasant, fruity smell. Plums, lemon, melon. The fruit his mother puts in the juicer and drinks in the morning. To be healthy. To keep her skin, or her eyes, or her hair like Lori's. He could eat a piece of Lori. He gets even more of a hard-on.

'Fucking hell, it's cold. Aren't you cold?' Lori complains again, and she rubs her arms.

Guille sees, close up, two big buttons under Lori's top. Her nipples are protruding, standing out almost shamelessly. On purpose, Guille thinks. *She's doing it on purpose, she does everything on purpose, they're plump, like a woman's, like Trini's mother's when she gets out of the pool in her orange bikini.* If he ran his hand over his trousers, just twice, he could come. Like a wet dream.

'Here, warm yourself up.' Cabello places one of the joints from the tray between the girl's lips. He lights it.

She inhales deeply, holds it in and then, with her eyes half closed, she smiles and releases a smooth veil of smoke. Guille observes the wonderful gap between her two front teeth. *If only I could be that smoke.* Lori's eyes are gleaming, almost tearful. *To go in and out, to rub against those two teeth like Samson between the columns of a temple.* Cabello has the joint now and is smoking it. Fast and intense. *Everything tumbling down, the idiot in that film, older than Samson's great-grandfather, the cardboard columns tumbling, and me leaning against those teeth and lips, look at them, yes, her swallowing me.*

'Let's share it with our friend, OK, Lori?' Cabello passes the joint to Guille. 'You can't keep it all to yourself, that's selfish.'

Guille's sorry that the joint has come to him via Cabello's lips and not directly from Lori's mouth.

'We have to cheer up our friend Guille. He needs cheering up today, OK, Lori?' Cabello smiles, touches the girl's naked thigh, stares openly at her cleavage and touches her thigh again, very softly, barely touching it with his fingertips.

Guille smokes. A shadow's finding its way into his chest. His dead father. His mother, hospitals, hassles. An open window. An enormous boat on the horizon.

Tuli appears with two bottles and plonks them noisily down on the table.

'Courtesy of my father.'

'Hey, your father's so generous towards us, fucking hell, he's a good mate. Next time I see him I'll give him a kiss on his forehead.' Juno pushes his quiff back using his fingers as a comb and at the same time stretches his neck as though trying to escape from his tie.

'Aren't you going to take that off? You're going to stay dressed up like that the whole time?' Lori asks, looking at Juno with a frown, grim faced.

'Fuck you, Lori,' Juno mumbles, not looking back at her. He lifts up one of the bottles, 'Wow! Macallan! Only the best!'

'Stupid prick. Fuck you, he said. Fuck you, too, stupid prick.'

'Lori, shhh, Lori, look at me. Ignore him.' Cabello is holding her face, looking into her eyes.

'What about this one?' Isidro, with a lighted spliff between his lips, has picked up the other bottle. 'Knockando Whisky, that's what my brother drinks. He says it's the business.'

'This one's better, isn't it, Lori?' Juno smiles, holding the bottle of Macallan in his hands.

'Shitty little queer.' Lori holds her arm out to Guille, demanding the joint.

Guille takes another draw and obeys. Lori's fingers, nails painted black. They leave his hand: her fingers, nails, Lori, the joint. His father. Cemeteries. Now they belong to him, too.

'Yeah, yeah, little queer, just as you like them.' Juno's still smiling, not looking at her.

'Hey, you can cut it out, too.' Cabello looks at Juno seriously, calmly. Guille sees his fangs.

'OK, OK, cool it.' Juno's head does a couple of backward flips, hard enough to send his quiff flying into the wall behind him. He's not looking at Cabello, he's looking at Tuli, 'Yeah, cool. Where's the glasses, Tuli?'

'What?' Tuli, standing up, looks at Juno absent-mindedly, with a soft smile, half gone.

'Glasses for the tipple.' He lifts up the whisky bottle level with Tuli's eyes. 'And some ice.'

'Tough guy,' Lori murmurs, 'and some ice . . . what a loser.'

Cabello runs his hand over her thigh again and smiles at her. Lori exhales a cloud of smoke that now appears to Guille to be dark, almost brown. He feels everything starting to get distorted, starting to look more real, or much less real. Better.

He's almost tempted to ask. To ask Lori or Cabello what's their problem with Juno. But he's not quite stoned enough. He's sure it's not something that's happened here and now. Guille knows they do things. That there's stuff going on between them, arguments, affections, mysteries. They live in this world and another parallel world that Guille can't access. Like that film about outer space, they're in another dimension at the same time as in this one. They come in and out through a mirror.

Guille watches their gestures, their expressions. Their voices don't sync with their lip movements. Juno's voice sounds like it's coming from Lori's mouth, Isidro's like it's coming from Loberas's, who's now there beside the window, doubled up laughing and clutching the back of the sofa because of something Isidro said or something he said himself. And over here are Lori's nipples, now a bit more sedate. Little beasties in their lair, now just showing their snouts. Looking out through the cloth.

'They must be seeing everything all blurred,' says Guille, suppressing the urge to laugh.

Cabello frowns at him for a moment and then carries on talking to the girl. Hand on thigh. The sea creature's tentacles. Juno throws some ice in a glass, several cubes skate across the table and fall on the floor. His grandmother's pearls rolling on to the floor that day. The dark furniture. Closed drawers. Dead man's clothes in the drawers. His grandfather. The house on the Alameda like a pantheon. Bad vibes. He looks out at the sea. The large boat has disappeared; perhaps it's that dot glimmering on the edge of the horizon, beyond the cement works tower. The sun's glare bouncing off the glass, or maybe the boat's lights are already turned on. The night will come from that direction.

Better to look inside the flat. Loberas also drops several ice cubes as he tries to throw them into a glass. Tuli kicks one, and it crashes against the marble skirting board on the other side of the room. The ice cube explodes and Tuli shouts 'Goal!' and pretends to be a footballer, fingers pointing upwards to the sky – or, at least, the ceiling. Cabello is speaking into Lori's ear. She looks very serious; he's got a hint of a smile on his face. Guille wonders if it's true what they say. Loberas told him. Tuli is moaning, now, clutching the foot he kicked the ice cube with and he drops on to the sofa, rolling over the backrest, almost crushing Isidro, who hardly complains or moves with his friend lying on top of him.

'I've broken a toe, I swear it, shitty fucking ice cube. Juno, you're a loser. Fucking ice.'

'It's a pity you didn't head it.' Juno smiles sarcastically and calmly takes a sip of whisky.

Lori passes the joint to Guille, glowing hot, straight from her hand. She looks at him for a few seconds with a new intensity and then carries on whispering with Cabello. *She's so gorgeous with those slightly almond-shaped eyes, no, I mean, nicer than that, they're green, with a hint of blue or grey, and look how she opens her mouth, like a strawberry, I bet she's just the same between her legs.* He glances at her tight crotch. Throbbing, pounding. *There it is. That's where it is.*

Guille draws on the spliff but doesn't take it right down. He looks at everyone's expressions, their hands, their eyes. Clearer than ever. He has the sense that he's seeing them for the first time, the first time he's really seen them. That's how they really are. They were hidden behind a curtain before. Now they're real, like the people who appear in dreams, just as real. And now it's as though they're the ones who are sailing in a boat, unaware of the destination, not caring, just going out to sea. The flat, the whole building. Cabello asks him for the spliff, what's left of it.

Yes, they do things. Cabello, Lori, Juno, Tuli, perhaps Isidro, too, he's like a sheep with that face and his fair hair and sleepy blue eyes. That what they say, that's what Loberas told him. They play a game with a bottle, they sit in a circle and spin it around. The person it points to goes off to a bedroom with Lori. Loberas is certain, he swears it's true. Cabello told him one night and promised to ask him along. Will they do it today, will they do it now? Lori is like a statue, an ancient Egyptian statue, a marble lioness. Her thighs are so smooth, the hem of her shorts makes a perfect curve, like a fence, the denim on one side and her naked skin on the other. Her pale fingers with nails painted black, moving through the air. Like puppets, ten little fingers wearing black hoods. Executioners.

And suddenly he feels Cabello's gaze and breath on him, yanking him back into the world.

'What do you say? Do you fancy it?' Cabello looks at him, genuinely curious.

'What?'

'She'll do it for you.' Cabello's eyes are serious, he's smiling, he surreptitiously taps Guille's leg with his knee.

Lori looks at him sidelong. Her eyes are brighter than ever.

'Do you fancy it, or what? What's up, Guillermo?' Another tap with his knee.

Guille thinks he understands, he senses that it's not a joke. His father has died, they're not going to take the piss like that. Any other day maybe, but not today. He's not sure what Cabello's talking about or why Lori's looking at him like that, frowning, but he says yes.

'Yeah, sorry, yeah. Yeah.'

Cabello looks at Lori, flips his hands, palms facing upwards. Business sorted.

'It's just I'm, you know, what with my father . . .' Guille tries to justify himself, renew his dramatic credentials.

Lori stands up, almost reaching the ceiling. Guille, still sitting down, sees her towering above him. They say that Egyptian sculptures are metres high, enormous. That's how Guille sees her, a goddess at the doors of a temple. Her mouth and eyes peering over the two protrusions under her black top, her hair a frozen black waterfall *Niagara Falls by night. Diving over the edge in a canoe, cascades of hair, vertigo, falling, coming up for air.* Guille reacts. He manages to stand up.

He's almost as tall as Lori. She gives him a sweet smile and starts walking. Guille follows her. They skirt around the sofa. Seen from the rear, rather than walking, Lori looks like she's skating on ice. She slides across the marble floor. Confident, smoothly, she knows where she's going. No one except Cabello seems to notice anything. They leave behind them an echo of laughter and voices bouncing off the windows. Now Guille does feel the cold, he's almost shivering.

Fátima Perea Pemán, La Penca. From the narrow corridor she can see her father's bare feet hanging over the edge of the bed. Since La Penca's mother died her father hadn't wanted to go back to sleeping in the marital bed, and now it's her, La Penca, who occupies the master bedroom and double bed. Her father says that the bed has the same decorative ornamentation as his wife's coffin. It's true that the headboard looks rather funereal, but the thing about the ornamentation is just one of her father's obsessions. Along with his drinking, thinks La Penca, and along with his other interests. He's never been bothered which bed she slept in, the bed was the least of it.

Her father's feet are pointing up at the ceiling. They are grey with a greenish tinge. They look like two animals guarding something. They're guarding the rest of his body while it sleeps. The sight of him makes La Penca feel sad and a little bit frightened. Not to mention disgusted. She turns around, hugging the wall. She's put on a clean thong. She doesn't want to remember what happened in Nene Olmedo's place and nor does she want to give in to that kind of torpor, that stickiness lapping at her whole body, made more intense by her father's presence. She hears the sound of her brother's PlayStation. The dog comes up to her, wagging his tail a bit, lower than usual, almost at floor level. Trying to cover something up. 'What have you done, you bastard,' La Penca asks him, and the dog wags his tail a bit faster now, genuinely happy, thinking that everything's been sorted out.

'Get off, you idiot.' La Penca knees the dog in the head, catching one of his eyes which blinks manically, like a frenetic indicator. Despite everything, he follows in his mistress's footsteps towards El Yubri's bedroom.

La Penca's brother is slumped in a leatherette armchair. Although he's got a number-1 or number-2 crop and has a scraggly beard from several days' growth, his face looks like a little boy's, rounded, flabby. His agile fingers race across the PlayStation controller. Killing barbarians. On the screen a musclebound figure is shooting a highly sophisticated weapon at individuals wearing turbans. El Yubri's alter ego. The arms of the leatherette armchair look like they've been shot to pieces by enemy fire: the green material ripped open and yellow sponge exposed to the room's stale air.

El Yubri doesn't look at his sister; he carries on with his mission of on-screen extermination. He's wearing bright-red sports shorts that reach almost to the knee. That's all he's wearing. There are breadcrumbs on his belly, in among a light fuzz that looks like it might have been shaved off a week or so ago. The dog tries his luck with him, prodding his arm with his muzzle in search of affection. El Yubri tries to elbow him away without taking his eyes off the street full of half-demolished buildings that his hero is passing through. The dog dodges his elbow and trots out of the room.

'Aren't you hot?' La Penca scans the room, looking for something.

El Yubri shrugs his shoulders. His sister stares at his neck, bathed in sweat, and El Yubri's glistening shoulders. The minefield of pimples, blackheads, moles and body hair disappearing down his back, squashed against the leatherette. On top of the chest of drawers, in among some crumpled clothes and cheap glass tumblers, La Penca spies a packet of Fortuna cigarettes. She climbs on to the bed, crawls to the other side and picks up the packet.

'Have you got a light?'

'Over there.' El Yubri nods towards the bedside table.

La Penca picks up a blue plastic lighter. She looks at the screen as she takes a cigarette from the packet. The back of her brother's neck. She lights the cigarette, stretches out on the bed, hot and queasy, ready to lose herself in that sleepy stickiness enveloping her. What the fuck did she do with Nene Olmedo? That bastard does whatever he wants with her, drains her of all her willpower the moment he claps those shifty eyes on her. And that other creep?

'I got the notice.' El Yubri carries on slaughtering the enemies of Western civilization.

Her father's feet. La Penca narrows her eyes. She slips into hot water, a swamp, animals moving around in the slime. She opens her eyes and, back in the room, takes a long drag on her cigarette and asks, 'What?'

'The notice, it came.' El Yubri breaks off from the slaughter. He turns the television off and looks back at his sister. 'What's up?'

'It's the heat.'

'What have you taken? Have you taken something?'

'No, nah, no. A gin and tonic, which I'm sure was dodgy, and this heat.' A small column of ash falls on her chest, clinging to her yellow top.

'I've got to go in the day after tomorrow.'

La Penca draws on her cigarette then blows the smoke out feebly. She opens her eyes, looks up at her brother.

'What have you taken, Penqui?'

'You mean the notice from the court? The day after tomorrow, that soon?'

'Yeah.'

La Penca sits up a bit, still leaning on one elbow, her head resting against the headboard. She looks at her brother, still not quite understanding.

'That soon?'

'It arrived three or four days ago, but I only opened it today.' The two siblings look at one another. 'I didn't want to go off on one.'

'Have you told him?' La Penca asks, nodding to the doorway, the corridor, supposedly the place where their father is sleeping.

'No, what for? Anyway . . .'

'What a load of shit, Yubri.'

'Anyway, he already knew. Like I did and you did, or are you saying you didn't know? I was always going to go inside for it, and now I'm going inside. Just like that.'

'What a load of shit, Yubri.'

'The lawyer's a dickhead, only interested in himself. He was just after money. He washed his hands of me. He knows I didn't do it, but what am I going to do about it, there's nothing I can do, they might as well pin a bank robbery on me like the Daltons. That's what I should have done, teamed up with them, and if I'd got caught it would have been for something that was worth the hassle and not for this stupid piece of crap.'

'That's hardcore. What about the business with the fire, the hearses?'

'That hasn't come up yet. They made the other stuff up, and at the hearing they put a guard on either side of me all tooled up, and I'd been in the cell for two days, they might as well have put a sign around my neck saying "thief". They made it all up so they could say "how clever we are, we're always nicking these crooks". They don't care if you're innocent.'

'You've got form.'

'For nicking a bit of cable, for fuck's sake.'

La Penca lies back down on the bed, puts her feet up in the air. She's like a light fitting with her head hanging down, all that heat concentrated in her body, her filaments glowing red hot. Her brother looks at her, distressed.

'For nicking a bit of cable, Penqui.'

El Yubri remembers that night in the Field of Mars, that's what he and Jerónimo called it. The patch of waste ground with those semi-urban olive trees covered in dust. The half-finished building, bare concrete, and he and Jerónimo dragging away the copper cables. Tight lipped, sweating. Jerónimo saying to him, 'It's like we're ploughing a field, Yubri, we could go and work in the countryside.' Loading the copper into the van and the torch beam lighting them up and a hoarse voice shouting, 'Stay where you are, stay where you are or you're dead meat, you bastards!' Jerónimo running, getting into the cab, starting the engine, him jumping in on top of the cables.

Yubri examines the scar on his right cheek. A little bit of missing flesh. He remembers the voice behind them shouting, 'I'll kill you. I'll shoot. Stop, you bastards!' The pain in his leg, the blood weighing his trousers down, a dull pain that was difficult to locate, lots of blood, feeling slightly faint when he thought he'd burst a big vein and was going to bleed out on those cables surrounded by the smell of pigs or grain or chickens there in the back of the van. Lurching around, unable even to sit up. Jerónimo going at full pelt, as fast as that ancient Ebro van would take them, as old as the hills it was, along that track full of ruts and potholes.

He caught two heavy blows in the face, bounced around and thought he'd broken several teeth before the big one. Jerónimo couldn't avoid one pothole, almost a ditch, and the van gave two massive jolts and then left the track and ended up nose first in an abandoned irrigation ditch. At first El Yubri thought they'd rolled over, until he pulled himself together among all the tools and managed to get out. One of the back doors had come off and was lying next to some bits of cable. Jerónimo had already got out.

El Yubri was hobbling, but his mouth hurt more than his leg. His leg made him scared, that soft part, he didn't dare touch it. The man with the torch who was doing all the shouting was back in the distance. All you could hear were the cicadas. Jerónimo was breathing heavily and kept on saying they were nearly at the road, they were nearly there. And he was thinking it would be better to get off the road when those two figures appeared. He didn't even know where they'd come from. Two municipal policemen. They shouted a bit and shone a torch on them from close up, and they had their pistols out. Jerómino made as if to run off, but it was enough for one of the cops to say 'Hey' for him to stop in his tracks. Afterwards he told El Yubri that he'd stopped running so as not to leave him high and dry. Yeah, yeah.

The patrol car was less than twenty metres away. Like Jerónimo said when they put them in the car, those policemen must have got there as fast as a flying saucer.

La Penca manages to open her eyes. She nearly burns her fingers on the cigarette butt.

'Ashtray,' she says.

El Yubri hands her a dessert plate with several cigarette ends and a few sweet wrappers in it. La Penca props herself up again on her elbow. She blows the ash off her chest and it lands on the bed.

'Now it'll just be me here on my own with him.'

El Yubri looks to where their father is, supposedly. He shrugs his shoulders.

'I'll swap with you.'

La Penca narrows her eyes. El Yubri insists, 'You go to the nick, and I'll play happy families with him. I'll swap with you.'

'Yeah, and I'll swap the other business with you. Then you get pissed off when I hang around with El Nene.'

'The other business?' El Yubri screws his eyes up. 'Don't say that stuff. The other business is over with, Penqui, since I put him in his place, Penqui.'

La Penca bites her lip. Swallows saliva. Lies back on the bed.

'You don't even have to think about that any more, it's over.'

Silence.

'You've come over all dopey, I don't know what's up with you. What have you taken? Have you been with El Nene this afternoon?'

'I haven't taken anything. But yes, I've been over at his place.'

El Yubri sits there staring at the crumpled bedspread by his sister's feet. Her toenails are painted the same colour as coagulated blood. He gently bites his bottom lip. A boy's face with mousy eyes.

'We'll see what the guys are like inside. I'm thinking of signing up for a course.'

His sister breaks his train of thought. 'One these days that bastard will get me pregnant.' Her eyes narrow with loathing.

'Enough of that shit, for fuck's sake, Penqui!' Yubri's calm shatters, he jumps to his feet, turns around and squeezes between the furniture in the narrow room. They hear a cough from his father's room. The dog's claws on the tiles in the corridor.

'I'll smash his face in.'

'Either him or one of his mates will get me pregnant. Or this bastard here,' Penca looks at the corridor out of the corner of her eye, almost furtively, almost in the same way as she said 'or this bastard here' in barely a whisper.

El Yubri stops moving. He looks at his sister. He looks at her in the same way as when Bastián sets his Rottweiler on Viberti's Dobermann.

La Penqui, one eyebrow raised, fiddles awkwardly with the Fortuna packet, looking for another cigarette, which her clumsy fingers can't quite manage to extract from its hiding place.

'So what the fuck do you want?' El Yubri, not understanding or not wanting to understand, finally asks her.

His sister smiles. 'As if I knew.'

'I'll do him. Do you want me to smash his face in? El Nene doesn't frighten me.'

La Penca gets the cigarette out and blows on her chest, even though there's no more ash on it.

'Bastard, I'll find him and I'll kill him, Penqui.'

'Kill, kill, you're going to kill. So much killing. Who are you going to kill, your father?'

El Yubri freezes like a pillar of salt.

'I'll poison him first, and that'll be the end of it.' La Penca clicks the lighter, which refuses to work. 'I really will kill him.'

Céspedes comes out of the bathroom. He's taken off his newly acquired suit and tie. They're screwed up in a ball in a plastic bag. He's wearing his Hawaiian shirt again in all its splendour along with his Bermuda shorts. He walks across the lounge in El Espejo, watches himself cross the room, sees his feet in the oval mirror that's embedded in the art nouveau bar. Out on the pavement he waits for two or three cars to go past. He crosses the road and goes into the terrace enclosure.

Green. Glass. There's Carole at the back, ensconced in a red bench seat. As she watches him approach she takes a long sip of her iced tea. Céspedes can sense that she's bored. He breathes in, deep down into his lungs.

'You're kitted out like a bad boy again,' she says.

'As if you'd ever liked hanging out with the good boys.'

'I had a boyfriend once who trained to be a priest.'

'They're the worst.'

'No, he joined the seminary afterwards. I was very young when I was living in Lille.'

'In Lille. So that's how you'd leave him. Only fit for the seminary. He must still be getting over the pain of you dumping him.'

'He left me.'

'I don't believe you. I bet it's not true.'

'No.'

'There, you see. A venial sin. And so predictable.' Céspedes takes a sip of his whisky. He feels free. And he feels he's going down the wrong path with her.

She confirms his suspicion. 'What time's the return train?'

'Whenever you like.'

'Really? Are you going to put on a train just for me? Are you going to pay for it, too?'

'Easier than that, darling. I bought tickets for the last train, which we can change for any of the earlier ones. There are loads of them. Loads of trains to everywhere.'

'Don't tell me you want to go somewhere else on some kind of world tour.'

'The best trains . . . let's see if I can get this right, yes . . .' Céspedes refreshes his memory with another sip, while Carole watches him with her head tilted back. 'Yes, that's right: *the best trains to take are the ones that go nowhere.* Luis Mateo Díez.'

'Who's he? Another friend of yours?'

'One of the best. No, I wish he were. He's a magnificent writer.'

'It's strange, isn't it?'

'What's strange?'

'It's strange that being, I mean, doing what you do, you like books so much, literature.'

'You mean, you have to choose between money or poetry?'

'More or less. You said it.'

'The stock exchange or real life.'

'The stock exchange or real life.' Carole raises her eyebrows, takes a sip of tea. She's tired. She leaves the glass on the side table, pauses, looks at him. 'What, what are you disguised as?'

'Now?'

'No, not now, I mean what are you disguised as? Perhaps it's what I don't know that makes you seem attractive. You know that and you weaponize it. But since we're travelling together, tell me, what are you disguised as?'

'Too many different things.'

She makes another gesture of exhaustion. *It's not exhaustion, it might be disappointment, the disappointment that's bred and nurtured like a weed when someone asks what am I doing here, why on earth did I say yes,* Céspedes thinks to himself. *She still thinks she's the mistress of her own life, enclosed in her tiny cage, running on the wheel that she thinks will make the world dance to her tune. Beautiful and lonely. So lonely, it's tempting to be cruel, to play with her like a cat plays with a defenceless little bird with its retractable claws. Carole, little girl lost.*

'Do you mean you wear one disguise on top of another, depending on the situation and who you're with?'

'Onion or chameleon? I'm afraid I'm both,' Céspedes elucidates.

'And at the moment?'

'I suppose the first disguise is still there, frayed and worn, and I think it's my real skin after all this time. And that's what I want to show you. But, who knows?'

She looks at him distrustfully. And he feels tender. Céspedes feels tender. Towards her. Towards himself, towards everyone. Towards those isolated figures crossing the street, dodging the heat today and the cold tomorrow, towards people driving their cars past the windows and towards those faceless, nameless people behind the walls of those buildings surrounding them, all believing they control their own destinies, hallucinating, chasing visions, illusions. Laboriously weaving a spider's web with no thought that a gust of wind will blow it away. Innocent, warm hearted, trying their best. All those people, better than him. He's known them, he's lived with them. And he's forgotten about them. Céspedes feels something melt, not only inside himself but in the earth's crust. *In the end everyone will be jumbled up and everyone an orphan, all of us crammed on board the raft of the Medusa,* he thinks, more or less. *The night surrounding us all, the cold black water where she's lurking, and she'll bite us and take us down to the depths, make herself blind and will blind us, too. There at the bottom of the sea, once again speechless, once again nameless.*

'And now, what are you disguised as? When I met you yesterday, what disguise were you wearing?'

'The same one as now.'

'Yes, and what is it?'

'Nakedness.'

'Nakedness? Do you think you're being naked now or are you just showing off your rags?'

Céspedes breathes in through his nose noisily and smiles.

'I know very little about myself these days.'

And she responds by raising her right eyebrow a little bit more.

Céspedes pictures her deep in the French provinces. Lille, those fields strewn with blood, where he'd also been when he was still a young man. Three months or more working on a contract relating to Eurostar that never came to anything. Days out in the open air. The church at Méteren, the fields of Flanders, trips with his wife, the small flat in the Rue d'Angleterre where he was happy for a while without realizing it.

He's tempted to talk, Céspedes is tempted to tell Carole that he knows Lille, the city where she lives. He probably knows the small town where she was born, too. When he asked her a few hours back, she'd simply described it as 'a small town which you'd never have heard of'. Bailleul, Saint-Jans-Cappel, Béthune? Fields with corpses and shrapnel under the surface, so many dead and so much metal, slow-moving mist that left a grey patina when it lifted and gradually started turning green, as if the ghosts of those old soldiers were rising out of the ground and were still evaporating into the fog and the clouds.

'As for me,' Céspedes begins after taking a long sip, not knowing where he's going, 'me, my family was a poor family, we lived in a place in the city that was known as The Fort. I don't know if they still call it that or who lives there now. At that time the people living in there had almost all come from somewhere else. My father was . . . my father had come from the north and worked on the railway – don't laugh, don't ask me if that's why I love trains.'

'No, that hadn't even occurred to me, but who knows?' Carole almost manages a smile, overcoming her tiredness.

'My father inherited a small business that came down to him from his brother who drowned when he was fishing on a small boat that never made it back to the shore. He was a bachelor, a mild-mannered man, very reserved. Well, the business was an ironmonger's. Am I boring you?'

Carole shakes her head, still wondering where Céspedes is heading. 'No. You were saying: the ironmonger's and you.'

'Yes, but you know, I don't want to bore you. That's the last thing I want.'

'Or make excuses for yourself?'

'No, not that either, I don't think so. Make excuses for what? Yes, I know there are a lot of things I ought to make excuses for, but not now, not to you. It's just to show you a few snaps from the family album or look at them myself through your eyes, through the eyes of someone I don't know.'

'I'm someone you don't know.'

'Exactly. We can't be anything else. That's what we want to be and what we are.'

Something flickered in Carole's eyes. 'How do you mean?'

'Things went well for my father. They worked hard, my mother as well. My mother learned all there was to know about thinners, paints, detergents and suppliers, deferred payments and banks. My mother spent a lot of time there because my father didn't leave his job on the railway for several years.'

'What about you?'

'What about me?'

'Didn't you help out?'

'No. I was a child. And then, when I was a teenager, I didn't help either. They wanted me to stay out of it.'

'And you let them?'

'Yes.' Céspedes sighs. 'When, that is, when I was really old enough to lend a hand everything was running almost like clockwork. My father opened another business, bathtubs, washbasins, WCs. There, you see.'

'What?'

'Nothing too sophisticated.'

Carole breaks into a sad, ironic, distant smile.

'They'd sent me off to study at what was considered a good school, and I was the first one from my branch of the family to go to university ever since millions of years ago my ancestors came down from the trees and stood up on their back legs.'

'And you felt that was a responsibility?'

'I also made concessions, or that's what I thought. My father wanted me to be an economist. I think that word sounded to him like, I don't know how to explain it, something epic. A son of his with the title of "economist".'

'Your concession was that you wanted to be something else, a poet, and that's where your love of books comes from, the poor boy made a sacrifice to satisfy his family who didn't appreciate a free spirit.'

Céspedes raises his hand and signals to a waiter that he wants more of the same, another whisky. He looks at Carole, shrugs his shoulders. *Yes, maybe I was a dickhead, but who knows where you'd have been, what you were doing when you were my age, coming from a good family, the luxury of being a rebel and being able to throw stones at bourgeois windows because you were so thoroughly bourgeois, because your very essence, your hair, those perfect eyes of yours, that natural delight in moving your chin in perfect time with your eyelids or tying a scarf around your neck so elegantly, all that comes from a long-established bourgeois tradition, built up over generations, and look at you, there, so scornful and yet still so perfect in spite of it.*

'That might be one way of looking at it even if it wasn't quite like that. It would never have occurred to me to be a poet. I know you said that sarcastically, but I was happy, just a few years later, I was happy I'd gone along with my father's veneration for the word "economist". And yes, I was a dickhead, if you want to put it like that. I came here, went to university – the Complutense. I met Carlos Moya, a sociologist, a real intellectual, and I made friends with two of his disciples, Carlos Cañeque and Enrique Montoya. And, you know, we had some wild nights, lots of reading, lots of philosophizing, as Cañeque liked to say. I wouldn't have wanted to be a poet, that never even occurred to me or anything like that, but I could have lived like one, been connected to other worlds.'

The waiter places a fresh glass of whisky on the side table, takes away the old glass, its contents diluted by the ice, and asks, 'Would madam like anything else?'

Carole shakes her head. *Rude, very tired,* Céspedes thinks. *This adventure's wearing a bit thin on her.*

'I came home with what's known as a decent set of intellectual baggage, my university degree and a certain amount of confusion.'

'Daddy must have been happy.'

'Daddy was dead.'

Carole's right eyebrow shoots up again, indicating surprise and a sense of mourning.

'Heart attack.'

'So he hardly got to see your economist strapline.'

'That's right. He missed out on it. He died at a time when my head was all over the place. The last time we met wasn't much fun. Let's just say he'd lost faith in me.'

Céspedes takes a long sip. The intensive-care unit. His father's drooping eyelids, half closed, swollen, a drowning man trying to stay afloat amid all the flotsam. Tubes, machines, everything that a shipwrecked life spits out, floating around him. The dark cave of a mouth without its dentures, face unshaven, a field of stubble. One grey eyelid opening, that one eye staring at him, finally focusing, recognizing him, the nurse looking at his father, slightly surprised. 'He's going to say something.' And the words that followed, as that eye was fixed on him, clear and hoarse, 'Stupid crazy lunatic.' His mouth twisted and his eye still looking at him until it closed and he slipped back into that sort of lethargy that would end in his death a few hours later. Daddy's last words. The bewildered nurse trying to apologize on behalf of the dying man, 'You know, sometimes they say things they've heard, it's not what they're really thinking, it's delirium, perhaps he didn't even see you.'

'So suddenly the poetry was over for you. That's tough.'

'Tough? You're not joking! You've really managed to stir up my prehistoric, my antediluvian resentment. Class resentment. And I thought I didn't have a trace of it left.'

'Who, me?'

'Yes, you. So used to humiliating people, even when you're not trying. It's in your blood, isn't it? I bet you don't even realize. It's your caste. Yes, you were suckled on it. Don't tell me what to do.'

'That's the last thing I need, to tell you what to do.'

'I'm beginning to realize now, you're taking me back to another time, another time when I could be fascinated by an unattainable woman at the same time as her very remoteness told me where my place was, clipped my wings.'

'And then you got what you wanted, didn't you? When you made some money and got over your inferiority complex . . .'

'When people like you started to believe that I was one of you, or rather, that I could join you without ruining the landscape. You and your parents, your mothers making allowances for me, accepting me. Excusing me in exchange for money, a lot of money. And you know what those allowances were worth? Do you know?' Céspedes pauses and looks from side to side, as though he's about to reveal a big secret, and then in a low but emphatic voice he says, 'Nothing. They weren't worth a bean.'

'Poor boy. And you only just realized?'

'As if you were royalty, but it's not even that, now, how ridiculous it all is.' He finishes off his whisky. 'Starting with me.'

'So I'm the last guilty party, the incarnation of the sins of who knows how many millions of ancestors.'

'How ridiculous, everyone – you, me, all of us.'

'How many people are you going to summons to your private Nuremberg, how many millions of people have abused you and kept you down in the ghetto?'

'Are you Jewish?'

'Obviously.'

'With a name like Carole?'

'Do I have to be called Rachel or Sarah or have a shaved head?'

'Your father was Spanish. And your mother?'

'You're the one who was going to get the family album out, not me. Remember?'

All out of kilter. Too much whisky. No, too many hours with no sleep, too much rubble, too much. Céspedes shakes his head. 'Well, you've almost seen me without my disguise, as you wanted. Letting me ramble on.'

'What a pathetic striptease. And, like I said, showing more rags than nudity.'

'It was unrehearsed. Not what I'd planned.'

Carole looks at her watch. Céspedes also looks at Carole's watch, the present, the absurdity. She sighs and says, 'I suppose so. We lose control of things. That's how it is, am I right, oh wise man? You'd like to be a bohemian or whatever and you end up being an economist, you'd like to have a family *comme il faut* and you get yourself tangled up with mistresses, you'd like to spend a day in a bubble and you end up stirring up your past.'

'Yes, that's how it all seems. We're swept along by the river. And how about you?'

'Me?'

'Yes, why are you here? Today.'

'I'm not going to do a striptease. But . . .' she frowns, purses her lips and starts speaking again, 'let's just say that I lose control of things, too. You don't have an exclusive on things going wrong.'

'A boyfriend? A row?'

Carole looked at him intensely.

'A breakdown?'

'Let's change the subject.'

Cars pass silently by on the other side of the plate glass. *The witching hour. Clocks have no pity. Inexorable. The most inhumane invention. So many absurd ideas caught in the spider's web. When I was a child I thought about how many times the hour hand would have to go around the clock before I died, sums in an exercise book, twice a day, seven hundred and thirty times a year, my father winding up that clock and me trying to calculate the number of times he'd have to wind it up again, I wasn't far out, sixty years seemed like going down a dead-end street back then, and now I'm nearly there myself, and here I am, my father and his clocks, crazy, idiot, famous last words.*

Céspedes looks up. Takes a sip of the dregs of the whisky. Liquid oxygen. Trees, peace, the street almost empty. And a memory of a different street, beneath different trees. It was early one morning, and he was walking on a street skirting the park, and he heard voices as he was going past a bar called La Vieja Aduana where they sometimes used to meet up. And there they were, the three of them: Garriga Vela, Taján and Soler. They'd just left the bar. Alexandra, the owner, was pulling down the blinds and saying good night to them. They were drunk. She was laughing. The three of them were trying to walk in a straight line. And suddenly, something bizarre. A cart appeared, an old cart, drawn by a single horse, driven by a very old man wearing a cap. In the back was a pile of old furniture and scrap metal. The horse's hooves echoed on the asphalt (like a black lung) in the early morning. The old man was a knife-grinder and, in the middle of the night, when he saw those three, he started playing the miniature pan pipes typical of his trade. Those sharp, insidious notes. The cart passed in front of Céspedes on the way towards the Customs House, which stood out in the night like an enormous monument of marble or ivory, and after a few yards crossed in front of the glowing, bewildered faces of the cavorting trio. The knife-sharpener started making sparks fly from the grinding stone beside him, the metal screeched, the horse slowed his already slow pace and, just as the cart passed them, Taján, Garriga and Soler grabbed hold of it and jumped up into the back with a mix of groans and stifled laughter. The tall palm trees outside the Customs House were like arrows pointing to the heavens, behind the outlandish silhouette made by the knife-grinder, the furniture, the scrap metal and the three stowaways. Wobbling, Taján managed to stand up among the grubby furniture. The knife-grinder emitted a muted cackle, seeing that human figure with his two companions looking up from below. Taján let out a howl and stood on top of an old washboard, with his legs apart and his arms outstretched into the December night that peered over the tops of the dormant orange trees. Taján threw back his head, and with a gaze as haughty and distant as Chancellor Otto von Bismarck, illuminated by the knife-grinder's sparks, he shouted out an exhortation at the top of his voice for the city to wake up.

Taján: 'Time to open your eyes. Time to wake up!'

The only response was the sound of the horse's hooves, the rattling of the furniture and scrap metal and the rasping knife-grinder's stone.

Taján: 'I summon you to the Resurrection! The time for lethargy is over. No more sleep. No more anaesthesia. I am the king of the city!'

Soler: 'In the absence of Rafael Pérez Estrada!'

Taján: 'Naturally! By all his mercy!'

Garriga: 'Hallelujah!'

Knife-grinder: 'Hallelujah!'

Wobbling just as much as Taján, the cart disappeared around the bend, heading for the town hall and the wooded darkness of the park. The echo of the horse's hooves on the asphalt and shouting and laughter could just be heard floating on the night air after the grinding noise and humble glow of the grindstone had already disappeared. Céspedes stood immobile beneath the winter orange trees.

The cars pass by silently on the other side of the glass. *Life's great mincing machine. Other people. Freedom that never returned, water between our fingers.* Céspedes looks at Carole's perfect eyebrows, the thick curtains of hair hanging on either side of her face. *The curtain falls. The party's over.* He takes a sip of the dregs of the whisky and looks at the woman, who's not saying a word.

'I think we'd better go back, don't you?'

'Yes,' she says, without returning his look.

yr snatch wants a stab?

Jorge rereads Nene Olmedo's WhatsApp. What the fuck does he mean? He's going to send him one back, ask what he means, when he sees that El Nene is writing to him and a new message appears on his screen.

yr girl wants stab or cock?

Bastard. Jorge's about to write to him to ask what that means and stops. He writes:

Nene

He deletes that and starts again:

hey whatsup? all ok

He sends it. Then he writes and sends:

ok bruv?

He receives:

bruv my ars wake up

And then immediately:

or if not want I stab

Fucking bastard. His cousin comes over. Jorge turns the phone over to hide the screen.

'For Christ's sake, can you put that phone down for one minute?'

'It's my mother. About my brother.'

'Your mother?'

'Yes, she . . .'

'When it's not your mother it's your girlfriend and when it's not her it's the pope. Mate, try working a little bit. It's not going to do you any harm, for fuck's sake.'

Pedroche looks over from his desk without lifting his head.

Head like an egg, stupid bastard, we'll see if Nene gives you a good slapping and wipes that smug vampire look off your shitty face, fat fuck.

'I'll send a quick reply and then I'll start work on the big picture, the one Manrique brought.'

'The big one? What big one? Fucking hell, start on it now.'

'I've already started, I've trimmed off the sides. I'll just reply and like you say, and' (lowering his voice) 'are you staying here when he goes to see that priest? Is he going now or what?'

'What's that got to do with it? No, apparently now the priest is saying he's got to go to some thing with some nuns, and he'll give him the stuff back later.' Floren, who's not a great actor, looks at Pedroche out of the corner of his eye and carries on in a jocular tone, 'Let's hope the priest doesn't decide to keep it all.'

Pedroche looks over again without looking up, as if he wants to make sure the plaster and cuts on his head are on permanent display.

'What a hassle. He'll end up keeping him hanging around until midnight,' Jorge stammers, his phone vibrating in his hand with another message. 'What a hassle.'

'No, mate, when I leave here I'm going to have a beer in La Esquinita to kill some time and hang around with him for a bit until he goes and sees the priest, and then I'll go home and have some dinner, and, I don't know, he can do whatever he wants.' Floren looks back at Pedroche, their eyes cross, and he gets flustered, raises his voice, he really doesn't know how to act. 'Well, come on then, get cracking with whatever Manrique brought in, OK?'

'I'll just reply to my mother then I'm on it.' Two bad actors in a pitiful performance with Pedroche as the silent critic.

As soon as his cousin moves away, Jorge looks at his phone:

no reply wnkr?

He writes and sends:

It's delayed

He writes more:

I thnk meet priest @ 10
soon as knw wll say
am on case

Nene Olmedo is writing. Jorge receives:

not telling stories wnkr?

Bastard pain in the arse.

fck no Nene on case wll let U knw

u btr coz she nice snatch

Jorge's still looking at his phone. Nene Olmedo is offline. Jorge looks around, feeling disorientated, slides his finger across the screen. He's just about to send a message to his girlfriend when he receives one from his mother:

know where yr brother is?

How the fuck am I supposed to know? Yes, I know he woke me up this morning thumping on my door and then cut up half the house, I know that. And that I'm up to here with him and you, too. I know that much.

His mother looks at her phone, leaning against the shelf in the bathroom as she puts on her make-up in front of the mirror. She knows that Jorge has read the message. She does the eyeliner carefully with a black pencil. Thickens up her eyelashes with mascara. Dark eyeshadow. Combs her eyebrows into a perfect arch. Runs her tongue timidly over her upper lip. Rafi likes her with heavy eyeliner. She looks at her phone. Takes a step back. Tilts her head back a bit. Dark-red bra. Smooth skin. Still almost perfect, slightly tanned, pronounced collar bones, shoulders, well, a little bit, ever so slightly, fleshier than they should be. Breasts, hidden beneath her bra and lifted up by the under-wiring, yes, they're perfect. She knows what effect they have. In the hotel, in the street. Looks that she pretends to ignore and that bolster her with strength and power. What about when her looks fade? Best not to think about the challenges the future holds. She'll have grandchildren by then. She'll have overcome other, different challenges. She'll be happy. She'll forget. Her date with Rafi today is what matters now.

She looks back at the screen. And writes again:

know where yr brother is?

She looks at herself in the mirror, touches up her hair a bit using her fingers as a comb. A whistle announces a reply:

no idea

Amelia spends a short time staring at the two words. She feels sad all of a sudden. Almost like the tenderness you feel when you're ill, a porosity, a worm tunnelling through your gut, threatening to weaken you. She holds it in check:

Dinner in fridge 4 U both

She doesn't know whether to put on the top with the blood-red straps or the red blouse with a printed pattern. She gets caught up in this dilemma. She wants this to be the most important thing in her life at this moment. The only thing.

In spite of this she writes:

XXXXX

Then she wishes she hadn't. Reflecting on Jorge's emotional stinginess. And Ismael nothing but a black hole.

Ismael is on his third gin and ice in Las Camborias. The waitress serves them short, and he's shaking his head observing the short measure. But he doesn't say anything. Except the second time he asked her, 'Do you charge for this the same as a normal one?'

And the waitress, feigning indifference and turning her back on him, replied, 'That is a normal one. That's how we serve them here.'

'And I bet you charge the normal price, too.'

Silence. The waitress carries on taking glasses out of the sink. Ismael squints. Once he saw a few frames of some film in which the actor pulled that expression and he liked it, the way it looked. Head down and eyes looking up, a smile on his mouth that wasn't really a smile. 'Who's he?' he asked his mother. 'Jack Nicholson,' she replied. 'Do you want to watch it? It's a really good film.'

No, he didn't want to watch it. Ismael can't stand more than five minutes on the same channel. He doesn't understand how people can spend hours watching the same thing. His brother and his girlfriend can sit on the sofa watching films that might last two hours. Not saying a word to each other, holding hands as if they were in the doctor's surgery. The most they'd do would be to get up to fetch a beer from the fridge. The rest of the time they'd sit there mesmerized like the living dead. They don't come to the flat any more. She doesn't come to the flat any more. Since that one time. Jorge said he was staring at her. Him, staring at her. Little shit. She's just a snotty brat. She was the one who told Jorge that he was staring at her. Ismael noticed her saying something to him under her breath – 'Your brother's looking at me' or something like that – and the stupid moron only believes her. As soon as she stopped whispering, Jorge turned around suddenly and looked at him with his dickhead face. Girls like it when things like that happen. She was the one staring at him. Girls like you to be all over them, and if you're not they make a scene. They'll make something up, whatever they want. They'll set brother against brother, whatever, they don't care. That's what the shitty little brat did and his dickhead of a brother went off on one. 'What's going on?' he said. Moron. Swallowing the bait. That's what wound him up more than anything.

And then what happened in the corridor. That's when it all kicked off. Their mother was at home that day. Just as well because otherwise something would have happened, he would have wrung Jorge's neck, and he'd have given that little bitch a lesson she wouldn't forget, so they'd forget about trying to take the piss again. It was dark in the corridor, and he couldn't see a thing. He'd just woken up and was looking down at the floor, he didn't see her or anything else. He was more shocked than anyone when she started calling out to Jorge like that. She nearly made him deaf. And then putting on a performance, how he'd stood in the middle of the corridor and wouldn't let her past, that she'd tried to go around him and he'd moved from side to side. How's he going to be moving? Like people move when they've just woken up. And the stuff about his dick. Saying he had a hard-on. That really is a joke, that little whore saying he had a hard-on. Why not say he was jerking himself off? Not to mention all the cocks she must have sucked, with a face like she never stops sucking cocks. The number of times the two of them were in there in Jorge's room with the door closed, and guess what they were up to. Saying a prayer? 'Course they were. That's why they wedged a chair against the door. Fucking themselves stupid. That's if his brother knows how to fuck. Or whatever. Seeing is believing. Maybe the thing with her is she wants to be fucked properly. And she's begging for it. He's got a hard-on. 'Ismael had a hard-on, Amelia.' That's what the little bitch said, bursting into tears, clinging to his mother.

That was the worst thing, the little whore dragging his mother into it. And she said his dick was hanging out. Fucking hell, he was in his underpants and he'd just got up. 'And you're having a siesta at eight o'clock in the evening?' she said, not letting go of his mother. He wanted to smash her face in. Give her a good slapping and throw her off the balcony. See her flattened on the pavement with her legs all twisted like they do when they fall off a high building, and her face stuck to the tarmac. He could also picture her splattered on top of a car. 'Oh, so I should have a sleep when it suits you, OK, so tell me when I should have a sleep, go on, tell me, dumbo.' Just as well that his mother told the truth, that he does sleep at strange times, that she's always having a go at him for just that reason. And then about him having his dick out, in the end she admitted, she admitted it, that he didn't have his dick out. Almost hanging out, she said. Oh, so it wasn't actually out, so I might as well have been wearing an overcoat.

And now the little bitch was getting up a head of steam. Since the thing about his dick wasn't clear, and she admitted it was dark in the corridor, and she couldn't stop going on about the same thing, and since his mother was protecting her and short-arse Jorge was there, shaking his head like a chicken trying to have a peck, she started on about the thing in the bathroom. Give me a break. Another made-up story. She was obviously bored with watching films one after another, the stupid whore. So one day, she said, one day she was in the bathroom with the door half closed because she thought it was only her and Jorge in the flat, and she was looking at herself in the mirror after having a wee, that's what she said, 'having a wee', she was looking at herself in the mirror, and what a shock she got when she noticed Ismael was spying on her. She could see him in the mirror. She jumped back and looked straight at the door, and he'd gone, but she ran out and saw his bedroom door closing, Ismael's bedroom. And then she said that she'd heard his footsteps, Ismael's bare feet running down the corridor. Always that fucking corridor. And his mother saying, 'What are you saying? What are you saying, darling?' That's all we needed, calling her 'darling' like she was her own daughter, our little sister.

'So was he looking at you all the time, didn't you realize? Tell me what happened.' And she was going, 'No, I don't know how long he was there, and I don't know if he'd been watching me all the time I was having a wee. How long he stayed there.' Watching a girl having a wee, give me a break. Not even Consuelo. Well, maybe Consuelo, but that little brat, do me a favour. 'Having a wee.' So when she's at home, in Portada Alta, they all say 'having a wee' – pull the other one. At least Consuelo would say 'pissing', and that would be something else, a real turn-on, a piss and a half and a proper cunt, not the little toy pussy on that stupid bitch.

And his idiot brother saying to the bitch, 'You didn't tell me about that,' and looking at him as if he were a wasp with a sting, 'Ooo, no, it's going to sting me,' pretending he was really angry and his mouth going like he was going to burst into tears instead of hitting someone. 'You didn't tell me about that,' said the birdbrain. And she was saying, 'Yes, I felt like my heart was in my mouth, but I didn't want to stir things up, that's why I didn't say anything.' And, worst of all, his mother. His mother saying, 'So Ismael, what happened?' 'What happened? You're really asking me that? What happened?' And his brother repeating Ismael's words. 'Yes, what happened?' 'It's not about what happened, it's about what she wants to happen, can't you see that?'

His mother taking her side. Not entirely, but she didn't say, 'Listen, honey, you'd better go. Don't come here trying to stir up trouble. Just because that idiot Jorge's got the hots for you. You'd better not set foot in this house again.' But no. Instead she went, 'So, Ismael, what happened?' It's all very well if Jorge dances to that little brat's tune, but his mother? Winding him up even more, telling him that Jorge's girlfriend is like his sister and that's how he should treat her, like a sister, and everyone should get on nicely with each other. The only thing she didn't say was 'kiss and make up' and all that crap. They almost managed to get him to flip, to really flip. He was hoping his brother would come at him, lay one finger on him. That was the finale he was hoping for. All because of that stupid little bitch. He could also picture her lying on the kitchen floor with a load of stab wounds and her top all covered in blood.

And there was the waitress. In Las Camborias. With her fleshy back. And not much gin left. The third one.

The sea looks like a watercolour with a yellowish tint, delightfully faded. We can also say that the long August evening is stretching across it when Guille emerges from the bedroom holding La Lori by the hand. They return to the living room, and it's then that they see the sea and the day expiring over it.

No one notices their return. Only Cabello, now sitting at the other end of the sofa, watches them closely and tries to guess what they've been up to. Guille relaxes. He was expecting a round of whistles, questions and laughter. La Lori is full of confidence, as always. *She doesn't waste time speculating about what other people would do*, thinks Guille. *Or maybe she'd worked it out even before she left home and she knows what she has to do. Watch and learn.*

La Lori lets go of Guille's hand. She approaches the table in the centre of the room, takes a cigarette from a packet, turns her head and lights up. Juno offers her a spliff and at the same time asks her where she's been. She refuses it and places both her hands on the back of her neck, as if a policeman had suddenly pointed his gun at her. With the cigarette hanging from her lips and one eye squinting she gathers up her hair, gives it a couple of twists and makes a sort of bun. With extreme dexterity.

Guille has been watching her. Not only out of admiration but to avoid meeting Cabello's eyes. His questioning eyes. He doesn't want to give any explanations. Once he heard his uncle say that what happens between a man and woman is no one else's business. It sounded like something out of the Middle Ages, like swords and wigs and all that stuff. But it would be a good one to use today. Except he knows he can't and that sooner or later word will get around that he's been in one of the bedrooms with La Lori and they'll ask him. They always do.

La Lori told him. It's true they play the bottle game and she's been to bed with a few of them. Not with him. It had been very different with him. His father had died.

As they went into El Tuli's parents' bedroom and he saw that enormous bed, Guille felt as if he was melting inside. He was scared, but he went up to La Lori from behind. Being so close he caught her full aroma, her full range of aromas. La Lori turned around, her tits brushing his arm. He had an erection. She realized and looked down at his trousers. And then at his face. 'Are you feeling bad?' she asked. It wasn't what Guille was expecting. He was almost about to look down at his trousers as well, not understanding. Bad? What did she mean? He thought about it but didn't say anything, biting his tongue. Looking into La Lori's eyes from so close, almost brushing her face. He realizes she's taller than him. Bummer. Seeing him lost for words, La Lori says, 'About your father, I mean. Is it true that he died today, or is it just bullshit?'

What was all this? Was there someone listening behind the door? The idea stuck in Guille's head. El Tuli, Juno, that Isidro guy and Cabello, choking back the laughter. He looked towards the door. La Lori asked him again. 'Are you feeling bad?' He turned his head towards her, the room started swimming, the bed nearly touched the ceiling, skating, like a bar of soap in the bathtub. And at the same time every drop of blood in his body rapidly slid down towards his feet in free fall. He felt drained. If she'd wanted to, La Lori could have folded him up, just like an inflatable mattress after the air's been let out.

But instead of folding him up, La Lori took him by the arm and sat him on the edge of the bed. And she blew on him. Leaning over him, La Lori took a deep breath and blew into his face. She opened her mouth, displaying the gap between her two front teeth and breathed in. Guille wanted to follow the trusted path of air, to enter La Lori's mouth, to fly past her tongue and descend along that dark cavity from which there suddenly sprang a sweet mouthful of air, with a slight scent of marijuana and spearmint gum.

La Lori stopped blowing and sat there looking at him. All the colours of her eyes, the green, grey and honey-coloured flecks there in front of Guille's. 'Is that better?' she asked. He swallowed saliva and said, 'Yes.' Looking serious with one eyebrow raised, she carried on staring at him for a short while longer. Guille looked down and, thanks to the way she was leaning forward, he saw her tits almost in their entirety. La Lori looked down at her own cleavage, and then into Guille's eyes. She displayed the gap between her teeth again, but this time she didn't blow or say anything. She sat next to him and he could see the picture they made in the mirror opposite, which until then had been shielded by La Lori.

It was difficult to recognize himself. He'd never imagined that anyone could look so pale. And the rings around his eyes looked as if they been painted on, like when he dressed up as a zombie. La Lori looked at him in the mirror. *Ave Maria Purissima.* That's what Guille thought she'd whispered. He saw himself turning his head in the mirror. In front of his face was La Lori's long hair, that forest, that impenetrable thicket. He sent commands to his hand to move up towards her tits. But his hand didn't obey. It barely lifted itself off the bedcover and then came to rest on his own thigh. New commands, an almost telepathic effort, interrupted by the girl.

'What happened to your father?'

'Bloody hell, Lori,' is all he managed to reply in a whisper.

At that moment Guille would like to have remembered what a person who's attracted to dead people is called. He'd heard it once in a film. Those people who get aroused thinking about dead women or men and even have sex with them. It made him want to laugh, he had to control the urge. He thought of his father, on a metal table, naked, his cock exposed like that day on the beach when a wave pulled his trunks down, he thought of his father and about who would want to have sex with him, and that got rid of his urge to laugh, put a brake on the convulsions that he thought he'd contained before they became obvious, but which led the girl to ask him, 'Are you going to throw up?'

Guille shook his head.

'There's a bathroom over there,' said La Lori, pointing out the half-open door. 'This guy's parents have a fantastic lifestyle. Yours do, too, I bet? Your people have money, don't they?'

She sounds like a housemaid, Guille thought, *but even so she's really hot.*

'What happened to him?'

'What you said,' Guille dug deep inside trying to find a new way of saying that people die, and it had been his father's turn today. That was something that even children understood. 'What you said, Lori, for Christ's sake.'

'So he died?' she confirms.

Guille replies again by shrugging his shoulders and letting out a sigh, a kind of dull hissing.

'But you don't want to tell me what happened.'

'The thing is, I don't know, I don't really know.'

La Lori looks at him, so close up. 'And you're here,' she says.

Now Guille replies by raising his eyebrows and thinking, *Is she really that crazy, or is it the dope?*

They look at each other in the mirror. They hear laughter in the background. Juno's voice louder than the rest, probably doing an impression. He's the only one who does good impressions. Guille no longer thinks there's anyone spying on them on the other side of the door. No. What he's thinking, what he's scared of, is that La Lori, attracted by the laughter and now she's sure that she can't find out anything about his father's death or dead people in general, will decide to go and see what's going on and leave him there sitting on the edge of the bed.

But no. The girl has a highly developed spirit of solidarity. Their eyes cross in the mirror and she asks him, 'Do you want me to toss you off?'

Silence. A moment of doubt until Guille turns his head a little by way of acceptance, or resignation, thinking, *Goodbye to having a fuck. She fucks everyone – or nearly everyone – except me. Is it because of my father? Because he's dead or because I didn't tell her what he died of?*

'Hey? Do you want me to toss you off?'

La Lori, judging by her tone, was understanding, although not to the extent that Guille can find the courage to raise the stakes. So, while he was thinking of saying, 'How about a fuck?' he ends up saying, 'Cool.'

So that's how it was. And now in the living room, while La Lori has made a knot in her hair and Guille is avoiding Cabello's gaze and possible interrogation, he turns around and sees her. *Oh my God!* Up until that moment he hadn't realized that Mónica Ovejero is there. Mónica Ovejero and Piluca, sitting on one end of the sofa near where he'd been before he left the room with La Lori.

Guille raises his hand in a wave but is met by an angry look from Mónica and Piluca with her chin raised. Inquisition. He looks at La Lori instinctively. Shit. They saw him, they saw him come into the living room holding hands with La Lori. He coughs, trips over the carpet and heads over to where the two girls are sitting, away from the racket being made by Juno, Isidro and El Tuli with their laughter, Juno doing an impression of El Tuli's father talking like Chiquito de la Calzada, an old-time stand-up comedian.

'How's it going? When did you get here? There's whisky,' says Guille, not knowing why he mentioned the whisky.

Mónica looks out to sea, tense and dignified, her beautiful long hair silkier than ever. Piluca answers him, 'When you were with that slut, that's when we got here.'

'Who, me? Oh. What do you mean?' Guille forces a laugh, looks over at La Lori as if he's only just noticed that she was there in the flat or on Planet Earth. 'What's up?'

'Let's go,' Mónica says to her friend.

And Guille sees the girl's eyes glistening with moisture, a hint of a pool, a life, and suddenly glimpses the meaning of love, redemption, the future, children, a car and even a job, coming back home and a thirty-year-old Mónica Ovejero there to greet him with a kiss and not a care in the world. He loved her. He loves her.

'But, where are you going? Why? There's whisky . . .' *The fucking whisky again.* 'Where are you off to?'

The two girls get to their feet. Guille, too, and once again the room, the window and the sea itself all start turning as if the room were a ball and was bouncing back and forth with them inside. He wants to throw up, and he wants to tell them both, tell Mónica, 'All she did was toss me off, Mónica, I swear, she tossed me off, because of my father.' His father who's lying on a metal slab.

The two girls walk ahead of him, and everyone else is laughing, not at them, not at him, but laughing for the sake of it, for no reason. *Everything we do is for no reason, like fish in goldfish bowl, swimming to get to the glass and staying there. God, I'm feeling really shit.* Guille walking behind Mónica's swaying tresses and Piluca's almost perfectly square head, saying to one of them or other 'I'll come, too' and more laughter behind them.

Walking down the corridor feeling that he was descending into a cave, towards the centre of the earth, sinking, remembering La Lori's hand on his cock, so slow, so disgustingly knowledgeable, and him touching her tits through her top, smelling the scent of her hair as she shakes her head, a scent that now almost makes him retch, a wave of repugnance, her hand moving *like an industrial machine*, so he thought at the time, La Lori lubricating her hand with her own saliva, pulling a hair from the side of her mouth *how can she be aware of such an insignificant detail while she's doing what she's doing, as if it were unimportant, she's so used to doing it?* and him starting to come, his vision clouding over, seeing his father laughing, the sun, his mother hugging him again, La Lori's scent, her mouth, the gap in her teeth, her nipples showing through her top in the living room, Cabello's laughter, bones turning into water, losing shape, melting, and when he opened his eyes he saw her with her hand in the air, sticky, getting up and going to the bathroom without looking at him, like the nurse who gave him stitches when he cut his leg. 'You wouldn't believe how good the soap they've got here smells,' she half yelled from the bathroom over the noise of the running water.

Guille not daring to stretch out on the bed or to get up. Shrivelling, falling apart, disappearing, like a sheet of paper thrown on to a fire. Not wanting to see himself in the mirror in front of him, the image that had brought him to the point of orgasm just a moment earlier, the whole image of the scene, La Lori beside him, her tits bouncing, her hand moving not up and down but in a sort of circular motion from the wrist, her gaze fixed on her manual labour and a sceptical expression on her face, that expression of professionalism that made him shoot his load. And now saying something else from the bathroom, something about the towels and the bath tub and the hydromassage. *What a slut.*

And now Mónica was leaving, all because of that. All because of a silly wank, a wank he could have done for himself, just because of that he was watching Mónica and Piluca getting into the lift. And there he was, not knowing what to say, not knowing how to ask for her love or how to keep it, asking her, in the same meaningless way as when he'd previously mentioned the whisky, 'Are you going to see my mother?'

Mónica replies, but she's looking at Piluca rather than him, 'I don't believe it.'

And Piluca gives the definitive order, 'Close the door.'

'Tell her . . .'

'I don't believe it.' Mónica looks like she's going to cry.

It wasn't such a big deal. He didn't say anything outrageous. After all, it was his father who'd died, not her father or anyone else's father. Now everyone wanted to have someone who'd died, for Christ's sake. Where did that come from?

'Close it now!'

He lets go of the door. *All because of a wank.* It almost makes him laugh, at any other time it would have made him laugh. 'All Because of a Wank' sounded like the title of a film, and he pictures himself joking about it with Juno. Only now he knows that he isn't going to mention it, ever. Among other things because he isn't about to confess that the only thing he'd done with La Lori was that and because he felt a vibrant, ferocious hatred towards Juno and his laughter. The echo of his cackling makes him wonder what to do next.

Go home. See his mother. That hazy mass of people. His father's presence. Much stronger than when he was alive. It had multiplied and was now in every corner of the house, hanging around everyone's neck, some of whom had never even met him. Perhaps they were already at the cemetery or the hospital or wherever they had to be. Yes, go home. And suddenly the image of La Lori returns, her hand engaged in that almost circular movement, slow, meticulous, and a new rush of desire flashes across some part of his body, like a shadow, still mixed with that feeling of disgust but also desire.

Yes, go and see his mother. He looks at the stairs. He can hear footsteps down below. Mónica's and the hideous Piluca's. He looks at the closed lift door. His mother. Yes. Later. And he goes back into the flat, hearing the laughter and boisterous voices of Juno and El Tuli coming closer and closer. Better to get there before Cabello asks La Lori what had happened. He has to tell her that what goes on between a man and woman is something that only they should know, that's what a real man would do. She'd understand. And then he'll go home. Maybe Mónica would be there. And she'd watch him give his mother a hug, which is where he ought to be. Like a real man, too. Comforting his mother. At the forefront of everything.

His mother is reclining comfortably on the bed, her back against the wall, her arms are crossed. She's looking out towards the horizon, and she says to Julia that perhaps with time she'll be able to make sense of it all. 'I might be able to make sense of what's happened, my life over the last ten, fifteen, almost twenty years, but then, once I do understand it, it might not matter much. All I hope is that then, between now and then, I can find something, something real in my life.'

Her friend, sitting on the edge of the bed (they're in Ana Galán's bedroom) is about to say something. Ana doesn't let her, she knows they'll be comforting words, something along the lines that she's got real things now, too. And it's Ana who carries on talking.

'What scares me most now is emptiness. Not the emptiness ahead of me, being on my own, I mean, I'm not scared of that, what scares me is the emptiness behind me, that all those years might come back to bite me, it's all so meaningless, so hollow. Do you know what I'm feeling? It's as if I'm on the edge of a very high precipice, but the precipice is right behind me, my heels are right on the edge and the slightest movement would make me topple backwards. Swallowed up by that void. And if that happens, if they see me looking depressed, people will say poor thing, she couldn't cope with her husband's death, but if it does happen it won't be because he's dead and I'm alone but rather because of all those years I've lived with him. I can tell *you* this, but I don't think I can tell anyone else.'

She stops talking. She's sniffling. She wipes away a tear that's just forming and looks out of the window. Dusk is slowly falling on the roofs, enveloping the tops of the palm trees like cotton. The sea is petrol blue. It's all so soft, so much beauty suspended in the air. She swallows. Julia has the impression that her friend is swallowing down the tears that aren't welling up in her eyes. And, looking vacantly straight in front of her and thinking out loud, Dr Galán carries on talking. 'That's what I'm scared of. What else would I be scared of? Being alone?'

She looks at Julia contemptuously. Blind, belated, caustic, retrospective rebellion. She shakes her head. 'I could never, ever have been more alone than I've been recently. It's a dense loneliness as heavy as lead and I can honestly tell you that I've only realized that today. I knew before today, of course I knew, but it's only today seeing him there covered in ants that I've realized how alone, how abandoned I've been all these years. And that I don't deserve it.'

She shakes her head again looking out of the window. They're short movements but very insistent, with contained energy and as if she's telling herself this, that she needs to persuade her inner being. Then she looks again at her friend, who's still sitting on the edge of the bed and knows that if she values Ana's respect for her at all, she can't try sugar coating the moment again with well-worn clichés. Or at least not with any cliché she's come across. So the best thing she can do is to hold Ana's gaze as she speaks to her.

'I have never, ever deserved this. I know that Dioni didn't either, and I can imagine everything he's suffered, but I didn't deserve it. I've deserved other stuff, but not this. And that's what the people out there (she looks towards the bedroom door) don't suspect. Who do I tell? Do I tell my brother, my sister-in-law, that the only thing they've really wanted all these years is not to know? And, my God, they've done a good job. You can't begin to imagine, well actually, yes you can begin to imagine it. Starting with my son or, actually, starting with me. And what do I do now? Do I tell Guille? He ran away at the first sign of danger, at the merest whiff of anything that could upset the natural order of things.'

The open wound. Let it all drain away, let all the putrid matter come out. Julia thinks that a medical approach rather than a sentimental one would make sense right now, but she keeps quiet and lets Ana continue with her flow of ideas.

'And is that being selfish? Yes, it is, very selfish. Each to his own. Hasn't Dioni been selfish? Up until yesterday – or until he decided to kill himself – wasn't that being selfish? Suffering, beating himself up. But did he stop doing what he wanted? Even what he's just done, did he do it for us, for his son, for me? Don't talk to me about being selfish.' There's a faint smile with a sad gesture. And she asks her friend, 'Have you seen Guille? Is he downstairs?'

'He was going out with some friends when I arrived.'

Ana Galán looks down at the floor and asks, 'Can I have a cigarette?'

She goes over to her friend and takes one from Julia. She picks up a lighter from the chest of drawers. But she doesn't light it, she just looks out of the window. There's no wind, the tops of the palm trees are becoming shrouded in darkness, motionless, not the slightest wind, the horizon has come to a complete standstill. The days that Dioni will no longer see. They don't belong to him.

Dr Galán is holding the lighter in one hand and the cigarette in the other. So this is where it was all leading up to. She remembers how unsure her mother always felt about Dioni. How she resigned herself to it and accepted their relationship and the wedding. 'It's God's will,' that's what she said, missing the other potential son-in-law, the doctor with a pedigree.

God's will. All those ants crawling over his face, pouring out of his hair, from behind his neck, as if their nest were inside his body. Tiny, stubborn, crawling over his eyelids, twitching their miniscule antennae over that body, which they'd thought of for some time as their own personal territory. Edible territory, an endless quarry. Coming out of his belly button, his ears, from between his legs in their hundreds. Disorientated but always hardworking, determined, robotic.

Dr Galán finally lights her cigarette. She opens the glass door leading to the small terrace, and a gust of hot air instantly pervades the room. It was God's will that she arrived home unexpectedly one afternoon. She'd been relieved of her duties thanks to the flu that had given her a temperature of almost thirty-nine degrees. She heard the laughter from the stairs. And from the moment she heard that sound she knew that trouble was just around the corner and would stay with her for some time.

More than simply being aware of it, that fact pierced her very being in the same way as the flu virus. But no medicine would be able to cure it. It pierced her brain and lodged there like a nebulous malaise, like a disturbance that her powers of reasoning were unable to identify. Perhaps because she believed in some part of her consciousness that it would never develop properly and would remain there dormant without ever actually coming to anything. Until death came unexpectedly for a different reason. No. Death came precisely for that reason, Dr Galán thinks now.

That afternoon, when she reached the top of the stairs and went into the living room, she found a young man lying on the sofa. His hands were behind his head and his legs were crossed, resting on the other arm of the sofa. He looked at her unperturbed, as if *she* were the stranger, in complete contrast to Dioni's nervousness as he immediately stood up and started stuttering.

He got a foot caught under the rug and tripped up comically. It was so comical that the young man started chuckling again, without taking his hands away from the back of his neck or his feet from the arm of the sofa. Dioni, reverting to adolescence, asked Ana what she was doing there and at the same time pointed to his friend and said his name was Vicente, and he told Vicente she was his wife.

'I'd already guessed she wasn't the maid because I've seen the maid before, and I've seen her picture in those frames.' And then he did get up, slowly and obligingly, and went over to Ana to give her a kiss on the cheek, which she avoided by putting out her hand. The rather unfriendly gesture made the stranger laugh again, and he shook her hand and even made as if to put it to his lips.

'We were chatting,' Dioni explained, like a teenager caught in flagrante smoking or masturbating in the bathroom. Ana understood. She saw it all in that Vicente's smile, the grin on his lips looking like a type of wave. Defiant. More than anything, she saw it in Dioni's hesitant gaze.

She looked into her husband's eyes and realized he was making a big effort not to look away. Ana said she was going to bed. And when her husband asked her if she was all right, she simply repeated that she was going to bed. She started walking towards the bedroom. 'Lovely to meet you,' said Vicente. Ana Galán saw him smiling out of the corner of her eye, but she didn't turn around and she didn't reply.

Just a few minutes later she thought she heard the sound of the front door closing. And fifteen or twenty minutes later *he's building up his strength, he's proving to me he's guilty, coward, queer* the bedroom door opened slightly, just a crack. Although at first Ana Galán, in a reflex action, pretended to be asleep, the next moment she turned around and looked straight at the bedroom door.

The door opened wide, and there was Dioni. From the doorway *coward* he asked, 'Are you all right?' There was no response. A rock, a stone that needs neither food nor emotion. Becoming harder and more inaccessible with every passing moment. That's how Ana suddenly felt. There was no way she needed to talk. She could have turned over and tried to sleep, focus on her feverishness, let herself fall into that not entirely unpleasant emptiness enveloping her.

But fear made Dioni go into the room, sit down on the edge of the bed and look at his wife in surprise. 'What's wrong?' The performance, the beginning of a game of chase, cats and mice, police and thieves. 'Tell me what's wrong. Did something happen at the hospital?'

Ana Galán saw through the infantile strategy. Don't talk about the visitor, act as if the visitor being there was so normal that only some other reason could explain his wife's refusal to speak. That was the drop of acid. The corrosive element. It punctured her granite-like skin and stirred up her anger. 'Stop, for one minute, for one second stop pretending, for one second in your life look at what's in front of you. For once in your life. Don't make me keep looking away, don't make me complicit in your theatrical performance. It's enough if you just don't say anything, let's both not say anything, please.' That's what she said to him, propped up on her elbow. Fully aware that her husband's response would be to keep the farce going, try another escape.

And yes, he said what she expected. 'What are you saying? What do you mean, Ana? Please.' That's the kind of thing Dioni said. Ana had just got up so that she would be at the same level as him, at least to be standing up straight in front of him. 'For Christ's sake, stop pretending, Dioni. Don't humiliate me.' 'Don't humiliate you? Where has that come from? What do you know about humiliation?' *Something of the truth at the very least, the tiniest shred of acknowledgement.* 'Really? Didn't you see that triumphant look on his face? The only thing he didn't say was, "He's mine, not yours. I've taken him away from you."'

Dioni's mask of amazement, his fake surprise together with real astonishment was what had made his wife react like that. Ana's silence, her eyes shining with her high temperature and with resentment. A silence that Dioni could only interpret as the beginning of calmness, a possible reconciliation.

'I met him. He's the friend of a client. He's not the brightest spark, but he's nice, despite today, despite the fact that you saw him like that . . .' the gullible Dionisio Grandes Guimerá was saying when the leap into the void happened.

'It's OK to be a queer but not to be a coward.'

That's what Ana Galán said. That's what had an impact on her husband's face and crumpled it. The muscles in his face melted away.

Ana had taken the leap. The irresistible attraction of the void. Breaking free from the bonds. A momentary loss of control. One of those moments in life when there's a fork in the road and a choice has to be made right then between the two paths.

Ana Galán will never know, she will never be sure, however much she thinks she can sense it, but her husband was on the point of accepting the challenge right then, saying 'Yes' and accepting that he had taken a wrong turn in his life, in both their lives. But he chose the other path, and what Dioni did was to shake his head and get up from the edge of the bed and look at his wife's face as if a nest of worms had just opened up in it.

He went out of the bedroom. He slept in the guest room. He left early for work. After managing to get to sleep a little before dawn, Ana Galán woke up mid-morning, feeling quite a bit better from her flu. The images and thoughts from the time she couldn't sleep, from all her tossing and turning, from her sleepiness, were all jumbled up in her head. It took her a few seconds to untangle the different twisted threads. Life taking on an unknown burden.

Ana didn't go to work. She wandered around the house. Her mood went up and down, or, to put it better, it was like a roulette wheel. Fear, embarrassment, regret, pride and anger once more. She helped Guille with his homework. The boy became a receptacle for her emotions and her fears. The past and the future personified in that child.

Dioni came home late. They didn't give each other a kiss. They didn't look each other in the eye. The three of them sat down to dinner. They spoke to their son and didn't speak to each other at all. When the meal was over, and this wasn't what usually happened, she stayed sitting at the table, and he took the plates out to the kitchen. Ana told Guille she was going to put him to bed and that she was going to bed, too, as she wasn't well and needed to get some rest. The boy complained and asked his father for help, and he replied with a gesture of resignation. She took him by the hand. A stage play. And also a hint of doubt. Had it all really happened like that? Had that man really been so arrogant, had he really been lying down on the sofa for so long, had he really looked at her so sarcastically? Was everything as she'd imagined? Were he and Dioni what she thought they were? Yes. She knew. That's how it was. That's how it all was. But that shadow of doubt was there. Was it really there, or had she herself created it to have some peace of mind? Or a little bit of hope. A door through which she could flee, a doubt. Was it all definitive? Better to sleep. Sleeping pills.

She went to sleep relatively early. And at some vague time in the night, particularly blurry because of sleepiness and her high temperature, she realized that Dioni was in bed sleeping beside her. When she woke up in the morning she was alone. She listened hard. The house was empty. They would talk tonight. He left a message on the answerphone halfway through the afternoon. He had a business dinner and would be late home. He also said, 'I hope your flu's better.' A bit of a truce. She wasn't going to negotiate. No. But she also knew that the threads or the bridges or whatever you want to call those connections that tied her to her husband weren't completely cut. Not all of them. Her temperature went up again. She tossed and turned in her sleep with a jumble of unconnected dreams, but she slept deeply. When she woke up, he was the one who was asleep. When she came out of the shower, he was still asleep. Dawn was rising. She went to the hospital. They would talk tonight. No. They didn't that night either. Nor the next day. Nor the rest of the week, nor the next few months. Actually, they never talked. The time had come for acceptance and resignation.

They started rebuilding their lives out of pieces of rubble. Debris can make for a good building material. Threads, words, suspension bridges being moved by a gust of wind. Holding each other's gaze for longer, less frightened, with less suspicion, more oxygen entering their lungs. He wasn't a bad man. They loved each other. She loved him. Of course she loved him. The first smile. Light. And the concrete wall of silence doing its job.

Looking out of the window of La Esquinita, Jorge spots Vane from the Famita shoeshop going past. She's wearing the same white leggings as she was this morning. She's changed her top, maybe at midday. Now she's wearing a sleeveless blouse. Fuchsia. Her brown arms are clutching the same blue folder. She's got blonde highlights in her dark hair. Her sunglasses are on top of her head, like a diadem. She's walking along the side of the patch of waste ground looking for her car.

There aren't many vehicles left in the parking area, only dust and weeds and the scorching ground. The girl's walking in her high heels as though she were wearing stilts, with none of this morning's energy. The light has also lost its intensity; it's now like translucent fabric letting the shadows seep through.

Floren places a glass of beer in front of his cousin Jorge, distracting his attention from the street. 'That's enough eyeing up the talent for now,' he says. 'They'll only end up giving you grief. Isn't that right, Pedroche? You tell him.'

'No, but I wasn't, I was looking over there,' says horny little Jorge, trying to make excuses.

Pedroche restricts himself to picking up the glass of beer his partner brought over and making a sort of dull grunt that serves to indicate his disapproval both of the joke and the existence of the entire female population of the planet. The beer's left little clusters of foam hanging off the ends of his grey-blond moustache. The injuries to his face stand out more under the bar's fluorescent light, which has been turned on prematurely. When he saw him, the barman asked him what had happened. 'Stairs,' he said. 'I fell down some stairs,' he elaborated when he noticed the barman still looking at him.

Jorge sees the girl from the shoeshop drive out of the parking area. She looks left and right up the street before she sets off. Her window's open, and even though there's not much light left she's wearing her sunglasses. *Off home. I don't know if she's got a boyfriend, she's not married*, Jorge is thinking, when the telephone starts vibrating in his pocket. He's afraid it will be Nene Olmedo. He looks. It's Nene Olmedo:

wots up?

He replies:

with him now

?

hving a beer

He's about to write that the priest is going to call Pedroche when he notices him struggling to get his phone out of his pocket, look at it and say to Floren, 'It's the priest.'

hang on – spking to priest

Jorge listens to Pedroche whispering. The words barely make it past his moustache. On top of that, the noise in the bar makes it impossible for Jorge to understand anything the poor man says. Only the last word reaches his ears clearly, 'OK.'

The telephone vibrates again, and the same message from Nene Olmedo appears:

?

Floren's asking Pedroche, 'What did the priest say? Is he keeping the cash or giving it back?' Pedroche looks up at him with a grim expression as he puts his phone away, then smiles and says, 'He's giving it back, obviously, all of it.'

'Today?' asks Jorge, also smiling. Pedroche looks at him suspiciously and doesn't reply. He takes another sip of his beer, getting more foam on his moustache.

'When's he handing it over?' It's Floren asking now.

Pedroche tries to swallow, almost chokes. 'He hasn't finished what he had to do. When he's finished he'll go home and pick it up and hand it over to me.'

'At his place?' asks Floren, waving his empty glass in the air and showing it to the waiter, who nods.

'By the entrance to the church, I don't know where he lives, so we're meeting at the church. The bugger is that he says he won't get home until at least ten o'clock. So he says at the entrance to the church at half ten.' Pedroche's running his mouth, perhaps at the prospect of getting the money and the jewellery back, perhaps because of the three beers he's swallowed.

Jorge sends a message to Nene Olmedo:

10.30

He receives:

that late?

He replies:

priest has problem

He receives:

def? 10.30?

He replies:

wot he said

'In that case I'll go with you, if that's when it is, I'll come, too,' Floren says to his partner.

'You don't have to,' says Pedroche.

'It's right next to my place. I'll come with you, then I'll go home.'

'OK.' Pedroche turns his head, appreciative.

Jorge opens his mouth, he's about to say something, he holds his tongue, then he says, 'Didn't you say your wife was waiting for you? To have supper, you said earlier.'

'Yes, we'll have supper a bit later, it's not a problem,' Floren replies, turning his back and taking his fresh glass of beer from the barman's hand. He carries on talking to Pedroche. 'You need to make sure that this is the last time. You've got to stop her messing you around. I don't know, mate, talk to the doctor, for Christ's sake. Her mother knows a psychologist or two, doesn't she?'

Jorge hesitates. The telephone vibrates in his hand again, and while he nods he looks down at several question marks and the letters wher.

He writes:

church door but my cuz go too

'You know, you wouldn't believe the problem he's got at home, too, with his brother, eh, Jorge? How is he, these days?'

Jorge shrugs his shoulders. 'He's still around.'

Pedroche, staring wistfully at the stuffed eggs on the counter, as though he was talking to them, says, 'Yes, Belita's been seeing doctors since she was a little girl, that's right, since she was a little girl, the thing is, it's a waste of time. I'm convinced that once they said that the outlook wasn't going to change, that's when they stuck her on me.'

wtf yr cuz?

Jorge replies:

it's his ptnr – cuz gd guy

so btr keep away

'Has your brother been up to anything recently?' Floren asks Jorge, in a happy mood.

Jorge shrugs his shoulders. Pedroche looks at him. 'The usual stuff,' Jorge says eventually.

Floren gets all excited and says, 'Once, well apart from all the times he's ended up in A&E, God knows how many times, with all the fights he gets involved in, once he put his mother's shoes in the oven, at home, in their own kitchen. He was going to cook them.'

Pedroche raises his eyebrows and for the first time looks at Jorge straight in the eye. 'That's right, isn't it?' says Floren, then he polishes off his beer and says, 'Fuck me, that goes down well what with how hot it's been today. You couldn't make it up, his mother's best shoes, with high heels and all that, and the guy goes and sets fire to them in the oven.'

'He burned them all, the high-heeled ones and even her slippers,' says Jorge, trying to make himself heard, to be noticed.

'Lucky he didn't burn the place down,' adds Floren.

'Did he burn them all?' Pedroche asks Jorge directly.

'Apart from two or three pairs he couldn't find because they were somewhere else. You wouldn't believe the smoke and the stink, and this morning he went and cut up all the curtains in the flat.'

'The curtains?' Floren signals to the barman again, this time drawing a little circle with his index finger to signify that he wants three beers.

'Yes, curtains, towels, sheets off my own bed, too. I saw it when I went home for lunch, with a pair of scissors, all in little pieces, he cut them all up into little pieces, triangles.'

'Well, the psychologists your mother knows can't be much good, I reckon, judging from his behaviour,' said Pedroche.

'He's going to a different one now, isn't he? A better one,' says Floren.

Jorge shakes his head. 'No, these days he's not seeing anyone because he refuses to go.'

'And he gets hammered, too. Not like us, really hammered,' Floren laughs, a fresh beer in his hand.

'Yeah,' says Jorge, looking at his beer and adding, 'Hadn't you better be off home? Your wife's going to be mad at you, cuz.'

'I'm going along with Pedroche. I'll get some fresh air, and I'll be good as new by the time I get home. I've had three beers not a bottle of gin like your brother.'

'You've had at least five,' says Jorge with a grin.

'Fancy a stuffed egg, Pedroche?' Floren replies. 'And what about you, do you want one?'

Jorge shakes his head. He looks over at the waste ground through the window. *They're all going now.* Empty cars. Steamy light. The heat's still smothering everything. He opens WhatsApp and writes:

nene I shld have a cut
gvng 2 U all sewn up mate

A few seconds later he receives an emoticon. A smiling turd. He looks at Pedroche wolfing down a stuffed egg, the mayonnaise sticking to his moustache-cum-taxman, retaining a portion of everything that goes in his mouth. He writes:

ok but pse care w my cuz
& fget abt my grl

One second later he receives the same emoticon, this time in duplicate. He picks up his glass of beer. Swallows. It will all be over by tomorrow. That's how you have to live, his father used to say. One day at a time.

Let that shithead go off with the money and then leave him and his girlfriend in peace. An ambulance passes in front of the bar, leaving flashes of orange light glowing over the dusty ground of the waste patch. A fairground flicker.

The light is also beginning to break up in the alleys and throughout the sluggish suburbs. A worm is chewing its way through the outlines of solid objects. Lines soften and lose their form, the naked window-bars at ground-floor level in the empty alleyways, the traffic lights (bent over from a long-forgotten collision), the window recesses floating like dead mirrors in the unadorned façades.

The Runner pulls up the blind and looks out at the balconies on the other side of the alley that his bedroom window overlooks. A woman disappears from the shadows of one bedroom and appears in the one next door, lit up by the diffused light of an electric bulb. The woman is wearing a light dressing-gown that exposes her thick upper arms, like a pair of hams. She's talking on the phone, gesticulating, and looks him in the eye.

The Runner looks away, opens the window and a wave of asphyxiating heat invades the room, crashes into his chest and envelops him. He closes the window, making the glass resonate. The woman is still looking at him, no longer gesticulating, just listening, with the telephone stuck to her ear and her bare arm reminiscent of a butcher's display. Two little girls in summer dresses are playing a hopping game on the ash-coloured pavement in front of the hairdresser's. Oblivious to the desolation.

Is desolation something I'm putting into the mix myself, or is it something that's there already, in those stacked-up buildings, in that weak light coming from the hairdresser's that's sticking to the pavement like an egg stain? It must be me. Those little girls playing hopscotch are laughing, hopping and laughing, they're not looking up, and they don't realize that tomorrow they'll be like that woman who's looking at me from the other side of the alley. It's me. I'm playing hopscotch, too.

The city's getting dark. On the patch of waste ground where Dionisio Grandes Guimerá greeted the dawn, the thistles, the earth, the desiccated branches are beginning to lose their ochre colour and are turning dark. The edges are blurring. The drops of blood that dripped on to the scorched ground from the first hypodermic needle that the doctors stuck in his veins are smudgy. Intubated. The ants are searching among the cigarette butts, faded plastic wrapping, flattened beer cans, leaves, crumpled paper, and, looking down on all this, above this brown desert, in the fading light of day, there's an enormous photo of a man with his arms wrapped around a woman from behind presiding over this imminent kingdom of darkness. REDISCOVER YOUR PASSION WITH A NEW MATTRESS, the advertisement hoarding still reads. Beside it is the half-torn-off poster showing a glimpse of a white vehicle, and a little further on a large photograph of an idyllic beach, which is also getting dark. **Spirit of the** MEDITERRANEAN. On the other side of the roundabout, between two lights, the petrol station's green neon signs are beginning to stand out. Cars, men crossing between the pumps, already inhabiting another place, a universe in which the discovery of a dying man on the adjacent waste ground is just a rumour that's breaking up, mutating, dissolving like the day itself.

Only the heat persists. Renewed, stubborn, reluctant to withdraw along with the light and the sun. Flickering street lamps, people going out in search of a freshness that hasn't yet arrived. Sleepwalkers, drifters. Father Sebastián has stepped out of the shower. A humble bathtub, half a metre square, a miniature bath lined with pale-yellow tiles, some of them cracked. He crosses the room with a towel tied around his waist and peers out of the window.

He lives in a sleepy neighbourhood with no greenery and too much asphalt, too much concrete, too many people on top of one another. Yes, people adrift and people seeking salvation, he thinks. And he also thinks about Belita, her jewellery and her husband. *Sometimes I also feel that I'm walking in the dark and that I'm one of those people adrift, my brothers.* Learning not to judge. It was only in the seminary that he thought he was on firm ground, secure, a cog in the right place. And then everything fell apart. He sees the envelope with the money on the table. The maroon velvet bag containing the jewellery. He hasn't even untied the ribbon to see what's inside, knowing that the husband or some other member of that poor lunatic's family was bound to turn up to claim it back.

His bare feet walk over the mottled tiles. It's barely six steps to the bedroom. The bed's unmade. He can still sense Lorena's presence in the room. He can't even remember the excuse he gave Belita's husband to delay their meeting, knowing that Lorena was going to have some free time and could come to see him. The wrinkles in the sheet are clearly visible. The image of Lorena lying face down, her tanned back exposed, her buttocks, the pale triangle left by her bikini and her hair spilling over her cheeks. Father Sebastián lowers his face to the sheet, but he can't pick up any scent.

Inner rooms already conquered by the gloom, footsteps. La Penca is dozing in her bedroom. They're her father's footsteps, and the light from the corridor comes into her room like a tame dog. She hears her father talking to El Yubri in his cracked voice. She can't make out what they're talking about, just her father's croaking and her brother's whispering. Her brother puts his stuff into a plastic bag. The clothes he's going to take to prison. 'I'm hungry,' La Penca hears her father announce. 'Fridge,' is the only word she can understand from what her brother is saying. And then she hears her father's footsteps approaching. Despite the stifling heat La Penca covers her bare legs, shoulders, her whole body with the sheet. She closes her eyes. She hears her father hesitate for a moment outside her bedroom door, his hoarse breathing, she imagines him staring at her, the white bulk at the back of the room, and then she hears him continue on his way towards the kitchen, followed by the clickety-click of the dog's claws on the tiles.

La Penca imagines, sees, the dog slashed open from head to toe, like the animals in the abattoir when she went to see her father at work. Slashed open from head to toe but with its head intact and talking, the dog talking the way La Segueta talks, with that voice they used to give to their dolls when La Penca was a little girl and used to play out there in the street. She'd play at preparing the dinner with leaves from the trees and gravel from the building sites. That was even before El Yubri was born. When Nene Olmedo first arrived in the neighbourhood and slashed that deaf and dumb boy across the hand along his life line with a knife. Because he didn't like the faces he pulled.

Night arrives here earlier in these narrow streets, these rows of windows, lines of washing, window bars and TV aerials, where the sun barely touches the ground for half an hour a day. Now they're having supper. The Runner, with his notebook perched on his knees, writes another sentence: *I know that with her I'll be a long way from here, a long way from me.* Then he crosses it out. Too twee. He looks at his watch. In a few minutes' time he'll go to meet her. He carries on browsing older pages of his notebook. This is what he reads:

THE RUNNER'S DIARY

Distance. Is it self-defence? That's how I used it. I can't remember when I actually started putting distance between myself and everyone else. It could all be down to pessimism, accepting defeat in advance. Certain that I wouldn't get very far trying to join in, that it was a dead end. Scratching at glass.

Better to lose myself in my head. Better to go off down all those unknown paths inside my head. Creating a map, finding my way. There are whole regions I've never explored. Empty buildings. Rooms with the door ajar. Corners.

Running helped me to create that distance. Running. The intense loneliness. Focused. Running with no destination in mind. Going around in circles. Going nowhere, even as an athlete. Running. Just running. Keeping everyone else at a distance but actually staying in the same place. Everyone else was keeping a distance. Everyone else was moving away.

Writing also made me feel removed from everyone else. Closer to myself, that's all. This diary. All these stories slumbering in the circuits of my computer and in a few notebooks. Bits of plastic and paper storing my emotions. Writing. Going around in a different type of circle. Have I actually been anywhere?

Or could it all be down to arrogance? I don't need any of you. Not one of you milling around me can give me anything I don't already have. I was only acting out of innocence. No, not innocence, naïvety. I was never innocent. Naïve and blind. Not realizing how long the path would be (a badly run marathon, miscalculating the distance and effort required). Not realizing how high the walls created by loneliness can be (and how they solidify, and then it's impossible to knock them down – it's much worse scratching at those stone walls than scratching at glass, the ground littered with fingernails).

(Lack of innocence.) Even as a child I never felt innocent. Never. Back then, less than ever. I would hide things, I hid my emotions. I tried to manipulate people. I was defending myself, that was as close as I came

to innocence. I did things in self-defence. Lying, keeping my mouth shut, calculating. Spying on people.

I don't know why. But I do know that at some point, when I was a teenager I saw distance as an option, as one path I could take, and it seemed right for me. A good disguise. One that fitted.

My friends back then, Sergio, Padín, El Mono, they all said how calm I was, how cool and collected. It was all calculated. Keeping my mouth shut, letting them do the talking. Not wearing myself out (like a good marathon runner). Pessimism again. What was the point of saying anything? I watched them yacking away. Boiling, bubbling, getting sidetracked. I followed a different path. I focused. I got smaller and smaller. I took up less space.

What's worse, much worse than pessimism or exhaustion, is resignation. Do I get that from my mother as well? She's always come out the loser in everything she's done. Perhaps I've been infected. Lost words that burrowed under my skin, found their way into my bloodstream and lodged in the recesses of my brain. They're still there. Transmitting messages, criticizing what they don't like. Cutting me off at the knees.

My mother clings to me like her one and only hope. She's already decided that I'm not going to disappoint her. She pretends she understands me. When I let her know she's annoying me she covers it up. One day, sitting on the edge of the bed, she burst into tears at something I said. I don't remember what it was, but I do remember that she dried her tears with the corner of the sheet. She messed up the bed to grab that corner of the sheet and wipe away her tears. She must have been really distraught to have done that. Bursting into tears. Messing up the bed. That's what I saw, that's the most distant corner of the universe that my eyes have reached, like tears in rain, Orion and all that stuff in the film about the replicant. My mother sitting on the edge of the bed, her shoulders heaving as she wept in silence. A black hole.

I didn't say a word. I held my tongue. I stood there, looking at her askance. Inside, I felt my whole skeleton and insides turning into fine dust, like the sand inside an hourglass trickling down, and then someone turned me up the other way.

The same sand going up and down. That's what it was like until I met Lucía. She paid no attention to my distance. She thought my weakness was almost comical. She was touched that I was so helpless when everyone else saw me as being too strong. A child in a suit of armour that he can barely walk around in. They all think she tamed the snappy dog. She put some salve on his wounds, she pacified his fear, nothing more. It was more than enough.

At the beginning I found that horizon outside myself disturbing, that open space without any walls. It was as if I had gone off the rails and was groping around blindfold. In a room I knew but blindfold. Dazzled. Unaccustomed. And now I know that if she ever disappeared, the whole world would be nothing more than an enormous room in the dark. Fear.

She cornered my fear, that old, wounded dog. She could see it in the light of the day, that's how she saw it, skeletal, with blunt fangs, slavering. Ridiculous. But a new kind of great raging fear started growing in the shadows, with rows and rows of sharp fangs. There's always room for shadows. I've always got a little corner ready for them. The fear of losing her. That everything would come to an end.

Light would never reach the ground in that alleyway. The walls would get covered in the mould that I would breathe in. Rusty beams, rusty bones. I need a stroke of luck to free me from it all. To be certain that the people living around her, the people working with her or in the nearby businesses, the people who go there shopping, the ones who have breakfast together, the ones who ask her out and she refuses, that none of those people make her look at me differently and make her reconsider, think what they're all thinking. What are you doing with that waster? Why him?

I've never dared to say what I dream about out loud. My sister's always asking me why I've got so many books stacked up that don't fit on the bookshelves. Why am I always writing? Why am I always running? My mother's sisters are always asking her the same thing, too. They look at me with pity. Lucía laughs. She knows how to handle them. They like her but also have their suspicions about her. They think it won't be long before she leaves me. I'm sure they've spoken to each other about it. About how little I can offer anyone.

Every day is a miracle.

The Runner closes the notebook. He'll do it. He'll carry on writing, and it will be a vaccine against fear. He looks at the time on the shabby clock. A kitchen clock his mother put in his room because nobody dared to drill holes in the tiles in the kitchen. Better get dressed and set off walking to the supermarket. Wait on the opposite pavement for Lucía to come out. Together with some of her workmates. With the store manager, that Ricardo with his Audi and his leering face and his half-cocked smile. One day he'll put an end to all that, too.

It's getting dark. People have come out of their sweltering homes. They're searching for any trace of relief beneath the scrawny trees, lit up in orange by a municipal street lamp. There are chairs and armchairs on the pavements, men in open short-sleeved shirts, guts hanging out, children running up and down and chasing each other, women talking in low voices. Calle Cruz Verde is an inhospitable ravine, a long scar that people are determined to bring to life. Raimundo Arias and Eduardo Chinarro are walking along the right-hand side of the road. A fat woman in a tight-fitting strappy top, her hair gathered into a lank ponytail, calls out to Eduardo, 'Eduardo, sweetheart!'

Eduardo turns around and his face lights up. 'Remedios! Great to see you, Remedios!'

The woman has moved away from the group she was with and gives Eduardo a hug. 'So what brings you to these parts, Remedios? Great to see you, Remedios!'

'I came around to see my niece. Her baby's not well.' With a nod of her head she points out the group of women who are sitting around on deckchairs.

'Oh, cool. And how's your daughter? How's Merceditas?'

The woman smiles grimly. 'Same old, same old, you know how it is.'

'Depression?'

'Same old thing.'

'She'll get over it one day.'

'I told her she should come with me to see her cousin, but not on your life. It's as much as she'll do to walk to the end of the street. But tell me, Eduardito, how are you, sweetheart? You look a bit rough, if you know what I mean. Or is it because of the heat?'

'That'll be it. You wouldn't believe the day we've just had, me and Rai here. This is my friend Raimundo, and she was my mother's neighbour.'

Rai makes a grimace of acknowledgement. He rests the base of his guitar on the pavement and wishes Eduardo would wrap up the tittle-tattle.

'I was more like your mother's sister than a neighbour, Eduardito.'

'Yes, it's true, Remedios, I remember it all so well.'

'And your mother was more than a sister to me, not even my mother looked after me like your mother used to.'

'She was, my mother was so good, I realized that later.'

'This is such a fucking drag,' Raimundo mumbles.

'You what?' asks Remedios defiantly.

'It's too hot to be hanging around here. My feet are going to melt.'

'Well, walk around a bit, you might catch a bit of fresh air.'

Raimundo looks at the woman through narrowed eyes. Eduardo ignores him and carries on, 'I remember when you didn't have a TV and . . .'

'My husband threw it down the stairwell – he was a nasty piece of work.' She spits to one side, and Rai moves his foot, even though the spittle landed some distance from him. 'We sweated hard enough for it, and he goes and throws it away.'

'Yes, Lucas was something else. Even worse when he was on the booze.'

'He was always even worse. He'd either come back steaming drunk or if not he'd be thinking up another stupid scheme. Hell's too good a place for him.' She spits on the pavement again, and this time Rai doesn't bother moving his foot.

'I remember seeing your clothes flying out of the window, too, but when you didn't have a TV . . .'

'My clothes and Merceditas's school things, everything, books, exercise books, even her little smock, I mean, he threw it all out of the window, chucked it all in the street, the rotten bastard.'

'It's a wonder he didn't throw himself out,' Raimundo notes in a low voice, but loud enough to be heard.

'Is your friend trying to be funny, or what's his problem? Because yours truly put up with all of Lucas's shit, but I'm not going to take it from anyone else.'

'Hey, he doesn't have a problem, everything's cool. We've had a bad day, Remedios. But listen, I was saying, I remember about the television. I remember . . .' He turns to Raimundo. 'You'll never guess what, Rai, I remember when Remedios used to come to ours and watch the bull-fights on the TV.'

'Yes, it's all true.' Remedios slaps her thighs. 'Tell me about it, sweetie, oh what a laugh.'

'She used to love the bullfights, but since she was scared that the bullfighter might be gored she'd wear a pair of sunglasses as big as this, there in front of the TV.'

'Obviously, you could see everything much worse.'

'Jumping around left and right, it was like you were doing the bull-fighting yourself, and Merceditas, I remember her crying and saying what's wrong mummy, what a laugh. And you were crossing yourself and telling the guy with the pole, stick him one till it comes out his arse, stick him a bit more 'coz the bastard's going for that poor boy. That's what you used to say, that's what she'd say, Rai.'

'Hilarious,' says Rai with a deadpan face.

A fat little boy, about eight years old and wearing a lemon-yellow sleeveless top comes up to them. His head's shaved up to the temples and he's got a sort of Mohican crest with some strands dyed a sort of orangey blond.

'Auntie, Mummy says can you take me upstairs.'

Remedios turns towards the group of women. 'I'm chatting a moment with Eduardito, for Christ's sake. Can't a woman have a moment of fun? Can't you get off your fat arse and take your own son upstairs?'

One of the women says something back that neither Rai nor Eduardito can make out.

'Yeah, yeah. You just keep on smoking that stuff and you'll soon find out what it does to your head.'

'Please can you, Auntie?' The little boy's clamping his knees together and writhing a bit, looking at Remedios plaintively.

'Yeah, yeah. Try not to piss your pants, cheeky little pup. Well,

Eduardito, sweetheart, I'd better take this one up. So what are you doing around here, why did you come here?'

'We're going to see a friend of Rai's who lives around here, Remedios. And then we'll be off.'

'Are you going to see La Pasoslargos?'

'Pasoslargos? No. Boris killed her on his motorbike, didn't he?'

'She threw herself under a train.'

'On the motorbike?'

'Auntie!' moans the little fat boy.

'No, hang on a minute. She threw herself under a train.'

'On the motorbike? What I heard,' says Eduardo, scratching his head, 'what I heard was that she got killed on the bike.'

'I don't know if she was on the bike, but she definitely went under a train because her sister told me so herself.'

'Are you going to take the boy upstairs? Otherwise he's going to piss himself,' Remedios's niece reminds her.

'OK, OK. It won't hurt him to hold on for a bit, fucking hell, what with the child himself and the child's mother! That's all I'm good for. Well, Eduardito, I'm off.'

Remedios and Eduardo give each other a hug. She turns around and says to her niece, 'And you might have taught the boy to do his business on his own by now. He's old enough. Even to save yourself the bother. Come on, son, let's go.' She takes hold of his hand and the fat little boy waddles alongside his great-aunt who, without stopping again, says to Eduardito, 'How I used to love your mother, Eduardito, and she loved me. Now, you keep your nose clean, Eduardito, sweetheart.'

Raimundo Arias picks his guitar off the floor, slings it over his shoulder and says, 'What an old bitch. She never stops, does she?'

'What do you mean, Rai? You don't know her. I can't tell you how good she's been to me.'

'Yeah, and your mother to her and her to your mother, you were the little house on the prairie right there in Carranque, I've just heard all about that, every last detail, mate.'

And with the shadows now blurring the corners and entrances to the buildings, Rai and Eduardo turn into Calle Melgarejos, short and steep. They walk down towards the cluster of trees in Plaza Miguel de los Reyes. The street smells of stale bleach. Eduardo looks pensive as he follows a couple of steps behind Rai, who's walking with a sense of urgency, agitated rather than fast, guitar shaking on his shoulder almost like a maraca.

And there, beneath the sleepy trees in the square, is where Rai meets up with his dealer. She's a little old lady, barely a metre and a half tall, wearing an apron, a housecoat with a grey print and a little boy of about six or seven by her side. You could almost call this chapter 'Kindergarten'.

'Antoñito, what are you up to?' Eduardo asks.

'I'm with my granny,' the boy says, grabbing a fistful of the woman's apron. Large eyes, body as small and fragile as his granny's. The boy looks stealthily from side to side.

'Do you like football, Antoñito?' asks Eduardo.

The boy shakes his head in disgust, bored with a question that must be one of Eduardo's standards.

Raimundo and the old lady talk to each other in whispers, about debts and IOUs. Rai mentions that this morning he's had to ditch what he had on him in the toilets at a petrol station.

'You see I found a dead body out in the middle of the countryside. Isn't that right, Eduardo?'

'Yes, that's right, Juana. Someone that Rai didn't know from Adam.'

'And there were cops everywhere. Over the top. I don't know what he died from.'

The boy looks from side to side.

'What about the beach, do you like the beach, Antoñito?'

'No.'

'No? But what with this heat, don't you like going to the beach and having a dip and digging holes in the sand?'

The boy stares at Eduardo, clinging on to his grandmother's apron, while she's still having a whispered conversation with Raimundo.

'Shall I sing you a song?'

'No.'

'No? It's a nice little song about a little boy who went to the moon in a rubber rocket.'

'No.'

'What about the guitar. Do you want to play the guitar?'

The child looks at Raimundo's guitar, resting on the ground, and nods his head.

Eduardo goes up to Rai to fetch the guitar, but, right then, the boy's grandmother and Eduardo's companion come to an agreement and the old woman gives him a small bag. Rai opens it, looks inside and counts and says, 'You know you can trust me, and you won't regret it, Juana.'

'Just as well. Because if I regret it, you'll be having a chat with Gregorio,' says the little old lady in her squeaky voice.

And as soon as she's said the last sentence she's started walking off towards Calle Lagunillas, the boy still clinging to her apron. Eduardo watches them until the boy and his grandmother disappear around the corner.

'What a drag. She's hard, that one. Let's head for Calle Capuchinos.' Rai puts the guitar over his shoulder.

'I don't know, Rai, I think I'm done for today.'

'What do you mean? Let's go to El Monegro's place, and then we can do another round.'

'I don't know, Rai, my old bones are knackered. It must be the heat.'

'Come on, let's go.' Rai starts up the hill.

Eduardo stands there, watching the tall, bony figure. He looks towards the far corner of the square, where the child and his grandmother disappeared. A street lamp is flickering on the corner and making the trees cast weird shadows. Eduardo sighs and starts walking.

'Hey, Rai, hang on, Rai.'

Two hundred and ninety-three kilometres per hour. The train is a glow-worm. On the other side of the windows the purple reflections and lonely dark clouds floating in the sky like Zeppelins have disappeared. A dark landscape. The windows have turned into mirrors. Céspedes sees his own reflection. He'd like to make fun of himself out loud, give himself a dressing down. He lets himself off. Lets it ride.

Carole's head is under his chin, resting against his chest. She's dozing. He smells her scalp. Perfumed pollen. He wants another whisky. He had two more at Atocha while Carole looked on indifferently. Scornfully?

In the window Céspedes watches Carole's eye movements. She's dreaming. His eyes meet the eyes of the passenger opposite in the window. They're sitting in a pair of seats facing another pair. The passenger looks away. Céspedes looks straight at him rather than his reflection in the window. The man makes an expression that might have been the trace of a smile, of complicity. Respect to Céspedes for having a woman like Carole snoozing on his chest. The top buttons on her blouse are undone, and you can see the top half of her breasts. Céspedes narrows his eyes and mutters, '*Pogue mahone.*'

They arrived in this carriage when the train was already moving. They'd got on three carriages back, and when they found their seats this passenger was already sitting there. He apologized, Céspedes tripped up, nearly fell on top of him, dropped the plastic bag carrying the suit he'd bought a few hours earlier. He didn't try to pretend he wasn't drunk. He wanted to provoke Carole, get her to blow her top finally. Céspedes told the man (about forty years old, a lightweight jacket hanging on the window hook, business traveller) that he'd taken his niece shopping. Carole studied the industrial landscape, the long, low-lying buildings, the first expanses of uncultivated land, the dark shadows of the electricity pylons stretching out across the bare fields.

Céspedes asked the man if he had any friends who were the same age as his niece. 'She needs friends, people her own age who understand her.' Carole told the passenger, 'Yes, I hope you'll find me someone because my uncle's a real bore.' The man smiled, replied evasively, looked at Carole, weighed her up. Céspedes felt like he was on the edge of a roof. *Too chicken to jump, too chicken to go inside and behave with decorum. Here, on the edge, making a fool of myself, knowing that tomorrow or the following day I'll have to come back and pick up the tab. I'm just the delivery boy, and tomorrow I'll pick up the pieces of everything I've broken today and pay for them.*

The phone rings in Carole's bag. She lifts her head off Céspedes's chest. She rummages in her bag, sleepily. She retrieves her telephone, stares at the screen. Breathes in and slides her finger to pick up.

'Yes?'

—

'On the train. Yes, on a train.'

—

'What does it matter? On my own. Do I cross-examine you?'

—

'No, I told you I didn't know.'

—

Céspedes's eyes cross with Carole's in the window. She holds his gaze.

'Tu n'aimes pas ça? Qu'est-ce que tu n'aimes pas?'

—

'Oui, peut-être oui, demain aussi.'

—

'Tu peux y resister.'

'A lovesick little friend?' Céspedes forces a smile. Carole glances at him fleetingly. 'You didn't tell me about him.'

'Personne. Le train. Je n'aime pas quand les trains s'arrêtent.'

'Are you a lovesick little lovebird?' Céspedes has leaned over towards Carole's phone, towards her mouth, 'Un petit oiseau?'

Carole lowers the phone, places it on the seat. Her eyes are shining. 'What are you doing?'

Céspedes makes excuses. He says sorry, raises one hand. Carole starts speaking into the phone again.

'Oui, non, pas de tout.'

'She's not very friendly.' Céspedes is speaking to the passenger opposite them. 'French girls are like that. Before you know it they get very prickly.'

'Ça vaut la peine de risquer le coup.'

—

Another orphan, another lost soul, he'll be asking her for a day of grace, one more chance, who knows.

'Ah, si tu veux, mon ami, mais tu sais, la géographie et moi . . .' Carole tries to be sarcastic but doesn't quite pull it off; her voice is about to crack. 'Ça m'a fait mal moi aussi. M'a fait mal. Beaucoup.'

Carole is sitting there with the phone stuck to her ear. Céspedes doesn't know if they've hung up at the other end or if they're still talking and she's decided that the conversation's over. She moves the phone away from her face. Closes it. Looks into the darkness passing by the window, that blackness flying past at three hundred kilometres per hour. Céspedes can see her eyes shining in the window's reflection.

'Everything OK?' he asks her.

'You men, you're all paranoid.' Carole tries to go back to the realm of sarcasm.

'And how are you?'

'Me? Can't you tell?'

'I think you're not doing so well, although the way you feed me information about yourself in such small doses I can only guess, so I don't really know, Carole. I don't know how you are.'

'And what about you, how do you think I am?' Carole asks the passenger opposite them.

'You look fine to me. But as for the rest, inside, I mean, only you would know.'

'But she looks fine to you on the outside, doesn't she?' Céspedes asks him, looking down at Carole's cleavage in her half-unbuttoned shirt.

The passenger smiles, shrugs his shoulders, looks into Carole's eyes. She holds his gaze.

'I don't know, that's your affair.'

'That's our affair,' Céspedes whispers into Carole's ear, his lips brushing against it. She doesn't recoil. Céspedes can see the edge of an areola, the weight of her breast. *Why not?* he says to himself, as though he was saying to himself that he shouldn't have drunk so much, because whisky dries up his mouth and his thoughts. 'There, you see, you're unknown territory, a mystery.'

'Is that all you have to say? So much reflection, such a desire to get to the bottom of things, a whole day travelling in pursuit of the truth, and at the end of it all you've nothing to say, Céspedes. Tiny, capricious Céspedes. That sums you all up.'

'Don't try putting me in a club. It's enough to cope with seeing my own boat sinking.'

'Self-pity, complacency. Last night when I saw you and you started talking to me I said to myself, well at least he's not a coward.'

'And now you think you were mistaken.'

'Now, like you, I don't know.'

Céspedes sits there looking into her eyes. That sadness. *Defenceless sister, welcome to the world of the hapless, although you do have an exit visa.* And without knowing why he lets slip the words he's been keeping to himself all day, 'You know we won't see each other again, don't you?'

'Are you going to get all emotional?'

'Yes, I'm already all emotional, Carole.'

Carole looks at the glass, sees her face reflected in the middle of the darkness. She looks away from the window, looks at Céspedes's crotch.

'Yes, how could you not be? But you're referring to a different type of emotion.'

'All types of emotions. That type and all the others. You're conscious of the power you have. You're going to have it for many years.'

'You've had enough of being a gentleman, is that it? Thus far and no further, is that what you're trying to say?'

'I don't know what I was hoping to gain, and maybe I've offended you by doing so. Offended your beauty.'

'Obviously, I'm provoking you, aren't I? I'm getting provocative, isn't that right?'

'We can spare ourselves the sermons.' Céspedes brushes Carole's ear as he whispers into it. He kisses it.

'It's what you've been planning since you saw me last night. Tell me, out of curiosity about the human species, have you thought about anything else since then? Is that the only thought you've had in your head?'

'I've had at least three other ideas.'

Carole is still looking at him. She doesn't think it's an honest answer. Céspedes obeys her, replies, 'It's the thought in my head right now. Forget about last night, this morning and everything. Ten minutes.' Céspedes kisses on her earlobe.

'Ten minutes. A quick one, is that what you want?'

Céspedes pulls his head away, looks into Carole's eyes, feels the weight of the passenger's gaze on them, turns his head towards him and the other man looks away.

'I want whatever you want. Whatever you want to give me. That's it.'

'Liar. Can't you try harder?'

'No. It's all the same to me to lose whatever dignity I have left. I can't think of a better way to spend it, I can assure you.'

Céspedes comes closer, kisses Carole's lips. She lets herself be kissed. A few seconds. She looks into his eyes. Pulls away slowly. Looks at the window, sees herself and Céspedes reflected there, and the passenger who's watching them discreetly. Carole's jaw is clenched. She could be about to laugh or cry.

She doesn't do either. She stands up, her expression unchanging. She leaves her seat, brushing her buttocks against Céspedes's chest. The glass door at the end of the carriage opens automatically. Carole leaves the compartment. Céspedes stands up, treads on the bag in which he put the suit he bought a few hours ago, loses his balance, is about to fall on top of the other passenger, regains his balance. He leaves the compartment.

Carole has gone into the toilet cubicle. The light shows that she hasn't locked the door. Céspedes sees his reflection in the window, rings around his eyes, tired, his Hawaiian shirt crumpled, his Bermuda shorts *the hunter's last rounds.*

He opens the toilet door. Carole is balanced on the tiny basin. They go into a tunnel; the train seems to compress violently and then fill out again. Céspedes closes the door behind him, slides the bolt, and the light becomes slightly more intense. Céspedes, pressed up against Carole, tries to kiss her. She turns her head away and whispers, 'No. Get it out.' Céspedes sees his eyes in the mirror over the metal washbasin, and Carole's hair, her shoulders, her back. He knows he's making a mistake. But he tells himself that nothing matters any more. He is master of nothing.

He opens his flies. Carole's eyes are close to his. She moves her arm. Céspedes notices her slender feminine fingers taking hold of his semi-erect organ. A gentle warmth, a promise. Carole moves her hand slowly, all the time looking into his eyes. Céspedes is about to say 'Leave it,' but he only manages to separate his lips. Carole crouches down, sits on the toilet, pulls Céspedes towards her. *It wasn't for this, I swear it. Don't touch her, don't contaminate her with my life. For her to be an island, that's what I wanted.* He closes his eyes, remembering Carole's outline from the previous morning, her profile, alone in the garden, and he can't work out whether it's from his memory or his imagination, his haziness from the alcohol, he sees her in the shade of those huge trees, also clutching a telephone and with tears running down her cheeks.

The humidity, saliva, the wet warmth of her tongue. *Two animals full of blood, leave it, yes, stop, just a little bit more then stop.* Céspedes doesn't want to look down, he can barely make out Carole's hair swinging rhythmically, he feels buffeted by the speed, the train is running inside him, dismembering him, the speed entering and exiting his body, someone turns the door handle, tries to come in, gives up, another tunnel, another compression, another expansion, Carole working with tongue and lips, touching, swallowing, licking, sucking, *she's trying to do an expert job, poor girl, get her diploma in blow jobs, what a disaster, what madness, and yet, when will I grow up? Only when she stops giving me a hard-on, death sentence.* Céspedes buries his fingers in the girl's hair like a garden rake, the other hand seeking out her breasts, he recalls the image of her tired breast, the hint of an areola, such smooth, silky skin, he feels her nipple with his fingertips, tiny, a little pink animal, he might come, he might now, but he opens his eyes and sees the mechanical movement of her head once again, her amateurish commitment, that sexual handicraft thanks to which a few young men must have told her, 'I've never had a blow job like that before.' Such pride. And Céspedes is overcome by another wave of sadness, the night out there, those fields consumed by the blackness, the abandoned houses in the middle of those fields, and here they are in this plastic cubicle, flying along at three hundred kilometres per hour towards the absurd.

No, that was definitively not what he'd wanted, he knows that now, and he knows that if he ejaculates in her face or her mouth it will be worse, much worse. Depression, emptiness. Face to face with the void. With his own profound misery. Yes, better to resist the temptation, better not to recall that image of her breasts, her dormant breast, the cream-coloured outline announcing her nipple, better to put a stop to this misunderstanding, the misunderstanding he provoked in the small hours of the previous day when he approached this woman and that he's maintained throughout the day, wanting to ignore reality, to leapfrog it, defy it, a pointless exercise. Not even narcissistic, not even pleasurable. The reaffirmation of the void, that's all.

'No.'

That's what he says when he opens his eyes, returning from another world. No. And he finds Carole's cloudy eyes, gleaming, tearful.

Everything seems to take on a new meaning. As if they were waking from a dream. Carole sitting on the metal toilet bowl, Céspedes buffeted by the speed of the train, holding on to the walls, his Hawaiian shirt, his erect penis, the tears in Carole's eyes. *But what is this?* They see themselves from the outside. And Céspedes knows that everything has already been broken for ever. That the persona he's been creating for this woman for the last fifteen or twenty hours is already a scarecrow, a sack filled with straw. *My stuffing's coming out at the seams, it's the end of the road.* And that her character has also reached the end of its performance.

Céspedes withdraws as much as he can within the confines of the compartment. He bangs the back of his neck against a shelf. He quickly tucks away his organ, which has become the evidence of all this stupidity. He zips up his Bermuda shorts and tries to speak. But he can only say her name. Carole. Where's that fellow gone who was so full of confidence, sarcasm, culture, the corporate raider, man of the world? 'Carole, listen,' says Céspedes.

Carole has stood up. She has an absent look and is showing her bottom teeth, as though obeying some doctor's orders. Slowly she shakes her head. She raises an eyebrow. That beauty.

Céspedes makes a clumsy attempt at irony. 'Shall we go? The man in the seat opposite will be missing us.' Carole lifts up one arm and pushes back her hair, and the watch on her wrist becomes the central point of the cubicle. Céspedes guesses what's going to happen.

Carole places her arm on her chest, as if it were in a sling, and unclasps the watch. She holds it by the end of the strap, between two fingers. The speed of the train makes it swing from side to side.

'Here, take it.'

Céspedes shakes his head.

'Don't you want it?' asks Carole.

Céspedes shakes his head and then, smiling, says, 'No. It's yours.' He shrugs his shoulders and, with a smile on his face, looks over to the metal toilet bowl.

Carole turns around, lifts the lid. She looks sidelong at Céspedes, who's still wearing a smile, now a little broader, more a like a genuine smile, and she opens her fingers. The watch falls and gets stuck in the small metal bowl. It looks like a black lizard down there, glistening, breathing. Carole pushes a button on the wall. A jet of blue liquid accompanied by a brusque noise is ejected under pressure and splashes over the watch before it's swallowed down into the entrails of the train, which has gone into another tunnel, and it feels like the walls of the carriage are going to contract, to fold in on each other.

It's the first night since his father died. There's still a green glow floating in the sky to the west, a pale light burning behind the horizon that refuses to be extinguished. A fresh breeze is blowing in from the sea, and more and more people are bustling around the tightly packed terraces of the seafront promenade at Pedregal. A beauty like broken glass. People are eating, drinking, breathing, laughing and strutting about, glad to have ridden out this torrid, choking day. Sons and daughters of this land and this sea, they know that night-time promises hope and release.

Guille follows a few paces behind Cabello and La Lori. They might be talking about him. Loberas is walking beside him, bumping into his shoulder; the stupid idiot can't walk in a straight line. Behind him is Juno in his funereal suit and tie, along with Isidro and El Tuli. That's where the whistle that brings them all to a halt comes from. Confusion. They ask each other what's going on. 'Let's go to La Chancla.' 'Why have you stopped?' 'It's El Tuli, he says to wait.' Guille feels like throwing up. They form a group behind him. Loberas breaks away, laughing, doubling up with laughter, saying, 'You'd never dare!' He pushes Guille. 'The old ladies.' 'What?' asks Guille. 'Those old ladies, over there.' Guille sees three elderly women sitting in Cremades, an ice cream parlour. He doesn't understand. He'd like to jump over the low wall separating them from the beach, walk along the sand and lie down near the seashore. Wake up in two months' time or maybe four. When everything's over, when this day which he knows will last much longer than twenty-four hours has finally come to an end.

'Lori! Lori!' It's that idiot Isidro calling out to her. She's still talking to Cabello very seriously, as if they hadn't smoked anything or had anything to drink. 'Come on, Lori, you're so good at fronting. Come on. El Tuli's treating you to an ice cream.'

Cabello comes over to Guille. 'Are you OK?' he asks. 'Yeah, a bit out of it but OK.' 'Aren't you going back home?' Cabello looks at him steadily. 'Yeah, yeah, I'll be off now,' Guille replies, looking away from Cabello's dark, all-absorbing eyes and fixing on La Lori, who's sitting with Isidro, Juno and El Tuli at a table in the ice cream parlour close to the three old ladies. 'She's fit, La Lori, isn't she?' says Guille, sounding out Cabello, trying to discover what he might know about what went on between him and the girl at El Tuli's house. Cabello nods gently. 'You should head back home, to your mother, don't you think?' And then, looking uncomfortably at his group of friends, he wonders, 'What are those guys up to?' And he pauses, watching as La Lori asks one of the women for a light.

'They're going to mug her,' says Cabello. 'What?' Guille doesn't understand, he just wants to escape, run away from his life. 'You'd better go home. I'm off.' Cabello turns around and starts walking up the sea-front promenade.

Yes, he'll just take three steps, cross over to the other side of the low wall, walk along with his feet sinking in the sand and lie down there, near the freshness, near the water's edge. And then go home, yes, call his mother, lie down on his bed with the air conditioning. Wait for it all to be over with.

That's when Loberas approaches him and says, 'Come over! We're going to nick her bag. What a laugh! El Tuli's really amazing!' And so Guille goes over with Loberas and sits among his friends, who are all excited. La Lori's speaking to one of the women, there's music and children shouting in the background, the night's hot breath is sweeping away the fresh sea air. Guille's telephone vibrates in his pocket. It'll be his mother, best not pick up, yes, best not to, let it vibrate, she'll soon get tired. And that's why Dr Galán is there with her phone stuck to her ear. Her house is also an ants' nest. The question is, where to go?

Trains shatter the night. From the darkness, the figures in the windows look like ghosts, people from another age travelling in another dimension. In the morgue an ant has survived the cold and is staggering around in a daze across the dead man's groin, tears off a flake of skin and retraces its steps, sluggishly, half keeling over, not knowing where the nest is, where to take the winter provisions. Another ant is rummaging and searching inside Dionisio Grandes Guimerá's inner ear, and it's now completely disorientated.

The Runner goes down the stairs without turning on the lights, crosses the narrow entrance hall and walks into the heat outside. There's a ballet of mosquitos and butterflies fluttering around the lamp-post near the entrance. His grandmother watches him leave, her head trembling from the Parkinson's and her sadness at seeing her favourite grandchild go downhill. 'Tell Lucía to come and see me soon,' she says, but the door has already closed, leaving a dull echo and a silence that the old lady fears will be broken by her daughter's voice from the kitchen. But nothing happens. The only voices are the ones blaring out from the neighbours' televisions, the sounds from the street coming through the windows, open in the hope of a cool breeze that doesn't arrive.

Heading up Calle Cruz Verde, Eduardo Chinarro is walking ten paces behind his colleague with the guitar. The temperature seems to be increasing and the walls and the asphalt are releasing the heat that they've absorbed throughout the day.

'Look at me,' La Penca says to her brother before she says goodbye. 'If he lays a finger on me, I'll kill him,' she confesses in a whisper, looking sidelong down the corridor, where her father's shadow is wandering around. And El Yubri looks at the floor, the cracked and mottled tiles, the dog with its glaucous eyes. 'That's not going happen,' he says, 'not any more, Penqui.'

on way

writes Jorge on his phone and presses the arrow that sends his message to Nene Olmedo. His cousin Floren and Pedroche go off on foot, walking parallel to the expanse of barren land where now only two or three cars are parked. Their voices are lost in the darkness, and Jorge writes to his girlfriend:

wher R U?

He receives an asterisk from Nene Olmedo, which he assumes denotes approval, or maybe it's a threat. Nothing from his girlfriend. He sees the two little blue ticks that indicate she's read his message, but then she goes offline straight away.

wher R U xx?

This time his girlfriend doesn't even bother opening the message and Jorge stops on the edge of the waste ground, not knowing where to go. He feels like the night is full of cracks. The outlines of Floren and Pedroche have already disappeared in the distance. The priest goes down the stairs in his block of flats. He feels good. Yes, there's no reason why he should get bogged down in those dark thoughts that every now and then envelop him like a sticky spider's web. Miracles don't happen, but life is still a tribute, the path is open and there's fruit by the side of the road. *El Sol Sale Para Todos* – the sun shines for everyone – that's the name of the local grocer's shop. As ordained by God. He goes out into the street, into the sultry, scorching air, a vagabond licking the walls. He's carrying that poor man's money and his velvet bag of jewellery in a small fake-leather briefcase. There are many other people who are worse off. His life is full of consolations. And he does good works. Yes, at the end of the day he does a modicum of good. A place at the right hand of the Lord. A stool.

Dr Galán observes her brother. Emilio's accompanying a small group, comprising Trini's mother, Asunción Arnedo and her husband, Montse and Carlos San Emeterio, Dioni's partner in the firm, to the front door. They say goodbye. Before they leave they look at her with renewed affection. Faces of condolence. Once they go through the gate they'll be back among the living. San Emeterio, deeply affected, will glimpse in the midst of sorrow what the office might be like without Dioni. Asunción and her husband will head down the hill, grateful for the comforts of life in this corner of paradise. Trini's mother and Montse will plan what to have for dinner, delayed by this tragedy, and will make some comment about Dioni's strange death and the calamity it means for Ana and how upset they've been today because of his death, how everything can change in an instant and what they'll do tomorrow, the swimming pool, the beach, an aperitif, all depending on the timing of the funeral. The enormous, essential trifles that make up the fabric their lives.

Julia asks her if she wants anything. Dr Galán looks at her distractedly and says no. Julia's standing up. She goes up to her, bends down, places a knee on the sofa and gives her a kiss on the cheek. Says she's off. She'll be back early tomorrow. Dr Galán says yes to everything. She watches her friend crossing the living room, hears her talking to Emilio near the door. Funeral preparations. Emilia, on the terrace, looks on from the other side of the window, like a goldfish in a bowl. This lethargy, like time run aground, all the wheels at a standstill.

The photos on the lacquered sideboard seem more voiceless than ever. Can this really be all his curriculum vitae amounts to? Can it really be so ridiculous? A double portrait of Ana and Dioni in Vienna on their honeymoon, the giant Ferris wheel in the Prater behind them. Ana and her mother walking arm in arm in front of a row of shops. Umbrellas, raincoats, laughing. Guille wearing a motorcycle helmet, riding on his uncle's shoulders. Guille in a judo suit. Ana talking at a medical conference, looking over the top of her glasses intelligently, both hands on the lectern. And that other photo in a silver frame, that photo that Dioni always wanted to save from all the fires and all the makeovers. A photo of him, eight or nine years old, in front of a window, holding on to the window bars with one hand and looking sadly at the photographer, who must have been his father.

Yes, all too ridiculous, thinks Dr Galán. Much more like a caricature than a proper curriculum vitae. She thinks of the photos that are missing, the pieces of a jigsaw that have been lost, making the picture incomplete. What isn't on display there and never saw the light of day. The gaps, the ghosts, the absences that marked all of their lives. The underground streams. The scaffolding behind the decorative façade.

A photo for Vicente. Yes, there ought to be one for him, the other member of the family. If it weren't for him, thinks Dr Galán, it's more than likely that Dioni wouldn't be dead, that his life would have taken a different path. She knows that after that encounter in their house Dioni continued to see him. She knows he was a very important person in her husband's life. And she wonders why he was really so important. If in some way that young man could compete with her on an emotional level or if it was just an urge. An attraction much stronger than Dioni ever felt for her and stronger than he could feel for any woman.

An irrepressible, all-consuming urge. The apex of desire. But was it just desire? How far did that love go? And to what extent was it reciprocated? Did that young man ever really love Dioni? What was it really like, all that business that she never wanted to know about? That she'll never know about now. The truth, or the closest thing to the truth, is there now, locked in a morgue on a cold tray. As inaccessible as he ever was. Just as remote.

This is what Ana will never know:
Yes, there was a period of happiness, a time when Dioni coped almost naturally with that double life and was relaxed about it. He gave his family everything that any other upstanding man would do. Staying up at night for his son, there was affection for his wife, education, care, stability, attention, security. And he kept up his parallel relationship with Vicente without this having the slightest negative impact on his family life, at least that's how it looked. Once he began his relationship with Vicente Dioni put an end to his encounters with rent boys and also to playing those games with self-destruction that sometimes turned violent.

Vicente understood that discretion was an essential requirement and almost always complied with that rule. No scenes in public, no more visits to their house, whether Ana was in town or not. He very rarely showed up at his office and only did so when he was worried, thought they might be breaking up or was desperate. He only showed up at the office once for financial reasons. Dioni helped him out with that side of things. There was nothing routine or fixed in stone about it, but Vicente had his little whims, and his lack of financial-management skills and his precarious job situation meant that he couldn't indulge them, but Dioni allowed him to. He was also there to help out in a crisis.

Vicente went with him on some of his business trips. He would stay in the room next door at the hotel, and they would have dinner in separate restaurants. He knew how to give Dioni what he needed. Affection, sex, a sense of humour and lack of inhibition.

It all fell apart quite naturally. It began with a small confession. A woman. A girl who was rather too young. Vicente said he felt nothing for her. Perhaps, yes, perhaps some kind of attraction, mixed in with other feelings, a little tenderness. As he said to Dioni, 'Perhaps I'm doing it to remember how it used to be, what I'm like with a woman, what I'm like now - you're the master wordsmith, call it what you want.' And when Dioni showed some concern, 'I'll tell her it's over, it's over and done with.' And with his best smile, he asked, 'Happy? It's Vicente's word of honour.'

The girl got pregnant, and the emotional roller-coaster was set in motion. It was a long and exhausting rigmarole, like a marathon. Dioni's strength or his love or his need ended up playing against him. If he'd broken loose, if he hadn't put up with so much frustration and disappointment, he would have survived. It's not entirely clear if he was too strong or too weak. It all lasted for years.

First of all there was the pregnancy. Vicente swinging back and forth like a pendulum. The imminent abortion was postponed. Vicente felt sorry for the girl. And how could he not when there was the chance of becoming a father, the joy of having a child. He didn't necessarily have to live with the girl, but he had to acknowledge his child, see him from time to time, let the child know he was his father. Why should he give all that up? Dioni had to understand, he had a son, too. It wasn't any different. Dioni couldn't hide behind that selfish argument. 'Why is it any different, because the child will be mine and not yours? You've already got a child, you've got it all, let me have something as well.'

Insomnia. Dioni going out alone. Bars where he felt out of place. One night with a rent boy. Rough sex. The edge of an abyss, and he refused to look down into it.

The birth of the child. Vicente was thrilled. His happiness found a way into Dioni's heart. They hugged, they loved each other more than anything else in the world. Everything was going to be different. Everything was going to be possible. Dioni almost believed it. He brushed up against it. Vicente's enthusiasm and love for life were almost infectious.

Vicente was right in a way. Everything was possible. Although in a very different way than his words had suggested. Shortly after the baby was born he went to live with the girl, Gema. Dioni met her. Vicente had told Gema that he had a very special friend. Who knows what Gema might have understood about how special that friendship was. Dioni never knew. The girl was friendly towards him. She had reason to be friendly. Apart from a few other bills, Dioni paid for the first few months' rent on the flat that the new family had taken on. A flat near Calle Bolivia. Vicente thought it was absolutely essential for the child's health to grow up beside the sea. The sun, the beach, walks. So Dioni put up with it. Selflessly or very selfishly, you know how it is.

But his financial generosity or his emotional need didn't exempt him from suffering. Probably not Vicente either. Dioni began spending time away in earnest. At first for a night then for a day or two at a time. Beginning to dig his own grave. His taste for rough sex grew. Perhaps he saw it as the path to be free of it all. Completely free of it all. A slow dark path. He brought back proof of that darkness whenever he returned. A bruise, scratches down his back, anal tearing.

Ana Galán wasn't aware of his intimate injuries. His obvious injuries were excused as stumbles or carelessness. Fuel for suspicion. Hint of a chasm that was too deep to be credible. Vicente did discover some of the injuries that Dioni was able to hide from his wife.

Those injuries suddenly turned Vicente into a decent, upstanding man, into a censor. He called Dioni's attention to the life he couldn't lead and told him he had better put a stop to it, and quickly, too. Dioni had his counter-attack ready. 'You've abandoned me, you've thrown me aside for an illiterate and pathetic little slut, not for a child like you say, but for a little pussy. You don't care about the child, you don't care about anyone but that slut.' Vicente's hand grasping Dioni's neck, his powerful, hairless arm tense, a beam that was squashing him against the wall. 'Hit me, go on, that will round it off nicely. Hit me.' The little boy who was probably two years old at the time, was watching them wide-eyed, expectant, almost smiling, from his playpen.

They went for a walk along the beach. Just the three of them, Dioni, Vicente and Quilín. Gema had found a job in a hairdresser's. She specialized in nails, manicures. They had a grown-up conversation. People facing up to the facts with no bitterness and who knew how to accept life for what it is, without going around in circles. At least that's what the naïve Vicente was trying to say. 'Look at it like this, we're a family,' he said sitting on a stone bench on the seafront in Pedregalejo as he looked out to sea and Quilín was playing on the beach a few metres away. 'We're a family, Gema, Quilín, you and me. You, your wife and Guille, you're another family, but you're also part of this one. Gema accepts you. Quilín loves you.' 'Gema accepts me? Does she know we're screwing – or that we used to? That you couldn't live without me or at least that's what you used to say. Does she know that?' Vicente shook his head a little, not as an answer to Dioni but rather in disapproval at his behaviour. 'She knows what she needs to know, and she accepts you, look at it like that, Dioni, a family, that's what we are.' And he blew some cigarette smoke out of his mouth and turned to look out to sea again, just like an actor in a bad film.

And Dioni thought, yes, perhaps he was the one who was wrong, perhaps Vicente had simply been an invention, a mirage that he'd created and fed to combat his absolute loneliness. A safety net protecting him from the horror of emptiness. But the abyss was there, and there was no safety net. And there was that man, smiling down at his son, and perhaps that's really all he was, a local hairdresser's perfect partner. Turning over a new leaf in his own way, leaving his riotous youth behind and trying to adopt him, Dioni, as his ridiculous family's godfather.

'I don't need a family. I've already got my own. I want you, and you're the only one who knows what you want.' Dioni felt like he was caught up in a melodrama, too, when he said those words, or something very similar, before he left.

There's a term in cycling that describes the moment a cyclist starts falling behind the group as it climbs a steep hill and catches up again and then falls behind again in a whole series of agonizing efforts to stay with the group, suffering painful changes in rhythm. That's what happened to Dionisio Grandes Guimerá. He fell behind Vicente and then caught up with him again. But climbing up that incredibly steep hill lasted for years. And Dioni never reached the summit. Quite the opposite.

Downhill. Abyss. Disintegration. Nothing like calm and nothing at all like peace. That's what happened. Perhaps what Dioni was searching for was similar to silence, the silencing of those internal voices that never stopped nagging in every imaginable tone.

There were reconciliations, fights, separations that threatened to become permanent. On one occasion Gema, the hairdresser who specialized in manicures, went to see him at his office. She said nothing at all that might indicate she was aware of the relationship between Dioni and Vicente, but she was very clear when she told him that Vicente was depressed, that he needed him, that whether he believed it or not, Dioni was very important to him. 'You're the person who lights up his life,' she said. Gema asked him to go and see him. He did. It was the final reconciliation. Behind all that, there were financial problems, too. Vicente swore on his knees that he didn't need him for that. And that he would never have allowed Gema to go and see him. She hadn't told him that the hairdresser's had sacked her or that they were about to be evicted. Depression was eating away at Vicente, at least that was Dioni's amateur diagnosis.

They went on a trip. The four of them. Vicente, Gema, Quilín and Dioni. Three days in a Parador. A golf course, a beach, a swimming pool where Gema and Quilín spent almost all their time. The little boy had a crocodile rubber ring, and she downed cocktails by the dozen. Dioni found out that she was an alcoholic and that was why the hairdresser's had sacked her. She nearly took off half a client's finger when she tried to cut away a loose piece of skin. It was the last time Dioni and Vicente had a sexual encounter. Mid-morning. Dioni sodomized Vicente for the first time as he said to him 'slut, queer, pretty boy'. He took pleasure in the humiliation. He subjected Vicente to what had been his accustomed role. Compared with his activities with the rent boys, it was gentle sex.

Dioni always remembered the last day at the Parador and the journey back in his car as the very dramatization of torture. Drunk hairdresser, child with crocodile, Vicente. At the Parador everything was part of the same mix. Time stood still. He worked out how many minutes were left to get back home: 1,560 from the moment he ejaculated inside Vicente's rectum. Twenty-six hours. Each hour with its sixty minutes and each minute with its sixty seconds. After the sexual encounter – Vicente with his face buried underneath the pillow, his back (reddened by the sun and almost greasy) that years before had rippled with sculpted muscles (now gone) – everything was an agonizing countdown. To get home. To the emptiness.

Ana, Guille. The sad stage play. From a distance it looked like a refuge, but it barely met the conditions for an old TB sanatorium. Rotten lungs, infected air. A magic mountain with no clear summit and no philosophy other than concealment. He found himself watching Ana inquisitively. Was she really never going to say anything to him that touched on reality, on what he felt? *Ask me. Ask me. Here I am. I'm an open book right in front of you. Have a flick through every single page, wherever you want. Even if it's just out of curiosity, ask me. But she doesn't. She's as much of a coward as I am.* That was the problem. And he loved her. And he felt sorry for her. And he felt horribly ashamed.

The deep post-coital dysphoria he felt at the Parador turned into a well that he couldn't climb out of for God only knows how long. He didn't answer Vicente's calls. Dioni could still see his disconsolate face after they'd had sex. Would he ask him now what he hadn't dared back then? Why he'd behaved like that and why he'd been so contemptuous towards him, wanting to humiliate him. He was grown-up enough to understand.

Dioni came home early for a few days, for quite a few days. Dinner with Ana and some friends. A weekend away in the countryside with Ana, Guille and Dr Quesada's family. Quesada's wife was a chemistry teacher, and she understood human beings just as well as she understood the elements in the periodic table, how they all reacted together. Their twelve-year-old son, a kind of computer engineer, was full of fun. Happy people. He wasn't comparing himself with Quesada's family for a minute, but Dioni did think that perhaps he could become an upstanding man, that all the shadiness could be consigned to the past. That lifted his spirits, and, as his spirits lifted, his appetites and his needs returned. The beginning of a new vicious circle.

It was a rapid descent. He no longer had Vicente to control him emotionally. Serious disappearances. Nights and days when no one knew where he was or who he was with. Returning home pathetically, dismally. The utmost secrecy. His friend and partner, Carlos San Emeterio, gave him every possible opportunity. His wife, powerless, sometimes on the alert and sometimes running away from reality. Dioni had rejected any possibility of changing course. The only thing now was to sink to the very depths and as quickly as possible. And that's what he did. As you know, the path led to a patch of waste ground near Avenida Ortega y Gasset. Beside a nest of voracious Argentine ants. That's the end of the story.

The end of the story, the end of the details that Ana Galán will never know. She never really knew how much her husband suffered, how he took his pleasure, the great heights he fell from or how insalubrious and asphyxiating were the wells into which he sank. She never knew about and will never know about the existence of that fake family that Vicente wanted to give her husband. Nor about the existence of Gema the hairdresser or Quilín the little boy. All she knew was that after she found them in their house that day, her husband and Vicente carried on seeing each other. She heard Vicente's name being mentioned at the end of a telephone conversation, she saw the letter V jotted down in her husband's diary, she had her suspicions and intuitions, but she had already given up. She once saw actual proof that they were still involved. Vicente's son hadn't been born yet. It was during the period when Dioni was still managing to balance his two lives. One winter's afternoon Ana took Dioni to the airport. He was going on a business trip to Amsterdam. They said goodbye to each other. When Ana was close to the exit she realized that Dioni's glasses were in her handbag. She'd picked them up in a rush as they were leaving home. She retraced her steps and thought that with a bit of luck she might catch up with her husband in the queue for security. It didn't work out like that. Dioni had already gone through and that young man was next to him, smiling. She watched them disappear as they walked to the boarding gate. Aeroplanes flying high in the sky, air vibrating, noises and echoes growing faint. The electricity of silence.

They were caught by a municipal policeman in plain clothes. He grabbed Guille and Loberas around their necks. Off-duty officer Alberto Marín had gone out to stretch his legs after dinner. He was wondering whether to have a gin and tonic on the terrace of La Chancla when he heard someone screaming and saw the little brats fleeing.

The first one got away, a little rich kid of about sixteen wearing a suit and tie. He caught the other two following him, shiny eyed with deranged grins, mid-flight. He literally grabbed their necks. A fish in either hand. One little no-hoper reeking of marijuana and alcohol who wouldn't stop squirming, and the other one, the moment he was caught, started whimpering and saying that his father had died.

After he'd held them there for a minute, even before he could call a patrol car to take charge of the two delinquents, a woman appeared, completely out of breath, pale, and the front of her blue-rinsed hair stained dark red, a streak of the same colour running down her forehead. She pointed at them. 'That's them. There were more of them, but that's them, and there was also a girl, she was distracting us so the others could rob me.'

They'd taken her handbag. El Tuli had come up with the plan. Isidro was the artist who, while La Lori was asking them for a light and chatting to the woman and her two friends, snatched the bag and ran off. Or tried to run off. The bag's straps were wrapped twice around the arm of the chair. It took two strong tugs to yank it away and leave the straps hanging off the chair, and the woman collapsed on the floor. Enough time for a waiter to grab La Lori by the hair but not enough for the two English tourists sitting at a neighbouring table to collar any of the makeshift gang.

Isidro, carrying the bag like a rugby ball, passed it to El Tuli – a perfect spin pass – before jumping over the low wall on to the beach and running off across the sand. El Tuli, hugging the bag to his stomach, fled through the side streets, heading towards Calle Bolivia. Juno, Guille and Loberas went the wrong way, straight up the promenade towards Municipal Police Officer Alberto Marín Marcos, off duty but always ready to uphold the law and earn some brownie points on his way up the greasy pole.

The waiter at Cremades, the ice cream parlour, accompanied by the friends of the handbag's owner, delivered La Lori into the hands of Municipal Police Officer Marín. La Lori, calm as you like, insisted that she didn't know those snotty little rich kids. It was pure coincidence that they had sat down next to her when they arrived at the ice cream parlour. She tried to convince the municipal police officer by softening her voice and making him fully aware of her attributes in the breast department. She was helped by the steamy evening and her generously low-cut top, but the presence of the handbag's owner, the expectations of the other onlookers and the police officer's dedication to duty made the seduction difficult and, ultimately, impossible. Two of Marín Marcos's colleagues, in uniform and with handcuffs at the ready, manacled the three youngsters accused of robbery and marched them to a patrol car, turning a deaf ear to Loberas's incoherent pleading, Guille's wailing or La Lori's requests for mercy, her eyes bright with tears.

Yes, the night was spreading, spiralling around and around in ever-decreasing circles, slowly reaching its very centre, that keyhole containing all the mysteries in the world. Focusing people's minds, confronting them with their labyrinths.

Some people unpardonably abandoned themselves to this fate, either distressed or delighted by this path towards the unfathomable. Others fought against it, trying to mingle with other people and thereby diluting what was burning inside them. The way each person reacted was the least important thing. Happiness or frustration, drifting or bonding, suspicion or hope. Violence and desire. The ways of the Lord are infinite.

Father Sebastián had arrived, quite late. Pedroche and Floren were waiting on the church steps. Too much beer to be lucid. Too much heat. Too much stickiness on El Yubri's hands. La Penca's brother. His father's blood.

'God's blood poured into the chalice. You can laugh, but that's what drove Belita crazy,' Pedroche says to Floren as they waited outside the church door. 'To a sickly child like her, that's what made her completely unhinged, Floren, and that's the truth; she got it stuck in her brain, which must have been half rotten already, moth eaten and dried out like those pictures old people bring us so we can change the frame. But that's what drove her completely mad, she's told me loads of times, she's spoken loads of times about God's blood and how it's going to save us. Some of us, it's only going to save some of us. She's first in line. That's why we're here, that's why she wants to give everything to that priest, because of what got stuck inside her crazy brain when she was a little girl. In order to save herself.'

Pedroche talks, and his friend and partner, Floren, the innocent, listens to what he's saying without believing half of it. And, on the other side of the street, hiding behind a large sign that says **Terés y García**, Nene Olmedo and El Tato are watching in silence. 'That's the loser there,' El Tato had said when they arrived and they saw Pedroche in the distance. 'And the other one's the little shit's cousin,' Nene Olmedo's assistant added, El Nene confining himself to a clipped affirmation, 'Hmm' or something like that. El Nene had the shiv in his pocket. An enormous screwdriver. More suited to undoing lives than screws.

The two accomplices watched as a tall man walked towards the church, in a short-sleeved shirt and with an old-fashioned look about him. 'The priest,' El Tato guessed correctly. Nene Olmedo nodded in agreement, watching as the priest bounded up the church steps with a briefcase under his arm and shook hands with Pedroche and Floren, smiling in the way that only priests know how to smile.

Yes, blood on his hands. Blood on the floor and blood on the wall. El Yubri used a pair of scissors to stab and kill his father. The large pair of scissors that his seamstress mother had used to cut out so many clothes, so many dresses, so many armholes, so many patterns, necklines and sleeves, those scissors she'd used to earn a living and feed little Penqui and little half-retarded Yubri and, most of the time, her lazy, incestuous husband who used to abuse his daughter.

His father was on the floor. He was wearing white cotton underpants and a vest, also white, also cotton, and nothing else. His feet were bare, with large, thick toenails tinged with green. A dark liquid was oozing out of his flabby belly and staining his vest. He raised his right hand, moved it feebly as though he were sleeping and having a nightmare, his eyes rolling back in his head. The scissors were no longer in El Yubri's right hand, they were stuck in the back of his father's head.

Slumped there, his shoulders propped against the Formica cupboard and with the scissors poking out from the back of his head like a post-modern ornamental comb, his father was blowing bubbles of blood out of his mouth, shaking with nervous convulsions, and he looked more like a drunk than a man in his death throes. The dog, frightened, looked back and forth between the man, El Yubri and the puddle of blood that was spreading across the floor. Tempted to lick it but holding himself back.

El Yubri had decided that his father wasn't going to fuck La Penqui again. Never again. He was going to prison in any case. Right then he didn't give a damn if they gave him a longer sentence. Not being the brightest spark, he thought that he would never get out of jail in any case. And, if he did, it would only be so he could go back the following month. So he might as well be hanged for a sheep as a lamb.

He told his father before the first onslaught. The old man was in the kitchen, fingering some pieces of fruit, undecided which one he was going to eat first. None of them.

'You're never going to eat anything again, and you're not going to do anything else to La Penqui either.' That's what El Yubri said. To which his father, hair ruffled and still looking half asleep, replied, 'What the fuck are you on about?' He still hadn't seen the scissors. In fact, he only saw their formless reflection glinting under the fluorescent light in the kitchen when El Yubri was already thrusting them towards his belly with all the strength the boy could muster.

The dog jumped backwards. His claws, which were too long, made him skid and bang his snout on the floor just as the steel ripped through El Yubri's father's sweaty vest and tore his skin open, punctured his intestines, resulting in the first flow of blood. Splashing. That's what those blows sounded like, or something very similar. The impact of a solid object in wet mud. A dog that can't get out of a puddle.

La Penca had a premonition. Rather, she had the ghost of a premonition, because just as the sense of foreboding was beginning to trickle through to her consciousness she heard her father yell. A lot of screaming. Excruciating. At first it almost put El Yubri off his task. The man was screaming as loudly and insistently as a siren on an ambulance or a fire engine. Repeatedly, stridently. Howling. Waving his hands in the air. The dog twirled around in a circle twice with his tail between his legs, watching as El Yubri ignored the racket his father was making and concentrated on the job at hand. Three, four powerful stabs. Sticking the scissors in and out of his father's gut and then stepping back from him. Like a painter stepping back to see the result of his brushstrokes more clearly. Taking two steps back and seeing the horror-stricken face of the man who'd given life to him. Strange things spilling out of his gut and him slumping down against the cupboard, his back propped up against the Formica and still screaming, but not quite so loud. He only stopped when El Yubri, coming at him once more, stuck the scissors in his head. Kuki saw this as the moment to party. He jumped forwards and backwards, wagging his tail happily and looking avidly at the tasty treat that was spreading over the denim-coloured tiles but, maybe not hungry, still undecided as to whether to dip his tongue in.

It was then that La Penca's shadow appeared at the door to the kitchen. She didn't go in. All she saw were her father's dirty feet. Those two thick, lifeless, livid appendages under the fluorescent light were all she needed to know that she was free. In the frosted windowpane she could see the blurred reflection of her brother's silhouette. Calm, engrossed. Beyond the window, in the building opposite, a comedian was chatting on the television and the night was trembling.

In that corner of Parque Litoral, however, the night's breath was heavy. The plants were breathing, transpiring. The air was becoming thick and seemed to be getting hotter and hotter. Rafi Villaplana was waiting for her in his car. Amelia had seen him arrive, with his head bent and the glow from the screen of his phone lighting up part of his face.

It wasn't going to be easy. Amelia knew that before she arrived. The past few days and what Rafi had said on the telephone didn't augur well. But she couldn't believe that things were going to pan out like that. The day hadn't started well, with her curtains, sheets and towels cut up into triangles. There was no reason why it should end well either.

Her son Ismael was wandering around Calle Refino and Calle Carrión looking for trouble. He'd had a row on Calle Refino with a car driver who was coming out of the car park and who, according to Ismael, nearly ran him over. He kicked the driver's door twice. The driver, held back by his wife, exchanged a few insults with him. Ismael ended the argument by thumping the bonnet and ostentatiously grabbing hold of his private parts through his trousers.

He stumbled on his way, jumped over the wall into the empty plot at the start of Calle Carrión and threw up in the bushes, all over a piece of foam that some rough sleeper must have been using as a bed. Exaggerating the noise, emphasizing the retching. He wandered around the site, trampling bushes and kicking cans. Then he tried to masturbate, thinking about Consuelo. He imagined he was taking off her green housecoat in the lift. And that she was wearing a pair of black lace knickers. Large ones, almost reaching her belly button. But he couldn't concentrate. Choking from the heat, lit up by the alcohol pulsing through his arteries, he was convinced that very soon Consuelo would take off her clothes for him. Her tiny teeth, dark eyes, whore's mouth saying, 'Ismael, fuck me.' He started pummelling his cock again.

His mother got into Rafi Villaplana's car on the front passenger's side. Rafi barely looked up from his phone to give her a sideways glance. 'Just a moment,' he said. He tapped away at the screen, sending and receiving messages. Amelia thought he was texting his English fiancée. She'd never seen her. She saw her photo just once, on Rafi's phone, when he had her on his WhatsApp profile for a week or so. Dark hair, the pair of them with their heads together, smiling. Afterwards he switched back to his usual picture. Sunglasses, a moustache she'd never seen on him and an expression that looked vaguely like a smile.

Amelia was expecting him to talk about his fiancée once he'd finished texting. He didn't. He sat there looking at his phone with the screen still lit up. He turned it off, put it in the door compartment and then, looking out at the darkness of the Parque Litoral, he sighed and said, 'What a shitty day I've had with that piece of crap Céspedes, the stupid moron.' And it was only then that he turned to face her and sized her up. 'What a skimpy top,' he said, looking at Amelia's cleavage. 'Some days are just not worth it,' Amelia contended, clumsily showing solidarity with Rafi and remembering her own day. 'Every life is in many days,' Amelia concluded. 'Hmm,' the ambitious Villaplana affirmed, reflecting that his own mother or any of the old biddies in the neighbourhood could have said the same thing not knowing, as Amelia also didn't know, that the last bit had been written by Joyce.

'Philosophy's not your strong suit, Amelia,' Rafi whispered with a smile. 'Isn't it?' Amelia asked, happy about the course the conversation had taken and because the presence of Rafi's fiancée was disappearing into the shadows of the park in front of them. 'So what is my strong suit?' she asked provocatively. 'This is,' said Villaplana, stretching out his left hand and fondling, weighing and squeezing Amelia's left breast. She parted her lips slightly, displaying a row of teeth like small beads. They looked into each other's eyes and held their mouths very close to one another. Each of them could feel the other's breath. 'Did you put that on just for me?' asked Rafi, looking at Amelia's top half, supposedly as a reference to her blouse. She responded with an ambiguous expression, contorting her face a little. Possibly, the expression suggested.

She's so cheap. Rafi Villaplana's response was to grope her breast more urgently and enthusiastically. He tilted back his head and looked up and down her face, in the same way as he would look at someone he was berating or someone he despised.

And now Kuki did move his snout closer to the blood and started licking. Timidly. The velvety blood spread across the cheap tiles. The fluorescent light flickered, and the flicker snapped El Yubri out of his trance. Back to reality. This wasn't going to disappear like a dream. His father was no longer having spasms, the fingers of one hand were quivering ever so slightly, the scissors, sticking out of the back of his head, looked like a bit of plumbing. He pushed the dog away with his foot and saw his reflection in the frosted windowpane. He wondered if the same barber as last time would still be at the prison. He was a pain in the arse, and he'd refused to shave his head.

Night had fallen throughout the city now, and the lights were shining under the hot black vault of the sky. 'Nandita's a good woman,' the priest said, 'you just have to be patient with her, don't lose heart and try to understand her, not as a Christian or a husband but as a man, as a human being.' Pedroche turned his head to one side, wondering whether to confess to the priest that those injuries on his face and head had been made by his wife. But he reflected that the priest couldn't care less about his wife or him or his injuries, because if he cared at all he would have asked him how he'd got those injuries, and, as he was twenty-five centimetres taller than Pedroche, he must have seen them from every angle as he gave his sermon. So the only thing that Pedroche said was, 'Not Nandita, Belita. Her name's Belita. My wife's name is Belita. Maribel Bermúdez Covaleda,' he said, giving her full name.

The priest looked up to the heavens and half closed his eyes. Of course, there's another woman whose name is Nandita, and what with this confusion, this heat and the day that it's been, it's easy to get their names mixed up, but not the women themselves, of course not. And from the corner, like a pair of B-movie hoodlums, Nene Olmedo and El Tato were watching the performance and how the priest opened the plastic briefcase and took out an envelope and a cloth bag, which from a distance you could see contained small but weighty items. And then there was an even hotter gust of wind, and in the patrol car Loberas was babbling and now it was Guille who kept his mouth shut and watched the palm trees, the buildings and the night pass by through the window. They'd already called his home, he'd already stopped insisting that his father had died that day, everything was now in motion, and he had the sensation that time was no longer stuck and was flowing again.

'This is how I want you to do it, like this, nice and slow,' Rafi Villaplana said to Amelia, 'like this.' And then he said what he'd been desperate to say, what turned him on most on of all. 'And, of course, I'll pay you.' 'What?' Amelia wanted to turn her face but he held her there and said, 'Do it like this, the way I like it, and I'll give you money, just for trying it out. Come on, suck.' Amelia resisted, she stopped moving her face and mouth towards Rafi's erect penis, but he forced her down, pushing her head downwards with his hand and repeating, 'This is how I want you to do it,' adding in a whisper, 'like this, you slut.'

The Runner's back is leaning against the blistering hot wall. Cars are passing in front of him in a slow procession, and he watches as they pull down the supermarket's last metal shutter on the other side of the street. He sees the man from the delicatessen counter come out; it must be just his fiancée left inside and the manager, that bastard. The two checkout ladies have passed close by to him, one of them saying hello with a flick of the head and the other, not noticing him, talking as usual about the abusively long hours they have to work and the stock-taking, and keeping them there until all hours for ten euros, what a cheek.

La Penca has advanced down the corridor with cautious steps, like someone walking along a ship's passageway in the middle of a storm. And, almost without trembling and without wanting to look at her mother's photograph, she's gone to sit down on the edge of her bed. With her knees together and her hands pressing against the mattress. She's been sitting there staring at the floor tiles, and she feels increasingly that the corridor, her room, the entire flat will suddenly turn upside down, just like a fairground ride.

'It feels like it's getting hotter and hotter and it's not going to stop getting hotter, know what I mean, Rai? It's like they've put a great big heater right on top of the world, you know?' Eduardo Chinarro is agitated. He's crossing the room from one side to another. He doesn't need methadone any more and he doesn't want to watch his partner. He doesn't want to see. Not the spoon or the silver foil or his friend's arm. Rai doesn't reply. He sticks the needle in. He draws out a little blood and the blood mixes with the whitish liquid in the syringe barrel. 'Is this the room your friend lends you? It's cool, Rai, even though it's really hot, today it's really hot everywhere.' 'He rents it to me, he doesn't lend it out; he doesn't lend anything out, nobody lends me anything.' Eduardo stretches his neck. It's his nerves, it's like an outside force rather than him making his neck contort. He straightens up. 'My neck hurts,' he moans, and then he responds, 'Yeah, that's right, he rents it to you, Rai, eighty euros, isn't it?' 'Ninety.' One on top of the other.

Eduardo looks at the foam mattress that Raimundo Arias is sitting on, guitar at his feet, leaning against the wall and serving as a hanger for the bird's-eye-print shirt that Rai had been wearing until they got there.

'I'm off, Rai.' Rai flicks the syringe plunger. His eyelids are drooping as he asks Eduardo where he's going. 'It's really hot, Rai, this room you've got here's the best, really cool, but I'm off now. I'm going to get something to eat,' the singer continues. And just in case Rai hasn't noticed the sweltering heat that's bouncing off the walls or the sweat dripping off Eduardo's face and making patches on his shirt, his friend blows ostentatiously down the top of his own shirt and flaps it around. 'Aren't you going to eat, Rai?' 'It's very late and anyway, I'm having a feed right now,' says Rai, tapping his arm, his swollen vein. 'See you tomorrow, Rai, I've got a hole in here,' Eduardo Chinarro says, smiling and showing the gaps in his teeth and touching his sternum. 'It's like I'm missing the bones in my chest or like they've melted on me.'

And so, with that grimace clamped to his face, that rictus grin that looks more like an expression of horror than a smile, Eduardo Chinarro, the tone-deaf singer, the boy from Carranque, the survivor, goes down the stairs and out into the night's hot, dry air. 'If you'd had a sponsor and they looked after you like they looked after others, you could've gone all the way as a performer, Eduardito, even a dummy knows that, you sing so good, but it's all down to luck, Camarón.' For some reason he can't figure out, he remembers his friend Moreno Peralta and the night he told him that. It was almost as hot then as it is now.

Eduardo's short of breath, as if he's been running. He's now in Calle Postigos, inertia taking him downhill, thinking over what Moreno Peralta had told him two or three years earlier. He didn't know whether his friend was still the trainer at Olímpica Victoriana FC. Maybe not. The world of football is very tough, everyone says so, one day you're up, and tomorrow no one remembers your name. It's all down to luck in that environment, too. Best just to carry on going downhill, best not to remember anything, as if the night were the belly of that whale his teacher was always on about at school and he'd been stuck inside it, letting time and everything else pass by on the outside.

*

She's swallowing Rafi's penis, hard and slippery with saliva. Amelia absorbs, sucks and licks, but she does it apprehensively because they've never done anything in a car before, because she doesn't know why they've come to this place and because she's noticed that Rafi is different, more uptight. Spiteful. Is this goodbye? His fingers are still pressing into her neck, gripping her head more out of violence than desire since he mentioned money. 'I'll pay you, I'll give you money,' he'd said. He hasn't spoken since, he's just held her there. He breathes out heavily, tenses his legs, and whispers something she can't make out.

The night is one long whisper in Amelia's ears. A gust of hot air is making the trees in the Parque Litoral quiver, and, as they quiver, the leaves' shadows draw a strange hieroglyphic on the car window that she can only see out of the corner of her eye, like everything else apart from Rafi Villaplana's penis, his crumpled trousers and the keyring with a feather that's hanging from the ignition key. She's frightened. In La Alameda Julia is held at a traffic light and can also see the giant fig trees quivering. A day to forget, a day we'll never forget, those are the words running through her exhausted brain in a fragmented thought, while the red light holds her stationary on her way back home. A shower. Tomorrow, the funeral. And the next day? Ana will go to the hospital as if nothing had happened. Keeping her distance so that nobody asks her anything, so that no one offers her their condolences. She's an expert at it. And she'll look after other sick people, other people in their death throes in the room where her husband died, and no one will realize a thing. The ants, that pale body invaded by insects and Ana's gaze. The lights turn green, and the image of Dr Galán disappears from Julia's head. A shower. The car advances smoothly along the deserted street. The city stretches out, everything is beginning to be left behind, the street lights pass by the window like a muted merry-go-round.

They watch as the priest shakes hands with the pair of losers and goes down the church steps. El Tato nudges Nene Olmedo and nods towards the two idiots. 'They've got the dough,' he affirms. Nene Olmedo looks straight ahead and breathes through his mouth, waiting for Pedroche and Floren to make a move. They are talking together without moving away from the church. 'Let's see where they head,' says El Tato, assuming the role of commentator because of his nerves. Pedroche seems to be saying, 'Yes.' Floren is pointing to a side street. They go down the steps. Nene Olmedo puts his hand in his tracksuit pocket and touches the screwdriver. Too many people. El Tato looks left and right. 'Let's see which way they go, Nene. There are a lot of people around here.' Nene Olmedo takes a step forward; El Tato follows behind.

The train speeds through the night, ripping it open as it passes, the tear closing up again immediately in its wake. As it passes it leaves a vacuum, a dull sound floating in the air, a few blades of dry grass and bits of rubbish suspended momentarily before falling back between the tracks. The train is now flying through an orange grove, above the treetops. You can see the straight lines of trees in the darkness. End of the line. The flight is over. Once again Céspedes has Carole's head resting on his shoulder. Sleeping, given over to weariness. Traces of perfume, the scent of her hair, everything that will vanish when they arrive at the station within the next few minutes and their lives separate for ever. Closed bracket. Farewell to this absurd dream, to this flight, which is now concluding. Once again the solid wall of the days to come, his wife, a house he can't enter, lawyers, attempts at reconciliation, more hatred, more words, insults and that long list of reproaches, the obligation to revive the bitterness in order to get a better share of the carve-up. The passenger opposite looks Carole up and down. She has her hands between her knees like a little girl, and she's breathing softly, her hair falling over her shoulder. 'Would you like to swap places with me?' Céspedes asks him, and the man, the ogler, caught in the act, apologizes clumsily. 'I thought you were asleep.' 'No, I just had my eyes closed. Would you like to change places with me?' And the man smiles and looks towards the window. There they are, the three of them, reflected sharply. *Sometimes there's no way out*, thinks Céspedes, and he looks at the man via the reflection in the window and then closes his eyes again. He rests his cheek on Carole's hair.

El Yubri goes into his sister Aurora's room. La Penca. 'Penqui, he's stopped moving,' he says in a low voice. The dog comes in behind him and lies at La Penca's feet, wagging his tail shyly, aware of the disaster. 'I've closed the kitchen door so Kuki can't touch him,' says El Yubri by way of consolation. A man with his heart in the right place. Always wanting to be admired by his sister. They say nothing. A car's headlights beam through the window and pass over the ceiling. They disappear. 'Penqui, I'm going to go . . .' and Aurora looks up, her eyes large and bright like two new pennies, and her brother adds, 'to the police.' And Penqui makes an enormous effort to move her lips and say, 'Don't go, call them. Better to call them.' She doesn't want to be left alone with the body. 'Call them, Yubri.' And now everything's on the move, yes, Guille feels that everything's flowing, it's only his father who's stopped, it's only him there somewhere, calm and immobile, but life goes on and passes by him, sweeps him along; it's there in Loberas's childish, doped-up wailing, in La Lori, who looks at him and smiles, in those policemen who walk past him and tell him to sit down and wait and tell him to repeat his name and address and his father's name and his mother's name and he says it again, now almost as a joke, 'My father died this morning.' 'But he's still got a name,' says Loberas unexpectedly, and he laughs. La Lori looks at Guille with a smile, and the policeman whispers to himself, 'And you said you didn't know each other, didn't you? Spoiled brats.' 'You could've been a contender. You could have been somebody.' Eduardo Chinarro's walking down Calle Cruz del Molinillo. Moreno Peralta was his friend. The last time he saw him he gave him a card. There was a drawing of a football next to his name. He should have kept it. He could go and see him tomorrow at Olímpica Victoriana's ground. 'If the TV people ever saw you you'd be made, Eduardo.' Yes, it could have happened that way. But that was back then. His voice had burned out, wasted on the streets, and now all he had left was his art. Tomorrow, he'll go there tomorrow. A legend in his time. Eduardo the singer walks on down the empty street, the paving stones scorching the rubber soles of his trainers. He's going to call in at the Monasterio de la Merced. That's what he's going to do. Yesterday, when they saw him sleeping on the steps in the sun, they brought him out some water. Tonight they might give him something to eat, if there's anyone still awake. Priests and nuns go to bed early, everyone knows that. Just a few hundred metres away Ismael is walking along Calle Montaño. He stops in front of a house with shuttered windows and a white door. He goes up and tries the door handle. He feels another wave of nausea. That piece of shit in that bar in Calle de la Cruz Verde has given him that dodgy gin again. He'll sort him out later. He gives the door a kick. A dog barks in a neighbouring house. The door doesn't give. He kicks it again, the dog barks twice as hard, and a light goes on in the house opposite. Ismael spits on the locked door, looks up and down the street and takes the opposite direction, going down towards Calle Madre de Dios. The Onda Pasadena might still be open, and there are girls there. The liquid is thick and bitter, and although Rafi's still squeezing her head, Amelia lets some of it dribble from her mouth. Rafi Villaplana, as stiff as a plank, snorts and groans, spills his semen over the mouth and neck and shoulder of Amel the Rebel, she of the stupid name who doesn't fulfil his penultimate wish, who pulls herself free and with her hair in her face sits up and looks at him while he's still shuddering, still having spasms, white blobs spattered over his trousers and thigh, the reddened cyclops, still ejaculating one last white dribble, almost liquid, spilling feebly over his belly, a veined column. Yes, Floren and Pedroche are going down the church steps and into Calle Pedro de Paz while Nene Olmedo and El Tato come out from behind the **Terés y García** sign and cross Calle de la Unión, following in the steps of the two jokers. 'Let's go to El Maqui, come on, mate, for Christ's sake, we'll have one for the road, you've got it back now, the money and the other stuff, what else are you going to do? Go back home and see her?' Floren convinces his partner, who shrugs and says, 'Floren, you were the one who wanted to go home early to have dinner with your wife.' 'She'll have had something to eat with the little one. They'll both be asleep, and anyway, what the hell.' The street is badly lit, and that's where the shadows get longer, and their footsteps resound with a soft echo. His girlfriend isn't replying to his messages and Jorge has another look at her photograph on the screen. His girlfriend smiling on the beach. Her cream-coloured nipples, staring at him like two sleepy eyes. A silent face. Better go to bed, better turn off the phone once he's sent her one last message. Telling her again that it's all sorted out, not to worry about El Nene or anyone else, that he's there for her. Gloria, I'm there for you, you'll always have me there. Yes, all sorted. Jorge wanders around the empty flat, his mother at work and his brother Ismael who knows where, the further away the better, better if he doesn't come home until the morning, when he'll be gone already, better if he never comes home at all. Not that he should die, just never come home. He opens the drawers in the chest in his mother's bedroom. He's looking for some sheets that haven't been cut to pieces by his brother. His were in shreds. He must have cut them up after he'd gone to work. His mother's bras. Carefully folded. Soft. Lace knickers. He almost doesn't dare touch them. They smell. He starts to get an erection. He closes the drawer. Lucía, the Runner's girlfriend, comes out through the side door, comes out of the dark entrance accompanied by Ricardo, the manager, the smiley manager with the car. She's smiling, too, tilts her head by way of saying goodbye to her work colleague, and she breaks into a broad smile when she sees him leaning against the wall on the other side of the street, and she goes towards him, stopping at the far kerb. Several cars heading in the direction of the city centre pass between them, and the Runner and his girlfriend look at each other across the double headlights and red rear lights. It's the miracle, the impossible dream that happens every day. He draws oxygen down to the bottom of his lungs again. They look at each other, and there's a trace of shyness about her that the Runner identifies with sex, the way Lucía looked at him the last time, deep into his eyes, revealing the existence of a new being inside her, and she said, 'More I want more give me more give me harder fuck me like I'm not me give me give me.' The Runner crosses the street, brushing against the back of the last car. There's her body, her scent and the sound of her voice. Everything reborn with a quick kiss, a fleeting hug. A short toot on a car horn makes them turn around. Lucía's boss has his window wound down, and he winks at them, 'Night night, lovebirds.' His teeth showing in a smile, the car's gleaming glass and paintwork, all disappear in the same burst of speed. 'Silly idiot,' says Lucía smiling, and the Runner says nothing, watching how the brake lights illuminate their surroundings with red, and the car comes to a halt at the last set of traffic lights, almost at the end of the street. Melanthius. You'll be eaten by the dogs. Ana Galán sinks down into the sofa, closes her eyes and, faced with the horror of the images that come into her mind, Dioni, the ants, Guille also intubated, also eaten by a million ants, opens her eyes again and takes a deep breath. She's floating in the silence of her house. The palm tree on the other side of the window is perfectly still, as though its branches were in plaster, and the night air is thick, hot and tranquil. The house is calm again. It took too much effort, to the point of exasperation, to get them to leave her on her own. Her brother tried to persuade her to let Emilia stay so she wouldn't be on her own while he went to the police station to sort out Guille. 'That poor lost boy who'll now need you twice as much, who'll need us all,' Emilia, her sister-in-law, the wisest of all women, had said to her. 'He'll need what he's always needed. I'll give it to him, and he'll take it and complain about it as usual,' Ana had said, cutting short her sister-in-law's sermon. And then she'd convinced her brother that his wife should go with him. She's a lawyer, too, and I need a minute, at least one minute, of peace and quiet. They exchanged glances, and she gave her some final pieces of advice before leaving her on her own. They won't be long, they'll have their phones on. Yes, yes. Sweet vultures, soft vultures, kind vultures, who'll be there when death arrives. All that friendliness, all that generosity of spirit that Dr Galán has seen so many times at the hospital and that she'd now like to dump in one of those strong plastic bags where the gardener puts dry branches, weeds and recently pruned shoots, still oozing sap, still palpitating. That's how people expect to see her. Oozing sap, letting out all that pain until the flow gradually solidifies, creating a barrier to contain the haemorrhaging. Except that the haemorrhage and the scar, the sap and the broken shoots, all that happened a long time ago, and she's now just an empty vessel, and Amelia, too, is an empty woman, the taste of semen in her mouth, that bitter liquid staining her chin. 'Why?' she asks. 'What was that all about?' And Rafi Villaplana, now with his trousers done up but still with the stains and spots on his thigh, hands her a blue banknote and says, 'Because it turns me on, because I told you right from the start, you suck me off and I'll pay you, it turns me on and that's all there is to it, or what the fuck's going on? What did you expect from me?' Amelia shakes her head, Pedroche shakes his head in the dark street, Nene Olmedo shakes his head when El Tato says, 'Now, let's go for them.' 'No.' El Nene says there's too much light in that part of the street where Floren and Pedroche are now, so El Nene and El Tato stop and watch the two losers go into Bar Maqui, and Eduardo Chinarro shakes his head when he thinks back on his friend Moreno Peralta and knows that he'll never go to see him, not at Olímpica Victoriana FC or anywhere else. Delusions. Self-deception. La Penca shakes her head gently, saying 'No' to herself. Céspedes shakes his head with his eyes closed, and Belita shakes her head. 'No,' she says in a whisper, lying in the marital bed, unable to sleep. 'No, that man's not going to live here, he's not going to sleep in this bed, he's not going to ask me for any more sacrifices. I know why I have to sacrifice myself and who for, and it's not for that filthy man, that pig,' and she gets up. Belita throws back the sheet that was covering her heavy, dormant (almost dead) white thighs and her bulky breasts, she gets up and walks down the dark corridor, barefoot, her nightie making her body look like a bell, and at the end of the corridor she can see the darkness of the living room, the glow coming in through the window, and Belita heads there. She's not whispering any more. Now she's thinking that miracles still happen, they're not something from the past, they're not just about the Roman circus and martyrs and dark paintings in churches, when the apostles and the Lord had to be present in a physical form, no, they're still happening now, on a daily basis, beneath all the noise of the everyday world, here in the streets, in the doorways, on the stairs, in the flats around Cruz de Humilladero or Plaza San Andrés, on the industrial estates, between the lines of washing, among the crying babies, in the shops and kiosks. Every day, everywhere, miracles exist and you can find the Truth, and all the evil can be swept away. The evil thoughts can be banished from her head, the evil presences, everything noxious. Belita shakes her head again, going up to the window. Her tiny mouth, her thin lips are moving in the middle of those flabby cheeks and she says in a low voice, 'No. I was pregnant, and they said "No".' Her bare feet are walking on the lentils she scattered there a while ago. There are lights in the distance, tiny points in the darkness. Below her, ten floors down, is a straight line, the illuminated street, toy cars going up and down the ramp to the bridge. 'They don't know where they're going, they don't know where they're going,' Belita repeats with her mouth brushing against the glass. Down there below. Nene Olmedo and El Tato wait, flattened against the wall of a monastery, the Venerable Brotherhood of Christ's Humility and Patience. 'They won't get away from us now. Now we'll get what's ours, Nene,' El Tato says, beginning to doubt his boss's authority. Too calm, too cautious. And El Nene replies with composure, 'We'll do it when they leave the bar because it's better that way, and they'll be so pissed they won't know what's hit them.' Jorge opens a different drawer and takes out some sheets, and underneath he sees an envelope. It's been torn open and on the front is his mother's name and address and a stamp. On the back, just one word, his father's name, Ernesto. He opens the envelope and finds a short, handwritten letter. *You won't hear anything more from me, and I'm not going to listen to any more of your insults or your spiteful remarks like on the telephone yesterday. Just so you're clear it's my decision and my life. You and me don't have a future, we haven't had one for a long time, and you know full well why. And if all this is hurting you now think about how much it hurt me back then. Eloísa is pregnant. That's what you didn't let me tell you or made me not want to tell you yesterday with all your tantrums and insults that I'm not going to listen to ever again. It's my life and that's what I'm going to do. And I'm going to be happy with her. I'm sorry about Ismael and Jorge. If they knew the whole story they'd understand. Maybe they will one day. Just because I'm going to have another life and another child and I'm leaving for ever doesn't mean I don't love them.* A brother. Somewhere he's got a half-brother. That's what Jorge thinks, and then he looks back and rereads the words that have made him most uncomfortable: *back then. Think about how much it hurt me back then.* And Jorge, troubled, abandoned little Gorgo, has the same feeling as when he touched his mother's underwear. He puts the letter back in the envelope with the same sense of disgust, covers it over with the sheets he'd taken out and closes the drawer. He takes a step backwards and looks at the cursed piece of furniture, so much like that well he peered into when he was small and his father said, 'Look, can you see what's down there? Down at the bottom?' He turns out the light. The room smells of his mother. He goes out. The train approaches the station. A female voice announces their arrival over the speakers and thanks the passengers for travelling by rail. Carole lifts her head off Céspedes's shoulder, and only then, when she's sitting up entirely straight, does she open her eyes. She looks around the carriage as if in a dream, in the centre of a stage she doesn't recognize. She looks at Céspedes in the same way, and Céspedes's mouth breaks into a huge smile. *I am your nightmare,* he thinks, *but don't worry, I won't last long.* 'We're here,' he says. The trip's over. Julia arrives at her garage. She parks between two columns, opens the car door, and the scalding-hot night air dissolves the air-conditioned bubble she's been wrapped in and envelops her entirely. She feels an instinctive urge to close the door again, but she resists, grabs her handbag, gets out of the car and heads towards the lift between the sleeping cars and the burning-hot concrete of the garage. One more step, one last effort, that's what she always tells herself after a hard day's work or at difficult times when she's about to leave all the effort or pain behind her and she's already cherishing a moment's rest. The first police officers arrive at La Penca's entrance hall. Monreal, Deusto, Montero, Arias and Faneca the motorbike cop. El Yubri, the obedient servant of his sister's wishes, called them. The national and the municipal police. He told them both the same thing. I've killed my father. Short and snappy. And then he gave them the address. After that, at the end, he told the municipal police, 'At least, I think he's dead.' He doesn't want to take on medical responsibilities, to tell them something that's not right. So that's why there are two patrol cars plus Faneca's motorbike lighting up, with their blue flashing lights, the humble façades of Portada Alta and the scrawny trees, sadly neglected in their flower beds. Curtains twitch and windows open, regardless of letting out the cool air from the electric fan or the air-conditioning unit. That doesn't matter now. Faces peer out, contorted by sleepiness and curiosity, rumpled hair, string vests, naked torsos and dressing-gowns askew, scenting a tragedy that promises to increase in proportion to the arrival of a silent ambulance in the small square, adding its orange glare to the blue radiance. 'It's El Yubri's block,' says El Viberti from his terrace, holding on to the collar of his Dobermann, Jiler (the only way he knows to pronounce the dog's real name, Hitler). A man and a woman get out of the ambulance and walk quickly towards the entrance. Things are getting exciting. Reporters arrive – Juan Cano and Álvaro Frías, a pair of top-flight journalists, Riverita (son of the legendary Corbata), Gross Gross and his photographer Julián Rojas. A whole conference of writers ready to dip their pens in blood. The windows and terraces of the neighbouring blocks are now full of people talking in the gloom, their voices getting louder and louder. Stories about what's happened start to circulate. El Yubri's hanged himself rather than go to prison, his father's had a heart attack, La Penca was drunk and has drowned in the bath. Mariano Villaplana is the first to arrive, along with the ambulance. Unable to sleep because of a long siesta and not working the night shift tonight, he was smoking a cigarette on a bench in the square when he saw the first police car arrive and another one five seconds later. With his perfect manners he says 'Good evening' to the ambulance driver, offers him a cigarette, which is refused with a wave of the hand, and talks about the downside of working nights, something he's well accustomed to, he says. 'Bad things almost always happen at night,' he says, following a protocol that will soon lead to the fundamental question, 'Do you know what's happened?' To which the driver will respond with a shrug of the shoulders and, wanting to shake off the bore, 'It's serious, that's all I know.' Other neighbours arrive in their eccentric pyjamas: Don Anselmo wearing Donald Duck on his chest, Carmeli almost showing her tits, Osuna with his hair standing on end and Manolo el Cojo chewing on a piece of bread, and they all ask Rafi Villaplana's father the same question. 'Something deadly serious,' he replies, nodding his head, grave, reserved, when he hears a familiar whistle from the entrance at the back. It's Encarnación, La Segueta, his wife, who waves him over to come and tell her what's going on. She's not going to mix with the local riff-raff with their appetite for crime and disorder at this time of night, with her dressing-gown hanging off her shoulder. Mariano walks towards the crowd, knock-kneed, cursing under his breath. It's a night of hoarse throats and hungover breath. Too hot to sleep. 'I don't want it. What's got into you? Don't give me that.' Amelia rejects the twenty-euro note proffered by Rafi Villaplana, La Segueta's illustrious son, worthy descendant of Mariano the Knock-Kneed. 'What's got into me is what I said.' Rafi sucks his gums and stares at Amelia. 'It turns me on to pay you for it, so take the money for the blow job you've given me. I've wanted to do this for a long time, that's what.' 'Twenty euros?' Amelia tries to smile. 'Are you having a laugh, or what the fuck's got into you?' 'Yes, cheap,' Rafi replies impassively, 'you're cheap.' 'Give that to your fiancée,' is what Amelia tells him, and she makes a sudden move to get out of the car, but not so fast that Villaplana doesn't have time to rub the banknote over the patch of semen on his trousers and place it in the palm of his lover's hand before closing her fist, squeezing it shut. 'You bastard, you piece of shit, don't imagine that I'm, that I'm . . .' Amelia, now out of the car, is bending over to speak to Rafi. She's left the door open. 'You've earned it,' Rafi replies, 'and wait and see, you'll come to like it, you'll do it to other punters, and you'll come to like it. I'm doing you a favour, I've done you a lot of favours, don't forget.' He breathes in through his nose and issues a command, 'Close the door.' 'Piece of shit, pig.' 'That's right, have your say, and then when you're out on the street you'll come crawling on your knees to beg me for a job.' Rafi leans over the front passenger seat, reaches the open door and pulls it towards him, closes it, turns the ignition key. He sees Amelia's expression, vaguely catches the stream of insults, repetitive now, sees her turn around, showing her figure, her back. Rafi slips it into first and whispers to himself, 'She's hot stuff, the bitch, that's the worst thing, she's hot.' Amelia watches the car pull slowly away. She makes an effort not to cry. No, don't cry over that bastard. But she knows she's going to cry, she alone is to blame for this wave of misery washing over her, buffeting and dragging her, this wrench, this filth, as if a sewer had opened up inside her body. 'You've earned it,' the miserable bastard said, but he might just as well have said, 'You were looking for it.' And that's what hurts most, she desperately needs to bury that thought and those words, tamp them down with anger so that they never come out of that deep, dark cesspit again. She's holding the crumpled banknote in her hand, crushed and sticky. She opens her fingers and lets it fall to the ground. She looks around. The empty park. Above the treetops there are lights in some of the windows. Most of them are dark; they've become holes. She walks towards her car. She doesn't want to cry. Not any more. The smell inside the car is comforting, a familiar womb, protective. Her son Ismael, *God has listened*, enters Onda Pasadena. He goes down the stairs. The place is almost empty. There's a couple sitting inside, their heads close together. Another pair of lovebirds dancing reluctantly, probably friends of the other two. At the bar a short man is standing on tiptoe to speak to the barmaid, a Russian. Too early, not many people yet. The doorman read him the rule book before he let him in. 'Not one word or one look, if you so much as look at anyone I'll kick you out on your arse. I don't need complications, Chumi.' He'd told the doorman that his name was Chumi, just to take the mickey. He often does that. Chumi, Quini, Fini, sometimes Gorgo, his brother's nickname. Ismael promised to behave himself, and he reminded the doorman that he was a model customer the last time he was there. 'The only thing I didn't do was wash the glasses and clean the toilets wearing a gas mask, mate,' is what he told him. And also that the business over the fight with the two dickheads was all their fault. He's a good guy, the doorman. A man in a striped shirt comes out of the toilets. He looks like El Bocas, the wanker who always used to bully him at school. Perhaps it is him. The man goes to the other end of the bar. Ismael goes up to the one who's talking to the barmaid. A pain in the arse. 'Are you really Russian or is that a put-on?' he's asking her. The girl replies, 'From Kyiv.' 'And where's that?' 'Ukraine.' 'Yeah, well, it's all the same thing, modern Russia, isn't it?' The barmaid turns to Ismael, 'What would you like?' 'Is this guy bothering you?' he asks her back. The short man backs away from the bar a little, observing the new arrival. 'What did you say?' 'I wasn't talking to you.' The barmaid puts her hand on Ismael's arm, 'It's OK, we were just chatting.' 'Let me know if he bothers you.' 'What's wrong with this guy?' The short man's head is twisted around, frowning. The man who resembles El Bocas smiles from a distance. The night is spreading, the darkness is curdling like blood. Eduardo Chinarro knocks once more on the door of the Monasterio de la Merced with the palm of his hand. His face is contorted, as if he's going to start singing. *Cane sugar, rum and salt water* . . . No. The one his mother used to sing would be better, gentler, yes, gentler and also praising God. Chinarro looks at the door, his face just a few centimetres from the wood. How did that song go? He doesn't remember. He rifles through his memory for his mother's face, lighting up the yard. *God in his power gathered up four sunbeams . . . God made a woman . . . God in his power . . .* They won't open the door. Even if he starts singing they won't open up. He could go behind the Hospital Civil where his friend Antonio died ages ago. If El Moderno's place is open he's bound to play ball. He'll make him a sandwich and let him sleep in the attic, even though it's really hot. Their fingers intertwined, walking under the trees, they can already feel the coolness of the sea. The Runner and Lucía emerge on the seafront promenade, the water licks the shore, and the tiny waves sound like gentle pan pipes. 'Today I felt like I was losing my grip on it all, that I was going to end up with nothing, and I was scared,' says the Runner, and she looks at him with a frown on her forehead and a smile on her lips. *Is that a genuine smile or is it fear or boredom because of what I'm saying?* the Runner thinks. 'But when I saw you, even before I saw you, when I really thought of you, I stopped feeling scared, and I know that everything will work out fine, that I'm going to be what I want to be.' She rests her head on his shoulder in a display of affection, but he's still thinking, *The more I talk the worse I'll make it, and she might think I'm weaker than I really am, other people seem stronger because they keep things to themselves more, they talk but they keep things to themselves more, they keep everything to themselves, that smartarse with the car wouldn't say any of the things I say, he'd say he's going to take her out to dinner at a very expensive place on Saturday, that he's going to take her in his car and that his car cost him thirty thousand euros, but it's worth it because it's a hundred and fifty horsepower and it could take them to the ends of the earth, wherever, he says, wherever she wants.*

Ismael's hapless younger brother Gorgo, Jorge, the coward, shuffles down the corridor in his bare feet. He doesn't turn on the lights, he doesn't want to open any more drawers. He gets to his bedroom. He puts the chair against the door to barricade it. He lies down on the sheetless bed. He'd like to wake up tomorrow and be somewhere else. He's tempted to go and fetch his phone, but he doesn't even lift his head off the pillow. Better just to forget, better not to think. About his mother, about the letter in the drawer, about his girlfriend, about his cousin Floren, about Nene Olmedo, about the forged invoice he left in the shop today. Better to imagine or remember pleasant things. Finally overtaking the Runner on Sunday in the 200 metres. The new motorbike he's thinking of buying in October. Vane, the shop assistant in Calzados Famita, the shoeshop, getting out of her car this morning in her white leggings, the look she gave him, she must have been wearing a thong, and that mouth of hers. Walking so slowly. Where is she right at this moment? Humping, probably. Yes. In the derelict plot behind the Ben Gabirol secondary school, El Tato has picked up a large stone, and he's holding it, weighing it up ostentatiously as he reaches Nene Olmedo's side. 'I had to go for a dump, Nene,' he explains. Nene doesn't look at him. 'They're still in there,' El Tato affirms rather than asks. Nene nods his head in a barely perceptible movement: yes. He's staring straight ahead, at the light that's leaking from Bar Maqui. Yes. Two elderly women emerge from the darkness, arm in arm. Carmen Marcos Díaz and Elena Moreno Úbeda pass close by to the two delinquents. Carmen is saying, 'How many days have gone by?' Elena asks, 'Where has my life gone?' They pass without looking at them, without even noticing the two partners in crime. 'Only they know what they're talking about,' El Tato whispers. 'Obviously they do,' replies Nene Olmedo grudgingly. The two figures disappear up the street, their voices fading away. 'I was quite the wild one in my youth, you know,' it sounds like one of them says. 'My problem is I've got an overdose of madness,' the other one replies, and their footsteps fade away and are extinguished in the darkness. The alleyway breathes. The light from Bar Maqui flickers. The night's different parts expand and contract, each with its own rhythm. Head, trunk and a thousand extremities. A sticky, crowded, hot, extended, empty, hollow, overflowing, lit-up, counterfeit, circular, devastating, inextinguishable and rotten, genuine, tall, dubious and dense, weak, beautiful, cowardly, arid, rounded, sonorous, asphyxiating, chock-a-block night. Belita's breath mists up the glass. Belita slides back the window, and there, ten storeys up, the burning air brushes against her body, her face, her naked arms, the air envelops her like a lecherous hand, and there before her is that nameless expanse, the dubious outline of the industrial estates, the bubbles of light and in the distance the horizon's black screen, fields that are not in the countryside, and gripping both sides of the window with her swollen fingers Belita spreads her legs and lets her urine run towards the floor, hot, down her thighs, Belita's small, almost ridiculous mouth opens to swallow all the night's air. 'I had a life inside me,' she says, 'I had a life inside me, Father,' the passengers walk along the suffocating platform not saying a word, with a rumble of wheels and suitcases, speechless voices, weariness and heat, the blazing heat around the track, the train lying flat on the ground like a dog after a long run, silently panting and spitting out more people, Céspedes walking in silence and Carole beside him like a coin spinning on its edge just before it falls, before everything falls, Floren and Pedroche leave Bar Maqui haltingly, with wide grins, a scream comes from La

Penca's building that silences the onlookers' chattering, the still trees, empty of birds, are also holding their breath, it was just one scream, all on its own, a dark beam, and then nothing, nothing apart from the growing whispers among the spectators, the scream was from La Penca, the dog watches her with his ears pinned back and his tail hidden between his legs, moving away, slinking, almost twisted, everything moves away and contracts, the water slides down Julia Mamea's body, lukewarm, restorative, the water runs down the slope of her breasts, over the crest of her nipples and drops into the shower tray, a procession of drops, a cascade mixed with soap bubbles and scented foam, the images of Dioni lying dead, the ants, Ana Galán's voice, her friend about to be evicted, Céspedes's messages, everything slides over her body and is lost down the drain, *just stay vacant, sleep, nothing matters, wash it all down the drain like the water*, the doctor certifies the death, La Penca's father is slumped on the floor like a sack, full of things that no longer work, remains that need to be disposed of, rubber gloves, bloody footprints, crackling voices coming out of those black gadgets policemen wear, faces lit up by the blue lights, dead people's hands, El Yubri is sitting on the arm of the sofa, steel rings on his wrists, and a policeman asks him again if the female in the next room is his sister, if he knows what she's taken, 'Penqui, my sister', and Father Sebastián tosses and turns in the heat of his bed, lips and nose stuck on the bottom sheet, which he thinks still retains a hint of Lorena, the scent that she'll be wrapped in at this very moment without being aware of it, that essence blended from her body, her skin and her perfume, her sweat and her innards, her fluids, hair dyes and creams, fermented food inside her, varnished nails, soap, hair, everything she consists of and that envelops her, that's what they blindly labelled sin at the seminary, the abyss that makes a man hesitate and drags him back, makes him affirm: that is the centre of his life, that is the true miracle, the true path, the divine essence, hope, earth versus heaven, darkness versus light, El Tato raises the stone, before speaking, before saying anything, taking Nene Olmedo by surprise, making Pedroche turn around slowly, wiping the smile off his partner Floren's face, 'Do I know you from somewhere?' Ismael asks the man in the striped shirt, now at the other end of the bar, now right beside him, and the man in the striped shirt shrugs his shoulders, 'Didn't you used to go to Mercedes secondary school and you used to be called El Bocas?' Belita's feet are treading in the warm puddle of urine, 'I had a life, I had a life,' Guille is looking at the floor, his Uncle Emilio and Aunt Emilia are talking to the man with the grey moustache in plain clothes, they're talking to him, and every now and then they look up and look over at him, they've taken Loberas and Lori away, the tunnel's getting narrow again, the man with the moustache is opening his mouth like a fish, and his moustache looks as if it's doing a contortionist's act on his upper lip, 'Life depends on others,' Guille had heard his father say, he'd heard him say it many times, too many times, that's what cowards do, thought Guille, let their lives be run by other people, a hard blow, the stone falls out of El Tato's hand after he hits Pedroche on the forehead, using the strip of plaster already there as a target, the blow makes a dull thud, like something squashing, like a pumpkin or a melon falling on to the floor and bursting open, Floren's hands are flailing about in the night, they look white, 'His father died this morning, he's confused, and he didn't commit the robbery or injure the lady, and quite apart from any offence that might have been committed you need to consider the context,' the light is too bright and makes the office seem like a goldfish bowl, the skin of the man with the moustache is transparent around his temples, veins, blue worms, the street is an empty vault, the humble stained glass of a traffic light on amber, Amelia is driving as if she were part of the vehicle, as if she were a cog in the machine, and the disgust, the hatred and the rage, the humiliation are all part of the mechanism, too, things that are external to her and form part of the landscape, part of those buildings she's leaving behind, posters, reed beds, empty stretches on either side of the road, the city disintegrating, neon signs turned off or on, glowing, AUTO CENTER, CEPSA, OLYMPIAN SEDUCERS, Carrefour, Pizzas 2×1 Every Day, lights criss-crossing, Pedroche slumps to one knee, snorts, Nene Olmedo pulls out the screwdriver, shaking, El Tato spits and lets out a shrill scream like a rat as he gives Pedroche a kick in the ribs, and Floren jumps at him and the screwdriver follows an irregular trajectory in the air like a broken streamer and also falls to the ground in front of El Tato, who's dribbling, green lights, taxi queues and stale cigarette smoke at the station entrance, Céspedes strides onwards, the plastic bag with his suit banging against his right leg with each step, Carole now just a head of hair walking in front of him, someone who's going away and who will soon melt into the hollow landscape of the night, his memories, this day stolen from time, the hazy sketch of what was meant to be a parenthesis and which has only been another ridiculous scrawl, yet one more in his life, welcome to the collection, welcome, Carole, the taxi queue is moving slowly, he can almost smell her body, almost brush against her, if he stretched out his fingers he could touch her, the air has suddenly blown in a breath of coolness, and Belita narrows her eyes, down there the lines of the road form a picture that wants to tell her something, she stops gripping the metal window frame and realizes that her fingers are hurting, there are marks on them, white and purple indentations, her nightie is sticking to her thighs, it's wet, her feet are standing in the puddle of urine, she steps back, there are the lentils, she takes another step back and shivers, 'Chiqui,' he says, Father Sebastián. 'Chiqui?' he turns and asks again in the darkness of the living room, 'Chiqui, are you there?' his Chiqui, Pedroche is on the ground on all fours, breathing heavily, there's a stream of blood pouring out of his head and running down his nose, he sees a large screwdriver fall to the ground beside him, they're going to kill him, *they're going to kill me*, he makes a move to pick the screwdriver up, but a bony brown hand beats him to it, he feels himself being pulled backwards, feels something tearing and something coming down on him and crushing him, 'Are you sure you didn't used to be called El Bocas?' Ismael is wearing a bovine smile flitting back and forth between his mouth and his eyes, he lifts the glass of gin to his mouth, the barmaid from Kyiv looks on from a distance, some new customers come in, the music gets louder, Ismael is the king of the night, he drinks, taking a great big slug, emptying the glass, the ice sticking to his upper lip, and after finishing his drink he says to him, his voice now a bit slurred, 'I don't know whether or not you're El Bocas, but I'm the King of Onda Pasadena, I'm the one with the balls around here,' 'Ah, so you like tennis, do you?' the man suspected of being El Bocas asks, indifferently, Eduardo Chinarro watches the cars passing along the street every now and then, leaving behind a smell of burned rubber in the air and a thundering noise that echoes off those old buildings, he has a finely tuned ear, and he's a born musician, he could have gone far, with a sponsor he could have been a contender, and he's sitting on the steps of the monastery, like he did yesterday in the heat, and seeing him lying there they came out and gave him something to drink, and he tries to remember the words that his mother used to sing as she hung the washing out of the window, *gather up four sunbeams and make them into a woman*, there were pots of geraniums on the windowsill, all around his mother, and the sheets were like sails, Julia Mamea wraps herself up in a fluffy dressing-gown, looks at herself in the mirror, raises her eyebrows and pushes back her wet hair, likes what she sees, goes out of the bathroom, picks up her phone, looks at it, reads the latest messages, no news, and turns it off, disconnects it, Lucía points to the lights on a boat floating on the blackness of the sea and asks, 'Would you like to go on that boat?' the Runner looks up and out to sea at the lights, that promise, and says, 'Yes,' 'Where to?' his girlfriend asks, and he replies, 'Wherever it's going; the boat is you,' and the two of them watch in silence as the lights move off into the distance on that inky darkness and the silence caresses and binds them together, 'Goodbye,' Céspedes puts his hand on Carole's shoulder, the taxi marshal hurries them along, 'This one's yours, sir, and that one's yours,' Carole, tired, with rings around her eyes like a little girl, stands on tiptoes and kisses Céspedes on the cheek, very close to his ear, 'Don't let them crush you, buccaneer,' she says, and without giving him a second glance she goes towards the taxi she was directed to, 'Excuse me, sir, if you're not going to take one please stand aside, sir,' and Céspedes takes a step back, leaves the queue, sees Carole's hair disappear into the taxi, the door closes, and behind the glass and fleeting reflections he watches her go, the vehicle makes a turn and heads towards the darkness of the port and the cranes, and Céspedes turns around, people are still coming out of the station, their suitcases slashing the night with the noise of their wheels on the ribbed pavement, *You knew you would end up here*, he says to himself, clutching the bag with the crumpled suit, wearing his Bermuda shorts, boat shoes and the incongruous shirt, *Time traveller*, he adds, the best shipwreck, find a hotel, yes, maybe that would be best, he takes a few hesitant steps along the pavement, gets to the corner of Calle Héroe de Sostoa, the road is silent and steamy, the trees sleepy, almost as tired as he is, everything is spinning, the heavy weight that fell on top of Pedroche's back was Floren, his friend and partner Florencio Ferrer Pérez, pushed over by the desperate, agitated Nene Olmedo, the night oscillates in a nauseous wave, a shadow emerges from Bar Maqui and asks, 'What's going on?' Floren makes an enormous effort, turns over and gets to his feet, 'What's going on there?' the voice coming from the bar is more of a threat than a question, 'What's going on?' and the voice asks, 'Floren, Floren, is that you?' and the shadows start moving, the shadows multiply and move back and forth, and they don't say anything, they just grunt and pant, choke and splutter, and that's when Floren turns around, shouts, and as he shouts El Tato's hand with the screwdriver in his fist hits him hard in the darkness, piercing his upper thigh, almost his groin, and Floren feels something literally turning his stomach, his back, his head, like an electric cable, still unaware that he's been injured, and two new shadows emerge from Bar Maqui, Ignacio and Popeye, the last clients of the night, and they walk towards that muted scuffle and the figures moving around in the half-light, Belita runs the towel under the tap in the washbasin, wrings it out and uses the damp cloth to wipe down her thighs and crotch, her nightie's on the floor, her whitish, pinky-green body transformed in the mirror into a soft mass, she runs the towel down her legs, Our Father, Our Father, who art in heaven, don't leave me here, don't leave me here like this, bring me hope, bless me, too, bless me like you did when I was a little girl and I got dressed up all in white and they made a cross on my forehead and I took flowers to the altar, I'm your daughter, Father Sebastián, your messenger, give me your blessings, come to me, have pity on me just as I have pity on the poor and needy, little defenceless Gorgo is sleeping on the sheetless bed, sleeping with his arms raised as if a gangster or a gunman had told him to put his hands up in his dreams, the chair's wedged against the door, Father Sebastián is sleeping, his mouth half open, a trail of saliva dripping on to the same place where he'd found the last trace of Lorena's perfume, the last vestige of that afternoon that is now flowing, now travelling through the recesses of his brain in the form of an electric impulse and settling in his prefrontal cortex like a light silt, layers, impulses, mechanics and chemistry transporting the image of her back to him, her hips, Lorena lying on her side, the blurred reflection of her gaze and her desire itself travelling through that liquid, amphibious world, while his dreaming revives other images, combining these memories with the impossible in its laboratory, his fingers twitching on the sheets, the room shrinking and expanding as slowly and firmly as his lungs, Father Sebastián, give me life, free me from my persecutors who have tied me to this rock that is wounding my body and spirit, take pity on me, the whole bar is teetering on the edge, the man in the striped shirt, who isn't El Bocas, is quicker off the mark, and before Ismael can raise a hand, before he can even let loose an insult to kick off the fight, he's headbutted Ismael who's drunker than he thought he was, slower, weaker and heavier, and he tumbles, falls down in slow motion, holding on to the bar at first and then collapsing, slipping down the counter until he's sitting on the floor, the bar spinning around him, the man with the grey moustache looks at the sheet of paper, reads Tuli's and Juno's full names, the ones who got away, and just Isidro's first name because Guille, who wants to cooperate, who only made a silly mistake because he was shaken up by the terrible news of his father's death, doesn't know the boy's surname, and he's also given them Cabello's full name and address, Alberto Cabello Mendoza, Calle Ortuño de Prados 3, that'll teach him to look down his nose at him, to think that he's more of a man than anyone else or that he owns La Lori and everything else around him, the man with the grey moustache nods his head slowly and then says, 'OK, take him home,' El Tato and Nene Olmedo run up the street, Nene fast and with a steady stride, El Tato haphazardly, foaming at the mouth, and behind them there's shouting, Ignacio giving chase and then suddenly running out of breath and clutching his side, Popeye issuing threats and Adolfo, the owner of Bar Maqui, now out of earshot, leaning over Pedroche and getting blood on his hands from the wound on his customer's forehead, 'They've done something to me,' says Floren, more out of surprise than concern, 'They've done something to me, fuck, it hurts, here in my groin or down there, in my groin,' Popeye arrives on the scene and uses the torch on his phone to provide lighting, Pedroche's on all fours, as if he's going to play horse-rides with the son he never had, Floren's standing up, bent over, balancing on one leg and holding the other as if he had cramp, Pedroche, slightly cross-eyed, looks up through the dripping blood and is lucid enough to state, 'The screwdriver, they stuck him with the screwdriver,' 'Fucking bastards come back here,' shouts Popeye to the empty street, the sleeping flats, the drunkenness that fills him with frustration, 'Get the car,' the owner of Bar Maqui instructs, 'Bring your car,' and Popeye starts off, Amelia's driving slowly along Camino de Doña María, greenery hanging over the narrow street, the car's headlights dragging long, distorted shadows out of the darkness, she looks at the clock on the dashboard, she's late, even though she'd asked Félix to cover the first hour of her shift for her, she's gone too slowly by the longest route, and she's had to stop twice, trying not to think, trying to empty her head and body of feelings, and a new fear starts to grow inside her, like dog's breath, she knows that Rafi might call her again, and she knows that she might say yes, however certain she may be now that she wouldn't even answer the phone, that she'll never speak to him again, but there's a nagging doubt gnawing inside her like a tiny animal, never quite in the same place, moving around, changing size, issuing commands when the fancy takes it, and she obeys, blind impulses, doing things she doesn't want to do, 'That's what brought me here,' Amelia says to herself, desolate, invaded, choked, yes, she's covered by a river, it's a monster she has to travel along, she is the animal, *it's me, and this is my body*, the night is her body, the car's headlights are her eyes scrutinizing the darkness that's breathing, it's the monster we feed, that feeds us, and her son, her son Ismael has a bleeding nose, and he spits out a sticky gob, the doorman throws him into the street, 'I warned you, dickhead, piss off home and start a fight there,' Ismael stumbles, drags his feet, they buckle under him, he tries to say, 'Don't you touch me,' but he only manages to make a sort of gurgling sound, a squelchy noise with his tongue caught in the middle, his drunkenness exacerbated by the blow, by the headbutt that bastard El Bocas who's not El Bocas gave him, he takes a couple of steps towards the road, turns, spits, wipes the blood from his nose and finally manages to tell the doorman, who's still looking at him menacingly, 'I'm going to have that bastard; you go inside and tell him I'm waiting out here for him, and when he comes out I'll kill him,' the doorman goes towards him looking determined and only stops when a voice comes from the entrance to the bar, 'Carlo, leave him, let it go,' it's the Ukrainian barmaid, who's come out and nods her head in the direction of the bar, 'Leave him and come back in,' Ismael smiles, 'Lucky for you she's here,' he says to the doorman, 'hiding behind a woman, you're *so* tough,' the barmaid's now got the doorman by the arm, 'You can see how drunk he is,' 'Yeah, yeah, so tough, all of you, we'll meet again, you and me, tough guy,' Ismael swings around, the street is a ship traversing dark waters, the asphalt a river of tar, his feet pattering along the ground, and he's like a puppet with too many broken strings, he lurches away from the bar, 'I've been here before, I've been here before today,' and he feels like laughing and shouting, but all he does is spit more saliva, 'I'll kill him,' he mumbles, Céspedes is rooted to the edge of the pavement, motionless beside the motionless trees, a car passes with the window open and a dance beat, and after the music's thud, the sound and echo of voices still hang in the air, belonging to two thugs who were travelling in the car, a whiff of hashish, 'One more bullet,' thinks Céspedes, holding his telephone in his hand, prolonging the trip, delaying his return to reality, he searches for Julia's name in his contacts list, *why not? nothing to lose*, and he presses on the icon and a green arrow shows on the screen, Céspedes lifts the phone to his ear, and an automated voice tells him the number he's calling is switched off or there's no coverage, a stone landing in the water, the bottom of a well, Céspedes sighs, looks up and down the street, *send her a message?* he bites his lip, lets go of the bag with the suit, it lands softly at his feet, *bloody hell, where's she got to?* he looks at the telephone's silent screen again, flicks his thumb, calls again, automated voice, once again as still as a tree, once again the demagnetized compass, the weathervane without wind, the empty street, an empty room in an empty hotel, he kicks the bag, it's swept down the road, tearing as it goes, and it ends up right in the middle of the street with a jacket sleeve hanging out of the top like the arm of a drowning man, end of the journey, Pedroche crawls on all fours, refuses the hand offered to him by Ignacio and finally manages to get to his feet, blood still pouring from his forehead, half his trousers hanging out behind him in shreds, he turns around on the spot twice, like a fat spinning-top with a broken point, 'One of my shoes is missing,' he says, 'and the jewellery,' Popeye pulls up beside the injured men, gets out, helps Ignacio put Floren in the back of the car, 'Fucking hell, why do I feel so cold?' says Floren apologizing, and he feels like throwing up, and Pedroche, in his cups, is still staring at the ground, 'Can we get some light here?' he asks, 'Hang on,' says Popeye as Floren sticks his head out of the window and releases a jet of warm beer through his mouth, the palm trees rustle over the heads of the Runner and Lucía, he's thinking about his home, his diary, everything that's written there as if it were a far-flung place, a bad dream he's awakening from now, 'Shine some light over here, the jewellery, the bastard,' Pedroche crouches down, more blood spills from his forehead, raking over the ground with his fingers, 'What the hell are you saying?' Popeye asks him, but Floren's partner doesn't reply, he just gropes about in the darkness, scratching his fingertips on the rough asphalt, and when Popeye arrives with his torch the only thing they find there is Nene Olmedo's screwdriver and Pedroche's scuffed shoe, 'They've robbed me,' he decides, 'Come on, for fuck's sake,' Ignacio pleads, worried by the way Floren is shaking, 'They've stolen the jewellery, Floren,' Pedroche tells his partner as he gets into the car, 'Bummer,' Floren replies, 'Hold this to your head,' says Popeye, handing Pedroche a filthy rag, 'But it's all dirty,' 'What? Do you think this is an ambulance? Let's go,' says Adolfo, who's just come running out after locking up the bar, and he jumps into the front passenger seat as the car's already started to move off, Julia tosses and turns in bed, with the air conditioning on and clean sheets, *tomorrow*, she thinks, *tomorrow, forget about these past few days, which are so heavy they feel like a lead weight, tomorrow*, she turns on the bedside lamp, her bedroom's a bubble, Ismael, God has listened, he looks up and can see the trees in the square bending over him and then, straightening up, pointing towards the sky, the dark tunnel, that barrel where the lift is always going up with Consuelo trembling inside it, opening her mouth and saying his name, Ismael, 'But why me?' Mariano Villaplana, the knock-kneed, heartbroken, asks his wife La Segueta, Encarnación, 'Why am I the only one who can't go over there?' 'Because it's none of your business,' his gap-toothed wife replies, watching the throng of people and the merry-go-round of lights on top of the police cars suspiciously, fearfully, with the ancient terror of a frightened little girl, superstitious of the dead, La Segueta makes the sign of the cross twice, once over the doorway and once over the heartbroken Mariano's chest, and then orders him upstairs, 'Does it hurt?' Ignacio asks Floren, and Floren lowers his head, not knowing what to say, 'It's uncomfortable more than anything else,' 'And are you bleeding a lot?' Popeye enquires as he drives the car, 'No, just the usual,' Ignacio replies on behalf of the injured man, 'What's the usual for when you've been stabbed with a screwdriver? You crack me up, Ignacio, the things you come out with,' Adolfo comments, still breathless from running, Popeye swings the car into Calle de la Unión, 'We don't even know what we're doing,' says Ignacio, who's drunk as well, 'I know what I'm doing,' says Pedroche in a low voice, pressing the filthy rag against his forehead, 'That's the worst of it,' Popeye, who's heard him, replies, driving the wrong way up the road and arriving at Avenida Juan XXIII, the car moving under the light of the tall street lamps up the deserted street, so empty and still that it all feels like a life-size model, a stage set of hollow houses, Eduardo Chinarro walks along wearily, screwing up his face like he does when he's singing, goes past La Goleta School and starts crossing the Puente de Armiñán, two cars driving side by side go past him, the occupants chatting from one vehicle to the other through the open windows, Eduardo comes to a halt when he gets to the middle of the bridge and leans on the side rail, beneath him the stony, dry riverbed goes down towards the sea through a jumble of dried-out weeds, balls of dirty cotton in the middle of the night, dormant buildings on either side, and the Puente de Aurora at the end, Eduardo feels the metal floor of this bridge beneath his feet and remembers when, years back, on his way from Carranque, he was coming down Calle Mármoles and crossing that bridge, and all the time singing in a low voice, warming up his vocal cords ready to start earning his living singing in the streets in the city centre, the Puente de Aurora was the frontier of his dreams, and there it is, with its metal decoration, lost in that world that no longer belongs to him, between unfamiliar buildings, with no water and no mud below, just concrete, lights that in the emptiness of the night look like prison floodlights, better carry on walking, better go and see if El Moderno's still open and they might give him something to eat and let him sleep in the attic, Eduardo spits over the side rail, and before his saliva has touched the ground he's already started walking in search of something to eat and a bed for the night, El Tato comes to a halt, out of breath, and calls out to Nene Olmedo, who looks back without stopping and sees his partner bent double, his hands on his knees, Nene looks down to the end of the street and only stops when he's sure no one's following them, then his lungs, his bronchial tubes and his racing heart suddenly make themselves felt, all at the same time, and he, too, doubles over and stays in this position until El Tato starts coming over, proudly holding up a small, heavy bag, 'Here are the jewels, Nene,' Nene has a trickle of spit running from his open mouth, El Tato watching him, half content, half exhausted, triumphant, and asks him, 'Did you get the envelope?' and Nene Olmedo straightens up, tries to find his voice of authority, 'What envelope?' 'The money, Nene, the cash,' Nene Olmedo shakes his head, spits to the side, 'It was really dark,' 'Fucking hell, it was really dark, but I got this,' El Tato lifts up the bag of jewellery again, 'Why didn't you do the wanker some damage like I did, I stuck him in the guts with the screwdriver you dropped with your butter fingers,' 'You stuck the other one who wasn't even important,' a motorbike goes by on the Camino de San Rafael, they watch it until it disappears from view, 'I stuck him because otherwise we'd still be there with the shiv on the floor and you pulling the wanker's hair,' 'Why don't you go and call on the entryphone and tell the whole block just in case they didn't hear you the first time? Shut your mouth, dickhead,' El Tato looks up at the building next to them, two or three windows with lights on, Nene Olmedo gestures to him to show him the bag, El Tato hands it over apprehensively, Nene opens it slowly, looks up and down the street, crouches down and empties the contents on to the pavement, earrings with purple stones, some gold chains, rings, a few bracelets, two or three holy medals, a ring with a red stone, Amelia looks in the rear-view mirror, making sure that there's no trace of Villaplana, dry semen, a scratch or running mascara, wipes away a tear before it can fall, gets out of the car, the gentle sound of the sea and the sweet smell of vegetation reach her, and there, in the middle of the night, illuminated, unreal, the hotel building rises up before her, a hive of balconies and windows, and the obedient Amelia walks towards it, crunching over the gravel, and the gravel seems to be climbing up her ankles and filling her lungs with its weight, with its darkness, the important thing is not to cry, La Penca's mouth is wide open, she's breathing like an asthmatic, she looks around, the packet of Fortuna's still in El Yubri's room, it might as well be at the other end of the universe, where Nene Olmedo's Martians live, and it's as if she can see them, as if she can see Nene's lips on top of her, opening very slowly, this afternoon or this morning (Aurora, La Penca, can't quite remember, before all this happened), asking her, 'Do you like that?' and her closing her eyes, sinking down, letting herself go with the current of a river, under the water but not drowning, being rocked by the current, 'Any good?' El Tato asks as his partner's index finger flicks through the pile of jewellery, separating out the pieces, nodding to say yes, 'We'll take them to the Dalton gang, see what they'll give us for them,' 'The Daltons don't do that stuff; we should take them to El Cararropero's brother-in-law,' 'As long as he doesn't rip us off,' 'He's a mate,' 'I stuck him with the blade, fucking hell, it felt like butter,' El Tato looks up, a man in a vest is watching them from a first-floor balcony, 'What's up with you. Can't you sleep? Go to bed, people have got to get up early tomorrow, or do you want me to come up there and put you to bed?' the man coughs, spits a half-chewed piece of orange on to the street and disappears, the police officer tells El Yubri to stand up, 'Let's go,' El Yubri is staring at a fixed point on the floor, he wants to say something, hesitates and finally looks up and asks if he can see his sister, the police officer looks at the man in plain clothes who shakes his head, 'Not at the moment,' the policeman tells him, and El Yubri replies, 'OK,' and stands up and looks around the room, 'What about the dog?' he asks, the uniformed policeman looks at the plain clothes man, 'He's shut away in the bathroom,' he says, 'OK,' El Yubri replies in a low voice, he goes into the corridor with the policeman, there are people he doesn't know, the flat is full of people, some of them look at him, he doesn't know whether to say good evening and decides to just look straight ahead, he used to play football with Penqui in this corridor with a tennis ball, and their mother complaining, white light coming from the kitchen, he wonders if they've put a sheet over his father or whether he's still there with that bewildered look on his face, staring at his feet with the scissors sticking out of his head, like a robot, El Yubri thinks, sinking into the bed, fondling the clean nightie she's just put on, Belita's eyes are wide open, the flat is in darkness, she turns on the light on the alarm clock, lighting up her face in green, it's late, her husband should have been back by now, the black mass in the corridor seems to be moving, there could always be someone behind the curtain, when she was a little girl her cousin used to put shoes behind the curtains, and when she saw them Belita would have an attack of the shivers, so bad she'd be frozen to the spot like a statue, the corridor's breathing, evil can also work miracles, dark miracles, she peers into the darkness, it looks as if it were full of spiders' webs, 'Chiqui? Chiqui are you there? Don't scare me, don't p unish me, I've forgiven you,' the only response is the menacing silence of the walls, the furniture floating in the darkness, the hospital building is straight ahead, growing out of the night, Popeye announces, 'Carlos Haya, nearly there,' Pedroche presses the filthy rag to his forehead, it's stopped pouring blood, just a few drops now, and for the first time since they were attacked he shows some concern for his partner, 'Does it hurt?' Floren says he's thinking about Carmen and Carmencita and he should have gone to have supper with them as soon as he'd finished work, 'So it goes,' says Popeye as he drives up the ramp to A&E, 'Tell them I'm allergic to penicillin,' Floren requests, 'You tell them, for fuck's sake, you're not going to die or lose your tongue,' Adolfo replies, 'You've hardly lost any blood,' Guille walks down the corridor between his Uncle Emilio and his Aunt Emilia, on either side there are empty offices and rooms with the lights turned on, and as he passes in front of one of these rooms Guille sees La Lori and Loberas sitting on a bench, Loberas with his head to one side, leaning against the wall, asleep, the girl looks at Guille hopefully, feels the urge to stand up, talk to him, but Guille's already disappeared, on his way out, Julia succumbs to sleep, a book resting on her chest, the taxi driver asks Céspedes for the second time where he wants to go, 'Hotel Las Vegas', Eduardo Chinarro looks up, sees the illuminated sign for El Moderno in the distance, the branches of a giant fig above his head like a plant-based womb, the night quivering, 'Chiqui, is that you?' Belita cower s in her bed, Ismael is sitting on a bench in the Plaza de la Merced, imagining the dark bedroom in which Consuelo is sleeping, breathing heavily, body naked inside a rucked-up nightie and her husband lying beside her, the concierge asleep, the lift door will open slowly, and she'll say, 'Come up, come up with me,' the hospital corridor is a labyrinth of lights, Floren says goodbye to his friends, 'Silly bastard, anyone would think he was going on holiday,' Ignacio and Popeye smile, Amelia crosses the hotel reception, makes a sign of apology to her colleague for being late, her footsteps echoing as if the whole world were hollow, 'A psychologist's on her way,' police officer María Eloy tells La Penca, sitting on the edge of the bed, the same bed where she was raped for the first time, where she'd sometimes wondered if it was her fault, if she'd ever encouraged her father without realizing it, the dog is scratching at the door, the flat smells of blood, Pedroche's ripped trousers are dragging on the floor behind him, 'Look at him with his bridal train!' says Popeye, and Pedroche walks on towards the treatment room, holding the filthy rag to his head, Nene Olmedo and El Tato look left and right and cross Paseo de los Tilos, 'We're not going to Portada Alta or to my place tonight, we'll head for Cararropero's,' Nene Olmedo announces, and El Tato goes along with it, there's a reflection of blue lights, El Yubri goes down the stairs slowly, through one of the windows on the staircase he sees the crowd pressing around his block, the murmuring, the flashing lights, he puffs out his chest, feels important, the Runner places his lips on Lucía's lips, a gust of fresh wind blows in from the sea, the breeze increases and blows softly, invisible veils flutter and brush against her skin, her eyes half closed, El Yubri goes out into the street, screws his face up and looks around him, all these people, Eduardo Chinarro steps off the pavement, and in the distance he sees a patch of light in El Moderno, it's open, he quickens his pace, Guille and his uncle and aunt go out into the street, the modern city, buildings, traffic lights, cars motionless at the side of the curb, geometric patterns on the road surface, the glass window of a bank, darkened shop windows in the distance, everything makes sense and everything is perfect, all roads are open.

Ana Galán is sitting on the sofa and notices the screen on her phone light up. A message from her brother. 'All sorted.' Yes, all sorted. Guille's problem sorted, Dioni's sorted, hers sorted. Tomorrow and the days and months after tomorrow, sorted. An annoying joke, almost macabre. Here's hoping they take ages coming home, here's hoping they get lost or stop to give Guille a talking-to, to build his spirits up and his sense of responsibility, whatever. Now you're the man of the house, you have to look after your mother, too, you two have to band together more than ever. All sorted.

It would be a release to sleep. To be cleansed of everything that's happened, of everything she's been feeling since she got the call at the hospital this morning. Since Dioni disappeared days before, since her life has been enclosed in a capsule inside a locked room for years now. File away at the sharpest edges of grief, that's what all her efforts will focus on in the coming months. *A task that must begin tonight, which I actually began the moment I knew that the man on the patch of waste ground was him.* Carry on anaesthetizing, extending the emptiness.

She gets up from the sofa. She rummages around in a Chinese chest of drawers. One of Dioni's fountain pens, a glasses case, also his. The idea of emptying the house, the cupboards, his clothes, his documents flashes through her brain like a dark mushroom that immediately pervades her very being and takes control of her breathing. *As soon as possible, tomorrow, the day after tomorrow, in the space of a week, the house will only contain the essential traces of Dioni, the ones chosen by me, the ones that are inescapable.* She opens another drawer, then a different one. She finds a packet of Winston and a lighter. Once again she's faced with another group of family photographs on top of the chest. Guille in swimming trunks pretending to be a surfer, her in Perugia ten years ago, Dioni raising his arms to the heavens, laughing, her mother in a black-and-white photo, perhaps before Ana was born, wearing black-framed glasses, head up, looking haughty. *What were you so proud of? Your run-of-the-mill life? What gave you pleasure, what was the night you conceived me like, what did you think of my father and what did you feel during your last few months? Did you talk to anyone about how frightened you were, which carpet did you sweep everything under? Am I like you, Mum? I could ask you anything under the sun tonight, and I could even strip myself naked in front of you.*

What would her mother think if she knew what Dioni was really like? If she knew what her daughter's life was really like? They might have suspected something at some point, her mother or her father, thinks Ana Galán. In any case, they would forget all about it, they would never have spoken about it between the two of them. Really? No, definitely not. Everything shut away, everything under lock and key. *I would never ask her those kinds of questions if she were actually here in front of me, I wouldn't strip myself naked either, no, it would be the same old thing, guessing, postulating, suspecting and keeping quiet, the other stuff is pure fantasy, perhaps in a different life with a different mother, being me but behaving differently, I would blurt everything out, for once in my life. And what if Vicente turns up at the funeral?*

Unlikely, but not impossible. Ana Galán pictures him, in a corner, to one side, alone. She would have to go up to him, pluck up her courage and go up to him, give him a hug. The two people that Dioni loved, it doesn't matter how. She wouldn't have to explain anything to anyone. But she knows she would never do it. It would be an acknowledgement that her whole life has been a sham, piling denial on top of denial. And to end up accepting it all in one fell swoop now that nothing matters any more. Or perhaps when everything really does matter. A moment when life is weighed up and measured.

No. If he did turn up, he would stay there to one side. A street dog sniffing around at the door to the butcher's. In vain. There are no bones or scraps for you.

Ana Galán walks slowly across the living room. She doesn't even know where to go in her own house. What will her new routine be like now? What will her stamping ground consist of from now on? And, standing in the middle of the living room, she wonders who it was who last saw Dioni before he ended up in the state in which he was found. Who spoke to him for the last time? Was Dioni desperate? Did he reveal anything? How did he get to that far-off patch of waste ground? How much did he suffer? What was he thinking, and when did he decide to do what he did? Did he really decide? Was it really a decision, reasoned thought, a plan? Or did he just go towards the abyss blindly, blindfold, without thinking? Without leaving behind a souvenir for anyone, the only message being his own end. Closing a door, nothing more.

Seeking peace and quiet. Finally, peace and quiet. Getting rid of the weight that was crushing him, although no one had forced him to carry it. He had forced himself. He made the choice, with or without a blindfold, just as we all make a choice, he chose much more than me, a lot more. I chose to keep my mouth shut, he chose to lie and then to keep his mouth shut, too; he made a lot of choices, he's suffered more, I also need that peace, that peace and quiet, but down a different path, in the opposite direction. He's got no right to drag me along with him, not any longer, not one centimetre further.

Ana Galán opens the glass door and goes out on to the terrace. She's hit full in the face by a gust of hot wind carrying the moisture of the climbing greenery. The plants seemed to hold their breath, to have stopped moving as their mistress arrived. She walks slowly over to the balustrade. There's the night laid out before her, like the enormous skin of a hunted animal that's just been brought down and is still bleeding. The night does breathe, the night does have a pulse, it's a black lung expanding and contracting over us all.

The jagged palm trees against the blackness of the sea and the hazy outline of the coast, the invisible mountains. Out there, somewhere out there, lost in the darkness is the patch of waste ground where he was found. The ants will still be out there, implacably criss-crossing the ground. Yes, out there on that rough, dried-out piece of land are the advertising posters faded by the sun, the gigantic photograph of the couple sleeping on the best mattress in the world, the idyllic beach with white sand and those two concrete monoliths with the letters **BUEST, WAS** painted on them. And beneath them, at their feet, are the withered bushes, the plastic, the faded tin cans, the insects dragging themselves along the arid and scorched ground, among dried-out, spikey thistles, cigarette butts, surgical gloves, pieces of gauze, the outline left by Dioni's body where the ants are still moving around looking for food, rummaging around in the bodies of other insects, carrying off bits of wings, antennae, elytra, larvae, seeds, going in and out of that never-ending ants' nest, that dark labyrinth that is spread out underground much further than anyone could ever imagine. Millions. As if the dreams of men were the opposite of this world, a barely glimpsed nightmare that trapped Dioni and took him away with it.

Ana Galán lets out a long sigh and focuses on the tarry, shiny, distant view of the sea. Reflections are flitting darkly over the blackness of the water. A gentle, almost cool breeze is coming in from the sea, which sweeps over her like a shadow. Ana Galán lights a cigarette and leans her elbows on the balustrade, her torso bent over it, her head up. She's smoking peacefully. And from a nearby house an anonymous neighbour is secretly watching her, as he has on so many other nights.

DRAMATIS PERSONAE

Since most of the characters are referred to in the novel by their first names or nicknames, they are listed here in that order (ignoring the definite article, if used).

The characters in the story of 'The Calle Molinillo Vampire' told by the Runner's grandmother appear after the general Dramatis Personae.

Alberto Marín Marcos. Municipal policeman who arrests Guille, Loberas and La Lori. In the line of duty he resists La Lori's overtures, which, once she is handcuffed and on her way to the station, become direct propositions. Marín Marcos passes the arduous test that Providence has placed in his path on this humid night in the heat of the *terral.* One could say that it left a bittersweet taste on his tongue.

Alexandra (Hornbostel). Owner of La Vieja Aduana bar from which, one strange morning, Garriga Vela, Taján and Soler emerge, right in front of Céspedes, all three of them climbing on to a scrap-metal cart. Alexandra waves them off with a smile.

Alfonso Pallarés. One of Juanmi's friends in the Faculty of Arts. Despite a vocation as a scoundrel, he's a diligent and brilliant student.

Álvaro Frías. Accomplished reporter on the *Sur* daily newspaper. Son of the legendary and much-loved José Antonio Frías. He goes to the Portada Alta district when he hears that a murder has been committed there.

Amelia (Martínez Robles). Mother of Ismael and Jorge (also called Gorgo). Rafi Villaplana's lover. She likes to be called Amel. She thinks that abbreviating her name in that fashion makes it sound romantic and even thrilling. She works as a receptionist at the

Hotel Los Patos. She's scared of ending up alone, a last survivor. Her husband (Ernesto) has left her and (as far as one can gather from a letter she keeps in her underwear drawer) she was unfaithful to him back in the day.

Ana Galán. Doctor at the emergency department at the hospital. Dioni's wife and Guille's mother. Smokes cigarettes leaning on her terrace balcony.

Ángel López. 800-metres athlete who used to train with the Runner and with Santi Cánovas. He had a powerful stride – you might say he was Carranque's own version of Alberto Juantorena. He works as an inspector for the city street-cleaning company. He has pale eyes and looks at you like a child. He still trains but doesn't enter competitions.

Ángeles (Aragón Sixto). Dioni's first girlfriend, with whom he shared his first sexual experiences. Dark hair, blue eyes, prominent cheekbones. Like Dioni himself, studied law. High court judge.

Anita. The Runner's neighbour, who dies from a heart attack at the age of twenty-nine and becomes the neighbourhood symbol for the brevity of life.

Anselmo (Don). Resident of Portada Alta. Sixty-six years old and the worse for wear. He wears pyjamas with a picture of Donald Duck on the front. He goes out in the street to investigate when El Yubri kills his father and the police cars and the ambulance give the neighbourhood a festive feel.

Antoñito. Juana's grandson (Juana is Raimundo's drug dealer). Antoñito is shy, clinging to his grandmother's apron. He doesn't like talking to Eduardo Chinarro, however much the latter tries.

Asunción Arnedo. Friend of Dr Galán. Present in Dr Galán's house when Dioni's death is announced. Married to Mark Aldrich, the Blue-Haired American. Teaches at Dickinson College, Pennsylvania. On holiday in Málaga.

Azulay (Carlos). One of the old-time athletes people tell Jorge (Gorgo) about. 400-metres and 400-metres-hurdles specialist. Also the high jump. The most rounded athlete to run on the track at the Carranque stadium. Curly hair.

Bartolo. Employee at the BP petrol station on Avenida Ortega y Gasset, where Rai goes when he discovers Dioni's body being eaten by ants. Wears the company's official green overalls and has a face like a fish, no chin, hardly any neck, piggy eyes and a bad temper. He's been working the pumps for eight years. Before that he was a lorry driver. He was a happy man driving his Iveco Stralis 420. An accident in which his lorry caught fire, his colleague Andrade died and he was left unable to drive as a result of a problem with his hip made him embittered. He considers it demeaning to wear the green overalls. Raimundo Arias sneers at his name.

El Bastián. Resident of Portada Alta. Owner of a Rottweiler called Boss. Sometimes he sets it on Viberti's Dobermann. El Bastián was a childhood friend of Rafi Villaplana. They used to dig holes in the sand on Playa de Sacaba and cover them with sugarcanes, newspapers and a dusting of sand. They enjoyed watching people fall in. They used to put bangers down drain holes. When Rafi started work at the hotel they grew apart. Now they don't even say hello. El Bastián has a greengrocer's stall at Huelin Market. He weighs 110 kilos.

Belita Bermúdez Covaleda. Pedroche's wife, who suffers from various mental issues. She gave Father Sebastián Grimaldos 1,800 euros and the family jewels as a donation. She fries eggs for her husband's supper several hours in advance.

Benito. Young man. Single. One of the regulars at La Esquinita. The poor boy goes out to get laid at the weekend at the expense of his liver and his finances, according to Boss-Eyed Manolo.

Blasco (Luisa). Nurse at the hospital where Dr Galán and Julia Mamea work. Younger sister of the actress Maite Blasco. Like her sister, Luisa was born in Madrid and also started a career in the world of theatre. Less fortunate than her sister, she didn't progress beyond the amateur stage. Her star role was playing Anna Balicke in Bertoldt Brecht's *Drums in the Night*.

The Blue-Haired American (Mark Aldrich). Asunción Arnedo's husband. Present in Dr Galán's house when Dioni's death is announced. Born in Boston. Left handed. Brilliant pitcher with the Red Sox Juniors. Forced out of baseball by a serious injury to his left hand while he was practising his other passion, karate. These days he runs road marathons. Teaches literature at Dickinson College, Pennsylvania. Friend of Daniel Murphy and Grace Jarvis and used to be a very close friend of Rafael Pérez Estrada.

Boss-Eyed Manolo. Divorcee. One of the regulars at La Esquinita. Likes to expound on the good life, which basically consists of eating, fornicating and getting the right amount of sleep on a regular basis.

Boy in the white swimming trunks. Boy who arouses Dioni when he sees him on the beach at El Candado. Homosexual. Apprentice welder. He died four months after Dioni saw him on the beach. In a motorbike accident.

Cabello (Alberto Cabello Mendoza). Friend of Guille. Self-assured teenager, a natural leader, partly down to his precocious facial hair and his gift with the girls. Friend of Lori, friend of Tuli and, as mentioned, friend of Guille, whom he looks after on the day his father dies. Gets on with everyone and a cut above the rest.

El Canijo. Mysterious individual who acts as a link between the Runner and Ismael. The Runner used to lend him books back in the day, and Ismael searches him out on Playa de Sacaba, although no one knows what peculiar traits two such different characters have in common. But that's life.

El Cararropero (Hipólito Fernández Miramón). Nene Olmedo's 'godfather', whom he goes to after he's stolen Belita Bermúdez's jewellery. Retired fisherman. Has a stall in the various flea markets around the province. He sells trinkets and deals in odds and ends. Was a friend of Nene Olmedo's father; his affection for Nene stems from there. El Cararropero has a wide jaw and has gone deaf.

El Cararropero's brother-in-law (Constancio Patrana). Expert.

Carlo. Doorman at the Onda Pasadena. He at first allows Ismael into the bar, and then he throws him out. Muscly. Carefully groomed hair. He spent two years studying physics at the University of Kraków.

Carlos Cañeque. Childhood friend of Céspedes in Madrid. Adherent of the theory and practice of immobilism. Writer, film director, multifaceted actor and trumpet player without a trumpet. Winner of the Premio Nadal for his writing and has published books of interviews with Borges, Cioran and Berlanga, together with Maite Grau.

Carlos San Emeterio. Lawyer. Friend and partner of Dioni's. Level headed and generous. Dioni's occasional confidant. Apart from law and his wife Adriana, his passion is aeronautics. He's published several books on the subject. Expert on the life and works of Antoine de Saint-Exupéry.

Carmeli. Thirty-two years old. Resident of Portada Alta who goes outside to check what's happened when El Yubri kills his father by stabbing him several times in the stomach and once in the back of the head with a giant pair of scissors. Foul mouthed, sometimes friendly. Works in Gino's, a brothel with a glorious past and a pitiful present. She wasn't at work on the day in question as she had her period. She has a son with Down's syndrome (Javierín, aged six). She was asleep and was woken up by the lights from the police cars and ambulance. When she first woke up she thought she was in a disco and that Rodolfo, Javierín's father, was saying that he'd won the lottery. When she went out to see what was going on she was wearing a green strappy top with such large armholes you could almost see her breasts.

Carmencita (Ferrer). Floren's daughter. She just *lurves* it in the swimming pool. Fussy eater. Poor appetite (a bit squeamish).

Carole Benoit. Meets Céspedes at the party held the previous night in a house in Los Pinares de San Antón. Half-French, half-Spanish. Born in Lille. Plays at being a doomsayer but doesn't quite pull it off. Swordswoman with a rubber-tipped foil. Beautiful, young, lost her way in the maze. Has a broken heart that she tries to cover up but doesn't pull that off either. From a very good family. One of her ancestors was a successful businessman, and she inherited the fruits.

Céspedes. Economist, businessman. Married. His wife (Marta Giménez Landau) has thrown him out of the house after finding him fornicating with some tramp (Natalia Ibáñez, known as La Ibáñez). Has been carrying on an extramarital relationship with Julia Mamea for many years. He is pestered by the overly ambitious Rafi Villaplana, who tries to involve him in deals that, at this complicated time in his life, are of no interest to Céspedes. He meets Carole at the party held the previous night in a house in Los Pinares de San Antón. It occurs to him to invite her to lunch in Madrid. He buys her a watch worth 8,850 euros which ends up in the toilet on the train. This is not the best day of his life. He drinks malt whisky.

Céspedes's father (Lorenzo Céspedes). Railway worker. Inherited an ironmonger's from his brother. A meticulous man. A saver. Keeps a careful note of all the money he's ever earned, since he started as an apprentice in a bicycle workshop (1942) up until two days before he suffered the heart attack that ended his life (1979).

Céspedes's mother (Miguelina Roncero). Slim, eyes very close together around a pointy nose, which earned her the nickname La Grajilla (the Jackdaw) in the El Fuerte neighbourhood. The nickname disappeared when she moved to a new neighbourhood and with the prosperity the family began to enjoy when her husband inherited his deceased brother's ironmonger's and Doña Miguelina took over the reins of the business.

Consuelo (also known as La Giganta). Ismael's neighbour, about forty-five years old, on whom he spies continuously so he can go up in the lift with her and fantasize about having carnal relations with her. She's tall with small teeth and dark eyes. Marilyn Monroe haircut, dyed accordingly; usually wears a flimsy green dress. Husband is shy. They have a son (Manolo). From his flat Ismael sometimes manages to see La Giganta's armpit as she hangs out the washing.

Consuelo la Giganta's husband. Lathe operator. Tall, energetic, rough manners. Jealous, completely unaware of Ismael's harassment of his wife. Just as well.

Consuelo la Giganta's son (Manolo). Scatterbrained teenager who Ismael hates because he bears a certain resemblance to his mother. Ismael is upset and outraged when he detects some of Consuelo's features in this boy.

El Corbata (Augustín Rivera). Journalist who, in his time, uncovered the famous case of the murder at the El Pomelo singles bar among other scoops. Mad keen Barça fan. Despite the devotion and gratitude he feels towards Iniesta, Ronaldinho and Messi, his idols are still Asensi and Marcial. Friend of Daniel Murphy. Father of Riverita, also a journalist.

Cortés. One of the old-time athletes people tell Jorge (Gorgo) about. Decathlon specialist. Blond, blue eyed; had a moustache and a sense of humour.

Covaleda. Former Chupa Chups salesman who was made redundant and was hired by Rafi Villaplana to work in the Hotel Los Patos. Made some remarks at a meeting of the management committee that Rafi took the wrong way and became his enemy.

Cumpián (Alberto). Old friend of the Runner. Easy-going surrealist. Used to work in a Seat showroom while his other friends were studying. Generous. Subsidized Padín's purchase of a 22-year-old Triumph motorcycle.

Currito Cabeza. Curro Cabeza and Maica Terés Soler's son and Maiquita Cabeza's brother. Junior *padel* champion. Present in Dr Galán's house when Dioni's death is announced. Big aficionado of *salchichón* and *fuet*.

The Daltons. Group of bank robbers along the lines of a classic outlaw gang. When they're not going about their day job, one of them sings flamenco at local *tablaos*, another is a karate black belt and yet another competes in amateur cycle races.

Danielín. Owner of the bar of the same name that Ismael visits occasionally and in which he starts a brawl with two men. Danielín is fifty years old. Despite Ismael's aggressive character and unpredictable behaviour he lets him in the bar because he was a friend of his father's. Also, it weighs on his conscience that it was he, Danielín, who introduced Ismael's father to Eloísa, the woman he's currently living with and with whom he has a son.

Dioni (Dionisio Grandes Guimerá). Lawyer. Dr Galán's husband, father of the soon-to-be-fatherless Guille. Vicente's lover. The moribund man who is found on a patch of waste ground covered in thousands of Argentine ants. Closet homosexual. When he was alive his smile had a hint of melancholy.

Dioni's father (Ramón Grandes). Humble man, persecuted for his politics in his youth and imprisoned for two years. Never wanted to discuss anything to do with this at home or, as far as we know, with anyone else. When he got out of prison he worked as a bricklayer's labourer. Saved his money to set up a shop selling fruit.

Doctor Torrecillas. Eminent urologist who nevertheless could do nothing to save the life of Juanmi's father.

Domínguez. Hotel employee. Enemy of Rafi Villaplana. Such was the hatred Domínguez felt for Rafi when he saw him for the first time, just for existing, it made him believe in reincarnation. Domínguez reasoned that such loathing could only be the result of a deep unresolved conflict in a previous life.

Dori (Salvadora Heredia). Bored friend of Amelia, from a period following the latter's divorce. They went to see films together and out to dinner. Dori encouraged Amelia to go on walks in the countryside. At the cinema, Dori ate popcorn and cried over romantic scenes. She always talked about the same thing over dinner. When they were walking along country paths she would keep on about how much she loved taking walks in the countryside.

Eduardo Chinarro. Raimundo (Rai) Arias's friend and begging partner. Never stops singing 'Cantinero de Cuba'. The veins and arteries on his neck swell up noticeably when he sings, owing to his passion and professionalism. He tries to remember what his mother used to sing as she hung up the washing over pots of geraniums when the sheets looked like sails. With a bit of luck he could have gone far in the music world, according to Moreno Peralta, an old friend of his. Heart of gold.

Elisa. Céspedes's wife. Childhood wrapped in cotton wool, although some of it didn't smell too good. Went to school in Switzerland. Moved to London and was slightly wild until she settled down and married Céspedes, a young man who came from nowhere and seemed to be going somewhere.

Elvira. Friend of Céspedes on drunken nights out in Barcelona. Blonde, lawyer, left handed and, to a certain extent, Julia's predecessor.

Emilia (Pujol). Wife of Emilio Galán and therefore Ana Galán and Dioni's sister-in-law. Lawyer. Wears glasses. Aloof. After much expiation and a period of unrelenting revenge, she accepted her husband's infidelity with Montse in a civilized fashion.

Emilio (Galán). Ana Galán's brother and therefore Dioni's brother-in-law. Emilia Pujol's husband. Lawyer. Had an extramarital affair with Montse, present in Dr Galán's house when Dioni's death is announced. The affair was discovered one day by Emilio's wife and created a serious crisis in their marriage. Fortunately they got through it, although beneath the scars it has left a strange undercurrent in their relationship.

Enrique Montoya. Friend of Céspedes from the days of his youth in Madrid. Born in Mexico, educated in France. Sociologist, expert in deviant and disturbed behaviour. Sounds good on the radio; that is, he speaks very well. Both caring and intelligent.

Enrique Rodríguez. Childhood friend of Dioni. A pleasant lad who likes to indulge in life's sinful pleasures. Reckless within certain limits.

Ernesto. Absentee father of Ismael and Jorge (Gorgo). He left his wife Amelia and his sons in order to rebuild his life with a woman named Eloísa, with whom he has another son and lives peacefully. Ernesto is a salesman.

Estefanía Villaplana Molledo. Daughter of Mariano Villaplana and Encarnación Molledo (La Segueta). Rafi's sister. Friend of Gloria, Jorge's (Gorgo's) fiancée. She has a boyfriend who is supposedly a poet.

Faneca. Motorcycle cop from Barcelona who responds to Yubri's call after the latter attacks his father.

Federico, El de la Primitiva. Manages a government betting and lottery shop in Ismael's neighbourhood. Listens patiently while Ismael fantasizes about the money he's going to win on the lottery and the crimes he's going to commit when everyone least expects it.

Felipe Vicaría. 400- and 200-metres athlete, whom the Runner considers the best ever to take to the track at Carranque.

Felix. Amelia's work colleague at the Hotel Los Patos. Has a pencil moustache. Blond. Used to be a singer. Unlucky.

Fernando Arcas. Friend of José Damián Ruiz Sinoga. Historian, aficionado of contemporary dance. Acquaintance of Céspedes, who considers him the soul of integrity.

Floren (Florencio Ferrer Pérez). Pedroche's friend and partner at Molduras y Marcos Ferrer. Married to Carmen. Carmencita's father. Home loving and contented. He's Ismael and Jorge's cousin and employs the latter at his business.

Fonsi (Alfonso Corbalán). Friend and current lover of Montse. She would have gone to the beach with him if it hadn't been for Dioni's misfortune. Fonsi is five years younger than Montse. Businessman in the construction industry.

Gabi (Gabriel Muñoz). Policeman who speaks to Raimundo at the petrol station and is kind enough to give him a lift in his car. A few days earlier he rescued two children from drowning at Playa de la Misericordia. Amelia (Amel) was there and was impressed by the policeman's bravery.

Gabriel (Muñiz). Gloria's father. Irritating individual who likes to put pressure on his future son-in-law Jorge (Gorgo), and boast about all his possessions, whether it's his sons José Manuel and Gabriel or his air-conditioning unit.

Gabriel (Muñiz Muñoz). Gloria's brother. He went to Mexico to take part in an advertising campaign as a model and decided to stay there to live and where his refined manners landed him work as a model for photonovels. He scrapes by in an apartment in Mexico City with his boyfriend Jairo Jesús. According to his father he's about to sign a contract with a television channel in Miami. It's not very likely to happen.

Gamal. A Moroccan. Hotel employee, whom Rafi Villaplana generously defended.

Garriga Vela (José Antonio). Novelist whom Céspedes once saw climbing on to a scrap-metal cart early one morning long ago, together with Taján and Soler. Writes magnificent novels when his passion for football allows. Dyed-in-the-wool Real Madrid fan, he watches their matches wearing a number-7 shirt in honour of his idol. He is a knight of the tumultuous Order of Finnegans.

Gema (Moncada). Vicente's girlfriend (Vicente as in Dioni's lover). Hairdresser with a tendency towards alcoholism. A nice girl who likes to wear porcelain fingernails like old-school porn stars. Because of her great figure, for a time she used to wiggle her hips in the boxing ring at the Carranque stadium with a board announcing the rounds, wearing a bikini and a big smile. Now she's a bit tubby, and her hair's frazzled from too much peroxide.

Gloria (Muñiz Muñoz). Jorge's (Gorgo's) fiancée. She has a small scar in the corner of her mouth. Likes to sleep all through the morning. Her father's a bore and her mother's a cockatoo, according to Jorge. One brother is an aggressive headcase, and the other one's gay (again, in Jorge's opinion). Gloria has a nice purple top.

Gloria's mother. Soulless and insincere woman, in the opinion of her potential future son-in-law Jorge (Gorgo). Avid consumer of tranquillizers.

Grace Jarvis. Very close friend of Dioni. North American. Guille stayed at her house for a year while he was a pupil at Carlisle High School. Grace teaches at Dickinson College in Carlisle, Pennsylvania.

Granero. Bank employee with whom Jorge (Gorgo) sometimes goes running. He likes talking about local athletes from the old days: Carlos Azulay, Cortés, Padilla, Soler, Santi Cánovas, Felipe Vicaría, Pedro Delgado, etc.

Gross Gross. Accredited journalist with *El País*, who goes to Portada Alta when he learns that there's been a tragic event.

Guille (Guillermo Grandes Galán). Son of Dioni Grandes Guimerá and Dr Ana Galán. His family is very fond of the letter G. Teenager in the process of losing his father. Disorientated. Confused. Typical problems of someone weak bodied and weak spirited. Platonically in love with Mónica Ovejero. La Lori jerks him off.

La Ibáñez (Natalia Ibáñez). Loose woman whom Rafi Villaplana introduces and offers to Céspedes as a goodwill gesture and to try to achieve his objective. Tall and dark. Has a fringe. Unhappy childhood. Played with dolls until a very late age. Worked for a short time in a roadside bar in El Bierzo. Discovered that set-up was not for her. Although business is slack, she prefers to freelance. Lisps.

Ignacio. Customer of Bar Maqui. Goes to help Floren and Pedroche when they're attacked. Born in Tomelloso, fifty-six years old, early retirement from banking and passionate about *frontenis* – a version of tennis played on a *frontón* court. He's had a lot to drink.

Inmaculada Berruezo. Childhood friend of Dioni, Enrique Rodríguez, Meliveo and Vicky Leyva.

Isaías Abril, Father. Priest. Member of the Order of St Augustine. Teaches natural science at the Colegio Los Olivos. Used to be one of the Runner's teachers. Sunglasses, big quiff, blondish hair. Used to pay a modest fee to pupils who brought him live centipedes and scorpions. He'd spend time on the long afternoons at the weekend making acrylic paperweights with these in the school laboratory, which he'd sell at a reasonable profit through a shop in Calle Compañía.

Isidro. Friend of Tuli, Juno and Cabello's gang. Dreamy blue eyes, possibly down to continuous consumption of cannabis. Woolly hair.

Isidro, Father. Priest who used to warn Céspedes in his early adolescence about the sins of the flesh. Former Spanish legionnaire. Sports a vicious scar on his neck. Schoolboy rumours attributed it to an attack he received in Africa by an Arab who was jealous of him and tried to cut his throat.

Ismael. Amelia's son and Jorge's brother. He used to call Jorge 'Gorgo' when he saw him in his cot and still couldn't talk properly. Back then Ismael was affectionate. Now he aspires to have sexual relations with Consuelo la Giganta, on whom he constantly spies. Violent with alcoholic tendencies. Mentally unbalanced. Often invokes (to himself) the biblical meaning of his name: God has listened.

Ismael and Jorge's (Gorgo's) grandfather. Army officer, Artillery Corps. Easy going and honest. Since he retired he sees the world as a strange place, different from what he always thought it was or ought to be. Military discipline has been lost. He's a sceptic.

Jane (Rice). Rafi Villaplana's current girlfriend. Daughter of a wealthy businessman. In love with the type of Latin lover embodied by Rafi. Also loves horses. Goes to horse-riding lessons. Rafi's family finds her enchanting, in an exotic way.

Jane's father (Edward S. Rice). Rafi Villaplana's potential future father-in-law. Businessman. Started off in the metallurgy sector. Keeps Rafi at arm's length.

Jane's mother (Alice Rice). Potential future mother-in-law of Rafi Villaplana. There's still something clearly attractive about her. Had a sexual relationship with her golf coach several years back. Contrary to what Rafi thinks, within the Rice family she's the one who dislikes him most.

Jerónimo. Yubri's friend and partner in crime. They steal copper wire in the Field of Mars and are arrested when Jerónimo crashes the old van he's driving. Pock-marked face, beady eyes, broad back. Walks with a stoop.

Jesús. Young employee at the BP petrol station close to the place where Dioni is found.

Jiler. Dobermann owned by Viberti. His name is derived from Hitler.

El Jirafa. Concierge of the building where Ismael and his family live. A man of few words. Long neck. Slow witted. He watches Ismael's manoeuvres to coincide with Consuelo in the entrance hall without understanding what he's up to. With his limited intelligence El Jirafa thinks that there's some financial reason behind it all (illegal betting on dogfights or cockfights that the flaky Ismael probably goes to and on which Consuelo places bets behind her husband's back). He fancies Saray, the 25-year-old who lives on the third floor.

Jorge (also called Gorgo). Amelia's son, Ismael's brother. Gloria's fiancé. Works in his cousin Floren's framing-and-mouldings business. Sensual. Short. Cowardly and intimidated. Pilfers from his cousin. Thinks that everything will work out fine tomorrow.

José Damián Ruiz Sinoga. Geologist whom Rafi Villaplana tries to involve in a murky urban-development deal. Céspedes, who has reports on Ruiz Sinoga, mocks Rafi's idea.

José Manuel (Muñiz Muñoz). Gloria's brother and Jorge's (Gorgo's) possible future brother-in-law. A ghost, in Jorge's opinion. Studies at the Military Academy. Before he joined up, he was a friend of Nene Olmedo. He smoked his excellent spliffs, and they also did two burglaries together, one targeting a shop selling electronics in El Palo and another a house in El Candado. Now he's a fervent believer in Law and Order and a true patriot.

JuanCa. The person everyone's waiting for. Much admired friend of Guille, Loberas and Juno who never turns up. The Godot of Málaga.

Juan Cano. Highly regarded reporter on the *Sur* daily newspaper. He's the first on the scene at Portada Alta when Yubri commits his crime, as he was talking to Faneca the motorcycle cop when he received the call from base.

Juana (Señora Juana). Small-time drug dealer. Supplies drugs to Raimundo Arias. Seventy-nine years old, one and a half metres tall, forty-six kilos in weight but has a commanding presence. Born in La Chancla, Almería. As a child she joined her mother trading on the black market. Emigrated to France in 1956 when she was barely twenty years old and held various jobs: assistant in a butcher's shop, barmaid, extortionist and occasional prostitute. On her return to Spain at the age of forty she set up home in the El Bulto neighbourhood. There she discovered the financial attractions of the drug scene. She gained a reputation working with Machine-Gun Cristóbal and subsequently went her own way. She only cuts her merchandise by 30 per cent. El Gregorio acts as her collector and bodyguard. She often goes about her business accompanied by her grandson Antoñito, aged nine.

Juanmi (Juan Manuel Ares Ruiz). Accidental heroin addict, acquaintance of Eduardo Chinarro and Nene Olmedo. Son of ear, nose and throat specialist Juan Ares Gonzaga and teacher Brígida Ruiz Beltrán. Studied philology for one and half years. Suffers from fair-weather friends. Laughs a lot.

Julia Mamea. Nurse, friend of Dr Ana Galán. Has a longstanding friendship/sexual relationship with Céspedes and occasionally with Ortuño (and, one imagines, with one or two others). Curiously, her name coincides with one of the Roman Emperor Septimius Severus' nieces, who was the mother of another emperor, Alexander Severus. She died, like her son, at the hands of the emperor's own soldiers, who mutinied. That Julia had three breasts; the one in this story only two.

Julián Rojas. Photographer working for *El País* who goes to Portada Alta when Yubri commits his crime. Self-made career on the strength of his talent. As a child he used to play on a vacant plot in Calle Mármoles, with Pompo, Castillo and El Muelas. The others carried knives; he preferred pacifism. I suppose you could say a heart of gold is mightier than a steel blade.

Juno. Friend of Guille, Montse's son. Impressive set of muscles and a stunning quiff that he's very proud of. He shows it off by stroking it or flicking it backwards with ferocious jerks of his neck. Mónica Ovejero is in love with him. He claims to be an expert on whiskies. Despite the heat, he rushes off to put on a dark suit and tie so that he's ready for death. Born leader.

Knife-sharpener (Francisco Pérez). Knife-sharpener and scrap-metal merchant who unexpectedly turns up early one morning in the city centre with an old horse pulling a cart. Born in Santo Estevo, Orense, in north-west Spain. Son and grandson of knife-sharpeners. A decent man. Descendant through his mother's line of Romasanta, the Wolf Man of Allariz.

Kuki. La Penca and El Yubri's dog. Gets kicked. Chews table legs out of frustration.

Lago (Eduardo). Friend of Céspedes when he was a student in Madrid. Lives in New York. Member of the tumultuous Order of Finnegans.

Leandro. Mechanic. Owns a shop that is both a workshop and motorcycle salesroom near the Runner's home. He comes from a village. Manic depressive. Sometimes he wonders how long it would take to asphyxiate himself if he closed the shop blinds, started up the eight or ten motorbikes in the shop and left the engines running.

Liébana, Father. Priest whom Rafi Villaplana used to assist as an altar boy at Saturday masses. Taught Rafi the art of speculation, conviction and mending one's ways. Whereas Father Liébana had heavenly visions in mind, Rafi applied the technique to earthly matters.

Loberas. Friend of Guille, Juno and JuanCa the Godot. Also of Mónica Ovejero and even Piluca. Likes to play the fool.

La Loren. Fifty-nine colourful years of age. Runs a brothel frequented by Boss-Eyed Manolo and, apparently, one or two other locals from La Esquinita. Advertises her wares on the internet. La Loren earned her stripes as a madam in brothels mostly on the Levante coast.

Lorena. 42-year-old blonde who has a secret relationship with Father Sebastián Grimaldos, three years younger than her. Has a slight limp because of an old fracture of the tibia and fibula.

La Lori. Friend of Cabello and acquaintance of Guille, with whom she has a sexual encounter. Resident of La Granja de Suárez. Typical girl-next-door with abundant, long, curly hair, gap teeth and prominent feminine attributes. Friendly with a number of rich kids from the east side of the city having met Cabello at a spiritual retreat two years back. Cabello was there because he was having one of his periodic mystical crises; La Lori because the food was free and they went on trips. Wears a strappy black top and very skimpy shorts fitting tightly over a pair of thighs so generous that they might spin out of control in three years' time and descend into chaos in six or seven.

El Lucas. Former neighbour of Eduardo Chinarro. Alcoholic with violent tendencies. When he got home drunk he was partial to throwing domestic items out of the window so that a shower of humble dishes, clothes, sheets and even chairs was a familiar sight in the neighbourhood. Also his daughter Merceditas's school books and exercise books.

Lucía. The Runner's fiancée. Works in a supermarket. The Runner's inspiration and spiritual guide. His hope.

Maica Terés Soler. Friend of Dr Galán. Mother of Maiquita Cabeza Terés and Currito Cabeza Terés. Goes to Ana Galán's house with her children when she learns of the tragedy that's about to descend on her. Her uncle is Soler, the 400-metres athlete whom the Runner tells Jorge (Gorgo) about.

Maiquita Cabeza Terés. Daughter of Curro Cabeza and Maica Terés. Goes with her mother and younger brother to Ana Galán's when they learn of the tragedy that's occurred there. Teenager, ballet dancer.

Malcolm (Otero). Friend of Céspedes when he was a student in Madrid. Editor. Member of the tumultuous Order of Finnegans, like Jordi Soler and Enrique Vila-Matas.

El Manolín. Goes to bed with La Roberta, Eduardo Chinarro's girlfriend, sort of. Doesn't like getting up early, which is why he left his job as a fishmonger and started selling illegal lottery tickets. Sneak thief. Three convictions for robbery. Has a gravelly voice and always carries a knife, just in case. And it's true what Chinarro says: his eyes bulge like a pair of eggs.

Man wearing a striped shirt in Onda Pasadena. Young man who drinks alone at the bar in Onda Pasadena and who reminds Ismael of a boy at school they used to call El Bocas. In fact, the man wearing a striped shirt is called Jacinto Castro, and he recently arrived in the city from Bilbao, where he was born and went to school. He took a photography course there with Ricky Dávila.

Manolo. Regular customer at the BP petrol station near the patch of waste ground where Dioni is found. Forty years old. Wears a gold signet ring on the little finger of his left hand.

Manolo el Cojo. Resident of Portada Alta who goes out on the street when he hears the police cars and ambulance around Yubri's front door. Chews on a piece of bread. He's a hungry man. Bricklayer.

María del Carmen. Floren's wife. Dressmaker. Kind. Dark haired. Floren is happy they're together. She is, too.

María Eloy (García). Member of the National Police Force who tells Penca that a psychologist is on her way following the murder of her father. Writes poetry at night.

Mariano Villaplana. Husband of Encarnación Molledo (La Segueta). Father of Rafi, Miguel, Estefanía and Pepe Villaplana. A man who likes watching television in his underpants and who, as well as his night shift, also sleeps in the doorway of La Amistad, a grocer's shop. Fond of one-arm bandits. As he frequently asserts, he studied for his Senior School Certificate.

La Marquesa. Resident of Calle Juan Sebastián Bach, whom Ismael hates for no reason at all. Seventy-eight years old. Slim. Feels the cold and usually wears a coat with fake fox fur, which earned her the nickname La Marquesa.

Mateo. The Runner's sister's boss. Understanding, fair minded, although not understanding or fair minded enough in the opinion of the Runner's sister. Mateo likes making model aeroplanes, photography and jazz, which his father calls negro music. He's done a wine-tasting course. When he orders a glass of wine he swirls it around in the glass a lot.

Medina. The Runner's sister's work colleague. The Runner says he's a bore, pedantic and stifling at work.

Meliveo (Antonio Carlos Sebastián Meliveo Mena). Childhood friend of Dioni, Enrique Rodríguez, El Pajarito, Inmaculada Berruezo and Vicky Leyra. He used to dress all in white and straighten his hair with an ordinary steam iron. A bad man with a heart of gold.

Merceditas. Former neighbour of Eduardo Chinarro. Daughter of Remedios and El Lucas. She suffers from severe depression and the occasional nervous breakdown.

Miguel Villaplana Molledo, El Migue. Son of Mariano Villaplana and Encarnación Molledo (La Segueta). Rafi's younger brother. Likes his friends to call him Jaime. Tries to imitate Rafi's worldly manners, ineptly.

Milagros. Fellow student of Dioni at the Faculty of Law. Very pretty girl. Short. Deep eyes, strawberry mouth. Sweet natured. Attracted by the shy Dioni, who can barely manage to exchange a few words with her in the student bar. Didn't finish her studies. Married a sergeant in the US Navy whom she met when his aircraft carrier *Coral Sea* made a stopover call in Málaga. Lives in Annapolis, Maryland.

El Moderno (José Parejas Blanco). Owner of a dive bar with the same name near the Hospital Civil, where Eduardo Chinarro wants to sleep. El Moderno, a kind man with a raspy voice as a result of a painful condition of the vocal cords, served a ten-year prison sentence for killing his wife, Rosalía Fernández, in a fit of jealousy that later turned out to be unjustified. His kindness stems from that act of meanness. While in prison he tried to hang himself twice (the cause of his throat condition). Hanging in his bar above the dusty bottles of Ponche Caballero, Licor 43 and Marie Brizard is a picture of the deceased Rosalía (sadly encrusted with fly droppings).

Mónica Ovejero. Close friend of Piluca, friend of Guille and his gang. Half in love with Juno. Shares his obsession with hair.

El Mono. Former friend of the Runner. His nickname – *mono* means 'monkey' – comes from his thick eyebrows and snub nose. Tall as a gorilla.

Montse. Friend of Dr Galán. Had a relationship with Ana's brother Emilio at a time when he was already married to Emilia and Montse was married to José Ramón Méndez, from whom she is currently divorced. Juno's mother. Present at Dr Galán's house when Dioni's death is announced. Gives Trini's mother a hug.

Moreno Peralta. Trainer for the Olímpica Victoriana football team. Former acquaintance of Eduardo Chinarro, to whom he gave advice on music. He claimed to be au fait with the subject because, in his own words, in Moreno Peralta's family there was a lad who could sing just as well as Pablo Alborán.

Nani. Owner of a newspaper kiosk near Father Sebastián Grimaldos's parish church. Thirty-five years old, almond-shaped eyes, hair ritually gathered in a high, tight ponytail. At one stage it was rumoured that she and the priest were having an affair. False.

El Negre (Francisco Hernández Negre). Friend of Raimundo Arias. Some nights, when Raimundo is up for it, Negre sings while Rai plays guitar. Eduardo Chinarro looks down his nose at the performance and always comes out with the same comment, 'Wow, they're every bit as good Camarón and Tomatito.' Then he has a go at Negre, 'Hey, if you like singing flamenco so much why don't you go with Rai and spend the whole day at it, out on the streets, all day and night?' To which Negre, completely composed, replies, 'I've got my own business to attend to.' All this happens in a place called La Polivalente.

Nene Olmedo. Friend of Tato. La Penca's lover (intermittently). Attractive, feline petty thief with pretensions to play in the criminal first division, although the opportunity has yet to present itself. Involved in robberies, handbag snatches, swindles and shady deals. Fervent believer in extra-terrestrial life forms and in the presence of aliens on our planet. He can prove it scientifically.

Niño del Sordo. Mechanic to whom the Runner likes to take his motorbike. Blond, blue eyes – almost translucent. One of his front teeth is broken. A bad fall back in the day when he aspired to race motorbikes. El Sordo is his boss, which is where he gets the nickname everyone in the neighbourhood knows him by.

La Nuri. Former lover of Rafi Villaplana. She bore a passing physical resemblance to Amelia, but otherwise La Nuri was quite a lot coarser. She piled on the make-up, used to wear chiffon, lace and see-through tops, but for Rafi that was all just a thin disguise. Who knows what became of her.

Ortuño. Friend of Céspedes and occasional lover of Julia Mamea. Clumsy lover; horny and awkward. Many people can't understand why Céspedes is his friend. He's quite fat and has a tendency to lurch to the right as he walks.

Osuna (José Luis Osuna Vallejo). Resident of Portada Alta who goes out on to the street when he hears the police cars and ambulance around Yubri's front door. Happily married to María Urbieta. Delivery man for a cake-and-pastries factory using his own van. Thirty-six years old. His hair is sticking up because he'd been asleep since 11 p.m. He starts his delivery round at 5.30 a.m.

Padín (José Manuel Capparós Padín). Old friend of the Runner. Circumspect, serious, ironic. Sometimes uses silences to communicate with the Runner.

El Pajarito *see* Soler.

Palmiro. Owner of the variety shop called La Amistad. Socializes with Mariano Villaplana and lets him have a deckchair to sit on to read the paper in the shop doorway and have serious snoozes.

Paloma (Aguilera Somarriba). Former fiancée of Rafi Villaplana. Sweet-natured woman. Educated at the Colegio el Monte. Her parents are small-business owners. For Rafi Villaplana this engagement represented a step up socially. When he met Jane, he thought that this was going to be his real take-off, an Apollo XI that would definitively take him beyond the orbit of Portada Alta, and he left sweet Paloma behind.

Paquito Arteaga. Childhood friend of Dioni, Enrique Rodríguez, Meliveo, El Pajarito, Inmaculada Berruezo and Vicky Leyva. Also known as Kesko, Van de Kesko or Van der Rayo. Cousin of the journalist Mar Arteaga.

Pedroche. Belita's husband. Floren's partner and friend. Born in a village. Introspective. Short, chubby, bald, ruddy complexion with blond moustache. Small eyes with long eyelashes (they actually look like a toy doll's eyes embedded in the face of a brute). Resigned to his fate but dreams of the life that could have been. His wife has attacked him more than once, although not as violently as this time. The image he carries of his wife in his head is of a whale, and that's how he refers to her mentally, as the Whale or the Sperm Whale. He feels he's been cheated. He dutifully eats the fried egg and chips that his wife has cooked for him hours earlier.

La Penca (Aurora Perea Pemán, sometimes known in the neighbourhood as Aurori). Yubri's (Calixto Perea Pemán's) sister. She's Raimundo the guitar man's Dulcinea. Has intermittent sexual relations with Nene Olmedo. Endures her father's attentions. Abused. Misses her deceased mother, whose photo she keeps in an imitation-silver (a poor imitation) plastic frame. She's stuck some white flowers (also plastic) in the frame.

Her mother was a dressmaker and had some amazing scissors that Yubri uses to kill his father.

La Penca's father (Andrés Perea Tejedor). Father of La Penca (Aurora Perea Pemán) and Yubri (Calixto Perea Pemán). Slaughterhouse worker with long periods of unemployment during which he was helped financially by his wife (now deceased). Likes wearing sweaty vests and two days' growth on his chin. Curly hair, whimsical expression, prominent belly. Like his son and sad heir, he has hairy shoulders and back.

La Penca's mother. Deceased. Her daughter keeps her photograph in a cheap frame with plastic flowers as an undying testimony of her affection. Also Yubri's mother.

Pepe Villaplana Molledo (El Pepe). Son of Mariano Villaplana and Encarnación Molledo (La Segueta). Good-for-nothing who thinks he's smart and profoundly knowledgeable about the world, arts and sciences because he studied economics for a year and passed in two subjects. Now, at the age of thirty-six, he knows it all. Lives in a house in the country with a withdrawn vegan woman. Has a small market garden in which he tries to grow vegetables. Wears a straw hat and a pair of thick sandals, which Rafi Villaplana finds offensive. El Pepe calls his ramshackle house and garden 'my smallholding'.

Pérez Palmis (Pepe). Friend of Dioni. He was something of a mentor during Dioni's first years in the profession. Economist, humanist. Childhood friend of Miguel Espinosa and well versed in his literary output.

Peruana (Eusebia Reátegui Romero). Housemaid in Ana Galán and Dionisio Grande's house. Native of Arequipa. She worked from the age of eleven in a canning factory in Lima where her mother was working when she was widowed. At the age of eighteen she emigrated to Spain. She worked in a bread shop for six months and for two months in a paint shop, where she was sexually harassed by owner. Then she went into domestic service and worked for a year and a half in the house of a lady who looked after her almost as if she were her daughter. The above-mentioned lady died in her sleep three months ago. Eusebia has only been working for the Grandes Galán family for three weeks.

Piluca (María del Pilar Bravo Ruiz). Close friend of Mónica Ovejero, whom she adores for her beauty. Sees herself in the same light. Out of the sixteen hours a day she spends awake she spends fifteen with her friend, or at least she tries to. She is short and tubby. Not even her stunning blue eyes can spare her the cruel tag with which Guille and his friends have damned her: Callo (Ugly). Despite that, she doesn't have any hang-ups, or at least she behaves as if she doesn't. Affected, mature beyond her years, she talks as an equal to women twice or three times her age. Although she doesn't yet know it, she has a defective ovary.

Policemen (Monreal, Deusto, Montero, Arias). Policemen who respond to the emergency call that Yubri makes after killing his father, whose surnames are, curiously, the same as those of some of the members of the amazing team at Club Deportivo Málaga during the 1970s.

Popeye (Miguel Ruiz González). Customer of Bar Maqui. Goes to help Floren and Pedroche when they're attacked. Fifty-eight years old, bricklayer. He's had a lot to drink but drives to the hospital smoothly and skilfully.

Quesada, Dr. Doctor and colleague of Ana Galán's and friend to Ana and Dioni.

Queta. Employee in the Hotel Los Patos. Colleague of Amelia's. Had a troubled sexual relationship with Rafi Villaplana for several months. Advises Amelia not to follow in her footsteps. In vain.

Quilín (Vicente Gómez Moncada). Stuttering son of Vicente and Gema.

Quino. The Runner's sister's fiancé. Works in IT for a successful company. Patronizing towards the Runner's family, although he prefers not to mix with them too much. Deep down, considers himself to be the knight in shining armour rescuing the princess from society's dark underbelly.

Quintana. Owner of the restaurant of the same name where Boss-Eyed Manolo goes on Friday nights before going to the brothel. Comes from a village and has a criminal record as a serial poacher. Emigrated to Germany (Stuttgart) where he worked in the sewers. When he came back from abroad he opened the restaurant. Passionate about greyhound racing.

Quintana (Señora de). Excellent cook in the restaurant owned by her husband. She met him in Germany, where she worked in the box office at a sleazy theatre club. She was having an affair with the owner of the club, a married man. Something her current husband has never even suspected.

Rafael de la Fuente. Rafi Villaplana mentions him as the last word in linguistic excellence. Director of major organizations in the hospitality world. Polyglot. Educated. Exquisite manners and a sharply honed sense of irony.

Rafi Villaplana Molledo. Amelia's (Amel's) lover. Fiancé to Jane, with whose father he aspires to do business deals. To achieve this he thinks it is important to involve Céspedes, whom he pesters. Ashamed to be the son of Mariano Villaplana, Encarnación Mollego (La Segueta) and of the entire Portada Alta neighbourhood. A man of aspirations and ambition. Completed his compulsory military service in the Army of Africa (Tetuán de Ceuta company).

Raimundo Arias (Rai). Guitarist. Eduardo Chinarro's begging partner. Prominent cheekbones, geometric face like a cubist portrait. Finds Dioni covered in ants on a patch of waste ground off Avenida Ortega y Gasset. In love with La Penca, his Dulcinea.

Ramírez. Gloria's father speaks to Jorge (Gorgo) about Ramírez and Toto Villanueva. People no one knows anything about. The only details (which may not be accurate) are that Ramírez is a welder and works (or lives) near the Plaza de los Mártires.

Ramiro González (Achucarro). Male nurse who, together with Dr Galán, attends to Dioni when he arrives at the hospital. Thirty-six years old. Panamanian. Studied at the California State University, Channel Islands, in Camarillo, California. Descended from exiled Spanish Republicans. His great-grandfather was a member of Manuel Azaña's cabinet when Azaña was minister of war.

Ramón Ranea. Fellow student of Dioni's at the Faculty of Law. Initiates him into homosexual practices. Pock-marked face and frizzy hair. Always has a cigarette glued into the corner of his mouth. Owns a 74 cc Bultaco Lobito bored out to 125 cc. Son of an antiques dealer.

Remedios. Former neighbour of Eduardo Chinarro's, whom he meets by chance in Calle Cruz Verde. She loved his mother like she was her sister. Short. Hair tied back very tightly into a bun of nondescript colour – thanks to the cumulative effects of various rinsed-out hair dyes – with grey roots showing. She goes around in a strappy khaki vest that accentuates her rolls of fat. She used to watch a few bullfights on the television at Eduardo's house, always with sunglasses on in order not to see any potential goring too clearly. Her daughter, Merceditas, is mentally unstable.

Ricardo. Manager of the supermarket in which Lucía, the Runner's fiancée, works. He asks her out and flirts with her. He's tall but inelegant, with blue eyes and dark skin. His speech is somewhat slurred, which Lucía finds unpleasant and which she's mentioned to the Runner, although the Runner thinks that Lucía's just saying this to reassure him. Ricardo has a red Audi A3 and a fake Rolex Datejust 41. He has a quiff and goes to the gym three times a week.

Riverita. Accredited reporter for *El Confidencial.* Son of Augustín Rivera, also a journalist, better known as El Corbata. Goes to Portada Alta when he hears that a tragic event has occurred there.

La Roberta. Eduardo Chinarro's former girlfriend, sort of. Reddish hair with pale skin and blue eyes. Office cleaner. Explosive character. When she was still with Chinarro she was also sleeping with El Manolín, a vendor of illegal lottery tickets with bulging eyes like a pair of eggs. Eduardo Chinarro doesn't know that Roberta has been dead for two years after falling down the stairs at home.

The Runner. Former athlete who still trains. He runs countless kilometres to go nowhere, or at least that's what some of the people who know him think. Sometimes he trains with Jorge (also called Gorgo). The Runner is engaged to the lovely Lucía. Chronically and semi-voluntarily unemployed. Owns a motorbike that is always breaking down. Has a grandmother he loves and a mother he's scared of being too much like. His sister is about to get married and leave home. Writes a diary. Although he doesn't admit it, deep down he wants to be a writer one day, and that's why his aunts, his cousins, the man who's brazenly courting his mother and all the men who swarm around Lucía treat him with something like respect. Or, at least, not with pity or contempt.

The Runner's grandmother. The Runner's maternal grandmother. She admires him and tries, within the constraints of her limited capacity, to protect him. (She gives him fifty euros a month from her meagre pension. This is the Runner's only regular income.) She suffers from Parkinson's and her daughter's relentless carping. She gets on with people. With her qualities she should have had a better life. But it wasn't possible, a question of lack of resources and difficult times. She tells her grandchildren the story of 'The Calle Molinillo Vampire'.

The Runner's father. Deceased. The Runner refers to him in his diary as an enigma. One night, when the Runner was a little boy, his father gave him an enormous bowl with coloured fish.

The Runner's mother. A woman ground down by Life. To her, Life is a personality, someone who attacked her from behind. She refers to it with bitterness, as if it were someone who had defrauded her. Perhaps because she brought her into the world or because she didn't make her life pleasant enough, she's resentful of her own mother. She protects her son and forgives him every fault. Also has a daughter.

The Runner's sister. Office worker. Independent, about to leave the family home and squabbles because she's about to marry Quino. Smug.

Santi Cánovas. 3,000-metres steeplechaser who, back in the day, would train with the Runner and with Ángel López. He gave the Runner his first pair of running spikes, blue Munichs with a white cross and one wobbly spike. Running hundreds of kilometres alongside the Runner, the two men became good friends.

Sarah (Callahan). Irish girl whom Guille met the previous summer in Dalkey, Ireland, and whom he hopes to see again during the two weeks following this day in August. Taller than Guille, red hair, blue eyes. He kissed her near the sea.

Saray. Amelia, Ismael and Jorge's (Gorgo's) neighbour. She's twenty-five years old with two children and a boyfriend who works in a metal workshop. Saray is malicious gossiper and busybody. Fond of making cutting remarks, always with a smile on her lips.

Sebastián Grimaldos, Father. Priest. Belita is in love with him and has given him 1,800 euros and all the family jewellery. Born in Salamanca, he trained at the Junior Diocesan Seminary in Ponferrada, where his father was stationed as a Civil Guard. He's been carrying on a love affair with Lorena since the previous summer. Grimaldos's father, Sergeant Grimaldos Guindos, had a scar in the form of a half-crescent running down from his right temple to his chin, caused by an exploding grenade during the Civil War, as a result of which he was known in Ponferrada and throughout El Bierzo as the Grimaldos Ogre.

La Segueta (Encarnación Molledo Muñoz). Wife of Mariano Villaplana, mother of Rafi, Miguel, Estefanía and Pepe Villaplana. Her gums are mostly toothless. Hates bras. Her breasts hang down like soft bells underneath her tops, which are usually decorated with tomato sauce, splashes of cooking oil and stains from fry-ups and stews. She drags around an enormous shopping trolley and drinks vast quantities of beer.

Seoane. Hotel employee favoured with several promotions by Rafi Villaplana. Likes scuba diving and is relatively grateful to Rafi.

Sergio (del Alcázar). Old friend of the Runner. Noisy and outrageously entertaining.

Soler (Antonio, also known as El Pajarito). Former 400-metres athlete mentioned by the Runner. Also a childhood friend of Dioni/Dionisio when he was friendly with Enrique Rodríguez, Meliveo, Inmaculada Berruezo and Vicky Leyva. Also a writer who many years later Céspedes saw in the early hours one morning climbing on to a scrap-metal cart together with Garriga Vela and Taján. Author of a novel entitled *Sur*.

La Sorda. Eduardo Chinarro's cousin. She lost 80 per cent of her hearing in her right ear and 50 per cent in her left as a result of a childhood illness. Sixteen years older than Eduardo, she brought him home with her once or twice a month after his mother died so that he could have a hot meal. Eduardo stopped going, frustrated at having to shout into his cousin's ear. According to Eduardo, his cousin's hearing capacity is only 1 per cent in both ears.

Taján (Alfredo). Writer whom Céspedes saw in the early hours one morning long ago climbing on to a scrap-metal cart together with Garriga Vela and Soler. Writes amazing books of poetry and novels when his other activities allow. Wears expensive ties and a fine ring on his right hand with a special compartment for hemlock.

El Tato (Marcelino Inestrosa). Nene Olmedo's partner in crime. He pokes around, pilfering a little bit here and a little bit there. One minor conviction for theft. Very thin and missing two front teeth in his lower jaw.

Taxi driver who picks up Céspedes, Julia and Ortuño (Domingo Conejo). Peaceable individual. Has seen lots of things in his taxi, but not many have aroused him as much as the night he saw Julia Mamea in between Céspedes and Ortuño in the back of his taxi. The two men draped over her, eating her up, half stripping her. 'And the whore was looking at me, she didn't take her eyes off me in the rear-view mirror, I mean, I was on the verge of stopping the taxi and getting in the back myself.' That's what he's told his fellow taxi drivers a few dozen times.

Taxi driver who takes Céspedes and Carole to the station (Rafael Recalde). Shaven head, wide mouth, bad breath. Twenty years driving a taxi. Hates rich kids and all their bullshit, he just can't help it. Vicente's brother-in-law. (Vicente as in Dioni's lover.)

Toto Villanueva. Gloria's father talks to Jorge (Gorgo) about Toto Villanueva and Ramírez. People no one knows anything about.

Trini's mother. Friend of Dr Galán. We don't know her name. The teenagers regard her as a legendary sex goddess. Conscientious woman. Dark hair. Takes Guille home when she discovers that his father might die. She's in the house when they learn of Dioni's death. Gives Montse a hug.

El Tuli (Gonzalo Trujillo McManus). Friend of Juno, Cabello, Loberas and Guille. Dishes out whiskies and spliffs to his friends in his father's house.

La Turbia. Employee in the laundry at the Hotel Los Patos. Sixty-two years old. Widow. One eye clouded over, hence her nickname (*turbia* means 'cloudy'). She's seen Rafi Villaplana's career trajectory at close hand. She saw him arrive as a bellboy. In her own words, he knows which side his bread's buttered.

Valderrama. Friend of Miguel (Jaime) Villaplana. The only thing known about him is that he married very young and that there were lots of gaudy shirts and bow ties and cheap perfume at his wedding.

Vane (Vanesa Ramírez). Shop assistant in Calzados Famita shoe-shop. Bottle blonde, fake tan. Arouses the lustful Jorge (Gorgo). Wears white leggings. Jorge (Gorgo) reckons she wears a thong.

Veloso. Friend of Juanmi at the Faculty of Arts. Minor poet.

El Viberti. Owner of Jiler (derived from Hitler) the Dobermann. He originally thought of calling the dog Adolfo, but the name sounded a bit soft and flabby. He was snooping from his balcony when the police came to Yubri's home. He didn't dare go down into the street because he has some outstanding issues with the legal system.

Vicente (Gómez Peña). Dioni's lover, Gema's partner and Quilín's father. A man with no clear profession; opportunistic waiter, occasional car-rental employee. In his youth he thought he was the bee's knees; with the passage of time he's become less full of himself.

Vicente, the idiot from the butcher's shop (Ortiz Burgos). Unhappy, mentally challenged individual who spends his days in the butcher's shop next to Floren's workshop. The butt of numerous jokes on the part of the workers from the nearby businesses.

Vicky Leyva. Childhood friend of Dioni, Enrique Rodríguez, Meliveo and Inmaculada Berruezo. Coincidentally, she was a close friend of Céspedes in his Madrid years. A short time later, her hair now dyed blonde, she would work for a season in a nightclub of dubious repute called El Pomelo.

Víctor Calero. Friend of Juanmi in the Faculty of Law. Does a poor imitation of Alfonso Pallarés, and in a botched-up way introduces Juanmi to using heroin.

Vilches (José). Bank employee, assistant branch manager. The Runner's mother's suitor. Diabetic. Sixty years old. He backcombs his grey hair, revealing a forehead mottled with dark patches. Pretentious, thrifty, meticulous. Thinks the Runner is a wastrel. Studied for the priesthood. Has a collection of novels by Nobel literature laureates (1901–85).

Waitress from Kyiv. Waitress at the Onda Pasadena who serves Ismael. Pours drinks and puts up with drunks. Violinist with aspirations to turn professional. She has a particular hold on Carlo the doorman.

Yolanda. Head of reception at the Hotel Los Patos. Amelia owes her promotion to her. A lesbian, she's always acted as Amelia's undisclosed guardian, not for emotional or sexual reasons but simply because she likes her and recognizes her professionalism and will to succeed.

El Yubri (Calixto Perea Pemán). La Penca's brother. Has a criminal record for stealing copper wire. Convicted for the armed robbery of a petrol station, a crime for which he maintains his innocence. Has also set fire to several hearses. He's about to go prison. His IQ on the Wechsler Scale is seventy-four.

'The Calle Molinillo Vampire'

Doña Agueda. Angelita's grandmother. Widow. She is saved from her financial difficulties by the pharmacist Don Laureano Andrade Andrade.

Amancio. Glassware shop owner. A stunted and servile man. With the passage of time it would be revealed that he was a kleptomaniac.

Angelita. Teenager who, one rainy night, is found murdered on a patch of waste ground close to Calle de la Cruz del Molinillo.

Antonio. Owner of a local grocer's shop. A resourceful man. He sells stale bread as if it were freshly baked, chickpeas instead of lentils and chorizo when someone asks him for salchichón, forever juggling with his profit margins and stock levels. Antonio is so clever, pleasant and engaging that his customers, almost all women, leave his shop satisfied.

Aurelio. Electrician who discovers Angelita's corpse on the patch of waste ground. For months afterwards, whenever he closes his eyes, he sees the girl's face, drenched by the rain and looking like marble.

Daniel Murphy. American with a busy lifestyle. Visits the neighbourhood after Angelita's death, interested in the mystery of the Vampire. Expert on the poetry of Vicente Aleixandre, translator, employee in a small shipping company on the river Susquehanna, waiter in the El Pomelo nightclub and actor in several horror films (also horrendous owing to budgetary constraints), this perhaps being the reason for his interest in the story of the Calle Molinillo Vampire.

Jiménez (Manuel Jiménez Pineda). Butcher. His shop is known locally as the Establishment. No one really knows why.

Laureano Andrade Andrade (Don). Pharmacist who often visits Doña Agueda and Angelita's house.

Machuca. National policeman with the spirit of a bulldog. Few scruples and fewer friends. As well as this one, during that dark period in society he investigated other infamous crimes, including the sad case of Azucena Beltrán.

Márquez, El Tenazas. Notorious policeman. Torturer. Interrogates Jiménez on multiple occasions. In vain. Spent the whole Civil War hidden behind a false wall. Three square metres. 'One square metre for each year,' he would say with a bitter expression.

Niño, Jiménez's nephew or cousin. Sixteen years old, although he doesn't look more than fourteen. Actually, he's Jiménez's second cousin. Helps him out in the butcher's shop. On rainy nights and given the rumours about the Vampire, he has fun putting on his cousin's cape and walking through the neighbourhood in the early hours of the morning in the heavy rain. Epileptic.

El Rata. Bootblack. Out of spite or ignorance people say he's a police informer, partly because Machuco is one of his customers. A non-paying customer. He was in prison for five years for a little-known case of aggravated burglary, of which he was probably innocent. Small. Darting eyes. A survivor.

Roche (Antonio). Famous journalist who goes to the neighbourhood to research and write about Angelita's murder and the identity of the mysterious Vampire.